Praise for *Blonde*

"Oates may have created the most important novel of her career."

—*Newsday*

"Grimly compelling. . . . A portrait of Hollywood as terrifyingly hallucinatory as Nathaniel West's *The Day of the Locust*."

—*Wall Street Journal*

"A fascinating imagining of the hellish battles that Monroe fought with herself."

—*Playboy*

"In *Blonde*, Oates has found a character and a narrative mode that exploit all her strengths as a writer . . . a narrative intensity often found in her stories but never sustained so successfully in a long novel and an exuberant mastery of language that suggests a writer at the peak of her power."

—*Atlanta Journal and Constitution*

"*Blonde* is a true mythic blowout, in which Marilyn is everything and nothing—a Great White Whale of significance, standing not for the blind power of nature but for the blind power of artifice."

—*GQ*

"Ms. Oates has hit another one of her targets. This vengeful history is about the majesty of imagination. Marilyn's self-imaginings were cruelly curtailed. Come now the artist to accord Marilyn her rightful status, as artist. The artist uses flesh and fact, the artist transcends them."

—*New York Observer*

"Joyce Carol Oates takes the boldest path to comprehending 'the riddle, the curse of Monroe' by proceeding directly and frankly to fiction. Her novel *Blonde* is fat, messy, and fierce. It's part Gothic, part kaleidoscopic novel of ideas, part lurid celebrity potboiler, and is seldom less than engrossing."

—Laura Miller, *New York Times*

"In Oates' corpus, *Blonde* lands near the top. It is an ambitious, complex, and powerful novel."

—*Greensboro News and Record*

"If you are prejudiced against biographical fiction . . . or if you simply think that there are too many books about Marilyn Monroe . . . now is the time to lay aside your prejudices—or, rather, to allow them to be swept aside by a torrentially imaginative, compulsively readable tour de force. . . . *Blonde* brings this near-mythic tale triumphantly and terribly to psychological life."

—*Sunday Telegraph*

"Joyce Carol Oates' precise and inspired writing is close to witchcraft. With mastery, she unravels the story of the mythical blonde, the overly adored and despised Marilyn Monroe. Breathlessly, I followed the intricate and passionate emotions surrounding the sweet and complex Norma Jeane, whose blazing 'aura' suffused the whole world and frightened the men who loved her most."

—Jeanne Moreau

"The novel may be more than 700 pages long, but you're hard pressed to put it down from the moment you turn to the first page. Oates has forged a book of irresistible and terrible locomotion, and it little matters that we know—oh how sorrowfully we know—how it will end."

—*Commercial Appeal*

"Joyce Carol Oates' scary and rhapsodic novel about the life of Marilyn Monroe is saturated with the mysteries of eye and camera. . . . It's eccentric, exhausting—and remarkable."

—*Salon.com*

"*Blonde* is at once epic and impressionistic, even lyrical, all snippets that seem intimate, a catalog that accumulates into something public and grand."

—Brian Bouldrey

"Oates is as diverse as she is driven. She has tackled topics ranging from the aesthetics of boxing to the misadventures of toxic twins. But rarely is she so intriguing as when she strays into a genre best described as 'faction.' It's as unsettling as it is worthwhile to take a fresh look at a much-publicized event or personality through Oates' eyes."

—*Times* (London)

Blonde

A NOVEL BY JOYCE CAROL OATES

NOVELS BY JOYCE CAROL OATES

With Shuddering Fall (1964)

A Garden of Earthly Delights (1967)

Expensive People (1968)

them (1969)

Wonderland (1971)

Do With Me What You Will (1973)

The Assassins (1975)

Childwold (1976)

Son of the Morning (1978)

Unholy Loves (1979)

Bellefleur (1980)

Angel of Light (1981)

A Bloodsmoor Romance (1982)

Mysteries of Winterthurn (1984)

Solstice (1985)

Marya: A Life (1986)

You Must Remember This (1987)

American Appetites (1989)

Because It Is Bitter, and Because
It Is My Heart (1989)

Black Water (1992)

Foxfire: Confessions of a
Girl Gang (1993)

What I Lived For (1994)

We Were the Mulvaneys (1996)

Man Crazy (1997)

My Heart Laid Bare (1998)

Broke Heart Blues (1999)

Blonde (2000)

Middle Age: A Romance (2001)

I'll Take You There (2002)

The Tattooed Girl (2003)

The Falls (2003)

Missing Mom (2005)

Black Girl / White Girl (2006)

The Gravedigger's Daughter
(2007)

My Sister, My Love (2008)

Little Bird of Heaven (2009)

Mudwoman (2012)

The Accursed (2014)

The Sacrifice (2015)

A Book of American Martyrs
(2017)

Hazards of Time Travel (2018)

My Life as a Rat (2019)

20th Anniversary Edition

A NOVEL

JOYCE CAROL OATES

ecco
An Imprint of HarperCollinsPublishers

For Eleanor Bergstein, and for Michael Goldman

BLONDE 20TH ANNIVERSARY EDITION. Copyright © 2020 by The Ontario Review. All rights reserved. Printed in the United States of America. No part of this book may be used or reproduced in any manner whatsoever without written permission except in the case of brief quotations embodied in critical articles and reviews. For information, address HarperCollins Publishers, 195 Broadway, New York, NY 10007.

HarperCollins books may be purchased for educational, business, or sales promotional use. For information, please e-mail the Special Markets Department at SPsales@harpercollins.com.

First Ecco edition published in 2001. Reissue published in 2009.

FIRST ECCO PAPERBACK EDITION PUBLISHED 2020

Library of Congress Cataloging-in-Publication Data has been applied for.

ISBN: 978-0-06-296845-6 (pbk)

20 21 22 23 24   LSC   10 9 8 7 6 5 4 3 2 1

AUTHOR'S NOTE

Blonde is a radically distilled "life" in the form of fiction, and, for all its length, synecdoche is the principle of appropriation. In place of numerous foster homes in which the child Norma Jeane lived, for instance, *Blonde* explores only one, and that fictitious; in place of numerous lovers, medical crises, abortions and suicide attempts and screen performances, *Blonde* explores only a selected, symbolic few.

The historic Marilyn Monroe did keep a journal of sorts and she did write poems, or poem-fragments. Of these, only two lines are included in the final chapter ("Help help!~"); the other poems are invented. Certain of the remarks in the chapter "The Collected Works of Marilyn Monroe" are taken from interviews, other are fictitious; the lines at the end of the chapter are the conclusion to Charles Darwin's *Origin of Species*. Biographical facts regarding Marilyn Monroe should be sought not in *Blonde,* which is not intended as a historic document, but in biographies of the subject. (Those consulted by the author are *Legend: The Life and Death of Marilyn Monroe* by Fred Guiles, 1985; *Goddess: The Secret Lives of Marilyn Monroe* by Anthony Summers, 1986; and *Marilyn Monroe: A Life of the Actress* by Carl E. Rollyson, Jr., 1986. More subjective books on Monroe as a mythic figure are *Marilyn Monroe* by Graham McCann, 1987, and *Marilyn* by Norman Mailer, 1973.) Of books consulted about American politics, especially in Hollywood in the Forties and Fifties, *Naming Names* by Victor Navasky was most helpful. Of the books on acting cited or alluded to, *The Thinking Body* by Mabel Todd, *To the Actor* by Michael Chekhov, and *An Actor Prepares* and *My Life in Art* by Constantin Stanislavski are genuine books, while *The Actor's Handbook and the Actor's Life* and *The Paradox of Acting* are invented. *The Book of the American Patriot* is invented. A passage from the conclusion of H.G. Wells's *The Time Machine* is twice cited, in the chapters "Hummingbird" and "We Are All Gone into the World of Light." Lines from Emily Dickinson appear in chapters titled "The Bath," "The Orphan," and "Time to Get Married." A passage from Arthur Schopenhauer's *The World as Will and Idea* appears in "The Death of Rumpelstiltskin." A passage from Sigmund Freud's *Civilization and Its Discontents* appears, in paraphrase, in "The Sharpshooter." Passages from Blaise Pascal's *Pensées* appear in "Roslyn 1961."

· · ·

Parts of this novel have appeared, in differing versions, in *Playboy*, *Conjunctions*, *Yale Review*, *Ellery Queen Mystery Magazine*, *Michigan Quarterly Review* and *TriQuarterly*. My thanks to the editors of these magazines.

Special thanks to Daniel Halpern, Jane Shapiro, and C. K. Williams.

CONTENTS

THE AFTERLIFE 1959–1962

INTRODUCTION

Published in the millennial year 2000, Joyce Carol Oates's *Blonde* was conceived on a grand scale, using the legendary Marilyn Monroe as an emblem of twentieth-century America. The novel opens with a breathless prologue, dated August 3, 1962, the day before Monroe's death, as a teenage bike messenger speeds at dusk through the L.A. traffic with a special delivery for

"MM" OCCUPANT
12305 FIFTH HELENA DRIVE
BRENTWOOD CALIFORNIA
USA
"EARTH."

He is "Death-in-a-hurry. Death furiously pedaling" and also Death, the messenger from the poem by Emily Dickinson, who kindly stops for the restless person who cannot wait for him. With this hallucinatory passage, Oates pulls us into a book about the fate of a female star in the Hollywood world of mirrors, smog, and shadows, a world where women's bodies are commodities traded for titillation and profit. In her most ambitious novel, Oates uncannily channels the inner voice of Monroe and demands that Monroe be given recognition, compassion, and respect.

Oates first had the idea for this book when she saw a photograph of a radiant fifteen-year-old Norma Jeane Baker, not yet looking anything like Marilyn Monroe, winning a beauty contest in California in 1941, with a crown of artificial flowers on her curly brown hair and a girlish locket around her neck. Oates identified with Norma Jeane's innocence, as she recalled in an interview with her biographer, Greg Johnson: "I felt an immediate sense of something like recognition; this young, hopefully smiling girl, so very American, reminded me powerfully of girls of my childhood, some of them from broken homes." Such girls, many of whom she had known growing up in rural Upstate New York, had become characters in her short stories and novels, where their dreams usually ended in defeat. Initially, Oates planned to write a novella about the metamorphosis of an ordinary high school girl into a star; she loses her real name and is given a studio name that will obliterate her history and identity. The book would end with the words *Marilyn Monroe*. But as she watched all of Monroe's movies, learned more about her intelligence and humor, her determination to be seen as a serious actress, and the intersection of her career with multiple strands of mid-twentieth-century American culture—sports, religion, crime, theater, politics—Oates realized she needed a larger fictional form to explore a woman who was much more than a victim.

As the book evolved and grew over two years of research and writing, Oates told Nikolas Charles, a journalist from *Time* magazine, in 2015, she began "half seriously" to think of Monroe "as my Moby Dick, the powerful galvanizing image about which an epic might be constructed, with myriad levels of meaning and significance." Building an epic novel around a woman, let alone a celebrity out of popular culture, gossip, and fan magazines, was a bold undertaking, but Oates saw profound aspects to Monroe's story that made it possible to think of her seriously as a tragic and representative American figure. And in the words of one reviewer, who did not know Melville had been one of her models, Oates succeeded completely: "*Blonde* is a true mythic blowout, in which Marilyn is everything and nothing—a Great White Whale of significance, standing not for the blind power of nature but for the blind power of artifice."

The myth of Marilyn Monroe was special because it combined three feminine personae: First, there was Norma Jeane Baker, the wholesome normal girl with a naive, vulnerable heart. An illegitimate child growing up in an orphanage and foster homes who longed for Daddy, family, education, romance, money, and security, her first memories are of sitting rapt in a dark theater, the church of Hollywood, where she goes to worship stars instead of saints.

The second persona was Marilyn Monroe, the pinup, bombshell, sex symbol, and movie goddess. She is the artificial creation of the Hollywood studio system, with a "sexy murmurous" name and a whispery, babyish voice. Voluptuous and seductive, her natural beauty transformed with braces, peroxide, false eyelashes, bright-red lipstick, tight clothes, and wobbly stiletto heels that make it hard for her to run away, Marilyn is all body. Yet, paradoxically, behind that glittering, glamorous image, Marilyn bears the shame and self-hatred of living in a female body in a misogynist culture—fear of being unclean; disgust with her sexuality; a lifetime of menstrual cramps, gynecological problems, miscarriages, and abortions.

The third persona, the Blonde, is a symbol, the pure and virginal creature of fairy tale and religious parable. In popular culture and advertising, she stands for the upper-class, tidy, and stainless existence Oates calls a "blond life." You don't have to be born blond. Blondness is attainable, but it can't guarantee a flawless life. Desired and worshipped as an ideal image of white beauty and class, the Blonde is nonetheless despised and defiled as a whore in pornography and fantasy.

Oates found herself obsessed by the intricate riddle of Marilyn Monroe. *Blonde* expanded to be her longest novel, and indeed the original manuscript is almost twice as long as the published book. As she writes on the copyright page, *Blonde* is not a biography of Monroe, or even a biographical novel that follows the historical facts of the subject's life. Indeed, Monroe's dozens of biographers have disagreed about many of the basic facts of her life. *Blonde*, however, is a work of fiction and imagination, and Oates plays with, rearranges, and invents the details of Monroe's life in order to achieve a deeper poetic and spiritual truth. She condenses and conflates events in a process she calls "distillation," so that in place of numerous foster homes, lovers, medical crises, and screen performances, she "explores only a selected, symbolic few." At the same time, Oates develops and deepens background themes inherent in Monroe's story, including the growth of Los Angeles, the history of film, the House Un-American Activities Committee's witch hunt for Communists in the film industry, and the blacklist. Each of these story lines could be a novel in itself, but like the chapters on cetology and whaling in *Moby-Dick*, they heighten the epic quality of the novel.

Of the hundreds of characters who appear in the book, some are identified by their real names, like Whitey, the make-up artist who created and maintained Monroe's iconic look, although the name also ironically suggests the white-skinned, platinum-haired blond doll he crafted. Others, including two sons of Hollywood stars, Cass Chaplin and Edward G. Robinson Jr., are given fictionalized stories. Monroe's famous husbands are given allegorical names—The Ex-Athlete and The Playwright—and are fictional characters rather than portraits of Joe DiMaggio and Arthur Miller. Similarly, fragments of poems by Emily Dickinson, W. B. Yeats, and George Herbert appear along with bits of poetry attributed to Norma Jeane that Oates composed herself.

Two major themes help to structure the vast sweep of narrative detail. First, acting as a metaphor, profession, and vocation. Oates quotes from classic handbooks of acting by Constantin Stanislav-ski and his disciple Michael Chekhov, who was a nephew of the playwright. Monroe was photographed studying his book *To the Actor.* Among the epigraphs is a passage from *The Actor's Free-dom* by Michael Goldman: "The acting area is a sacred space . . . where the actor cannot die." Goldman, to whom *Blonde* is dedi-cated, along with his wife, novelist and screenwriter Eleanor Berg-stein, is a drama theorist and scholar. Oates also quotes works on acting she has invented, allowing her to emphasize the differences between the individual religious dedication of the theater, an art to which Monroe aspired, and the collective process of film, where the director, editor, costume designer, and cameraman are cocre-ators. Monroe tries to bring the intensity of stage performance to the more technical medium of the screen.

Oates also drew on the literary traditions of the fairy tale and Gothic novel. In a 1997 essay on fairy tales, she noted their lim-ited view of female ambition and promotion of simplistic wish-fulfillment. Competition between women is inherent in all the plots: "In the great majority of the tales, to be a heroine . . . re-quires extreme youth and extreme physical beauty; it would not be sufficient to be merely beautiful, one must be 'the greatest beauty in the kingdom'—'the fairest in the land.'" But these tales also of-fer "an incalculably rich storehouse of . . . images, a vast Sargasso Sea of the imagination."

The Hollywood version of that fairy tale is the romance of the Fair Princess and the handsome Dark Prince, the plot of the first movie Norma Jeane ever sees, and the recurring fantasy of her life. Her first agent, I. E. Shinn, tells her that to be a star means to compete: "There must be a Fair Princess exalted above the rest." The dark side of the successful Fair Princess is the excluded Beg-gar Maiden, the outsider trying hopelessly to break in. Moreover, in the Gothic version of the fairy tale, the Dark Prince is also a powerful male who imprisons the princess in a haunted castle. The Studio stands for this macabre space, as Norma Jeane works

through a system run by ruthless, predatory men she
fy, satisfy, and serve. Being "groomed for 'stardom,'"
iously writes, is "a species of animal manufacture, like
breeding." At its lower levels, The Studio is staffed by employees
who look like fairy tale gargoyles and trolls. I. E. Shinn is Rumpelstiltskin, compared to "the ugly little dwarf man who taught
the Miller's daughter to spin gold out of straw." Beyond the walls
of The Studio are The Magi: gossip columnists, writers for fan
magazines, and the tabloids. They are quasi-religious figures of the
Church of Hollywood, but also like the evil witches of fairy tales,
"there at the birth of the star and . . . there at the death."

These themes come together in a chapter called "Hummingbird," narrated as Norma Jeane's diary of September 1947, when
she was twenty-one and heading to her first movie audition at The
Studio. She is the only girl in her acting class invited to audition,
and to meet the producer Mr. Z, and she thinks it's because her
talent has been recognized. She has also been invited to Mr. Z's famous aviary, which she believes is a collection of beautiful tropical
birds; but when she goes into the room, she sees instead a collection of dead stuffed birds in a glass case. *All dead birds are female,*" she thinks; *"there is something female about being dead."*
Mr. Z quickly takes her into the private apartment behind his office, where he orders her to get down on a white fur rug and brutally rapes her. Norma Jeane tries to justify what has happened:
*"he was not a cruel man I believe but one accustomed to getting
his way of course & surrounded by 'little people' there must be the
temptation to be cruel when you are surrounded by such & they
cringe . . . before you in terror of your whim."*

Humiliated and in pain, she gets up to go to her audition. But
the rape was the audition, and she gets the part. What's left is for
them to give her a new name. The chapter ends with her ecstatic,
terrible declaration of rebirth: *"My new life! My new life has begun! Today it began! . . . It's only now beginning, I am twenty-one
years old & I am MARILYN MONROE."*

When *Blonde* was published in 2000, it was nominated for literary prizes and widely reviewed as Oates's masterwork. But it was also called lurid, eccentric, and fierce. Darryl F. Zanuck, the model for Mr. Z, had been called a cynical sexual predator—but that was just rumor. Readers of *Blonde* today, however, will recognize in that hellish rape scene a script from the casting couch of Harvey Weinstein and other Hollywood moguls, whose years of molestation, harassment, abuse, and sexual assault of aspiring actresses were brought to light in 2017, when women accusers came forward to create the #MeToo movement. *Blonde* now looks more realistic, and its feminist fury stands justified.

We know from the first sentences of the novel, as well as all the books and movies that have been made about her, that Marilyn Monroe's story ended with her death at the age of thirty-six, a death that has become part of her legend. *Blonde* too has been written about and filmed for television and movies. Just a few years ago, it could still be read as sensationalizing the story of Monroe. Now it must be seen as a passionate and prophetic defense.

—ELAINE SHOWALTER

Blonde

A NOVEL BY JOYCE CAROL OATES

In the circle of light on the stage in the midst of darkness, you have the sensation of being entirely alone. . . . This is called solitude in public. . . . During a performance, before an audience of thousands, you can always enclose yourself in this circle, like a snail in its shell. . . . You can carry it wherever you go.

—*Constantin Stanislavski,*
An Actor Prepares
(translated by Elizabeth Reynolds Hapgood)

The acting area is a sacred space . . . where the actor cannot die.

—*Michael Goldman,*
The Actor's Freedom

Genius is not a gift, but the way a person invents in desperate circumstances.

—*Jean-Paul Sartre*

Prologue

3 AUGUST 1962

SPECIAL DELIVERY

There came Death hurtling along the Boulevard in waning sepia light.

There came Death flying as in a children's cartoon on a heavy unadorned messenger's bicycle.

There came Death unerring. Death not to be dissuaded. Death-in-a-hurry. Death furiously pedaling. Death carrying a package marked *SPECIAL DELIVERY HANDLE WITH CARE* in a sturdy wire basket behind his seat.

There came Death expertly threading his graceless bicycle through traffic at the intersection of Wilshire and La Brea where, because of street repair, two westbound Wilshire lanes were funneled into one.

Death so swift! Death thumbing his nose at middle-aged horn honkers.

Death laughing *Screw you, buddy!* And you. Like Bugs Bunny flying past the gleaming glittering hulks of expensive new-model automobiles.

There came Death undeterred by the smoggy spent air of Los Angeles. By the warm radioactive air of southern California where Death had been born.

Yes, I saw Death. I'd dreamt of Death the night before. Many nights before. I was not afraid.

There came Death so matter-of-fact. There came Death hunched over rust-stippled handlebars of a clumsy but stolid bicycle. There came Death in a Cal Tech T-shirt, laundered but unironed khaki shorts, sneakers, and no socks. Death with muscled calves, dark-haired legs. A curvy knucklebone spine. Adolescent bumps and blemishes on his face. Death nerved-up, brain-dazzled by sunshine flashing like scimitars off windshields, chrome.

More horn honking in Death's flamboyant wake. Death with a spiky crew cut. Death chewing gum.

Death so routine, five days a week, plus Saturdays and Sundays for a higher fee. *Hollywood Messenger Service*. Death hand-delivering his special packages.

There came Death unexpectedly into Brentwood! Death flying along the narrow residential streets of Brentwood near-deserted in August. Here in Brentwood the touching futility of meticulously tended "grounds" past which Death pedals briskly. And routinely. Alta Vista, Campo, Jacumba, Brideman, Los Olivos. To Fifth Helena Drive, a dead-end street. Palm trees, bougainvillea, red climber roses. A smell of rotting blossoms. A smell of sun-scorched grass. Walled gardens, wisteria. Circular driveways. Windows with blinds drawn tight against the sun.

Death bearing a gift with no return address for

"MM" OCCUPANT
12305 FIFTH HELENA DRIVE
BRENTWOOD CALIFORNIA
USA
"EARTH"

Now on Fifth Helena, Death was pedaling more slowly. Death was squint-ing at street numbers. Death hadn't given the package so strangely addressed a second glance. So strangely gift-wrapped in candy-cane-striped tinsel paper with a look of having been used before. Adorned with a ready-made white satin bow affixed to the box by transparent adhesive tape.

It was a package measuring eight inches by eight inches by ten. Weighing only a few ounces, as if empty? Stuffed with tissue paper?

No. If you shook it, you could tell there was something inside. A soft-edged object made of fabric, perhaps.

There came, in the early evening of August 3, 1962, Death ringing the doorbell at 12305 Fifth Helena Drive. Death wiping his sweaty forehead with his baseball cap. Death chewing gum rapidly, impatiently. Hearing no footsteps inside. And he can't leave the goddam package on the doorstep, has to get a signature. Hearing just the vibratory hum of a window air-conditioning unit. Maybe a radio inside? This is a small Spanish-style house, a "hacienda," just one floor. Fake adobe walls, glaring orange tile roof, win-dows with drawn venetian blinds, and a look of grayish dust. Cramped and miniature like a dollhouse, nothing special for Brentwood. Death rang the doorbell a second time, pressing hard. And this time, the door was opened.

From Death's hand I accepted the gift. I knew what it was, I think. Who it was from. Seeing the name and address I laughed and signed without hesitation.

The Girl

1942–1947

THE KISS

This movie I've been seeing all my life, yet never to its completion.

Almost she might say *This movie is my life!*

Her mother first took her when she was two or three years old. Her earliest memory, so exciting! Grauman's Egyptian Theatre on Hollywood Boulevard. This was years before she'd been able to comprehend even the rudiments of the movie story, yet she was enthralled by the movement, the ceaseless rippling fluid movement, on the great screen above her. Not yet capable of thinking *This was the very universe upon which are projected uncountable unnameable forms of life.* How many times in her lost childhood and girlhood she would return with yearning to this movie, recognizing it at once despite the variety of its titles, its many actors. For always there was the Fair Princess. And always the Dark Prince. A complication of events brought them together and tore them apart and brought them together again and again tore them apart until, as the movie neared its end and the movie music soared, they were about to be brought together in a fierce embrace.

Yet not always happily. You couldn't predict. For sometimes one knelt beside the deathbed of the other and heralded death with a kiss. Even if he (or she) survived the death of the beloved, you knew the meaning of life was over.

For there is no meaning to life apart from the movie story.

And there is no movie story apart from the darkened movie theater.

But how vexing, never to see the end of the movie!

For always something went wrong: there was a commotion in the theater and the lights came up; a fire alarm (but no fire? or was there a fire? once, she was sure she smelled smoke) sounded loudly and everyone was asked to leave, or she was herself late for an appointment and had to leave, or maybe she fell asleep in her seat and missed the ending and woke dazed as the lights came up and strangers around her rose to leave.

Over, it's over? But how can it be over?

Yet as an adult woman she continued to seek out the movie. Slipping into theaters in obscure districts of the city or in cities unknown to her. Insomniac, she might buy a ticket for a midnight show. She might buy a ticket for the first show of the day, in the late morning. She wasn't fleeing her own life (though her life had grown baffling to her, as adult life does to those who live it) but instead easing into a parenthesis within that life, stopping time as a child might arrest the movement of a clock's hands: by force. Entering the darkened theater (which sometimes smelled of stale popcorn, the hair lotion of strangers, disinfectant), excited as a young girl looking up eagerly to see on the screen yet again *Oh, another time! one more time!* the beautiful blond woman who seems never to age, encased in flesh like any woman and yet graceful as no ordinary woman could be, a powerful radiance shining not only in her luminous eyes but in her very skin. *For my skin is my soul. There is no soul otherwise. You see in me the promise of human joy.* She who slips into the theater, choosing a seat in a row near the screen, gives herself unquestioningly up to the movie that's both familiar and unfamiliar as a recurring dream imperfectly recalled. The costumes of the actors, the hairstyles, even the faces and voices of the movie people change with the years, and she can remember, not clearly but in fragments, her own lost emotions, the loneliness of her childhood only partly assuaged by the looming screen. *Another world to live in. Where?* There was a day, an hour, when she realized that the Fair Princess, who is so beautiful because she is so beautiful and because she is the Fair Princess, is doomed to seek, in others' eyes, confirmation of her own being. *For we are not who we are told we are, if we are not told. Are we?*

Adult unease and gathering terror.

The movie story is complicated and confusing, though familiar or almost familiar. Perhaps it's carelessly spliced together. Perhaps it's meant to tease. Perhaps there are flashbacks amid present time. Or flash-forwards! Close-ups of the Fair Princess seem too intimate. We want to stay on the outsides of others, not be drawn inside. *If I could say, There! that's me! That woman, that thing on the screen, that's who I am.* But she can't see ahead to the ending. Never has she seen the final scene, never the concluding credits rolling past. In these, beyond the final movie kiss, is the key to the movie's mystery, she knows. As the body's organs, removed in an autopsy, are the key to the life's mystery.

But there will be a time maybe this very evening when, slightly out of breath, she settles into a worn, soiled plush seat in the second row of an old theater in a derelict district of the city, the floor curving beneath her feet like the earth's curve and sticky against the soles of her expensive shoes; and the audience is scattered, mostly solitary individuals; and she's relieved that, in her disguise (dark glasses, an attractive wig, a raincoat) no one will recognize her and no one from her life knows she's here, or could guess where she might be. *This time I will see it through to the end. This time!* Why? She has no idea. And in fact she's expected elsewhere, she's hours late, possibly a car was scheduled to take her to the airport, unless she's days late, weeks late; for she's become, as an adult, defiant of time. *For what is time but others' expectations of us? That game we can refuse to play.* So too, she's noticed, the Fair Princess is confused by time. Confused by the movie story. You take your cues from other people. What if other people don't provide cues? In this movie the Fair Princess is no longer in the first bloom of her youthful beauty, yet of course she's still beautiful, white-skinned and radiant on the screen as she climbs out of a taxi on a windswept street; she's in disguise in dark glasses, a sleek brown wig, and a tightly belted raincoat, closely tracked by the camera as she slips into a movie theater and purchases a single ticket, enters the darkened theater, and takes a seat in the second row. Because she's the Fair Princess, other patrons glance at her but don't recognize her; perhaps she's an ordinary woman, though beautiful, no one they know. The movie has begun. She gives herself up to it within seconds, removing her dark glasses. Her head is forced back by the angle of the screen looming over her, and her eyes are cast upward in an expression of childlike, slightly apprehensive awe. Like reflections in water, the movie light ripples across her face. Lost in wonderment she's unaware of the Dark Prince having followed her into the theater; the camera broods upon him as, for several tense minutes, he stands behind frayed velvet drapes at a side aisle. His handsome face is veiled in shadow. His expression is urgent. He is wearing a dark suit, no necktie, a fedora hat slanted over his forehead. At a music cue he comes quickly forward to lean over her, the solitary woman in the second row. He whispers to her and she turns, startled. Her surprise seems genuine though she must know the script: the script to this point, at least, and a little beyond.

My love! It's you.

Never has it been anyone except you.

In the reflected shimmering light from the gigantic screen the faces of the lovers are charged with meaning, heralds from a lost age of grandeur. As if, though diminished and mortal, they must play out the scene. *They will play out the scene.* Boldly he grips her by the nape of her neck to steady her. To claim her. To possess her. How strong his fingers, and icy; how strange, the glassy glisten of his eyes, closer than she's ever seen them before.

Yet another time, she sighs and lifts her perfect face to the Dark Prince's kiss.

THE BATH

It is in early childhood that the born actor emerges,
for it is in early childhood that the world is first
perceived as Mystery. The origin of all acting is
improvisation in the face of Mystery.

—T. Navarro,
The Paradox of Acting

I

"See? That man is your father."

There was a day, it was Norma Jeane's sixth birthday, the first day of June
1932, and a magical morning it was, blinding breathless whitely dazzling, in
Venice Beach, California. The wind off the Pacific Ocean fresh and cool and
astringent, smelling only faintly of the usual briny rot and beach debris. And
borne, it seemed, by that very wind came Mother. Gaunt-faced Mother with
her luscious red lips and plucked and penciled brows who came for Norma
Jeane where she was living with her grandparents in a pockmarked old ruin
of a beige stucco building on Venice Boulevard—"Norma Jeane, come!"
And Norma Jeane ran, ran to Mother! Her pudgy little hand caught in
Mother's slender hand, that feel of the black-net glove strange to her and
wonderful. For Grandma's hands were chafed old-woman's hands, as
Grandma's smell was an old-woman smell, but Mother's smell was so sweet
it made you dizzy, like a taste of hot sugary lemon. "Norma Jeane, my love—
come." For Mother was "Gladys," and "Gladys" was the child's *true
mother.* When she chose to be. When she was strong enough. When the
demands of The Studio allowed. For Gladys's life was "three dimensions

verging into four" and not "flat as a Parcheesi board" like most lives. And in the face of Grandma Della's flustered disapproval, Mother led Norma Jeane in triumph out of the third-floor apartment reeking with onions, lye soap, and bunion ointment, and Grandpa's pipe tobacco, ignoring the older woman's outrage like a frantic-comic radio voice—"Gladys, whose car are you driving this time?"—"Look at me, girl: Are you hopped up? Are you *drunk*?"—"When will you be bringing my granddaughter back?"—"Damn you, wait for me, wait till I get my shoes on, I'm coming downstairs too! *Gladys*!" And Mother called out in her calmly maddening soprano voice, " '*Qué sera, sera.*' " And giggling like naughty pursued children, Mother and Daughter hurried down flights of stairs as down a mountainside, breathless and gripping hands, and so out! outside! to Venice Boulevard and the excitement of Gladys's car, never a predictable car, parked at the curb; and on this bright-dazzling morning of the first of June 1932 the magical car was, as Norma Jeane stared, smiling, a humpbacked Nash the hue of dishwater when the soap has gone flat, the passenger's window cracked like a spiderweb and mended with tape. Yet what a wonderful car, and how young and excited Gladys was, she who rarely touched Norma Jeane now lifting her with both net-gloved hands into the passenger's seat—"Whoops, baby-love!"—as if lifting her into the seat of the Ferris wheel at Santa Monica pier to bear her, wide-eyed and thrilled, into the sky. And slammed the door beside her, hard. And made certain it was locked. (For there was an old fear, a fear of Mother for Daughter, that during such flights, a car door might open, as a trapdoor might open in a silent film, and Daughter would be lost!) And climbing into the driver's seat behind the wheel like Lindbergh into the cockpit of the *Spirit of St. Louis*. And revved the motor, and shifted gears, and pulled out into traffic even as poor Grandma Della, a mottled-faced fattish woman in a faded cotton housecoat and rolled cotton "support" stockings and old-woman shoes, burst out onto the front stoop of the building like Charlie Chaplin the Little Tramp in frantic-comic distress.

"Wait! Oh, you wait! Crazy woman! Hophead! I forbid you! I'll call the *po*-lice!"

But there was no waiting, oh, no.

Hardly time to breathe!

"Ignore your grandmother, dear. She is silent film and we are talkies."

For Gladys, who was this child's *true mother*, would not be cheated of Mother Love on this special day. Feeling "stronger, at last" and with a few bucks saved, so Gladys had come for Norma Jeane on the child's birthday (her sixth? already? oh, Jesus, depressing) as she'd vowed she would. "Rain or shine, sickness or health, till death do us part. I vow." Not even a seizure of the San Andreas Fault could dissuade Gladys in such a mood. "You're mine. You look like me. No one is going to steal you from me, Norma Jeane, like my other daughters."

These triumphant, terrible words Norma Jeane did not hear, did not hear, did not, blown away by the rushing wind.

This day, this birthday, would be the first that Norma Jeane would remember clearly. This wonderful day with Gladys who was sometimes Mother, or Mother who was sometimes Gladys. A slender darting bird of a woman with sharp prowling eyes and a self-described "raptor's smile" and elbows that jabbed you in the ribs if you got too close. Exhaling luminous smoke from her nostrils like curving elephant tusks so you dared not call her by any name, above all not "Mama" or "Mommy"—those "pukey-cute titles" that Gladys had long ago forbidden—or even look at her too intensely—"Don't squint at me, you! No close-ups. Unless I'm prepared." At such times Gladys's edgy brittle laugh was the sound an ice pick makes stabbing into blocks of ice. This day of revelation Norma Jeane would recall through her life of thirty-six years, sixty-three days, which was to be a life outlived by Gladys as a doll baby might be fitted snug inside a larger doll ingeniously hollowed out for that purpose. *Did I want any other happiness? No, just to be with her. Maybe to cuddle a little and sleep in her bed with her if she'd let me. I loved her so.* In fact, there was evidence that Norma Jeane had been with her mother on other birthdays of hers, at least Norma Jeane's first birthday, though Norma Jeane could not recall except by way of snapshots— HAPPY 1ST BIRTHDAY BABY NORMA JEANE!—a hand-lettered paper banner draped like a bathing beauty's sash around the blinking damp-eyed infant with the chubby-cute moon face, dimpled cheeks, curly dark-blond hair, and satin ribbons drooping in the hair; like old dreams these snapshots were blurred and creased, taken evidently by a man friend; there was a very young very pretty though feverish-looking Gladys in bobbed hair, kiss curls, and bee-stung lips like Clara Bow gripping her twelve-month infant "Norma Jeane" stiff on her lap as you might grip an object breakable and precious, with awe if not with visible pleasure, with steely pride if not with love, the date scrawled on the backs of these several snapshots June 1, 1927. But six-year-old Norma Jeane possessed no more memory of that occasion than she had of being born—wanting to ask Gladys or Grandma, How do you *be* born, was that something you did yourself?—to her mother in a charity lying-in ward at the Los Angeles County General Hospital after twenty-two hours of "unremitting hell" (as Gladys spoke of the ordeal) or carried in Gladys's "special pouch" beneath her heart for eight months, eleven days. She could not remember! Yet, thrilled to be staring at these snapshots whenever Gladys was in a mood to display them tumbled across whatever bedspread atop whatever bed of Gladys's in whatever rental "residence," she never doubted that the infant in the snapshot was her *as all through my life I would know of myself through the witnessing and naming of others. As Jesus in the Gospels is only seen and spoken of and recorded by others. I would know my existence and the value of that existence through others' eyes, which I believed I could trust as I could not trust my own.*

Gladys was glancing at her daughter, whom she hadn't seen in—well, months. Saying sharply, "Don't be so nervous. Don't squint as if I'm going to crash this car in the next minute, you'll make yourself need glasses and that's the end for you. And try not to squirm like a little snake needing to pee. *I* never taught you such bad habits. *I* don't intend to crash this car, if that's what you're worried about, like your ridiculous old grandma. *I promise.*" Gladys cast a sidelong glance at the child, chiding yet seductive, for that was Gladys's way: she pushed you off, she drew you in; now saying in a husky lowered voice, "Say: Mo-ther has a birthday surprise for you. Waiting up ahead."

"A s-surprise?"

Gladys sucked in her cheeks, smiling as she drove.

"W-where are we going, M-mother?"

Happiness so acute it was broken glass in Norma Jeane's mouth.

Even in warm humid weather, Gladys wore stylish black-net gloves to protect her sensitive skin. Gaily she thumped both gloved hands against the steering wheel. "Where are we going? Listen to you. As if you've never been in your mother's Hollywood residence before."

Norma Jeane smiled in confusion. Trying to think. Had she? The implication seemed to be that Norma Jeane had forgotten something essential, that this was a betrayal of a kind, a disappointment. Yet it seemed Gladys moved frequently. Sometimes she informed Della and sometimes not. Her life was complicated and mysterious. There were problems with landlords and fellow tenants; there were "money" problems and "maintenance" problems. The previous winter, a brief violent earthquake in an area of Hollywood in which Gladys lived had left her homeless for two weeks, forced to live with friends and out of touch completely with Della. Always, however, Gladys lived in Hollywood. Or West Hollywood. Her work at The Studio demanded it. Because she was a "contract employee" at The Studio (The Studio was the largest movie production company in Hollywood, therefore in the world, boasting more stars under contract "than there are stars in the constellations"), her life didn't belong to *her*— "The way Catholic nuns are 'brides of Christ.' " Gladys had had to *board out* her daughter since Norma Jeane was an infant of only twelve days, mostly with the child's grandmother, for five dollars a week plus expenses, it was a damned hard life, it was grueling, it was *sad*, but what choice had she, working such long hours at The

Studio, sometimes a double shift, at her boss's "beckon-call"—how could she possibly take on the care and burden of a young child?

"I dare anyone to judge me. Unless he's in my shoes. Or *she*. Yes, *she*!"

Gladys spoke with mysterious vehemence. It may have been her own mother, Della, with whom she was feuding.

When they quarreled, Della spoke of Gladys as a "hot-head"—or was it "hop-head"?—and Gladys protested this was a downright lie, a slander; why, she'd never even smelled marijuana being smoked, let alone smoked it herself—"And that goes double for opium. Never!" Della had heard too many wild and unsubstantiated tales of movie people. True, Gladys sometimes got excited. *Fire burning inside me! Beautiful.* True, at other times she was susceptible to "the blues," "down in the dumps," "the pit." *Like my soul is molten lead, leaked out and hardened.* Still, Gladys was a good-looking young woman, and Gladys had lots of friends. Men friends. Who complicated her emotional life. "If the fellows would let me alone, 'Gladys' would be fine." But they didn't, so Gladys had to medicate herself regularly. Prescription drugs or maybe drugs provided by the fellows. Admittedly she lived on Bayer aspirin and had developed a high tolerance for it, dissolving pills in black coffee like tiny sugar cubes—"Can't taste a thing!"

This morning, Norma Jeane saw at once that Gladys was in an "up" mood: distracted, flamey, funny, unpredictable as a candle flame flickering in agitated air. Her waxy-pale skin gave off waves of heat like pavement in summer sun and her eyes!—flirty, slip-sliding and dilated. *Those eyes I loved. Couldn't bear to look at.* Gladys was driving distractedly, and fast. In a car with Gladys was like being in a bumper car at the carnival, you hung on tight. They were driving inland, away from Venice Beach and the ocean. North on the Boulevard to La Cienega, and at last to Sunset Boulevard, which Norma Jeane recognized from other drives with her mother. How the humpbacked Nash rattled as it sped along, prodded by Gladys's restless foot on the gas pedal. They clattered over trolley tracks, braked at the last second for red lights, causing Norma Jeane's teeth to rattle even as she giggled nervously. Sometimes, Gladys's car skidded into the midst of an intersection like a movie scene of honking horns, shouts, and fists waved by other drivers; unless the drivers were men, alone in their automobiles, when the signals were friendlier. More than once, Gladys ignored a traffic policeman's whistle and escaped—"See, I didn't do anything wrong! I refuse to be intimidated by bullies."

Della liked to complain in her jokey-angry way that Gladys had "lost" her driver's license, which meant—what? She'd lost it, the way people lost things? Misplaced it? Or had one of the policemen taken it from her, to punish her, when Norma Jeane hadn't been around?

One thing Norma Jeane knew: She didn't dare ask Gladys.

Off Sunset they turned onto a side street, and then another, and finally onto La Mesa, a narrow, disappointing street of small businesses, diners, "cocktail" lounges, and apartment buildings; Gladys said this was her "new neighborhood I'm only just discovering, and feeling so *welcome in*." Gladys explained that The Studio was "only a six-minute drive away." There were "personal reasons" she was living here, too complicated to explain. But Norma Jeane would see—"It's part of your surprise." Gladys parked the car in front of a cheap Spanish-style stucco building with decaying green awnings and disfiguring fire escapes. THE HACIENDA. ROOMS & EFFICENCY APTS WEEKLY MONTHLY RENTAL INQUIRE WITHIN. The street number was 387. Norma Jeane stared, memorizing what she saw; she was a camera taking snapshots; one day she might be lost and have to find her way back to this place she'd never seen before until this moment, but with Gladys such moments were urgent, highly charged and mysterious, to make your pulse beat hard as with a drug. *Like amphetamine it was, that charge. As through my life I would seek it. Making my way like a sleepwalker out of my life back to La Mesa to the Hacienda as to the place on Highland Avenue where I was a child again, in her charge again, under her spell again, and the nightmare had not yet happened.*

Gladys saw the look on Norma Jeane's face that Norma Jeane herself could not see, and laughed. "Birthday girl! You're only six once. You might not even live to be seven, silly. Let's *go*."

Norma Jeane's hand was sweaty so Gladys declined to take it, instead prodding the child to move with her gloved fist, lightly, of course, playfully directing her up the slightly crumbling outside steps of the Hacienda and inside into an oven-hot interior, a flight of gritty linoleum-covered stairs— "There's someone waiting for us, and I'm afraid he may be getting impatient. Come *on*." They hurried. They ran. Galloping upward. Gladys in her glamorous high heels, suddenly panicked—or was she playing at being panicked? was this one of her *scenes*? Upstairs, both mother and daughter were panting. Gladys unlocked the door of her "residence," which turned out to be not very different from the former residence Norma Jeane vaguely recalled. There were three cramped rooms with stained wallpaper and stained ceilings, narrow windows, sheets of loose linoleum on bare floorboards, a couple of Mexican rag rugs, a leaky-smelly icebox and a double-burner hot plate and dishes in the sink and shiny black roaches like watermelon seeds scuttling away noisily at their approach. Tacked to the kitchen walls were posters of films with which Gladys had been involved and of which she was proud— *Kiki* with Mary Pickford, *All Quiet on the Western Front* with Lew Ayres, *City Lights* with Charlie Chaplin, at whose soulful eyes Norma Jeane could

stare and stare, convinced Chaplin was seeing *her*. It wasn't clear what
Gladys had had to do with these famous films, but Norma Jeane was mesmerized by the actors' faces. *This is home! This place I remember.* Familiar,
too, was the airless heat of the apartment, for Gladys didn't believe in leaving windows open even a crack while she was away, the pungent odor of
food smells, coffee grounds, cigarette ashes, scorch, perfume, and that mysterious acrid chemical odor Gladys could never entirely wash away even if
she scrubbed, scrubbed, scrubbed at her hands with medicinal soap and
made them raw and bleeding. Yet these smells were comforting to Norma
Jeane *for they meant home. Where Mother was.*

But this new apartment! It was more crowded and disordered and strange
to her than the others. Or was Norma Jeane older now, and able better to
see? As soon as you stepped inside there was that suspended terrible moment
between the first tremor of the earth and the next more powerful tremor that
would be unmistakable and undeniable. You waited, not daring to breathe.
Here were many opened but unpacked boxes stamped PROPERTY OF STUDIO.
There were piles of clothes on the kitchen counter and clothes on wire hangers on a makeshift clothesline stretching across the kitchen, so it looked at
first as if there were people crowded into the kitchen, women in "costumes"—Norma Jeane knew what "costumes" were, that they differed from
"clothes," though she could not have explained the distinction. Some of these
costumes were glitzy and glamorous, flimsy "flapper" dresses with tiny skirts
and string straps. Some were more somber, with long trailing sleeves. There
were panties and bras and stockings washed and neatly placed over the
clothesline to dry. Gladys was watching Norma Jeane, as she stared open-
mouthed at these clothes dangling overhead, and laughed at the child's confused expression. "What's wrong? Do you disapprove? Does Della? Has she
sent you to *spy*? Go on—in here. Through here. *Go on.*"

She prodded Norma Jeane with her sharp elbow into the next room, a bedroom. It was small, with a badly water-stained ceiling and walls, and a single window, and a partly drawn, cracked, and stained shade over the
window. And there was the familiar bed with its gleaming if slightly tar-
nished brass headboard and goose-down pillows, a pine bureau, a bedside
table piled with pill bottles, magazines, and paperback books, an overflowing ashtray perched atop a copy of *Hollywood Tatler*; more clothes strewn
about, and on the floor more opened but unpacked boxes; and a large gar-
ish movie still of *The Hollywood Revue* of 1929 with Marie Dressler in a
diaphanous white gown on a wall beside the bed. Gladys was excited, breathing quickly and watching as Norma Jeane glanced anxiously around—for
where was the "surprise" person? Hiding? Beneath the bed? Inside a closet?
(But there wasn't a closet, just a beaverboard wardrobe leaning against a

wall.) A lone fly buzzed. Through the room's single window there was visible only the blank smudged wall of the adjacent building. Norma Jeane was wondering *Where? Who is it?* even as Gladys nudged her lightly between the shoulder blades, chiding, "Norma Jeane, I swear you're half blind sometimes as well as—well, half *dumb.* Can't you *see?* Open your eyes and *see?* That man is your father."

Now Norma Jeane saw where Gladys was pointing.

It was not a man. It was a picture of a man, hanging on the wall beside the bureau mirror.

2

On my sixth birthday seeing his face for the first time.

And not having known before that day—I had a father! A father like other children.

Always thinking the absence had to do with me. Something wrong, something bad, in me.

Had no one told me before? Not my mother, not my grandmother or grandfather. No one.

Yet never to look upon his actual face, in life. And I would die before him.

3

"*Isn't* he handsome, Norma Jeane? Your father."

Gladys's voice, which was sometimes flat, toneless, subtly mocking, was thrilled as a girl's.

Norma Jeane stared speechless at the man said to be her father. The man in the photograph. The man on the wall beside the bureau mirror. *Father?* Her body was hot and tremulous as a cut thumb.

"Here. But, no—mustn't touch with sticky fingers."

With a flourish, Gladys removed the framed photo from the wall. It was a real photo, Norma Jeane could see, glossy, not something printed like publicity posters or a page torn from a magazine.

Gladys cradled the photo in her glamorously gloved hands, at about Norma Jeane's eye level yet far enough from the child that she couldn't have touched it without effort. As if at such a time Norma Jeane would have wished to touch this!—knowing from past experience, too, not to touch Gladys's special things.

"He—he's my f-father?"

"He certainly *is*. You have his sexy blue eyes."

"But—where is—"

"Shh! *Look*."

It was a movie scene. Almost, Norma Jeane could hear the excited skittering music.

How long, then, mother and daughter stared! In reverent silence contemplating the man-in-the-picture-frame, the man-in-the-photograph, the man-who-was-Norma-Jeane's-father, the man who was darkly handsome, the man with sleek oiled wings of smooth thick hair, the man with a pencil-thin mustache on his upper lip, the man with pale shrewd just-perceptibly drooping eyelids. The man with fleshy almost-smiling lips, the man whose gaze coyly refused to lock with theirs, the man with a fist of a chin and a proud hawk nose and an indentation in his left cheek that might have been a dimple, like Norma Jeane's. Or a scar.

He was older than Gladys, but not much. In his mid-thirties. He had an actor's face, a certain posed assurance. He wore a fedora tilted at a jaunty angle on his proudly held head, and he wore a white shirt with a soft flaring collar, like a movie costume from some other time. The man who seemed to Norma Jeane about to speak—yet didn't. *Listening so hard. It was like I'd gone deaf.*

Norma Jeane's heartbeat was so fluttery, a hummingbird's wings. And noisy, filling the room. But Gladys didn't notice and didn't scold. In her exaltation staring greedily at the man-in-the-photograph. Saying, in a voice rushing and ecstatic as a singer's, "*Your* father. His name is a beautiful name and an important name but it's a name I can't utter. Not even Della knows. Della may think she knows—but she doesn't. *And Della must not know.* Not even that you've seen this. There are complications in both our lives, you see. When you were born, your father was away; he's at a great distance even now, and I worry for his safety. He's a man of wanderlust who in another era would have been a warrior. In fact, he has risked his life in the cause of democracy. In our hearts, he and I are wed—we are husband and wife. Though we scorn convention and would not wish to acquiesce to it. 'I love you and our daughter and one day I will return to Los Angeles to claim you'—so your father has promised, Norma Jeane. Promised us both." Gladys paused, wetting her lips.

Though she was speaking to Norma Jeane she seemed scarcely aware of the child, staring at the photograph from which, it almost seemed, a splintery light was reflected. Her skin was clammy-hot and her lips appeared swollen, as if bruised, beneath bright red lipstick; her net-gloved hands trembled slightly. Norma Jeane would recall trying to concentrate on her mother's words despite a roaring in her ears and a sick, excited sensation deep in her belly, as if she had to go to the bathroom badly but dared not speak or even move. "Your father was under contract to The Studio when we first met—eight years ago on the day following Palm Sunday; I will always remember!—and he was one of the most promising young actors but—well, for all his natural talent and his screen presence—a 'second Valentino' Mr. Thalberg himself called him—he was too undisciplined, too impatient and devil-may-care to be a film actor. It isn't just looks, style, and personality, Norma Jeane, you must be obedient too. You must be humble. You must swallow your pride and work like a dog. It comes more easily for a woman. *I* was under contract too—for a while. As a young actress. I transferred to another department—voluntarily! For I saw that it was not to be. *He* was rebellious, of course. He was a stand-in for Chester Morris and Donald Reed for a while. Eventually he walked away. 'Between my soul and my career I choose—my soul,' he said."

In her excitement Gladys began to cough. Coughing, she seemed to give off a stronger scent of perfume, mingled with that faint sour-lemon chemical odor that seemed absorbed in her skin.

Norma Jeane asked where her father was.

Gladys said irritably, "Away, silly. *I told you.*"

Gladys's mood had shifted. It was often this way. The movie music, too, shifted abruptly. It was saw-notched now, as were the rough, hurtful waves thrown onto the beach, where Della, short of breath from "blood pressure" and scolding, walked with Norma Jeane on the hard-packed sand for the sake of "exercise."

Never would I have asked why. Why I hadn't been told until then.

Why I was being told now.

Gladys rehung the photo on the wall. But now the nail sunk into the plasterboard wasn't so secure as it had been. The lone fly continued to buzz, striking itself repeatedly and yet hopefully against a windowpane. "There's the damn fly 'buzzed when I died,' " Gladys remarked mysteriously. It was Gladys's way often to speak mysteriously in Norma Jeane's presence, though not necessarily to Norma Jeane. Rather, Norma Jeane was a witness, a privileged observer like the eye of the movie watcher of which the principals, in the movie, pretend to be unaware—or are in fact unaware. When the nail was in, and seemed not about to fall out, it took some fussing to ascertain that the frame was straight. In such household matters Gladys was a perfectionist, scolding Norma Jeane if the child left towels hanging crooked or books unevenly aligned on shelves. When the man-in-the-photograph was safely back up on the wall beside the bureau mirror, Gladys stepped back, relaxing just a little. Norma Jeane continued to stare up at the photo, transfixed. "So, your father. But it's our secret, Norma Jeane. Enough for you to know that he's away—for now. But he'll return to Los Angeles one day soon. *He has promised.*"

4

It would be said of me that I was unhappy as a child, that my childhood was a desperate one, but let me tell you I was never unhappy. So long as I had my mother I was never unhappy and one day there was my father, too, to love.

And there was Grandma Della! Norma Jeane's mother's *mother.*

A sturdy olive-skinned woman with eyebrows thick as brushes and a sly glimmering of a mustache on her upper lip. Della had a way of standing in a doorway or on the front stoop of her building, hands on her hips like a double-handled jug. Shopkeepers feared her sharp eye and sarcastic tongue. She was a fan of William S. Hart, the straight-shooter cowboy, and she was a fan of Charlie Chaplin, the genius of mimicry, and she boasted of being of "good American pioneer stock," born in Kansas, moved to Nevada, then to southern California and met and married her husband, who was Gladys's father, gassed, as Della said reproachfully, in the Argonne in 1918—"At least, he's alive. That's something to be grateful for to the U.S. government, eh?"

Yes, there was a Grandpa Monroe, Della's husband. He lived with them in the apartment and Norma Jeane was given to know he didn't like her, but somehow Grandpa wasn't *there.* When asked about him, Della's response was a shrug and the comment, "At least, he's alive."

Grandma Della! A neighborhood "character."

Grandma Della was the source of all Norma Jeane knew, or imagined she knew, of Gladys.

The primary fact of Gladys was the primary mystery of Gladys: She could not be a *true mother* to Norma Jeane. Not at the *present time.*

Why not?

"Just don't blame me, any of you," Gladys said, agitatedly lighting a cigarette. "God has punished me enough."

Punished? How?

If Norma Jeane dared to ask such a question, Gladys would blink at her with beautiful slate-blue bloodshot eyes, in which a scrim of moisture continually shone. "Just don't *you.* After what God has done. Understand?"

Norma Jeane smiled. Smiling meant not that you understood but you were happy not-understanding.

Though: it seemed to be known that Gladys had had "other little girls"—

"two little girls"—before Norma Jeane. But where had these sisters disappeared to?

"Just don't blame me, any of you, *God damn you*."

It seemed to be a fact that Gladys, though very young-looking at thirty-one, had already been the wife of two husbands.

It *was* a fact, which Gladys herself cheerfully acknowledged, in the way of a movie character with a comical habit or tic, that her last name was often changing.

Della told the story, it was one of Della's aggrieved-mother stories, of how Gladys had been born and baptized Gladys Pearl Monroe in Hawthorne, Los Angeles County, in 1902. At seventeen she'd married (against Della's wishes) a man named Baker so she'd become Mrs. Gladys Baker, but (of course!) that hadn't worked out for even a year and they'd divorced and she'd married the "meterman, Mortensen" (the father of the two vanished older sisters?), but that hadn't worked out (of course!) and Mortensen was gone from Gladys's life, and good riddance. Except: Gladys's name was still Mortensen on certain documents she hadn't changed, and would not change, since anything to do with records, legal matters, frightened her. Mortensen was not Norma Jeane's father, of course, but Mortensen had been Gladys's name at the time of Norma Jeane's birth. Yet—and this was a fact that infuriated Della, it was so perverse—Norma Jeane's last name was officially Baker, not Mortensen.

"Know why?" Della might inquire of the neighborhood, of whomever might be listening to such folly. "Because Baker was the one my crazy daughter 'hated less.' " Della went on, working herself up into genuine upset. "*I* lie awake nights grieving for this poor child, all mixed up who she's supposed to be. *I* should adopt the child and give her my own name that's a good decent uncontaminated name—'Monroe.' "

"Nobody is adopting my little girl," Gladys said vehemently, "while I'm alive to prevent it."

Alive. Norma Jeane knew how important it was, to remain *alive*.

So it happened that Norma Jeane Baker was Norma Jeane's legal name. At the age of seven months she'd been baptized by the renowned evangelist preacher Aimee Semple McPherson in her Angelus Temple of the International Church of the Foursquare Gospel (to which, at the time, Della belonged), and this would remain her name until such time as her name would be changed by a man, a man acquiring Norma Jeane as his "wife," as eventually her full name would be changed by a decision of men. *I did what was required. What was required of me was that I remain alive*.

In a rare moment of maternal intimacy, Gladys informed Norma Jeane that her name was a special name: " 'Norma' is for the great Norma

Talmadge, and 'Jeane' is—who else?—Harlow." These names meant nothing to the child, but she saw how Gladys shivered at their very sound. "You, Norma Jeane, will combine the two, d'you see? In your own special destiny."

5

"So, Norma Jeane! Now you know."

It was wisdom blinding as the sun. Profound as the back of a whipping hand. Gladys's red-lipsticked mouth, which so rarely smiled, smiled now. Her breath came short as if she'd been running.

"You've looked upon *his face*. Your true father, who isn't named Baker. But you must never tell anyone, d'you hear? Not even Della."

"Y-yes, Mother."

Between Gladys's fine-penciled brows the sharp crease appeared.

"Norma Jeane, *what*?"

"Yes, Mother."

"*That's* more like it!"

The stammer was still inside Norma Jeane. But it had shifted from her tongue to her hummingbird heart, where it would be undetected.

In the kitchen Gladys removed one of her glamorous black-net gloves, and this she drew against Norma Jeane's neck, as a tickling caress.

That day! A haze of happiness like warm damp fog drifting over the flatlands of the city. Happiness in every breath. Gladys murmured, "Happy birthday, Norma Jeane!" and, "Didn't I tell you, Norma Jeane, this is your *special day*?"

The telephone rang. But Gladys, smiling to herself, didn't answer.

The blinds at the windows were carefully drawn to the sills. Gladys spoke of "inquisitive" neighbors.

Gladys had removed her left glove but not the right. She seemed to have forgotten her right glove. Norma Jeane noted how the slightly reddened skin of her bare left hand was stippled with small diamond shapes imprinted from the tight-fitting net glove. Gladys wore a maroon crepe dress with a tightly cinched waist, a high collar, and a full skirt that made a breathless swishing sound when she moved. It was a dress Norma Jeane had not seen before.

Each moment invested with such significance. Each moment, like each heartbeat, a warning signal.

At the table in the kitchen alcove, Gladys poured grape juice for Norma Jeane and a strong-smelling "medicated water" for herself into chipped coffee cups. The surprise was an angel-food birthday cake for Norma Jeane!

Whipped vanilla icing, six little pink wax candles, syrupy crimson frosting that spelled out—

HAPPY BIRTDAY
NORMAJEAN

The sight of the cake, its wonderful smell, made Norma Jeane's mouth water. Though Gladys was fuming. "The hophead bastard of a baker, spelling 'birthday' wrong, and your name—*I told him.*"

With a little difficulty, her hands shaking, though maybe the room was vibrating, or the earth strata far beneath (in California you never know what is "real" or what is "just yourself"), Gladys managed to light the six little candles. It was Norma Jeane's task to blow out the pale, nervously flickering flames. "And now you must make a wish, Norma Jeane," Gladys said eagerly, leaning forward so that she nearly touched the child's warm face. "A wish for you-know-who to return to us soon. Come on!" So Norma Jeane, shutting her eyes, made this wish and blew out all but one of the little candles in a single breath. Gladys blew out the remaining candle. "There you are. Good as a prayer." It took awhile for Gladys to locate an adequate knife with which to cut the cake, rummaging through a drawer; finally she found a "butcher knife—don't be scared!" and the blade of this long sharply glinting knife shone like sunshine on the surf at Venice Beach, hurting the eyes, yet you couldn't not look, but Gladys did nothing with the knife except to sink it into the cake, frowning in concentration, steadying her gloved right hand with her gloveless left hand as she cut large pieces of cake for each of them; the cake was slightly damp and sticky at the center, and the pieces spilled over the edges of the saucers Gladys was using as plates. *So good! That cake tasted so good. Let me tell you there was never a cake in my life that tasted so good.* Mother and daughter both ate hungrily; for each this was breakfast, and already the day had careened beyond noon.

"And now, Norma Jeane: your presents."

Another time the telephone began to ring. And Gladys, brightly smiling, didn't seem to hear. She was explaining that she hadn't had time to wrap Norma Jeane's presents properly. The first was a pretty pink crotcheted sweater in light cotton wool, tiny embroidered rosebuds for buttons, a sweater for a younger child maybe since it was tight on Norma Jeane who was small for her age, but Gladys, exclaiming over the sweater, didn't seem to notice— "Isn't that charming! You're a little princess." Next were smaller items of clothing, white cotton socks, underwear (price tags from the dime store still attached). It had been many months since Gladys had provided her daughter with such necessities; also, Gladys was several weeks behind on payments to Della, so Norma Jeane was excited to think that Della would be pleased about this. Norma Jeane thanked her mother, and Gladys said, with a snap of her fingers, "Oh, this is just preliminary. *Come.*" With a dramatic flair Gladys led Norma Jeane back into the bedroom, where the handsome man-in-the-photograph hung prominently on the wall, and teasingly tugged open the top bureau drawer—"Presto, Norma Jeane! Something for *you.*"

A doll?

Norma Jeane stood on tiptoe, eagerly, clumsily lifting out a doll, a golden-haired doll, a doll with round blue glass eyes and a rosebud mouth, as Gladys said, "D'you remember, Norma Jeane, who used to sleep in here—in this drawer?" Norma Jeane shook her head, no. "Not in this apartment but in this drawer. *This* very drawer. Don't you remember who used to sleep in here?" Again, Norma Jeane shook her head. She was becoming uneasy. Gladys stared at her so, with widened eyes as if in mimicry of the doll, except Gladys's eyes were a pale washed-out blue and her lips were bright red. Gladys said, laughing, "*You. You*, Norma Jeane. *You* used to sleep in this very drawer! I was so poor then I couldn't afford a crib. But this drawer was your crib when you were a tiny infant; it was good enough for us, *wasn't it?*" There was a shrill edge to Gladys's voice. If there was music in this scene it would be a quick staccato music. Norma Jeane shook her head, no, a sullen look settled over her face, her eyes clouded with not-remembering, will-not-remember, as she didn't remember wearing diapers or how hard it had been for Della and Gladys to "potty-train" her. If she'd had time to examine the topmost drawer in the pine bureau *and the way the drawer could be shoved shut* she would have felt sickish, that sickish-scared sensation in her belly she felt at the top of a flight of stairs or looking out a high window or running too close to the edge of the surf when a tall wave broke, for how could she, a big girl of six, have ever fitted into so small a space?—and *had someone shoved the drawer shut, to muffle her crying?*—but Norma Jeane hadn't time to think such thoughts for here was her birthday doll in her arms, the most beautiful doll she'd ever seen close up, as beautiful as Sleeping Beauty in a picture book, wavy golden hair to her shoulders, silky-soft as real hair, more beautiful than Norma Jeane's wavy fair-brown hair and wholly unlike the synthetic hair of most dolls. The doll wore a little lace nightcap and a flannel nightgown in a floral print, and her skin was rubbery-smooth, soft, perfect skin, and her tiny fingers were perfectly shaped! And the small feet in white cotton booties tied with pink ribbons! Norma Jeane squealed with excitement and would have hugged her mother to thank her, but Gladys stiffened just perceptibly so the child knew not to touch her. Gladys lit a cigarette and exhaled the smoke luxuriously; her brand was

Chesterfields, which was Della's brand (though Della believed smoking was a dirty, weak habit she was determined to overcome), saying, in a teasing voice, "I went to a lot of trouble to get that doll for you, Norma Jeane. Now I hope you'll accept the responsibility of the doll." *The responsibility of the doll* hung strangely in the air.

How Norma Jeane would love her blond baby doll! One of the great loves of her childhood.

Except: it made her uneasy that the doll's arms and legs were so clearly boneless, and loose, and could be made to flop about oddly. If you laid the doll down on her back, her feet just *flopped*.

Norma Jeane stammered, "W-what is her name, Mother?"

Gladys located a bottle of aspirin, shook several out onto her palm, and swallowed them dry. Calling out in her swaggering Harlow voice, and with a droll movement of her plucked eyebrows, "That's up to you, kiddo. She's *yours*."

How hard Norma Jeane tried to think of the doll's name. She tried and tried; but it was like stammering, in her thoughts: she couldn't think of any name at all. She began to worry, sucking at her thumb. Names are so important!—you must have a name for someone or you couldn't think of that person, and they must have a name for you, or—where would you *be*?

Norma Jeane cried, "Mother, what is the d-doll's name? *Please*."

More amused than annoyed, or seeming so, Gladys shouted from the other room, "Hell, call the thing Norma Jeane—it's about as bright as *you*, sometimes. I swear."

So much excitement, the child was exhausted.

Time for Norma Jeane's nap.

Yet: the phone rang. As the afternoon waned into early evening. And the child thought, anxiously, *Why doesn't Mother answer the phone? What if it's Father? Or does she know it isn't Father and how does she know this, if this is what she knows?*

In the Grimms' fairy tales that Grandma Della read to Norma Jeane, things happened that might be dreams, that were strange and scary as dreams, but were not. You would like to wake from such things but *you could not*.

How sleepy Norma Jeane was! She'd been so hungry and eaten so much cake, a piggy-piggy eating so much birthday cake for breakfast, leaving her sickish now and her teeth aching and maybe Gladys had poured a bit of her special colorless drink into Norma Jeane's grape juice—"Just a thimbleful, for fun"—so her eyes wouldn't stay open, her head lolled on her shoulders like a wooden head, and Gladys had to walk her into the hot, airless bedroom and lay her on the sagging bed, where Gladys didn't much like her to sleep, on the chenille spread, so Gladys tugged off her shoes and, ever fastidious about such things, placed a towel beneath Norma Jeane's head, "So you won't drool onto my pillow." The pumpkin-colored chenille spread was one that Norma Jeane recognized, from previous visits to other residences of her mother's, but its color had faded; it was stippled with cigarette burns and mysterious smears and smudges, of the hue of rust or of old faded bloodstains.

On the wall beside the bureau, there Norma Jeane's father looked down upon her. She watched him through half-closed eyes. She whispered, "Dad-*dy*."

The first time! On her sixth birthday.

The first time to have uttered the word: "Dad-*dy!*"

Gladys had drawn the blind down over the window, to the top of the sill, but it was an aged, cracked blind, inadequate to keep out the fierce afternoon sun. The blazing eye of God. The wrath of God. Grandma Della had been bitterly disappointed in Aimee Semple McPherson and the Church of the Foursquare Gospel, yet she believed, still, in what she called God's Word, the Holy Bible—"It's a hard teaching, and we are mostly deaf to its wisdom, but *it is all we have*." (But was this so? Gladys had her own books, and Gladys never mentioned the Bible. What Gladys spoke of with a look of passion and awe was The Movies.)

The sun had shifted downward in the sky when Norma Jeane was half wakened by the telephone ringing in the next room. That jarring sound, that sound of mockery, that angry-adult sound, that sound of male reproach. *I know you're there, Gladys, I know you're listening; you can't hide from me.* Until at last Gladys snatched up the receiver in the next room and spoke in a high, slurred voice, half pleading. *No! I can't, not tonight I told you, I told you it's my little girl's birthday, I want to spend it with her alone*—and a pause and then more urgently in half cries and screams like a wounded animal—*Yes I did, I did tell you, I have a little girl, I don't care what you believe, I'm a normal person, I'm a real mother I told you, I've had babies, I'm a normal woman and I don't want your filthy money, no I said I can't see you tonight, I will not see you, tonight or tomorrow night, leave me alone or you'll regret it, if you walk in here using that key I'll call the police you bastard!*

6

When I was born, on June 1, 1926, in the charity ward of the Los Angeles County Hospital, my mother wasn't there.

Where my mother was, no one knew!

Later they found her hiding and they were shocked and disapproving, say-ing *You have a beautiful baby, Mrs. Mortensen, don't you want to hold your beautiful baby? It's a girl baby, it's time to nurse.* But my mother turned her face to the wall. Her breasts leaked milk like pus, but not for me.

It was a stranger, a nurse, who taught my mother how to pick me up and hold me. How to cup the tender back of the infant's head with one hand and support the spine with the other.

What if I drop it.

You won't drop her!

It's so heavy, and hot. It's . . . kicking.

She's a normal healthy baby. A beauty. Look at those eyes!

At The Studio where Gladys Mortensen had been an employee since the age of nineteen there was the world-you-see-with-your-eyes and the world-through-the-camera. The one was nothing, the other was everything. So in time Mother learned to perceive me through the mirror. Even to smile at me. (Not eye-to-eye! Never.) In the mirror it's like a camera eye, almost you can love.

The baby's father, I adored. The name he told me, there is no such name. He gave me $225 and a telephone number to GET RID OF IT. *Am I really the mother? Sometimes I don't believe I am.*

We learned mirror-looking.

There was my Friend-in-the-Mirror. As soon as I was big enough to see. My Magic Friend.

There was a purity in this. Never did I experience my face and body from the inside (where there was numbness like sleep), only through the mirror, where there was sharpness and clarity. In that way I could see myself.

Gladys laughed. *Hell, this kid isn't half bad-looking, is she? Guess I'll keep her.*

It was a daily decision. It was not permanent.

In the blue smoke haze I was being passed about. Three weeks old, in a blanket. A woman cried drunkenly *Oh, her head! Careful, put your hand beneath her head.* Another woman said *Jesus, it's smoky in here, where's Gladys?* Men peeked and grinned. *She's a little girl, eh? Like a silk purse down there. Smooooth.*

Another, later time one of them helped Mother bathe me. And then her-self and him! Squeals and laughter, white-tile walls. Puddles of water on the floor. Perfumy bath salts. Mr. Eddy was rich! Owned three "hot spots" in L.A., where the stars dined and danced. Mr. Eddy on the radio. Mr. Eddy a practical joker leaving $20 bills in joke places: on a block of ice in the ice-box, rolled up inside a window shade, in the mutilated pages of *The Little*

Treasury of American Verse, taped to the inside of the lowered filth-splattered toilet seat.

Mother's laughter was shrill and piercing like breaking glass.

7

"But first you must be *bathed*."

The word *bathed* was slowly, sensuously drawn out.

Gladys was drinking her medicated water, unable to sit still. On the turntable, "Mood Indigo." Norma Jeane's hands and face were sticky from birthday cake. It was almost night, on Norma Jeane's sixth birthday. Then it was night. Water from both faucets splashed noisily into the rust-stained old claw-footed tub in the tiny bathroom.

Atop the icebox the beautiful blond doll stared. Glassy blue eyes opened wide and rosebud mouth always about to smile. If you shook her, the eyes opened even wider. The rosebud mouth never changed. Tiny feet in soiled white booties were turned outward at such a strange angle!

Mother taught Norma Jeane the words. Humming and swaying.

You ain't been blue
No   no   no
You ain't been blue
Till you got that Mood Indigo

Then Mother was bored with music, searching now for one of her books. So many books still unpacked. Gladys had had elocution lessons at The Studio. Norma Jeane loved being read to by Gladys because it meant more calm. Not sudden outbursts of laughter, or cursing, or tears. Music could do that. But there was Gladys with a reverent look searching through *The Little Treasury of American Verse*, which was her favorite book. With her thin shoulders lifted and head raised like a screen actress holding the book above her.

Because I could not stop for Death,
He kindly stopped for me;
The Carriage held but just Ourselves
And Immortality.

Norma Jeane listened anxiously. When Gladys finished the poem she would turn to Norma Jeane with bright glistening eyes. "What's that about, Norma Jeane?" Norma Jeane didn't know. Gladys said, "One day when your mother isn't around to save you, *you will know*." Pouring more of clear strong liquid into a cup and drinking.

Norma Jeane was hoping for more poems, poems with rhymes, poems could understand, but Gladys seemed to be through with poetry for the ni̧ Nor would she be reading from *The Time Machine* or *The War of the Worlds,* which were "prophetic books"—"books that would soon come true"—as she sometimes did in an intense, tremulous voice.

"Time for Baby's *baaath*."

It was a movie scene. Water splashing from the faucets was mixed with music you could almost hear.

Gladys stooped over Norma Jeane to undress her. But Norma Jeane could undress herself! She was six. Gladys was in a hurry, pushing Norma Jeane's hands away. "For *shame*. Cake all over you." Waiting for the tub to fill, and it was a long wait. Such a big tub. Gladys removed her crepe dress, pulling it over her head so her hair lifted in snaky tufts. Her pale skin slick with sweat. Mustn't stare at Mother's body, which was so secret: pale freckled skin, the bones beneath pushing out, small hard breasts like clenched fists straining at the lacy slip. Almost, Norma Jeane could see fire in Gladys's charged hair. In her moist staring lemony eyes.

The wind in the palm trees outside the window. Voices of the dead, Gladys called them. Wanting always to get *in*.

"Inside *us*," Gladys explained. "Because there aren't enough bodies. At any given time in history there is never enough *life*. And since the War—you don't remember the War because you weren't born yet, but I remember, I'm your mother, and I came into this world before you—since the War where so many men and women, too, and children died, there's a scarcity of bodies, let me tell you. All those poor dead souls wanting to push *in*."

Norma Jeane was frightened. Push in where?

Gladys paced, waiting for the tub to fill. She wasn't drunk, nor was she high. She'd removed the glove on her right hand and now both slender hands were bare and reddened in patches, the skin scaling; she didn't want to admit it was her work at The Studio, sixty hours a week sometimes, chemicals absorbed into her skin even through her latex gloves, yes, and into her hair, the very follicles of her hair, and her lungs, oh, she was dying! America was killing her! Once she began coughing she couldn't stop. Yes, but why then did she smoke? Well, everyone in Hollywood smoked, everyone in the movies smoked, a cigarette calmed the nerves, yes, but Gladys drew the line at marijuana, what the papers called *reefer*; God damn, she wanted Della to know she was no *hophead*, and she was no *junkie*; she was no *round-heels* God damn it and she'd *never done it for money*, or almost never.

And that only when she'd been laid off for eight weeks from The Studio. After the Crash of October 1929.

"Know what that was? The Crash?"

Norma Jeane shook her head in wonder. No. What?

"You were three years old at the time, baby. I was desperate. All that I did, Norma Jeane, I did to spare *you*."

Lifting Norma Jeane then in her arms, her thin sinewy-muscled arms, lifting her with a grunt, lowering the startled child, kicking and thrashing, into the steaming water. Norma Jeane whimpered, Norma Jeane didn't dare to scream, the water was so hot! burning hot! scalding hot, rushing from the faucet Gladys had forgotten to shut off, she'd forgotten to shut both faucets off, as she'd forgotten to test the temperature of the water. Norma Jeane tried to climb back out of the tub but Gladys pushed her back. "Sit still. This has to be done. I'm coming in too. Where's the soap? Dir-*ty*." Gladys turned her back to the sniveling Norma Jeane and quickly stripped off the rest of her clothes, slip, brassiere, panties, flinging them down onto the floor gaily, like a dancer. Naked then, boldly she climbed into the big old claw-footed tub, slipped and regained her balance, and lowered her lean hips into the water, which smelled sharply of wintergreen bath salts, seating herself facing the frightened child, knees opened as if to embrace, or to secure, the child to whom six years before she'd given birth in an agony of despair and recrimination—*Where are you? Why have you forsaken me?*—addressed to the man who was her lover, whose name she would not reveal even in the throes of labor. How clumsy, mother and daughter in this tub, with water surging in choppy waves overflowing the rim; Norma Jeane, nudged by her mother's knee, sank in water past her mouth, began to choke and cough, and Gladys quickly yanked her up by the hair, scolding—"Now stop that, Norma Jeane! Just *stop*." Gladys groped for the bar of soap and began to lather vigorously between her hands. Strange for her who shrank from being touched by her daughter to be naked now, crowded in a tub with her daughter; and strange the rapt, ecstatic expression on her face, which was flushed and rosy with the heat. Again Norma Jeane whimpered that the water was too hot, please Mother the water was too hot, so hot almost her skin couldn't feel it, and Gladys said severely, "Yes, it has to be hot, there's so much dirt. Outside us, and *in*."

Far away in another room, muffled by splashing water and Gladys's chiding voice, there came the sound of a key turning in a lock.

This was not the first time. It would not be the last time.

CITY OF SAND

I

"Norma Jeane, wake up! *Hurry*."

Fire season. Autumn 1934. The voice, Gladys's voice, was charged with alarm and excitement.

In the night the smell of smoke—of ash!—a smell like burning trash and garbage in the incinerator behind Della Monroe's old apartment building in Venice Beach, but this wasn't Venice Beach, this was Hollywood, Highland Avenue in Hollywood, where mother and daughter were living alone together at last, just the two of them *as it was meant to be until he summons us*, and there came the sound of sirens and this smell like burning hair, like burning grease in a frying pan, like damp clothes carelessly scorched by the iron. It was a mistake to have left the bedroom window open, for the smell permeated the room: a choking smell, a gritty smell, a smell that stung the eyeballs like windblown sand. A smell like the hot-plate coils when Gladys's teakettle, its water steamed away without Gladys's noticing, melted onto it. A smell like the ash from Gladys's perpetual cigarettes and the scorch burns in the linoleum, in the rose-patterned carpet, in the double bed with the brass headboard and goose-down pillows shared by mother and daughter, the unmistakable scorch smell of bedclothes the child recognized immediately, in her sleep; a smoldering Chesterfield fallen from Gladys's hand as, reading in bed late at night, a compulsive and insomniac reader, Gladys drifted off to a light doze to be wakened suddenly and rudely and, to her, mysteriously and unaccountably by a spark igniting pillow, sheets, comforter, which sometimes flared up into actual flames to be desperately pounded out with a book or a magazine or, in one instance, an *Our Gang* calendar hurriedly snatched from the wall, or Gladys's own hammering fists; and if the flames persevered Gladys would rush cursing into the bathroom to get a glass of water and fling it onto the flames, wetting the bedclothes and mattress— "God *damn*! What *next*!" There was an antic slapstick rhythm to such episodes, pre-talkies. Norma Jeane, who slept with Gladys, would have awakened immediately to scramble from the bed panting and alert as any animal primed for self-survival; and often, in fact, it was the child who ran to fetch water. For though this was a true alarm and upset in the middle of the night it had become familiar enough to be a routine ritual emergency and to have evolved a methodology. *We were used to saving ourselves from being burned alive in bed. We'd learned to cope.*

"I wasn't even asleep! My mind is too restless. In my brain it's bright day. What seemed to happen was, my fingers suddenly went numb. It's been happening lately. I was playing piano the other night and *nothing came*. I never work without rubber gloves in the lab but the chemicals are stronger now. The damage may already have been done. Look: the nerve ends in my fingers are practically dead, my hand doesn't even *shake*."

Gladys held the offending hand, her right, out for her daughter to examine, and it did seem to be so; strangely, after the alarm of smoldering bedclothes and middle-of-the-night distress, Gladys's slender hand didn't shake, just hung limp from her wrist as if it were nothing of hers, nothing volitional, nothing of her responsibility, the faintly lined palm held open and outward, pale yet roughened and reddened skin, a beautifully shaped hand, empty.

There were other such mysteries in Gladys's life, too many to enumerate. Monitoring them required constant vigilance yet, paradoxically, an almost mystical detachment— "It's as every philosopher from Plato to John Dewey has taught: you don't go until your number's up, and when your number's up, you *go*." Gladys snapped her fingers, smiling. To her, this was optimism.

Which is why I'm a fatalist. You can't quarrel with logic!

And why I'm so good at emergencies. Or was.

It was normal life day-to-day I couldn't play.

But that night the fires were real.

Not miniature fires in bed to be pounded out or doused with glasses of

water but fires "raging" in southern California after five months of drought
and high temperatures. Brush fires posing a "serious danger to life and property" within even the city limits of Los Angeles. The Santa Ana winds would
be blamed: blowing in off the Mojave Desert, gentle at first as a caress, then
more protracted, more intense, bearing heat, and within a few hours
firestorms were reported erupting in the foothills and canyons of the San
Gabriel Mountains, pushing west toward the Pacific. Within twenty-four
hours there had erupted hundreds of fires, separate and congruent. There
were searing-hot winds whipped to velocities of one hundred miles an hour
in the San Fernando and Simi valleys. Walls of flame twenty feet high were
observed leaping across the coastal highway like rapacious living creatures.
There were fields of fire, canyons of fire, fireballs like comets within a few
miles of Santa Monica. Sparks, borne by the wind like malicious seeds,
erupted into flame in the residential communities of Thousand Oaks, Malibu, Pacific Palisades, Topanga. There were tales of birds bursting into flame
in midair. There were tales of stampeding cattle shrieking in terror and running ablaze like torches until they dropped. Enormous trees, hundred-year-
old trees, burst into flame and were consumed within minutes. Even
water-soaked roofs caught fire, and buildings imploded in the flames like
bombs. Despite the effort of thousands of emergency firefighters, brush fires
continued to "rage out of control" and heavy, sulfurous white-gray smoke
obscured the sky for hundreds of miles in all directions. You would think,
seeing the darkened sky by day, the sun reduced to a sickly thin crescent, that
there was a perpetual solar eclipse. You would think, the mother told her
frightened daughter, that this was the end of the world promised in the Book
of Revelation in the Bible: " 'And men were scorched with great heat, and
blasphemed the name of God.' But it's God who has blasphemed *us*."

The sinister Santa Ana winds would blow for twenty days and twenty nights
bearing grit, sand, ash, and the suffocating smoke odor, and when at last the
fires subsided, with the onset of rain, seventy thousand acres of Los Angeles
County would be devastated.

By that time, Gladys Mortensen would have been hospitalized in the State
Psychiatric Hospital at Norwalk for nearly three weeks.

She was a little girl and little girls aren't supposed to *think hard*, especially
pretty little curly-haired girls aren't supposed to *worry, fret, calculate*; still,
she had a way of frowning like a midget adult, pondering such questions as:
How does fire *begin*? Is there a single spark that's the first spark, the first-
ever spark, out of *nowhere*? Not from a match or a lighter but out of
nowhere? But *why*?

"Because it's from the sun. Fire is from the sun. The sun *is* fire. That's what God is—*fire*. Put your faith in Him and you'll be burnt to a cinder. Put your hand out to touch Him, your hand will be burnt to a cinder. There's no 'God the Father'; I'd sooner believe in W. C. Fields. *He* exists. I was baptized in the Christian religion because my mother was a deluded soul, but *I'm no fool*. I'm an agnostic. I believe in science to save mankind, maybe. A cure for TB, a cure for cancer, eugenics to improve the race, and euthanasia for the hopeless. But my faith isn't very strong. Yours won't be either, Norma Jeane. The fact is we weren't meant to live in this part of the world. Southern California. It was a mistake to settle here. Your father"—and here Gladys's husky voice softened as it invariably did when she spoke of Norma Jeane's absent father, as if the man himself might be hovering near, listening—"calls Los Angeles the 'City of Sand.' It's built on sand and it *is* sand. It's a desert. Rainfall below twenty inches a year. Unless there's too much rain and flash floods. Mankind isn't meant to live in such a place. So we're being punished. For our pride and our stupidity. Earthquakes, fires, and the air smothering us. Some of us were born here, and some of us will die here. It's a pact we've made with the devil." Gladys paused, out of breath. Driving a car, as she was now, Gladys quickly became breathless, as if being in rapid motion were a physical exertion, yet she'd been speaking calmly, even pleasantly. They were on a darkened Coldwater Canyon Drive above Sunset Boulevard and it was 1:35 A.M. of the first full night of the Los Angeles fires and Gladys had screamed to wake Norma Jeane and pulled her, in her pajamas and barefoot, out of the bungalow and into Gladys's 1929 Ford, urging her to *hurry, hurry, hurry* and be very quiet so the other tenants didn't hear. Gladys herself was in her black lace nightgown, and over this she'd hastily flung a frayed green silk kimono, a gift from Mr. Eddy of years ago; she, too, was barefoot and bare-legged and her disheveled hair was tied back in a scarf, her slender face masklike and regal in cold cream only just beginning to be sullied by wind-borne ash and dust. What a wind, what dry, heated, malevolent air rushed along the canyon! Norma Jeane was too terrified to cry. So many sirens! Men's shouts! Strange high-pitched cries that might have been the shrieks of birds or animals. (Coyotes?) Norma Jeane had seen the lurid firelight reflected upon clouds in the sky, the sky at the horizon beyond the Sunset Strip, the sky over what Gladys called "the healing waters of the Pacific—too far away"; the sky silhouetted in the foreground by wind-agitated palm trees, trees whose dried, desiccated leaves were being shredded, and she'd been smelling smoke (*not* just scorch burns in Gladys's bed) for hours, but it hadn't struck yet, nor did it exactly strike her now *for I wasn't a questioning child, you could say I was an accepting child, I mean a desperate hopeful child* that her mother was driving the Ford in the wrong direction.

Not away from the fire-splotched hills but toward them.

Not away from the stinging suffocating smoke but toward it.

Yet Norma Jeane should have known the signs: Gladys was speaking calmly. In that voice of hers that was pleasant, logical.

When Gladys was herself, her truest self, she spoke in a flat, toneless voice, a voice from which all pleasure and all emotion had been squeezed, like the last drop of moisture wrung with force from a washcloth; at such times she didn't look you in the eye; it was her power to look through you, the way an adding machine might look if it had eyes. When Gladys was not-herself, or easing into that not-self, she began to speak rapidly in snatches of words inadequate to keep pace with her racing bubbling mind; or she spoke calmly, logically, like one of Norma Jeane's schoolteachers saying things everyone knows. "It's a pact we've made with the devil. Even those of us who don't believe in the devil."

Gladys turned sharply to Norma Jeane to ask if she'd been listening.

"Y-yes, Mother."

Devil? A pact? How?

By the side of the road there was a pale glimmering object, not a human baby but possibly a doll, a discarded doll, though your first panicked thought was that it *was* a baby, abandoned in the fire emergency, but of course it must've been a doll. Gladys didn't seem to notice as the car swung past but Norma Jeane felt a stab of horror—she'd left her doll behind, on the bed! In the confusion and upset, wakened from sleep by her agitated mother and hurried outside to the car, sirens and lights and the smell of smoke, Norma Jeane had left the golden-haired doll behind to burn; the doll wasn't so golden-haired now as it had once been, and its fair rubber-smooth skin not so spotless, the lace cap long vanished and the floral-print nightgown and the little floppy feet in white booties irrevocably soiled, but Norma Jeane loved her doll, her only doll, her doll-with-no-name, her birthday doll she'd never named except to call her "Doll"—but, more often, tenderly, just "you"—as you'd speak to your mirror self, needing no formal name. Now Norma Jeane cried, "Oh, what if the house burns down, M-mother? I forgot my doll!"

Gladys snorted in contempt. "That doll! You'd be fortunate if it did burn. It's a morbid attachment."

Gladys had to concentrate on her driving. The 1929 tarnished-green Ford was second- or third-hand, purchased for $75 from a friend of a friend expressing "sympathy" for Gladys, a single divorced mother; it wasn't a reliable car, and the brakes were peculiar, and she needed to grip the steering wheel tight with both hands near the top of the wheel, and lean far forward, to see clearly through the windshield, with its faint weblike cracks, and over the hood. She was in a calm state, a premeditated state, she'd swallowed down half a glass of a potent drink, a drink to soothe, to provide certainty, *not* gin, *not* whiskey, *not* vodka, but driving on the Strip and up into the hills was a challenge tonight, for there were emergency vehicles with their blaring sirens and blinding lights, and on Coldwater Canyon Drive there were other cars on the narrow road headed in the opposite direction, downhill; their headlights were so blinding that Gladys cursed, wishing she'd worn her dark glasses; and Norma Jeane, squinting through her fingers, caught a glimpse of pale, anxious faces behind windshields. *Why are we going uphill, why into the hills, why on this night of fires?* was a question the child did not ask, though possibly thinking how when her grandmother Della had been alive she'd warned Norma Jeane to watch out for Gladys's "changes of mood" and made Norma Jeane promise that if things got "dangerous" Norma Jeane should telephone her at once— "And I'll come in a taxi if I have to, if it costs five dollars," Della had said grimly. It wasn't Grandma Della's actual telephone number she'd left with Norma Jeane but the number of Della's apartment building supervisor, since there was no phone in Della's apartment, and this number Norma Jeane had memorized since coming to live with Gladys, brought in triumph to live with Gladys more than a year ago in Gladys's new residence on Highland Avenue, near the Hollywood Bowl, this number Norma Jeane would recall through her life— VB 3-2993—though in fact she never dared call it, and on this night in October 1934 her grandmother had been dead for many months, and her grandfather Monroe had been dead even longer, and there was no one at that number she could call had she dared to use it.

There was no one, at any number, that Norma Jeane could call.

My father! If I'd had his number, no matter where he was, I would call him. Saying, Mother needs you now, please come help us, and I believed he would have come, I believed this.

Ahead, at the entrance to Mulholland Drive, there was a fire barricade. Gladys cursed— "God *damn!*" —and braked her car to a jolting stop. She'd intended to drive them high into the hills, high above the city, no matter the fire risk, no matter the sirens, the sporadic flashes of fire, the whistling heat-borne Santa Ana wind buffeting the car even along sheltered stretches of Coldwater Canyon Drive. In these secluded prestigious hills, as in Beverly Hills, Bel Air, and Los Feliz, there were the private residences of film "stars" past whose gates Gladys had frequently driven Norma Jeane on Sunday excursions when she could afford the gasoline, happy times for both mother and daughter *it was what we did together instead of church* but now it was the middle of the night and the air was thick with smoke and you couldn't see any houses and possibly the private residences of the stars were burning and that was why the road was barricaded. And that was why, a few minutes later when Gladys tried to turn north onto Laurel Canyon Drive, where flares had been set in the roadway and emergency vehicles were parked, she was stopped by uniformed officers.

Asking her rudely where the hell did she think she was going, and Gladys explained that she lived on Laurel Canyon, her residence was there and she had a right to drive home, and the officers asked where exactly did she live, and Gladys said, "That's my business," and they came closer, shining a flashlight virtually into her face; they were suspicious, skeptical, asking who was in the car with her, and Gladys said, laughing, "Well, not Shirley Temple." One of the officers came to speak with her, he was a Los Angeles County sheriff's deputy, he was staring at Gladys, who even in her greasy cold-cream mask was a woman of poise and beauty, a woman in the classic mode of the enigmatic Garbo, if you didn't look too closely; her dark-dilated eyes were enormous in her face, her nose long, fine-boned, and waxy-tipped, and her mouth was swollen and lipstick-red; before fleeing into the night on this night of all nights she'd taken time to apply lipstick for you never know when you'll be observed and judged; and the deputy understood that something was wrong, here was a distraught youngish woman only partly dressed, in a falling-off-the-shoulder silky green kimono and what appeared to be a tattered black nightgown beneath, small breasts hanging loose and limp, and beside her a frightened child with uncombed curly hair, in pajamas and barefoot; a small-boned chubby-faced child with a fevered skin and cheeks streaked with sooty tears. Both the child and the woman were coughing, and the woman was muttering to herself—she was indignant, she was angry, she was coquettish, she was evasive, she was insisting now that she'd been invited to a private residence at the very top of Laurel Canyon: "The owner has a fireproof mansion. My daughter and I will be safe there. I can't say this man's name, officer, but it's a name you all know. He's in the film industry. This little girl is his daughter. This is a city of sand and nothing will long endure *but we're going.*" There was a belligerent edge to Gladys's husky voice.

The deputy informed Gladys he was sorry, she'd have to turn back; nobody was being allowed up into the hills tonight, they'd been evacuating families to lower ground, she and her daughter would be safer back in the city: "Go home, ma'am, and calm down, and put your little girl to bed. It's late." Gladys flared up. "Don't you condescend to me, officer. Don't you tell me what to *do*." The deputy demanded to see Gladys's driver's license and auto registration, and Gladys told him she didn't have these documents with her—this was a fire emergency, what did he expect—but she handed over to him her studio pass, which he examined briefly and handed back, saying that Highland Avenue was in a safe part of the city, at least for the time being, so she was lucky and should return home immediately; and Gladys smiled angrily at him, and said, "Actually, Officer, I want to see Hell up close. A preview." She spoke in her sexy-husky Harlow voice; the abrupt change was disconcerting. The deputy frowned as Gladys smiled seductively and loosened her hair from the scarf, shaking it onto her shoulders. Once so self-conscious about her hair, Gladys hadn't had it trimmed or styled for months; there was a vivid snowy-white streak, jagged as a cartoon lightning bolt, above her left temple. Embarrassed, the deputy told Gladys she had to turn back, they could provide her with an escort if she needed one, but this was an order or she'd be placed under arrest. Gladys laughed. "Arrested! For driving my car!" Then said more soberly, "Officer, I'm sorry. Please don't arrest me." And in a murmur, not wanting Norma Jeane to overhear, "I wish you could shoot me." The deputy said, losing patience, "Lady, go home. You're drunk or doped up and nobody's got time for it tonight. You're saying things to get you into trouble." Gladys clutched at the deputy's arm, you could see he was just a man in a uniform, middle-aged, with sad-pouchy eyes and a tired face, and that glinting badge, and that uniform, and that heavy leather belt around his waist, and the pistol hidden in its holster; he felt sorry for this woman and her little girl, the smeary cold-cream face, the dilated eyes, and a smell of alcohol on the woman's breath, and that breath in any case stale, not healthy, but he wanted them gone, the other deputies were waiting for him, they'd be up through the night. Politely the deputy detached Gladys's fingers from his arm and Gladys said, playfully, "Even if you shot me, Officer, if I tried to run that barricade, for instance, you wouldn't shoot my daughter. She'd be left an orphan. She *is* an orphan. But I don't want her to know it even if I loved her. I mean, if I don't love her. We all know it's nobody's fault, being *born*."

"Lady, you're right. Now go home, OK?"

The L.A. County deputies watched as Gladys in the tarnished-green 1929 Ford struggled to turn in the narrow canyon road, they shook their heads, bemused and pitying, and how like a striptease it was, Gladys fumed, strange men looking on: "Thinking their private, dirty, men thoughts."

But Gladys did manage to turn the car around and drove south on Laurel Canyon, back toward Sunset and into the city. Her face shone with grease and her red-lipsticked mouth was trembling with indignation. Beside her, Norma Jeane sat stricken with a confused adult shame. She'd heard, but hadn't quite heard, what Gladys had told the deputy. She believed, but wasn't quite sure if this was true, that Gladys had been "acting"—as Gladys often did, in these incandescent states in which she wasn't herself. But it was a fact, an incontestable fact, like a movie scene, and others had witnessed it, too, that her mother, her mother Gladys Mortensen, who was so proud and independent and loyal to The Studio and determined to be a "career woman" accepting charity from no one, had been, just now, *so stared at, so pitied and crazy*. It was so! Norma Jeane wiped at her eyes, which stung from the smoke, wouldn't stop watering, but she wasn't crying; she was mortified with a shame beyond her years, but she wasn't crying; she was trying to think: Could it be true that her father had invited them to his house? All these years, he'd lived only a few miles away? At the top of Laurel Canyon Drive? But why then had Gladys wanted to turn up Mulholland Drive? Had Gladys intended to mislead the deputies, to throw them off the trail? (It was a frequent fond expression of Gladys's—"Throw them off the trail.") When, on their Sunday drives, Gladys drove Norma Jeane past the mansions of the stars and others "in the film industry," she sometimes hinted that *your father* might just be living close by, *your father* might just have been a guest at a party here, but Gladys never explained further; it was meant to be taken lightly, as some of Grandma Della's warnings and prophecies were meant to be taken—if not lightly, at least not literally—these were hints, like winks; you were meant to feel a stab of excitement but only that. So Norma Jeane was left to ponder what the truth was, or if in fact there was "truth," for life wasn't anything like a gigantic jigsaw puzzle really; in a puzzle all the pieces fit together, neatly and beautifully together, it didn't even matter that the landscape-in-the-puzzle was beautiful, like a fairyland, only just that the completed picture was *there*: you could see it, you could marvel over it, you could even destroy it, but *it was there*. In life, she'd come to see, even before the age of eight, nothing was *there*.

Yet Norma Jeane could remember her father leaning over her crib. It was a white wicker crib with pink ribbons. Gladys had pointed it out to her in a store window: "See that? You had one just like it when you were a baby. Remember?" Norma Jeane had shaken her head silently; no, she hadn't remembered. But later it came to her in a kind of dream, daydreaming at school, risking being scolded as often she was (in this new school in Hollywood, where nobody liked her), that she did remember the crib, but mostly she remembered her father leaning over her and smiling, and Gladys beside him leaning on his arm. Her father's face was full and strong-boned and handsome and inclined to gentle irony, a face like Clark Gable's, and his thick dark hair lifted from his forehead in a widow's peak, like Clark Gable's. He had a thin, elegant mustache, and his voice was a deep, rich baritone, and he'd promised her *I love you, Norma Jeane, and one day I will return to Los Angeles to claim you.* Kissing her then lightly on the forehead. And Gladys, her smiling loving mother, looking on.

So vivid in her memory!

So much more "real" than what surrounded her.

Norma Jeane blurted out, "W-was he here? Father? All this time? Why didn't he come to see us? Why aren't we with him now?"

Gladys didn't seem to hear. Gladys was losing her incandescent energy.

She was perspiring inside the kimono and gave off a powerful odor. And there was something wrong with the car's headlights: the beams had weakened, or the outer glass was coated with grime. The windshield, too, was covered in a fine ashy film. Hot winds buffeted the car, snaky spirals of dust flew past. North of the city, massed clouds were turbulent with a flamey light. Everywhere was a sharp acrid smell of burning: burning hair, burning sugar, burning rot, decayed vegetation, garbage. She was close to screaming. *She could not bear it!*

It was then that Norma Jeane repeated her questions in a louder voice, an anxious childish voice of the timbre she should have known her distraught mother *could not bear*. Asking where her father was? Had he been living so close to them all along? But why—

"You! Shut *up*!" Quick as a rattlesnake Gladys's hand leapt from the steering wheel, a sharp backhand blow to Norma Jeane's feverish face. Norma Jeane whimpered and hunched in a corner of the seat, drawing her knees up to her chest.

At the foot of Laurel Canyon Drive there was a detour, and when Gladys followed this detour for several blocks she came to a second detour, and when at last, indignant, sobbing to herself, she came to a larger street, she didn't recognize it, didn't know whether this was Sunset Boulevard and, if so, where on the Boulevard; which way should she turn to get to Highland Avenue? It was 2 A.M. of an unknown night. A desperate night. A crying sniveling child beside her. She was thirty-four years old. No man would ever again look at her with longing. She'd given her youth to The Studio, and now what a cruel reward! Driving out into the intersection, rivulets of sweat on her face, looking from left to right to left—"Oh, God, which way is home?"

2

Once upon a time. At the sandy edge of the great Pacific Ocean.

There was a village, a place of mystery. Where the light was golden upon the sea surface. Where the sky was inky-black at night winking with stars. Where the wind was warm and gentle as a caress.

Where a little girl came to a Walled Garden! The wall was made of rock and was twenty feet high and covered in beautiful flaming-red bougainvillea. From inside the Walled Garden came the sound of birds singing, and music, and a fountain! And voices of unknown persons, and laughter.

Never can you climb over this wall, you're not strong enough; girls aren't strong enough; girls aren't big enough; your body is fragile and breakable, like a doll; your body *is* a doll; your body is for others to admire and to pet;

dy is to be used by others, not used by you; your body is a luscious fruit... others to bite into and to savor; your body is for others, not for *you*.

The little girl began to cry! The little girl's heart was broken.

Then came her fairy godmother to tell her: There's a secret way into the Walled Garden!

There's a hidden door in the wall, but you must wait like a good little girl for this door to be opened. You must wait patiently, and you must wait quietly. You must not knock on the door like a naughty boy. You must not shout or cry. You must win over the doorkeeper—an old, ugly, green-skinned gnome. You must make the doorkeeper take notice of you. You must make the doorkeeper admire you. You must make the doorkeeper desire you. And then he will love you and will do your bidding. Smile! Smile, and be happy! Smile, and take off your clothes! For your Magic Friend in the mirror will help you. For your Magic Friend in the mirror is very special. The old, ugly, green-skinned gnome will fall in love with you, and the hidden door in the Walled Garden will swing open for you, only for *you*, and you will step inside laughing with happiness; inside the Walled Garden will be gorgeous blossoming roses, and hummingbirds and tanagers, and music and a splashing fountain, and your eyes will widen with wonders, for the old, ugly, green-skinned gnome was really a prince under an evil enchantment, and he will kneel before you and ask for your hand in marriage, and you will live with him happily forever in his Garden kingdom; *never will you be a lonely, unhappy little girl again.*

So long as you remain with your Prince in the Walled Garden.

3

"Norma Je-ane? Come home *now*."

The summer before, there was Grandma Della calling Norma Jeane often, too often, from the front step of her apartment building. Cupping her hands to her mouth and practically bellowing. The old woman seemed to be worrying more and more about her little granddaughter as if she knew a truth rushing at them no one else knew.

But I hid away. I was a bad girl. The last time Grandma called me.

It was like any other day. Almost. Norma Jeane was playing with two little girlfriends on the beach; and there came, out of the sky like a swooping bird, that voice—"Norma Jeane! NORMA JE-ANE!" The two little girls looked at Norma Jeane and giggled, feeling sorry for her maybe. Norma Jeane thrust out her lower lip, and continued digging in the sand. *I won't! Can't make me.*

In the neighborhood, Della Monroe, a Tugboat Annie character, was known by all. A familiar sight in the Christian Church Reborn, where (onlookers swore!) her bifocal glasses steamed when she sang. And afterward how shamelessly Della would push Norma Jeane forward, ahead of others, so that the youngish blond minister could admire Norma Jeane in her Shirley Temple curls and prissy Sunday dress, as invariably he did. Smiling, "God has blessed you, Della Monroe! You must be real grateful to him."

Della laughed and sighed. She wasn't one to accept even a heartfelt compliment without giving it a sly twist. "*I am*. If not Norma Jeane's momma."

Grandma Della didn't believe in spoiling children. She did believe in putting them to work at a young age, as she'd worked, herself, all her life. Now her husband had died and his pension was "measly"—"small potatoes"—Della continued to work. "No rest for the wicked!" She did specialty ironing for an Ocean Avenue laundry and specialty sewing for a local seamstress and, when she couldn't avoid it, she watched babies in her apartment: she *coped*. She'd been born on the *frontier* and was no silly *fainting lily* like some of these ridiculous females in the movies and like her own neurotic daughter. Oh, Della Monroe hated "America's Sweetheart" Mary Pickford! She'd long supported the nineteenth amendment giving women the right to vote and had voted in every election since fall 1920. She was shrewd, sharp-tongued, and quick-tempered; though hating movies on principle because they were phony as a plugged nickel, she admired James Cagney in *The Public Enemy*, which she'd seen three times—that tough little bantam quick to strike out against his enemies but accepting of his fate, to be wrapped in bandages like a mummy and dumped on a doorstep, once he knew his number was up. The same way she admired killer-boy "Little Caesar," Edward G. Robinson, talking crooked out of his girl mouth. These were men enough to accept death when their number was up.

When your number's up, it's up. Grandma Della seemed to think this was a cheerful fact.

Sometimes after Norma Jeane had been working with Della all morning, cleaning the apartment, washing and drying dishes, Della took her on a special outing to feed wild birds. Norma Jeane's happiest time! She and Grandma scattered bits of bread on the sandy soil of a vacant lot and stood watching from a short distance as the birds flew in, cautious yet hungry, a flurry of wings, quick darting little beaks. Pigeons, mourning doves, orioles, noisy scrub jays. Clusters of black-capped sparrows. And in the bushes, hovering amid trumpet vine, hummingbirds no bigger than bumblebees. Della identified the tiny bird as one that had the ability to fly backward and sideways, unlike any other bird, a "tricky little devil" that was almost tame but wouldn't eat bread crumbs or seeds. Norma Jeane was fascinated by these iridescent crimson- and green-feathered birds that glittered like metal in the sun, beating their wings so rapidly you saw only a blur; sticking long needle-thin beaks into tubular flowers to suck out nourishment, hovering in the air. Then darting away so swiftly! "Oh, Grandma, where do they *go?*"

Grandma Della shrugged. The mood of being grandma and humoring a lonely child had passed. "Who knows? Where birds go."

It would be commented on, after her death, that Della Monroe had aged since her husband's passing. Though when he'd been alive, she'd complained of him to anyone who would listen: his drinking, "bad lungs," "bad habits." Heavy as Della was, her face flushed with high blood pressure, she hadn't taken sensible care of her health.

Like a windblown sail swinging around the neighborhood looking for her granddaughter. No sooner letting Norma Jeane out to play than she wanted her back indoors. Saying she was saving the little girl from the mother— "That one, that broke her own mother's heart."

That August afternoon, blinding sun and heat and no one was out except a few children behind the apartment building. Grandma Della had a sudden premonition something was going to happen, something bad, so she ventured out into the heat calling, "Norma Jeane! Norma Je-ane!" in that way of hers like the butcher's cleaver striking, one-two-three, one-two-three, calling from the front walk, and calling from the alley beside the building, and calling from the vacant lot, and Norma Jeane and her girlfriends ran away giggling to hide *and I didn't answer, she couldn't make me!* Though Norma Jeane loved her grandmother, who was the only living person who truly loved her, the only living person who loved her without wishing to hurt her, only just to protect her. Except neighborhood boys said of Della Monroe, *That fat old elephant!* and Norma Jeane, hearing, was ashamed.

So Norma Jeane hid. Then, after a while, not hearing Della calling her, she decided she'd better go home after all; came up from the beach looking like a wild girl, blood pounding in her ears, and an old woman Grandma's age scolded *You! Your grandma's been calling you, miss!* Norma Jeane hurried inside the building and ran up the stairs to the third floor, as so many times she'd done, yet knowing this time would be different, for how quiet everything was, that stillness in movies before a surprise, and so often a surprise that made you scream, that you couldn't prepare for. Oh, look!—Grandma's apartment door was open. Which was wrong. Norma Jeane knew it was wrong. And inside, Norma Jeane knew what she would find.

For Grandma had fallen before, when I was home. Losing her balance, suddenly dizzy. I'd find her on the kitchen floor dazed and moaning and breathing hard not knowing what had happened and I'd help her up, she'd sit in a chair, and I'd bring her her pills and a cloth with ice chips wrapped inside to press against her face that was so hot and it was scary but after a while she'd laugh, and I knew it was all right.

Except this time when it wasn't. When her grandmother was lying on the bathroom floor, a sweating bulk of a body wedged between the tub and the toilet, both scrubbed clean that morning, the smell of cleanser a rebuke to human weakness, there was Grandma Della on her side like a beached fish, face huge and mottled-red, eyes partly open and unfocused and her breath wheezing. "Grandma! *Grandma!*" It was a movie scene and yet it was real.

Grandma Della reached blindly for Norma Jeane's hand as if wanting to be pulled up. She was making a choked guttural sound, at first unintelligible. Not angry and not scolding. Oh, this was wrong! Norma Jeane knew. She knelt beside her grandmother, smelling that odor of sickly doomed flesh, of sweat and intestinal gas and bowels, recognizing it immediately, the odor of death, and she was crying, "Grandma, don't die!" even as the stricken woman gripped Norma Jeane's hand in a spasm that nearly cracked her fingers, managing to say, each word labored and percussive as a nail driven with tremendous force, "*God bless you child I love you.*"

4

It was my fault! My fault Grandma died.
Don't be ridiculous. It was nobody's fault.
I wouldn't come when she called me! I was bad.
Look, it was God's fault. Now go back to sleep.
Mother, can she hear us? Can Grandma hear us?
Christ, I hope not!
It's my fault what happened to Grandma. Oh, Mommy—
I am not Mommy, you disgusting little idiot! Her number came up, is all.
Using her pointy elbows to fend off the child. Not wanting to slap her because not wanting to use her chapped, reddened hands.

(Gladys's hands! She had a terror the cancer had seeped into her bones, from the chemicals.)

And don't touch me, damn you. You know I can't bear it.

An uneasy time for those born under the sign of Gemini. The tragic twins.

When the call came for Gladys Mortensen in the negative-cutting lab she'd had to be led haltingly to the phone, she was so frightened. Her supervisor, Mr. X—who'd once been in love with her; yes, he'd pleaded with her to marry him, he'd have left his family for her when she'd been his assistant in '29 before she'd been demoted by illness *not her fault*—handed her the receiver in silence. The rubbery cord was twisted as a snake. The thing was alive but Gladys stoically refused to acknowledge it. Her eyes were watering from the virulent chemicals with which she'd been working (on a work detail that should have gone to another, lower-ranked employee of the lab, but Gladys refused to give Mr. X the satisfaction of complaining) and there was a faint roaring in her ears as of movie voices murmuring *Now! now! now! now!*— and this, too, she ignored. She'd become adept, since the age of twenty-six, when the last of her girl babies was born, at ignoring, filtering out, the numerous intrusive voices in her head that she knew were not-real; but sometimes she was tired, and a voice protruded, like a radio station suddenly beamed in loud. She would have said, had she been asked, that this "emergency call" was about her daughter Norma Jeane. (The other two daughters, living in Kentucky with their father, had disappeared from her life. The father had simply taken them. He'd said she was a "sick woman," and maybe that was so.) *Something has happened to. Your child. So sorry. It was an accident.* Instead, the news was of Gladys's mother! Della! Della Monroe! *Something has happened to. Your mother. So sorry. Can you come as quickly as possible?*

Gladys let the receiver fall to the end of its snaky twisty cord. Mr. X had to catch her, to prevent her fainting.

My God, she'd forgotten about Della. Her own mother, Della Monroe. She'd allowed Della to become vulnerable to harm, having pushed her out of her thoughts. Della Monroe, born under the sign of Taurus. (Gladys's father had died the previous winter. Gladys had been sick at the time with one of her violent migraines and hadn't been able to attend the funeral, or even get to Venice Beach to see her mother. Somehow, she'd managed to forget Monroe, her father, reasoning that Della would mourn for them both. And if Della was disgusted with her, that would help Della not-think about being a widow. "My poor father died in the Argonne. Gassed in the Argonne," Gladys had been telling friends for years. "I never knew the man really.") Gladys hadn't been able to love Della in recent years, loving was exhausting and required too much strength, but she'd assumed that Della, being Della, would outlive her. Della would outlive the orphan daughter Norma Jeane who was her charge. Gladys hadn't loved Della because she was frightened of the old woman's judgment. *An eye for an eye, and a tooth for a tooth. No mother can abandon her babies without being required to pay.* Or, if she'd loved Della, it was a squabbling sort of love inadequate to protect her mother from harm.

For that is what *love is*. A protection from harm.

If there is harm, there was *inadequate love*.

The child Norma Jeane, whom it was difficult not to blame, who'd found her grandmother dying on the floor, hadn't been harmed at all.

It was like "lightning struck" Grandma, Norma Jeane would say.

But the lightning had missed Norma Jeane; and for this, Gladys resolved to be grateful.

Supposing it to be a sign: as it was a sign that both she and Norma Jeane had been born Geminis, in the month of June, while Della with whom it was impossible to get along had been born under the sign of Taurus, at the farthest distance from the Gemini. *Opposites attract, opposites repel.*

Her other daughters had been born under very different signs. It was a relief to Gladys that, a thousand miles away in Kentucky, they'd passed beyond the sphere of their sick mother's influence; they belonged now wholly to their father. They would be spared!

Of course, Gladys brought Norma Jeane home with her. She wasn't about to give up her own flesh and blood to foster care or to the L.A. County Orphanage—as Della was always darkly hinting would be the little girl's fate except for *her*. Almost, Gladys would have liked to believe in the Christian heaven, and Della looking down at her and Norma Jeane in the bungalow on Highland Avenue, disgruntled that her prediction hadn't come true. *You see? I'm not a bad mother. I've been weak. I've been sick. Men have misused me. But now I'm well. I'm strong!*

Still, the first week with Norma Jeane was a nightmare. Such cramped quarters, at the rear of the musty-smelling bungalow! Trying to sleep in the same sagging bed. Trying to sleep at all. It infuriated Gladys that her own daughter should seem to be frightened of her. Should flinch from her and cringe like a kicked dog. *It isn't my fault your precious grandma died. I didn't kill her!* She couldn't bear the child's weeping and her runny nose and the way, like a movie waif, she clutched at her doll, now worn and soiled. "That thing! You've still got that thing! I forbid you to talk to it! That's the first step to—" Gladys paused, trembling, not wanting to give a name to her fear. (Why, Gladys wondered, did she hate the doll so much? It had been her birthday present to Norma Jeane, after all. Was she jealous of the attention Norma Jeane paid it? The golden-haired doll with the blank blue eyes and frozen smile *was* Norma Jeane—was that it? Gladys had given her daughter the doll almost as a joke; a man friend of hers had given it to her saying he'd picked it up somewhere, though probably, knowing what she knew of that hophead, he'd lifted it out of a car or off a porch, strolled off with some little girl's beloved doll and broke her heart, vicious as Peter Lorre in *M*!) But she couldn't take the damned thing away from Norma Jeane. At least not yet.

5

They were living together bravely, mother and daughter. At the time of the Santa Ana winds, the smothering smoke-tinctured air, and the fires of Hell of the autumn of 1934.

They were living together in three rented rooms of a bungalow-boardinghouse at 828 Highland Avenue, Hollywood—"A five-minute walk to the Hollywood Bowl," as Gladys frequently described it. Though in fact they never walked to the Hollywood Bowl.

The mother was thirty-four years old and the daughter was eight.

There was a subtle distortion here, as in a fun-house mirror that's *almost normal* so you trust it, and you shouldn't. That Gladys was thirty-four years old!—and her life hadn't yet begun. She'd had three babies and they'd been taken from her and in a sense erased, and now this eight-year-old with the mournful eyes, the young-old soul, a reproach to her she couldn't bear yet must bear, for *We are all we have of each other* as Gladys told the child repeatedly *as long as I am strong enough to hold it together.*

The fire season was not unexpected. Fit punishments are never unexpected.

Yet long before the Los Angeles fires of 1934 there was menace in the air of southern California. You didn't require winds blowing off the Mojave Desert to know that chaos would soon be raging out of control. You could see it in the baffled, corroded faces of vagrants (as they were called) on the streets. You could see it in certain demonic cloud formations at sunset above the Pacific. You could sense it in the cryptic veiled hints, suppressed smiles, and muffled laughter of certain persons at The Studio you'd once trusted. Better not to listen to radio news. Better not to even glance at the news sections of any paper, even the *Los Angeles Times*, which was frequently left lying about the bungalow (deliberately? to provoke the more sensitive tenants, like Gladys?) for you would not want to know the alarming statistics pertaining to American unemployment, evicted and homeless families across the country, or the suicides of bankrupts and of World War I veterans who were disabled and without jobs and "hope." You would not want to read about news in Europe. In Germany.

This next war, we'll be fighting right here. No escape this time.

Gladys shut her eyes, in pain. Swift as the first stroke of a migraine. This conviction had been uttered in a voice not her own, a male radio voice of authority.

For such reasons Gladys brought Norma Jeane to the bungalow on Highland Avenue to live with her. Though she still worked long hours at The Studio and was in perpetual terror that she would be laid off (throughout Hollywood, studio employees were being laid off or permanently dismissed), and there were days when she could barely force herself to crawl out of bed, so heavy the weight of the world was upon her soul. She was determined to be a "good mother" to the child in the short time remaining. For if there wasn't a war launched from Europe or from the Pacific, there might well be a war launched from the sky: H. G. Wells had prophesied such a horror in

The War of the Worlds, which for some reason Gladys had nearly committed to heart, like parts of *The Time Machine*. (It was her vague belief that
Norma Jeane's father had given her an omnibus containing these and other
novellas by Wells along with some volumes of poetry, but in fact these were
given her "for her edification" by a Studio employee who'd been a friend of
Norma Jeane's father, himself a Studio employee for a brief period of time
in the mid-1920s.) A Martian invasion: why not? When she was in one of
her excitable moods, Gladys believed in astrological signs and in the powerful influence of the stars and other planets on humankind. It made sense that
there were other beings in the universe and that these, in the image of their
Maker, harbored a cruel predatory interest in humankind. Such an invasion
would fit in with the Book of Revelation, in Gladys's opinion the only book
of the Bible that convinced, in southern California. Instead of wrathful angels
with flaming swords, why not ugly fungoid Martians wielding beams of
invisible heat that "flashed into flame" when striking their human targets?

But did Gladys really believe in Martians? In a possible invasion from
the sky?

"This is the twentieth century. Times have changed since the reign of Yah-
weh, and so have cataclysms."

No one knew whether Gladys was being playful and provocative or deadly
serious. Making such pronouncements in her sexy Harlow voice, the back
of her hand on her lean hip. Her glittering stare was level and unflinching.
Her lips looked swollen, moistly red. Norma Jeane saw uneasily that other
adults, especially men, were fascinated by her mother, the way you'd be fascinated by someone leaning too far out of a high window or bringing her
hair too close to a candle flame. Even with the streak of gray-white hair lifting from her forehead (which, out of "contempt," Gladys refused to dye),
and the bruised, creepy shadows beneath her eyes, and the fevered restless-
ness of her body. In the bungalow foyer, on the front walk, and in the street,
wherever Gladys found someone to listen, Gladys *did scenes*. If you knew
movies, you knew that Gladys was *doing scenes*. For even to *do a scene* that
made no clear sense was to capture attention, and this helped to calm the
mind. It was exciting, too, that much of the attention Gladys drew was erotic.

Erotic: meaning you're "desired."

For madness is seductive, sexy. Female madness.

So long as the female is reasonably young and attractive.

Norma Jeane, a shy child, often an invisible child, liked it that other adults,
especially men, stared with such interest at this woman who was her mother.
If Gladys's nervous laughter and incessantly gesturing hands hadn't driven
them away after this initial interest *she might have found another man to
love her. She might have found a man to marry her. We might have been*

saved! Norma Jeane didn't like it that, after one of these exhilarating public scenes, when Gladys was back home she might swallow down a handful of pills and fall onto the brass bed to lie shuddering and insensible, not even sleeping, eyes clouded over as if with mucus, for hours. If Norma Jeane tried to loosen her clothing, Gladys might curse and slap at her. If Norma Jeane tried to tug off her tight-fitting pumps, Gladys might kick her. "No! Don't touch! I could give you leprosy! Leave me alone."

If she'd tried harder with those men. Maybe. It might've worked!

6

Wherever you are, I'm there. Even before you get to the place where you are going I'm already there, waiting.

I am in your thoughts, Norma Jeane. Always.

Such good memories! She knew herself privileged.

She was the only child at Highland Elementary to have "pocket change"—in a little strawberry-red satin change purse—to buy her own lunch at a corner grocery. Fruit pies, orange soda pop. Sometimes a packet of peanut-butter crackers. So delicious! Her mouth watered to recall such treats, years later. Some days after school, even in winter when dusk came early, Norma Jeane was allowed to walk by herself two and a half miles to Grauman's Egyptian Theatre on Hollywood Boulevard, where, for only ten cents, she could see a double feature.

The Fair Princess and the Dark Prince! Like Gladys, they were always waiting to console.

"These 'movie days.' Don't tell anyone." Gladys warned Norma Jeane not to confide in anyone; you couldn't trust anyone, even friends. They might misunderstand and judge Gladys harshly. But Gladys often had to work late. There were tasks in "developing" that only Gladys Mortensen could do, her supervisor depended upon her; without Gladys, such box-office hits as Dixie Lee's *Happy Days* and Mary Pickford's *Kiki* might have been disasters. Anyway, Gladys insisted it was safe at Grauman's Egyptian. "Just sit near the back, on the aisle. Look straight forward at the screen. Complain to the usher if anyone bothers you. And don't talk to strangers."

Returning home at dusk after the double feature, disoriented as if still in the rapturous movie dream, Norma Jeane followed her mother's directive to walk "quickly, as if you know where you're going, near the curb and under the streetlights. Don't make eye contact with anyone and don't accept rides from strangers, *ever*."

And not a thing ever happened to me. That I recall.

Because she was always with me. And he was, too.

The Dark Prince. If the man was anywhere, he was in the movie dream. Your heart quickened approaching the cathedral-like Egyptian Theatre. Your first glimpse of him would be in the posters outside, handsome glossy photos behind glass like works of art to be stared at. *Fred Astaire, Gary Cooper, Cary Grant, Charles Boyer, Paul Muni, Fredric March, Lew Ayres, Clark Gable.* Inside he would be gigantic on the screen, yet intimate, so close you could reach out your hand and touch him—almost! Speaking to others, embracing and kissing beautiful women, still he was defining himself to *you.* And these women, too—they were close enough to be touched, they were visions of yourself as in a fairy-tale mirror, Magic Friends in other bodies, with faces that were somehow, mysteriously, your own. Or would one day be your own. *Ginger Rogers, Joan Crawford, Katharine Hepburn, Jean Harlow, Marlene Dietrich, Greta Garbo, Constance Bennett, Joan Blondell, Claudette Colbert, Gloria Swanson.* Like dreams dreamt in confusing succession their stories melded together. There were bright brassy musicals, there were somber dramas, there were "screwball" comedies, there were sagas of adventure, war, ancient times—dream visions in which the same powerful faces appeared and reappeared. In different guises and costumes, inhabiting different fates. There he was! *The Dark Prince.*

And his Princess.

Wherever you are, I'm there. But this was not always true at school.

The bungalow-boardinghouse at 828 Highland Avenue was all adults except for curly-haired little Norma Jeane, who was a favorite among the tenants. ("Hardly an atmosphere for children, with such characters traipsing in and out," a woman tenant remarked to Gladys. "What d'you mean, 'characters'?" Gladys asked, annoyed. "We all work for The Studio." "That's what I mean," the woman said, laughing suggestively. " 'We all work for The Studio.' ") But school was children.

I was afraid of them! The strong-willed ones, you had to win over fast. You didn't get a second chance. Without brothers or sisters you were alone. I was strange to them. I wanted them to like me too much, I guess. They called me Pop Eyes and Big Head, I never knew why.

Gladys told her friends she was "obsessed" with her daughter's "poor public education," but she visited Highland Elementary only once in the eleven months Norma Jeane was a student there and then only because she'd been summoned.

The Dark Prince had no presence there at all.

Even in daydreams, even with her eyes shut hard, Norma Jeane could not imagine him. He would be waiting for her in the movie dream; this was her secret happiness.

7

"I have plans for you, Norma Jeane. For *us*."

A white Steinway spinet piano that was so beautiful Norma Jeane stared at it in astonishment, touched its polished surface with wondering fingers: oh, was this for *her*? "You'll take piano lessons. As I'd wanted to." The sitting room in Gladys's three-room flat was small and already crowded with furniture but space was made for this piano, "formerly owned by Fredric March," as Gladys frequently boasted.

The distinguished Mr. March, who'd made his name in silent films, was under contract to The Studio. He'd "befriended" Gladys in the studio cafeteria one day; he'd sold her the piano at a "considerably reduced price" as a favor to her, knowing she hadn't much money; or, in another version of Gladys's account of how she'd come to acquire such a special piano, Mr. March had simply given it to her "as a token of his esteem." (Gladys took Norma Jeane to see Fredric March in *I Love You Truly*, with Carole Lombard, at Grauman's Egyptian; in all, mother and daughter saw this film three times. "Your father would be jealous if he knew," Gladys remarked mysteriously.) Since Gladys couldn't afford a professional piano teacher for Norma Jeane just yet, she arranged for her to take casual lessons from another tenant in the bungalow, an Englishman named Pearce who was a stand-in for several leading men, including Charles Boyer and Clark Gable. He was of medium height, handsome, with a thin mustache. Yet he exuded no warmth—no "presence." Norma Jeane tried to please him by practicing her lessons dutifully; she loved playing the "magic piano" when she was alone, but Mr. Pearce's sighs and grimaces made her self-conscious. She quickly acquired the bad habit of compulsively repeating notes. "My dear, you must not *stammer* the keys," Mr. Pearce said in his clipped, ironic accent. "It's unfortunate enough you *stammer* the English language." Gladys, who'd managed to "pick up" a bit of piano, tried to teach Norma Jeane what she knew, but their sessions at the spinet were even more of a strain than those with Mr. Pearce. Gladys cried, exasperated, "Don't you hear when you strike a wrong note? A *sharp*, a *flat*? Are you *tone-deaf*? Or just *deaf*?"

Still, Norma Jeane's piano lessons continued sporadically. And she had occasional voice lessons with a woman friend of Gladys's, also a tenant in the bungalow, who worked in the music department at The Studio. Miss Flynn told Gladys, "Your little girl has a sweet, sincere personality. She tries

very hard. Harder than some of the young singers we have under contract!
But right now"—Jess Flynn spoke softly, so that Norma Jeane might not
hear—"she really has no voice at all."

Gladys said, "She will."

It was what we did together instead of church. Our worship.

On Sundays when Gladys had money to buy gas or a man friend to supply it, she drove with Norma Jeane to see the homes of the "stars." In Beverly Hills, Bel Air, Los Feliz, and the Hollywood Hills. Through the spring
and summer of 1934 and into the drought-stricken autumn. Gladys's voice
was a mezzo-soprano's, swelling with pride. The palatial home of Douglas
Fairbanks. The palatial home of Mary Pickford. The palatial home of Pola
Negri. The palatial homes of Tom Mix and Theda Bara—"Bara married a
multimillionaire businessman and retired. Smart." Norma Jeane stared.
What enormous houses! They were truly like palaces or castles in the illustrated fairy-tale books she'd seen. Never so happy, mother and daughter, as
at these magical times cruising the glittering streets. Norma Jeane was in no
danger of stammering and annoying her mother because Gladys did all the
talking. "The home of Barbara La Marr, 'The Girl Who Was Too Beautiful.' (Just a joke, sweetie. You can't be too beautiful, like you can't be too
rich.) The home of W. C. Fields. There, the former home of Greta Garbo—
beautiful, but smaller than you'd expect. And there, through that gate, the
Spanish-style mansion of the incomparable Gloria Swanson. And there, the
home of Norma Talmadge, 'our' Norma." Gladys parked the car so she and
the child could stare at the elegant stone mansion in which Norma Talmadge
had lived with her film-producer husband in Los Feliz. Eight magnificent
Metro-Goldwyn-Mayer lions in granite guarded the entrance! Norma Jeane
stared and stared. And the grass so green and lush. If it was true that Los
Angeles was a city of sand, you couldn't have guessed this in Beverly Hills,
Bel Air, Los Feliz, or the Hollywood Hills. Rain hadn't fallen in weeks and
everywhere else grass was burnt out, dying or dead, but in these storybook
places the lawns were uniformly green. Crimson and purple bougainvilleas
were in continuous bloom. There were exquisitely shaped trees Norma Jeane
saw nowhere else—Italian cypress, Gladys called them. Not stunted, shabby
palm trees of the kind that grew everywhere, but court palm trees taller than
the peaks of the tallest houses. "The former home of Buster Keaton. Over
there, Helen Chandler. Behind those gates, Mabel Normand. And Harold
Lloyd. John Barrymore. Joan Crawford. And Jean Harlow—'our' Jean."
Norma Jeane liked it that Jean Harlow, like Norma Talmadge, lived in a
palace surrounded by green.

Always above such houses the sun shone mildly and did not glare. If there were clouds they were high vaporous fluffy white clouds on a perfect painted blue sky.

"There, Cary Grant! And so young. And there, John Gilbert. Lillian Gish—only one of her former mansions. And there, the corner house, the late Jeanne Eagels—poor thing."

Norma Jeane promptly asked what had happened to Jeanne Eagels.

In the past, Gladys had said simply, sadly, *She died.* This time she said contemptuously, "Eagels! A hophead drug fiend. Skinny as a skeleton, they say, at the end. Thirty-five, and *old.*"

Gladys drove on. The tour continued. Sometimes Gladys began in Beverly Hills and looped her way back to Highland Avenue by the late afternoon; sometimes she drove directly to Los Feliz and looped back to Beverly Hills; sometimes she drove up into the less populated Hollywood Hills, where younger stars lived, or personalities-about-to-become-stars. Sometimes, as if drawn against her will, like a sleepwalker, she turned onto a street they'd already cruised that day and repeated her remarks: "See? Through that gate, the Spanish-style home of Gloria Swanson. And over there, Myrna Loy. Up ahead—Conrad Nagel." The tour seemed to be growing in intensity even as Gladys drove slower, staring through the windshield of the tarnished-green Ford, which always needed washing. Or perhaps the glass was permanently covered in a fine film of grime. There would seem to be some purpose to the tour, which, as in a movie with a knotty, complicated plot, would shortly be revealed. Gladys's voice conveyed reverence and enthusiasm as always, but beneath it there was a calm, implacable rage. "There—the most famous of all: FALCON'S LAIR. The home of the late Rudolph Valentino. *He* had no talent for acting at all. He had no talent for life. But he was photogenic, and he died at the right time. Remember, Norma Jeane—*die at the right time.*"

Mother and daughter sat in the 1929 tarnished-green Ford staring at the baroque mansion of the great silent film star Valentino and did not want to leave, ever.

8

Both Gladys and Norma Jeane dressed for the funeral with fastidious care and taste—though stranded among more than seven thousand "mourners" thronging Wilshire Boulevard in the vicinity of the Wilshire Temple.

A temple was a "Jewish church," Gladys told Norma Jeane.

A Jew was "like a Christian" except of an older, wiser, more tragic race. Where Christians had pioneered the West in the actual soil of the earth, Jews had pioneered in the film industry and had made a revolution.

Norma Jeane asked, "Can we be Jews, Mother?"

Gladys began to say no, then hesitated, laughed, and said, "If they wanted us. If we were worthy. If we could be born a second time."

Gladys, who'd been speaking for days of having known Mr. Thalberg "if not well, in admiration for his film genius," was striking in a glamorous black crepe dress in a modified twenties style with a dropped waist, a swishy layered skirt to mid-calf, and an elaborate black lace collar. Her hat was black cloche with a black veil that lifted and fell, lifted and fell with her quickened warm breath. Her gloves appeared new: black satin to the elbow. Smoke-colored stockings, high-heeled black leather pumps. Her face was a waxy-pale cosmetic mask like a mannequin's face, the features highlighted, exaggerated in the bygone style of Pola Negri; her perfume was sharply sweet, like the decaying oranges in their mostly iceless icebox. Her earrings might have been diamonds or rhinestones or an ingeniously faceted glass that winked as she turned her head.

Never regret going into debt for a worthy purpose.

The death of a great man is always a worthy purpose.

(In fact, Gladys had purchased only accessories. She'd "borrowed" the black crepe dress from The Studio's costume department, unauthorized.)

Norma Jeane, frightened of the milling crowd of strangers, uniformed policemen on horseback, a procession of somber black limousines along the street, and waves of cries, shouts, screams, and even outbursts of applause, was wearing a dress of midnight-blue velvet with a lace collar and cuffs and a plaid tam-o'-shanter, white lace gloves and dark ribbed stockings, and shiny patent-leather shoes. She'd been made to miss school that day. She'd been fussed over, and chided, and threatened. Her hair had been washed (by Gladys, grimly and thoroughly) very early that morning, before dawn, for it had been one of Gladys's difficult nights: her prescription medicine made her sick to her stomach, her thoughts were "all in a whirl, like ticker tape," and so Norma Jeane's snarled hair had to be forcibly unsnarled, with a pitiless rat-tailed comb, and then brushed, brushed, brushed until it gleamed—and with the aid of Jess Flynn (who'd heard the child crying at 5 A.M.) neatly braided and wound about her head so she looked, despite her teary eyes and mangled mouth, like a storybook princess.

He'll be there. At the funeral. One of the pallbearers or ushers. He won't speak to us. Not in public. But he'll see us. He'll see you, his daughter. You'll never know when but you must be prepared.

A block from the Wilshire Temple, a crowd was already forming on both sides of the street. Though it wasn't yet 7:30 A.M. and the funeral was scheduled for 9 A.M. There were mounted police, and police on foot; there were photographers milling about, eager to begin taking pictures of the historic event.

Barricades had been set in the street and on the sidewalks, and behind these a vast seething throng of men and women would wait avidly, with a strange concentrated patience, for film stars and other celebrities to arrive in a succession of chauffeur-driven limousines, enter the temple, and depart again after a lengthy ninety minutes, during which time the murmurous crowd—barred from the private service as from any direct communication, let alone intimacy, with these celebrities—continued to swell at its edges; and Gladys and Norma Jeane, pushed against one of the wooden sawhorses, clutched at it and at each other. At last there emerged out of the temple's front entrance a gleaming black coffin borne aloft by elegantly dressed, solemn-faced pallbearers—through the staring crowd their names were uttered in excited recognition: *Ronald Colman! Adolphe Menjou! Nelson Eddy! Clark Gable! Douglas Fairbanks, Jr.! Al Jolson! John Barrymore! Basil Rathbone!* And behind them swaying with grief the dead man's widow Norma Shearer, the film star, clad head to toe in sumptuous black, her beautiful face veiled; and behind Miss Shearer a surge of celebrities began to spill from the temple like a stream of golden lava, somber in grief as well, their names evoked in a litany that Gladys repeated for Norma Jeane's benefit, as the child crouched against the sawhorse, excited and frightened, hoping not to be trampled—*Leslie Howard! Erich von Stroheim! Greta Garbo! Joel McCrea! Wallace Beery! Clara Bow! Helen Twelvetrees! Spencer Tracy! Raoul Walsh! Edward G. Robinson! Charlie Chaplin! Lionel Barrymore! Jean Harlow! Groucho, Harpo, and Chico Marx! Mary Pickford! Jane Withers! Irvin S. Cobb! Shirley Temple! Jackie Coogan! Bela Lugosi! Mickey Rooney! Freddie Bartholomew* in his velvet suit from *Little Lord Fauntleroy! Busby Berkeley! Bing Crosby! Lon Chaney! Marie Dressler! Mae West!*—and here photographers and autograph seekers broke through the barricades as mounted police, cursing, nudging with their billy clubs, tried to drive them back.

There was a confused melee. Angry shouts, screams. Someone may have fallen. Someone may have been struck by a billy club or trampled by a horse's hooves. Police shouted through bullhorns. There was a sound of automobile engines, a swelling roar. The commotion subsided quickly. Norma Jeane, her tam-o'-shanter knocked askew, too panicked to cry, clung to Gladys's rigid arm *and Mother didn't shake me off, she allowed it.* By degrees, the pressure of the crowd began to diminish. The handsome black hearse like a chariot of death and the numerous chauffeur-driven limousines had departed and only onlookers remained, ordinary people of no more interest to one another than a flock of sparrows. People began to drift away, free to walk now in the very street. There was nowhere to go, but there was no point in remaining here. The historic event, the funeral of the great Hollywood pioneer Irving G. Thalberg, was over.

Here and there women were wiping at their eyes. Many onlookers appeared disoriented, as if they'd suffered a great loss without knowing what it was.

Norma Jeane's mother was one of these. Her face seemed smudged behind the damp, sticky veil and her eyes were watery and unfocused like miniature fish swimming in divergent directions. She was whispering to herself, smiling tensely. Her gaze raked Norma Jeane without seeming to take her in. Then she was walking away, unsteady in her high-heeled pumps. Norma Jeane noticed two men, not standing together, watching her. One of the men whistled to her, questioningly; it was like the opening of a sudden dance scene in a Ginger Rogers and Fred Astaire movie, except there was no burst of music and Gladys did not seem to be aware of the man and the man almost immediately lost interest in her and turned yawning to stroll away. The other man, tugging absentmindedly at his crotch as if he were alone and unobserved, was drifting in the other direction.

A clatter of hooves! Norma Jeane looked up astonished to see a uniformed man, riding a tall handsome chestnut horse with enormous bulging eyes, peering down at her. "Little girl, where's your mother? You aren't here alone, are you?" he asked. Stricken with shyness, Norma Jeane shook her head, no. She ran after Gladys and took Gladys's gloved hand and was again grateful that Gladys didn't throw off her hand, for the mounted policeman was watching them closely. *It was going to happen soon. But not yet.* Gladys, dazed, couldn't seem to remember where she'd parked the car but Norma Jeane remembered, or almost remembered, and eventually they found it, the tarnished-green 1929 Ford parked on a commercial street perpendicular to Wilshire. Norma Jeane thought how strange it was, and this, too, like something in a movie that turns out right, that you have a key for a certain car; out of hundreds, thousands of cars your key is for only one car; a key for what Gladys called the "ignition"; and when you turn the key, the "ignition" starts the engine. And you aren't lost and stranded miles from home.

Inside, the car was hot as an oven. Norma Jeane squirmed with the need to go to the bathroom, badly.

Gladys said petulantly, wiping at her eyes, "I only just want not to feel grief. But I keep my thoughts to myself." To Norma Jeane she said with sudden sharpness, "What the hell happened to your dress?" The hem had snagged on a splinter in the sawhorse and ripped.

"I—don't know. *I* didn't do it."

"Then who did? Santa Claus?"

Gladys had the intention of driving to the "Jewish cemetery" but didn't know where it was. When she stopped several times on Wilshire to ask directions, no one seemed to know. She drove on, now smoking a Chesterfield.

She'd removed the cloche hat with the sticky veil and tossed it into the back-seat of the car with the accumulation—newspapers, screen magazines, and paperback books, stiffened handkerchiefs, and miscellaneous items of cloth-ing—of months. As Norma Jeane squirmed in discomfort she said, musing, "Maybe if you're a Jew like Thalberg, it's different. There must be a differ-ent perspective on the universe. The calendar isn't even the same as ours. What is a perpetual surprise to us, so new, is not new to them. They live half in the Old Testament, all those plagues and prophecies. If we could have that perspective." She paused. She glanced sidelong at Norma Jeane, who was trying to hold in her pee, but the pressure was so strong there was a hurt between her legs sharp as a needle. "*He* has Jewish blood. That's part of the barrier between us. But he saw us, today. He couldn't speak but his eyes spoke. Norma Jeane, he saw *you*."

It was then, less than a mile from Highland Avenue, that Norma Jeane wet her panties—in mortification, in misery!—but there was nothing to be done once it started. Gladys smelled the pee at once and began slapping and punching at Norma Jeane as she drove, furious. "Pig! Little beast! That beau-tiful dress is ruined and it isn't even *ours*! You do these things deliberately, don't you?"

Four days later, the first of the Santa Ana winds began to blow.

9

Because she loved the child and wished to spare her grief.

Because she was poisoned. And the little girl was poisoned.

Because the city of sand was collapsing in flame.

Because the smell of burn was saturating the air.

Because by the calendar those born under the sign of Gemini must now "act decisively" and "display courage in determining their lives."

Because it was past her time of month, and the blood in her had ceased to flow. And she would no longer be a woman desired by any man.

Because for thirteen years she had worked in the film lab at The Studio and thirteen years a reliable loyal devoted employee helping to make possi-ble the great films of The Studio promoting the great stars of the American screen transforming the very soul of America, and now to discover her youth drained away, now she was deathly sick in her soul. They lied to her in the Studio infirmary, the Studio-hired doctor insisting her blood was not poi-soned when her blood *was* poisoned, chemical poison seeping through even the double-strength rubber gloves and into the bones of her hands, those hands her lover had kissed saying they were beautiful delicate "hands of solace," and into the marrow of her skeleton, coursing through her blood and into her brain and the poison fumes seeping into her unprotected lungs. And her eyes, the wavering vision. The eyes aching even in sleep. And her co-workers refusing to acknowledge their own sicknesses for fear of being fired—"unemployed." Because it was a season of hell, 1934 in the United States and a season of shame. Because she had called in sick, and called in sick, and called in sick until a voice informed her she was "no longer on Studio payroll, Studio pass canceled, and admittance at security will be denied." After thirteen years.

Because never again would she work for The Studio. Never again work for a pittance selling her soul for mere animal survival. Because she must cleanse herself and the afflicted child.

Because the child was her own secret self, exposed.

Because the child was a freak of deformity, in disguise as a pretty little curly-haired girl. *Because there was deception.*

Because the very father of the child had wished it not to be born.

Because he had said to her he doubted it was his.

Because he had given her money, scattering bills across the bed.

Because the sum of these bills was but $225, the sum of their love.

Because he told her he'd never loved her; she had misunderstood.

Because he told her not to call him again, not to follow him on the street. *Because there was deception.*

Because before the pregnancy he had loved her, and after he had not. Because he would have married her. She was certain.

Because the child had been born three weeks before expected, that it must be a Gemini like herself. And so accursed as she.

Because no one would ever love a child so accursed.

Because the brush fires in the hills were a clear summons and a sign.

It would not be the Dark Prince who came for my mother.
All the rest of my life, the horror that one day strangers would also come for me to bear me away naked and raving and a spectacle of pity.

She was made to stay home from school. Her mother would not allow her to go among their enemies. Jess Flynn was sometimes trusted and sometimes not. For Jess Flynn was an employee of The Studio and possibly a spy. Yet Jess Flynn was a friend bringing them food. Dropping by with a smile "just to see how things are." Offering to lend Gladys money if it was money Gladys needed, or the carpet sweeper in Jess's apartment. Gladys lay most of the time in bed, naked beneath the soiled sheet, the room darkened. A flashlight on the bedside table for the detection of scorpions, of which Gladys was very afraid. The blinds in all the rooms had been pulled to the windowsills so you could not tell night from day, dusk from dawn. A smoke haze in even bright sunshine. A smell of sickness. A smell of soiled bedclothes, undergarments. A smell of stale coffee grounds, rancid milk, and oranges in the icebox that contained no ice. The gin smell, the cigarette smell, the smell of human sweat, fury, and despair. Jess Flynn did "a little tidying up" if allowed. If not, not.

From time to time Clive Pearce rapped on the door. Talked to Gladys or to the little girl through the door. Though it wasn't clear what was said. Unlike Jess Flynn, he would not enter. The piano lessons had ceased over the summer. He would say it was a "tragedy," yet "might have been a worse tragedy." Other tenants of the boardinghouse conferred; what to do? All were employees of The Studio. They were stand-ins and extras but also an assistant cinematographer, a masseur, a costumer, two script timers, a gymnastics instructor, a film-lab technician, a stenographer, set builders, and several musicians. Among them it was generally known that Gladys Mortensen was "mentally unstable"—unless she was just "temperamental, eccentric." It was known by most of the tenants that Mrs. Mortensen lived with a little girl who, except for her curls, looked "uncannily" like her.

It was not known what to do, or whether to do anything. There was a reluctance to become involved. There was a reluctance to incur the Mortensen woman's wrath. There was the vague presumption that Jess Flynn was a friend of Gladys Mortensen's, and in charge.

The child, naked and sobbing, crawled to hide behind the spinet piano, defying her mother. Eluding her mother. Scrambling then across the carpet like a panicked animal. The mother struck at the piano keyboard with both fists, an outcry of sharp treble notes, a vibrating sound as of quivering nerves. And this too slapstick. In the spirit of Mack Sennett. Mabel Normand in *A Displaced Foot*, Gladys had seen as a girl.

If it makes you laugh, it's comedy. Even if it hurts.

Scalding-hot cleansing water rushing into the tub. She'd stripped the child naked and was herself naked. She'd half carried the child, tried to lift her and force her into the water, but the child resisted, screaming. In the confusion of her thoughts, which were mixed with the acrid taste of smoke and jeering voices too muffled by drugs to be heard clearly, she'd been thinking the child was much younger, it was an earlier time in their lives and the child was only two or three years old weighing only—what?—thirty pounds, and not distrustful of her mother, and not suspicious, cringing and shoving away and beginning to scream *No! No!* this child so grown, so strong and *willful*, possessed of a will contrary to her mother's, refusing to be led and lifted and set into the scalding-hot cleansing water, fighting free, running from the steamy bathroom and out of her mother's bare clutching arms.

"You. You're the reason. He went away. He didn't want *you*"—these words, almost calmly uttered, flung after the terrified child like a handful of stinging pebbles.

And the child, naked, ran blindly along a corridor and pounded at a neighbor's door crying, "Help! Help us!" and there was no answer. And the child ran farther along the corridor and pounded at a second door crying, "Help! Help us!" and there was no answer. And the child ran to a third door, and pounded on it, and this time the door was opened, and an astonished young man, tanned and muscular in an undershirt and beltless trousers stared down at her, he had an actor's face but he blinked now in unfeigned astonishment at this frantic little girl who was totally naked, her face streaked with tears, crying, "H-help us, my mother is sick, come help my mother she's sick," and the first thing the young man did was to snatch up a shirt of his from a chair to wrap quickly about the child, to cover her nakedness, saying then, "All right now, little girl, your mother is sick? What's wrong with your mother?"

AUNT JESS AND UNCLE CLIVE

She loved me; she was taken from me but she loved me always.

"Your momma is well enough to see you now, Norma Jeane."

It was Miss Flynn speaking. And Mr. Pearce behind her in the doorway. Like pallbearers they were. Gladys's friend Jess Flynn with her reddened eyelids and her twitchy-rabbit nose and Gladys's friend Clive Pearce stroking his chin, nervously stroking his chin and sucking a mint. "Your momma has been asking for you, Norma Jeane!" Miss Flynn said. "The doctors say she's well enough to see you. Shall we go?"

Shall we go? This was movie talk; the child was alerted to danger.

Yet as in a movie you must play out the scene. You must not show your suspicion. For of course you don't know beforehand. Only if you'd stayed through the feature to see the movie a second time would you know what the strained smiles, the evasive eyes, the clumsy dialogue really mean.

The child smiled happily. The child was trusting and wanted you to see it.

Ten days had passed since Gladys Mortensen had been "taken away." Hospitalized at the State Hospital at Norwalk, south of L.A. The city air was still hazy-humid and made your eyes water, but the canyon fires were beginning to subside. Fewer sirens screamed in the night. Families evacuated from the canyons north of the city were being allowed to return to their homes. Most schools had resumed. Though Norma Jeane had not returned to school and would not return to Highland Elementary, to fourth grade. The child cried easily and was "nervous." Slept in Miss Flynn's sitting room on Miss Flynn's pull-out sofa on loose, untucked-in sheets from Gladys's apartment. Sometimes she was able to sleep for as many as six or seven hours in a row. When Miss Flynn gave her "just half" of a white pill that tasted like bitter flour on the tongue, she slept a deep dazed stuporous sleep that made her little heart pound like slow measured blows of a sledgehammer and turned her skin clammy as a slug. And when she wakened from this sleep she recalled nothing of where she had been. *I wasn't seeing her. I wasn't there to see her taken away.*

There was a fairy tale Grandma Della used to tell Norma Jeane; maybe it was a story Grandma Della had made up herself: a little girl who sees too much, a little girl who hears too much, a crow comes to peck out her eyes, a "big fish walking on his tail" comes to gobble up her ears, and for good measure a red fox bites off her pointy little nose! See what happens, miss?

The promised day. Yet it came as a surprise. Miss Flynn kneading her hands, smiling with her mouth and her teeth that didn't quite fit in her mouth, explaining that Gladys "had been asking for her."

It was cruel of Gladys to have said of Jess Flynn that she was a thirty-five-year-old virgin. Jess was a voice instructor and music assistant at The Studio, she'd been recruited years ago as a graduate of the San Francisco Choir School with a soprano voice lovely as Lily Pons's. Gladys said, "Jess's bad luck! There are as many 'lovely' sopranos in Hollywood as there are cockroaches. And cocks." But you mustn't laugh, you mustn't even smile when Gladys "talked dirty" and embarrassed her friends. You mustn't even let on you were listening unless Gladys winked at you.

So there came, that morning, Jess Flynn smiling with her mouth, her moist sad eyes, and twitchy nose. She'd had to take the day off from work. Saying she'd been on the phone with the doctors and Norma Jeane's "momma" was well enough to see her, and she and Clive Pearce would be driving her, and they'd be bringing "some things in suitcases" which Jess would pack; Norma Jeane could go out into the backyard and play and didn't have to help. (But how could you "play" when your mother was sick in the hospital?) Outside, wiping her eyes that stung in the gritty air, the child didn't allow herself to think that something was wrong; *momma* was a wrong name for Gladys, as Jess Flynn must know.

Didn't see her carried away. Arms in sleeves tied behind her back. Strapped naked to the stretcher and a thin blanket thrown over her. Spat, screamed, tried to tear herself free. And the ambulance attendants, sweaty-faced, cursing her in turn, carrying her away.

They'd explained to Norma Jeane that she hadn't seen, she hadn't been anywhere near.

Maybe Miss Flynn had put her hands over Norma Jeane's face? That was ever so much nicer than a crow pecking out her eyes!

Miss Flynn, Mr. Pearce. But they were not a couple unless a movie couple in a comedy. Gladys's closest friends in the boardinghouse. They were very fond of Norma Jeane, truly! Mr. Pearce was upset by what had happened and Miss Flynn had promised to "take care of" Norma Jeane, and so she had, for ten difficult days. Now the diagnosis was official, now a decision had been made. Norma Jeane overheard Jess weeping and sniffing, talking at length on the telephone in the other room. *I feel so terrible! But it could not go on permanently. God forgive me, I know I promised. And I meant it, I love this little girl like my own child, I mean—if I had a child. But I have to work, God knows I have to work, I have no money saved, there is nothing else to be done.* In the beige linen dress already showing half-moons of perspiration at her underarms. After weeping in the bathroom she'd vigorously brushed her teeth as she did when she was nervous; now the pale gums leaked blood.

Clive Pearce was known in the boardinghouse as the "gentleman Brit." An actor under contract to The Studio, in his late thirties but still hoping for a break; as Gladys said with a droll downturning of her mouth, "Most of our 'breaks' are *broke*." Clive Pearce was wearing a dark suit, a white cotton shirt, and an ascot tie. Handsome, but he'd nicked himself shaving. His breath smelled of fumes and of chocolate peppermint, a smell Norma Jeane recognized with her eyes shut. Here was "Uncle Clive"—as he'd suggested she call him, but she'd never been able to say that for it didn't seem right, for *he was not my uncle really.* Still, Norma Jeane liked Mr. Pearce, very very much! Her piano instructor she'd tried so hard to please. Just to coax a smile from Mr. Pearce made her happy. And she liked Miss Flynn very much, too, Miss Flynn who'd urged her, just these past few days, to call her "Aunt Jess"—"Auntie Jess"—but the words stuck in Norma Jeane's throat for *she was not my aunt really.*

Miss Flynn cleared her throat. "Shall we go?"—and that ghastly smile.

Mr. Pearce, guilt-stricken, noisily sucking his mint, hoisted up Gladys's suitcases, two smaller suitcases in the grip of one big hand, the third in the other. Not looking at Norma Jeane, muttering *What's to be done, what's to be done, nothing else to be done, God help us.*

There was a movie in which Aunt Jess and Uncle Clive were married and Norma Jeane would be their little girl. But this was not that movie.

Broad-shouldered Mr. Pearce carried the suitcases out to the automobile at the curb, which was his own. Chattering nervously, Miss Flynn led Norma

Jeane out by the hand. It was a warm-oven day in which the sun, hidden by smoky clouds, seemed to be everywhere. Mr. Pearce was to drive of course, for men always drove cars. Norma Jeane begged for Miss Flynn to sit in the back with her and her doll, but Miss Flynn sat in front with Mr. Pearce. It would be a drive of perhaps an hour, and not many words were exchanged between the front and back seats. The rattling noise of the motor, air hissing through opened windows. Miss Flynn sniffed as she read directions to Mr. Pearce from a sheet of paper. Only at this time would the drive be "going to visit Mother in the hospital"; in retrospect it would be something else. If you could see the movie twice, that is.

Always it's important to be costumed correctly, whatever the scene. Norma Jeane was wearing her only good school clothes: a plaid pleated skirt, a white cotton blouse (ironed by Jess Flynn herself that morning), reasonably clean mended white socks, and her newest undies. Her curly-snarly hair was brushed, though not combed. ("No use!" Miss Flynn sighed, letting the hairbrush fall onto her bed. "I'd be tearing half the hair out of your head, Norma Jeane, if I persisted.")

Embarrassing to Miss Flynn and Mr. Pearce that Norma Jeane clutched so desperately at her doll. That doll was so shabby, its skin fire-scorched and most of its hair burnt away and its glassy-blue eyes fixed in an expression of idiot horror. Miss Flynn had promised Norma Jeane she would purchase her another doll but there'd been no time or else Miss Flynn had forgotten. Norma Jeane was prepared to hug her doll tight and never let her go—"This is *my doll*. My mother gave me."

The doll had been spared by the fire in Gladys's bedroom. In a fury, Gladys had managed to start a fire on her bed, in the bedclothes, after Norma Jeane had escaped the scalding-hot bath to run for help to a neighbor; this was wrong to do, Norma Jeane knew, it was always wrong to "go behind your mother's back" as Gladys called it; but Norma Jeane had had to do it, and Gladys bolted the door behind her and started a fire with matches, burning most of the glamorous black crepe dress and the midnight-blue velvet dress Norma Jeane had been made to wear on the day of the funeral on Wilshire Boulevard, several ripped-up photographs (one of them Norma Jeane's father? Norma Jeane would never see that handsome photograph again), and shoes, cosmetics; in her rage she'd have liked to burn everything she owned, including the spinet piano that had once belonged to Fredric March and of which she was so proud, and her very own self she'd have liked to burn, but the emergency medics had broken down the door to prevent it, smoke billowing out of the apartment, and there, Gladys Mortensen, a sallow-skinned naked woman, so thin her bones nearly protruded through her skin, a woman with a lined, contorted witch's face, screaming obscenities and clawing and kicking at her rescuers, who'd had to be wrestled down and "put into restraint for her own good"—as Norma Jeane would hear Miss Flynn and others in the boardinghouse repeatedly describing the scene—which Norma Jeane had not seen because she hadn't been there, or someone had covered her eyes.

"Now, you know you weren't there, Norma Jeane. You were safe and sound with *me*."

Your punishment if you're a woman. Not loved enough.

This was the day Norma Jeane was taken to "visit momma" in the hospital. But where was Norwalk? South of Los Angeles, she was told. Miss Flynn cleared her throat as she read off directions for Mr. Pearce, who seemed anxious and annoyed. He was not Uncle Clive now. At piano lessons Mr. Pearce was sometimes quiet and sad-sighing and sometimes lively and funny, it had to do with the smell of his breath; if his breath smelled *that way*, Norma Jeane knew they'd have a good time, no matter how awkwardly she played. With a pencil Mr. Pearce beat time on the piano *one-two, one-two, one-two* and sometimes on his little pupil's head, which made her giggle. Leaning his warm whiskey breath to Norma Jeane's ear to hum loudly like a bumblebee and beating time louder with his pencil *one-two, one-two, one-two* and playfully there came poking Mr. Pearce's snaky tongue into Norma Jeane's ear!—she squealed and giggled and would have run away to hide except Mr. Pearce scolded saying don't be silly—and she came back to the piano bench shivering and giggling, and so the lesson continued. *I loved being tickled! Even if it hurt sometimes. I loved being smooched like Grandma Della would do, I missed Grandma so. I never minded if my face was scratched.* Then there were piano lessons when Mr. Pearce, breathing quickly, and anxious, suddenly shut up the keyboard (which was never shut by Gladys and which looked strange, being shut), declaring, "No more lessons for today!" and walked out of the apartment without a backward glance.

Strange, too, how one evening that summer when Norma Jeane, up past her bedtime, nudged and burrowed persistently against Mr. Pearce, who'd dropped by to have a drink with Gladys, crowding between Gladys and her visitor on the sofa, trying like a puppy to push her way into his lap, and Gladys, staring, said sharply, "Norma Jeane, behave yourself. You're being disgusting." Then to Mr. Pearce she said, in a lower voice, "Clive, what's this?" And the naughty giggling little girl was banished to the bedroom, where she couldn't overhear the adults' conversation, except after a few excited minutes it seemed they were laughing companionably again; and there came the reassuring *click!* of a bottle against glass. And from that hour Norma Jeane understood that Mr. Pearce was not always the same person and you were silly to expect otherwise; as Gladys was not always the same person. In fact, Norma Jeane was getting to be a surprise to herself: sometimes she was happy-silly, sometimes quick to cry, sometimes far off and prone to playacting, sometimes "nerved up," as Gladys defined the state, and "scared of her own shadow like it's a snake."

And always there was Norma Jeane's Magic Friend in the mirror. Peeking at her from a corner of the mirror or staring boldly, full-faced. The mirror could be like a movie; maybe the mirror *was* a movie. And that pretty little curly-haired girl who was *her*.

Clutching her doll, Norma Jeane regarded the backs of the heads of the adults in the front seat of Mr. Pearce's automobile. The "gentleman Brit" in handsome dark suit and ascot tie was not Mr. Pearce on the piano bench lost in rapturous concentration playing Beethoven's brief heartbreaking "Für Elise"—"note by note the most exquisite music ever written," Gladys extravagantly claimed—nor was he Mr. Pearce humming loudly like a bumblebee and tickling Norma Jeane beside him on the piano bench, spidery fingers "playing" piano up and down her shivery body; nor was Miss Flynn, shading her eyes against migraine, the Miss Flynn who'd hugged her and wept over her and begged her to call her "Aunt Jess"—"Auntie Jess." Yet Norma Jeane did not believe these adults had purposefully deceived her, any more than Gladys had deceived her. These were different times and different scenes. In film there is no inevitable sequence, for all is present tense. Film can be run backward as well as forward. Film can be severely edited. Film can be *whited out*. Film is the repository of that which, failing to be remembered, is immortal. One day when Norma Jeane would come permanently to dwell in the Kingdom of Madness she would recall how logical, if still hurtful, was this day. She would recall, erroneously, that Mr. Pearce had played "Für Elise" before setting out on their journey. "One last time, my dear." Soon she would learn the teachings of Christian Science and much would become clear that was unclear that day. *Mind is all, truth makes us free, deception and lies and pain and evil are but human illusions caused by ourselves to punish ourselves and not real; only out of weakness and ignorance do we succumb to such.* For always there was a way to forgive, through Jesus Christ.

If only you could comprehend what the hurt was, you must forgive.

This was the day Norma Jeane was taken to visit with her "momma" in the hospital at Norwalk except this was the day Norma Jeane was taken instead to a brick building on El Centro Avenue bearing a sign above its front entrance that would imprint itself permanently upon Norma Jeane's soul even as, at the moment she first sighted it, she did not "see" it at all.

LOS ANGELES ORPHANS HOME SOCIETY
EST. 1921

Not a hospital? But where was the hospital? *Where was Mother?*

Miss Flynn, sniffing and scolding, excitable as Norma Jeane had never seen her, had to pry the terrified child out of the backseat of Clive Pearce's automobile. "Norma Jeane, please. Be a good girl please, Norma Jeane. *Don't kick me, Norma Jeane!*" Turning his back on the struggle, Mr. Pearce quickly strode away to have a smoke in the open air. He'd had mostly walk-on roles for so many years—often he was posed in profile, with an enigmatic-Brit smile—he had no idea how to manage an actual scene; his classic Brit training at the Royal Academy had not included improvisation. Miss Flynn shouted to him, "At least bring the suitcases inside, Clive, damn you!" In Miss Flynn's recounting of this traumatic morning, she'd had to half-carry, half-drag Gladys Mortensen's daughter into the orphanage. She'd alternately begged and scolded, "Please forgive me, Norma Jeane, there's no other place for you right now—your mother is *sick*, the doctors say she's *very sick*—she tried to hurt you, you know—she can't be a mother to you just now—*I* can't be a mother to you just now—oh, Norma Jeane! Bad girl! That *hurts*." Inside the dank, airless building Norma Jeane began to tremble uncontrollably and in the director's office she wept, stuttering as she told the stout woman with a carved-looking face that she wasn't an orphan, she had a mother. *She wasn't an orphan. She had a mother.* Miss Flynn hastily departed, blowing her nose into a hankie. Mr. Pearce had delivered Gladys's suitcases into the vestibule and hastily departed also. The teary-faced runny-nosed Norma Jeane Baker (for so documents identified her: born June 1, 1926, Los Angeles County General Hospital) was left alone with Dr. Mittelstadt, who'd summoned into her office a slightly younger matron, a frowning woman in a stained coverall. Still the child protested. *She wasn't an orphan. She had a mother. She had a father living in a big mansion in Beverly Hills.*

Dr. Mittelstadt regarded the eight-year-old ward of the County of Los Angeles Children's Services through wavy bifocal lenses. She said, not cruelly, perhaps kindly, with a sigh that for a moment lifted her prominent bosom, "Child, save your tears! You may need them."

THE LOST ONE

If I was pretty enough, my father would come and take me away.

Four years, nine months, and eleven days.

Through the vast continent of North America it was a season of abandoned children. And nowhere in greater numbers than in southern California.

After hot dry winds blew out of the deserts for days, unrelenting and pitiless, there began to be discovered infants blown with sand and debris into parched drainage ditches, into culverts and against railroad beds; blown against the granite steps of churches, hospitals, municipal buildings. Newborn infants, bloody umbilical cords still attached to their navels, were discovered in public rest rooms, in church pews, and in trash bins and dumps. How the wind wailed, days on end—yet this wailing, as the wind subsided, was revealed as the wailing of infants. And of their older sisters and brothers: children of two or three wandering dazed in the streets, some with smoldering clothes and hair. These were children lacking names. These were children lacking speech, comprehension. Injured children, many badly burned. Others even less lucky had died or been killed; their little corpses, often charred beyond recognition, were hastily swept off Los Angeles streets by sanitation workers, collected in dump trucks to be buried in unmarked mass graves in the canyons. Not a word to the press or radio! No one must know.

"The lost ones," these were called. "Those beyond our mercy."

Heat lightning had flashed in the Hollywood Hills and a firestorm came rolling down like the wrath of Jehovah and there was a blinding explosion in the very bed Norma Jeane and her mother shared, and next thing she knew, her hair and eyelashes singed, her eyes seared as if she'd been forced to stare into a blinding light, she was alone without her mother in this place for which she had no name other than *this place*.

Through the narrow window beneath the eaves, how many miles away she could not calculate, if she stood on the bed assigned to her (barefoot, in her nightgown, in the night), she saw the pulsing-neon lights of the RKO Motion Pictures tower in Hollywood:

RKO   RKO   RKO

Someday.

Who had brought her to *this place* the child could not recall. There were no distinct faces in her memory, and no names. For many days she was mute. Her throat was raw and parched as if she'd been forced to inhale fire. She could not eat without gagging and often vomiting. She was sickly-looking and sick. She was hoping to die. She was mature enough to articulate that wish: *I am so ashamed, nobody wants me, I want to die.* She was not mature enough to comprehend the rage of such a wish. Nor the ecstasy of madness such rage would one day stoke, a madness of ambition to revenge herself upon the world by conquering it, somehow, anyhow—however any "world" is "conquered" by any mere individual, and that individual female, parentless, isolated, and seemingly of as much intrinsic worth as a solitary insect amid a teeming mass of insects. *Yet I will make you all love me and I will punish myself to spite your love* was not then Norma Jeane's threat, for she knew herself, despite the wound in her soul, lucky to have been brought to *this place* and not scalded to death or burned alive by her raging mother in the bungalow at 828 Highland Avenue.

For there were other children in the Los Angeles Orphans Home more wounded than Norma Jeane. Even in her hurt and confusion, she perceived this fact. Retarded children, brain-damaged children, handicapped children—you could see at a glance why their mothers had abandoned them—ugly children, angry children, animal children, defeated children you would not wish to touch for fear the clamminess of their skin would permeate your own. There was the ten-year-old girl whose cot was next to Norma Jeane's in the girls' third-floor dorm whose name was Debra Mae who'd been raped and beaten (what a hard, harsh word "rape" was, an adult word; Norma Jeane knew instinctively what it meant, or almost knew: a *razor* sound and something shameful to do with between-a-girl's-legs-which-you-are-never-supposed-to-show, where the flesh is soft, sensitive, easily hurt, and it made Norma Jeane faint to think of being struck there, let alone something sharp and hard pushed *in*); and there were the five-year-old boy twins found nearly dead of malnutrition in a canyon in the Santa Monica Mountains, where they'd been left tied up by their mother as "a sacrifice like Abraham in the Bible" (as the mother's note explained); and there was an older girl who would befriend Norma Jeane, an eleven-year-old called Fleece, whose original name might have been Felice, who told and retold with lurid fascination the story of her year-old sister who'd been "banged against a wall until her brains spilled out like melon seeds" by their mother's boyfriend. Norma Jeane, wiping her eyes, conceded *she hadn't been hurt at all*.

At least, not that she could remember.

If I was pretty enough, my father would come and take me away had to do somehow with the neon-flashing RKO sign miles away in Hollywood Norma Jeane would see from the window above her bed and, at other times, from a roof of the orphanage, a beacon out of the night she would have wished to believe was a secret signal except others saw it as well and perhaps even interpreted it as she did. *A promise—but of what?*

Waiting for Gladys to get out of the hospital so they could live together again. Waiting, with a child's desperate hope overlaid with a more adult fatalist knowledge *she will never come, she has abandoned me, I hate her*, even as she was obsessed with worrying that Gladys wouldn't know where she'd been taken, where this red-brick building behind the eight-foot mesh-wire fence was—the barred windows, steep stairs, and endless corridors; the dorm rooms in which cots (called "beds") were crowded together amid a mix of odors in which the acid stink of pee was predominant; the "dining hall" with its mix of equally strong odors (rancid milk, burnt grease, and kitchen cleanser) in which, tongue-tied and shy and frightened, she was expected to eat, to eat without gagging and vomiting, to "keep her strength up" so she wouldn't become ill and be sent to the infirmary.

El Centro Avenue: where was that? How many miles from Highland?

Thinking *If I went back there. Maybe she would be there, waiting.*

Within a few days of her new status as a ward of Los Angeles County, Norma Jeane had wept away all the tears she'd had. Used them up too soon. No more could she cry than her battered blue-eyed doll, unnamed except as Doll, could cry. The ugly-friendly woman who was director of the orphanage, whom they were instructed to call "Dr. Mittelstadt," had warned her. The heavyset flush-faced matron in the coverall had warned her. The older girls—Fleece, Lois, Debra Mae, Janette—had warned her. "Don't be a crybaby! You're not so special." You could say, as the shiny-faced joyous minister at Grandma Della's church had said, that the other children in the orphanage, far from being strangers she feared and disliked, were in fact sisters and brothers of hers unknown until now *and the vast world populated by how many more, countless beyond reckoning as grains of sand, and all possessing souls and all equally beloved by God.*

Waiting for Gladys to be discharged from the hospital and come and get her but in the meantime she was an orphan among one hundred forty orphans, one of the younger children, assigned to a girl's third-floor dorm (ages six to eleven) with her own bed, an iron cot with a thin lumpy mattress covered in stained oilcloth that smelled nonetheless of pee, her place beneath the eaves of the old brick building in a large rectangular and crowded room that was dimly lit even by day, airless and stifling on hot sunny days, and chill, drafty, and damp on sunless rainy days, which constituted much of the Los Angeles winter; she shared a chest of drawers with Debra Mae and another girl; she was allotted two changes of clothing—two blue cotton jumpers and two white cotton batiste blouses—and much-laundered "linen" and "underthings." She was allotted towels, socks, shoes, galoshes. A raincoat and a light wool coat. She'd attracted a flurry of attention, but it was a fearful attention, brought into the dorm on that first terrible day by the matron hauling Gladys's suitcases with their semblance of glamour (if you didn't examine them too closely), packed with strange, fanciful items of clothing, silk dresses, a ruffled pinafore, red taffeta skirt, plaid tam o'-shanter and satin-lined plaid cloak, little white gloves and gleaming black patent-leather shoes, and other things gathered up in guilty haste by the woman who'd wished Norma Jeane to call her "Aunt Jess"—or was it "Auntie Jess"—and crammed into the suitcases, and most of these items, despite stinking of smoke, were stolen from the new orphan within days, appropriated even by those girls who gave evidence of liking Norma Jeane and would come, in time, to befriend her. (As Fleece explained unapologetically, it was "every man for himself" in the orphanage.) But no one wanted Norma Jeane's doll. No one stole Norma Jeane's doll, which was bald now, naked and soiled, her wide-open glassy-blue eyes and rosebud mouth frozen in an expression of terrified coquetry; this "freaky thing" (as Fleece called it, not unkindly) with which Norma Jeane slept every night and hid in her bed during the day like a fragment of her own yearning soul, weirdly beautiful in her, laughed at and ridiculed by others.

"Wait for the Mouse!"—so Fleece cried to her friends, and indulgen, they waited for Norma Jeane, youngest and smallest and shyest of their circle. "Come on, Mouse, shake your cute li'l ass." Long-legged scar-lipped Fleece with the coarse dark hair, coarse olive skin, restless sharp-green eyes, and hands that could hurt, she'd taken on Norma Jeane out of pity maybe, out of big-sisterly affection if frequent impatience, for Norma Jeane must have reminded her of her lost baby sister whose brains had been so spectacularly spilled "like melon seeds running down a wall." Fleece was the first of Norma Jeane's protectors at the orphanage and, along with Debra Mae, the girl she would recall with most emotion, a kind of anxious infatuation, for with Fleece you never knew how she'd react, you never knew what cruel, coarse words might spring to Fleece's lips, and how her hands, quick as a boxer's, might leap out as much to call attention as to hurt, like an exclamation point at the end of a sentence. For when at last Fleece coaxed out of Norma Jeane a few stumbling, stammered words and a measure of trust—"I'm not an orphan really, my m-mother is in the hospital, I have a mother, and I have a f-father, my father lives in a big mansion in Beverly Hills"—Fleece laughed in her face and pinched her arm, so hard the red mark would show for hours like a pernicious little kiss on Norma Jeane's waxy-pale skin. "Bullshit! Li-ar! Your mother and father are dead like everybody else. *Everybody is dead.*"

THE GIFT GIVERS

The night before the night before Christmas they came.

Bringing gifts to the orphans of the Los Angeles Orphans Home Society. Bringing two dozen dressed turkeys for Christmas Day dinner and a magnificent twelve-foot Christmas evergreen erected by Santa's elves in the visitors' room of the Home, where it transformed that musty-smelling space into a shrine of wonder and beauty. A tree so tall, so full, lighted, alive; smelling of the forest far away, a sharp odor of darkness and mystery; sparkling with glass ornaments, and on its topmost branch a radiant blond angel with eyes uplifted to heaven and prayerful clasped hands. And beneath this tree, *mounds of gaily wrapped presents*.

All this amid a blaze of lights. Amid amplified Christmas carols from a sound truck in the drive out front: "Silent Night," "We Three Kings," "Deck the Halls." Music so suddenly loud, you felt your heart kick into its rhythm.

The older children knew, they'd been so blessed at previous Christmases. The younger children and the children new to the Home were mystified, frightened.

Quiet! quiet! keep to your row! Briskly the children were marched out of the dining hall, where they'd been made to wait without explanation for more than an hour following their evening meal, marched in double columns.

Yet this was not a fire drill, it seemed, and it was too late in the day for play-ground recess. Norma Jeane was confused, jostled by children pushing from behind—what was happening? who was here?—until she saw, on a raised platform at the far end of the visitors' room, a sight that stunned her: the darkly handsome Prince and the beautiful blond Princess!

Here, at the Los Angeles Orphans Home Society!

At first I thought they'd come for me. Only for me.

Here was a confusion of cries, amplified voices, and laughter, Christmas music played to a cheery staccato beat so you had to breathe more quickly just to keep up. And everywhere glaring blinding lights, for there was a cam-era crew in attendance upon the royal couple as they handed out gifts to the needy, and there were numerous photographers with flash cameras crowd-ing and jostling for position. There was the sturdy-bodied director of the Home, Dr. Edith Mittelstadt, accepting a *gift certificate* from the Prince and the Princess, her raddled face caught by camera flashes in an awkward smile, an unrehearsed smile, as the Prince and the Princess, on either side of the middle-aged woman, smiled their beautiful rehearsed smiles so you wanted to stare and stare at them and never look away. "Hel-lo, children! Mer-ry Christmas, children!" the Dark Prince cried, lifting his gloved hands like a priest giving a blessing, and the Fair Princess cried, "Hap-py Christmas, dear children! *We love you.*" As if these words must be true there came a roar of happiness, a waterfall of worship.

How familiar the Dark Prince and the Fair Princess looked!—yet Norma Jeane could not identify them. The Dark Prince resembled Ronald Colman, John Gilbert, Douglas Fairbanks, Jr.—yet was none of these. The Fair Princess resembled Dixie Lee, Joan Blondell, a bustier Ginger Rogers—yet was none of these. The Prince wore a tuxedo with a white silk shirt and a sprig of red berries in his lapel, and on his stiffly lacquered black hair a jaunty Santa's cap, red velvet trimmed in fluffy white fur. "Come get your presents, children! Don't be shy." (Was the Dark Prince teasing? For the children, especially the older ones, pushing forward, determined to get their gifts before the supply ran out, were anything but shy.) "Yes, *come!* Wel-*come!* Dear children—*God bless you.*" (Was the Fair Princess about to burst into tears? Her painted eyes shone with a glassy gaze of utmost sincerity and her glossy crimson smile slipped and slid like a creature with its own wayward life.) The Princess wore a brilliant red taffeta dress with a full shimmering skirt, a tiny cinched-in waist, and a red-sequined bodice that fitted her ample bosom like a tight glove; on her stiffly lacquered platinum-blond hair was a tiara—a diamond tiara?—for such an occasion, at the Los Angeles Orphans Home? The Prince wore short white gloves, the Princess white gloves to her elbows. Behind and beside the royal couple were Santa's elves, some with white whiskers and bristly white paste-on eyebrows, and these helpers passed presents to the royal couple in a continuous stream from beneath the Christmas tree; it was wonderful, like magic, how the Prince and the Princess were able to snatch presents out of the air without so much as looking for them, let alone stooping to pick them up.

The mood in the visitors' room was merry but frantic. The Christmas carols were loud; the Prince's microphone emitted sparks of static that displeased him. In addition to the presents, the Prince and Princess were giving away candy canes and candied apples on sticks, and the supply of these was running low. Last year, it seemed, there hadn't been enough presents for all, which accounted for the older children pushing forward. *In your places! Keep to your places!* Briskly the uniformed matrons were yanking troublemakers out of line to send away upstairs to the dormitories, giving them vigorous shakes and cuffs; it was lucky that the royal couple took no notice of this, or the camera crew and photographers, or if they noticed they gave no sign: *whatever isn't in the spotlight isn't observed.*

At last it was Norma Jeane's turn! She was in the line to receive a gift from the Dark Prince, who, up close, looked older than he'd looked from a distance, with a strangely ruddy, poreless skin like Norma Jeane's doll had once had; his lips appeared rouged, and his eyes as glassily bright as the Fair Princess's. But Norma Jeane had no time to concentrate as she stumbled in a haze of excitement, a roaring in her ears, someone's elbow in her back; shyly she lifted both hands for her present, and the Dark Prince cried, "Little one! Precious lit-tle one!" and before Norma Jeane knew what had happened, as in one of Grandma Della's fairy tales, he'd seized her hands and lifted her up onto the platform beside him! Here, the lights were truly blinding; you could hardly see at all; the roomful of children and adult staff members was no more than a blur, like agitated water. With mock gallantry the Dark Prince gave Norma Jeane a red-striped cane and a candied apple, both terribly sticky, and one of the red-wrapped gifts, and turned her to face a barrage of camera flashes smiling his perfect, practiced smile. "Mer-ry Christmas, little girl! Mer-ry Christmas from San-ta!" Nine-year-old Norma Jeane must have gaped in utter panic, for the photographers, who were all men, laughed at her in delight; one cried, "Hold that look, sweetheart!" and it was *flash! flash! flash!* and Norma Jeane was blinded and would not have a second chance, unable to smile for the cameras (for *Variety*, the *Los Angeles Times*, *Screen World*, *Photoplay*, *Parade*, *Pageant*, *Pix*, the Associated Press News Service) as she might have smiled, as watching her Magic Friend in the mirror she smiled in a dozen special ways, secret ways, but her Friend-in-the-Mirror had abandoned her now, so taken by surprise *and I would never be surprised again I swore.* In the next moment hauled down from the platform, the only place of honor, and again an orphan, one of the younger, smaller orphans, and a matron shoved her rudely along with a shuffling column of children headed upstairs for the dormitories.

Already they were tearing open their Christmas presents, scattering tinsel paper in their wake.

It was a stuffed toy, for a child of maybe two, three, four years old; Norma Jeane was twice that age yet deeply moved by the "striped tiger"—kitten-sized, made of a soft fuzzy fabric you would want to rub against your face, you would want to hug, hug, hug in bed, golden button eyes and a funny flat nose and springy tickly whiskers and orange-and-black tiger stripes and a curving tail with a wire inside so you could move it up, down, into a question mark.

My striped tiger! My Christmas present from him.

The candy cane and the candied apple were taken from Norma Jeane by girls in the dorm. Devoured in a few quick bites.

She didn't care: it was the striped tiger she loved.

Yet the tiger, too, disappeared after a few days.

She'd taken care to hide it far inside her bed, with her doll, yet one day when she came upstairs from work duty, her bed had been torn open and the tiger was gone. (The doll was untouched.) Through the Home in the wake of Christmas there were numerous striped tigers—as there were pandas, rabbits, dogs, dolls—these gifts earmarked for younger orphans while the older ones received pens, pencil boxes, games, but even if she could have identified her own striped tiger she would not have dared to claim it out of another's hand, nor would she have wished to steal it, as someone had stolen from her.

Why hurt another person? It's enough to be hurt yourself.

THE ORPHAN

And these signs shall follow them that believe:
In my name shall they cast out devils;
they shall speak with new tongues;
they shall take up serpents;
and if they drink any deadly thing, it shall not hurt them;
they shall lay hands on the sick, and they shall recover.

—Christ Jesus

Divine Love always has met and always will meet
every human need.

—Mary Baker Eddy,
Science and Health with Key to the Scriptures

I

"Norma Jeane, your mother has requested one more day to consider."

Another day! But Dr. Mittelstadt spoke encouragingly. She was not one to show doubt, weakness, worry; in her presence, you were meant to be optimistic. You were meant to dispel negative thoughts. Norma Jeane smiled as Dr. Mittelstadt spoke of having heard from the head psychiatrist at Norwalk that Gladys Mortensen was not so "delusional" and "vindictive-minded" as she'd been; there was the hope this time, the third time that Norma Jeane was up for adoption, that Mrs. Mortensen would be reasonable and grant permission. "For of course your mother loves you, dear, and wants you to be happy. She must wish the best for you—as we do." Dr. Mittelstadt paused and sighed, an eager catch in her voice as she said what she'd been leading up to say: "So, child, shall we pray together?"

Dr. Mittelstadt was a devout Christian Scientist but she did not press her religious beliefs upon any but her favored girls, and upon these girls very lightly, as one might offer morsels of food to starving persons.

Four months before, on Norma Jeane's eleventh birthday, Dr. Mittelstadt had called the girl into her office and given her a copy of Mary Baker Eddy's *Science and Health with Key to the Scriptures.* Inscribed on the inside cover was, in Dr. Mittelstadt's perfect hand:

To Norma Jeane on her birthday!

"Though I walk through the Valley of the Shadow of Death, I will fear no evil." Psalms xxiii, 4.

This great American Book of Wisdom will change your life as it has changed mine!

Edith Mittelstadt, Ph.D.
June 1, 1937

Every night, Norma Jeane read in the book before bed, and every night she whispered aloud the inscription. *I love you, Dr. Mittelstadt.* She would think of this book as the first true gift of her life. And of that birthday, her happiest day since she'd been brought to the Home.

"We will pray for a right decision, child. And for the strength to abide with whatever the decision is, granted us by the Father."

Norma Jeane knelt on the carpet. Dr. Mittelstadt, joints stiff with arthritis, remained behind her desk, head bowed and hands clasped in passionate prayer. She was only fifty years old yet reminded Norma Jeane of her grandmother Della: that mysteriously bulky female flesh, shapeless but for the restraint of a corset, the immense sunken bosom, the raddled kindly face, hair faded gray, fattish legs vein-splotched inside thick support hose. Yet those eyes of yearning and hope. *I love you, Norma Jeane. Like my own daughter.*

Had she uttered these words aloud? She had not.

Had she embraced Norma Jeane and kissed her? She had not.

Dr. Mittelstadt leaned forward in her creaking chair with a sigh to lead Norma Jeane in the Christian Science prayer that was her greatest gift to the child, as it had been God's great gift to her.

Our Father which art in heaven,
   Our Father-Mother God, all-harmonious,

Hallowed be Thy name.
   Adorable One.

Thy Kingdom come.
   Thy kingdom is come, Thou art ever-present.

Thy will be done on earth, as it is in heaven.
Enable us to know—as in heaven, so on earth—God is omnipotent, supreme.

Give us this day our daily bread,
Give us grace for today; feed the famished affections.

And forgive us our debts, as we forgive our debtors.
And Love is reflected in love.

And lead us not into temptation, but deliver us from evil;
And God leadeth us not into temptation, but delivereth us from sin, disease, and death.

For Thine is the kingdom, and the power, and the glory, forever.
For God is infinite, all-power, all Life, Truth, Love over all, and All.

Amen!

Norma Jeane dared to murmur, in a softer echo, "Amen."

2

Where do you go when you disappear?
And wherever you are, are you alone?

Three days of waiting for Gladys Mortensen to make her decision. Whether to release her daughter for adoption. Days that might be broken down into hours and even minutes to be endured like an indrawn breath.

Mary *Baker* Eddy, Norma Jeane *Baker*. Oh, that was an obvious sign!

Fleece and Debra Mae, knowing how Norma Jeane was scared, told her fortune with their stolen deck of cards.

You were allowed to play hearts, gin rummy, and fish at the Home but not poker or euchre, which were men's gambling games, nor were you allowed to tell fortunes, which was "magic" and an offense to Christ. So the girls' fortune-telling was done after lights out, in thrilling stealth.

Norma Jeane didn't really want her fortune told by her friends because the cards might interfere with her prayers and because, if the fortune was bad, she'd rather not know until she had no choice except to know.

But Fleece and Debra Mae insisted. They believed in the magic of cards a lot more than they believed in the magic of Jesus Christ. Fleece shuffled the deck, had Debra Mae cut, and Fleece reshuffled, dealing cards in front of

Norma Jeane, who waited without daring to breathe: a queen of diamonds, a seven of hearts, an ace of hearts, a four of diamonds—"They're all red, see? That means good news for Mouse."

Was Fleece lying? Norma Jeane adored her friend, who teased and often tormented her but protected her at the Home and at school, where the younger orphan girls required protection, but Norma Jeane didn't trust her. *Fleece wants me to stay in this prison with her. Because nobody will ever adopt her.*

It was true, sad but true. No couple would ever adopt Fleece, or Janette, or Jewell, or Linda, or even Debra Mae, who was a pretty freckle-faced red-haired twelve-year-old, for these were no longer children but girls; girls who were too old, girls with "the look" in their eyes giving away they'd been hurt by adults and weren't going to forgive. But mainly they were just too old. They'd been in foster homes that hadn't "worked out" and they'd been returned to the orphanage and would be wards of the county until they were old enough to support themselves at sixteen. To be older than three or four, in the orphanage, was old. Adoptive parents wanted babies, or children so young they had no distinct personalities, no speech, and therefore no memory. It was a miracle, in fact, that anyone wanted to adopt Norma Jeane. Yet since she'd been made a ward of the county, she'd been requested by three couples. These couples had fallen in love with her, they'd claimed, and were willing to ignore the fact that she was nine years old, and ten years old, and now eleven years old; and that her mother was living and identified, committed to the California State Psychiatric Hospital at Norwalk, where her official diagnosis was, "Acute chronic paranoid schizophrenia with probable alcoholic and drug-induced neurological impairment" (for such records were available to prospective adoptive parents upon request).

It did seem a miracle. Except if you observed, as did the staff, the way that little mouse Norma Jeane lit up in the visitors' room! Though she might have been sad-faced just before, truly Norma Jeane turned on like a lightbulb in the presence of important visitors. Her sweet face, a perfect moon face, and her eager blue eyes, and her quick shy smile and manners that made you think of a more subdued Shirley Temple—"Just such an angel!"

There was the pleading in those eyes: *Love me! Already, I love you.*

The first couple who'd applied to adopt Norma Jeane Baker were from Burbank, where they owned a thousand-acre fruit farm; they'd fallen in love with the girl, they said, because she looked just like the daughter Cynthia Rose they'd lost at the age of eight to polio. (They'd showed Norma Jeane the dead child's snapshot and Norma Jeane came to believe that maybe she was their little girl, maybe it was possible; if she went to live with the couple her name would be changed to Cynthia Rose and this she looked forward to! "Cynthia Rose" was a magic name.) The couple had hoped for a younger child, but as soon as they'd laid eyes on Norma Jeane, "It was like Cynthia Rose reborn, restored to us. A miracle!" But word came from Norwalk that Gladys Mortensen refused to sign papers releasing her daughter for adoption. The couple had been heartbroken, it was like "Cynthia Rose being taken from us a second time," but there was nothing to be done.

Norma Jeane hid away to cry. She'd wanted to be Cynthia Rose so badly! And live on a thousand-acre fruit farm in a place called Burbank with a mother and father who loved her.

The second couple, from Torrance, who boasted of being "comfortably well off" even in this rotten economy, since the husband was a Ford dealer, had plenty of children of their own—five boys!—but the wife yearned for just one more, a girl. They, too, had wanted to adopt a younger child but when the woman laid eyes on Norma Jeane she was *it*: "Just such an angel!" The woman asked Norma Jeane please to call her Mamita—maybe this was Spanish for "Momma"?—and so Norma Jeane did. The very word was magic to her: Mamita! *Now I will have a real Momma. Mamita!* Norma Jeane loved this fattish fortyish woman who'd come searching for her, as she said, out of loneliness, living in a household bursting with males: she had a sunburnt, creased face yet a smile hopeful and radiant as Norma Jeane's; she was in the habit of touching Norma Jeane often, squeezing the girl's little hand and giving her gifts, a child's white handkerchief embroidered with the initials *NJ*, a box of colored pencils, nickels and dimes, chocolate kisses wrapped in tinfoil that Norma Jeane couldn't wait to share with Fleece and the other girls, to make them less jealous of her.

But this adoption, too, Gladys Mortensen had blocked, in the spring of 1936. Not in person but by way of a Norwalk administrator who told Dr. Mittelstadt that Mrs. Mortensen was very sick, with intermittent hallucinations, one of them that Martians had landed in spaceships to take away human children; another that her daughter's own father wanted to take her away to some secret place, where she, the girl's true mother, would never see her again. Mrs. Mortensen's "only identity is that of Norma Jeane's mother and she isn't strong enough just yet to surrender that."

Another time Norma Jeane hid away to cry. But this was more than a broken heart! She was ten years old, old enough to be bitter, and angry, and to feel the injustice of her fate. She'd been cheated of Mamita, who loved her, by the cruel, cold woman who'd never allowed her to call her Momma. *She would not be my mother. Yet she would not let me have a real mother. She would not let me have a mother, a father, a family, a real home.*

There was a secret way to crawl out onto the roof of the orphanage, outside the third-floor girls' lavatory, and to hide behind a tall stained brick chimney. By night the RKO flashing neon came direct to this place; you could feel its pulsing heat on your outstretched hands and shut eyelids. Panting Fleece caught up with Norma Jeane to hug her in lean, strong arms like a boy's. Fleece whose underarms and greasy hair you could always smell, Fleece with rough comforting ways like a big dog. Norma Jeane began to cry helplessly. "I wish she was dead! I hate her *so*."

Fleece rubbed her warm face against Norma Jeane's. "Yeah! I hate the bitch too."

Did they plot, that night, how they'd hitchhike to Norwalk, to set the hospital on fire? Or did Norma Jeane remember this wrong? Maybe it was a dream. And she'd been there: the flames, the screams, the naked woman running, and her hair aflame, and her eyes mad yet knowing. Those screams! *All I did was, I pressed my hands against my ears. I shut my eyes.*

Years later when she visited Gladys at Norwalk and spoke with the ward nurses, Norma Jeane would learn that in the spring of 1936 Gladys had tried to commit suicide by "lacerating" her wrists and throat with hairpins and had lost "a good deal of blood" before she was discovered in the furnace room of the hospital.

3

October 11, 1937

Dear Mother,

> I'm Nobody! Who are you?
> Are you—Nobody—too?
> Then there's a pair of us!
> Don't tell! they'd banish us—you know!

This is my favorite poem in your book, remember the Little Treasury of American Verse? Aunt Jess brought it to me and I read it all the time and think of how you read the poems to me, I loved them so. When I read them I think of you Mother.

How are you? I think about you all the time and hope you are feeling much better. I am well and would surprise you how tall I am! I have made many friends here at the Home and at my school which is Hurst Elementary. I am in 6th grade and one of the tallest girls. There is a very nice Director at our Home and a nice staff. They are strict sometimes but it is necessary, there are so many of us. We go to church and I have been singing in the choir. You know I am not very musical!

Aunt Jess comes to see me sometimes and takes me to the movies and school is a little hard for me, arthmetic [sic] especially but *fun*. Except for arthmetic my grades are all B's, I am ashamed to say what my arthmetic grade is. I think that Mr. Pearce has been here to see me, too.

There is a very nice couple named Mr. and Mrs. Josiah Mount who live in Pasadena where Mr. Mount is a lawyer and Mrs. Mount has a big garden mostly of roses. They have taken me on Sunday drives and to visit their house which is very large overlooking a pond. Mr. and Mrs. Mount are asking that I come home with them to live as their daughter. They are hoping that you will say Yes and I hope so, too.

Norma Jeane couldn't think of anything more to write to Gladys. She showed the letter shyly to Dr. Mittelstadt for criticism, and Dr. Mittelstadt praised her, saying it was a "very nice letter" with just a few mistakes she would correct, but she believed that Norma Jeane should end with a prayer. So Norma Jeane added,

I am praying for us both Mother hoping that you will give permission for me to be adopted. I will thank you from the bottom of my heart and pray for God to bless you forever Amen.

Your loving daughter Norma Jeane

Twelve days later came the reply, the first and the last letter Gladys Mortensen would write to Norma Jeane in the Los Angeles Orphans Home. A letter on torn-out yellow paper, in a downward-slanted shaky handwriting like a procession of staggering ants:

Dear Norma Jeane, if you are not ashamed to say thats who you are in the eyes of the World—

I have rec'd your filthy letter & so long as I am alive & able to fight this insult will never be allowed my Daughter to be adopted! How can she be "adopted"—she has her MOTHER who is living & will be well & strong enough soon to bring her home again.

Please do not insult me with these requests as they are hurtful & hateful to me. I have no need of your shitty God for his blessing or his curse I thumb my nose! I hope I still have a nose to thumb, & a thumb! I will retain a Lawyer you can be sure to keep what is mine until Death.

"Your loving mother" YOU KNOW WHO

THE CURSE

"Look at the ass on that one, the little blonde!"

Hearing, yet blushing and indignant not-hearing. On El Centro returning to the Home from school. In her white blouse, blue jumper (tight at the bust and hips, overnight it seemed), and white anklet socks. Twelve years old. Yet in her heart hardly more than eight or nine, as if her true growth ceased at the time she'd been expelled from Gladys's bedroom to run naked screaming for help from strangers. Running from steam and scalding water and a burning bed meant to be her funeral pyre.

Shame, shame!

There came the day. The second week of September when she'd just started seventh grade. She wasn't wholly unprepared, though she was disbelieving. Hadn't she been hearing for years older girls speaking of this, and the crude jokes of the boys? Hadn't she been repelled, fascinated by the ugly blood-stained "sanitary napkins" wrapped in toilet paper, and sometimes not wrapped, in the trash containers in the girls' lavatories?

Hadn't she, made to carry trash downstairs to the rear of the Home, been sickened by the stink of stale blood?

A curse in the blood Fleece was always saying with a smirk *you can't escape.*

But Norma Jeane inwardly rejoiced in her knowledge. *Yes you can escape. There is a way!*

Among her friends at the Home and at school (for Norma Jeane had friends among children with families, "real" homes) she never spoke of *the way* which was *the way of Christian Science*, which was a wisdom revealed to her by Edith Mittelstadt. That God is Mind, and Mind is all, and mere "matter" does not exist.

That God heals us through Jesus Christ. If only we believe utterly in Him.

Yet now, this day, a weekday in mid-September, she'd felt a strange dull ache in the pit of her belly in gym class, in her middy blouse and bloomers playing volleyball—Norma Jeane was one of the bigger girls among the seventh-graders, one of the better athletes, if sometimes hesitant and clumsy out of shyness, fumbling the ball so the others grew impatient with her, you couldn't rely upon Norma Jeane, and how hard she tried to refute this judgment, with what determination—yet this afternoon in the muggy heat of the gym she'd dropped the volleyball as a hot liquid seeped into the crotch of her panties; she was dazed with a sudden headache and afterward, changing into her slip, blouse, jumper in the locker room, she was determined to ignore it, whatever it was; she was shocked, insulted; *this was not happening to her.*

"Norma Jeane, what's wrong?"

"What? Nothing is wrong."

"You're looking kind of"—the girl meant to smile, meant to be sympathetic, yet it came out pushy, coercive—"sick."

"Nothing is wrong with *me*, is something wrong with *you*?"

She'd left the locker room trembling with indignation. *Shame, shame! But in God there is no shame.*

Hurrying home from school, avoiding her friends. Where usually she walked with a small gang of girls, prominent among them Fleece and Debra Mae, today she made certain she was alone, walking in quick tight steps with thighs pressed together, a kind of duckwalk, the crotch of her panties was damp but the hot seeping in her loins seemed to have stopped *she'd willed it to stop! refused to give in!* her eyes lowered to the sidewalk, not-hearing the whistles and calls of the boys, high school boys and others even older, in their twenties, cruising El Centro Avenue. "Nor-ma Jeane, that your name, honey? Hey, Nor-ma Jeane!" Wishing her jumper hadn't grown so tight. Vowing she would lose weight. Five pounds! Never would she be fat like certain of the girls in her class, never heavy like Dr. Mittelstadt *but flesh is not real, Norma Jeane. Matter is not mind and only mind is God.*

When Dr. Mittelstadt carefully explained this truth to her, she understood. When she read Mrs. Eddy's book, especially the chapter called "Prayer," she halfway understood. But when she was alone, her thoughts were confused as a jigsaw puzzle knocked to the floor. There was order there, but—how to find it?

Now, this afternoon, the thoughts inside her skull, how like a cascade of shattered flying glass. What ordinary unenlightened people called a headache was but an illusion, a weakness; yet by the time Norma Jeane walked nine blocks from Hurst Junior High to the orphanage, her head pounded so terribly she could barely see.

Craving an aspirin. Just one aspirin.

The nurse in the infirmary routinely gave out aspirins if you were sick. When girls had their "periods."

But Norma Jeane vowed *she would not give in*.

It was a test of her faith, a trial. Had not Jesus Christ said, *Your Father knoweth what things ye have need of, before ye ask him?*

She recalled with disgust how her mother had broken up aspirins to put into fruit juice when Norma Jeane was just a little girl. And out of her unmarked bootleg bottle a teaspoon or two of "medicinal water"—vodka, it must have been—into Norma Jeane's glass. When she was a child of three—or younger!—too small to defend herself against such poison. Drugs, drink. The way of Christian Science was to repudiate all unclean habits. One day she would denounce Gladys for such cruel practices against an unknowing child. *She wanted to poison me as she poisoned herself. I will never take drugs and I will never ever drink.*

At supper faint with hunger yet sickened when she tried to eat, macaroni and clotted cheese, scorch scrapings from the baking pan, all she could force herself to eat was doughy white bread slowly chewed and slowly swallowed. And clearing the table afterward she nearly dropped a tray laden with dishes and cutlery, saved only by a girl rushing to support it. And in the stifling kitchen scouring pots and the grease griddle under the frowning eye of the cook, of all work duties the most disgusting, bad as scrubbing toilets. For ten cents a week.

Shame, shame! But ye shall triumph over shame.

When at last she would be released from the orphanage, placed with a foster family in Van Nuys, in November of that year, 1938, she would have saved $20.60 in her "account." As a going-away gift, Edith Mittelstadt would double this sum. "Remember us with kindness, Norma Jeane."

Sometimes yes, more often no. One day she would compose the story of her own orphan life. Her pride wasn't to be purchased so cheaply.

Truly I had no pride! And no shame! Grateful for any kind word or any guy's stare. My young body so strange to me like a bulb in the earth swelling to burst. For certainly she was well aware of her chubby growing breasts and the widening of her thighs, hips, "ass"—as that part of the anatomy, when female, was called with approval and a kind of jocular affection. *What a sweet ass. Look at that sweet ass. Oh, baby baby! Who's she? Jailbait.* Frightened of such changes in her body, for should Gladys know, Gladys would be disdainful; Gladys who was so slender and svelte, Gladys who most admired slender "feminine" film stars like Norma Talmadge, Greta Garbo, the young Joan Crawford and Gloria Swanson, not fleshy-chunky females like Mae West, Mae Murray, Margaret Dumont. Since she hadn't seen Norma Jeane for so long, surely Gladys would disapprove of her having *grown*.

It didn't occur to Norma Jeane to wonder what Gladys looked like after years of incarceration at the Norwalk hospital.

Since her letter refusing to sign adoption papers for Norma Jeane, Gladys hadn't written again. Nor had Norma Jeane written to her, except to send, as usual, Christmas and birthday cards. (And receive nothing in return! But as Christ has taught, it is better to give than to receive.)

Norma Jeane, normally so docile and unassertive, shocked Edith Mittelstadt with her angry tears. Why was her nasty mother, her sick mother, her *nasty sick crazy mother* allowed to ruin her life? Why was the law so stupid, keeping her under the thumb of a woman in a mental hospital who would most likely never get out? It was unfair, it was unjust, it was only because Gladys was jealous of Mr. and Mrs. Mount, and hated *her*. "And after I prayed," Norma Jeane sobbed. "I did like you told me and prayed and *prayed*."

Here, Dr. Mittelstadt spoke severely to Norma Jeane, as she might have spoken to any orphan in her charge. Reprimanding her for "blind, selfish" emotion; for failing to see, as *Science and Health* made clear, that *prayer cannot change the Science of being, only bring us into better harmony with it*.

Then what good, Norma Jeane silently fumed, was prayer?

"I know you're disappointed, Norma Jeane, and very hurt," Edith Mittelstadt said, sighing. "I'm disappointed myself. The Mounts are such good people—good Christians, if not Scientists—and so very fond of you. But your mother, you see, is still clouded in her mind. She is a distinctly 'modern' type—the 'neurotic'—she is sick because she makes herself sick with negative thoughts. *You* are free to cast off such thoughts and should give thanks to God every minute of your precious life that you *are*."

She had no need for that shitty God, his blessing or his curse.

Yet swiping at her eyes, childlike in emotion, nodding as Dr. Mittelstadt spoke persuasively. Yes! It was so.

The director's forceful yet warm voice. Searching gaze. Her soul shining in her eyes. You scarcely noticed that her face was so slack and creased and worn; close up, though, you saw liver spots on her flaccid arms, which she made no attempt to hide with sleeves or makeup as another woman might have done out of vanity; wiry hairs bristled at her chin. With movie eyes Norma Jeane saw these startling imperfections. For, in movie logic, aesthetics has the authority of ethics: to be less than beautiful is sad, but to be willfully less than beautiful is immoral. Seeing Dr. Mittelstadt, Gladys would have winced. Gladys would have jeered at her behind her back—and what a broad back it was, in navy blue serge. But Norma Jeane admired Dr. Mittelstadt. *She's strong. She doesn't care what other people think. Why should she?*

Dr. Mittelstadt was saying, "I was misled too. The staff at Norwalk misled me. Perhaps it was no one's fault. But, Norma Jeane, we can place you in an excellent foster home; we don't need your mother's permission for that. I will find a Science home for you, dear; I promise."

Any home. Any home at all.

Norma Jeane murmured softly, "Thank you, Dr. Mittelstadt."

Wiping her reddened eyes with a tissue the woman offered her. She'd become physically smaller, it seemed; docile again, with her child's posture and voice. Dr. Mittelstadt said, "By Christmas of this year, Norma Jeane! With God's help, I promise."

Basking again in the knowledge it could hardly be a coincidence that Mary Baker Eddy's middle name was *Baker*, and Norma Jeane Baker's last name was *Baker*.

In a reference book at school Norma Jeane looked up MARY BAKER EDDY and learned that the founder of the Christian Science Church was born in 1821 and died in 1910. Not in California, but that wouldn't matter: people traveled across the continent by train and airplane all the time. Gladys's first husband "Baker" was a man who'd traveled out of Gladys's life, and it was possible—probable?—that he was related to Mrs. Eddy, for why would Mrs. Eddy have the middle name "Baker" unless she, too, was a Baker in some respect?

In God's universe, as in any jigsaw puzzle, there are no coincidences.

My grandmother was Mary Baker Eddy.
My step-grandmother I mean.
Because my mother married Mrs. Eddy's son.
He was not my actual "father" but adopted me.
Mary Baker Eddy was my stepfather's mother
and my mother's stepmother-in-law
but she didn't know Mrs. Eddy.
Personally I mean.

I never knew Mrs. Eddy
who is the founder of the
Christian Science Church.
She died in 1910.

I was born on June 1, 1926.
This fact I know.

Shrinking from the older boys' eyes. So many eyes! And always waiting. The junior high school was adjacent to the senior high and now going to school was nothing like it had been in sixth grade.

Norma Jeane hid in the midst of other girls. That was the only way. In her blue jumper tight at the bust and hips. Riding up her hips so the hem was crooked. What if her slip showed? You had to wear a slip, and the straps got twisted and soiled. Underarms had to be washed twice a day. And sometimes that wasn't enough. The joke at school was *orphans stink!* and a guy pinching his nose shut making a face was assured always of a laugh.

Even kids from the orphanage laughed. The ones knowing it didn't apply to them.

Nasty jokes about girls. Their special smell. *The curse. Blood curse.* She would not think of it, no one could force her to think of it.

For weeks she'd postponed asking the matron for a next-larger-size jumper because the woman would make a snide comment as usual. *Gonna be a big girl, eh? Runs in the family I bet.*

You went to the nurse in the infirmary for "sanitary napkins." All the older girls went. But Norma Jeane would not go. No more than she would beg for aspirin. Such measures did not apply to her.

One thing I know, that, whereas I was blind, now I see.

These words from the New Testament, the Gospel According to John, Norma Jeane whispered often to herself. As Dr. Mittelstadt in the privacy of her office had first read to her of the healing of the blind man by Jesus which was so simple. *Jesus spat on the ground, and made clay of the spittle, and he anointed the eyes of the blind man with the clay*, and the blind man's eyes were opened. So simple. If you have faith.

God is Mind. The Mind alone heals. If you have faith, all will be granted you.

Yet—she would never tell Dr. Mittelstadt this, or even her girlfriends!— there was a daydream she loved, a daydream that played continuously in her head like a film that never ceases, of tearing off her clothes to be *seen*. In church, in the dining hall, at school, on El Centro Avenue with its noisy traffic. *Look at me, look at me, look at me!*

Her Magic Friend was not fearful. Only Norma Jeane was fearful.

Her Friend-in-the-Mirror who pirouetted in nakedness, did the hula, wiggled her hips and breasts, smiled smiled smiled, exulted in nakedness before God as a snake exults in its sinuous glittery skin.

For I would be less lonely then. Even if you all reviled me.

You could look nowhere except at ME.

"Hey, look at Mouse. Pret-*ty*."

One of them had found a compact with loose fragrant peach-colored powder inside and a badly soiled powder puff. Another had found a lipstick, bright coral pink. Such precious items were "found" at school or in Woolworth's, wherever you were lucky. Cosmetics were forbidden at the Home for girls younger than sixteen, but these girls hid away to dab powder on their scrubbed-shiny faces and apply lipstick to their mouths. There was Norma Jeane staring at her face in the clouded compact mirror. Feeling a stab of guilt, or was it excitement, sharp as pain between the legs. Not that hers was the only pretty face, but it was *her face* that was pretty.

The girls teased her. She blushed, hating to be teased. Well, she loved to be teased. But this was something new, something scary of which she was uncertain. She said, surprising her friends, for it wasn't like Mouse to be so angry, "I hate it. I hate how phony it is. I hate the *taste*." Pushing the compact away and rubbing the bright coral color off her mouth.

Though the waxy-sweet taste would linger, hours through the night.

Prayed, prayed, prayed, *prayed*. For the pain behind her eyes and the pain between her legs to cease. For the bleeding (if it was bleeding) to cease. Refused to lie down on her bed because it wasn't time for bed yet, because that would be giving in. Because the other girls would guess. Because they would claim her as one of their own. Because she was not one of them. Because she had faith, and faith was all she had. Because she must do homework. So much homework! And she was a slow hesitant student. She smiled in fear even when she was alone and there was no teacher to placate.

Now she was in seventh grade. Taking math. Homework was a nest of knots to be untied. But if you untied one, there was another; if you untied that, there was another. And each of the problems was harder than the problem before. "God *damn*." Gladys had torn at a knot that wouldn't untie, she'd taken a scissors to the string and *snip! snip!* Like combing snarls out of her little girl's hair, *God damn* it's easier sometimes just to get the scissors and *snip!*

Only twenty minutes before lights out at nine! Oh, she was anxious. After she'd finished with kitchen cleanup, nasty greasy pans, she'd hidden in a toilet stall and stuffed toilet paper into her panties without looking. But now the toilet paper was soaked with what she refused to identify as blood. Sticking a finger in she'd never do! Oh, that was disgusting. Fleece, reckless and show-offy, obnoxious Fleece in a stairwell as boys thundered downward, backed into a corner to stick her finger up inside her skirt and into her panties—"Hey, Abbott!" Seeing her period was started. Fleece held up her finger glistening red at the top so that the other girls could see, scandalized and laughing. Norma Jeane had shut her eyes, feeling faint.

But I am not Fleece.

I am none of you.

In secret Norma Jeane often crept into the lavatory in the middle of the night. The other girls in the dorm sleeping. It thrilled her to be awake at such a time. Awake and alone at such a time. As years ago Gladys, too, would prowl the night like a big restless cat unable or unwilling to sleep. Cigarette in hand, and maybe a drink, and often she'd end up on the phone. It was a movie scene comprehended through the cotton batting of a child's sleep. *Hey: h'lo. Thinking of me? Yeah, sure. Yeah? Wanna do something about that? Uh-huh. Where there's a will there's a way. But Baby makes three, know what I mean?* At such times the dingy foul-smelling lavatory was a place of excitement like a theater before the lights darken, the curtains part, and the movie begins, if Norma Jeane believed herself safely alone. Removing her nightgown, as capes, cloaks, clinging garments are removed in movies, and a subtle pulsing movie music beneath as her Magic Friend is revealed, as if hiding inside the drab garment only just waiting to be revealed. This girl-who-was-Norma-Jeane yet not-Norma-Jeane but a stranger. A girl so much more special than Norma Jeane could ever be.

The surprise of it was, where once she'd been thin-armed and her breasts tiny and flat as a boy's, now she was "filling out," as it was called with approval, hard little breasts getting larger by quick degrees, bouncier, and the creamy-pale skin so strangely soft. In her cupped hands she held both her breasts, staring and marveling: how amazing, the nipples and the soft brown flesh about the nipples; the way the nipples turned hard, like goose bumps; and how peculiar it was that boys, too, had nipples; not breasts but nipples (which they would never use, for only a woman could nurse); and Norma Jeane knew (too many times she'd been forced to see!) that boys had penises—"things," they were called, "cocks," "pricks"—ropy little sausages between their legs, and this made them boys, and important, as girls could not be important; and hadn't she been made to see (but this was a cloudy memory, she couldn't trust it) the fat turgid moistly hot "things" of adult men who were friends of Gladys's long ago?

Want to touch it, sweetheart? It won't bite.

"Norma Jeane? Hey."

It was Debra Mae, poking her in the ribs. Where she was hunched awkwardly forward onto the scarred tabletop panting through her mouth. Possibly she'd passed out, but only for a minute. The pain she didn't feel and the hot seeping of blood that wasn't hers. Feebly she pushed the girl's hand away but Debra Mae said sharply, "Hey, are you crazy? You're bleeding, don'tcha know it? All on the chair here. *Je*-sus."

Blushing with shame, Norma Jeane struggled to her feet. Her math homework fell to the floor. "Go away. Leave me alone."

Debra Mae said, "Look, it's *real*. Cramps are *real*. Your period is *real*. Blood is *real*."

Norma Jeane stumbled from the study room, her vision blinded, blotched. A trickle of liquid ran down the inside of her leg. She'd been praying and gnawing her lower lip and she was determined not to give in. Not to be touched and not to be pitied. Behind her, she heard voices. Hid in a stairwell. Hid in a closet. Hid in a stall in the lavatory. Climbed out a window when no one was watching. Crawling on hands and knees to the peak of the roof. The night sky opening ridged with cloud, and a pale quarter-moon beyond, and the fresh cool air, and miles away the RKO lights flashing. *Mind is the only Truth. God is Mind. God is Love. Divine Love has always met and always will meet every human need.* Was someone calling her name? She didn't hear. She was suffused with certitude and joy. She was strong, and she would be stronger. Knowing she had the power in her to withstand all pain and fear. Knowing she was blessed, Divine Love flooding her heart.

Already the pain throbbing in her body was becoming remote—as if belonging to another, weaker girl. She was climbing up out of it by an exertion of her will! Climbing up the steep roof and into the sky, where clouds were banked like steps, steps leading upward, ridged with light from the sun setting in the west at the very edge of the horizon. A misstep, a moment of doubt, and she might fall to the ground limp as a broken doll but this would not happen, *it was my will that it would not happen* and so it did not. She foresaw that her life from this point onward would be hers to direct, so long as Divine Love flooded her heart.

By Christmas, she'd been promised. In which direction, Norma Jeane's new home?

The Child

1932–1938

THE SHARK

There was the shape of the shark before it was the shark. There was the silence of the deep green water. The shark gliding in deep green water. I must've been underwater and out of the surf though not swimming, my eyes were open and stinging from the salt—I was a good swimmer in those days, my boyfriends took me to Topanga Beach, to Will Rogers, Las Tunas, Redondo, but my favorites were Santa Monica and Venice Beach, "Muscle Beach," where the good-looking body-builders and surfers hang out—and I was staring at it, at the shark, the shape of the shark poised, gliding in dark water, so I could not have guessed its size or even what it was.

When you least expect it, the shark lunges. God has granted it great tearing jaws, rows of fiery razor teeth.

Once we saw a shark strung up still living, streaming blood on the pier at Hermosa. My fiancé and me. We'd just gotten engaged, I was fifteen years old, just a girl. God, was I happy!

Yes, but the mother, you know the mother's at Norwalk.

I'm not marrying the mother, I'm marrying Norma Jeane.

She's a good girl. She seems so. But it doesn't always show itself when they're that young.

What doesn't?

What might happen later. To her.

I didn't hear! I wasn't listening. Let me tell you I was in seventh heaven, engaged at fifteen and the envy of every girl I knew, and I'd be married just after my sixteenth birthday instead of returning to high school for two more years and with the U.S. at war, like *The War of the Worlds,* who knew if there'd be a future?

"TIME TO GET MARRIED"

I

"Norma Jeane, know what I think? It's time for you to get *married*."

These happy surprised words just sprang out, like switching on a radio and there's a voice singing. She hadn't planned them exactly. She wasn't a woman to plan utterances. She knew what she'd meant to say when she heard herself say it. Rarely did she regret anything she said, for simply to say it was what she'd meant to do. Wasn't it? And then once it's said it's said. Pushing open the screen door to the back porch, where they'd set up the ironing board and the girl was ironing, most of the laundry basket emptied out and Warren's short-sleeved shirts on wire hangers overhead, and there was Norma Jeane smiling up at Elsie, not hearing her exactly, or if hearing not absorbing, or if absorbing assuming it was one of Elsie's jokes, Norma Jeane in short shorts, polka-dot halter top showing the pale tops of her chubby breasts, barefoot, a glow of perspiration on her skin, blond down on her legs and fuzz at her underarms and her curly-frizzy dirty-blond hair pulled back from her face in one of Elsie's old scarfs. What a sunshiny good-natured girl this one was, unlike others who, when you approached them even with a determined smile on your face, stared and flinched as if they were expecting to be walloped, yes, there'd been some, younger ones, boys and girls both, who'd wet their pants when you came up on them unexpectedly. But Norma Jeane wasn't one of these. Norma Jeane wasn't like anyone they'd ever taken in before.

That was the problem. Norma Jeane was a special case.

Eighteen months with them sharing a second-floor attic room with Warren's girl cousin, who was working at Radio Plane Aircraft. And from the first they'd liked her. Almost you could say, maybe it's an exaggeration, but almost you could say they loved her. So different from the usual run of kids sent up by the county. Quiet but paying attention and quick to smile, laugh at jokes (and there were plenty of jokes in the Pirig household, you bet!), and never failed to do her chores and sometimes other kids' chores, kept her half of the attic room neat and her bed made the way they'd been taught at the Home and lowered her eyes to say grace to herself before meals if nobody else said it, and Warren's cousin Liz laughed at her, saying she was down on her knees by her bed praying so much, you'd think whatever it was she was praying for would've showed up by now. But Elsie never laughed at Norma Jeane. This girl so fainthearted, if there was a mere mouse struggling in a trap in the kitchen dragging itself across the floor, or Warren squashed a roach beneath his foot, or Elsie herself hauled off and whacked a fly with the swatter, she'd look like it was the end of the world, not to say how she'd run from the room if there was talk of something hurtful (like certain details of the war news, men buried alive on the death march after Corregidor), and naturally she was squeamish helping Elsie pluck and clean chickens, but Elsie never laughed. Elsie was the one always wanted a daughter and Warren hadn't ever been one hundred percent sold on taking in foster kids except the money came in handy, Warren was the kind of man wanted kids of his own or no kids but he'd had only good things to say about Norma Jeane too. So how to spring this on her now?

Like wringing a kitten's neck! But God knows it had to be done.

"Yeah. I've been thinking. It's time for you to get married."

"Aunt Elsie, huh? What?"

There was somebody bawling out of the little plastic radio on the porch railing, sounded like—who was it?—Caruso. Elsie did what she never would do, switched the radio off.

"Ever think about it? Getting married? You'll be sixteen in June."

Norma Jeane was smiling at Elsie, perplexed, the heavy iron poised upended in her hand. Even in surprise, the girl knew enough to lift the hot iron from the board.

"*I* was married, almost that young. There was special circumstances there too."

Norma Jeane said, "M-married? Me?"

"Well"—Elsie laughed—"not *me*. We're not talking about *me*."

"But—I don't have any steady boyfriend."

"You have too many boyfriends."

"But no *steady*. I'm not in *l-love*."

"Love?" Elsie laughed. "You can get in love. Your age, you can get in love fast."

"You're teasing, aren't you? Aunt Elsie? I guess you're teasing?"

Elsie frowned. Fumbling for her cigarettes in her pocket. She was bare-legged, pale vein-splotched legs fat at the knees but still shapely below, and her bare feet in house slippers. Her housedress was front-buttoned, cheap cotton and not too clean, straining at the buttonholes. Sweating more than she liked, and her underarms smelly. She wasn't accustomed in this house-hold to having her word questioned except by Warren Pirig, so now her fingers twitched dangerously. *How about I slap your face you sly little bitch looking so innocent?*

There was so much rage in her so suddenly! Though she knew, sure, she knew, Norma Jeane wasn't the one to blame. Her husband was the one to blame, and even that poor bastard was halfway innocent.

So she believed. Judging from what she'd seen. But maybe she hadn't seen everything?

What she'd seen, what she'd been seeing for months till finally she couldn't not see it any longer and still respect herself, was Warren watching the girl. And Warren Pirig wasn't one to watch anybody. Talking to you, he'd swerve his eyes off into a corner, like you weren't worth his looking at because he'd seen you before and knew who you were. Even with the drinking buddies he liked and respected he'd be looking somewhere else half the time like there was nothing to see, exactly, nothing that warranted the effort. And this was a man with damaged vision in his left eye, from amateur boxing days in the U.S. Army in the Philippines, and twenty-twenty vision in his right eye, so he refused to wear glasses saying they "got in the way." To be fair to Warren, you had to grant he didn't look at himself either, not with care. In too much of a hurry to shave half the time, or put on clean shirts, unless Elsie laid them out for him and tossed the soiled shirts into the laundry where he couldn't fish them out; for a man who was a salesman, even if it was scrap metal and used tires and a few secondhand cars and trucks, he wasn't what you'd call concerned for the impression he made on others. Good-looking when he'd been young and lean and in uniform when Elsie first set eyes on him at age seventeen up in San Fernando, but he hadn't been young and lean and in uniform for a long time now.

Maybe if it was Joe Louis standing in front of him, or President Roosevelt, they'd get Warren Pirig's attention. But no ordinary person, and for sure no fifteen-year-old kid.

Elsie saw this man's eyes follow the girl like ball bearings moving in their sockets. She saw this man staring like he'd never stared at any other county kids except if one of them was making trouble or gave a hint of intending to make trouble. But Norma Jeane, this man was looking at *her*.

Not at meals. Elsie noticed that. Wondering, was it deliberate? The only time they were all seated together, facing one another in close quarters. Warren was a big man, a heavy eater, and meals were for eating, not gabbing as he called it, and Norma Jeane was likely to be quiet at the table, giggling at Elsie's jokes but never saying much of her own, she had little-lady table manners they'd taught her at county that were sort of comical, Elsie thought, in the Pirig household, so she'd stay sort of still and shy, though eating about as much as anybody excepting Warren. So, in these close quarters, Warren seemed never to look at Norma Jeane as he never looked at anybody, often reading the paper he'd folded back to a vertical strip; it wasn't rudeness exactly but just Warren Pirig's way. At other times, though, even with Elsie close by, Warren would watch that girl like he didn't know what he was doing, and it was this helplessness in him, a kind of sick drowning look in his face—and that face a banged-up face, a face like mountain terrain on a map—that lodged deep in Elsie so she began to brood on it and found herself thinking about it when she didn't realize she was thinking about anything at all, and Elsie wasn't the brooding type, there were relatives she'd been feuding with for twenty years and old ex-woman friends she'd cut dead on the street, but it was correct to say she never brooded over any of these persons; she simply didn't think about them at all. But now there was a smudged space in her brain that was her husband and this girl, and she resented it because Elsie Pirig wasn't the jealous type and never had been because she was too proud for such yet now discovered herself checking through the girl's things in her attic room hot as an oven already in April and wasps buzzing beneath the eaves, and all she found was Norma Jeane's red-leather diary the girl had already shown her, proud of this gift from the director at the L.A. orphanage; Elsie had leafed through the diary, her hands actually shaking (her! Elsie Pirig! this wasn't her!) in dread of seeing something she didn't want to see, but there was nothing of special interest in Norma Jeane's diary or in any case nothing that Elsie in her haste had time to ponder. There were poems, probably copied out of books or things she'd been assigned at school, carefully written in Norma Jeane's school-girl hand:

There was a bird flown so high
He could no longer say, "This is the sky."
There was a fish in the ocean so low
He could no longer say, "There is nowhere else to go."

And:

If the blind man can *see*
What about *me*?

Elsie liked that one but could make no sense of others, especially when they didn't rhyme the way a poem should.

Because I could not stop for Death,
He kindly stopped for me;
The carriage held but just ourselves
And Immortality.

Even less comprehensible were Christian Science prayers, Elsie guessed they were. The poor kid seemed actually to believe this stuff she'd copied out, a single prayer to a page:

Heavenly Father
Let me join Your perfect being
In all that is Eternal—Spiritual—Harmonious
And let Divine Love resist all Evil
For Divine Love is Forever
Help me to love as You love
There is no PAIN
There is no SICKNESS
There is no DEATH
There is no SORROW
There is only DIVINE LOVE FOREVER.

How could anybody make sense of this, still less believe it? Maybe Norma Jeane's mentally sick mother was Christian Science and that's where the girl had picked it up; you had to wonder whether stuff like this had pushed the poor woman over the edge or whether, already over the edge, you grabbed on to stuff like this to save your life. Elsie flipped another page and read:

Heavenly Father
Thank You for my new Family!
Thank You for my Aunt Elsie I love so!
Thank You for Mr. Pirig who is kind to me!
Thank You for this new Home!
Thank You for my new school!
Thank You for my new friends!
Thank You for my new life!
Help my Mother to become Well again
And Perpetual Light shine upon her
All the days of her life
And help my Mother to Love me
In such a way she will not wish to hurt me!
Thank You Heavenly Father AMEN.

Quickly Elsie shut the diary and thrust it back into Norma Jeane's underwear drawer. She felt as if she'd been kicked in the gut. She wasn't the kind
of woman to go through anybody's things and she hated a snoop and, God
damn, she resented it that Warren and the girl had pushed her to this.
Descending the steep stairs, she was so rattled she nearly fell. She'd made up
her mind to tell Warren the girl would have to go.
    Go where?
    I don't care where the hell. But out of this house.
    Are you crazy? Sending her back to the orphanage for no reason?
    You want me to wait till there's a reason, you bastard?
    Call Warren Pirig a bastard even if you're teary-eyed with hurt and you'd
be in danger of getting whacked across the face with his closed fist; she'd
seen him once (Warren was drunk and provoked; these were special circumstances for which she'd forgiven him) smash through a door locked
against him. Warren weighed two hundred thirty pounds last time the doctor weighed him, and Elsie, five foot two, weighed just under one hundred
forty. Figure the odds!
    Like they say in boxing, a mismatch.
    So Elsie decided to say nothing to Warren. Keeping her distance from him
like a woman already wronged. Like that song by Frank Sinatra you heard
a lot on the radio, "I'll Never Smile Again." But Warren was working twelve
hours a day hauling rotted tires over to East L.A. to a Goodyear plant, where
they were buying scrap rubber that, on December 6, 1941, the day before
Pearl Harbor, wasn't worth five cents a pound. ("So how much are they paying you now?" Elsie asked, excited, and Warren looked somewhere over her
head and said, "Just enough to make it worthwhile." They'd been married

twenty-six years, and Elsie had yet to know how much Warren made a year in actual cash.) This meant that Warren was out of the house all day and when he returned for supper he wasn't in any mood for chitchat, as he called it, washed face and hands and arms to the elbow and got a beer from the icebox and sat down to eat and ate and pushed away from the table when he was through and a few minutes later you could hear him snoring, flat out on their bed with only his work boots off. If Elsie was keeping her distance from Warren, purse-lipped and indignant, Warren took no notice.

And the next day was laundry day: meaning that Elsie kept Norma Jeane out of school for part of the morning to help her with the leaky Kelvinator washing machine and the wringer that was forever getting stuck and toting baskets of clothes outside to hang them on the backyard lines (admittedly, it was against county regulations to keep a child out of school for such a purpose but Elsie knew she could trust Norma Jeane never to breathe a word, unlike one or two other ungrateful little bitches who'd tattled to authorities in bygone years), and it wasn't the right time to bring up such a grave subject, not when Norma Jeane, cheerful and sweaty and uncomplaining as usual, was doing most of the work. Even singing to herself in her sweet, breathy voice, top tunes of the week from *Your Hit Parade*. There was Norma Jeane lifting damp sheets with her slender, surprisingly muscled arms and pinning them to the line while Elsie in a straw hat to protect her eyes from the sun, a Camel burning between her lips, panted like a worn-out old mule. Several times, too, Elsie had to leave Norma Jeane to go inside the house to use the bathroom, or have some coffee, or make a telephone call, leaning against the kitchen counter watching the fifteen-year-old hanging laundry on her tiptoes like a dancer: that sweet little ass of hers, even Elsie who was no lezzie could appreciate.

Marlene Dietrich they said was a lezzie. Greta Garbo. Mae West?

Staring at Norma Jeane out in the backyard struggling with laundry. Ratty-looking palm trees, and crap from their leaves underfoot. The girl taking care as she hung Warren's billowing sports shirt up to dry. And Warren's shorts big enough, when the breeze caught them just right, to practically wrap around the girl's head. God damn Warren Pirig! What was there between him and Norma Jeane? Or was it all just in Warren's head, in that dumb-ass sick yearning look Elsie hadn't seen from him, or from any man, in twenty years? Pure nature it was, a man stumbling unconscious. You can't blame him, can you? Can't blame yourself. Yet: she was the man's wife, she had to protect herself. A woman would have to protect herself against a girl like Norma Jeane. For there was Warren approaching the girl from behind in that strangely graceful way of his you didn't expect from a man of that size except if you recall he'd been a boxer and boxers have to be quick on their feet. Warren cupping the girl's ass like twin melons in his big hands and she turns to him astonished and he buries his face in her neck and her long curly dirty-blond hair falls like a curtain over his head.

Elsie felt the rush in the pit of her belly. "How can I send her away?" she said aloud. "We'll never get another one like her."

When all the laundry was hanging on the lines by about 10:30 A.M., Elsie sent Norma Jeane off to Van Nuys High with an excuse for her tardiness to take to the principal.

> Please excuse my daughter Norma Jeane, she was required by her mother to drive with me to a Doctors appointment I did not feel strong enough to drive both ways by myself.

It was a new, original excuse, one Elsie had never used before. She didn't want to overuse Norma Jeane's health problems; somebody at the high school might get nosy if Norma Jeane stayed out too frequently with what Elsie described as *migran headache* or *bad cramps*. (The headache and cramps were legitimate much of the time. Poor Norma Jeane really suffered from her period such as Elsie hadn't ever suffered at that age—or any age. Should take her to a doctor probably. If she'd go. Lying upstairs on her bed or downstairs on the wicker sofa to be closer to Elsie, gasping and moaning and sometimes crying softly, poor kid, a hot-water bottle on her belly (which it seemed Christian Science allowed) but, unknown to Norma Jeane, Elsie ground up aspirin in orange juice for her, as much aspirin as she could get away with, poor sweet dumb kid talked into believing medicine was "unnatural" and Jesus would "heal" you if you had enough faith. Sure, like Jesus would cure your cancer, or grow you a new leg if the old one was blown off, or restore perfect vision to an eye with retina damage like Warren's. Like Jesus would make amends for the maimed children in *Life*, victims of Hitler's *Luftwaffe!*)

So Norma Jeane went off to school while the laundry dried on the line. Not much breeze but a hot dry sun. It never ceased to amaze Elsie that as soon as Norma Jeane was finished with household chores one of her boyfriends would show up at the curb in his car, tap the horn, and off trotted Norma Jeane all smiles and bouncy curls. How did this guy in the rattletrap jalopy (looking older than high school age, Elsie thought, peering through the front blinds) even know that Norma Jeane had stayed home from school that morning? Did the girl send psychic signals? Was it some kind of sexual radar? Or (Elsie didn't want to think) was it an actual scent like a dog, a bitch in heat, and every damn male dog in the neighborhood shows up panting and scratching the dirt?

The way men stumble unconscious. Can't blame them, can you?

Sometimes more than one of them showed up in his car to drive Norma Jeane to school. Laughing like a little girl, she'd flick a penny to see which car, which guy, to take.

A mystery of Norma Jeane's diary was *not a single male name was listed*. Hardly any names at all except for hers and Warren's, and what did that mean?

Poems, prayers. Stuff you couldn't make sense of. That wasn't normal for a fifteen-year-old, was it?

They would have their talk now. It wasn't to be avoided.

Always Elsie Pirig would remember this talk. God damn, it left her resentful of Warren; it's a man's world and what the hell can a woman who's a realist do about that?

Shyly Norma Jeane said, in a way that allowed Elsie to know she'd been thinking about this since early that morning, "You were just joking about me getting married, Aunt Elsie—weren't you?" and Elsie said, picking a bit of tobacco off her tongue, "I wouldn't joke about such a thing." Norma Jeane said, worried, "I'd be afraid to marry anyone, Aunt Elsie. You'd have to love a boy really well for that." Elsie said lightly, "There must be one of them you could love, isn't there? I've been hearing some things about you, sweetie." Quickly Norma Jeane said, "You mean Mr. Haring?" and when Elsie looked at her blankly she said, "Oh, you mean Mr. Widdoes?" and still Elsie looked at her blankly and she said, a flush rising into her face, "I'm not seeing them anymore! I didn't know they were married, Aunt Elsie, I *swear*." Elsie smoked her cigarette and had to smile at this revelation. If she just kept her mouth shut long enough, Norma Jeane would fill her in on every detail. Staring at her with that sweet little-girl look, her darkish-blue eyes filled with moisture and her voice tremulous like she was trying not to stammer. "Aunt Elsie"—it had a nice sound to it, in Norma Jeane's voice. Elsie asked all the foster kids to call her "Aunt Elsie" and most of them did but it had taken Norma Jeane almost a year; she'd tried and stumbled over the word repeatedly. No wonder the girl hadn't been chosen to be in a play at the high school, Elsie thought. She was so honest—couldn't act worth a damn! But since Christmas, when Elsie gave her several nice presents including a plastic hand mirror with a woman's profile in silhouette on the back, at last Norma Jeane was calling her "Aunt Elsie" as if, in fact, they were *family*.

Which made this hurt all the more.

Which made her all the more pissed at Warren.

Elsie said, carefully, "It's going to happen to you sooner or later, Norma Jeane. So better sooner. With this terrible war started, and young men joining up to fight, you'd better grab a husband while there are guys available and still in one piece." Norma Jeane protested. "You're serious, Aunt Elsie? This isn't a joke?" and Elsie said, annoyed, "Do I look like I'm joking, miss? Does Hitler? Tojo?" and Norma Jeane said, shaking her head as if trying to clear it, "I just don't understand, Aunt Elsie, why should I get married? I'm only fifteen, I've got two years of high school to go. I want to be a—" and Elsie interrupted, incensed, "High school! *I* got married in my junior year and my mother never finished eighth grade. You don't need any diplomas to get married." Norma Jeane said, pleading, "But I'm too y-young, Aunt Elsie," and Elsie said, "That's exactly the problem. You're fifteen, you've got boyfriends and man friends and there's going to be trouble before we know it and Warren was saying to me just the other morning, the Pirigs have a reputation to uphold here in Van Nuys. We've been taking in foster kids from L.A. County for twenty years, and there've been girls now and then who've gotten into trouble under our roof, not always bad girls but good girls, too, girls running around with boyfriends, and it reflects badly on us. Warren says what's this I hear about Norma Jeane running around with married men and *I* said it's the first I heard of such a thing and *he* says, 'Elsie, we better take emergency measures fast.' " Norma Jeane said uncertainly, "Mr. P-pirig said that? About me? Oh! I thought Mr. Pirig liked me!" and Elsie said, "It's not a matter of liking or not liking. It's a matter of what the county calls emergency measures." Norma Jeane said, "What measures? What emergency? I'm not in trouble, Aunt Elsie! I—" and Elsie interrupted again, wanting to get this out quick, like spitting something foul out of her mouth, "The point is you're fifteen and could pass for eighteen in a man's eyes but you're a ward of the county until you're actually eighteen and unless you get married, the way state law is, you could get sent back to the orphanage at any time."

This came out in such a flood of words, Norma Jeane appeared dazed like someone hard of hearing. Elsie herself was feeling faint, that sickish sensation that rises up from the soles of your feet when there's a tremor in the earth. *It had to be done. God help me!*

Norma Jeane said, frightened, "But w-why should I go back to the orphanage? I mean—why should I be sent back? I was sent *here*." Elsie said, avoiding the girl's eyes, "That was eighteen months ago and things have changed. You know things have changed. You were like a child when you came here and now you're—well, a *girl*. And acting sometimes like a full-grown *woman*. There's consequences to all our behavior, especially that kind of behavior—with men, I mean." "But I haven't done anything wrong," Norma Jeane said, her voice rising in desperation. "I promise you, Aunt Elsie! I haven't! They're nice to me, Aunt Elsie, most of them, really! They say they just like to be with me and take me out and—that's all! Really. But I can tell them 'no' from now on; I can tell them that you and Mr. Pirig won't let me go out anymore. I'll tell them!" Elsie said, faltering, unprepared for this, "But—we need the room. The attic room. My sister and her kids are coming from Sacramento to live with us—" Norma Jeane said quickly, "I don't need an actual room, Aunt Elsie. I can sleep on the sofa downstairs or in the laundry room or—anywhere. I can sleep in one of Mr. Pirig's cars he has for sale. Some of them are nice, there're cushions in the backseats—" and Elsie said, shaking her head gravely, "Norma Jeane, the county would never allow that. You know they send inspectors," and Norma Jeane said, touching Elsie's arm, "You're not going to send me back to the Home, are you? Aunt Elsie? I thought you liked me! I thought we were like a family! Oh, Aunt Elsie, please—I love it here in this house! I love you!" She paused, panting. Her stricken face was damp with tears and a look of animal terror shone in her dilated eyes. "Don't send me away, please! I promise I'll be good! I'll work harder! I won't go out on dates! I'll quit school and stay home and help you out, and I could help Mr. Pirig, too, with his business! I would want to die, Aunt Elsie, if you sent me back to the Home. I can't go back to the Home. I'll kill myself if I'm sent back to the Home. Aunt Elsie, please!"

By now Norma Jeane was in Elsie's arms. Trembling, and breathless, and very warm, and sobbing. Elsie hugged her close, feeling the girl's quivering shoulder blades, the tension in her spine. Norma Jeane had grown taller than Elsie by an inch or so and she was stooping to make herself smaller, like a child. Elsie was thinking she'd never felt so bad in her adult life. Oh, shit, she just felt so fucking bad! If she could have she'd have kicked Warren out on his ass and kept Norma Jeane—but of course she couldn't. *It's a man's world and to survive a woman must betray her own kind.*

Elsie held the sobbing girl, biting her lip to keep from breaking down herself. "Norma Jeane, stop. Crying never helps. If it did, we'd all be better off by now."

2

I won't get married, I'm too young!

I want to be a WAC nurse. I want to go overseas.

I want to help suffering people.

Those little English children wounded and maimed and some of them buried in rubble. And their parents dead. And nobody to love them.

I want to be a vessel of Divine Love. I want God to shine through me. I want to help heal the wounded, I want to show them the way of faith.

I can run away. I can enlist in Los Angeles. God will answer my prayer.
She'd been transfixed with horror, her mouth open and slack and her breath quick as a panting dog's and a terrible roaring and pounding in her ears, staring at the photographs in the copy of *Life* left on the kitchen table: a child with swollen eyes and an arm missing, a baby so swathed in bloody bandages only his mouth and part of his nose were visible, a little girl of about two with bruised eyes and a dazed, emaciated face. What was the little girl clutching, a doll? A bloodstained doll?

There came Warren Pirig to take the magazine from her. Snatched it out of her numbed fingers. His voice was low and angry-sounding yet at the same time forgiving, as often it was when they were alone together. "You don't want to look at that," he said. "You don't know what you're looking at."

He never called her "Norma Jeane."

3

They were Hawkeye, Cadwaller, Dwayne, Ryan, Jake, Fiske, O'Hara, Skokie, Clarence, Simon, Lyle, Rob, Dale, Jimmy, Carlos, Esdras, Fulmer, Marvin, Gruner, Price, Salvatore, Santos, Porter, Haring, Widdoes. They were soldiers, a sailor, a marine, a rancher, a house painter, a bail bondsman, a trucker, the son of a Redondo Beach amusement park owner, the son of a Van Nuys banker, an aircraft factory worker, Van Nuys high school student athletes, an instructor at Burbank Bible College, an officer for the Los Angeles County Department of Corrections, a repairer of motorcycles, a crop duster, a butcher's assistant, a postal employee, a Van Nuys bookie's son and right-hand man, a Van Nuys High teacher, a Culver City Police Department detective. They took her to Topanga Beach, to Will Rogers Beach, Las Tunas, Santa Monica, and Venice Beach. They took her to movies. They took her to dances. (Norma Jeane was shy dancing "close" but a terrific jitterbugger, dancing with her eyes shut tight as if hypnotized, a gemlike glisten on her skin. And she could hula like a native Hawaiian!) They took her to church services and to the racetrack at Casa Grande. They took her roller-skating. They took her rowing and canoeing and were surprised that, a girl, she insisted upon helping to row, and so capably. They took her bowling. They took her to Bingo games and billiard parlors. They took her to baseball games. They took her on Sunday drives into the San Gabriel Mountains. They took her on drives along the coastal highway as far north sometimes as Santa Barbara and as far south as Oceanside. They took her on romantic drives by moonlight, the Pacific Ocean luminous to one side and dark wooded hills on the other and the wind rippling her hair and sparks from the driver's cigarettes flying back into the night, but in later years she would confuse these drives with scenes from movies she'd seen or believed she must have seen. *They didn't touch me where I didn't want to be touched. They didn't make me drink. They were respectful of me. My white shoes were freshly polished every week and my hair smelled of shampoo and my clothes of fresh ironing. If they kissed me it was closed-mouthed. I knew to keep my lips pursed tightly together. And my eyes closed when we kissed. Rarely would I move. My breathing was quickened but never panting. My hands were still in my lap though I might raise my forearm to push him away, gently.* The youngest was sixteen, a football player at Van Nuys High. The oldest was thirty-four, the Culver City detective she'd discovered belatedly was married.

Detective Frank Widdoes! A Culver City cop investigating a murder in Van Nuys in late-summer 1941. A man's bullet-ridden body had been found dumped in a desolate area near train tracks on the outskirts of Van Nuys and the victim was identified as a witness in a Culver City murder case and so Widdoes drove up to question area residents and as he was surveying the crime scene along a dirt lane there came a girl on a bicycle, a dark-blond girl pedaling slowly and dreamily and oblivious of the plainclothes detective staring at her, believing her at first glance to be about twelve years old, then seeing more clearly she was older, possibly as old as seventeen, with a bust like a woman, in a snug-fitting mustard-yellow jersey top, and she wore short shorts in a white cord material that outlined her little heart-shaped ass like that Betty Grable bathing-suit pinup, and when he stopped her to ask her if she'd seen anyone or anything "suspicious" in the area he saw that she had the most remarkable blue eyes, beautiful liquidy dreamy eyes, eyes that seemed not to see him but somehow inside him, as if he already knew her, and though she didn't know him she understood that he already knew her and had the right to question her, to detain her and sit with her in his unmarked police car for as long as he wished, as long as the "investigation" required, and she had a face he wasn't likely to forget, heart-shaped, too, with a widow's peak, her nose just a little long and her teeth just a little crooked, which added to her looks, he thought, gave her that look of placid normalcy, for after all she was only a kid even if she was also a woman, a kid wearing a woman's body like a little girl trying on an adult woman's clothes and seeming to know this and exult in it (the tight jersey top and the way she sat with perfect pinup posture, breathing deeply to expand her rib cage, and her tawny-tanned legs perfect, too, in those short shorts riding up nearly to her crotch) and yet not-knowing simultaneously. If he'd ordered her to remove her clothes she would have done so smiling and eager to please and she'd have been more innocent still, and more beautiful, and if he did such a thing—which of course he would not—except if he did, and the punishment was being turned to stone or torn apart by wolves, it might almost have been worth it.

So he'd seen the girl a few times. He'd drive up to Van Nuys and meet her near the high school. He hadn't touched her! Not in that way. Hardly at all, in fact. Knowing she was jailbait, and knowing the kind of professional trouble he could get into, not to mention deeper marital trouble since he'd cheated on his wife already and had gotten caught, that's to say he'd angrily confessed to his wife and had so gotten "caught." And he'd moved out, and was living alone now and liking it. And this girl Norma Jeane was a welfare kid, he'd discovered. A ward of L.A. County placed with a foster family on Reseda Street, Van Nuys, a street of shabby bungalows and grassless yards and her foster father owned a half acre of used cars, trucks, motorcycles, and other junk for sale, a stink of burning rubber perpetually in the air and a bluish haze over the neighborhood and Widdoes could imagine the interior of the house but decided not to investigate because, better not, it could backfire on him and in any case what could he do, adopt the kid himself? He had his own kids, costing him. He felt sorry for her, gave her money, one- and five-dollar bills so she could "buy something nice" for herself. It was all innocent, really. She was the kind of girl who obeys, or who wants to obey, so if you're responsible you take care what you tell her to do. When they put their trust in you, it's a temptation worse than when they're distrustful. And her age. And her body. It wasn't just his badge (she admired the badge, "loved" the badge, and wanted always to look at it, and at his pistol; she'd asked could she touch the pistol and Widdoes laughed and said sure, why not, as long as it remained in his holster and the safety was on), but his air of authority, eleven years as a cop and you get that air of authority, questioning people, bossing people around, that expectation that, if they resist, they'll regret it and they know it as by instinct we sense in the physical being of another a dominance that, pushed to a limit, and that limit not negotiable, we can be hurt. Yet it was all innocent, really. Things are never the way they look to outside eyes. As a detective, Widdoes knew this. Norma Jeane was only three years older than his daughter. But those three years were crucial. She was much smarter than you'd think at first glance. In fact, a few times she'd surprised him. The eyes and the baby voice were misleading. The girl could talk earnestly about things (the war, the "meaning of life") like any adult of Widdoes's acquaintance. She had a sense of humor. She laughed at herself—she wanted to be "a singer with Tommy Dorsey." She wanted to be a WAC officer. She wanted to join the Air Force Women's Flying Training Detachment she'd been reading about in the paper. She wanted to be a doctor. She told him she was "the only living grandchild" of a woman who'd founded the Christian Science church, and her mother, who'd died in an airplane crash over the Atlantic in 1934, had been a Hollywood film actress with The Studio, an understudy for Joan Crawford and Gloria Swanson, and her father whom she hadn't seen in years was a Hollywood producer, now a naval commander in the South Pacific, and none of these statements did Widdoes believe yet he listened to the girl as if he believed, or as if he was trying to believe, and she seemed grateful for such kindness. She let him kiss her if he didn't try to force her lips open with his tongue, and he didn't. She let him kiss her mouth, her neck, and her shoulders—but only if her shoulders were bare. She became anxious if he shifted her clothing or tried to unbutton or unzip anything. Such childish fussiness was touching to him, he recognized it as a trait similar to those in his own daughter. *Some things are allowed and some things not-allowed.* But Norma Jeane let him stroke her silky downy arms and even her legs to mid-thigh; she let him stroke her long, curly hair and even brush it. (Norma Jeane provided the hairbrush! Telling him that brushing her hair was something her mother did when she was a little girl and she missed her mother so.)

These months Widdoes saw a number of women. He didn't think of Norma Jeane as a woman. It might've been sex that drew him to her but it wasn't sex he got from her. At least, not in any way the girl knew or needed to acknowledge.

How did it end between them? Unexpectedly. Abruptly. Not an incident Widdoes would have wanted anybody to know about, especially his superior officers in the Culver City P.D., where already in Frank Widdoes's file there were several citizen complaints of "excessive force" in making arrests. And this wasn't an arrest. One evening in March 1942 he'd come to pick up Norma Jeane on a street corner a few blocks from Reseda and for the first time the girl wasn't alone. There was a guy with her; it looked as if they were arguing. The guy was possibly twenty-five years old, husky and looking like a garage mechanic in cheaply flashy clothes, and Norma Jeane was crying because this "Clarence" had followed her and wouldn't leave her alone though she'd begged him and Widdoes shouted at Clarence to get the fuck away and Clarence said something in response to Widdoes he shouldn't have said and might not have said if he'd been wholly sober and if he'd been able to get a good look at Widdoes; and without another word Widdoes climbed out of his car and as Norma Jeane looked on in horror calmly unholstered his Smith & Wesson revolver and pistol-whipped the fucker across the face, cracking his nose in a single blow and spraying blood; Clarence sank to his knees on the pavement and Widdoes rammed him on the back of the neck and down goes the fucker like a shot, his legs twitching, and he's out cold. And Widdoes pulls the girl into the car and drives away but the girl's scared stiff, literally scared rigid and unmoving, so scared she can hardly speak and can't seem to hear Widdoes's words meant to comfort that maybe sound angry, aggrieved. Even later she won't let him touch her, even her hand. And Widdoes has to admit he's scared, too, now he's had time to think it over. Things that are allowed and not-allowed and he'd crossed the threshold in a public place and if there'd been witnesses? if the kid had died? He sure as hell didn't want anything like this to happen again. So he didn't see little Norma Jeane again.

Never even saw her another time to say goodbye.

4

She was beginning to forget.

There was a magic way she linked *forgetting* with the monthly period she didn't think of as bleeding exactly but expelling poison. Every few weeks it would happen to her and it was a good, necessary thing, her headache and feverish skin and nausea and cramps were a sign of her weakness and not *real*. Aunt Elsie explained to her how it was natural and every girl and woman had to endure it. "The curse" it was called but Norma Jeane never called it that. For it was from God and could not be anything but a blessing.

The very name "Gladys" was not a name she now spoke aloud or even to herself. If she spoke of her mother in this new place (which she did rarely and then only to Aunt Elsie), she would say "my mother" in a calm, neutral voice the way you might say "my English teacher" or "my new sweater" or "my ankle." Nothing more.

One morning soon she would wake to discover all memory of "my mother" vanished the way, when her period ran its course after three or four days, it stopped as mysteriously as it began.

The poison gone. And I'm happy again. So happy!

5

Norma Jeane *was* a happy girl, always smiling.

Though her laugh was odd, unmusical: high-pitched and squeaky as a mouse (so poor Norma Jeane was teased) being stepped on.

No matter. She laughed often because she was happy and because other people laughed and in their presence so did she.

At Van Nuys High she was an average student.

Except for her looks, an average girl.

Except for something taut and nervous and excitable and flamelike in her face, an average girl.

Tried out for cheerleading. Only the prettiest and most popular girls with good figures and good athletic ability were chosen to be cheerleaders, but there was Norma Jeane sweating and queasy at tryouts in the gym. *I did not even pray because I believed God should not be prevailed upon where a prospect is hopeless.* For weeks she'd been practicing the cheers and knew each by heart and the leaps, contortions of the spine, outspread arms and legs; she knew herself capable as any girl at the high school yet as the hour approached she grew ever weaker and more panicked and her voice was choked and at last she could not speak at all and there was so little strength in her knees that she nearly collapsed on the mat. Among the forty or more girls who'd assembled in the gym that afternoon there was an embarrassed silence. Quickly the captain of the cheerleading squad said, in her brisk bright voice, "Thank you, Norma Jeane. Who's next?"

Tried out for Drama Club. Auditioned for Thornton Wilder's *Our Town.* Why? There must have been desperation in it. This need to be normal, and more than normal; this need to be chosen. And there was the anticipation that, in this play that seemed so beautiful to her, and in acting in this play, she, Norma Jeane, would find a home; she would be "Emily" and be called by that name by others. She'd read and reread the play and believed she understood it; there was a part of her soul that understood it. Though years from the realization *I have put myself into the very center of imaginary circumstances, I exist at the heart of an imaginary life, in a world of imaginary things and this is my redemption.* But standing on the stark lighted stage, blinking and squinting into the front row of seats where those who would judge her were sitting, she felt suddenly overcome by panic. The drama teacher called out, "Next? Who's next? Norma Jeane—begin." But she could not begin. She held the script in a trembling hand, the words blurred on the page, her throat seemed to close. Lines she'd committed to memory only the evening before now swirled in her head like demented flies. At last she began to read in a hurried, choked voice. Her tongue was too large for her mouth! She stammered and faltered and lost her way. "Thank you, dear," the drama teacher said, dismissing her. Norma Jeane looked up from the script and said, "P-please, can I try again?" and there was an awkward pause. She heard murmurs and muffled laughter. "I think I could be Emily. I k-know—I am Emily." *If I could take off my clothes. If I could stand before you naked as God created me, then— then you would see me!* But the drama teacher was unmoved. Saying, in a voice laced with irony, so that other, favored students might laugh at his wit and at the object of his wit, "Hmm. Is it—Norma Jeane? Thank you, Norma Jeane. But I doubt that Mr. Thornton Wilder would see it that way."

She left the stage. Her face was burning, but she meant to retain her dignity. So, in a film, you might be called upon to die. So long as others were watching, you must retain your dignity.

In Norma Jeane's wake came a single wolf whistle.

Tried out for girls' choir. She knew she could sing, she *knew!*—she was always singing at home, she loved to sing and her voice was melodic in her ears, and hadn't Jess Flynn promised that her voice could be trained? She was a soprano, she was certain. "These Foolish Things" was her best song. But when the choir director asked her to sing "Spring Song" by Joseph Reisler, which she'd never seen before, she'd stared at the sheet music unable to read the notes; when the woman sat at a piano, played through the song, and asked Norma Jeane to sing while she accompanied her, Norma Jeane lost her confidence and sang in a breathy, wavering, disappointing voice— not hers!

She asked please could she try a second time.

The second time, her voice was a little stronger. But not much.

The choir director dismissed her politely. "Maybe next year, Norma Jeane."

For her English teacher, Mr. Haring, she'd written essays on Mary Baker Eddy, the founder of Christian Science, and on Abraham Lincoln, "America's greatest president," and on Christopher Columbus, "a man not afraid to venture into the unknown." She'd showed Mr. Haring some of her poems, carefully written in blue ink on sheets of unlined paper.

Into the sky—so high!
I know that I will never die.

I know that I would never be blue
If I could love you.

If there is a way
for those on Earth to say—
"I love you!"
and make it always be true.

As God tells us "I love you—
and you—and you—"
and always IT IS TRUE.

When Mr. Haring smiled uneasily and told her the poem was "very good"—the rhyming "perfect"—Norma Jeane blushed with pleasure. It had taken her weeks to build up her courage to bring these poems in, and now—what a reward! And she had many more poems! Her diary was spilling over with poems! And she had poems her mother had written a long time ago as a young girl living in northern California, before she'd been married.

> The red blaze is the morning
> The violet is noon
> The yellow day is falling
> And after that is none.
>
> But miles of sparks at evening
> Reveal the width that burned
> The Territory Argent that
> Never yet consumed.

This peculiar poem Mr. Haring read and reread, frowning. Oh, if she'd made a mistake showing it to him! Her heart began to pound like a frightened rabbit's. Mr. Haring was a disciplinarian with his students though a young man of twenty-nine, wiry-thin, sandy-haired, beginning to go bald, and walking with a limp from a boyhood accident: a young husband struggling to support his family on a public-school teacher's salary. He looked like a weaker, less amiable Henry Fonda in *The Grapes of Wrath*. He wasn't always of a cheery disposition in class and was given to occasional outbursts of sarcasm. You never knew with Mr. Haring how he might react, what strange things he might say, but you hoped he would smile at you, at least. And usually Mr. Haring smiled at Norma Jeane, who was a quiet, shy girl, a startlingly pretty and precociously shapely girl who wore sweaters a size or two too small and whose manner was unconsciously provocative—at least, Haring supposed her manner was unconscious. *A fifteen-year-old sexpot yet not seeming to know it. And those eyes!*

Norma Jeane's mother's poem, lacking a title, did not seem to Haring to be a "finished" poem. At the blackboard with a stick of chalk (this was after school; Norma Jeane had come in for a private consultation), he demonstrated to her how the "rhyme scheme" was deficient. "Morning" and "falling" were meant to be A-rhymes, but as Norma Jeane could see they didn't really rhyme. The B-rhyme ("noon," "none") was even worse. In the second stanza, there was no C-rhyme at all ("evening," "that") and the D-rhyme ("burned," "consumed") was flat. Poetry is musical, after all, you hear it with the ear, you don't just see it with the eye. And what was

"Territory Argent"? He'd never heard of such a place and doubted it existed. "Obscurity and coyness": these were typical weaknesses in female poetry. A strong rhyme scheme is needed for strong poetry, and the sense of a poem should never be unclear. "Otherwise the reader shrugs his shoulders and says, 'Eh? *I* can write better than this.' "

Norma Jeane laughed, because Mr. Haring laughed. She was deeply embarrassed by the flaws in her mother's poem (though stubbornly she would continue to think it was a beautiful, strange, mysterious poem); but she'd have had to admit she didn't know what "Territory Argent" meant herself. Apologetically, she told her English teacher that her mother had not finished college. "Mom married when she was only nineteen. She wanted to be a real poet. She wanted to be a teacher—like you, Mr. Haring."

Haring was touched by this. The girl was so sweet! He kept the desk between them.

Something in Norma Jeane's quavering voice signaled him to ask, gently, "Where is your mother now, Norma Jeane? You don't live with her?"

Mutely Norma Jeane shook her head. Her eyes filled with moisture and her young face tightened as if in danger of shattering.

It came then to Haring that he'd heard this girl was a ward of L.A. County. Living with the Pirigs. The Pirigs! He'd had their foster kids in his English classes before. He was frankly surprised this one was so well-groomed, healthy, and intelligent. Her dark-blond hair wasn't greasy, her clothes appeared neat and clean if rather eye-catching: the cheap tight red sweater outlining her amazing little breasts and the cheap tight gray serge skirt that all but showed the crack of her buttocks. If he'd dared to look.

He hadn't looked and wasn't going to. He and his exhausted young wife had a four-year-old daughter and an eight-month-old son and that fact, stark and pitiless as the desert sun, hovered before his bloodshot eyes.

Yet he said, quickly, "Look, Norma Jeane. Bring in poems—yours, your mother's—any time. I'm happy to read them. That's my job."

So it happened in the winter of 1941 that Sidney Haring who was Norma Jeane's favorite teacher at Van Nuys High began to see her after class once or even twice a week. Tirelessly they talked of—oh, what did they talk of?—mainly novels and poems Haring gave Norma Jeane to read, Emily Brontë's *Wuthering Heights*, Charlotte Brontë's *Jane Eyre*, Pearl Buck's *The Good Earth*, slender volumes of verse by Elizabeth Barrett Browning, Sara Teasdale, Edna St. Vincent Millay, and Haring's own favorite, Robert Browning. He continued to "critique" her schoolgirl poems. (She never brought in another of her mother's—fortunately.) One winter afternoon it happened that Norma Jeane suddenly realized she'd stayed too late, she was expected home by Mrs. Pirig to do chores, and Haring offered to drive her home; after

that, when No
a distance of
together.

It was al
dent, an
door fo
and h
inha
ti

you'll notice he's only seen from the wais
I happen to know from a reliable sourc
job in Washington, D.C., he is." "I d
Haring laughed, enjoying this—"don't
Norma Jeane Baker out in Van Nuy
believe."
They were sitting in Haring's c
a five-minute drive from the Pi
the near distance were railroa
the Verdugo Mountains. R
Jeane seemed truly to see
fixed on his and the im
against himself and ho
whispered, "Oh! I h
Haring laughed
After he dropp
ken out in swea
rum his penis
But I did
Next ti
ited ag
ten. Nei
th

Yet in
of sexual flirta
the books Haring ga
believe held promise. If th
mysterious *you*, Haring could n
Haring. Only once did Norma Jeane
they'd drifted onto another subject. Haring
didn't trust FDR, he believed the war news wa
didn't trust any politicians on principle; and Norma Jea
no, no, that wasn't right—"President Roosevelt is different."
you know that Roosevelt is 'different'?" Haring asked, amused. "Y
know the man personally, do you?" "Of course not, but I have faith in hi
I know his voice from the radio." Haring said, "*I* know his voice from the
radio, and I think I'm being manipulated. Anything you hear over the radio
or see in the movies is scripted and rehearsed and played to an audience; it
isn't spontaneous and can't be. It may seem from the heart but it isn't. It can't
be." Norma Jeane said, excitedly, "President Roosevelt is a great man! He's
as great as Abraham Lincoln, maybe." "And how do you know that?" "I
have f-faith in him." Haring laughed. "D'you know my definition of faith,
Norma Jeane? 'Believing in that which you know isn't true.' " Norma Jeane
said, frowning, "That's not right! You have faith in something you know is
true even if you can't prove it." "But what do you 'know' about Roosevelt,
for instance? Only what you read in the papers and hear on the radio. I bet
you didn't know the man's a cripple." "A—what?" "A cripple. He had
polio, they say. His legs are paralyzed. He's in a wheelchair. In his photos,

up." "Oh, he is not!" "Well,
, an uncle of mine who has a
on't believe it." "Well, then"—
believe it. FDR is untouched by what
, California, believes or wishes not to

r on an unpaved road at the edge of town,
igs' ramshackle house on Reseda Street. In
tracks and farther away the hazy foothills of
used by opposition, for the first time Norma
im. She was breathing quickly and her eyes were
pulse to take hold of her to calm her, to pull her
d her still, was almost overwhelming. Wide-eyed she
te you, Mr. Haring. I don't like you at all."
nd turned the key in the ignition.
ed Norma Jeane at her home he would discover he'd bro-
t; his undershirt was damp, his head steamy. Out of his scro-
throbbed angry as a fist.
n't touch her, did I! I might've, and I didn't.
me they saw each other the emotional outburst would be forgot-
ther would mention it, of course. Their conversation would be lim-
books, poetry. The girl was his student; he was her teacher. Never
would they speak to each other in such a way and a damned good
ng, Haring thought; he wasn't in love with this fifteen-year-old girl but
here was no point in taking risks. He could lose his job, he could damage
his already shaky marriage, and there was his pride.

If I did touch her. What then?

She'd written her poems for him—hadn't she? Sidney Haring was the *you*
she adored—wasn't he?

Suddenly then, and mysteriously, Norma Jeane dropped out of Van Nuys
High School in late May. With three weeks to go in tenth grade. She would
leave no word for her favorite teacher. One day she simply failed to appear
in English class, and the following morning Haring was notified by the principal's office, like her other teachers, that she had officially withdrawn "for
personal reasons." Haring was stunned but dared not show it. What had
happened to her? Why would she have dropped out at such a time? And without any word to *him*?

Several times he picked up the telephone to call the Pirigs and ask to speak
with her but lost his courage.

Don't get involved. Keep your distance.

Unless you love her. Do you?

At last one afternoon, obsessed by thoughts of the girl now absent from his life as from his classroom, he drove to Reseda Street hoping for a glimpse of Norma Jeane, a sign of her, staring at the wood-frame bungalow badly in need of repair, the grassless front yard and the eyesore of a junkyard beyond, a stink of burning trash. What children, you would wonder, might be "fostered" here? In the stark noon sunshine the Pirig house was defiant in its shabbiness, and its peeling gray paint and rotted roof seemed to Haring charged with meaning, an emblem of the fallen world that it was an innocent girl's fate to inhabit by an accident of birth and from which she could not be delivered except by the brave intervention of one like himself. *Norma Jeane? I've come for you, to save you.*

It was then that Warren Pirig emerged from the garage beside the house, headed for a pickup truck in the driveway.

Haring pressed down on the gas pedal and quickly drove past.

6

Easy as pitching headfirst through a pane of glass.

But she'd had two beers that afternoon, and was nursing one now.

Saying, "She has to leave."

"Norma Jeane? Why?"

Elsie didn't reply at first. Smoking her cigarette. The taste was bitter and exhilarating.

Warren said, "Her mother's taking her back? That's it?"

They weren't looking at each other. Nor even toward each other. Elsie understood that Warren's good eye was shuttered against her and his damaged eye was cloudy. Elsie was sitting in her chair at the kitchen table with her cigarettes and a lukewarm bottle of beer from which she'd picked most of the Twelve Horse label. Warren, who'd just come inside, was on his feet, in his work boots. There was a fearful momentum in the man at such times, as in all large men only just entering a constricted and overheated and female-smelling place. Warren had removed his soiled shirt and tossed it onto a chair and was in his thin cotton undershirt and gave off an air of bristling heat, a powerful sweat smell. Pirig the Pig. Once they'd been that intimate, playful as kids. He was Pirig the Pig who was crazy for burrowing, rooting, ramming, snorting, and squealing. His fatty-muscled sides like slabs of raw meat in his young wife's grasping hands. *Oh! oh! oh! oh! War-ren! Jesus God.* That was years ago, longer ago than Elsie wished to recall. In the succeeding years her husband had grown into an even bigger man: shoulders, chest, belly. His massive forearms, his looming head. Wiry tufts of graying-black hair everywhere you could see. Even on his upper back, his sides, the backs of his big ruined hands.

Elsie wiped her eyes, turning the gesture into a negligent wiping of her nose.

Warren said loudly, "I thought the mother was nuts. She's better? Since when?"

"No."

"No, what?"

"It isn't Norma Jeane's mother."

"Who's it, then?"

Elsie considered how to say this. She wasn't a woman who prepares words yet she'd prepared these—so many times they now seemed flat, phony. "Norma Jeane has to leave. Before something happens."

"What the hell? What's gonna happen?"

This wasn't going as well as she'd hoped. He was such a big man, looming over her. Without his shirt, his furred body was larger than the kitchen could accommodate. Elsie fumbled for her cigarette. *You bastard. You're the one.* That afternoon she'd gone downtown and she'd rubbed rouge on her cheeks, picked at her hair with a comb, but last time she'd glanced into the mirror she looked sallow-skinned, tired. And there was Warren contemplating her from the side; Jesus, she didn't like to be scrutinized from the side, chin pudgy and nose like a pig's snout.

Elsie said, "She's got boyfriends. And older guys. Too many."

"Older guys? Who?"

Elsie shrugged. She wanted Warren to see she was on his side.

"I don't ask names, hon. These kind of guys, they don't come to the house."

"Maybe you should ask names," Warren said aggressively. "Maybe I should. Where is she now?"

"Out."

"Out where?"

Elsie was fearful of looking at her husband's face. That glaring blood-veined eye.

"I think just driving. Where those guys get gas, I don't know."

Warren made a blowing noise with his lips. "A girl her age," he said, in the slow way of a man in a speeding vehicle drifting off the road, "she'd have boyfriends; it's only natural."

"Norma Jeane has too many. And she's too trusting."

"Too trusting how?"

"She's too *nice*."

Elsie let that sink in. If he'd done anything to Norma Jeane when they'd been alone together it would only have been because Norma Jeane was too nice, too sweet, too docile, and too obedient to shove Warren away.

"Look, she's not in any trouble, is she?"

"Not yet. Not so far as I know."

Yet Elsie knew Norma Jeane had only just had her period the week before. Paralyzing cramps, a pounding headache. Poor kid bled like a stuck pig. Scared to death but refused to admit it, praying to Christ Jesus the Healer.

" 'Not yet'—what's that supposed to mean?"

"Warren, we have our reputation to think of. The Pirigs." As if he needed reminding of his own name. "We can't take chances."

"Reputation? Why?"

"With the county. With Children's Welfare."

"They've been nosing around? Asking questions? Since when?"

"I've had some calls."

"Calls? From who?"

Elsie was getting nervous. Flicking ash from her cigarette into a putty-colored ashtray. It was true she'd had calls, though not from L.A. County authorities, and she was beginning to worry that Warren could read her thoughts. A great boxer like Henry Armstrong, Warren claimed, whom he'd seen fight in L.A., could read his opponent's thoughts; in fact, Armstrong knew what his opponent was going to do, or try to do, before his opponent knew. There was that shrewd, mean look in Warren Pirig's good eye that, when he made it a point to actually look at you, you knew he was dangerous.

Looming over her, close now. The bulk of him. Gritty-sweaty smell of him. And there were his hands. His fists. If she shut her eyes she could recall the force of the blow against the right side of her face. And her face swollen, lopsided. Something to think about. Brood upon. You're never lonely that way.

Another time, he'd hit her in the belly. Made her puke all over the floor. The kids who'd been living with them at that time (scattered now, long out of touch) had run like hell, laughing, into the backyard. Of course, Warren hadn't hit Elsie hard by his standards. *If I wanted to hurt you, I would. I didn't.*

She had to admit she'd asked for it. Talking in a loud whining voice, which Warren didn't like, and while he was getting ready to answer her she'd started to walk out of the room, and Warren didn't like that either.

Then afterward, not immediately but possibly the next day, the next night, he'd be loving. Not apologetic in so many words but wanting to make it up. His hands, his mouth. What strange uses of the mouth. Not saying much to her because what's there to say at such times?

He'd never told her he loved her. But she knew—anyway, she guessed she knew—he did.

I love you the girl had said. Those damp frightened eyes. *Oh Aunt Elsie I love you don't send me away.*

Carefully Elsie said, "We just have to think about the future, hon. We've made mistakes in the past."

"Bullshit."

"I mean, mistakes were made. In the past."

"Fuck the past. The past ain't now."

"You know young girls," Elsie said, pleading. "Things happen to them."

Warren had gone to the icebox, yanked open the door and taken out a beer, and slammed the door and was now drinking deeply. He leaned against the kitchen counter beside the stained sink, picking at the caulking with the big blunt dirt-edged thumbnail he'd injured years ago. The caulking he'd put in himself only that winter and already, God damn it, was coming loose. And tiny black ants in the cracks.

Warren said uncomfortably, like a man trying on clothes that didn't fit, "She'll take it hard. She likes us."

Elsie couldn't resist. "Loves us."

"Shit."

"But you know what happened last time." Elsie began then to talk rapidly of a girl who'd lived with them a few years before—Lucille, who'd lived in that attic room and gone to Van Nuys High and gotten into "trouble" at the age of fifteen and hadn't even known with certainty who the baby's father was. As if this departed Lucille had some bearing upon Norma Jeane. Warren wasn't listening, distracted by his own thoughts. Elsie herself was scarcely listening. Yet this was a speech that seemed to her required at this point.

After Elsie finished Warren said, "You're gonna send the poor kid back to County? Back to—what?—the orphanage?"

"No." Elsie smiled. Her first true smile of the day. This was her trump card and she'd been saving it. "I'm going to get that girl married and out of here and *safe.*"

She flinched as Warren turned abruptly from her and without a word slammed out of the house. She heard the pickup motor start in the driveway.

Returning then late, sometime after midnight, after Elsie and the others had gone to bed. She woke from a thin agitated sleep to his heavy footsteps and the bedroom door shoved open and his harsh labored breath and the smell of alcohol. It was nearly pitch-dark in the bedroom and Elsie expected him to fumble for the wall switch but he didn't and by the time she managed to lean over to reach for the bedside lamp it was too late. He was on her.

Uttering no word of greeting or even of acknowledgment. Hot, heavy, swollen with need of her, or of any woman, grunting and grappling with her, tugging at her rayon nightgown and she was so astonished she neither thought to protect herself nor (for after all *she was this man's wife*) arrange herself in the sagging bed to accommodate him.

They had not made love—in how long?—in months; *making love* wasn't maybe the terminology she used, *doing it* was more likely, for always between them there had been a strange verbal shyness however sexually demanding and voracious and appreciative Warren had been as a young husband, and Elsie too was reticent, joking and teasing, an awkward way of speech, but to utter *love*, to say *I love you*, was difficult. How strange she'd always thought it that there were things you did every day of your life like going to the bathroom, picking your nose, scratching your body, and touching yourself and other people (if there were other people in your life for you to touch and be touched by), yet these were things you didn't talk about, things for which there were no adequate words.

Like what he was doing to her now, what word, how to speak of it or even to comprehend it, an assault, a sexual assault except *she was this man's wife so it was all right* and she'd provoked him so there was justice in it, wasn't there? Before climbing onto the bed Warren had unzipped and unbuckled his trousers and kicked them off, but he still wore his smelly undershirt. She would suffocate in the coarse hairs of his body. She would be crushed beneath his heaving bulk. Never had he weighed so much and never was his weight so dense, so furious. His penis was a thick squat rod that prodded against her belly, blindly at first. With his knees he shoved her flaccid thighs roughly apart and seized his penis to push it into her as she'd many times seen him attack a wrecked car with a rod to pry it apart, taking pleasure in overcoming resistance. Elsie tried to protest, "Oh, Jesus, Warren—oh, wait—" but his forearm was jammed against the underside of her jaw and desperately she tried to squirm free of its pressure against her throat for what if in his drunken obliviousness of her he suffocated her, smashed her windpipe or her neck? Taking hold then of Elsie's wrists and stretching her flailing arms perpendicular to her sides as if crucifying her, nailing her to the bed, pumping himself with furious yet methodical strokes and she could see in the dark his sweaty face contorted, lips drawn back from his teeth in a grimace as often she saw him while he slept, moaning in his sleep, reliving the fights of his youth when he'd been beaten badly but had also beaten other men. *I handed out my share of hurt*. Was that a kind of happiness, a man's happiness, to know *I handed out my share of hurt*, uttered not even boastfully but matter-of-factly? Elsie tried to position herself in such a way as to blunt the force of Warren's attack, but he was too strong and too shrewd. *He'll kill me if he can. Fuck me to death. Not Norma Jeane.* She was able to endure it, not scream or cry for help or even sob though she was gasping for breath, and tears and saliva leaked from her face as contorted as his. Between her legs she believed she must be torn, bleeding. Never had Warren been so big. Blood-engorged, demonic. *Wham!—wham!—wham!*—Elsie's poor head thudding against the headboard of the bed they'd had all their married life and the headboard in turn thudding against the wall and the very wall vibrating and shuddering as if the earth beneath were quaking.

She was in terror he'd break her neck, but that didn't happen.

7

"What'd I tell you, sweetie? It's our lucky night."

Seeming to know beforehand the bittersweet fact that it would be their last movie night together. Elsie took Norma Jeane to the Thursday night movies in town at the Sepulveda Theater, where *Stage Door Canteen* and *Caught in the Draft* were playing plus previews of a new Hedy Lamarr film and after the last showing there was a drawing for prizes and what a whoop Elsie Pirig let out when the second-prize number was called and it was Norma Jeane's ticket. "Here! We're here! We got the number here! My daughter's ticket! We're coming!"

The incredulous joyous cry of a woman who's never won anything before in her life.

Elsie was so excited, so childlike, the audience laughed good-naturedly at her and applauded and there were scattered wolf whistles directed at the daughter as the two shuffled onto the stage with the other prizewinners. "Too damned bad Warren isn't here to see *this*," Elsie whispered in Norma Jeane's ear. She was wearing her good rayon navy-and-white polka-dot dress with prominent shoulder pads and her last good pair of stockings and she'd rubbed rouge onto her cheeks and her cheeks were now aflame. The mysterious bruises and welts on the underside of her jaw she'd managed to disguise, or almost disguise, with face powder. Norma Jeane in a schoolgirl pleated skirt and red sweater worn with a strand of glass beads, dark-blond curly hair tied back in a scarf, was the youngest person onstage and the person at whom the audience stared most intently. She wore no rouge but her lips were very red, matching her sweater. Her fingernails were very red. Though her heart was beating wildly like a bird trapped in her rib cage she managed to stand straight and tall while the others, including Elsie, slouched self-consciously, nervously touched their hair, their faces, hid their mouths behind their fingers. Norma Jeane held her head at a subtly tilted angle and smiled as if this was the most natural thing in the world for her on a weekday evening, climbing up onto the stage of the Sepulveda Theater to shake hands with the middle-aged manager and accept her prize. At the Los Angeles Orphans Home years ago there'd been a frightened little girl hauled onto a lighted platform by the Dark Prince's white-gloved hands and she'd stared stupidly beyond the lights into the audience, but now she knew better. Now she resisted looking out into the audience, knowing there were faces she would recognize, individuals who knew her, some of them from Van Nuys High. *Let them look at me, look at me.* No more than voluptuous Hedy Lamarr would Norma Jeane break the movie spell and acknowledge those whose role it was to stare at her.

Elsie and Norma Jeane were given their prize: a twelve-piece set of plastic dinner and salad plates in a fleur-de-lis pattern. The five prizewinners, all women save for one plump, elderly man in a tattered U.S. Army fatigue hat, were generously applauded. Elsie hugged Norma Jeane right up there onstage and nearly burst into tears, she was so happy.

"Not just plastic plates! This is a *sign.*"

Elsie hadn't told Norma Jeane, but the boy she hoped to introduce her to, the twenty-one-year-old son of a woman friend from Mission Hills, was to be in the audience that night. The plan was, he could see Norma Jeane with Elsie at a discreet distance and give it some thought, whether he'd like to date her. There was the age difference, only six years, which would mean nothing to adults—in fact, it would be in the girl's favor to be six years younger—but at his age, his mother told Elsie, six years seemed almost too much. "Give my girl a chance. Just look at her," Elsie begged. She hadn't any doubt that if he'd been in the audience the boy must have been impressed with Norma Jeane up there onstage like a beauty queen. And it would be a sign for him too.

This girl brings good luck!

Out front beneath the darkened marquee Elsie lingered with Norma Jeane, expecting her woman friend and the boy to come up to them. But this didn't happen. (Elsie hadn't seen them anywhere in the audience. God damn, if they hadn't been there!) Maybe because too many other people were milling around wanting to talk to them. Some were acquaintances and neighbors but most were total strangers. "Everybody loves a winner, eh?" Elsie nudged Norma Jeane in the ribs.

By degrees the excitement subsided. The interior of the lobby was darkened. Bessie Glazer and her son Bucky hadn't showed up and what did that mean? Elsie was too elated to think much about it. She and Norma Jeane drove back toward Reseda Street, the box of plastic plates in the backseat of Warren's 1939 Pontiac sedan.

"We've been putting it off, hon. But tonight we'd better talk about you-know-what."

Norma Jeane said, in a quiet, resigned voice, "Aunt Elsie, I'm just so *afraid*."

"Of what? Of getting married?" Elsie laughed. "Most girls your age are afraid of *not* getting married."

Norma Jeane said nothing. She was picking at her thumbnail. Elsie knew the girl had wild notions of running away to join the WACs or some nurses' training program in L.A., but the fact was she was too young. She wasn't going anywhere except where Elsie intended her to go.

"Look, sweetie. You're making too much of it. You've seen a boy's—a man's—thing, haven't you?"

Elsie was so crude and blunt, Norma Jeane laughed, startled.

She nodded, just barely.

"Well, you know—it gets bigger. You know that."

Again, just barely, Norma Jeane nodded.

"It has to do with them looking at you. It makes them want to—you know—'make love.' "

Norma Jeane said, naively, "I never really looked, Aunt Elsie. I mean—at the Home, the boys would show us their things to sort of scare us, I guess. And here in Van Nuys, on dates. They wanted me to touch it, I guess."

"Who was this?"

Norma Jeane shook her head. Not evasively but with an air of genuine confusion. "I'm not sure. I mean, I mix them up. There was more than one of them. Different dates. And different times. I mean, if a guy was fresh with me one time he'd apologize and ask me to give him another chance and I always do, and the next time he's on his good behavior. Most guys, they can be gentlemen if you insist. It's like Clark Gable and Claudette Colbert: *It Happened One Night*."

Elsie grunted. "If they respect you."

Norma Jeane said earnestly, "But the ones who wanted me to touch their—things—I wasn't disgusted with them or mad because I can see that's how guys are, they're born like that. But I'd get scared and skittish and start giggling like I do, like I'm being tickled!" Norma Jeane giggled now, uneasily. She was sitting on the edge of the car seat as if on eggshells. "One time, this was at the beach at Las Tunas, I was in a guy's car and I jumped out and ran to this other guy's car parked a little ways away where he was with his date—we all knew one another, we'd come out together—and I asked the couple please to let me in and I rode back to Van Nuys with them, and the other guy, my date, was driving close behind us trying to ram us with his bumper! I made more of a fuss than I'd meant to, I guess."

Elsie smiled. She loved it, this teenage sexpot of hers making the horny bastards squirm. "Kid! You're too much. When was this?"

"Last Saturday."

"Last *Saturday!*" Elsie chuckled. "So he wanted you to touch it, eh? Smart girl, not to. That just leads to the next step." Elsie paused suggestively, but Norma Jeane didn't inquire about the next step. "The word for it is 'penis' and it's to make babies, as I guess you know. On the order of a hose. The 'seed' shoots through it."

Norma Jeane giggled suddenly. Elsie laughed, too. In a way, if you're talking about hydraulics, there's not much to say. Another way, there's so much you're paralyzed to begin.

Over the years Elsie had had to instruct her foster daughters about sex (the boys she didn't, figuring they knew already), and each time she abbreviated the telling more. Some girls looked shocked and scared when she told them; some burst into hysterical giggles; some stared at Elsie in disbelief. Others were only just embarrassed because they already knew more than they wanted to know about sex.

One girl who, it later turned out, had been raped by her own father and uncles, shoved Elsie and shouted into her face, "Shut up, you old bat!"

By age fifteen, and being a smart inquisitive girl, Norma Jeane surely knew a lot about sex. Even Christian Science had to acknowledge it existed.

Elsie was too edgy and excited to return home right away so she drove past Reseda toward the edge of town. Warren wouldn't be home, probably, and when Warren wasn't home you kept waiting for him to come home not knowing what mood he'd be in.

Elsie felt Norma Jeane quicken in anticipation, like a little girl. She'd told Elsie that years ago before her mother had gotten sick she'd taken Norma Jeane for long dreamy Sunday rides that were the happiest memories of her childhood.

Elsie persisted. "When you're married, Norma Jeane, and it's OK to do it, you'll feel different. Your husband will show you." She paused, unable to resist. "I've got him picked out and he's a nice sweet kid, he's had a number of girlfriends, and he's a Christian."

"You have him p-picked out, Aunt Elsie? Who is he?"

"You'll see soon enough. It isn't one hundred percent certain. Like I say, he's a normal red-blooded kid, a high school athlete, and he knows the score." Elsie paused. Again she couldn't resist. "Warren knew the score, or thought he did. Boy oh boy." She shook her head vehemently.

Norma Jeane saw Elsie stroke the bruised underside of her jaw. Elsie had asked Norma Jeane to help her disguise the bruises, claiming she'd gotten them from banging into the bathroom door in the middle of the night.

Norma Jeane had murmured, "Oh, Aunt Elsie. That's too bad." And not another word. As if knowing damned well what had caused the bruises. And Elsie's stiff limping around the house like somebody'd shoved a broomstick up her ass.

Knowing, too, a deeper female wisdom, not to speak of it.

These past several days, Warren had avoided looking in Norma Jeane's direction. If he had to be in the room with her he'd turn the blind side of his face toward her. A wounded tenderness was in his eyes when Norma Jeane spoke to him unavoidably but even then he wouldn't look directly at her, which must have puzzled and hurt her. He'd stayed away from evening meals lately, eating supper at one of his taverns or going without.

Elsie was saying, "On your wedding night, you could maybe get a little drunk. I don't mean drunk, but high on champagne. The man usually lies on the woman and pushes his thing in, and she's ready for him, or should be. So it doesn't hurt."

Norma Jeane shuddered. She was looking sidelong at Elsie, doubtfully. "It doesn't hurt?"

"Not always."

"Oh, Aunt Elsie! Everybody says it *hurts*."

Elsie relented. "Well. Sometimes. In the beginning."

"But a girl bleeds, doesn't she?"

"A virgin might."

"It must hurt, then."

Elsie sighed. "I guess you *are* a virgin, eh?"

Norma Jeane nodded solemnly.

Elsie said, awkwardly, "Well. Your husband sort of prepares you. Down there. You get wet and ready for him. Haven't you ever?"

"Ever what?" Norma Jeane's voice quavered.

"Wanted to. 'Make love.' "

Norma Jeane considered this question. "I like them to kiss me, mostly, and I love to cuddle. Like with a doll. Except I'm the doll." She giggled in her high-pitched, startled, squeaky way. "If my eyes are closed I don't even know who it is. Which one it is."

"Norma Jeane, what a thing to say!"

"Why? If it's only just kissing and cuddling. Why's it so important which guy you're with?"

Elsie shook her head, mildly shocked. Why was it important? Damned if she knew.

Thinking how Warren would've murdered her. If she'd so much as kissed another man, let alone had an affair. Sure, he'd been unfaithful to her plenty of times and she'd been hurt and mad as hell and she'd showed him what she thought of him, jealous and tearful, and he'd denied any wrongdoing but obviously liked it, his wife's reaction. That was part of it, part of marriage, wasn't it? When you're young, at least.

Elsie said, with a pretense of indignation, "You're supposed to be faithful to one man. 'In sickness and in health till death do us part.' It's a religious thing, I guess. They want to make sure that if you have kids it's your husband's kids, not somebody else's. You'll be married in a Christian ceremony, I'll make sure of that."

Norma Jeane bit at her thumbnail. Elsie, cruising the car, reached over to slap lightly at her hand. At once Norma Jeane dropped her hands into her lap and clasped them tightly together.

"Oh, Aunt Elsie! I'm sorry. I guess I'm just—scared."

"Hon, I know. But you'll get over it."

"What if I have a baby?"

"Well. That won't come till a little later."

"Not if I get married next month! I could have a baby inside a year."

This was true, though Elsie hadn't wanted to consider it just yet.

"You could ask him to use protection. You know—one of those rubber things."

Norma Jeane crinkled her nose. "One of those things like a little balloon?"

"They're nasty," Elsie agreed, "but the other's worse. His age, your husband would be going into the army or navy or whatever, maybe he's already signed up, and he wouldn't want his wife to get pregnant any more than you'd want it. And if he's overseas, you're safe."

Norma Jeane brightened. "He might go overseas? Yes. He'd be in the war."

"All the men are going."

"I wish I could go! I wish I was a man."

Elsie had to laugh at this. Norma Jeane, looking the way she did, with her pretty face and childlike ways, and so easily upset by hurtful things—wishing she was a man!

Don't we all. No such luck. Play the hand you're dealt.

Elsie had driven into the dead end of an unpaved road. In the near distance, though you couldn't see it in the dark, there were raised railroad tracks. The year before, the bullet-riddled body of a man from out of town had been found somewhere around here. A "gangland assassination," the papers called it. Now wind blew through the tall grass like the spirits of the dead. What men do to one another. Everybody's share of hurt. Elsie was thinking how, if this was a movie scene, her and Norma Jeane in the car in this desolate place, something would happen: there'd be a signal that something would happen in the movie music. In actual life, there was no music and there were no cues. You drifted into a scene not knowing if it was important or unimportant. If you'd remember it all your life or forget it within the hour. Just people alone together in a movie, and the camera watching them, it meant something crucial would happen; the fact of the camera meant that something would happen. Maybe it was the excitement of winning the plastic plates (which she could use, and Warren would be impressed) but her thoughts were flying in all directions tonight and she was having to suppress the urge to take hold of Norma Jeane's hand and squeeze and squeeze and *squeeze*. She said, as if they'd been talking about this, "Movies like the ones tonight are OK and make you feel good but they're a bunch of lies, y'know? Bob Hope's funny as hell but he's not, y'know, real. The movies I liked were *Public Enemy, Little Caesar, Scarface*—Jimmy Cagney, Edward G. Robinson, Paul Muni. Mean, sexy men that get theirs in the end." Elsie backed the car around and drove to Reseda. There was no forestalling returning to the house; it was getting late and she was thirsty for a beer, not in the kitchen but she'd take it into the bedroom with her and drink it slowly to put her in the mood for sleep. She said, in a brighter voice, as if in fact this was a movie scene but its tone was shifting, "You might actually get to like your hubby, Norma Jeane! And want kids. *I* did at one time."

Norma Jeane's tone, too, had shifted. She said suddenly, "I'd maybe like kids. It's the normal thing, isn't it? An actual baby. Once it's born and out of your body. Once it couldn't hurt you. I love cuddling with babies. It wouldn't have to be my own, even. Just any baby." She paused, breathless. "But if it was *my baby*, I'd have the right. Twenty-four hours of the day."

Elsie glanced at the girl, surprised at her change of mind. Yet this was like Norma Jeane: you'd see her brooding and turned in upon herself, then it was like a switch was thrown when she saw you and she became perky and sunshiny and quivering with good feelings as if a camera had been turned on her.

More emphatically, Norma Jeane said, "Yes! I'd like to have a b-baby. Maybe just one? Then I wouldn't ever be alone—would I?"

Elsie said sadly, "Not for a while." Sighing. "Not till she goes away and leaves you."

" 'She'? I don't want a girl baby. My mother had girl babies. I want a *boy baby*."

Norma Jeane spoke with such vehemence that Elsie glanced at her in alarm.

A strange, strange girl. Maybe I never knew her?

Elsie was relieved to see that Warren's battered pickup wasn't in the driveway; except this meant he'd be coming in late, no doubt drunk, and if he'd lost at cards as he'd been doing lately he'd be in a rough mood, but Elsie put off thinking about that just now. The buttercup-yellow plastic plates she would set prominently on the kitchen table for Warren to discover and wonder—what the hell? She could imagine the quizzical look on his face. And he'd like being told the good news. He'd smile, maybe. Anything you win for nothing, anything that falls into your lap, it's all gravy, right? Elsie kissed Norma Jeane good night. In a low voice saying, "All that I told you tonight, Norma Jeane—it's for your own good, hon. You need to be married because you can't stay with us and, God knows, you don't want to go back to—that place."

This revelation that had so stunned Norma Jeane only a few days before seemed now to have been calmly absorbed by the girl. "I know, Aunt Elsie."

"You have to grow up sometime. None of us can avoid it."

Norma Jeane laughed that sad squeaky little laugh. "I guess if my number's up, Aunt Elsie, it's *up*."

THE EMBALMER'S BOY

"I love you! Now my life is perfect."

There came the day, it wasn't quite three weeks after Norma Jeane's sixteenth birthday, June 19, 1942, a day when she exchanged sacred wedding vows with a boy she'd loved at first sight, as he'd loved her at first sight, gazing at each other in tender astonishment—*Hi! I'm Bucky* and *I'm N-norma Jeane*—as at a discreet distance Bess Glazer and Elsie Pirig looked on smiling and already teary-eyed, foreseeing this very hour. *It's a fact, every woman at the wedding in the First Church of Christ, Mission Hills, California, was crying that day at the sight of the beautiful young bride* looking perhaps fourteen years old as her bridegroom towered over her at six feet three, one hundred ninety pounds, appearing himself no older than eighteen, an awkward yet gallant boy, good-looking like a full-grown Jackie Coogan with spiky dark hair trimmed short to expose his protruding, pinkening ears. He'd been a high school champion wrestler and a football player and you could see how he'd protect that little girl who'd been an orphan. *Love at first sight on both sides. Hardly engaged a month. It's the times, the war. Everything speeded up.*

Just look at their faces!

The bride's face shone luminous-pale as mother-of-pearl except for her delicately rouged cheeks. Her eyes like dancing flames. Her gleaming dark-blond hair like captured sunshine framing her perfect doll face, part in ringlets and part braided by the bridegroom's own mother and twined with lily-of-the-valley upon which the gossamer bridal veil floated weightless as a breath. Everywhere in the small church the sweet aching innocence of lily of the valley *that scent I will recall through my life the scent of happiness fulfilled. And the terror that my heart would stop and God would gather me into His bosom.*

And the wedding gown, so beautiful. Yards of shiny white satin, a tight-fitted bodice, and long tight-fitted sleeves with ruffled cuffs, yards and yards of eye-dazzling satin, white folds and pleats and ribbons and lace and tiny bows and tiny white pearl buttons and a five-foot train and never could you guess the gown was secondhand belonging to Bucky's sister Lorraine; of course it had been altered to fit Norma Jeane's height and figure, dry-cleaned and spotless and lovely, and the bride's white satin high-heeled sandals spotless, too, though purchased at a Goodwill shop in Van Nuys for only five dollars. The bridegroom's oyster-shell dinner jacket fitted his broad shoulders tightly, you could see he was a strong, husky no-nonsense boy, scraped through at Mission Hills High, Class of '39, though he'd been absent many days hating textbooks, classrooms, blackboards, and having to sit, sit, sit in desks too small for him listening to old-maid teachers of both sexes drone on and on like they had some secret of life, which obviously they didn't, for sure. Bucky Glazer was offered sports scholarships from UCLA, Pacific University, San Diego State, and elsewhere but he'd turned them all down, preferring to earn some money and be independent, got a part-time job as an embalmer's assistant at the oldest most prestigious funeral home in Mission Hills so the Glazers went around boasting their boy was the next thing to an actual embalmer and an embalmer is the next thing to the medical doctor who does autopsies, a pathologist; but also Bucky worked night shifts at Lockheed Aviation on the assembly line, manufacturing miracle bombers like the B-17 destined to bomb the hell out of America's enemies.

Yes, Bucky planned to join up with the U.S. armed forces to fight for his country, and this he'd made clear to his fiancée, Norma Jeane, from the start.
Everything speeded up! It's the times.

It was commented on: most of the wedding guests were from the groom's side. The Glazers and their many relatives were big-boned pleasant-faced healthy Americans who resembled one another despite profound differences of age and sex and who gave the impression, seated together in pews in the small stucco church, of having been herded in. At a signal, they would rise together and be herded out. Many belonged to the First Church of Christ and were very much at home, nodding throughout the nuptial ceremony. On the bride's side were just her foster parents the Pirigs and two rawboned mismatched boys described as foster brothers and a scattering of high school girlfriends with bright made-up faces, and a stocky frizz-haired woman in blue serge who'd introduced herself before the ceremony as "Doctor" and who began to cry hoarsely when the Church of Christ minister sternly inquired of the bride, "Do you, Norma Jeane Baker, take this man, Buchanan Glazer, to be your lawfully wedded husband, for richer or poorer, in sickness and in health, till death do you part in the name of our Lord God and His Only Begotten Son Jesus Christ?" and the bride swallowed hard and whispered, "Oh!—*yes sir.*"

The orphan's quavering voice. For life.

Dr. Edith Mittelstadt gave the newlyweds a "family heirloom" sterling silver tea service—heavy ornamental teapot, cream and sugar bowls, and matching tray—which Bucky would pawn in Santa Monica for a disappointing twenty-five dollars.

And he'd have to suffer the indignity of being fingerprinted, too, as Norma Jeane looked on giggling and crimson with embarrassment.

Like I'm a crook or something. Gosh, that makes me mad!

Where was the bride's mother? Why wasn't the bride's mother at her own daughter's wedding? And where was the father?—no one wished to inquire.

Was it true, the bride's mother was committed to a state mental asylum? Was it true, the bride's mother was incarcerated in a state women's prison? Was it true, the bride's mother had once tried to kill her when she was a little girl? Was it true, the bride's mother had killed herself in either the mental asylum or the prison? No one wished to inquire on such a happy occasion.

Was it true, there actually was no father? No Baker? The bride was illegitimate? On her birth certificate the damning words FATHER: UNKNOWN?

Among these good-hearted Christian Americans on this happy occasion, no one wished to inquire.

As Bucky had said to his bride-to-be on the eve of their wedding, there was no shame to her circumstances. *Don't give it another thought, honey. Nobody in the Glazer family looks down on anybody else for such a reason that can't be helped, I promise you. I'll punch 'em in the nose if they do.*

Now Norma Jeane had grown pretty enough, a man had come for her.

Love at first sight to be treasured all our lives but maybe this wasn't one hundred percent true?

Fact was, Bucky Glazer hadn't much wanted to meet this girl Norma Jeane Baker. Seeing her at the Sepulveda Theater with that witchy Elsie Pirig, the two called up onstage, the girl looked to Bucky's hard-to-please eye like just another high school tart—plus too young—so he'd upset his mom by slipping out of the movie house and waiting for her in the parking lot, breezily lounging against the hood of his car smoking a cigarette like a character in a movie. Poor Mrs. Glazer, lurching in her high heels and scolding as if Bucky wasn't a grown-up twenty-one but a kid of twelve.

"Buchanan Glazer! How could you! So rude! Humiliating your own mother! What can I tell Elsie? She'll be calling me in the morning. *I* had to hide so she wouldn't see me! And that girl is perfectly *sweet*."

It was Bucky's maddening strategy to let his mother fuss and fume and blow her nose, assuming she'd get her way eventually like most of the women in the Glazer family. She had with Bucky's older brother and both his older sisters, coercing them into marrying young, the wisest course of action, otherwise you invite trouble; it's as dangerous for boys as for girls and poor Bess was frantic with wanting to break up Bucky's scandalous romance with a twenty-nine-year-old divorcée he'd met working nights at Lockheed, mother of a young child and a glamorous hard-faced woman who'd "got her hooks in my boy," as Bess lamented to anyone who would listen. Bucky had gone out with girls through high school and he was "dating" a number of girls at the present time, including the daughter of the funeral home director, but to Bess the divorcée was a serious threat.

"What's wrong with Elsie Pirig's girl? Why don't you like her? Elsie swears she's a good Christian girl who doesn't smoke or drink and she reads the Bible and she's a born homemaker and shy around boys and you know, Bucky, you should think about settling down. With a girl you can trust. If you have to go overseas, you'll need someone to come home to. You'll need a sweetheart to write to you."

Bucky couldn't resist. "Hell, Carmen can write to me, Mom. She's already writing to a couple of guys."

Bess began to cry. Carmen was the glamorous divorcée who'd gotten her hooks in Bucky.

Bucky laughed and repented and hugged his mother, saying, "Mom, I've got you to come home to, don't I? And write to me? Why would I need anybody else?"

Not long afterward Bucky scandalized a roomful of female relatives when he'd overheard his mother saying in her mournful martyr's voice, "My boy deserves a virgin, at least—" and leaned into the doorway to say loudly, with a deadpan expression, "What's a virgin? How'd I recognize one if I saw one? How'd *you*, Mom?" and continued on his way again, whistling. *That Bucky Glazer, isn't he something? Sharpest one in the family.*

Yet somehow it happened. Bucky agreed to meet this Norma Jeane.

Easier to give in to Bess than endure her nagging or, worse yet, her sighs and put-upon looks. He'd known Norma Jeane was young but they hadn't informed him she was only fifteen, so it was a shock seeing her close up. The stumbling way like a sleepwalker she moved toward him, then stopped stricken with shyness, half smiling, stammering her name. *Just a kid. But Jesus, look at her. That figure!* Even as he'd been preparing to joke about this "date" afterward with his buddies, he now felt so powerful an attraction to the girl his thoughts flashed ahead to the time when he'd be bragging about her. Showing her snapshot. Better yet, showing her off. *My new girl Norma Jeane. She's kind of young but mature for her age.*

The looks on his friends' faces, Bucky could imagine.

He took her to the movies. He took her dancing. He took her canoeing, hiking, and fishing. She surprised him by being an outdoor kind of girl, despite her looks. Amid his friends who were all his age she sat quiet and alert and sharp-eyed and smiling in appreciation of their jokes and horsing around, and it was clear as the nose on your face that Norma Jeane was just about the prettiest girl anybody'd ever seen outside the movies with her heart-shaped face and widow's peak and darkish blond hair spilling in curls down her shoulders and the way she carried herself in her little sweaters, skirts, pleated pants—now "pants" were allowed for women in public places.

Sexy like Rita Hayworth. But a girl you'd want to marry like Jeanette Mac-Donald.

It was a time of things-happening-fast. Ever since the shock of Pearl Harbor. Every day now was like an earthquake day you wake up wondering what's next. Headline news, radio bulletins. Yet it was exciting too.

You had to pity old guys past forty or whatever who'd had their chance in the armed forces and didn't get called upon to truly fight. Defend their country. Or if they had, like in World War I, it was so long ago and boring nobody even remembered. What was happening in Europe and in the Pacific was *now*.

Norma Jeane had a way of leaning toward him, almost shivering in anticipation of what he'd say; touching his wrist and her blue eyes lifting dreamy and unfocused and her breath quickened as if she'd been running, asking him what did he think the future would bring? Would the U.S. win the war and save the world from Hitler and Tojo? How long would the war last and would bombs ever fall on this country? on California? And if so, what would happen to them? What would be their fate? Bucky had to smile; nobody he knew would say such a strange word—*fate*. But here was a girl to make him think, and he appreciated that. Surprised sometimes to hear himself talking like somebody on the radio. He comforted Norma Jeane, telling her not to worry: if the Japs tried to bomb California or any of the "territorial United States" they'd be blasted out of the sky by antiaircraft weapons. ("Secret missiles we're making at Lockheed, if you want to know.") If they ever tried to land troops, they'd be sunk off the coast. And if they ever succeeded in getting on U.S. soil, every able-bodied American man would fight them to the death. *It just couldn't happen here.*

One strange conversation they had. Norma Jeane spoke of *The War of the Worlds* by H. G. Wells, which she said she'd read, and Bucky explained to her no, it was a radio program and it was by Orson Welles, a few years ago. Norma Jeane went quiet, saying she must've mixed it up with something else. Bucky saw the connection, the way it would figure in the girl's head. "You didn't hear it, I guess? Maybe you were too young. We heard it at our house. Oh boy, was that something! My grandpa thought it was real and just about had a heart attack and my mom, you know what she's like, she kept hearing Orson Welles saying it was a 'simulated newscast' yet still she was scared, everybody was panicking, I was just a kid and thought, sort of, it could be real though I knew it wasn't, it was just a radio program. But, hell"—Bucky smiled to see Norma Jeane gazing at him so urgently, like the next syllable he uttered was precious—"anybody who lived through that, that program that night, even if it wasn't real you came away thinking it could be; so when the Japs bombed Pearl Harbor a few years later it wasn't that different, was it?" He'd sort of lost the thread of what he was saying. He had a point to make and he believed it was an important point, but with Norma Jeane so close to him, and smelling like soap or talcum powder or whatever it was, something flowery, he couldn't concentrate. Nobody was near so he leaned quickly forward and kissed her mouth, and immediately like a doll's her eyes shut and a sensation like flame passed through his body, chest to groin, and he placed his outstretched fingers behind her tilted head, bunching up her curly hair, and he kissed her a little harder, his eyes, too, now shut; he was lost in a dream inhaling her fragrance and like a girl in a dream she was soft, docile, unresisting, and so he kissed her harder, prodding at her primly pursed lips with his tongue, knowing that one of these days Norma Jeane was going to open her mouth to him, and Jesus! he hoped he wouldn't come in his pants.

Love at first sight. Bucky Glazer was coming around to believe.

Already telling guys at Lockheed he'd first glimpsed his girl onstage at the movie theater. She'd won a prize, and boy oh boy *was she a prize* climbing up into the spotlight and the audience clapping like crazy for her.

"A guy deserves a virgin to marry. Out of self-respect."

Thinking about Norma Jeane a lot. They'd been introduced in May and her birthday was June 1; she'd be sixteen years old. Girls could get married at sixteen, there were examples in the Glazer family. *Now, Bucky, you don't want to do anything in haste,* his mother cautioned him but he perceived this as one of Bess's ploys: telling Bucky what *not* to do, knowing that's the very thing Bucky will *want* to do. Still he was thinking about Norma Jeane the way he'd rarely thought about any of his other girls. Even when he was with Carmen. Especially when he was with Carmen and making comparisons. *Face it, she's a slut. Nobody you could trust.* Thinking about Norma Jeane afternoons at the funeral home helping Mr. Eeley the embalmer prepare a corpse for the "viewing room." If the corpse happened to be a female, and halfway young. He was seized with a sense, new to him, of the brevity of time, of mortality; as the Bible said, *Ashes to ashes, dust to dust.* Every week in *Life* there were photos of the injured and the dead, G.I. corpses half-buried in sand on some godforsaken Pacific island you'd never heard of before, stacks of dead Chinese killed in Japanese bombing raids. Everybody was naked in death. *What would Norma Jeane look like naked?* He was almost overcome, needing suddenly to bend over to lower his head between his knees as Mr. Eeley, a droll mustached bachelor with eyebrows thick as Groucho Marx's, teased him for being "weak." During his night shift at Lockheed, amid the earsplitting din, he brooded over Norma Jeane, wondering if she'd had a date that evening though she'd promised him she would stay home and think of him. Guys only a few years older than Bucky on the line eager to get home to their wives, climb into bed at 6 A.M. The kinds of things they said, rubbing their hands. Rolling their eyes and smirking. Some of them showed snapshots of their young, pretty wives, girlfriends. One of them passed around a snapshot of his wife posed Betty Grable-style, back to the camera and peeking over her shoulder, wearing not a swimsuit like Betty Grable but just lacy underpants and high heels. Jesus. Bucky just about ground his teeth. She wasn't half so sexy as Norma Jeane would be in that pose. *Wait'll you see my girl.*

Was he falling in love? Well—God damn! Maybe he was. Maybe it was time. He wouldn't want to lose her to another guy.

In Bucky Glazer's opinion there were two categories of female: the "hard" and the "soft." And he was a sucker for the soft, he knew. Here was this sweet little girl looking up to him wide-eyed and trusting and agreeing with virtually everything he said; naturally he knew a lot more than she did, so it was only logical for her to agree, and he admired that; he didn't care for combative girls who thought it was the sexiest kind of flirting, getting on a guy's nerves like Katharine Hepburn in the movies. Maybe that did charge Bucky up, but this soft, pliant little Norma Jeane charged him up in a different way, so he found himself whispering to her in his sleep, shaping his arm around her in the bedclothes, kissing and stroking her. *It won't hurt, I promise! I'm crazy about you.* Waking in the middle of the night stricken with desire in the bed he'd been sleeping in since, God knows, age twelve, he'd outgrown it a long time ago, ankles and size-fourteen feet hanging over the edge of the mattress. *Time to get a bed of your own. A double bed.*

So that night it was decided. Three weeks after they'd been introduced. Well, it was a time of things-happening-fast. One of Bucky's young uncles had been reported missing on Corregidor. His closest friend from the Mission Hills wrestling team was starting out on solo bombing flights in southeast Asia, a navy pilot. Norma Jeane wept, saying yes she would marry him, she would accept his engagement ring, yes she loved him; if that wasn't enough she did next the strangest thing any girl had ever done, in the movies or out: took his big-knuckled chafed hands in her small soft hands, no matter that they smelled (he knew, couldn't get the stink scrubbed off) of the embalmer's fluid that was formaldehyde, glycerine, borax, and phenol alcohol, and lifted his hands to her face and actually inhaled the odor, as if it was a balm to her, or recalled to her an odor that was precious, her eyes shut and dreamy and her voice just a whisper. "I love you! Now my life is perfect."

Thank you God, thank you God, O thank you God. Never will I doubt You ever again in my lifetime I vow. Never will I wish to punish myself for being unwanted and unloved.

At last the solemn ceremony in the First Church of Christ, Mission Hills, California, was ending. Not only every woman in the church but a number of the men were dabbing at their eyes. The tall blushing bridegroom stooped to kiss his girl bride, shyly eager like a boy on Christmas morning. He seized her so tightly around the ribs, the satin dress bunched up at the small of her back and the bridal veil fell back at an awkward angle from her head.

Kissing the bride who was now Mrs. Buchanan Glazer full on the lips, and tremulously her lips parted for him. Just a little.

LITTLE WIFE

1

"No wife of Bucky Glazer's is going to work. Ever."

2

She meant to be perfect. He deserved nothing less.

In ground-floor apartment 5A of Verdugo Gardens, 2881 La Vista Street, Mission Hills, California.

In the early dreamy months of marriage.

First marriage, and nothing so sweet! You don't know it at the time.

Once upon a time, a young bride. Young housewife. Stealing time to write in her secret journal. *Mrs. Bucky Glazer. Mrs. Buchanan Glazer. Mrs. Norma Jeane Glazer.*

No "Baker" remaining. Soon there would be no memory.

Bucky was only five years older than Norma Jeane but from the first, cuddling in his arms, she called him Daddy. Sometimes he was Big Daddy, proud possessor of Big Thing. She was Baby, sometimes Baby-Doll, proud possessor of Little Thing.

She'd been a virgin, sure enough. Bucky was proud of that too.

How well they fitted together! "It's like we invented it, Baby."

Strange to think that, at sixteen, Norma Jeane had succeeded where Gladys had failed. To find a good, loving husband, to be married, a *Mrs.* That was what had made Gladys sick, Norma Jeane knew—not having a husband, and not being loved in the only way that mattered.

The more she thought about it, the more Norma Jeane concluded that Gladys possibly hadn't been married at all, ever. "Baker" and "Mortensen" might be pure inventions, to spare shame.

Even Grandma Della had been fooled. Possibly.

Strange, too, to remember that morning Gladys drove them to Wilshire Boulevard to witness the funeral of the great Hollywood producer. Waiting then, heartbeat by heartbeat, for Daddy to claim her. Yet it would be years.

"Daddy? Do you love me?"

"Baby, I'm crazy about you. Just look."

Norma Jeane had sent an invitation to Gladys inviting her to the wedding. Scared and excited and anxious and yearning to see the woman who was Mother. Yet terrified that Mother would appear.

Who on earth is that, that madwoman, oh, look! They would stare and stare.

Of course, Gladys hadn't come to Norma Jeane's wedding. Nor sent any greeting, or good wish.

"Why should I care? I don't."

As she'd told Elsie Pirig, it was more than enough to have a mother-in-law. No need of a mother. Mrs. Glazer. Bess Glazer. Urging Norma Jeane even before the wedding please to call her "Mother," except the word stuck in Norma Jeane's throat.

Sometimes she was able to call the older woman "Mother Glazer" in a soft sliding voice you almost couldn't hear. What a kind woman she was, a true Christian woman. Yet you couldn't blame her for sharply scrutinizing her new daughter-in-law. *Please don't hate me for marrying your son. Please help me to be his wife.*

She would succeed where Gladys had failed. This she vowed.

Loving it when Bucky made lusty vigorous love to her, calling her his sweetie, his honey, his baby, Baby-Doll, groaning and shivering and whinnying like a horse—"You're my little horsey, Baby! Giddy-*ap!*"—the bedsprings squeaking like mice being killed. And Bucky in her arms afterward, his chest heaving, body slick with oily oozy sweat she loved to smell, Bucky Glazer like an avalanche fallen upon her, pinning her to the bed. *A man loves me. I am a man's wife. Never to be alone again.*

Already she'd forgotten her prewedding fears. How silly she'd been, a child.

Now she was envied by unmarried women, unengaged girls. You could see it in their eyes. What a thrill! Magic rings on the third finger of her left hand. Glazer "heirlooms" they were called. The wedding band was a slightly dull gold worn smooth by time. *From a dead woman's finger.* The engagement ring had a tiny diamond. But these were magic rings that drew Norma Jeane's eye in mirrors and in reflecting surfaces, seeing them as others saw them. *Rings! A married woman. A girl who is loved.*

She was sweet, pretty Janet Gaynor in *State Fair, Small Town Girl, Sunny Side Up*. She was a young June Haver, a young Greer Garson. A sister to Deanna Durbin and to Shirley Temple. Almost overnight she'd lost interest in the sexy glamorous stars, Crawford, Dietrich, the memory of Harlow with her platinum-blond hair, so blatantly bleached, phony. For what is glamour but phony. Hollywood phony. And Mae West—a joke! A female impersonator.

Of course, these women were doing what they could to sell themselves. They were what men wanted. Most men. Not very different from prostitutes. But their price was higher, they had "careers."

Never will I need to sell myself! Not so long as I am loved.

Riding the Mission Hills trolley, Norma Jeane often saw with a thrill of pleasure how strangers' eyes, both women's and men's, dropped to her hand, her rings. Their eyes immediately identifying her as *a married woman, and so young!* Never would she remove her heirloom rings.

It would be death, she knew, to remove her heirloom rings.

"Like I've entered heaven. And I'm not even dead."

Except there began a nightmare of Norma Jeane's, new to her since her wedding: a faceless person (man? woman?) crouched over her as she lay in bed paralyzed and unable to escape and this person wanted the rings off her finger and Norma Jeane refused to give them up and the person seized her hand and began sawing at her finger with a knife so real Norma Jeane couldn't believe she wasn't bleeding, waking groaning and thrashing, and if Bucky happened to be asleep beside her, nights he wasn't working the graveyard shift, he'd wake groggily to comfort her, to hug and rock her in his strong arms. "Now, Baby-Doll. Only a bad dream. Big Daddy's got you safe and sound, OK?"

But it wasn't always OK, not immediately. Sometimes Norma Jeane was too frightened to sleep for the remainder of the night.

Bucky tried to be sympathetic, and he was flattered how his young wife desperately needed him, but he was uneasy too. He'd been a kid for so long himself. He was only twenty-one! And Norma Jeane was unpredictable, he was beginning to discover. When they'd dated she'd been sunny, sunny,

sunny, and now, these rocky nights, he was seeing another side of her. Like her "cramps" as she shamefacedly called her menstrual period, an alarming revelation to Bucky, from whom such female secrets had been mostly kept, for his own good; here was Norma Jeane not only bleeding (like a stuck pig, Bucky couldn't help but think) from her vagina, which was exactly the place for lovemaking, and she was virtually knocked out and useless for two or even three days, lying with a heating pad on her belly, often a cold compress on her forehead (she had "migraine" too), but to make matters worse she'd refuse medication, even aspirin, which Bucky's mother recommended, so he'd get annoyed with her—"Christian Science crap nobody takes seriously." But he didn't want to argue with her, that only made things worse. So he tried to be sympathetic, he sure tried, he was a married man and (as his older, married brother said dryly) he'd better get used to it, including the smell. But the nightmares! Bucky was exhausted and needed his sleep—he could sleep for ten hours straight if undisturbed—and here was Norma Jeane waking him, scaring the hell out of him, in an actual panic, her little nightie soaked in sweat. He wasn't used to sleeping with anyone. Not all night. And night after night. Someone as unpredictable as Norma Jeane. It was like there were two of her, like twins, and the night twin took over sometimes, no matter how loving the day twin was and how crazy he was about her. He'd hold her and feel her wild heartbeat. Like a frightened bird in his embrace, a hummingbird. Yet, God, that girl could hug *hard*. A panicked girl is strong as a guy, almost. Before he was fully awake Bucky would be thinking somehow he was back in high school, on the mat, wrestling with an opponent determined to crack his ribs.

"Daddy, you won't ever leave me, will you?" Norma Jeane begged, and Bucky said sleepily, "Uh-uh," and Norma Jeane said, "Promise you won't, Daddy?" and Bucky said, "Sure, Baby, OK," and still Norma Jeane persisted, and Bucky said, "Baby, why'd I leave *you*? Didn't I just marry you?" There was something wrong in this answer but neither could quite gauge what it was. Norma Jeane curled closer into Bucky, pressing her hot teary face against his neck, smelling of damp hair and talcum and armpits, and what he guessed was animal panic, whispering, "But do you promise, Daddy?" and Bucky muttered yes, he promised, could they please go back to sleep now? and Norma Jeane suddenly giggled—"Cross your heart and hope to die?"—making a cross with her forefinger over Bucky's big thumpy heart, tickling the wiry chest hairs over his heart, and suddenly Bucky was aroused, Big Thing was aroused, and Bucky grabbed at Norma Jeane's fingers and pretended to be eating them, and Norma Jeane kicked and squealed with laughter, feverish, squirming, "No! Daddy, *no!*" Bucky pinned her to the mattress, climbed onto her slender body, nuzzling and nipping at her breasts, her breasts he was crazy about, tonguing her, growling, "Daddy, yes. Daddy's gonna do what Daddy wants to do with his Baby-Doll 'cause Baby-Doll belongs to *him*. And this belongs to Daddy, and this—and *this*."

And I was safe then when he was inside me.
Wanting it never never to end.

3

She meant to be perfect. He deserved nothing less.

Packing Bucky's lunches. Big double sandwiches, Bucky's favorites. Baloney, cheese, and mustard on thick white bread. Deviled ham. Leftover meat slices with ketchup. A Valencia orange, the sweetest kind. Sweet dessert like cherry cobbler or applesauce gingerbread. With rationing getting worse, Norma Jeane saved her meat portions from supper for Bucky's lunches. He never seemed to take note, but Norma Jeane knew he appreciated it. Bucky was a big husky boy, still growing, with an appetite, Norma Jeane teased him, like a horse—"a really hungry horse." There was something about the ritual of rising early to pack Bucky's lunches for him that filled her with emotion, brought tears to her eyes. She slipped into his lunch box love notes adorned with garlands of red-inked hearts.

When you read this, Bucky darling, I will be thinking of YOU & how I ADORE YOU.

And,

When you read this, Big Daddy, think of Baby-Doll & the Red-hot LOVING she's going to give you when you get HOME!

These notes, Bucky couldn't resist showing the other guys on his shift at Lockheed. There was a handsome swaggering fellow, a would-be actor a few years older than Buddy, he hoped to impress—Bob Mitchum. But Bucky wasn't so sure about Norma Jeane's peculiar little poems:

When our hearts melt in love
even the angels above
are envious of us.

Was it poetry if it didn't rhyme? If it didn't rhyme *right*? These love poems Bucky folded up carefully and kept to himself. (In fact, he lost the poems and often hurt Norma Jeane's feelings by forgetting to comment on them.) There was that strange, dreamy, schoolgirl side to Norma Jeane that Bucky distrusted. Why wasn't it enough for her to be pretty and straightforward like other good-looking girls; why did she try to be "deep" too? It was related in some way, Bucky believed, to her nightmares and "female problems." He loved her for being special but half resented it too. As if Norma Jeane was only pretending to be the girl he knew. That way she had of speaking out unexpectedly and that squeaky, unsettling little laugh of hers and what you could only call morbid curiosity—asking about his work as Mr. Eeley's assistant at the funeral home, for instance.

The Glazers really liked Norma Jeane, though, and that meant a lot to Bucky. He'd married the girl to please his mom, sort of. Well, no: he was crazy about her too. He was! The way other guys turned to stare at her in the street, he'd have been crazy not to fall for her. And what a *good wife* she was, that first year and more. The honeymoon just went on and on. Norma Jeane hand-printed menus for the upcoming week on index cards, for Bucky's approval. She took down Mrs. Glazer's recommended recipes and eagerly clipped new ones out of *Ladies' Home Journal, Good Housekeeping, Family Circle*, and the other women's magazines Mrs. Glazer passed along to her. Even when she had a headache after a day of housework and laundry, Norma Jeane gazed adoringly upon her handsome young husband as he hungrily ate the meal she'd prepared for him. *You don't really need God so much if you have a husband.* They were like prayers: meat loaf with large chunks of raw red onion, chopped green peppers, and bread crumbs and a thick ketchup topping that baked to a crust in the oven. Beef stew (except the beef was likely to be fatty and gristly these days) with potatoes and other vegetables (except she had to be careful with vegetables, Bucky didn't like them) and dark gravy ("enrichened" with flour) on Mother Glazer's corn-bread biscuits. Deep-fried breaded chicken with mashed potatoes. Fried frankfurters on buns, dripping with mustard. Of course Bucky loved hamburgers and cheeseburgers when Norma Jeane could get the meat, served with large portions of french fries and lots and lots of ketchup. (Mother Glazer had warned Norma Jeane, if she didn't put enough ketchup on Bucky's food there was the danger he'd get impatient, take up the bottle, give it a wallop, and out would rush half the contents!)

There were casseroles that weren't Bucky's favorites, but if he was hungry—and Bucky was always hungry—he'd eat them with almost as much appetite as his favorite foods: tuna, cheese and macaroni, creamed salmon with canned corn on toast, chicken parts in cream sauce with potatoes, onions, and carrots. Corn pudding, tapioca pudding, chocolate pudding. Fruit Jell-O with marshmallows. Cakes, cookies, pies. Ice cream. If only there wasn't the war, and rationing! Meat, butter, and sugar were becoming so scarce. Bucky knew it wasn't Norma Jeane's fault but in a childlike way he seemed to blame her: men blamed women for meals that weren't fully satisfying as they blamed women for sex that wasn't fully satisfying; that's the way the world is and Norma Jeane Glazer, a bride of less than a year, knew this fact by instinct. But when Bucky liked a meal, he exuded enthusiasm and it was thrilling to her to watch him eat, as a long time ago (it seemed: in fact, not many months ago) she'd been thrilled watching her high school teacher Mr. Haring read her poems, aloud or even silently. There sat Bucky at the kitchen table, head slightly lowered toward his plate as he chewed, a faint glisten on his broad strong-boned face. If he'd come from work he would have washed his face, forearms, and hands and combed his hair damply back from his forehead. He would have changed out of his sweaty clothes, wearing a fresh T-shirt and chino trousers, or sometimes just boxer shorts. How exotic Bucky Glazer seemed to Norma Jeane, in his very maleness. His head that seemed, in certain facets of light, like a modeled clay head, his sturdy square chin, his grinding jaws, his boyish mouth and fair, frank hazel eyes— more beautiful, Norma Jeane swooningly thought, than any man's eyes she'd ever seen up close, outside the movies. Though one day Bucky Glazer would say of her, his first wife, *Poor Norma Jeane tried but she couldn't cook worth a damn, those casseroles of hers clogged with cheese and carrots and she'd drench everything with ketchup and mustard.* He would say frankly *We didn't love each other; we were too damned young to be married. Especially her.*

Seconds he'd have, of everything. Of his favorite foods he'd have thirds. "Honey, this is de-li-*cious*. You've done it again."

Lifting her then in his bulgy-muscled arms like Popeye's before she had time even to set the dishes in the sink to soak and she squealed in panicked anticipation, as if for a split second she'd forgotten who this two-hundred-pound lusty boy was, crowing, "Gotcha, Baby!" He'd carry her into the bedroom, his footsteps so heavy the floorboards trembled—surely neighbors on all sides would feel it, certainly Harriet and her apartment mates next door would know what the newlyweds were up to—her arms tight around his neck like a drowning girl's so Bucky's breath came quick and audible as a stallion's; and he laughed, she had a stranglehold on him practically, a choke hold like a wrestler, and she kicked and thrashed as with a shout of triumph he pinned her shoulders to the bed, tugging open her housedress or peeling up her sweater, nuzzling her bare, beautiful breasts, soft bouncy breasts with pinkish-brown nipples like jelly beans, and her rounded little tummy covered in a fine pale fuzz and always so warm, and the burnished chestnut hairs, so curly, damp, and ticklish at the base of her belly, a surprising bush for a girl of her age. "Oh, Baby-Doll. *Ohhhh*." Much of the time Bucky was so excited he came on Norma Jeane's thighs, it was a way, too, of birth control if he didn't trust himself to roll on a condom in time, for even in his passion Bucky Glazer was shrewdly alert to not wanting to start a baby. But like a stallion he'd become hard again within minutes, blood rushing into Big Thing as if a hot-water faucet had been turned on. He'd taught his teenage bride how to make love and she'd been a docile and then an eager pupil, and sometimes, Bucky had to admit, her passion scared him a little, just a little *wanting so much from me, from it: love*. They kissed, cuddled, tickled, poked their tongues into each other's ears. Clutched and grabbed at each other. If Norma Jeane tried to escape by scrambling off the bed, Bucky lunged at her and tackled her with a whoop—"Gotcha again, Baby!" He wrestled her back onto the bed into the churned-up bedclothes, shouting, laughing, panting, and moaning, and Norma Jeane, too, moaned and wept, yes, and the hell with nosy neighbors next door or upstairs or someone passing on the walk outside the screened window, beyond the carelessly drawn blind. They were married, weren't they? In a church of God? They loved each other, didn't they? Had every right to make love when and however often they wanted, didn't they? Damn right!

She was a sweet kid but so emotional. Wanting love all the time. She was immature and unreliable and I guess so was I; we were too young. If she'd been a better cook and not so emotional, it might've worked out.

4

To My Husband

My love for you is deep—
  deeper than the sea.
Without you, my darling,
  I would cease to be.

Already in the winter of '42–'43, the war going badly in Europe and the Pacific, Bucky Glazer was restless, talking of enlisting in the navy, or the marines, or the merchant marine. "God made the U.S. number one for a reason. We got to uphold that responsibility."

Norma Jeane stared at him with a bright, blank smile.

Soon draft boards would be calling up "childless" married men. It only made sense to enlist before he got drafted, didn't it? He was working forty hours a week at Lockheed plus one or two mornings at McDougal's Funeral

Home assisting Mr. Eeley. ("But it's weird: people aren't dying so much right now. So many men are gone and old folks want to hang on to see how the war turns out. And without much gas, you can't drive fast enough to crash.") His embalming experience would be useful in the armed services. Also his high school football, wrestling, track: Bucky Glazer had been a star athlete, he could help train weaker recruits. Also he had an aptitude for math, at least Mission Hills High School math, and radio repair, and maps. Every evening he listened to the war news and thoughtfully read the *L.A. Times*. He took Norma Jeane to the movies every week, mostly to see *The March of Time*. On the walls of their apartment he'd taped war maps of Europe and the Pacific and inserted colored pins in areas where men he knew were stationed—relatives, friends. He never talked about anyone reported dead or missing or taken prisoner, but Norma Jeane knew he was thinking plenty.

For Christmas 1942, one of Bucky's cousins in the army sent him a Japanese skull "souvenir" from an Aleutian island called Kiska. What a surprise! Unwrapping the package, lifting the skull in both hands like a basketball, Bucky whistled a long low whistle and called to Norma Jeane in the next room to come look. Norma Jeane hurried into the kitchen and looked. And almost fainted. What was that ugly thing? A head? A human head? A smoothly bald, hairless, and skinless *human head*? "It's a Jap skull. It's OK," Bucky said. A boyish flush colored Bucky's face. He poked his fingers into the enormous eye sockets. The nose hole, too, seemed abnormally large and jagged. Three or four discolored teeth remained in the upper jaw, but the lower jaw was missing altogether. Thrilled and envious, Bucky said several times, "Je*sus*! Trev's sure made an end run around ol' Bucky." Norma Jeane smiled her bright, blank smile like one who hasn't caught on to a joke or doesn't wish to acknowledge she's caught on, like those nasty jokes the Pirigs and their friends would tell to make her blush, and she hadn't blushed. She could see how excited her husband was and wasn't about to disturb his mood.

"Ol' Hirohito" was placed prominently on top of the RCA Victor console radio in the living room. Bucky seemed as proud of it as if he'd captured it, in the Aleutian Islands, himself.

5

She meant to be perfect. He deserved nothing less.

And he had such high standards! And a sharp eye.

Each morning thoroughly cleaning the apartment in Verdugo Gardens. Only three not-very-spacious rooms and a bathroom large enough to contain a tub, a sink, a toilet, and all these spaces entrusted to her she cleaned with the concentration and fervor of a religious mendicant. It did not echo ironically in her ears that *No wife of Bucky Glazer's is going to work. Ever.* She understood that a woman's work inside the home is not work but sacred privilege and duty. "The home" sanctified any expenditure of spirit or effort. It was a frequently voiced conviction of the Glazers, in some unclear way allied with their Christian ardor, that no woman, especially no married woman, should work outside "the home." Even during the Depression when some of the family (Bucky was vague about details, embarrassed and ashamed, and Norma Jeane would not have wished to inquire) lived in a trailer and a tent somewhere in the San Fernando Valley, even then only male members of the family "worked," though these included children, no doubt Bucky himself, younger than ten.

A matter of pride, male pride, that Glazer women didn't work outside "the home." Innocently Norma Jeane inquired, "But now it's wartime, isn't that different?" Her question hovered in the air, unheard.

No wife of mine. Ever!

To be the object of male desire is to know *I exist!* The expression of the eyes. Hardening of the cock. Though worthless, you're wanted.

Though your mother didn't want you, yet you are wanted.

Though your father didn't want you, yet you are wanted.

The fundamental truth of my life whether in fact it was truth or a burlesque of truth: when a man wants you, you're safe.

More vividly than she recalled her young husband's heated presence in their apartment, Norma Jeane would one day recall the long, deeply gratifying morning hours stretching into early afternoon in that place of shaded, near-secret seclusion, not quiet (for Verdugo Gardens was a noisy place, like a barracks, children shouting outside, babies crying, radios turned up higher than Norma Jeane's own): the rhythmic, repetitive, hypnotic pleasures of housework. How swiftly the animal brain takes to the instrument at hand: carpet sweeper, broom, mop, scouring pad. (The young Glazers couldn't yet afford a vacuum cleaner. But that would come soon, Bucky promised!) In the living room there was a single rectangular rug measuring about six feet by eight, royal blue, a remnant purchased for $8.98, and over this rug Norma Jeane ran the carpet sweeper in a trance of oblivion. A single shred of lint was exciting: now it was there, a blemish; now it was gone! Norma Jeane smiled. Perhaps she recalled Gladys in a mellow mood, a vague almost-loving mood, performing one or another task (not housework), drugged yet more than drugged, for Norma Jeane understood now that her mother's brain generated its own unique and purposeful chemistry. To be so utterly absorbed in the moment at hand. To become one with the action you are performing. *Whatever this is: this wonder that is before me* pushing the heavy carpet sweeper back and forth, back and forth. And then in the bedroom, a yet-smaller rug, oval in shape. Singing with the radio, a popular Los Angeles station. Her voice was soft, feathery, off-key, content. She recalled Jess Flynn's lessons and smiled to think of Gladys's grandiose hopes for her, Norma Jeane, to sing! That was funny, like piano lessons from Clive Pearce. The poor man wincing and trying to smile as Norma Jeane played, or tried to play. She felt a wave of shame for her more recent baffling attempt at the high school to audition for a role in a student play—what was it?—*Our Town*. It was harder to smile at that memory. The eyes of ridicule, the voice of a teacher's confident authority. *I doubt that Mr. Thornton Wilder would see it that way.* The man was right, of course! Now she loved the carpet sweeper, which was a wedding gift from one of Bucky's aunts. And she'd been given a wooden-handled mop with a wringer and a green plastic bucket, another useful present from a Glazer relative. These instruments to aid in her task of becoming perfect. She mopped and polished the badly scuffed linoleum floor of the kitchen, and she mopped and polished the faded linoleum floor of the bathroom. With her Dutch Boy scouring pads she deftly, fanatically, scoured sinks, counters, tub, and toilet. Some of these would never be clean, not even near-clean. Stained by previous tenants beyond reclamation. Briskly then she changed bedclothes, "airing out" the mattress, the pillows. Each week she hauled laundry to a Laundromat nearby. She returned with the damp clothes to hang on a line outside the apartment. She loved ironing, mending. Bucky was "hard on his clothes," as Bess Glazer gravely warned her daughter-in-law, and this challenge Norma Jeane was determined to meet with unflagging zeal and optimism, mending socks, shirts, trousers, underwear. In high school she'd learned to knit for British War Relief and now, when she had time, she was knitting a surprise for her husband, a hunter-green pullover sweater from a pattern Mrs. Glazer had given her. (This sweater Norma Jeane would never complete, for she kept ripping out what she'd done, dissatisfied with the way it looked.)

So long as Bucky was out of the apartment, Norma Jeane draped one of her scarfs over the Japanese skull on the radio. Shortly before he was due home, she'd remove it. "What's under here?"—so Harriet one day inquired, lifting the scarf before Norma Jeane could warn her. Harriet's pug nose crinkled when she saw it. But she only let the scarf fall back into place. "Oh, Christ. One of those."

More lovingly, Norma Jeane dusted the framed photographs and snapshots on display in the living room. Most of these were wedding photos, glossy and radiantly colored, in brass frames. Married less than a year, and already Bucky and Norma Jeane had accumulated many happy memories. A sign of good things to come? Norma Jeane had been struck by the numerous family photos in the Glazers' house, displayed proudly on virtually every suitable surface. Great-great-grandparents of Bucky's, and so many babies! Norma Jeane was enchanted to see how you could trace Bucky from his first appearance as a chubby gape-mouthed baby in youthful Bess Glazer's arms, in 1921, to the husky young bull of a man he was in 1942. What proof that Bucky Glazer existed and was cherished! She recalled from her infrequent visits to the homes of Van Nuys High School classmates how these families, too, proudly displayed images of themselves on tables, on pianos, on windowsills and walls. Even Elsie Pirig had a few select photos of the Pirigs' younger, sunnier selves. It was a shock to realize that only Gladys had never had any family photos framed and displayed, except that of the dark-haired man she'd claimed was Norma Jeane's father.

Norma Jeane laughed, lightly. Probably the photo had been a publicity still from The Studio. No one Gladys had even known well.

"Why should I care? I don't."

Now she was married, Norma Jeane rarely thought about her lost father or the Dark Prince. Rarely did she think about Gladys, except as one might think of any relative in chronic ill health. What was the need?

There were a dozen framed photos. Several were beach scenes, Bucky and Norma Jeane in their swimsuits, arms around each other's waist; Bucky and Norma Jeane with some of Bucky's friends at a barbecue; Bucky and Norma Jeane posed lounging against the grille of Bucky's newly purchased 1938 Packard. But it was the wedding photos that most fascinated Norma Jeane. That radiant girl bride in the white satin dress with the dazzling smile, the bridegroom in his formal jacket and bow tie, hair slicked back from his forehead, profile handsome as Jackie Coogan's. Everyone had marveled at how attractive the young couple was and how much in love they were. Even the minister had wiped at his eyes. *Yet how scared I was. And none of it shows.* In a daze Norma Jeane had been led up the aisle by a friend of the Glazer family (since Warren Pirig refused to attend the wedding), blood beating in her ears and a sick sensation in the pit of her belly. At the altar she swayed in high heels that pinched (a half size too small but a bargain at the second-hand shop), staring with her sweet dimpled smile at the minister of the Church of Christ intoning his rote words in a nasal voice, and it came to her that Groucho Marx would have played this scene with more pizzazz, wriggling his ridiculous fake eyebrows and mustache. *Do you, Norma Jeane, take this man . . . ?* She'd had no idea what the question meant. Turning then, or made to turn, for probably Bucky had nudged her, she saw Bucky Glazer beside her like an accomplice in crime, nervously licking his lips, and she managed to answer the minister's question in a whisper, *I-I do,* and Bucky answered more forcibly, in a voice loud enough to be heard through the church, *I sure do!* There was some fumbling then with the wedding band but it fitted Norma Jeane's icy finger perfectly, and Mrs. Glazer with her customary foresight had made sure that Norma Jeane's engagement ring had been shifted to her right hand, so that part of the ceremony went smoothly. *So scared. I wanted to run away. But where?*

Another favorite photo showed the bride and groom cutting into their three-tiered wedding cake. This was at the wedding party, at a Beverly Hills restaurant. Bucky's big capable hand over Norma Jeane's slender fingers on the long-bladed knife and both young people smiling broadly into the camera's flash. By this time, Norma Jeane had had her first glass or two of champagne and Bucky'd had both champagne and ale. There was a photo of the newlyweds dancing, and there was a photo of Bucky's Packard festooned with crepe-paper garlands and JUST MARRIED signs, the newlyweds waving goodbye. These photos and others, Norma Jeane had sent off to Gladys at the state hospital at Norwalk. She'd included a chatty, cheerful note on floral stationery:

We were all very sorry you could not attend my wedding, Mother. But of course everyone understood. It was the most wonderful, wonderful day of my life.

Gladys hadn't answered, but Norma Jeane hadn't expected an answer. "Why should I care? I don't."

She'd never had champagne before that day. As a Christian Scientist she didn't approve of drinking but a wedding's a special occasion, isn't it? How delicious the champagne, how magical the fizzy sensation in her nose, but she hadn't liked the light-headedness that followed, the giddy giggling and lack of control. Bucky got drunk on champagne, beer, and tequila and vomited so suddenly while they were dancing, he stained the skirt of the beautiful white satin wedding dress. Fortunately, Norma Jeane was planning to change out of the dress soon anyway, before she and Bucky left for their honeymoon hotel up the coast at Morro Beach. Hurriedly Mrs. Glazer wetted napkins and wiped away most of the smelly stain. Scolding, "Bucky! Shame on you. This is Lorraine's dress." Bucky was boyishly repentant and forgiven. The party continued. The hired band continued to play, loudly. Norma Jeane, now shoeless, was dancing with her husband another time. "Don't Get Around Much Anymore"—"This Can't Be Love"—"The Girl That I Marry." Sliding on the dance floor, careening into other couples, squealing with laughter. Cameras flashed. There was a swirl of confetti, balloons, and rice. Some of Bucky's high school friends were tossing around water-filled balloons, and Bucky's shirtfront got soaked. Strawberry short-

cake was served, with whipped cream. Somehow, Bucky dropped a spoon-
ful of syrupy strawberries on the flared skirt of the white linen dress into
which Norma Jeane had just changed. "Bucky, *for shame.*" Mrs. Glazer was
scandalized but everyone else (including the newlyweds) laughed. There was
more dancing. A heated, festive confluence of smells. "Tea for Two"—"In
the Shade of the Old Apple Tree"—"Begin the Beguine." Everyone clapped
to see Bucky Glazer, face gleaming like a car hubcap, attempt the tango!
*Sorry you could not attend my wedding. Do you think I give a damn?—I
don't.* Bucky and his older brother, Joe, were laughing together. Elsie Pirig
in acid-green taffeta, her lipstick smeared, was squeezing Norma Jeane's
hand in farewell and extracting from her the promise that she'd telephone
sometime the next day and that she and Bucky would drive over to visit Elsie
as soon as they returned from their four-day honeymoon. Norma Jeane was
asking again why Warren hadn't come to the wedding, though Elsie had told
her it was for business reasons—"He sends his love, sweetie. We're gonna
miss you, you know." Elsie, too, was in her stocking feet, shorter than
Norma Jeane by two inches. Suddenly she leaned forward to kiss Norma
Jeane on the lips, fiercely. Norma Jeane had never been kissed like this before
by any woman. She was pleading. "Aunt Elsie, I could come home with you
tonight. Just one more night. I could tell Bucky I didn't pack all my things,
OK? Oh, *please.*" Elsie laughed as if this was quite a joke, pushing Norma
Jeane away in the direction of her bridegroom. It was time for the newlyweds to drive off to their honeymoon hotel. Bucky wasn't laughing with Joe
but arguing. Joe was trying to take Bucky's car keys from him and Bucky
was saying, "I can drive—hell, I'm a married man!"

The drive up the coast was a little scary. Ocean fog drifting over the highway, and the Packard drifting over the center line. Norma Jeane was clear-
headed now and cuddled with her head against Bucky's shoulder to make
sure she could grab the steering wheel if necessary.

At the Loch Raven Motor Court above the fog-shrouded ocean, now at
dusk, Norma Jeane helped Bucky out of the gaily decorated Packard and they
slipped and slid and nearly fell together, in their good clothes, in the cinder
drive. The cabin smelled of insect spray and there were daddy longlegs scurrying across the bedspread. "Hell, these're harmless," Bucky said affably,
banging at them with a fist. "It's scorpions that'll kill you. Brown r'cluse spiders. Bite you in the ass, you're *bit.*" He laughed loudly. He needed to use
the bathroom. Her arm securely around his waist, Norma Jeane led him to
the toilet. She was so embarrassed. The first sight of her husband's penis,
which until now she'd only felt, nudged or pressed or rubbing against her,
was startling to her, engorged with urine, sizzling and steaming into the toilet bowl. Norma Jeane shut her eyes. *Only Mind is real. God is love. Love*

is the power of healing. Shortly afterward, this same penis was being nudged into Norma Jeane, into the tight slash of an opening between her thighs. Bucky was alternately methodical and frenetic. Of course Norma Jeane had been prepared for this at least in theory, and in fact the pain wasn't much worse than her usual menstrual cramps, just as Elsie Pirig predicted. Except it was sharper, like a screwdriver. Again she shut her eyes. *Only Mind is real. God is love. Love is the power of healing.* There was some bleeding onto the wadded toilet paper Norma Jeane had fastidiously placed beneath them, but it was bright fresh blood, not the darker and smellier kind. If only she could have a bath! Soak in a hot soothing bath! But Bucky was impatient, Bucky wanted to try again. He had a wilted-looking condom he kept dropping, cursing, "God *damn*," his face swollen red like a child's balloon blown near to bursting. Norma Jeane was too embarrassed to help him with the condom, this was only just her wedding night and she couldn't stop trembling and shivering and it was disorienting to her—nothing at all like what she'd expected—that she and Bucky were so awkward with each other's nakedness. Why, it was nothing like her nakedness in the mirror. It was nothing like any nakedness she'd expected. It was clumsy, skin-smacking, sweaty. It was *crowded.* Like there were more people than just her and Bucky in this bed. All the years she'd been thrilled, seeing her Magic Friend in the mirror, smiling and winking at herself and moving her body to imagined music like Ginger Rogers, except she didn't need any dance partner in order to dance and be happy. But it was different now. It was all happening too quickly. She couldn't see herself to know what was going on. Oh, she wished it was over so she could cuddle in her husband's arms and sleep, sleep, sleep, and maybe dream of her wedding day and of *him.* "Honey, can you help me? Please." Bucky was kissing her repeatedly, grinding his teeth against hers as if he had a point to prove in an argument. Somewhere close by, waves were breaking on the beach like applause with a jeering edge. "Jesus, honey, I love you. You're so sweet, you're so good, you're so beautiful. C'mon!" The bed rocked. The lumpy mattress listed and began to skid dangerously to one side. Fresh toilet paper was needed to slip beneath them, but Bucky wasn't paying attention. Norma Jeane squealed and tried to laugh, but Bucky wasn't in a laughing mood. One of the last pieces of advice Elsie Pirig had given Norma Jeane was *All you need to do, really, is stay out of their way.* Norma Jeane had said that didn't sound very romantic and Elsie snapped back *Who said it was?* Yet now Norma Jeane was beginning to understand. There was a strange impersonality about Bucky's urgent lovemaking, it wasn't anything like their avid, heated, protracted "necking" and "petting" of the past month. Between Norma Jeane's legs there was a searing-burning sensation, there were smears of blood on Bucky's thighs; you'd have thought this was enough for the night but Bucky was determined. He'd managed again to thrust himself into the slash between her thighs, Trojan or not, a little deeper than the first time, and now he was jiggling the bed and moaning and suddenly he reared up like a horse shot in mid-gallop. His face crumpled, his eyes rolled white in their sockets. A whimpering-whinnying sound escaped him—"Je-*sus*."

Sinking then in Norma Jeane's arms, into a deep, damply snoring sleep. Norma Jeane winced with pain and tried to maneuver into a more comfortable position. The bed *was* too small. Yet it was a double bed. Tenderly she stroked Bucky's sweat-glistening forehead, his muscled shoulders. The bedside lamp was on and the light hurt her tired eyes but she wasn't able to reach it without disturbing Bucky. Oh, if only she could take a bath! That was all she really wanted, a bath. And doing something practical about the tangled sheet that was so wet beneath them. Several times during the long night that yielded at last to June 20, 1942, and a nearly opaque morning fog, Norma Jeane woke from a thin headachy sleep and always there was Bucky Glazer, naked and snoring, pinning her to the bed. She tried to lift her head, to see the long length of him. Her husband. *Her husband!* Like a beached whale he was, naked, his hairy legs sprawled across the bedclothes. She heard herself laugh, a frightened little-girl laugh, reminded of her long-lost doll she'd loved so, the doll-with-no-name, unless the name was "Norma Jeane," the doll with the floppy boneless legs, the feet.

6

Tell me about your work, Daddy. But it wasn't Bucky's Lockheed-factory work she meant.

Curling up like a cat on Bucky's lap in her short nightie, no panties beneath, her arm around his neck and her warm breath in his ear distracting him from the new issue of *Life*, photo spreads of haggard G.I.s in the Solomon Islands, and in New Guinea there was General Eichelberger and his even more haggard men, gaunt and unshaven and some of them wounded, and there was a photo spread of Hollywood entertainers visiting troops abroad, "boosting morale": Marlene Dietrich, Rita Hayworth, Marie McDonald, Joe E. Brown, and Bob Hope. Norma Jeane flinched from looking too closely at the war photos, but she studied the other feature more carefully, then grew restless as Bucky continued to read the magazine. *Tell me about your work with Mr. Eeley,* she whispered, and Bucky felt a shiver of both dread and excitement, not that he was shocked exactly, not that he was a prude, for sure Bucky Glazer was no prude and he'd told plenty of grisly hilarious stories about his work as an embalmer's assistant to his buddies; but no girl or female relative of his had ever inquired, definitely you got the point that most people didn't want to know, no thanks! But here was this child wife of his wriggling on his lap, whispering in his ear *Tell me, Daddy!* like she had to know the worst, so Bucky spoke as lightly as he could manage, not going into much detail, describing a body they'd been working on that morning in preparation for a viewing: a woman in her mid-fifties who'd died of liver cancer, her skin such a sickish yellow color they'd had to cream it several times, applying layers of cosmetic tint with a little brush, and then the layers dried unevenly, so the poor woman looked like a wall peeling paint and they had to begin over again; her cheeks were so sunken they had to firm up her lower face from inside her mouth with cotton batting and they'd had to stitch the corners of her mouth shut and fix them into a peaceful expression—"Not a smile but an 'almost smile' Mr. Eeley calls it. You wouldn't want a *smile*." Norma Jeane shivered but wanted to know how they'd prepared the dead woman's eyes, did they "make up" the eyes? And Bucky said they'd mostly had to inject a solution with a syringe to fill out the hollows and cement the eyelids shut—"You don't want a dead body's eyes to pop open at a viewing." Bucky's basic job was to drain out blood and start the embalming fluid pumping through the veins. It was Mr. Eeley who did the artistic work once the body was firmed up—"restored"—primping the eyelashes, coloring the lips, manicuring nails that in some cases hadn't ever been manicured in life. Norma Jeane asked whether, when they'd first seen her, the dead woman had looked frightened or sad or in pain, and Bucky lied a little, saying no, she looked "like she was just asleep—they mostly all do." (In fact, the woman had looked as if she were trying to scream, her lips drawn back from her teeth and her face twisted like a rag; her eyes had been open, the focus clouded with mucus. Already, only hours after her death, she'd begun to emit a nostril-piercing smell as of rancid meat.) Norma Jeane hugged Bucky so tight he could hardly breathe but he didn't have the heart to dislodge her grip. He didn't have the heart to shift her off his lap and onto the sofa, though her warm fleshy weight on his left thigh was putting his nerve endings to sleep.

So needy. He couldn't breathe. He did love her. It was the formaldehyde smell absorbed into his skin, his hair follicles. If he wanted to escape, where?

She was asking him another time how the dead woman had died, and Bucky told her. She asked him how old the dead woman was, and Bucky picked a number out of the air—"Fifty-six." He felt his young wife tense as if counting out numbers in her head, subtracting her age from fifty-six. Then she relaxed a little, saying, as if thinking out loud—"It's a long way off then."

7

She laughed, it was so easy. A fairy-tale riddle, and she knew the answer. *What is it I am? A married woman is what I AM. What is it I'm not? A virgin is what I'm NOT.*

Pushing the squeaky-wheeled stroller through the scrubby little park. Or maybe it wasn't a park exactly. Palm-tree debris underfoot, and other litter. But she loved it! Her heart swelled with happiness knowing *this is what I am, what I am doing is what I am.* This early-afternoon routine she'd grown to love. Singing to little Irina strapped into the stroller. Popular songs, snatches of Mother Goose lullabies. Elsewhere it was the terrible season of Stalingrad, Russia: February 1943. A human slaughter. Here it was just winter in southern California: cool dry eye-aching sunshine most days.

What a beautiful baby! the faces would exclaim. Norma Jeane would murmur, smiling, blushing, *Why, thank you.* Sometimes the faces would say *Beautiful baby, and beautiful mother.* Norma Jeane only smiled. *And what is your little girl's name?* they would ask and Norma Jeane would say proudly *Irina—aren't you, honey?* leaning over the baby, stooping to kiss her cheek or catch at her flailing pudgy fingers that closed so swiftly and tightly around her own. Sometimes the faces would say pleasantly *Irina— that's an unusual name, is it foreign?* and Norma Jeane might murmur *I guess so.* Nearly always they would ask how old the baby was and Norma Jeane would tell them *Almost ten months, she'll be a year in April.* The faces would smile brightly. *You must be very proud.* And Norma Jeane would say *Oh, yes, I am—I mean, we are.* Sometimes, pushy, inquisitive, the faces would ask *Is your husband—?* and quickly Norma Jeane would say *He's overseas. Far away—in New Guinea.*

It was true, Irina's father *was* somewhere in a place called New Guinea. He was a lieutenant in the U.S. Army. In fact, he was "missing." He'd been officially "missing in action" since December. Of this, Norma Jeane was able not to think. So long as she could sing "Little Baby Bunting" and "Three Blind Mice" to Irina, that was what mattered. So long as the beautiful little blond girl smiled up at her, chattered, and squeezed her fingers, called her "Ma-ma" like a young parrot just learning to speak, that was what mattered.

In you
the world is born anew.

Before you—
but there was none.

. . .

Mother stared at the baby. For a long moment she could not speak and I was afraid she would burst into tears or turn away and hide her face.

Then I saw that her face was radiant with happiness. And the astonishment of happiness after so many years.

We were in a grassy place. The lawn behind the hospital, I think.

There were benches, there was a small pond. Most of the grass was burnt out. All the colors were hues of brown. The hospital buildings were blurred with distance, I couldn't see them clearly. Mother was so improved she had ground privileges, unsupervised. She would sit on a bench and read poetry, shaping the precious words to herself, whispering them aloud. Or she would walk for as long as they allowed. Her "captors" she called them. Yet not bitterly. She acknowledged she'd been sick, the shock treatments had helped. She acknowledged she had some distance to go before she was well.

Of course, there was a high wall around the hospital grounds.

It was a bright windy winter day when I arrived, to show Mother my baby. I trusted her with my baby. I placed my baby firmly in her arms.

At last Mother began to cry. Hugging the baby to her flattened breasts. But these were tears of happiness, not sorrow. Oh my darling Norma Jeane *Mother said* this time it will be right.

In Verdugo Gardens there were a number of young wives whose husbands were overseas. In Britain, in Belgium, in Turkey, in northern Africa. In Guam, in the Aleutian Islands, in Australia, in Burma, and in China. It was sheerly a lottery, where a man was sent. There was no logic to it and certainly no justice. Some men were stationed at bases permanently, in intelligence, in communications, or maybe they worked in hospitals, or as cooks. Maybe they were assigned to postal services. Maybe they were assigned to stockades. As the months and eventually the years passed it would become clear that there were two divisions of men in the armed services in World War II: those who actually fought in the war and those who did not.

It would become clear that there were two divisions of human beings in the wake of the war: those who were lucky and those who weren't.

If you were one of the unlucky wives you could make an effort not to be bitter or downcast and that would be to your credit. It would be said warmly of you *Isn't she brave?* But Norma Jeane's friend Harriet was beyond that. Harriet wasn't brave, and Harriet wasn't making any effort not to be bitter. Much of the time, when Norma Jeane took Irina out in the stroller, Irina's mother lay exhausted on the shabby sofa in the living room she shared with two other servicemen's wives, the shades drawn and no radio playing.

No radio! Norma Jeane couldn't bear to be alone in her apartment for five minutes without a radio playing. And Bucky no more than three miles away at Lockheed.

It was Norma Jeane's task to call out cheerfully, "Harriet, hi! We're back." And Harriet would make no audible reply. "Irina and I had a really nice walk," Norma Jeane would report, in the same determinedly upbeat voice, lifting Irina out of the stroller and carrying her inside. "Didn't we, honeybun?" She would take Irina to Harriet, lying immobile and heavy on the sofa dampened with tears of rage and anger if not actual sorrow, for perhaps she was beyond sorrow; Harriet, who'd gained twenty pounds since December, her skin puffy and chalky and her eyes bloodshot. In the unnerving silence, Norma Jeane heard herself chatter—"We did! Yes, we did. Didn't we, Irina?" At last Harriet took Irina (who was now beginning to fret, to whimper and kick) from Norma Jeane as she might have taken from her friend's hands a bundle of damp laundry to be tossed into a corner.

Let me be Irina's mother if you don't want her?

Oh, please.

Maybe Harriet wasn't Norma Jeane's friend any longer. Maybe in fact she'd never been Norma Jeane's friend. She was estranged from the "silly, sad" women with whom she shared the apartment, and often she refused to speak with her family, or her husband's family, on the phone. Not that Harriet had quarreled with them—"Why? There's nothing to quarrel about." Not that she was angry with them or distressed by them. She was just too exhausted to deal with them. She was bored with their emotion, she said. Norma Jeane was worried that Harriet might do something hurtful to herself and to Irina, but when she brought the subject up, hesitantly, elliptically, to Bucky, he scarcely listened, for this was "women's stuff" and of no interest to a man, and she didn't dare bring the subject up to Harriet herself. It was dangerous to prod Harriet.

Following a stuffed-toy pattern from *Family Circle*, Norma Jeane sewed a little striped tiger for Irina out of orange cotton socks, strips of black felt (for stripes), and cotton batting stuffing. The tiger's tail was cleverly made of coat-hanger wire covered with cloth. The eyes were shiny black buttons and the whiskers were pipe cleaners from Woolworth's. How Irina loved her baby tiger! Norma Jeane laughed excitedly as Irina hugged the little creature and crawled around on the floor with it, squealing as if it were alive. Harriet looked on indifferently, smoking a cigarette. *You could at least thank me,* Norma Jeane thought. Instead, Harriet remarked, "Well, Norma Jeane. Aren't we domestic! The perfect little wife and mother." Norma Jeane laughed, though this stung. With an air of gentle reproach, like Maureen O'Hara in the movies, she said, "Harriet, it's a sin to be unhappy when you have Irina." Harriet laughed loudly. She'd been sitting with half-shut eyes and she opened her eyes with exaggerated interest now and stared at Norma Jeane as if she'd never seen her before and didn't much like what she saw. "Yes, it's a sin, and I'm a sinner. So why don't you leave us now, Little Miss Sunshine, and go straight home to hell?"

8

"There's this guy I know, develops film? 'Strictly confidential,' he says. Over in Sherman Oaks."

In the hot, oppressive summer of 1943, Bucky had become restless. Norma Jeane tried not to think what it meant. Every day the big headline news was of U.S. Air Force bombing raids against the enemy. Heroic nighttime missions into enemy territory. A classmate of Bucky's from Mission Hills High was posthumously decorated for valor, flying a B-24 Liberator on a raid of German oil refineries in Romania, shot down in action. "He *is* a hero," Norma Jeane conceded, "but, honey, he's *dead*." Bucky was staring at the pilot's photo in the paper with a vacant, brooding expression. He surprised her, laughing so harshly—"Hell, babe, you can be a coward and wind up dead too."

Later that week Bucky acquired a secondhand Brownie box camera and began taking pictures of his trusting young wife. At first it was Norma Jeane in dressy Sunday clothes, white pillbox hat and white eyelet gloves and white high-heeled pumps; Norma Jeane in shirt and blue jeans, leaning on a gate with a leaf of grass held reflectively between her teeth; Norma Jeane on the beach at Topanga in her two-piece polka-dot swimsuit. Bucky tried to get Norma Jeane to pose Betty Grable-style, peeking coyly over her right shoulder and displaying her cute little rear, but Norma Jeane was too self-conscious. (They were on the beach, Sunday midday, people were watching.) Bucky tried to pose Norma Jeane catching a beach ball, with a big happy smile, but the smile was as forced and unconvincing as the almost smile of one of Mr. Eeley's cadavers. Norma Jeane begged Bucky to get someone to take pictures of both of them together—"It's no fun all alone here. Bucky, come *on*." But Bucky shrugged, saying, "What do I care about *me*?"

Next, Bucky wanted to take pictures of Norma Jeanne in the privacy of their bedroom, "Before" and "After" pictures.

"Before" was Norma Jeane as herself. First fully clothed, then partly unclothed, then naked—or, as Bucky called it, "nude." Nude in their bed with a sheet drawn up teasingly to hide her breasts, and by degrees Bucky would tug the sheet from her, taking pictures of Norma Jeane in awkward, kittenish poses. "C'mon, Baby. Smile for Daddy. You know how." Norma Jeane didn't know whether to be flattered or embarrassed, thrilled or ashamed. She was overcome by an attack of giggling and had to hide her face. When she recovered, there was Bucky waiting patiently, aiming the camera at her *click! click! click!* She pleaded, "Daddy, come *on.* That's enough. It's lonely here in this big old bed by myself." But when Norma Jeane opened her arms to her husband to entice him to her, he just clicked away with the camera.

Each *click!* a sliver of ice entering her heart. As if seeing her through the camera lens he wasn't seeing *her* at all.

But "after" was worse. "After" was humiliating. "After" was when Norma Jeane had to wear a sexy red-blond wig, Rita Hayworth-style, and lacy black lingerie Bucky brought home for her. To her alarm, he even made her up with cosmetics, exaggerating her eyebrows, her mouth, even "enhancing" her nipples with cherry-pink rouge applied with a tiny ticklish brush. Norma Jeane sniffed uneasily. "This makeup, is it from the funeral home?" she asked, with dread. Bucky frowned. "No, it is not. It's from an adult novelty store in Hollywood." But the makeup had that unmistakable smell of embalming fluid overlaid with something sweetish like overripe plums.

Bucky didn't take "after" pictures for very long. He quickly became aroused and excited, set the camera aside, and pulled off his clothes. "Oh, Baby. Baby-Doll. Je-*sus.*" He was as breathless as if he'd just emerged out of the surf at Topanga. He wanted to make love, and to make love fast, fumbling with a condom while Norma Jeane looked on in dismay like a patient contemplating her surgeon. It was as if her entire body was blushing. The thick, wavy, red-blond wig that fell to her bare shoulders, the sexy black bra and panties hardly more than wisps of fabric—"Daddy, I don't like this. I don't feel right." She'd never seen such a look on Bucky Glazer's face as she saw now. It was like that famous still of Rudolph Valentino as the Sheik. Norma Jeane began to cry, and Bucky said, annoyed, "What's wrong?" Norma Jeane said, "I don't like it, Daddy." Bucky said, stroking the wig hair, pinching her tumescent-pink nipple through the transparent lace of the bra, "Yes, you do, Baby. You *do* like it." "*No.* It isn't what I want." "Hell, I'll bet you Little Thing is ready. I'll bet you Little Thing is *wet.*" With rough prying fingers he touched her between the legs and Norma Jeane flinched and pushed at him. "Bucky, *no.* That *hurts.*" "Oh, come on, Norma Jeane. It never hurt before, you love it! You know you do." "I don't love this now. I don't like this at all." "Look, it's just fun." "It isn't fun! It makes me ashamed." Bucky said, exasperated, "But we're married, for Christ's sake. We've been married for over a year—we've been married forever! Guys do lots of things with their wives, there's no harm in it." "I think there is! I think there *is* harm in it!" "I'm telling you," Bucky said, losing patience, "it's just what people do." "We're not other people. We're us."

Flush-faced, Bucky began to stroke Norma Jeane again, more forcibly; most times if they'd been arguing and Bucky touched her, she immediately softened and acquiesced like a rabbit you could put into a trance by petting rhythmically and firmly. Bucky kissed her, and she began to kiss him back. But when Bucky tugged at the bra and panties, Norma Jeane pushed him away. She yanked off the synthetic-smelling glamour wig and threw it onto the floor and wiped away some of the makeup on her face, leaving her lips pale and puffy. Thin rivulets of mascara tears ran down her cheeks. "Oh, Bucky! This makes me so ashamed. It makes me not know who I *am*. I thought you loved *me*." She began to shiver. Bucky, crouching over her, Big Thing dangling now at half mast and the goddam condom bunched at the tip, glared at her as if he'd never seen her before. Who the hell did this girl think she was? Right now she wasn't even that pretty, her face damp and smudged. An orphan! A castoff! One of the Pirigs' white-trash foster kids! Her mother was a certified nut, whatever tales Norma Jeane told of her, and no father existed, so where'd she get her prissy airs, imagining herself superior to *him*? It came to Bucky in a flash how he'd disliked her the other evening at the movies when they'd seen Abbott and Costello in *Pardon My Sarong* and Bucky'd laughed so hard he nearly wet his pants, making the entire row of seats shake, and Norma Jeane cuddling against his shoulder stiffened and objected in this little-girl voice she didn't see what was so funny about Abbott and Costello—"Isn't the little fat man *retarded*? Is it right to laugh at a *retarded person*?" Bucky was pissed as hell but just shrugged off his wife's query. Wanting to yell at her *What's so funny about Abbott and Costello is they're funny for Christ's sake! Listen to this audience laughing like hyenas!*

"Maybe I'm tired of loving *you*. Maybe I'd like a little change once in a while from *you*."

In a fury of hurt and deflated masculinity Bucky climbed off the bed, stumbled into his trousers and threw on a shirt, and left the apartment, slamming the front door so that any of their nosy neighbors who wished could overhear. There were three sex-starved servicemen's wives next door cutting their eyes at Bucky Glazer whenever they saw him and no doubt standing with ears pressed against the bedroom wall at this very moment, so let them hear. Norma Jeane, panicked, called after him, "Bucky! Oh, honey, come back! Forgive me!" But by the time she'd slipped on a robe to run after him, he was gone.

Driving away in the Packard. The gas gauge was almost at empty but what the hell. He'd have gone to see his old girlfriend, Carmen, except he'd heard she'd moved and he didn't know her new address.

Yet the snapshots were a surprise. Bucky stared in astonishment. *This* was Norma Jeane, his wife? Though she'd been squirming in embarrassment as Bucky hung over their bed, clicking away, a few of the snapshots suggested a bold, complicitous girl with a sly, teasing smile; though Bucky knew very well that Norma Jeane had been miserable, he persuaded himself that she looked, in several of the snapshots at least, as if she'd been enjoying the attention—"Exhibiting her body like a high-priced whore."

It was the "after" poses that most intrigued Bucky. In one of these Norma Jeane lay sidelong on their bed, red-blond hair tumbling sensuously across the pillow, eyes sleepily half closed and the tip of her tongue showing between lips that had been made luscious and swollen by Bucky's little cosmetic brush. *Like a clit showing between the lips of the vagina.* Norma Jeane's erect nipples showed through the transparent black bra and her raised hand was blurred, passing across her stomach as if she were about to caress herself lewdly or had just done so. With a part of his mind Bucky knew the pose was an accident, he'd pushed Norma Jeane down into this seductive position and she was about to push herself back up, yet—what did that matter?

"Je-*sus.*"

Bucky felt a stab of desire imagining this exotic, beautiful girl, a stranger to him.

He selected a half-dozen snapshots showing Norma Jeane at her sexiest, and these he proudly passed around to his buddies at Lockheed. Amid the near-deafening factory din he had to raise his voice to be heard—"This is strictly confidential, OK? Not to go beyond us." The men nodded agreement. The looks on their faces! They were *impressed.* The snapshots were all of Norma Jeane in the red-blond Rita Hayworth wig and black lingerie. "*This* is your wife? Your *wife?*" "*Your* wife?" "Glazer, you're a lucky man." Whistles and envious laughter. Just as Bucky had anticipated. Except Bob Mitchum didn't respond the way he'd expected at all. Bucky was stunned when Mitchum leafed quickly through the snapshots, scowling, and said, "What kind of S.O.B. shows pictures like these of his *wife?*" Before Bucky could stop him, Mitchum tore the snapshots into pieces.

There would have been a fight if their foreman hadn't been close by.

Bucky skulked off, mortified. And furious. Mitchum was just jealous. A would-be Hollywood actor who'd never get further than assembly-line work. *But I have the negatives* Bucky gloated. *And I have Norma Jeane.*

9

Unknown to Norma Jeane, he'd taken to dropping by his parents' home on the way to his own. His raw aggrieved boy's voice echoed familiarly in the kitchen he knew so well. "Sure I love Norma Jeane! I married her, didn't I? But she's so *needy.* She's like a baby that always has to be held or she'll cry.

It's like I'm the sun and she's a flower that can't live without the sun and it's—" Bucky searched for the word, his forehead furrowed in pain— "*tiring.*"

Mrs. Glazer nervously chided him. "Now, Bucky! Norma Jeane is a good sweet Christian girl. She's *young.*"

"Hell, I'm young too. I'm twenty-two, for God's sake. What she needs is some older guy, a *father.*" Bucky glared at his parents' concerned faces, as if they were responsible. "She's sucking me dry. She's driving me away." He paused, on the brink of saying that Norma Jeane wanted to cuddle and make love all the time. Kissing and hugging in public. Sometimes Bucky liked it fine, and other times he didn't. *And the weird thing is, I don't think she feels much, in her actual body. The way a woman is supposed to feel.*

As if reading her son's thoughts, Mrs. Glazer said anxiously, a rashlike blush rising into her face, "Bucky, of course you love Norma Jeane. We all love Norma Jeane, she's like a daughter to us, not a daughter-in-law. Oh, that beautiful wedding!—it seems like it was only last week."

Indignantly Bucky said, "And she wants to start a family too. In the middle of this *war.* World War Two and the world's going to hell and my wife wants to start a *family.* Je-*sus!*"

Mrs. Glazer said weakly, "Oh, Bucky, don't be profane. You know how that upsets me."

Bucky said, "*I'm* upset. When I go home, there Norma Jeane *is.* Like she's been cleaning house and making supper all day long waiting for me to *come home.* Like without me she doesn't *exist.* Like I'm God or something." He paused in his pacing, breathing hard; Mrs. Glazer had spooned cherry cobbler onto a plate, and he began to eat hungrily. Mouth full, he said, "I don't want to be God, *I'm just Bucky Glazer.*"

Mr. Glazer, who'd been quiet until now, said flatly, "Well, son, you're staying with that girl. You were married in our church—'Till death do you part.' What d'you think marriage is, a merry-go-round? You ride around a few times, then get off and go back to playing with the other boys? It's for *life.*"

Eating cherry cobbler, Bucky made a noise like a wounded animal.

Maybe your generation, old man. But not mine.

10

"Baby, I have to go."

Almost, she couldn't hear. Newsreel machine-gun fire. Newsreel music. *The March of Time.* They were at the movies. Every Friday night, at the movies. It was the cheapest entertainment; they could walk downtown holding hands like high school sweethearts. Gas was too expensive now. If you could get it. A low near-inaudible rumble as of distant thunder out of the mountains. A dry wind that scorched your eyeballs and nostrils. You wouldn't want to walk far in such dry aching air. Downtown to the Mission Hills Capitol was far enough. Maybe they were seeing *Confessions of a Nazi Spy*—suave sophisticated George Sanders and Edward G. Robinson with his stricken bulldog face. Robinson's liquidy dark eyes shimmering with emotion. Who could so swiftly summon hurt, rage, outrage, terror, and futility as Edward G. Robinson did? Except he was a smallish man, unconvincing as a lover. Not the Dark Prince. Not a man you'd die for. Or maybe, that night, they were seeing *Action in the North Atlantic* with Humphrey Bogart. Coarse-skinned pouchy-eyed Bogart. Always a cigarette between his fingers, smoke drifting across his battered face. Yet Bogart was handsome. In uniform, on the giant screen, all men were handsome. Or maybe, that evening, they'd gone to see *The Battle of the Beaches* or *Hitler's Children*. Bucky wanted to see them all. Or another Abbott and Costello comedy, or Bob Hope in *Caught in the Draft*. It was Norma Jeane's choice to see musicals: *Stage Door Canteen, Meet Me in St. Louis, All About Lovin' You*. But Bucky was bored with musicals, and Norma Jeane had to concede they were frothy and silly, as phony as the Land of Oz. "People don't break into song in real life," Bucky grumbled. "People don't start dancing, for Christ's sake, *there's no music*." Norma Jeane didn't want to point out that there was always music in the movies, even in Bucky's war movies, even in *The March of Time*. Norma Jeane didn't want to disagree with Bucky, who'd grown so thin-skinned lately. Edgy and irritable like a big handsome dog you'd want to stroke but dared not.

She knew but didn't know. For months. Before the wig and the black lace underwear and the *click! click!* of the camera she'd known. She'd heard the things Bucky muttered, the hints he made. Listening to war news on the radio every night during supper. Urgently reading *Life, Collier's, Time*, the local papers. Bucky, who read with difficulty, pushing his fingers beneath rows of print and sometimes moving his lips. He took down outdated newspaper maps from the walls of the apartment and taped up new maps. A new configuration of colored pins. He was distracted and impatient, making love. No sooner beginning than ending it. *Hey, Baby, I'm sorry! G'night*. Norma Jeane held him as he sank swiftly into sleep like a rock sinking to the soft mucky bottom of a lake. She knew he would go soon. The country was hemorrhaging men. It was fall 1943 and the war had lasted forever. It was winter 1944 and high school boys were worrying that the war would end before they could sign up. Sometimes, though less often now, Norma Jeane drifted into her old dreamy dreams of being a Red Cross nurse or a girl pilot.

A girl pilot! Women who were qualified to fly bombers weren't allowed to fly them. Women who died in service weren't allowed funerals with military honors like men.

Norma Jeane could understand: men had to have rewards for being men, for risking their lives as men, and these rewards were women. Women at home, waiting for their men. You couldn't have women fighting alongside men in the war, you couldn't have women-men. Women-men were freaks. Women-men were obscene. Women-men were lesbians, "lezzies." A normal man wanted to strangle a lezzie or fuck her till her brains spilled out and her cunt leaked blood. Norma Jeane had heard Bucky and his friends ranting about lezzies, who were worse, almost, than fairies, fags, "preverts." There was something about these sick, sorry freaks that made a normal healthy man want to lay hands on them and administer punishment.

Bucky, please don't hurt me, oh please.

Ol' Hirohito's skull on the console radio in the living room, Bucky no longer saw. As often, it seemed to Norma Jeane, Bucky no longer saw *her*. But Norma Jeane was aware of the "souvenir" and shuddered when she removed the scarf. *I didn't kill and behead you. I'm not the one to blame.*

Sometimes in her sleep she saw the gaping eye holes of the skull. The ugly nose hole, the grinning upper jaw. A smell of cigarette smoke, the sound of hot angry water rushing from a faucet.

Gotcha, Baby!

In one of the rear rows of the Mission Hills Capitol, Norma Jeane slipped her hand into Bucky's hand sticky from buttered popcorn. As if the moviehouse seats were a wild ride that could precipitate them both into danger.

Strange how, since she'd become Mrs. Bucky Glazer, Norma Jeane didn't care so much for the movies. They were so—*hopeful*. In the way that unreal things are hopeful. You bought a ticket, took your seat, and opened your eyes to—what? Sometimes during the movies her thoughts wandered. Tomorrow might be laundry day, and what was she going to make Bucky for supper? And Sunday: if she could get Bucky to go to church instead of sleeping in. Bess Glazer had made a veiled allusion to the "young couple" not attending Sunday services, and Norma Jeane knew her mother-in-law was blaming *her* for not getting Bucky to church. Bess Glazer had seen her pushing little Irina in her stroller the other afternoon and called her right afterward to express surprise—"Norma Jeane, how do you have *time*? For another woman's *baby*? I hope she's paying you, that's all I can say."

That evening *The March of Time* thundered. The marching music was so loud and thrilling your heartbeat quickened. This was real-life footage. This was *real*. For the war news Bucky sat bolt upright, staring at the screen. His jaws ceased their popcorn grinding. Norma Jeane watched with fascination and dread. There was brave crusty "Vinegar Joe" Stilwell, unshaven, muttering, "We got a hell of a beating." But the music soared and zoomed. The screen flashed with hurtling planes. Grainy-gray skies, a foreign soil below. Duels in the air above Burma! The fabulous Flying Tigers! Every man and boy in the Capitol yearned to be a Flying Tiger; every woman and girl yearned to love a Flying Tiger. They'd painted their old Curtiss P-40s to resemble cartoon sharks. They were daredevils, they were war heroes. They pitted their planes against the faster, more technically advanced Jap Zeros.

In a single dogfight over Rangoon, Tigers downed twenty of seventy-eight Japanese fighters—and lost none!

The audience applauded. There were isolated whistles. Norma Jeane's eyes filled with tears. Even Bucky wiped at his eyes. It was astonishing to see such action in the sky. Spurts of antiaircraft fire, stricken planes dropping to the ground streaming fire and smoke. You would think this was forbidden knowledge. The knowledge of another's death. You would think that death was sacred and private, but the war had changed all that. The movies had changed all that. It wasn't just that you gazed with detachment at another's death but you were granted a vision the dying didn't have of themselves. *The way God must see us. If God is watching.*

Bucky was gripping Norma Jeane's hand so hard it was all she could do to keep from wincing. In a low urgent voice he said what sounded like, "Baby, I got to go."

"Go—where?"

The men's room?

"I have to join up. Before it's too late."

Norma Jeane laughed, knowing he must be joking. Fiercely she kissed him. They'd always necked on their movie dates, just getting to know each other. The Flying Tigers were gone from the screen; now it was G.I. weddings. Grinning soldiers on furlough and abroad at bases. "The Wedding March" was being played loudly. So many weddings! So many brides—of all ages. The rapidity with which the wedding couples flashed upon the screen and vanished suggested comedy. Church ceremonies, civil ceremonies. Lavish surroundings, stark surroundings. So many radiant smiles, so many vigorous embraces. So many passionate kisses. So much *hope.* The audience tittered. War was noble but love, marriage, weddings were funny. Norma Jeane's hand was a scrambling little mouse in Bucky's crotch. Taken by surprise Bucky mumbled, "Mmmmm, Baby, not now. *Hey.*" But he turned to her, kissing her hard. Opened her mock-resisting lips to push his tongue deep into her mouth, and she sucked at him whimpering and clutching. He gripped her right breast in his left hand as he'd have gripped a football. Their seats rocked. They were panting like dogs. Behind them, a woman thumped at their seats, whispered, "You two go home if that's what you want to do." Norma Jeane turned on her, furious. "We're married. So leave us alone. *You* go home. *You go to hell.*"

Bucky laughed; suddenly his sweet-tempered wife was a spitfire!

Though afterward realizing *That was the beginning, I guess, that night.*

I I

"But—where? Where did she go? Why don't you know!"

With no warning, Harriet disappeared from Verdugo Gardens. In March 1944. Taking Irina with her. And leaving behind most of their shabby belongings.

Norma Jeane was panicked: what would she do without her baby?

It seemed to her, confused as in a dream, she'd taken her baby to Gladys and received Gladys's blessing. But now there was no baby. There would be no blessing.

A half-dozen times Norma Jeane knocked on her neighbors' door. But Harriet's apartment mates were baffled too. And worried.

No one seemed to know where the depressed woman had gone with her little girl. Not back to her family in Sacramento, and not to her in-laws in Washington State. Her friends told Norma Jeane that Harriet had left without saying goodbye and without leaving a farewell note. She'd left having paid her share of the rent through March. She'd been thinking of "disappearing" for a long time. She "wasn't cut out to be a widow," she'd said.

She'd been "sick" too. She'd tried to hurt Irina. Maybe in fact she had hurt Irina in some way that didn't show.

Norma Jeane backed away, eyes narrowed. "No. That isn't true. I would have seen it. You shouldn't say such things. Harriet was my friend."

It made no sense that Harriet would leave without saying goodbye to Norma Jeane. Without having Irina say goodbye. *She would not. Not Harriet. God would not let her.*

"H-hello? I w-w-want to report a m-missing p-person. A m-mother and a b-b-baby."

Norma Jeane telephoned the Mission Hills police department but stammered so badly she had to hang up. Knowing it would do little good anyway, for Harriet had obviously left of her own volition. Harriet was an adult woman and Harriet was Irina's birth mother, and though Norma Jeane loved Irina more than Harriet loved her, and believed that love was reciprocated, there was nothing, there was absolutely nothing to be done.

Harriet and Irina had vanished from Norma Jeane's life as if they had never been. Irina's father was still officially "missing in action." His bones would never be found. Maybe the Japs had taken his head? When Norma Jeane concentrated with all her strength she saw a story taking place in a faraway room, unless it was a dream Norma Jeane couldn't see clearly, in which Harriet was bathing Irina in scalding water and Irina was screaming in pain and terror and there was no one but Norma Jeane to save Irina but Norma Jeane ran helplessly, trying to locate the room, up and down a doorless steamy corridor grinding her teeth in desperation and fury.

Waking, Norma Jeane crept into the cubbyhole of a bathroom, the blinding light overhead. She was so scared she crawled into the tub. Her teeth were chattering. Her skin tingled and smarted from the hot, hot water. This was where Bucky would discover her at 6 A.M. He'd have lifted her in the crook of his muscular arm and carried her off to bed except *the way she was looking at me, her eyes all pupil like an animal's, I knew not to touch her.*

12

"It's history, now. The time we're in."

There came then the day. Norma Jeane was prepared, almost.

Bucky informed her he'd enlisted that morning in the merchant marine. He informed her he'd probably be shipped out within six weeks. To Australia, he thought. Japan would soon be invaded, and the war would end. He'd been wanting to enlist for a long time, as he guessed she knew.

He told her this didn't mean he didn't love her because he did love her like crazy. He told her it didn't mean he wasn't happy, *he was happy. He was the happiest he'd ever been.* Except he wanted more from his life than just a honeymoon.

You're living in a time of history; if you're a man you have got to do your share. You have got to serve your country.

Hell, Bucky knew this sounded corny. But that's the way he felt.

He could see the pain in Norma Jeane's face. Her eyes swelling with tears. He felt sick with guilt yet triumphant too. Elated! He'd done it, and he was going; he was almost free! It wasn't just Norma Jeane but Mission Hills, where he'd lived all his life, his folks breathing down his neck, the Lockheed factory, where he was stuck in the machine shop, the sour stink of the embalming room. *I sure wasn't going to wind up being an embalmer! Not this boy.*

Norma Jeane surprised him with her composure. Saying only, sadly, "Oh, Bucky. Oh, Daddy. I understand." He grabbed her and held her, and suddenly they were both crying. Bucky Glazer, who never cried! Even when his ankle was broken on the football field, senior year. They knelt on the bumpy linoleum floor of the kitchen Norma Jeane kept so polished and clean and they prayed together. Then Bucky lifted Norma Jeane and carried her into the bedroom sobbing, her arms tight around his neck. That was the first day.

Out of a deep exhausted sleep after his Lockheed shift he was wakened by a child's clumsy fingers stroking his cock. In his dream the child laughed at him, the look of disgust on his face, for Bucky was in his football jersey, and his buttocks were naked, and they were in a public place, plenty of people were watching, so Bucky shoved at the child and managed to shake himself free and to his astonishment there was Norma Jeane panting beside him in the dark, stroking and pulling at Big Thing, her warm thigh over his as she pushed her belly and groin against him, moaning *Oh, Daddy! Oh, Daddy!* It was a baby she wanted, the hairs stirred on the back of Bucky's neck, the naked moaning female beside him single-minded in her desire, an impersonal desire chill and pitiless as any force bearing him onward to his possible death in the unimaginable dark waters of what he knew no better than to call history. Bucky pushed Norma Jeane roughly away, telling her to leave him alone, let him sleep for Christ's sake, he had to get up at 6 A.M. Norma Jeane seemed not to hear. She clutched at him, kissing him wildly; he shook her off, now like an animal in heat, a naked animal in heat, repulsive to him. His cock, erect while he'd been dreaming, was wilting now; Bucky shielded his groin, swung his legs off the bed, and switched on the lamp: 4:40 A.M. He cursed Norma Jeane again. The light exposed her hunched over, panting, her left breast hanging out of her nightie, face flushed and eyes dilated as he remembered them from the other night. *As if this was her night self. Her night twin I wasn't supposed to see. That she herself didn't see, knew nothing of.*

He was groggy, and he was shaken, but Bucky managed to say almost reasonably, "God damn, Norma Jeane! I thought we went through this yesterday. I'm *in*. I'm *going*." Norma Jeane cried, "No, Daddy! You can't leave me. I'll die if you leave me." "You aren't going to die any more than anybody else is going to die," Bucky said, wiping his face on a sheet. "Just calm down and you'll be OK." But Norma Jeane didn't hear. She was clutching at him, moaning, her breasts pressed against his sweaty chest. Bucky shivered in disgust. He'd never liked aggressive, sexy women, he'd never have married one; he'd thought he was marrying this sweet shy virgin—"And look at you." Norma Jeane then tried to straddle him, smacking her thighs against his, not hearing him or, if hearing, ignoring him, coiled tense and quivering, and he was yet more disgusted, shouting in her face, "Stop it! Stop it! You sad, sick cow." Norma Jeane ran from him and into the kitchen; he heard her sobbing, banging around in the dark; dear Christ he had no choice but to follow her, switching on the light and there she was with a knife in her hand, like a deranged girl in a melodramatic movie, except she didn't look like anyone you'd see in any movie, and the way she was stabbing at herself, at her bare forearm, wasn't what you'd see in any movie. Bucky rushed at her, fully awake now, and grabbed the knife out of her fingers. "Norma Jeane! Je-*sus.*" She'd been serious: she'd cut her arm, it was bleeding, a bright bracelet of blood, astonishing to Bucky, he'd remember it as one of the horrific revelations of his civilian life, until that moment an American boy's life, innocent and seemingly inviolable.

So Bucky stanched the blood with a kitchen towel. Half carried Norma Jeane into the bathroom, where tenderly he washed the shallow, smarting wounds, a surprise it seemed to someone who was accustomed to chill bodies that could not bleed no matter how stuck or jabbed or lacerated; he soothed Norma Jeane as you'd soothe a small distressed child and Norma Jeane wept quietly now, the wildness drained from her; she leaned against him murmuring, "Oh, Daddy, Daddy, I love you so, Daddy, I'm sorry, I won't be bad again, Daddy, I promise, do you love me, Daddy? Do you love me?" and Bucky kissed her, murmuring, "Sure I love you, Baby, y'know I love you, I married you, didn't I?"—putting iodine on the cuts, and gauze bandages, and tenderly then he half carried her unresisting back to their bed of churned sheets and creased pillows, where he held her in his arms, soothing and comforting her until by degrees like an exhausted child she sobbed herself to sleep and Bucky lay open-eyed, nerves jangling with misery yet in a kind of fearful elation, until it was 6 A.M. and time to slip away from her— who would continue to sleep slack-mouthed, breathing thickly as if comatose, and what a relief to Bucky! what a relief to shower her smell off him, the stickiness of her body! to shower and shave and take himself in the chill invigorating twilight of early morning to the merchant marine facility on Catalina Island to report to his assignment amid a world of men like himself. And that was the beginning of the second day.

13

"Bucky, darling—goodbye!"

On a balmy day in late April the Glazers and Norma Jeane saw Bucky off on the freighter *Liberty* bound for Australia. The precise terms of Bucky's first assignment were classified, and it wasn't yet known when he might be furloughed back to the States. Eight months at the earliest. There was talk of an invasion of Japan. Now she would have a blue star to place proudly in her window like other servicemen's wives and mothers. She smiled and was brave. She was looking "very sweet and very pretty" in a blue cotton shirtwaist, white high-heeled pumps, and a white gardenia in her curly hair so that Bucky, hugging her repeatedly, tears spilling down his cheeks, could inhale the sweet fragrance and would recall it, aboard the freighter amid men, as Norma Jeane's own.

It's history. What happens to us. No one to blame.

It wasn't Norma Jeane but Mrs. Glazer who was most emotional that morning, weeping and sniffing and complaining in the car as Mr. Glazer drove them from Mission Hills to the boat for Catalina. In the backseat Norma Jeane sat awkwardly wedged between Bucky's older brother Joe and his older sister Lorraine. The Glazers' words swirled about her head like gnats. Norma Jeane, numbed, faintly smiling, wasn't required to listen to most Glazer talk and wasn't required to respond. *She was sweet but practically a dummy. Except for her looks nobody'd have known she was there.* Norma Jeane was thinking that in a normal family there is rarely silence such as the silence that existed between Gladys and her. She was thinking calmly that she'd never belonged to any true family and it was being revealed now that she'd never belonged to the Glazers, though there was the polite pretense and she meant to be polite in return. The Glazers would praise her, in her hearing, for being "strong," "mature." For being "a good wife to Bucky." Possibly from Bucky they'd been hearing about her emotional episodes in the recent past, what Bucky was cruel enough to call female hysteria. But as actual eyewitnesses scrutinizing her carefully, the Glazers had to approve of Norma Jeane. *That girl grew up fast! Her and Bucky both.*

Saying goodbye to Bucky Glazer in his merchant marine uniform, his hair trimmed brutally short so that his boyish face looked almost gaunt. His eyes glistened with excitement and fear. He'd nicked himself shaving. He'd been away at the training camp only a short while but already he seemed older, different. Self-consciously he hugged his weeping mother, and his sisters, and his father, and his brother, but mostly he hugged Norma Jeane. Murmuring almost in anguish, "Baby I love you. Baby, write to me every day, OK? Baby, I'm gonna miss you." In her ear hotly he whispered, "Big Thing's gonna miss Little Thing, for sure!" Norma Jeane made a startled sound like giggling. Oh, what if the others overheard! Bucky was saying that, when the war was over, when he came home, they'd start their family—"As many kids as you want, Norma Jeane. You're the boss." He began kissing her the way a boy might kiss, hot wet smacky kisses, anxious kisses. The Glazers edged away to allow the young couple privacy, not that there was much privacy on the pier at Catalina that balmy morning in April 1944 as the freighter *Liberty* was preparing to ship out to Australia, one of a convoy of merchant marine freighters. Norma Jeane was thinking what good luck, the merchant marine wasn't a branch of the U.S. Armed Services as most people probably thought. The *Liberty* wasn't a warship and didn't carry bombers and Bucky would not be armed, Bucky would never be sent "into action" or "into combat." What had happened to Harriet's husband and to so many other husbands could not happen to him. That merchant marine freighters were continually being attacked by enemy submarines and planes was a fact she seemed not to acknowledge. She would say to whomever inquired, "My husband isn't *armed*. The merchant marine just carries *supplies*."

On the way back to Mission Hills, Mrs. Glazer sat in the backseat with Lorraine and Norma Jeane. She'd removed her hat and her gloves and gripped Norma Jeane's icy fingers, understanding that her daughter-in-law was in a state of shock. She'd ceased weeping but her voice was hoarse with emotion. "You can move in with us, dear. You're our daughter now."

WAR

"I'm nobody's daughter now. I'm through with that."

She didn't move in with the Glazers in Mission Hills. She didn't remain in Verdugo Gardens. The week following Bucky's departure on the *Liberty* she got an assembly-line job at Radio Plane Aircraft fifteen miles to the east in Burbank. She rented a furnished room in a boardinghouse near the trolley line and she was living alone by the time of her eighteenth birthday when the thought came to her as she lay exhausted, sinking into a dreamless sleep, *Norma Jeane Baker is no longer a ward of L.A. County*. The following morning the thought came to her yet more powerfully, like a flash of heat lightning illuminating a dark bruise of a storm sky above the San Gabriel Mountains, *Was that why I married Bucky Glazer?*

Amid a thunderous clatter of machinery at the aircraft factory beginning then to tell herself the story of why she'd become engaged at fifteen and dropped out of high school to marry at sixteen. And why in terror and exhilaration she was now living by herself for the first time in her life at eighteen, perceiving that her life would only now begin. And this she knew to be because of the War.

If there is no Evil
yet there is War
is War not-evil?
Is Evil not-War?

There came the day at Radio Plane when she who rarely read newspapers out of superstition overheard some of her female co-workers in the lunchroom talking of an event reported in the *L.A. Times*, one of the smaller front-page headlines below the usual war headlines, and a small accompanying photograph of an ecstatically smiling woman in white, and she stopped dead in her tracks and stared at the paper one of the women was holding and must have looked stricken for the women asked what was wrong and she stammered a vague reply nothing was wrong, the women's eyes sharp as icepicks upon her, scrutinizing and judging and not liking this young married girl so secretive-seeming and her shyness mistaken for aloofness and her fastidiousness about hair, makeup, clothes mistaken for vanity and her desperate zeal not to fail at her job mistaken for a predatory female wish merely to ingratiate herself with the male foreman, and she retreated in confusion and embarrassment knowing the women would laugh cruelly as soon as she was out of earshot, mimicking her stammer and hushed little-girl voice, and that evening she bought a copy of the *Times* to read in fascinated horror—

EVANGELIST McPHERSON DIES
CORONER RULES DRUG OVERDOSE

Aimee Semple McPherson was dead! Founder of the International Church of the Foursquare Gospel in Los Angeles where eighteen years before Grandma Della had taken the infant Norma Jeane to be baptized in the Christian faith. Aimee Semple McPherson, who'd long since been exposed and humbled as a fraud, her fortune of millions of dollars built upon hypocrisy and venality. Aimee Semple McPherson, whose very name was now notorious where once she'd been one of the most famous and admired women in America. Aimee Semple McPherson, a suicide! Norma Jeane's mouth had gone dry. She was standing at the trolley stop, hardly able to concentrate on the article. *I would not think that it meant anything, that the woman who baptized me had taken her own life. That the Christian faith might be no more than an item of clothing hastily slipped on, to be hastily slipped off and discarded.*

"But you're Bucky's *wife*. You can't just live *alone*."
The Glazers were shocked. The Glazers were severely disapproving and

angry. Norma Jeane shut her eyes, seeing a dreamlike succession of hypnotic days in her mother-in-law's kitchen amid gleaming utensils and a spick-and-span linoleum floor, smelling the rich odors of simmering stews and soups, roasting meats, baking bread and cakes. The comforting chatter of an older woman's voice. *Norma Jeane, dear, will you help me with this?* Onions to be chopped, baking pans to be greased. Stacks of dirtied plates after Sunday dinner to be scraped clean, rinsed and washed and dried. She shut her eyes, seeing a girl smiling as she washed dishes, arms sunk to her elbows in sparkling Ivory suds. A girl smiling lost in concentration running a carpet sweeper carefully over the living room and dining room carpets, dumping bundles of soiled laundry into the washing machine in the dank-smelling cellar, helping Mrs. Glazer to hang clothing on the line, to remove clothing from the line, to iron, to fold, to put away in drawers, in closets, and on shelves. A girl in a pretty starched shirtwaist dress, a hat and white gloves and high-heeled pumps, no silk stockings but carefully with an eyebrow pencil she'd drawn "seams" on the backs of her legs to simulate stocking seams in this time of war deprivation. Entering the Church of Christ with her in-laws, so many of them. The Glazers. *Is that—? Yes, the younger son's wife. Living with them while he's overseas.*

"But I'm not your daughter. I'm nobody's daughter now."

Still, she wore the Glazer rings. It was her truest intention to remain faithful to her husband.

You sad, sick cow.

Except living alone in her furnished room in Burbank in even such cramped shabby quarters and having to share a bathroom with two other boarders, living alone in this place new and strange to her where no one knew her, sometimes Norma Jeane laughed aloud in startled happiness. She was free! She was alone! For the first time in her life truly alone. Not an orphan. Not a foster child. Not a daughter, or a daughter-in-law, or a wife. It was a luxury to her. It felt like theft. She was *a working girl* now. She brought home a weekly salary, she was paid by check, she cashed her checks in a bank like any adult. Before she'd been hired at Radio Plane Aircraft she'd applied to several other small nonunion factories and they'd turned her down for lack of experience and being too young and even at Radio Plane they'd initially turned her down, but she'd insisted *Please give me a chance! Please.* Terrified, and her heart hammering, yet stubbornly insisting standing on tiptoe and straight-backed to display her healthy young capable body *I k-know I can do it, I'm strong and I don't get tired ever. I don't!* And they'd hired her, and so it was true: quickly she learned the mechanics of assembly-line work, robot-mechanical work, for how like the routine of housework it was except amid a clamorous exterior world of other people, a world in which if you worked hard you would be perceived as more efficient, more intelligent, and therefore more valuable than your co-workers, the watchful eye of the foreman upon you, and beyond him the plant manager, and beyond him the bosses known only by name, and those names never uttered by machine-shop workers like Norma Jeane. And returning home by trolley after her eight-hour shift, staggering with exhaustion yet like a greedy child counting up in her head the money she'd earned, less than seven dollars after taxes and social security but it was hers, to spend or to save if she could. Returning then to her quiet room, where no one awaited her except her Magic Friend in the mirror, a faint headache; very hungry, she was required to prepare no elaborate enormous meal for a famished husband but most evenings just Campbell's soup heated out of a can, and how delicious this hot soup, and maybe a piece of white bread with jelly, a banana or an orange, a glass of warmed milk. Falling then into her bed, which was a narrow cot of a bed with a mattress an inch thick, a girl's bed again. She hoped to be too tired to dream and often this was the case, or seemed so, yet sometimes she wandered confused through the unexpectedly long and unfamiliar corridors of the orphanage to find herself swinging on a swing in the sandy playground she would have said she'd forgotten, and a presence on the far side of the wire-mesh fence, was it him? the Dark Prince coming for her? and she hadn't seen him at the time, had not acknowledged; wandering then on La Mesa only partly clothed in her underpants, seeking the apartment building in which she and Mother were living yet unable to find it, unable to utter aloud the magic words that would bring her to it—THE HACIENDA. She was a child in the time of *Once upon a time*. She was Norma Jeane looking for her mother. Yet she was not a child truly for she'd been made a married woman. The secret place between her legs had been rent and bloodied and claimed by the Dark Prince.

My heart was broken. I cried and cried. When he left I considered how I might injure myself in righteous punishment. For the stab wounds in my arm swiftly healed, I was so healthy. Yet living alone she discovered she had no need to change towels more than once a week, if that frequently. She had no need to change the sheets on her bed more than once a week, if that frequently. For there was no vigorous sweaty young husband to soil them, and Norma Jeane kept herself scrupulously clean washing and bathing as often as she could, frequently washing out her nightie, underwear, and cotton stockings by hand. She had no carpet in her room, therefore no need of a carpet sweeper; once a week she borrowed her landlady's broom and always returned it promptly. She had no stove, no oven, to be kept scoured and clean. There were few surfaces in the room apart from the windowsills that could collect dust, so she had little need of dusting. (She smiled to recall ol' Hirohito. She'd escaped him!) When she gave up the apartment in Verdugo Gardens she'd left behind most of the household belongings for the Glazers to take away and keep at their house; the belief was, Bucky's family was "storing" these things until Bucky returned. But Norma Jeane knew that Bucky would never return.

At least not to her.

If you loved me you would not have left me
If you left me you did not love me

Except that people were dying and being injured and the world filling up with smoldering rubble, Norma Jeane liked the War. The War was as steady and reliable as hunger or sleep. Always, the War was *there*. You could talk about the War with any stranger. The War was a radio program that went on and on. The War was a dream dreamt by everyone. You could never be lonely during the War. Since December 7, 1941, when the Japanese bombed Pearl Harbor, for years there would be no loneliness. On the trolley, on the street, in stores, at work, and at any time you could ask with apprehension or eagerness or in a matter-of-fact voice *Did anything happen today?* for always something would have happened or might be going to happen. There were battles being "waged" in Europe and in the Pacific continuously. News was either good or bad. You would immediately rejoice with another person, or you would be saddened or upset with another person. Strangers wept together. Everyone listened. Everyone had an opinion.

After dusk, like an approaching dream, the world dimmed for everyone. This was a magic time, Norma Jeane thought. Car headlights were shuttered, lighted windows were forbidden and lighted marquees. There were earsplitting air raid warnings. There were false alarms, rumors of imminent invasion. Always there were food shortages and other shortages to complain of. There were black market rumors. Norma Jeane in her Radio Plane work clothes, slacks, shirt, and sweater, and her hair neatly tied back in a scarf, found herself talking to strangers with surprising ease. She'd been miserably self-conscious and inclined to stammering with her in-laws, sometimes even with her husband if he was in one of his picky moods, but rarely did she stammer with friendly strangers; and most strangers were friendly. Especially, men were friendly. Norma Jeane could see that men were attracted to her, even men old enough to be grandpappies; she recognized that intense warm staring look in the eyes that signaled desire, and this was comforting to her. So long as she was in a public place. For if they asked would she like to go out to dinner? to the movies? she could quietly indicate her rings. If she was asked about her husband she could quietly say, "He's overseas. In Australia." Sometimes she heard herself say he was "lost in action" in New Guinea, and sometimes she heard herself say he'd been "killed in combat" on Iwo Jima.

But mostly strangers wanted to talk about the ways in which the War had touched *their* lives. *If only the damned war would end* they said bitterly. But Norma Jeane thought *If only the War would go on forever*.

For her job at Radio Plane depended upon there being a shortage of male workers. Because of the War there were women truck drivers, women trolley conductors, women garbage collectors, women crane operators, and even roofers and painters and groundskeepers. There were women in uniform everywhere you looked. At Radio Plane, Norma Jeane calculated there must be eight or nine women to each man—except on the managerial level, of course, where there were no women. She owed her job to the War, she owed her freedom to the War. She owed her salary to the War and already within three months of working at Radio Plane she was promoted and given a twenty-five-cent-an-hour raise. She'd performed so skillfully on the assembly line, she was selected for more demanding work that involved coating airplane fuselages with a liquid plastic "dope." The smell was powerful and faintly nauseating. The smell penetrated her brain. Minuscule bubbles in her brain like champagne bubbles. The blood drained out of Norma Jeane's face and her eyes seemed to lose focus. "You'd better get some fresh air, Norma Jeane," the foreman said, but Norma Jeane said quickly, "I don't have time! I don't have time"—giggling and wiping at her eyes—"I don't have time." She was having trouble with her tongue, which seemed too large for her mouth. In terror of failing at her new job and being sent back to the assembly line or fired and sent home. For she had no home. For her husband had left her. *You sad, sick cow*. She dared not fail, and would not fail. At last the foreman took her arm to escort her out of the "dope" room and Norma Jeane took deep breaths of fresh air at a window but almost immediately returned to her work, insisting that she was fine. Her hands moved deftly with an intelligence of their own that would increase gradually with the hours, days, weeks even as her tolerance for the chemical mixture increased. As she'd been told—"Sometimes you'll hardly smell the stink." (Though her hair and clothes smelled of it, she knew. So she had to be extra careful, to wash thoroughly and to air out her clothes.) She did not want to consider that the fumes were permeating her skin, her nasal passages, her lungs, and her brain. She was proud of having been promoted so quickly and of being given a raise, and her hope was to be promoted yet again and given yet another raise. She impressed her foreman as a hard worker, a serious young woman who could be trusted with serious work.

She looked like a girl, but she did not act like a girl. Not at Radio Plane! Building navy bombers to be flown against the enemy. She perceived the factory as a kind of race, and she was a runner in this race, and in high school she'd been one of the fastest girl runners, she'd won a medal of which she was proud, though when she sent the medal to Gladys at Norwalk, Gladys never replied. (In a dream she'd seen Gladys wearing the medal pinned to the collar of her green hospital shift. Could it be possible this dream was real? *She would not give in* and she did not give in.)

That November morning, spraying dope and combating a sensation of light-headedness, she feared her period coming early for now to keep her job she had to take as many aspirins as she dared for her cramps, knowing it was wrong, knowing she could not heal herself if she succumbed to such weakness, and even then was forced to take one or two sick days, to her shame. That November morning spraying dope and determined not to be sick, or to faint, though the tiny bubbles in her brain were more distracting than usual and suddenly smiling she was able to see a delirious and seductive future.

The Dark Prince in formal black attire and Norma Jeane who was the Fair Princess in a long white dress of some shimmering material. Walking hand in hand on the beach at sunset. Norma Jeane's hair blew in the wind. It was the pale platinum-blond hair of Jean Harlow who'd died it was said because her Christian Science mother had refused to call a doctor for her when she was deathly ill only twenty-six years old but Norma Jeane knew better, for you only die out of your own weakness and she would not be weak. The Dark Prince paused to slip his jacket around her shoulders. Gently he kissed her lips. Music began, romantic dance music. The Dark Prince and Norma Jeane began to dance yet soon Norma Jeane surprised her lover. She kicked off her shoes and her bare feet sank into the damp sand and what a delicious sensation Norma Jeane felt, dancing as the surf crashed about her legs! The Dark Prince stared at her in astonishment for she was so much more beautiful than any woman he'd ever known, and even as he stared she eluded him, lifting her arms and her arms became wings and suddenly she was a beautiful white-feathered bird soaring higher, higher, higher until the Dark Prince himself was a mere figure on the beach amid crashing frothy waves looking after her in the wonderment of loss.

Squinting then, Norma Jeane looked up from her gloved hands gripping the dope canister to see a man watching her from the doorway. It was the Dark Prince, a camera in his hands.

PINUP 1945

Your life outside the stage is not your accidental life.
It will be defined as inevitable.

—From *The Actor's Handbook*
and the Actor's Life

Through that first year of wonders breaking upon her like the harsh stinging surf on the beach at Santa Monica when she'd been a child she would hear the calm metronome of that voice. *Wherever you are, I'm there. Even before you get to the place where you are going I'm already there, waiting.*

The look on Glazer's face! His buddies on the *Liberty* would rag the kid mercilessly how he'd been leafing through the December '44 *Stars & Stripes* with this peeved, bored expression until turning a page he stared, bug-eyed, and his jaw truly *dropped*. Whatever was in those pulp pages had the effect on Glazer like an electric shock might've had. Then this croaking noise from him, "Jesus. My wife. *This is my w-wife!*" The magazine was snatched from him. Everybody gawking at GIRL DEFENSE WORKERS ON THE HOME FRONT and this full-page photo of the sweetest-faced girl you'd ever seen, darkish curls springing out around her head, beautiful wistful eyes and moist lips in a shy-hopeful smile, she's wearing a denim coverall snug on her young sizable breasts and her amazing hips, with little-girl awkwardness she's holding a canister in both hands as if to spray the camera.

Norma Jeane works a nine-hour shift at Radio Plane Aircraft,
Burbank, California. She is proud of her work in the war effort—

*"Hard work but I love it!" Above, Norma Jeane in the fuselage
assembly room. Left, Norma Jeane in a pensive moment thinking of
her husband, Merchant Marine Seaman Recruit Buchanan Glaser,
currently stationed in the South Pacific.*

Ragging the poor kid, teasing him—the name was printed Glaser not
Glazer, how's he so sure this little girl is his wife?—and there's a struggle
over the magazine, almost it gets ripped, Glazer rushes over glaring-eyed and
excited—"You fucks! Cut it out! Gimme that! *That's mine!*"

And there was the March 1945 issue of *Pageant* confiscated from a sniggering cadre of boys in Sidney Haring's English class at Van Nuys High,
tossed cavalierly into Haring's desk without a second glance until sometime
later that day in private Haring examined it, leafed through it to where the
boys, dirty-minded he didn't doubt, had earmarked a page, and suddenly
Haring pushed his glasses against the bridge of his nose to stare, in astonishment—"Norma Jeane!" He recognized the girl at once despite her heavy
makeup and sexy pose, head tilted to one side, dark-lipsticked mouth open
in a drunken-dreamy smile, eyes half shut in ludicrous ecstasy. She was wearing what appeared to be a near-transparent ruffled nightie to mid-thigh, and
high-heeled shoes, and she was clutching beneath her strangely pointed
breasts what appeared to be a dumbly smiling stuffed panda: *Ready for a
cold winter night's warm cuddle?* Haring had begun to breathe through his
mouth. His eyesight was blurred by moisture. "Norma *Jeane*. My *God*." He
stared and stared. He felt a flush of shame. This was his fault, he knew. He
might have saved her. Might have helped her. How? He might have tried.
Tried harder. He might have *done something*. What? Protest her marrying
so young? Maybe she'd been pregnant. Maybe she'd had to get married.
Could he have married her himself? He was already married. The girl only
had been fifteen then. He'd been powerless, and it had been wisest to keep
his distance. He'd done the wise thing. Throughout his life, he'd done the
wise thing. Even getting crippled was a wise thing; he'd avoided the draft.
He had young children, and he had a wife. He loved his family. They
depended on him. Every year there were girls in his classes. Foster children,
orphans. Mistreated girls. Yearning-eyed girls. Girls who looked to Mr. Haring for guidance. For approval. For love. You can't help it, you're a high
school teacher, a man, relatively young. The War made it all more intense.
The War was a wild erotic dream. If you were a man. Perceived to be a man.
He couldn't save them all, could he? And he'd lose his job. Norma Jeane had
been a foster child. There was a doom in that. Her mother had been sick—
exactly in what way he couldn't remember. Her father had been—what?
Dead. What could *he* have done? Nothing. What he'd done, which was noth-

ing, was all he *could* do. *Save yourself. Never touch them.* He wasn't proud
of his behavior, but he had no reason to be ashamed either. Why ashamed?
He was not. Yet glancing guiltily toward the door of his classroom (it was
after school, no one was likely to barge in, yet a stray student or colleague
might look through the glass panel in the door) he tore the page out, discarded the copy of *Pageant* by shoving it into a used manila envelope (so the
janitor wouldn't take notice) and that envelope into his wastebasket. *Ready
for a cold winter night's warm cuddle?* Haring took care not to wrinkle the
full-page photo of his former student but slipped it into a folder kept at the
bottom of his bottom drawer, along with a half-dozen handwritten poems
the girl had written to him.

I know that I could never be blue.
If I could love you.

And there in February was Detective Frank Widdoes of the Culver City Police
Department searching the pigsty trailer home of a murder suspect—to be precise, a suspect in a sensational case of rape-murder, rape-mutilation-
murder, rape-mutilation-murder-dismemberment. Widdoes and his fellow
cops knew for sure they had their man, the bastard was guilty as all hell; now
they needed physical evidence linking him to the dead girl (she'd been missing
for several days, then found, dismembered, in a landfill in Culver City, a resident of West Hollywood and a Susan Hayward look-alike under contract to
one of the film studios but she'd been recently dropped and somehow met up
with this sicko and that was the end of her) and Widdoes was holding his nose
with one hand and with the other looking through a pile of girlie magazines,
and there in *Pix*, where the magazine was folded open to a two-page feature
he happened to see—"Jesus Christ! That girl." Widdoes was one of those legendary detectives who in the movies never forgets a face and never forgets a
name. "Norma Jeane—what? Baker." She was posed in a tight-fitting one-
piece swimsuit, which showed practically everything she had and left just
enough to the imagination, and ludicrous high heels; one of the shots was
frontal and the other the Betty Grable pinup stance, the girl peering coyly over
her shoulder at the viewer, hands on her hips, with a wink; there were bows
on the swimsuit and in the girl's hair, which was a darkish mass of shellacked-
looking curls, and the girl's still-childlike face appeared hardened with
makeup thick as a crust. In the full-front pose she was holding a beach ball
provocatively out to the viewer, a silly-simpering expression on her face and
lips pursed for a kiss. *What's the best cure for midwinter blues? Our Miss February knows.* Widdoes felt a dull pain in his heart. Not like a bullet but like
he'd been hit by a blank wadded-up piece of cardboard out of a gun barrel.

His partner asked him what he'd found over there, and Widdoes said savagely, "What d'you think I'm finding? In a shithole you find shit."

The copy of *Pix* he unobtrusively rolled up and stuck into an inside pocket of his coat for safekeeping.

And not long afterward in his trailer office back of the smoldering junkyard on Reseda was Warren Pirig, a cigarette burning fiercely in his mouth as he stared at the glossy cover of the new *Swank*. The cover! "Norma Jeane? Jesus." There was his girl. The one he'd given up and he'd never once touched. The one he still remembered, sometimes. Except she was changed, older, staring back at him as if now she knew the score. And liked what she knew. She was wearing a damp-looking white T-shirt with the words *USS Swank* across the front and high-heeled red shoes and that was all: the tight-fitting T-shirt to her thighs. Her darkish-blond hair had been swept atop her head and a few stray curls hung down. You could tell she wasn't wearing a bra, her breasts were so round and soft-looking. The way the T-shirt clung to her hips and pelvis, you'd conclude she wasn't wearing panties either. A flush came over Warren's face. He sat up abruptly at the battered old desk, his feet striking the floor hard. Last he'd heard from Elsie, Norma Jeane was married and moved away to Mission Hills and her husband was overseas. Never had Warren inquired after Norma Jeane since then, nor did Elsie volunteer information. And now this! The cover of *Swank* and two pages inside of similar shots in the white T-shirt. Showing her tits and ass like a whore. Warren felt a stabbing desire and at the same time a profound disgust, as if he'd bitten into something rotten. "God damn. I blame *her*." He meant Elsie. She'd broken up their family. His fingers twitched with the impulse to do hurt.

Still, he took care to preserve this special issue of *Swank*, March 1945, hiding it in his desk drawer beneath old financial records.

In Mayer's Drugs, with no warning, one April morning she would long remember (the eve of the death of Franklin Delano Roosevelt), Elsie heard Irma calling to her excitedly and went to see the new issue of *Parade* her friend was waving—"It's her, isn't it? That girl of yours? The one who got married a couple of years ago? Look!" Elsie stared into the opened magazine. There was Norma Jeane! Her hair had been plaited like Judy Garland's in *The Wizard of Oz* and she wore snug corduroy slacks and a powder-blue "hand-knit sweater set" and she was swinging on a country gate, smiling happily; in the background were horses browsing in a pasture. Norma Jeane was very young and very pretty but if you looked closely, as Elsie did, you could see the tension in that bright, broad smile. The girl's cheeks were dimpled with the strain. *Spring in the beautiful San Fernando Valley! For instructions on how to knit this charming sweater set in cotton wool, see p. 89.* Elsie was so stunned, she left Mayer's without paying for the magazine. Drove straight to Mission Hills to see Bess Glazer, without taking time to telephone beforehand. "Bess! Look! Look at this! Did you know about this? See who it is!"—thrusting the copy of *Parade* into the older woman's startled face. Bess saw it and frowned; she was surprised, yes, but not very surprised. "Oh, her. Well." To Elsie's bewilderment, Bess said nothing more, but led her through the house and into the kitchen, where, out of a drawer beside the stove, she retrieved the December 1944 issue of *Stars & Stripes* with the feature GIRL DEFENSE WORKERS ON THE HOME FRONT. And there was Norma Jeane—again! Elsie felt as if she'd been kicked in the belly—again. She sank onto a chair staring at Norma Jeane, her own daughter, her girl!— in snug-fitting coveralls, smiling at the camera in a way Norma Jeane had never smiled at anyone, so far as Elsie could recall, in real life. *As if whoever it was held that camera was her closest friend. Or maybe it was the camera that was her closest friend.* A wave of emotion washed over Elsie: confusion, hurt, shame, pride. Why hadn't Norma Jeane shared this wonderful news with *her?* Bess was saying, with her sour-prune look, "Bucky sent this home. He's proud of it, I guess." Elsie said, "You mean you're *not?*" Bess said huffily, "Proud of such a thing? Of course not. The Glazers think it's shameful." Elsie was shaking her head indignantly. "*I* think it's wonderful. *I'm* proud. Norma Jeane's going to be a model, a movie star! You just wait." Bess said, "She's supposed to be my son's *wife.* Her wedding vows come *first.*"

Elsie didn't storm out of the house; she stayed, and Bess made coffee, and the women talked and had a good cry over their lost Norma Jeane.

FOR HIRE

For the true actor, every role is an opportunity.
There are no minor roles.

—From *The Actor's Handbook*
and the Actor's Life

She was Miss Aluminum Products 1945, her first week with the Preene Agency. In a tight-fitting white pleated nylon dress with a dipping neckline, strands of costume pearls and pearl button earrings, white high heels, and elbow-length white gloves, a creamy white gardenia in her "highlighted" shoulder-length hair. A four-day convention in downtown Los Angeles, where she was required to stand for hours on an elevated platform amid a display of gleaming aluminum household products, passing out brochures to interested parties—mainly men. Paid $12 a day with (minimal) meals and carfare included.

Her second week, she was Miss Paper Products 1945. In a bright pink crepe-paper gown that rustled when she moved and wilted with moisture beneath her arms, and with a gilt crepe-paper crown atop her upswept hair. In a downtown convention hall passing out both brochures and sample paper products: tissues, toilet paper, sanitary pads (in plain brown unmarked wrappers). Paid $10 a day with (minimal) meals and trolley fare included.

She would be Miss Hospitality at a Surgical Appliances Convention in Santa Monica. Miss Southern California Dairy Products 1945 in a white swimsuit with big black Guernsey-cow spots and high heels. A "showgirl" hostess at the Luxe Arms Hotel opening in Los Angeles. A hostess at Rudy's

Steakhouse opening in Bel Air. In nautical attire—a middy blouse and short skirt, silk stockings and high heels—she was a hostess at the Rolling Hills Yacht Show. In jaunty cowgirl "rawhide" fringed vest and skirt, high-heeled boots, wide-brimmed hat, and a holster with a silver-plated (unloaded) six-shooter on her shapely hip, Miss Rodeo 1945 in Huntington Beach (where beneath bright lights she would be "lassoed" by the grinning master of ceremonies).

No dating of clients. Under no circumstances tips from clients. Clients will pay the Agency directly. Violating of such rules will result in suspension from the Agency.

For the pain and fever of cramps she took Bayer's aspirin. When that wasn't sufficient she began to take stronger pills (codeine?—what exactly was "codeine"?) prescribed by the Preene Agency's "attending" physician. Her heavy throbbing menstrual flow. Her throbbing head. Often the vision in one or both of her eyes faded. On the very worst days she couldn't work. Each loss of payment, if only $10, hurt her like a pulled tooth. What if she went blind? What if she had to grope her way to a trolley, stumble on and stumble off like an elderly woman? She was in terror of becoming the disheveled woman who'd once been her mother. She was in terror of failing at the simplest task. She was in terror of dogs sniffing at her wet crotch. Sanitary pads already fortified with layers of Kleenex soaked through within an hour. And where could she change? And how often? They would observe that she walked stiffly, a board between her thighs. She was desperate; she couldn't remain home in bed moaning and half conscious as she'd done in Verdugo Gardens and at the Pirigs', where Aunt Elsie would bring her a hot-water bag and warmed milk. *How's it going, hon? Just hang on.*

Now there was no one who loved her. Now she was on her own. She was saving to buy a secondhand car from a friend of Otto Öse's. She was renting a furnished room in West Hollywood within walking distance of Otto Öse's studio. She was sending five-dollar bills to Gladys at the State Psychiatric Hospital—"Just to say hello, Mother!" She was spoken of as one of the new "promising" Preene models. She was a "rising" model. The head of the Agency disliked her "dishwater-blond" hair. Unless it was "ditchwater-blond." She had to pay for a beauty parlor rinse—"highlighting" streaks. She had to pay for modeling lessons at the Agency. Sometimes she was provided clothes for her appearances, sometimes she had to provide her own. She had to provide her own stockings. She had to provide her own deodorant, makeup, underwear. She was making money, yet she was borrowing money: from the Agency and from Otto Öse and from others. She was in terror of getting a run in a stocking; she'd been observed (on a trolley, by strangers) bursting into tears, seeing the tiny telltale snag that was the beginning of a disastrous run. *Oh no. Oh no, please God. No.* Now she was a Preene model, all disasters were equivalent: the terror of sweating through deodorant on a hot steamy day, the terror of smelling, the terror of staining a dress. And everyone would see. For everyone was watching. Even when she wasn't being photographed in Otto Öse's studio beneath Otto Öse's cruel glaring lights and cruel unsparing gaze she was being watched. She had dared to step out of the mirror and now everyone was watching. There was no corner in which she could hide. In the Home, she could hide in a toilet stall. She could hide beneath her bedclothes. She could squeeze out a window and hide in a slanted corner of the roof. Oh, she missed the Home! She missed Fleece. She'd loved Fleece like a sister. Oh, she missed all her sisters—Debra Mae, Janette, Mouse. *She'd* been Mouse! She missed Dr. Mittelstadt to whom she still sent little poems sometimes. *In the Shadows of the Night the stars are more bright. In our hearts we know what is right.* Otto Öse who'd photographed her at Radio Plane Aircraft and saw into her heart laughed at such sentiments. Li'l Orphan Annie goo-goo eyes. Otto Öse told her point-blank she was being paid "damn good bucks" to be somebody special, so she better be somebody special—"Or get off the potty." She would, she would be somebody special! If it killed her. For hadn't Gladys believed in her, from the start? Voice lessons, piano lessons. Beautiful costume-clothes to wear to school.

Otto Öse, the Dark Prince. He'd swooped upon her in the dope room and took so many photographs of her for *Stars & Stripes*, Norma Jeane in her girl-defense-worker coveralls, no matter how she protested, no matter how shy she was, and, after Bucky's photo sessions, ashamed of having her picture taken; he'd pursued her around the fuselages, and wouldn't take no for an answer. He was in the employ of the official U.S. Armed Services magazine and that was a grave responsibility. For him, but also for her. The American G.I.s fighting overseas required their morale being boosted by shots of pretty girls in coveralls—"Don't want our boys to despair, do you? That's tantamount to treason." Otto Öse had made Norma Jeane laugh, though he was the ugliest man she'd ever seen. He *click click clicked* his camera hunched and staring at her like a hypnotist. "Know who my boss is at *Stars & Stripes*? Ron Reagan." Norma Jeane shook her head, confused. Reagan? That actor, Ronald Reagan? A third-rate Tyrone Power or Clark Gable? It was surprising to Norma Jeane that an actor like Reagan had anything to do with a military magazine. It was surprising that an actor could do anything real, at all. " 'Tits, ass, and leg, Öse—that's your assignment,' says Ron Reagan. Dumb ass don't know shit about factories if he thinks I can get *leg* in a place like this." The rudest, ugliest man Norma Jeane had ever met!

Still, Otto was right. He'd plucked her out of oblivion as he boasted, and he was right. The strangers who hired her had every right to expect somebody special, not just some Van Nuys hick. She'd learned not to take offense, still less burst into tears, when they examined her as if she were a mannequin. Or a cow. "That lipstick's too dark. She looks like a tramp." "Hell, get with it, Maurie: lipstick that shade is fashionable these days." "Her bust's too big. You can see her nipples through the cloth." "Hell, her bust is perfect! You want Dixie cups? What's wrong with nipples, you got a thing against nipples? Listen to this comedian." "Tell her not to smile so much, looks like she's got St. Vitus' twitch." "American girls are s'posed to smile, Maurie. What're we paying for, a moper?" "Looks like Bugs Bunny." "Maurie, you belong in vaudeville not women's quality apparel. The girl's scared for God's sake. This is costing us." "You're telling me, this is costing us." "Maurie, shit! You want me to send her back, she only just arrived? This innocent angel-face little girl?" "Mel, you crazy? We already paid twenty bucks up front, plus eight for the car, we'd lose that, think we're millionaires? She stays."

She was proud of that: always, she was allowed to stay.

Her first week at the Preene Agency, she encountered a glamorous red-haired girl leaving just as Norma Jeane was arriving; the girl was descending the stairs, striking her heels hard and angry against the steps, a girl with auburn-red hair falling across her eyes Veronica Lake style, in a tight-fitting black jersey dress with underarm stains, bright crimson lipstick and rouged cheeks, and a perfume so strong it made your eyes water. The girl wasn't much older than Norma Jeane but beginning to crack at the edges, and staring at Norma Jeane, whom she'd nearly shoved out of her way, she clutched at her arm—"Mouse! My God! You *are* Mouse, aren't you? Norma Jane—Jeane?"

It was Debra Mae, from the Home! Debra Mae, whose cot had been beside Norma Jeane's and who'd cried herself to sleep every night unless (for it was always unclear at the Home) it had been Norma Jeane who'd cried herself to sleep every night. Except now Debra Mae was "Lizbeth Short," a name she said bitterly she hadn't chosen and didn't like. She was a photographer's model on suspension from the Preene Agency. Or maybe (this was unclear to Norma Jeane, who would not want to ask) Debra Mae had been dropped from the Agency. And the Agency owed her money. She told Norma Jeane not to make the mistake she'd made, and Norma Jeane naturally asked what mistake was that, and Debra Mae said, "Taking money from men. If you do, and the Agency finds out, that's all they'll want from you." Norma Jeane was confused. "Want—what? I thought the Agency didn't allow that." "That's what they say," Debra Mae said, with a twisted mouth. "I wanted to be a real model and get an audition with a film studio, but"—shaking her red hair vehemently—"it didn't work out that way." Norma Jeane said, trying to figure this out, "You mean—you accept money from men? For dates?" Seeing a look on Norma Jeane's face she didn't like, Debra Mae flared up. "That's so *disgusting?* That's so *unknown?* Why? Because I'm not married?" (Debra Mae's eyes dropped to Norma Jeane's left hand, but Norma Jeane had removed her rings of course; nobody'd hire a married woman as a model.) "No, no—" "Only a married woman can take money from a man for fucking her?" "Debra Mae, no—" "Because I need the money, that's so disgusting? Go to hell." Debra Mae pushed past Norma Jeane in a fury, her back taut and her flamey-red head held high. Her high heels clattered on the stairs like castanets. Norma Jeane blinked after the orphan sister she hadn't seen in nearly eight years, stunned as if Debra Mae had slapped her in the face. In her hurt memory it would someday seem that in fact Debra Mae *had* slapped her in the face. Norma Jeane called after her, pleading, "Debra Mae, wait—do you ever hear from Fleece?" Meanly, Debra Mae shouted back over her shoulder, "Fleece is *dead.*"

DAUGHTER AND MOTHER

I wasn't proud yet, I was waiting to be proud. She sent carefully selected photo features of herself from *Parade, Family Circle,* and *Collier's* to Gladys Mortensen at the State Psychiatric Hospital. These weren't cheesecake photos like those in *Laff, Pix, Swank,* and *Peek* but fully clothed photos of Norma Jeane: in the hand-knit sweater set; in jeans and a plaid shirt and her hair in pigtails like Judy Garland in *The Wizard of Oz* as she knelt beside twin lambs, smiling happily as she stroked their soft white nubby wool; in *Back-to-School* coed clothing, pleated red plaid skirt, long-sleeved white turtleneck sweater, saddle shoes, white bobby sox, her honey-brown curly hair in a ponytail, smiling as she waved *Hello!* to someone on the other side of the camera, or *Goodbye!*

But Gladys never replied.

"Why should I care? I don't."

A dream she'd begun to have. Or maybe she'd always had it and could not recall. *Between my legs, a cut. A deep slash. Just that—a slash. A deep emptiness out of which blood drained.* In a variant of this dream which she would call the *cut dream* she was a child again and Gladys was lowering her into hot steamy water with a promise to cleanse her and "make it well," and

Norma Jeane was clinging to Gladys's hands, wanting to let go and in terror of letting go.

"But I guess I do care. I'd better admit it!"

Now she was earning money from the Preene Agency and as a contract player at The Studio, she began to visit Gladys in the hospital at Norwalk. In a phone conversation she'd been told by the resident psychiatrist that Gladys Mortensen was "as nearly recovered as she will be ever." Since her hospitalization a decade ago, the patient had had numerous electroconvulsive treatments, which had reduced her "manic seizures"; she was currently on a regimen of heavy medication to prevent outbursts of "excitation" and "depression." According to hospital records she had not tried to injure herself—or others—in a very long time. Norma Jeane asked anxiously if a visit to Gladys would be too upsetting and the psychiatrist said, "Upsetting to your mother or to you, Miss Baker?"

Norma Jeane hadn't seen her mother in ten years.

Yet she recognized her at once, a thin faded woman in a faded green shift with a crooked hemline, or maybe the dress was buttoned crookedly. "M-mother? Oh, Mother! It's Norma Jeane." Afterward it would seem to Norma Jeane, awkwardly embracing her mother, who neither embraced her in return nor resisted her, that both she and Gladys burst into tears; in fact, only Norma Jeane burst into tears, surprising herself with the rawness of her emotion. *In my early acting classes I could never cry. After Norwalk, I would be able to cry.* They were in a visitors' lounge amid strangers. Norma Jeane smiled and smiled at her mother. She was trembling badly and could not catch her breath. And her nostrils pinched, to her shame: for Gladys smelled, a sour yeasty unwashed smell. Gladys was shorter than Norma Jeane remembered, no more than five feet three. She wore filthy felt slippers and soiled bobby sox. The faded green shift was stained beneath the arms. There was a missing button, and you could see Gladys's flat concave chest through the loose neck, a dingy white slip. Her, hair, too, was faded, a dull grayish brown, oddly frizzed like shredded wheat. Her face, which had once been so quick with life, now seemed flattened, the skin sallow and minutely creased like crumpled paper. It was shocking to see that Gladys must have pulled out most of her eyebrows and lashes, her eyes were so naked and exposed. And such small watery untrusting eyes, of no color. The mouth that had always been so glamorous, sly, and seductive was now thin as a slit. Gladys might have been any age between forty and sixty-five. Oh, she might've been anyone! Any stranger.

Except the ward nurses were comparing us. They saw. Somebody'd told them that Gladys Mortensen's daughter was a model, a magazine cover girl, they'd wanted to see for themselves how alike mother and daughter were.

"M-mother? I've brought you some things." Edna St. Vincent Millay, *Selected Poems*, in a small hardcover volume she'd bought at a secondhand bookstore in Hollywood. A beautiful dove-gray knitted shawl delicate as cobwebs, a gift from Otto Öse to Norma Jeane. And a tortoiseshell compact with pressed powder. (What was Norma Jeane thinking of? The compact had a mirror inside, of course. One of the sharp-eyed ward nurses told Norma Jeane she couldn't leave such a gift—"The mirror might be broken and put to a bad use.")

But Norma Jeane was allowed to take her mother outside. Gladys Mortensen was well enough to have "ground privileges." Slowly and painstakingly they walked, Gladys's swollen feet shuffling in the worn felt slippers in a way Norma Jeane couldn't help think was exaggerated to the point of cruel comedy. Who was this sour, sickly old woman playing the role of Norma Jeane's mother, Gladys? Were you meant to laugh at her or cry? Hadn't Gladys Mortensen always been so quick on her feet, restless, impatient with "slowpokes"? Norma Jeane wanted to slip her arm through her mother's thin, flaccid arm but didn't dare. She feared her mother would flinch from her. Gladys had never liked being touched. The sour-yeasty odor was more pronounced as Gladys moved.

Her body turning rancid by slow degrees. I will always bathe, scrub myself clean. Clean! This will never happen to me.

At last they were outside in bright, windy air. Norma Jeane cried, "Mother! It's *so nice here*."

Her voice strangely lifted, childlike.

Even as she had to fight an impulse to break free of her burdensome mother and run, run!

Norma Jeane was glancing uneasily about at the weather-worn benches, the burnt-out dun-colored grass. A powerful sensation came over her: hadn't she been here before? But when? She'd never visited Gladys in the hospital, yet somehow she knew this place. She wondered if Gladys had sent her her thoughts, in dreams perhaps. Always Gladys had had such powers when Norma Jeane was a little girl. Norma Jeane was certain she recognized the open space behind the west wing of the old red-brick hospital. That paved area marked DELIVERIES. Those stunted palm trees, the scrubby eucalyptus. The dry rustling sound of palm leaves in the wind. *The spirits of the dead. Wanting to return.* In Norma Jeane's memory the hospital grounds were much larger and hillier, located not in a congested urban area but far out in the California countryside. Yet the sky was identical to the sky in her memory, bright patches of cloud blown inland from the ocean.

Norma Jeane was about to ask Gladys in which direction she wanted to walk but already, without a word, Gladys detached herself from Norma Jeane and shuffled to the nearest bench. There she sat immediately, like a collapsing umbrella. Folding her arms over her narrow chest and hunching her shoulders as if she were cold, or spiteful. Her eyes heavy-lidded as a turtle's. Her dry shredded-wheat hair stirring stiffly in the wind. Quickly and tenderly Norma Jeane drew the dove-gray shawl over her mother's shoulders. "Are you warmer now, Mother? Oh, this shawl is *so pretty on you!*" Norma Jeane couldn't seem to control her voice. She sat beside Gladys, smiling. She was tasting panic for she found herself in a movie scene yet had been given no words to speak; she must improvise. She dared not tell Gladys that the shawl was a gift to her from a man she didn't trust, a man she both adored and feared, a man who'd been her savior. He'd photographed her in "artful poses" with this shawl draped provocatively across her naked shoulders; she'd worn a strapless red dress made of a synthetic-stretch material, without a bra beneath, her nipples, rubbed with ice ("an old trick, but a good one" as Öse said), prominent as small grapes. The photo feature was for a new glossy magazine called *Sir!* owned by Howard Hughes.

Otto Öse claimed he'd bought the shawl for Norma Jeane, the first and only present from him to her, but Norma Jeane seemed to know that the photographer had found the shawl somewhere, in the backseat of an unlocked car, for instance. Or he'd taken it from another girl of his. It was Öse's belief as a "radical Marxist" that the artist had a right to make appropriations as he wished.

What would Otto Öse say if ever he saw Gladys!

He would photograph us together. That will never happen.

Norma Jeane asked Gladys how she was feeling, and Gladys murmured something unintelligible. Norma Jeane asked would Gladys like to come visit Norma Jeane sometime—"The doctor here says you can visit me anytime. You're 'nearly recovered,' he says. You could stay with me overnight, or just for an afternoon." Norma Jeane had only a small furnished room, a single bed. Where would she sleep if Gladys slept in the bed? Or could they both sleep in the bed? She was excited and apprehensive, only now recalling that her agent, I. E. Shinn, had cautioned her not to tell anyone she had a "mental case" mother—"The aura of it will attach to *you.*"

But Gladys didn't seem eager to accept her daughter's invitation. She grunted a vague reply. Norma Jeane had the idea, though, that Gladys was pleased to be invited, even if she wasn't ready to say yes. Norma Jeane squeezed her mother's thin, dry, unresisting hand. "Oh, Mother, it's been so l-long. I'm *sorry.*" How could she tell Gladys she hadn't dared come see her so long as she was married to Bucky Glazer? She'd been so frightened of the Glazers. She'd dreaded Bess Glazer's judgment. Fumbling, Norma Jeane removed a Kleenex from her handbag and dabbed at her eyes. Even on days when she wasn't modeling she was obliged to wear dark brown mascara, for a Preene girl-for-hire must always look her best in public; she was in terror of mascara running down her face like ink. Her hair was now a fair honey-brown, wavy and no longer curly; Norma Jeane's tight girlish curls and ringlets were "out"; at the Agency they told her she looked like "some Okie's daughter" dolled up to take her picture in Woolworth's. Of course, they were right. Otto Öse had told her the same thing. Her scanty eyebrows, her way of holding her head, her bargain clothes, even the way she breathed—they were all wrong and had to be corrected. (*What'd you do to yourself?* Bucky Glazer had demanded, the single time they'd met since his discharge. *What the hell are you trying to be, a glamour girl?* He'd been hurt and angry. He'd been shamed in his family's eyes. No Glazers ever got divorced. No Glazer wives ever *ran off*.)

Norma Jeane was saying, "I sent you my wedding pictures, Mother. I guess—I should tell you—I'm not married any longer." She held out her left hand, which trembled slightly and was barren now of all rings. "My h-husband—we were so young—he decided, he—he didn't want—" If this were a movie scene, the young newly divorced wife would burst into tears and her mother would comfort her, but Norma Jeane knew that could not happen, so she didn't allow herself to cry. She understood that tears would upset, or annoy, Gladys. "You c-can't love a man who doesn't love you, isn't that right, Mother? Because if you love somebody truly it's like your two souls are together, and God is in you both; but if he doesn't love you—" Norma Jeane fell silent, not certain what she meant to say. Oh, she'd loved Bucky Glazer, more than life itself! Yet somehow that love had drained away. She was hoping Gladys wouldn't ask any questions about Bucky and the divorce; and Gladys did not.

They sat in the splotched sunlight, cloud shadows passing over them like swift predator birds. There were few other patients outside on even this fair, fresh day. Norma Jeane wondered how her mother, who was so clearly superior to the other patients on the ward, was regarded. She wished Gladys had brought the poetry book with her, but Gladys must have left it in the visitors' lounge. They might have read poems together! What happy memories Norma Jeane had of the times Gladys read poetry to her. And their long dreamy Sunday drives into Beverly Hills and the Hollywood hills, Bel Air, Los Feliz. The homes of the stars. Gladys had known these men and women, many of them. She'd been a guest in some of those great houses, escorted by Norma Jeane's handsome actor father.

And now it's my turn. It is!

Mother, give me your blessing.

If her father was still living and in Hollywood, and if Gladys was discharged from the hospital, as seemed likely, and if she came to live with Norma Jeane—and if Norma Jeane's career "took off" as Mr. Shinn believed it would—Norma Jeane's mind spun with excitement as often it did in the middle of the night when she woke with her nightie soaked through and even the sheets damp.

Rummaging in her handbag, which was crammed with things (a small emergency makeup kit, sanitary pads, deodorant, safety pins, and vitamin pills and loose pennies and a dime-store notebook for jotting down thoughts), Norma Jeane brought out an envelope containing recent magazine features and photos of herself. These were exclusively "nice" poses, nothing cheap or vulgar. She'd prepared the photos to be presented one by one like gifts before her mother's startled eyes, which would fill gradually with pride and emotion. But Gladys only grunted "Huh!"—staring at the photos with an unreadable expression. Her thin bloodless lips grew thinner still. Afterward Norma Jeane would think *Maybe her first thought was this was herself? As a girl.* "Oh M-mother, it's been so exciting this past year, so w-wonderful, like one of Grandma Della's fairy tales, sometimes I almost can't believe it—I'm a *model.* I'm *under contract* at The Studio—where you used to work. I can make a living just being photographed. It's the easiest work in the world!" But why was she saying such things? The truth was, her life was hard work, anxious work, work to keep her awake at night worrying, work like none other she'd ever done, more of a strain on her nerves and more exhausting than her work at Radio Plane; it was like walking a high tightrope without a net below while the eye of the other—photographer, client, Agency, Studio—scrutinized her continuously. *The eye of the other* with its cruel power to laugh at her, jeer at her, reject her, fire her, send her back like a kicked dog into the oblivion from which she'd only just emerged.

"You can keep all these, if you want to. They're c-copies."

Gladys made a vague grunting sound. Continuing to stare at the photos Norma Jeane was showing her.

Strange how in each of the photos Norma Jeane looked different. Girlish, glamorous. Girl-next-door, sophisticated. Ethereal, sexy. Younger than her age, older than her age. (But what was Norma Jeane's age? She had to pinch herself to remember she was only twenty.) She wore her hair down, and she wore her hair up. She was sassy, flirty, pensive, yearning, tomboyish, dignified, fun-loving. She was cute. She was pretty. She was beautiful. Light fell revealingly upon her features or subtly shadowed them as in a painting. In the photo of which she was most proud, taken not by Otto Öse but by a Studio photographer, Norma Jeane was one of eight young women contract players signed on by The Studio in 1946, posed in three rows, standing, sitting on a sofa, and seated on the floor; Norma Jeane was gazing dreamily off-camera, lips parted yet not smiling as the others, her rivals, were smiling at the camera and all but begging *Look at me! Look at me! Only me!* Norma Jeane's agent Mr. Shinn disliked this publicity photo because Norma Jeane wasn't glamorously costumed like the others. She wore a white silk blouse with a deep V-neck and a bow, the kind of blouse worn by a refined young girl of good family, not a pinup sexpot; true, Norma Jeane was seated Indian-style on the carpeted floor as the photographer had positioned her, knees spread wide and silk-stockinged legs exposed; yet Norma Jeane's dark skirt and loosely clasped hands obscured her lower body. Surely there was nothing here to offend Gladys's fastidious eye? As Gladys frowned at the photo, turning it toward the light as if it were a puzzle, Norma Jeane said with an apologetic laugh, "I guess there isn't any 'Norma Jeane,' is there? Once I get to be an actress, if they let me—I'll have people to be. I hope I can work all the time. That way I'll never be alone." She paused, waiting for Gladys to speak. To say something flattering, or encouraging. "M-mother?"

Gladys frowned more severely and turned toward Norma Jeane. The sour-yeasty odor made Norma Jeane's nostrils pinch. Without meeting Norma Jeane's anxious gaze, Gladys muttered what sounded like "Yes."

Norma Jeane said impulsively, "My f-father was under contract to The Studio? You said? Around 1925? I've been sneaking around there trying to find his picture in the old files, but—"

Now Gladys did react. Her expression changed swiftly. She seemed to be seeing Norma Jeane for the first time, with her lashless, furious eyes. Norma Jeane was so frightened she dropped half the photos and stooped to pick them up, blood rushing into her face.

Gladys's voice sounded like a rusted door hinge. "Where is my daughter! They said my daughter was coming. I don't know *you*. Who are *you*?"

Norma Jeane hid her stricken face. She had no idea.

Still, stubbornly, she would return to Norwalk to visit Gladys. Again and again.

One day to bring Mother home with me. I would!

That bright windy day in October 1946.

In the parking lot of the California State Psychiatric Hospital at Norwalk, in the funky little black Buick roadster, Otto Öse slouched, waiting for the girl he'd talked up around town as his sweet little Okie cash cow. Add up this one's bust and hip measurements and you'd get her approximate IQ. And she adored *him*. And Jesus she was sweet, if goofy—sometimes trying to talk to him about "Marx-ism" (she'd been reading the *Daily Worker* he'd given her) and "the meaning of life" (she'd been trying to read Schopenhauer and other "great philosophers")—but the taste of her was like brown sugar on the tongue. (Had Otto Öse really tasted this girl? Among his friends this was debatable.) Waiting for her an hour as she visited her nutcase mother at Norwalk. Most depressing place in the world, a California state psychiatric hospital. Brrr! You didn't want to think—anyway, Otto Öse didn't want to think—craziness runs in the blood. In the genes. Poor sweet little Norma Jeane Baker. "Better for her she never has kids. She knows it too."

Otto Öse smoked his parchment Spanish cigarettes and fussed with his camera. Wouldn't allow anyone else to touch his camera. Like touching Otto Öse's genitals. No, you don't! And there came Norma Jeane at last, hurrying toward him. A blind look in her face and stumbling in high-heeled shoes on the pavement. "Hey, baby." Quickly Öse tossed away his cigarette and began shooting her. Climbed out of the Buick and went into a crouch. *Click, click. Click-click-click.* This was the joy of his life. This was why he was born. Fuck old-fart Schopenhauer, maybe life is blind will and purposeless suffering, but at such times who cares? Shooting a girl's ruined face and her breasts jiggling and her ass, and she's young-looking as a kid stuffed into a woman's body, innocent like something you'd want to smudge with your thumb just to dirty up. Poor kid's been crying, eyes puffy and sooty-dark mascara streaking her cheeks like a clown face. The front of her pink cotton-knit sweater was darkened with tears like raindrops and her oyster-white linen slacks, bought only that week in a consignment shop on Vine, where the studio executives' wives and girlfriends dumped their last year's wardrobes, were hopelessly wrinkled at the crotch. "The face of the Daughter," Öse intoned, in a priest's sacerdotal voice. "*Not* sexy." Coming out of his crouch, he sniffed at Norma Jeane. "You smell too."

FREAK

The way they quickly assured her *It's all right Norma Jeane, hey, Norma Jeane it's all right* she understood that it wasn't. She came back to this place where a girl was crying, laughing-sobbing—it was herself, being walked to a chair, one of the folding chairs arranged in a semicircle; she was hyperventilating, shaking as in a fit or convulsion.

It wasn't acting, what she did. It was deeper than acting. It was crude, it was too raw. We were taught technique primarily. To simulate an emotion, not to be the bearer of the emotion. Not to be the lightning rod through which emotion breaks loose into the world. She scared us, and that's hard to forgive.

They would say of her that she was "intense." The only one never to miss a class. Acting, dancing, singing. And always early. Sometimes before the room was unlocked. She was the only one to show up "perfectly groomed" day after day. Not looking like an actress or a model (we'd seen her *Swank* and *Sir!* covers; we were impressed) but more like a good-girl secretary. Hair set and brushed and shining. White nylon blouse with a bow at the collar, long sleeves and tight cuffs. Neat and crisp and ironed every morning. And a gray flannel skirt, narrow, tight-fitting, she must've steam-ironed every morning standing in her slip. You could just see her, frowning over the iron!

Sometimes she wore a sweater, and the sweater would be two sizes too small because that was all she owned. Sometimes a pair of slacks. But mostly the good-girl clothes. And stockings with perfectly straight seams, and high heels. She was so shy you'd have thought she was mute. Sudden movements and loud laughter startled her. She'd pretend to be reading a book before class started. Once it was *Mourning Becomes Electra* by Eugene O'Neill. Another time it was Chekhov's *The Three Sisters*. Shakespeare, Schopenhauer. It was easy to laugh at her. The way she'd sit at the edge of the semicircle and open her notebook and begin taking notes like a schoolgirl. And the rest of us in jeans, slacks, shirts, sweaters, and sneakers. In warm weather in sandals or barefoot. Yawning and our hair hardly combed and the guys unshaven because we were all good-looking kids, most of us from California high schools, where we'd been the stars of every school play and envied and praised and adulated from kindergarten. Some of us had family connections to The Studio. We had all the confidence, and little Norma-Jeane-from-nowhere had none. We speculated she was an actual Okie because she wasn't from anywhere around here. She'd trained herself to speak like the rest of us but her old accent kept breaking through. She had a stammer too. Not all the time but sometimes. At the beginning of an acting exercise she'd stammer a little, then push past it, and you could see her shyness melting away and that look in her eyes like another self was breaking through. But it was drummed into us *It isn't acting when you have no technique, when it's just you. Naked.*

So we had all the confidence. And Norma Jeane, who was one of the youngest in our class, had none. Only just her luminous pale skin and dark-blue eyes and that eagerness in her body like an electric current that couldn't be shut off and must've left her exhausted.

After one of her acting scenes, one of us asked her what she'd been thinking of—because God damn she'd devastated us watching it, and you couldn't have made yourself laugh at Norma Jeane any more than you could laugh at those Margaret Bourke-White photographs of Buchenwald—and she said in this little-girl breathy voice *Oh, I wasn't, I wasn't th-thinking. Maybe I was remembering?*

Yet she had no confidence. Each time she had to perform she came forward trembling as if it were the first time, and that would be her doom. She was nineteen or twenty then, and already you could see the doom in her. The most beautiful girl in the class, and yet the least talented of us could crush her with a word, a glance, the hint of a sneer. Or by ignoring her when she glanced up, smiling hopefully. Our acting instructor got impatient with her when she stammered answering his questions, and often she took minutes getting into a scene, like she was on a high diving board summoning the courage to dive and that courage came from a place deep inside her she had to grope for. We punished her the only way we knew. Letting her understand *We don't love you. You don't belong. You'd be more convincing as a tramp, a slut. You aren't what we want. You aren't what The Studio wants. Your insides don't match your outside. You're a freak.*

HUMMINGBIRD

Divine love always has met and always will meet
every human need.

—Mary Baker Eddy,
*Science and Health with
Key to the Scriptures*

Sept 1947   Hollywood Cal.

Woke early! couldn't sleep past 6 AM & all last night waking & sweating
& hearing voices of excitement & warning   This would be the day to
determine my FUTURE   & already my heart was beating against my ribs
like something small & feathered was trapped inside! But this is a *good
happy feeling* I think

Birds singing outside my window at the Studio Club   a good omen in the
tall grass & jimson weed   orioles, that liquidy call, & scrub jays harsh
& wakeful   & a remembered voice   that dream of a man (a stranger)
warning me something urgent in my life   & I'm scared I cant hear or dont
know the actual words as if they are in a foreign language

Today I am scheduled to be shown Mr Z's famed AVIARY   his prized collection of birds only the privileged have seen   & later my audition   *Scudda-Hoo! Scudda-Hay!* starring June Haver   Mr Shinn says
I am prettier & more talented than June Haver, I would like to believe
him   It's a fact I'm the only girl in my acting class invited to audition for
this movie   just a minor role of course

Pink plastic curlers covering my head   36 of them!   a torture to position my head on a pillow   my scalp aches & burns   but I will not take
sleeping pills like I'm advised   Shook out my "new" hair   brushed &
sprayed   not yet accustomed to it   *What has happened, my hair has
turned white* as with a terrible shock

Sick with nerves & worry   have not visited Mother in 5 months & must
send $$$ A good thing Bucky cant see me now he'd be disgusted   I
dont blame the Glazers its a shock to catch sight of myself unexpected   a
kewpie doll with such fluffed blond hair   & the red lipstick & tight
clothes Mr Shinn says I must wear

Mother once said *Fear is born of hope*   if you could excise hope from
your life you would excise fear   these 20 anxious minutes applying
makeup   botched it & wiped everything off with cold cream & began
again   Oh Christ these brown eyebrows flaring out & not inward like
my own   & how could I have brown eyebrows with such silver-platinum
hair its so FAKE   if Dr Mittelstadt could see me now   or Mr Har-
ing   Bess Glazer   Id be ASHAMED

On Hollywood Boulevard so many trees cut down   & Wilshire, & Sun-
set   L.A. is a new city now   since the War   Grandma Della would
not know it, even Venice Beach   after the War, Otto says there will be
new wars   capitalism requires new wars   always there is a War
except enemies change   These new buildings/ streets/ sidewalks/ pave-
ment   Clattering & whining & the earth quivering like an
aftershock   Bulldozers/ cranes/ cement mixers/ drills   the hills out in
Westwood leveled & new buildings & streets   "This used to be a coun-
try town" Otto says   he'd lived there when he first came to L.A.   You
can hear L.A. ticking almost   I LOVE IT   I am L.A.-born & a daugh-
ter of this city & nobody need know more than that   I WILL INVENT
MYSELF LIKE THIS CITY INVENTING ITSELF   & no backward look

At Schwab's for breakfast   & their eyes on me as I enter   in acting
class you must learn to be "blind" to the audience though paradoxically you
are "seeing" through the eye of the audience   & there above the foun-
tain & grill the long mirror   & my reflection inside   always it seems
jerky like a silent film   not graceful oh God the girl in the mirror at
Mayer's   Im thinking of Aunt Elsie who loved me   & betrayed
me   Yet: that girl in the mirror shy & fearful of seeing herself

oh God the life behind me I have lost

It's a mystery those tiny hummingbirds   youd think were bumblebees at
first   seeing them this morning behind the Studio Club & I was hearing
Grandma Della again   & she has forgiven me I think   she loves
me   A hummingbird is my favorite bird: so small & so hardy & bold &
fearless   (But wouldnt hawks kill them? crows? jays etc.) sticking their
long needle beaks into trumpet flowers to suck out the sweet juice   you
cant feed them by hand like other birds   three Ana's hummingbirds this
morning   they must eat continuously or burn out & die   tiny wings
beating so fast you cant see the wings   a whirring, a blur   & their
heartbeats so fast   & they can fly sideways & backward   I said
Grandma it's like thinking   your thoughts can fly anywhere

Do I love Otto Öse

do I love hurt/   fear

(Yet he would not hurt me Im sure   not truly   Through his camera
lens regarding me with more gentleness lately   as I am earning $$$ for
him   tho' that is not the only reason!)

At Schwab's it's a stage   *at all times say to yourself I am an actress I am
proud of being an actress for the secret of acting is control*   & I'm self-
conscious   & hesitate   their alert & hopeful eyes swinging upon
me   as upon anyone who enters   & a few smiles & hellos   heads
turning at my new hair & figure in this white sharkskin suit so carefully
ironed this morning   *Oh it's just her whats her name   Norma
Jeane*   only a contract player at The Studio & of no significance   no
influence   the female eyes narrowing   & two or three men frankly
staring   but mostly the eyes fall away disappointed   that spark of
hope fading like a flame blown out

Last Friday at Schwab's I'd come in after my morning exercises & the color
was up in my face & I was feeling so good & not-anxious & who was at the
counter having coffee & a cigarette but Richard Widmark   & he stared
at me & smiled   asking my name & was I at The Studio   he'd seen
me there, maybe   & we got to talking & I was breathless but didnt stam-
mer   & his eyes piercing as in his movies & I began to tremble   I
could see this man wanted more of me than I could give   backing away
with a smile & my new laugh which is light & bell-like   when I remem-
ber   *Well Norma Jeane!* says Widmark with his lopsided smile *maybe
we'll work together* someday   & I say *Oh I'd like that very much
Richard*   (he'd asked me to call him *Richard*   & he'd asked my
agent's name)

This morning in Schwab's nobody's here   quickly I scanned the counter
& the tables & booths   & in the mirror tremulous & shy the girl in the
white sharkskin suit   not-there, a ghost

Thank God then Mr Shinn came & I'm safe   my agent, I adore
him   Otto brought me to him   little humped man like a gnome with
heavy eyebrows & a dented forehead & nearly bald & he's combed a half-
dozen dyed-brown hairs across the crown   Rumpelstiltskin in the old
fairy tale Della told me   the ugly little dwarf-man who taught the miller's
daughter to spin gold out of straw   *Ha! ha! ha!* Mr Shinn's laugh is a
shovel striking rock   yet his eyes intelligent & strange/beautiful for a
man, I think   he is so restless drumming fingers on the tabletop   red
carnation he always wears in his lapel (fresh each morning!)   *Norma
Jeane the future may be very interesting for us both   don't forget your
appointment with Z at 11 yes?*

as if I wld forget   my God

Who's that blonde looking like a tramp one of my so-called friends reported
to me Mr Z had said of me   I'd come to The Studio in slacks & sweater
& he happened to see me I guess   not knowing my name he'd forget by
now, I hope

My "arty" feature in *U.S. Camera*, Otto is proud of   *A photograph is
composition/ light & dark gradations   it's not a pretty face*

Otto has given me *Human Anatomy* to study   & drawings by Michelan-
gelo & an artist of the 16th century Andreas Vesalius he says to
memorize   *Men desire you with their souls accessible only through the
body*

(But Otto does not touch me now   only as a photographer posing his
"model")

Mr Z is of an age you cant guess like certain of the older European immigrants   not so terribly old, I think   In the executive lounge where I've
served drinks I've stolen looks at him & pondered him   there are rumors
of him, of course   once I saw (I thought I saw) Debra Mae/ Lizbeth Short
with Mr Z   in dark glasses & a hat hiding half her face & they were in
Mr Z's Alfa Romeo exiting the lot   Mr Z is famous in California now
yet he was born in a small village in Poland & emigrated to this country w/
his parents when he was only a child   his father was a peddler in NYC
yet Mr Z by the age of only 20 (which is younger than me, now) had built
& managed Coney Island Amusement Park   & later Carnival   Mr

Z's genius it's said is for building talent & creating an audience for something that was not there previously & not anticipated   In his carnival Mr Z had an Indian fire-eater & a "yogin" (from India) who could walk & sit on burning coals & Tom Thumb & a Giant & a Dancing Hog & some poor Negro with certain of his insides on the exterior of his body   & by the age of only 22 Mr Z was a millionaire & began making silent films in a warehouse on the Lower East Side & moved to Hollywood in 1928 & went into partnership to found The Studio   creating such stars as Sonja Henie the champion ice skater & the Dionne Quintuplets & the German police dog Rin Tin Tin   & Myrna Loy & Alice Faye & Nelson Eddy & Jeanette MacDonald & June Haver   & so many others it left me dizzy to be told   (for tales are told of Mr Z & other Hollywood pioneers like fairy tales & old legends)   Mr Z's secretary stared coldly at me   making me repeat my name, & I stammered   & inside Mr Z was on the phone & called out *Come in & shut the door!*   in the voice you'd speak to a dog   & so I came inside   trembling & smiling

A blond girl entering a gentleman's office w/ tall draped windows & furniture gleaming teakwood & glass   & the gentleman behind the desk lifting his eyes suspicious & assessing   I listened for the music of this scene to cue me   & heard nothing

Behind Mr Z's office which is spacious as you'd imagine there is his private apartment few persons are allowed to enter   (Mr Shinn has never been inside, for instance   meeting with the great man only in his office or in the executive dining room)   & he led me across the threshold into this new place & I was afraid suddenly   I hoped he would not notice   I'd prepared my words to speak of course but was forgetting . for in such a situation I did not know Mr Z's lines as you would in a script in acting class   so knowing your own lines is inadequate   I was smiling seeing the blonde in a dark-tinted mirror above a sofa   in white sharkskin suit that showed her young shapely figure   & she looked good   & this was what Mr Z was seeing   I smiled happily hoping the panic wld not show in my eyes   tripped on the edge of a carpet & Mr Z laughed   *Are you doing this deliberately   d'you think this is a Marx Brothers movie*   I laughed though I did not comprehend the joke   if it was a joke

Mr Z is so revered at The Studio it's a surprise to see him at close range   not a tall man, & his expensive clothes loose-fitting   Mr Z's eyes behind his tinted bifocal glasses were bloodshot & yellow as with jaundice   he smelled of liquor & his Cuban cigars (some of us selected girls would present to Mr Z & his fellow executives & their guests in the Studio private lounge   drinks & cigars & we were costumed like nightclub girls   & it was a privilege, for we received tips   & there was the threat always that your contract wld not be renewed if you refused   & yet Mr Z had not seemed to favor me then, but redheads)   But still he'd invited me to see the AVIARY which was a more rare privilege

He nudged me into the farther room   & shut the door   *What d'you think of my* AVIARY   *This is but a fraction of my collection of course*   & what a shock, Mr Z's AVIARY was not of living birds as I had expected but of dead stuffed birds!   Many hundreds of them behind glass so far as I could see   I stared not knowing what to say (though the birds were beautiful I suppose   when you looked carefully through the pane of glass as in a museum)   Proudly Mr Z was speaking of his collection set in *a simulacrum of natural habitats*   nests & rock formations & twisted tree limbs & driftwood   grasses, wildflowers, sand, earth   & a strange sepia light like looking into the past   the AVIARY had no windows but was wood-paneled with little painted sets to make you believe you were in a forest or a jungle or desert or on a mountainside   yet at the same time underground, as in a cave   inside a box or a coffin   Yet I saw the AVIARY was fascinating the more I stared   for the birds were beautiful & lifelike not seeming to grasp that they were dead   I seemed to hear a voice like Mother's *All dead birds are female, there is something female about being dead*

Mr Z seemed pleased at my interest & was not so impatient with me   explaining he'd begun his collection as a young man just moved to California   & for years he searched out & captured the birds himself on expeditions   & eventually had to delegate to others for his life became too complicated   & so forth, & so on he was talking rapidly & the blond girl listening avidly & smiling   & wide-eyed   The prize specimens of the AVIARY were rare & near-extinct birds it was explained   Amazon parrots big as turkeys they seemed & gorgeously plumed green, red, yellow & their beaks curved like comical blunt noses made of bone   & South American songbirds of fantastical colors   & near-extinct North American goshawks   & a great golden eagle & a bald eagle & smaller falcons, all of them noble & powerful birds I had never seen before except in pictures

My eye was drawn to the smaller birds in another display   amid wildflowers & grasses   a flame-feathered tanager   cedar waxwings & silky flycatchers   the tanager reminded me of one of Mr Z's silent film stars   she'd been so beautiful & her career long over & even her name near-lost   I think Mother had driven us past her house in Beverly Hills   KATHRYN MCGUIRE it was!   & the shock of it made me smile   & another bird, a small owl with heartshaped face & feathers that looked curled & folded wings like arms   the face was that of MAY MCAVOY another silent screen star of Mr Z's   & in my confusion & fear I believed I saw the face of JEAN HARLOW in a mockingbird posed with wide-spread silver-gray wings as if in flight

Then like a magician Mr Z threw a hidden switch & suddenly there came birds songs into the silent cavernous room   how many dozens, hundreds of birds singing   & each song lovely & yearning & heart-rending   & yet the effect of so many songs at once was that of mere noise & frantic pleading *Look at me! Hear my song! Here I am! Here!*   My eyes flooded with tears of pity & horror   Mr Z laughed at me yet was flattered, & liked me

Stroking the nape of my neck & my hairs stirred in fright   he confided in me he'd learned taxidermy & found it the most restful of his hob-bies   someday he would show me   maybe   his laboratory not here on the lot but elsewhere   in the desert   *Oh I'd like that Mr Z thank you   this is so beautiful and so   mysterious*

Like a child tapping my red-painted nails on the glass   amid the birds frenzied songs   almost it seemed there was a stellar's jay on an evergreen branch only a few inches from me *seeing me*   & with that look of a fel-low captive *Help! help me*   I was relieved I did not see a single hum-mingbird in the AVIARY

How long we remained in the AVIARY amid the birds songs I cld not say   afterward

How long I remained in Mr Z's company I cld not say   afterward

How long the blonde smiled, smiled, smiled   her mouth aching as a happy-mask wld ache if it had flesh & nerves   there's a horror in happy-masks, no one will acknowledge   (& my teeth aching from the retainer I must wear at night   for my front teeth protruded a tenth of a tenth of an inch   & must be corrected The Studio informed me for profile shots wld be "sabotaged"   & my contract cld not be renewed   I was sent to the studio dentist & fitted with an ugly wire retainer to wear   & $8 deducted from my salary each week   a bargain it was explained to me & I suppose it was for if I'd gone to a private dentist I cld not afford it & my career would end)

Mr Z laughed saying *Enough of the Aviary, it bores you I see* & I
was surprised for I had not been bored, nor behaved that way & wondered if Mr Z must always play against the script a moviemaker would
wish to take others by surprise for he alone is in possession of the
script *Which one of them are you Blondie but dont tell me your
name what's your specialty?* Staring at me now with dislike as
if a bad smell emanated from me! I was so hurt, & surprised wanting to protest I have showered just this morning of course I woke early
& did my exercises & ironed this suit & showered only afterward & applied
Arrid to my underarms which are clean-shaven daily (though I know I
have a tendency to grow moist when I am anxious) I have powdered
myself with talcum powder smelling of lilac I have spent 40 minutes on
my makeup & this sharkskin suit is not a *tramp's* costume is it? How
cld you say such a thing of me not knowing me My hands are soft from
lotion & my nails manicured & glamorous yet not showy, I think It is
not my fault about the peroxide I was ordered by The Studio to have
my hair bleached "platinum blond" it was not my decision but I said
nothing of course Mr Z regarded me bemused as you wld regard a
trained dog or elephant or any freak removing his tinted glasses &
revealing his eyes so naked, lashless He was of my height if I was not
wearing these spike shoes Not fifty years old is he? which isn't old
for a man *Cmon let's drop the goo-goo routine you cant be as dumb
as you look* We'd left the AVIARY & were now in Mr Z's private apartment behind his office he'd switched off the AVIARY lights & the birds
songs abruptly ended as if all species were struck extinct

Mr Z pushed me toward a white fur rug saying *Get down Blondie* & only
then it came to me *Mr Z is my father—is he?* The secret heartbreak of
Gladys Mortensen's life yet the only happiness of her life

In bed that night past midnight unable to sleep I wld grope for one of
Mother's old watersoaked books from years ago the TIME TRAVELER by
H. G. Wells & the Time Traveler as he is solely called takes his seat with
courage & apprehension on the Time Machine of his invention &
presses a lever & plunges into the Future seeing suns & moons spin overhead I'd read it so many times, yet I'd move my finger along the printed
lines in dread of what must come & my eyes misting over with tears

*So I traveled, stopping ever and again, in great strides of a thousand years
or more, drawn on by the mystery of the Earth's fate, watching with a strange
fascination the sun grow larger and duller in the western sky, and the life of
the old Earth ebb away. At last, more than thirty million years hence, the*

huge red-hot dome of the sun had come to obscure nearly a tenth of the darkling heavens. . . .

Until I could not bear to read more, Id begun to shake   that thered be a time when we *will not be*, as there was a time when we *were not*   & not even films will preserve us as we would wish to believe   Even Rudolph Valentino lost finally to human memory!   & Chaplin, & Clark Gable (I'd wished to believe might be my Father, & Mother had sometimes hinted)   Mr Z was impatient   he was not a cruel man I believe but one accustomed to getting his way of course & surrounded by "little people"   there must be the temptation to be cruel when you are surrounded by such & they cringe & fawn before you in terror of your whim   I'd been stammering & now could not speak at all   I was on my hands & knees on the soft fur rug (Russian fox, Mr Z wld boast later) & my sharkskin skirt shoved up to my waist & panties removed   I dont need to shut my eyes to "go blind"   you'd learn in the Home   when you're "blind" time passes strangely   floating & dreamy in a way   yet in another way speeded up like the Time Traveler upon his machine   I would not remember Mr Z afterward except the small glassy eyes & dentures smelling of garlic & the sweat-film on his scalp visible through the wiry hairs   & the hurt of the Thing   of hard rubber, I think greased & knobby at the end shoved first between the crack of my buttocks & then   up inside me   like a beak plunging in   *In, in* as far *in* as it will go   I wouldnt remember how long was required for Mr Z to collapse like a swimmer upon the beach panting & moaning   I was in terror the old man wld have a heart attack or a stroke & I wld be blamed   you hear of that all the time, cruel crude funny stories   you laugh to hear yet wld not laugh if you were the victim   My contract was $100 a week & would soon be raised to $110 unless it was canceled   like other girls in our acting class   & they must move from the Studio Club no longer eligible   & I wld have to move out of the Studio Club too & live where, where wld I live?

Later that day the start of my NEW LIFE I wld see Mr Z & his friend George Raft & two other gentlemen in suits & expensive ties waiting for their limousine beneath the canopy   on their way to lunch (at the Brown Derby, where Mr Z has a table?)   & I wld be hurrying on an errand & their eyes drifting onto me bemused   *Like a silk purse down there*   *no hairs*   The infant Norma Jeane wrapped in a pink woolen blanket & passed among strangers   coughing & choking in the smoky air   How happy & young Mother was then, how hopeful   men put their arms around her praising her for the *beautiful baby*   & Mother was beautiful too but it's not enough   We dont have the same last name & who would know that Gladys Mortensen is my mother?   I promised Mr Shinn I would tell no one I had a mother in Norwalk but one day Mother would come to live with me   I vowed this

I had to leave Mr Z's office passing by his secretary   so sharp-eyed & disdainful   I was hobbling with pain & my makeup streaked & the woman called out to me in a low voice there's a powder room just outside   & I thanked her too ashamed to raise my eyes to hers

How long I hid in the powder room I would not recall afterward

Already I was forgetting Mr Z   begged codeine tablets from one of the makeup girls   my cramps had begun, so unfair this should happen at such a time   8 days early, & just before my audition yet I had no choice, did I   Fearful of codeine which is a strong analgesic   painkiller   I did not believe in pain & therefore not in "painkillers"   & Mr Shinn mentioned that Norma Talmadge my namesake was a notorious Hollywood *dope fiend* (!)   & that was why her career had ended as it had   she was still alive, a living skeleton it was said   in her Georgian mansion in Beverly Hills   *Please dont tell me more* I begged Mr Shinn who revels cruelly in such tales of bygone Hollywood stars   who had not been his clients

It was nearing time for my audition   & I was desperate to staunch the flow of ugly brown menstrual blood   hiding in the womens room my hands shaking fitting Kotex between my legs & within minutes the blood would soak through   I was in terror of staining my white sharkskin skirt   *& then what would I do*   & a searing pain in my anus I could not comprehend

When at last I was able to leave my hiding place & go to the audition in another building I was twenty minutes late & panting in terror   & before I could speak, stunned to be informed that I would not have to audition after all for *Scudda-Hoo! Scudda-Hay!*   nor even to read aloud the few lines of June Haver's girlfriend   I whispered I didn't understand & the casting director said with a shrug *You're in—you're cast. If your name is Norma Jeane Baker.* I stammered yes that's my name   but I couldn't understand this   & he repeated showing me his clipboard *You're in*   & told me to take a script & return at 7 AM the next morning   I was staring at this man not known to me, the bearer of such a message   *I'm in the m-movie? You mean I'm in the m-movie? My first m-m-movie? I'm cast, I'm IN?*   & the shock & the joy of it overcame me, I burst into tears embarrassing the casting director & his assistants

Through a roaring in my ears like a waterfall I heard congratulations   I was trying to walk, & nearly fainted   inside my clothes I was bleeding & it felt distant   my body numbed & distant   in a women's room I changed the blood-soaked Kotex which seemed wrong to me at such a happy time   & the throbbing cramps in my belly   & hot tears splashing down my face   By this time I'd forgotten Mr Z   & would not recall much of that visit except in flashes   certain of the birds of the AVIARY   their eyes snatching at mine & their piteous songs   yet even these I would shut out   the roaring in my ears of great happiness as after my wedding, when I'd drunk champagne   *I am so happy, I cant bear such happiness!*

I was in a daze intending to telephone Mr Shinn to inform him of this news   & should have known Mr Shinn would already know, & in fact was at The Studio already meeting with the executive producer of the movie   a summons came to me then to appear at once in Mr X's office   & when I arrived there was Mr X & Mr Shinn already trying out new names for me   "Norma Jeane" is a hick name, an Okie name they were saying   "Norma Jeane" has no glamour or allure   I was hurt wanting to explain that my mother had named me for Norma Talmadge & Jean Harlow yet of course I could not for Mr Shinn would silence me with a glare   The men ignored me speaking earnestly to each other as men do   as if I wasnt there   & I realized then that here was the mysterious voice of my dream   the voice of omens & premonitions   in fact two voices, mens voices talking not to me but of me   One of Mr X's assistants had given him a list of female names & he & Mr Shinn were conferring

Moira   Mona   Mignon   Marilyn   Mavis   Miriam   Mina

& the last name was to be "Miller"   I was upset they didnt consult me for there I was, now seated between them   yet invisible to them almost   I resented being treated like a child & thought of Debra Mae who'd been named against her will   & I did not like the name "Marilyn"   there'd been a matron at the Home of that name, hateful to me   & "Miller" was not a glamorous name at all   Why is it superior to "Baker" which they would not consider?   I tried to explain to them I would like to retain "Norma" at least   it was the name I grew up with   & would always be my name   but they refused to listen

Marilyn Miller   Moira Miller   Mignon Miller

wanting the "MMMMM" sound   they pronounced like rolling wine in

their mouths   & doubtful of the quality   & suddenly Mr Shinn
slapped his forehead saying Marilyn Miller is already an actress's name, she's
on Broadway   & Mr. X cursed for he was losing patience   & quickly
I said what of "Norma Miller"   & still the men weren't listening   I
was pleading saying my grandmother's name was "Monroe"   & Mr X
snapped his fingers as if he'd only just thought of it himself   & Mr Shinn
& he pronounced in unison as in a movie

Mari-lyn Mon-roe

savoring the sexy murmurous sound of it!

MARI-LYN MON-ROE

& several times again & they laughed & congratulated each other   &
me   & that was that!

MARILYN MONROE

would be my movie name & would appear in the credits for *Scudda-Hoo!*
Scudda-Hay!   Now you're a true *starlet* Mr Shinn said with a wink

I was so happy, I kissed him   & Mr X   & anybody close by   &
they were all happy for me   CONGRATULATING ME

Sept 1947 every dream of Norma Jeane Baker's realized   & every hope
of every orphan girl gazing out over the roof of the orphanage   at the
RKO tower & the lights of Hollywood miles away

To celebrate Mr Shinn wanted to take MARILYN MONROE out to dinner that
evening   & dancing   (though a little gnome of a man hardly coming
to my shoulder!)   & quickly I told him thank you Mr Shinn but I'm not
well this happiness has made me dazed & dizzy & I want to be alone   &
this was the simple truth   I staggered & fell & slept on a sofa in one of
the sound stages   & woke at evening & left the lot unobserved   &
caught a trolley at the usual corner smiling to myself telling myself I'm a *starlet*   I'm MARILYN MONROE   as the trolley clattered & swayed my mind
drifted off like startled birds scattering into the sky   & it was a sky
streaked with red like fire   the fires in the mountains & canyons fanned
by the Santa Ana winds   & that smell of burning sugar, burning hair &
ash was blown to our nostrils & Mother fled with me in the Nash driving
north toward the brush fires until the L.A. POLICE barricades stopped
her   but I would not think of that so long ago or even of the AVIARY that
morning & the man who'd taken me into it   I told myself *My new life!*
My new life has begun! Today it began! Telling myself *It's only now*

beginning, I am twenty-one years old & I am MARILYN MONROE   & a man spoke to me on the trolley as men often do   asking was I upset about something   could he help me, he asked   I told him excuse me, I must get off this is my stop   & hurriedly I got off the trolley   in fact I'd thought it was my stop at Vine but was confused, this sharp pain between my eyes & in the pit of my belly   on the pavement I stood swaying & bewildered glancing to the east, glancing to the west   somewhere in L.A. west of Hollywood yet not recognizing my surroundings & with no idea suddenly   *Which way is home?*

The Woman

1949–1953

Beauty has no obvious use; nor is there any clear cultural necessity for it. Yet civilization could not do without it.

—Sigmund Freud,
Civilization and Its Discontents

THE DARK PRINCE

The power of the actor is his embodiment of the fear
of ghosts.

—From *The Actor's Handbook
and the Actor's Life*

*I guess I never believed that I deserved to live. The way other people do. I
needed to justify my life every hour. I needed your permission.*

It was a season of no weather. Too early in the summer for the Santa Ana
winds yet the harsh dry air blown from the desert tasted of sand and fire.
Through closed eyelids you could see flames dancing. In sleep you could hear
the scuttling of rats driven out of Los Angeles by the crazed, continuous con-
struction. In the canyons north of the city the plaintive cries of coyotes. There
had been no rain for weeks yet day followed day overcast with a pale glaring light like the inside of a blind eye. Tonight above El Cayon Drive the sky
cleared briefly, revealing a sickle moon of the moist-reddish hue of a living
membrane.

*I don't want anything from you, I swear! Only just to say—You should
know me, I think. Your daughter.*

That night in early June the blond girl was sitting in a borrowed Jaguar at
the side of El Cayon Drive, waiting. She was alone and she appeared to be
neither smoking nor drinking. Nor was she listening to a car radio. The
Jaguar was parked near the top of the narrow graveled road, where there
was a fortresslike property, vaguely Oriental in design, surrounded by a

ten-foot cobblestone wall and protected by a wrought-iron gate. There was even a small gatehouse but no one was on duty inside. On lower ground, spotlights flooded properties and sounds of laughter and voices lifted like music through the warm night, but this property, at the summit of El Cayon, was mostly darkened. Around the high wall there were no palm trees, only Italian cypresses, twisted by the wind into bizarre sculpted shapes.

I don't have any proof. I don't need any proof. Paternity is a matter of the soul. I wanted just to see your face, Father.

A name had been given the blond girl. Tossed at her as carelessly as a coin tossed at a beggar's outstretched hands. Eager as any beggar, and unquestioning, she'd snatched at it. A name! His name! A man who'd possibly been her mother's lover in 1925.

Possibly?—probably.

Amid the debris of the past she'd been scavenging. As a beggar, too, might scavenge trash, even garbage, in search of treasure.

Earlier that night at a poolside party in Bel Air she'd asked please could she borrow a car?—and several of the men had vied with one another offering her their keys, and she was barefoot running and gone. If the Jaguar was missing for too many hours the "borrowing" would be reported to the Beverly Hills police but that wasn't going to happen for the blond girl wasn't drunk and she wasn't on drugs and her desperation was shrewdly disguised.

Why? I don't know why, maybe just to shake hands, hello, and goodbye if you want it that way. I have my own life of course. I won't be losing anything I'd actually had.

The blond girl in the Jaguar might have remained there waiting through the night except a private security guard in an unmarked car drove up El Cayon to investigate. Someone in the near-darkened mansion at the top of the hill must have reported her. The cop wore a dark uniform and carried a flashlight, which he shone rudely into the girl's face. It was a movie scene! Yet no music beneath to cue if you should feel anxiety, suspense, humor. The cop's lines were delivered flatly so you had no cue from him either. "Miss? What business d'you have here? This is a private road." The girl blinked rapidly as if blinking back tears (but she had no tears left) and whispered, "None. I'm sorry, officer." Her politeness and childlike manner disarmed the cop immediately. And he'd seen her face. *That face! I knew she'd got to be somebody, someday. But who?* He said, faltering, scratching at the underside of his slightly stubbled jaw, "Well. Better turn around and go home, miss. If you don't live up here. These are kind of special folks live up here. You're too young for—" His voice broke off, though he'd finished about all he had to say to her.

The blond girl said, starting her borrowed car, "No, I'm not. Young."

It was the eve of her twenty-third birthday.

"MISS GOLD DREAMS" 19...

"Don't make me into a joke, Otto. I beg you."

He laughed. He was delighted. It was revenge, and we know that revenge is sweet. He'd been waiting for Norma Jeane to come crawling back to him. He'd been waiting to shoot her in the nude since the first hour he'd seen her in her soiled coveralls cringing behind the fuselages with a canister of dope in her hands. As if she could hide from *him*.

From the eye of Otto Öse's camera, as from the very eye of Death, *nobody hides*.

How many females in his lifetime had Otto Öse stripped of their clothing and of their pretensions and "dignity" and each had initially vowed *Never!* as this girl imagining herself superior to her fate had vowed *Never, I will not, oh never!*

As if she'd been a virgin. In her soul.

As if inviolable. In a capitalist-consumer economy in which no body, like no soul, is inviolable.

As if the distinction between *pinup* and *nude* was all she had to cling to, for self-respect.

"Sooner or later, baby. You'll come to *me*."

Yet she'd refused his offers as long as she'd had a hope of a film career. When she'd been a new fresh face on the scene. *His* discovery. In every girlie

some of the glossy nationals and a few high-toned journals like *U.S.
era. His* work. It was solely because of Otto Öse she'd been signed on
a client by I. E. Shinn, a top Hollywood agent. And signed on by The Studio as a contract player and cast in an insipid "rural comedy" featuring June
Haver and a pair of matched mules and her four minutes of film footage ruth-
lessly edited back to mere seconds and those seconds depicting the blond
starlet "Marilyn Monroe" so far in the distance, in a rowboat with June
Haver, no one including possibly Norma Jeane Baker herself could have recognized her.

This was the film debut of "Marilyn Monroe." *Scudda-Hoo! Scudda-Hay!*
1948.

That was a year ago, and more. Since then she'd been cast in two or three
other low-budget low-quality films at The Studio in minor fleeting roles that
turned upon sight gags involving dumb-blond females with shapely figures.
(In the crudest film, "Marilyn Monroe" walks provocatively away from
Groucho Marx, who's ogling her buttocks.) Then rudely she'd been dropped
by The Studio. Her contract not renewed for another year.

"Marilyn Monroe" in a few short months had come to nothing.

It was rumored around town (falsely, Otto knew, but the very fact of the
rumor and its cruel tenacity was an ominous sign) that in desperation to further her career like so many other young starlets she'd slept with producers
at The Studio including the notorious womanizer–woman hater Mr. Z and
with an influential director whose influence she'd failed to enlist in her cause.
It was said of "Marilyn Monroe" that she slept with her dwarf agent I. E.
Shinn and with certain of his Hollywood friends to whom he owed favors.
It was rumored that "Marilyn Monroe" had had at least one abortion and
probably more than one. (Otto was amused to learn that in one variant of
the rumor he'd not only arranged for the illegal operation with a Santa
Monica doctor, he'd been himself the father. As if Otto Öse, of all men,
would be so careless with his sperm!)

For three years Norma Jeane had politely declined offers Otto had brought
to her to do nude features. From *Yank, Peek, Swank, Sir!* and some others
for far more money than she'd now be getting from Ace Hollywood Calendars: a measly fifty dollars. (Otto would receive nine hundred for the photo
shoot, and he'd keep the negatives, but he didn't need to tell Norma Jeane
that.) She'd gotten behind in rent now that she was no longer living at the
subsidized Studio Club but in a furnished room in West Hollywood; she'd
had to buy a secondhand car to get around L.A. and the car had been repos-
sessed, for fifty dollars, just that week. The Preene Agency was close to dropping her because The Studio had dropped her. Otto hadn't called Norma
Jeane in months, waiting for her to call him. For why the hell should he call
her? He didn't need *her*. Girls were a dime a dozen in southern California.

Then one morning the phone rang in Otto's studio and it was Norma Jeane and his heart leapt with an emotion he couldn't have defined: excitement, gratification, vindictiveness. Her voice was breathy and uncertain. "Otto? H-hello! This is N-norma Jeane. C-can I come see you? Is there any—work for me? I was h-hoping—" Otto drawled, "Baby, I'm not sure. I'll call around. L.A. is teeming with a fantastic new crop of girls this year. I'm in the midst of a shoot right now; can I get back to you?" He'd hung up the receiver gloating and later that day began to feel guilty, and a strange plea-sure in the guilt, for Norma Jeane was a sweet, decent girl who'd made money for him in halter tops and shorts and tight sweaters and swimsuits; she could make money for him stripped, why not?

I was not a tramp or a slut. Yet there was the wish to perceive me that way. For I could not be sold any other way I guess. And I saw that I must be sold. For then I would be desired, and I would be loved.

He was telling her, "Fifty bucks, baby."

"Only . . . f-fifty?"

She'd envisioned one hundred. Even more.

"Only fifty."

"I thought, once—you s-said—"

"Sure. And maybe we can get more later. For a magazine feature. But right now the only offer we have is Ace Hollywood Calendars. Take it or leave it."

A long pause. What if Norma Jeane burst into tears? She'd been crying a lot lately. She couldn't remember if Gladys had ever cried. And she dreaded the photographer's derision. And her eyes would be red and puffy and the shoot would have to be postponed for another day and she needed the money today.

"Well. All right."

Otto had the release form ready for her signature. Norma Jeane supposed it was because, if he waited until after the shoot, she might have changed her mind out of embarrassment or shame or anger and he'd be out his fee. Quickly she signed.

" 'Mona Monroe.' Who the hell's that?"

"Me, right now."

Otto laughed. "It isn't much of a disguise."

"*I* won't be in much of a disguise."

Removing her clothes with slow fumbling fingers behind the tattered Chi-nese screen, where on other occasions she'd changed into pinup costumes. In a flood of sunshine dirtied by the pane through which it rayed. There were no hangers for the clothes she kept freshly laundered, ironed: a white batiste blouse, a flared navy-blue skirt. Removing her clothes and standing at last naked except for her white sandals with a medium heel. Removing her dignity. Not that there was much dignity remaining. Every hour of every day since the terrible news had come from The Studio, a voice mocked *Failure! Failure! Why don't you die? Why are you alive?* To this voice, which she couldn't quite recognize, she had no reply. She hadn't realized how much "Marilyn Monroe" had meant to her. She'd disliked the name, which was concocted and confectionary, as she disliked her synthetic bleached-blond hair and the Kewpie-doll clothes and mannerisms of "Marilyn Monroe" (mincing steps in tight pencil skirts showing the very crack of her buttocks, a wriggling of her breasts as someone else in conversation might gesture with his hands) and the screen roles in which The Studio executives had cast her, but she'd hoped, and Mr. Shinn had supported her in this hope, that one day soon she'd be cast in a serious role and make a true screen debut. Like Jennifer Jones in *The Song of Bernadette*. Like Olivia de Havilland in *The Snake Pit*. Jane Wyman playing a deaf-mute in *Johnny Belinda!* Norma Jeane was convinced she could play roles like these. "If only they'd give me a chance."

She'd never told Gladys about her name change. She'd imagined that when *Scudda-Hoo! Scudda-Hay!* opened she would take Gladys to the premiere at Grauman's Egyptian Theatre and Gladys would be astonished and thrilled and proud to see her daughter on the screen, in however minor a role; at the conclusion of the movie she would have explained that "Marilyn Monroe" in the credits was *her*. That the name change hadn't been her idea but at least she'd been able to use the name "Monroe," which was in fact Gladys's maiden name. But her role in the silly movie had been cut back to a few seconds, and there was no pride in it. *Without pride I can't go to Mother. I can't expect her blessing without pride.*

If her father was aware of her as "Marilyn Monroe" he'd have been disgusted too. For there was no pride in "Marilyn Monroe"—yet.

Otto Öse was setting up the photo shoot, talking to Norma Jeane in a brisk excited voice. Plans for other "arty" shots after this one. For always there was a demand for—well, "specialty" photos. Norma Jeane listened numbly as if from a distance. Apart from his camera, Otto Öse was inclined to be lethargic and morose; with his camera he came alive. Boyish and funny. She'd learned not to be offended by his wisecracks. Norma Jeane was shy with him since they hadn't seen each other in months and their parting had been awkward. (She'd told him too much. About being lonely and anxious about her career and thinking of him—"an awful lot." She hadn't believed she'd said this. It was exactly the wrong thing to say to Otto Öse and she knew it. He hadn't answered at first, he'd turned away from her, smoking his foul-smelling cigarette, and finally he'd mumbled, "Norma Jeane, please—I don't want you to get hurt." His left eyelid was twitching and his mouth sullen as a boy's. He'd been silent for so long after that she knew she'd made a blunder for which there was no remedy.) Now she stood behind the tattered Chinese screen, shivering in the airless heat. She'd vowed never to pose in the nude because it was a *crossing over* and once you'd *crossed over* it was like taking money from a man for sex. You couldn't go back to what you'd been. There was something dirty about the transaction in the way of literal dirt, grime. She was obsessive about cleanliness. Fingernails, toenails. *I will never be like Mother: never!* At the film studio she'd sometimes showered after acting class if she'd been perspiring during a scene. Was it Orson Welles who'd said, "An actor sweats or he isn't an actor"? But no actress wants to stink! At the Studio Club, Norma Jeane was one of the girls who liked to soak in a hot bath for as long as she was allowed. But now, in her cheap furnished room, to her shame she had no bathtub or shower and had to wash awkwardly out of a small sink. Almost, she'd accepted an invitation to spend a weekend with a producer who lived in Malibu because she'd yearned for the luxury of a bath. The producer was a friend of a friend of Mr. Shinn's. One of so many "producers" in Hollywood. A wealthy man, he'd given Linda Darnell her start. In fact, Jane Wyman. Or that was his boast. If Norma Jeane had stayed with this man, that too would be a *crossing over*.

She didn't want money, she wanted work. She'd turned the producer down and now she was stripped bare in Otto Öse's cluttered studio, which smelled like copper pennies clutched in a sweaty hand. Underfoot were dustballs and the desiccated husks of insects she believed she recognized from the last time she'd been here months ago. *When I vowed I would never return. Never!*

She could not interpret the looks the photographer cast her: was he attracted to her or did he loathe her? Mr. Shinn had said Otto was Jewish and Norma Jeane hadn't ever known any Jews. Since Hitler and the death camps and the photographs of Buchenwald, Auschwitz, and Dachau she'd stared at for long stunned minutes in *Life*, she'd become fascinated by Jews, Judaism. Hadn't Gladys said that Jews are a chosen people, an ancient and fated people? Norma Jeane had been reading about the religion, which seeks no converts, and about the "race"—what a mystery, "race"! The origins of human "races"—a mystery. You had to have a Jewish mother to be born a Jew. Was it a blessing or a curse to be "chosen"?—Norma Jeane would have liked to ask a Jew. But her question was naive, and after the horror of the death camps she would certainly have been misunderstood. In Otto Öse's dark-socketed eyes she saw a soulfulness, a depth, and a history lacking in her own eyes, which were a clear, startling blue. *I'm only an American. Skin deep. There's nothing inside me, really.*

Otto Öse was unlike any other man Norma Jeane knew. It wasn't just that he was talented and eccentric. It was that, in a sense, he wasn't a *man*. He wasn't defined by *maleness*. His sexuality was a mystery to her. He didn't seem to like women on principle. Norma Jeane wouldn't have liked most women herself on principle, if she'd been a man. So she thought. Yet for a long time she'd tried to believe that Otto Öse might distinguish her from other women and love *her*. Might feel sorry for her and love *her*. For didn't he look with tenderness upon her sometimes, and always with intensity, through the eye of his camera? And afterward excitedly spreading out contact sheets and prints of Norma Jeane, or of the Norma Jeane he'd photographed in her pinup costumes, he would murmur, "My God. Just look. *Beautiful*." But it was the photographs he meant, not Norma Jeane.

Naked, except for her shoes. *Why am I doing this? It's a mistake.* She was looking desperately for a robe to slip into. Wasn't there always a robe for a nude model? She should have brought one herself. Shyly she peered around the edge of the screen. Her heart beat hard in dread and a curious kind of elation. If he looked upon her naked, wouldn't he desire her? Love her? She watched him, his back to her, in a shapeless black T-shirt, work pants that showed the painful narrowness of his hips, stained canvas shoes. None of the Preene models or young actresses at The Studio who knew Otto Öse truly knew anything about him. His reputation was for exacting, frequently exhausting work—"But it's worth it, with Otto. He never wastes time." His private life was a mystery—"You can't even imagine Otto as a *fag*." Norma Jeane saw that Otto's hair was turning metallic gray and thinning at the crown of his long narrow skull. His face in profile was more hawklike than Norma Jeane recalled. He looked so *hungry*, so *predatory*. She could imagine him soaring and swooping and diving at his terrified prey. There he was arranging a large crimson velvet cloth against a rickety cardboard backdrop; he hadn't noticed Norma Jeane watching. He whistled, muttered to himself, laughed. He turned to squint toward the rear of the studio,where amid the clutter there were battered pieces of furniture: a chrome kitchen table and chairs layered in grime, a hot plate, coffeepot, cups. There were six-foot plywood sections and corkboards upon which he'd tacked dozens of contact sheets and prints, some of them yellowed with age. Close by was a filthy toilet with only just a ragged strip of burlap for a door. Norma Jeane dreaded having to use this toilet and avoided it for as long as she could. Now it seemed to her she saw a shadowy movement beyond the burlap—was there someone inside? *He's brought someone to spy on me!* The thought was wild and absurd. Otto wasn't like that. Otto felt contempt for *pimps*.

"Ready, baby? Not shy, are you?"—Otto tossed Norma Jeane a piece of gauzy crinkled cloth, a former curtain. She wrapped it around herself gratefully. Otto said, "I'm using crushed velvet for a candy-box effect. You're a piece of candy, luscious enough to eat." Otto spoke casually, as if the situation were familiar to them both. He absorbed himself in setting the tripod in place, loading and adjusting the camera. He didn't so much as glance up as

Norma Jeane approached, slowly, numbly, like a girl in a dream. The crimson velvet cloth was badly frayed at the edges but the color was still vivid, throbbing. Otto had arranged the cloth so that its edges wouldn't show in the photo and the low stool on which Norma Jeane was to sit, framed by the throbbing color, was disguised by the cloth. "Otto, can I use the b-bathroom? Just for—"

"No. The toilet's broken."

"Just to wash my—"

"No. Let's get started with 'Miss Golden Dreams.' "

"That's what I'm supposed to *be?*"

Otto wasn't looking at Norma Jeane even now. Out of delicacy, maybe, or a worry the girl might panic and run away. Wrapped in the soiled curtain she was approaching the edge of the set and the near-blinding lights that were always intimidating. Only when she stepped hesitantly onto the cloth did Otto see, and said sharply, "Shoes? You're wearing shoes? Take them off." Norma Jeane stammered, "I c-can't wear my shoes? The floor is so dirty." "Don't be stupid. Have you ever seen a nude in *shoes?*" Otto snorted in derision. Norma Jeane felt her face burn. How fleshy she was, her breasts of which she was ordinarily so proud, her thighs and buttocks! Her smooth creamy buoyant nakedness was like a third party in the room with them, an awkward intrusion. "It just feels—my f-feet—they seem more n-naked somehow than—" Norma Jeane laughed, not in the new way she'd been trained at The Studio but in the old squeaking-startled way, like a mouse being killed. "Could you p-promise not to—show the bottoms? The soles? Of my feet? Otto, please!"

Why was it so important suddenly? The soles of her feet?

Unprotected and vulnerable and exposed. She couldn't bear to think of men staring lewdly at her, and the proof of her animal helplessness her pale naked feet. She recalled how at their last photo session, a pinup feature for *Sir!* in which Norma Jeane wore a red satin V-neck top, white short shorts, and red satin high-heeled shoes, Otto had told her that her thighs were "disproportionate" to her ass: too muscular. And he didn't like the scattering of moles like "tiny black ants" on her back and arms and made her cover them with foundation makeup.

"Let's go, baby. Everything *off.*"

Norma Jeane kicked off her shoes and let the gauzy curtain fall to the floor. Her body tingled, now she was naked in the presence of this man, who was both her friend and an utter stranger. She took her place amid the crushed velvet, sitting on the low stool with her legs tightly crossed, turned to one side. Otto had so arranged the cloth that the viewer wouldn't know with certainty whether the model was sitting up or lying down. Nothing would show but the field of vivid crimson and the model's naked body, as in an optical illusion in which dimensions and distance are unclear. "You w-won't, will you? Show the soles of my—"

Otto said irritably, "What the hell are you jabbering about? I'm trying to concentrate and you're getting on my nerves."

"I've never posed n-naked before. I—"

"Not naked, sweetheart—*nude*. Not smut, *art*. There's a crucial distinction."

Norma Jeane, hurt by Otto's tone, tried to joke in her ingenue voice as she'd been coached at The Studio. "Like photographer—not *pornographer*. That's it?"

She'd begun to laugh shrilly. Otto knew the danger signs.

"Norma Jeane, relax. Calm down. It's going to be a candy-box shot like I said. Take away your arms, d'you think Otto Öse hasn't seen plenty of tits? Yours are swell. And uncross your legs. We're not going to do a frontal shot, we won't even catch any pubic hair, we can't ship it through the U.S. mails and that would defeat our purpose. Right?"

Norma Jeane was trying to explain something confusing about her feet, the soles of her feet, how they would look from the *underside*. But her tongue was thick and numb. Speech was difficult, like breathing under water. She was aware of someone watching her from the rear of the studio. And there was the grimy window looking out onto Hollywood Boulevard; someone might be watching her from that window, peering over the windowsill. Gladys hadn't wanted them to look at Norma Jeane but they'd lifted the blanket and looked. It was impossible to prevent them.

Otto said patiently, "You've posed for me in this studio plenty of times. And out on the beach. What difference does a halter top the size of a handkerchief make? A swimsuit? You show your ass more suggestively in a pair of shorts or jeans than you do bare, and you know it. Don't play dumber than you are."

Norma Jeane managed to speak. "Don't make me into a joke, Otto. I beg you."

Otto said contemptuously, "You're already a joke! The female body *is* a joke. All this—*fecundity*. This—*beauty*. The aim is to drive men wild to copulate and reproduce the species like praying mantises with their heads bitten off by their female sex partners, and what *is* the species? After the Nazis, and the American collaboration in the slaughter of the Jews, ninety-nine percent of humankind doesn't deserve to live."

Norma Jeane quavered before Otto's assault. In the past he'd made remarks, part jocular, part serious, about the worthlessness of mankind, but this was the first time he'd alluded to the Nazis and their victims. Norma Jeane protested. "American c-collaboration? What do you mean, Otto? I thought we s-saved—" "We 'saved' the death-camp survivors because it was good propaganda, but we didn't prevent six million deaths. U.S. policy—meaning FDR—was to turn away Jewish refugees and send them back to the gas ovens. Don't look at me like that, this isn't one of your imbecile movies. The United States is a booming postwar fascist state (now that the self-declared Fascists are defeated) and the House Un-American Activities Committee is their Gestapo and girls like you are luscious pieces of candy for whomever's got the dough to buy them—so shut up about things you don't understand."

Otto was smiling his wide gleaming death's-head smile. Norma Jeane smiled anxiously to placate him. He'd several times given her the *Daily Worker* and crudely printed pamphlets published by the Progressive Party, and the American Committee for the Protection of the Foreign-Born, and other organizations. She'd read them, or tried to. How badly she wanted to *know*. Yet if she asked Otto about Marxism, socialism, communism, "dialectical materialism," the "withering-away of the state," he cut her off with a dismissive shrug. For it turned out (maybe) that Otto Öse didn't believe in the "naive religiosity" of Marxism either. Communism was a "tragic misreading" of the human soul. Or possibly a "misreading" of the tragic human soul. "Baby, for Christ's sake just look *sexy*. That's your talent and God knows it's a rare one. Worth every penny of your fifty-buck fee."

Norma Jeane laughed. Maybe she was only a piece of candy. *Pretty piece of ass* as she'd overheard someone (George Raft?) once commenting.

There was comfort in the photographer's contempt. It spoke of standards higher than her own. Far higher than Bucky Glazer's and higher even than Mr. Haring's. She fell into an open-eyed dream, thinking of these men and of Warren Pirig, who'd spoken little to her except with his eyes, and there was Mr. Widdoes, who'd pistol-whipped a boy with that air of "putting things right" that was a masculine prerogative inevitable as the tide. In a dream sometimes Norma Jeane recalled that Widdoes had beaten *her*.

Yet her own father had been so gentle! Never scolded her. Never hurt her. Cuddling and kissing his baby girl as Mother looked on smiling.

One day I will return to Los Angeles to claim you.

This photo session Otto Öse would remember through his life. This photo session that would be his claim on history.

Not that he knew, at the time. Except he was liking what he did, and that was rare. Mostly, he hated his girl models. He hated their naked-fish bodies, their anxious hopeful eyes. If you could tape over the eyes. Tape the mouths in such a way that, though exposed, the mouths couldn't speak. But Norma Jeane in her trance never spoke. He hardly needed to touch her, only just with his fingertips, to position her.

Monroe was a natural even as a girl. She had brains but operated from instinct. I believe she could see herself through the camera eye. It was more powerfully, more totally sexual to her than any human connection.

He was posing his model upright as the mermaid prow of an imaginary ship. Breasts bared, nipples big as eyes. Norma Jeane seemed unaware of the contortions he was putting her through. So long as he murmured, "Great. Ter-rific. Yes, like that. Good girl." Such words as you murmur at such a time. He came forward stalking his prey, but his prey registered no alarm. His prey was so thoroughly *his*. Strange, when Norma Jeane Baker was clearly the most intelligent of his models. Even shrewd, in a way you'd expect only a man to be shrewd, a gambler willing to risk X in the hope of winning Y, though in fact there is little hope of winning Y and every possibility of losing X. *Her problem wasn't she was a dumb blonde, it was she wasn't a blonde and she wasn't dumb.*

Isaac Shinn had told Otto it was such a shock to Norma Jeane when she'd been dropped by The Studio, he worried she might do something to hurt herself. Otto laughed in disbelief. "Her? She's the life force. She's Miss Weed Vigor." Shinn said, "It's the most dangerous kind of suicidal, the poor kid hasn't a clue herself. *I* have the clue." Otto listened. He knew that Isaac Shinn for all his bullshit never spoke somberly except he spoke truth. Otto said maybe it was for the best The Studio had dropped "Marilyn Monroe" (ridiculous name nobody was going to take seriously); now the girl could return to a normal life. She could finish her education and get a reliable job and remarry and start a family. A happy ending. Shinn said, appalled, "Don't tell her that, for Christ's sake! She shouldn't give up on a film career yet. She's got terrific talent and she's gorgeous and still young. I've got faith in her even if that fucker Z doesn't." Otto said with surprising earnestness, "But for Norma Jeane's own good she should get out of this shit. It isn't just the studios, but everybody's informing on everybody else, it's a hotbed of 'subversives' and police spies. Why doesn't she think of it herself?" Shinn, who perspired easily, was tugging at the collar of his custom-made white silk shirt. He was a dwarf with a humped upper back and a massive head and a personality you might define as phosphorescent, glaring in the dark. A controversial but generally respected Hollywood figure in his mid-forties, I. E. Shinn was rumored to have made more money betting on horses than he'd made as an agent; he'd been an early member of the left-leaning Committee to Preserve Individual Freedom, founded in 1940 in resistance to the right-wing California legislature's Joint Fact-Finding Committee on Un-American Activities. So he was courageous and stubborn; Otto Öse, briefly a member of the Communist Party until he'd become disillusioned, had to admire that. Shinn's eyes were thick-lashed and intense and gave the impression of inward suffering at odds with the jocular tics and twitches of his face. He was uniquely ugly as Otto Öse believed himself, in his vanity, to be uniquely ugly. *A pair. Twin brothers. Twin Pygmalions. And Norma Jeane our creation.* Otto would have liked to photograph Shinn in dramatic chiaroscuro, *Head of a Hollywood Jew*, like a portrait by Rembrandt. But Otto Öse's income was from girls. Shinn had said, shrugging, "She thinks she's too dumb. She thinks because she stutters sometimes, she's almost a moron. Believe me, Otto, she's happy enough. And she's going to have a career—I guarantee it."

Otto moved the tripod closer. Norma Jeane smiled up at him reflexively, as a woman might smile at a man advancing upon her to make love to her. "Great, baby! Now a little tip of the tongue. Hold it." She did as she was instructed. She was asleep with her eyes open. *Click!* Otto himself had become entranced. He'd photographed many nudes but none like Norma Jeane. As if in the act of staring at her he was consuming her, yet at the same time being consumed by her. *I live in your dreams. Come, live in mine.* Posed against the crinkled-velvet background, she was a luscious piece of candy you'd want to suck and suck. On a whim he'd given her a sixteenth-century Italian anatomical text with the cryptic advice that she should memorize it. She was so eager! She wanted—well, so much! *Love me. Will you love me? And save me.* It was difficult to believe that this young woman in the prime of health and beauty could ever age as Otto Öse knew himself aging. He was rail-thin, yet his flesh seemed to him flaccid inside his loose-fitting clothes. His head was a skull encased with skin. His nerves were tight-strung wires. He smiled to see Norma Jeane's toes curving under in a gesture of childlike modesty. What was this fixation of hers, not wanting him to photograph the soles of her feet? He had an idea. "Baby, I'm gonna try another pose. Get down from there." Without hesitation Norma Jeane obeyed. If he'd wished he could have photographed her from the front, her small rounded belly with its faint pale sheen, the triangle of dark-blond pubic hair at the fork of her legs that looked as if she'd (shyly, slyly) trimmed it: she'd become as unselfconscious as a small child, or a blind child. One of those malnourished Mexican migrant children urinating at the edge of a field scarcely bothering to squat, unself-conscious as a dog.

In excitement Otto repositioned the velvet drape, spreading it now flat on the floor. Like a picnic! Dragged a stepladder layered in cobwebs out of a corner of the studio so that, inspired, he could shoot Norma Jeane from several feet above her as she lay on the cloth below. "Baby, on your stomach. Now, on your side. Now *stret-ch!* You're a big sleek cat, aren't you, baby? A beautiful big sleek cat. Let's hear you purr."

The effect of Otto's words was immediate and astonishing. Norma Jeane obeyed Otto unquestioningly, laughing deep in her throat. She might have been hypnotized. She might have been a young bride unskilled in lovemaking beginning to enjoy love, her body responding instinctively. Naked on the crinkled velvet, stretching luxuriously, arms, legs, the sinuous-snaky curve of her back and buttocks as Otto *clicked! clicked!* the shutter of his camera, staring at her through the lens. Otto Öse, who boasted that no woman, and certainly no naked model, could surprise him. Otto Öse, whom sickness had both deprived and cured of his manhood. In this series of shots he was several feet farther from his subject, balanced on the ladder, aiming downward, so that the printed photo would place the girl surrounded by the velvet cloth, not dominating its space in the pose of the traditional nude as in her initial upright position. It was a subtle difference but a significant one. The upright alluring nude, gazing dreamily at the viewer, is an invitation to sexual love on the nude's terms: a female freely beckoning to the (invisible, anonymous) male. But the reclining nude, seen from a short distance, stretched out on her stomach and reaching out, is perceived as physically smaller, more vulnerable in her nakedness, and not the viewer's equal. She is to be dominated. Her very beauty suggests pathos. An exposed little animal, helpless, totally captured by the camera's probing eye. The graceful curve of shoulders, back, and thighs, the swelling of her buttocks and breasts, the curious animal yearning in her uplifted face, the pale, vulnerable undersides of her feet—"Fan-tas-tic! Hold it." *Click, click!*

Otto's breath was coming quickly. Perspiration broke out on his forehead and beneath his arms, stinging like tiny red ants. By this time he'd forgotten the beautiful model's name (if she had a name) and could not have said for whom he was taking these remarkable shots; still less could he have said how much he would receive for them. *Nine hundred. For selling her out. Why, when I love her? This is proof I don't love her.* He'd had two shots of rum with his former friend, former roommate, and former Commie comrade Charlie Chaplin, Jr., whose "filial identity" was synonymous with his "filial curse," to prepare himself for the shoot, a sinus-clearing potent medicine in scummy jam glasses. He wasn't drunk on rum but on—what? The blinding lights, the throbbing crimson color, the girl flesh luscious-as-candy stretched out before him writhing and stretching in the throes of sexual intercourse with an invisible lover. He wasn't drunk on rum but on the transgression he was committing, for which he would be not punished but handsomely paid. From his vantage point above her Otto saw the girl's life flow past him, from its squalid origins (she'd confided in him she was what she quaintly called *illegitimate* and her father who lived close by in Hollywood had never acknowledged her existence, and he knew that her mother was crazy, a paranoid schizophrenic who'd once tried to drown her—or was it scald her to death?—institutionalized at Norwalk for the past decade) to its equally squalid end (early death by drug overdose or alcohol, or wrists slashed in a tub, or a madman lover). The tragedy of the girl's anonymous life pierced Otto Öse's heart, who had no heart. She was a creature unprotected by society, no family, no "heritage." A piece of luscious meat to be marketed. In her prime, and her prime would not last. Though at twenty-three she looked six years younger, strangely untouched by time and ill usage but, like the proletariat subjects of Otto Öse's great mentor Walker Evans, the disenfranchised sharecroppers and migrant workers of the American south in the 1930s, she would one day begin to age suddenly and irrevocably.

I force no one. Of their own volition they come to me. I, Otto Öse, help them to sell themselves who would have little value on the market except through me.

How then was he exploiting Norma Jeane? Saying, tossing the rag of a curtain at her, "OK, baby. Done. You were terrific. Fan-tas-tic." Blinking, dazed, the girl looked at him as if for the moment not recognizing him. As a brothel girl doped and medicated would not recognize the man who's been fucking her, nor even exactly that she's been fucked, and that it has been going on for quite a while. "All over. And it was *good.*" Not wanting the girl to think how good it might be, how fantastic and even historic this session in Otto Öse's studio was. That the nude photos of Norma Jeane Baker a.k.a. "Marilyn Monroe" he'd taken that day would become the most famous, or infamous, calendar nudes in history. For which the model would earn fifty dollars, and millions of dollars would be earned by others. By men.

And the soles of my feet exposed.

Behind the tattered Chinese screen, Norma Jeane fumbled to dress quickly. Ninety minutes had passed in a drugged dream. Her head throbbed with pain confused with traffic outside on Hollywood Boulevard, the stink of exhaust. Her breasts ached with a ghostly milk-to-be-sucked. *If I'd had a baby with Bucky Glazer. Now I would be safe.*

She heard Otto talking to someone. He'd made a telephone call, probably. Laughing softly.

Now the lights were out, the frayed crimson velvet cloth carelessly folded up and shoved onto a shelf, the used rolls of film ready to be developed. Norma Jeane wanted only to be gone from Otto Öse. Waking from her dreamy trance beneath the blinding lights she'd seen in the photographer's skull face a gloating satisfaction that had nothing to do with her. She'd heard in his elated voice a happiness that had nothing to do with her. *Not humiliated now, baring myself to a man who doesn't love me. If I'd had a baby.* She had to acknowledge that stripping bare in Otto Öse's studio hadn't been done exclusively for money, though she desperately needed money and hoped to visit Gladys this weekend. She'd stripped bare and humbled herself in the hope that if Otto Öse saw her naked, her beautiful young body and her beautiful young yearning face, he could no longer resist loving her who had in fact resisted loving her for three years. Norma Jeane wondered if Otto Öse was impotent. In Hollywood, she'd discovered what *male impotence* was. Yet even an impotent man might love her. They could kiss, cuddle, hug each other through the nights. She would be happiest with an impotent man, in fact. She knew!

She was fully clothed now. In her medium-heeled shoes.

She checked her reflection in a compact mirror clouded with powder through which her blue eyes surfaced like minnows. "I'm still *here*."

She laughed her new throaty laugh. She was richer by fifty dollars. Maybe her luck, which had been running bad for months, would now change. Maybe this was a sign. And who would know?—calendar "art" was anonymous. Mr. Shinn was hoping to arrange for an audition at Metro-Goldwyn-Mayer. *He* hadn't given up on her.

She smiled in the little round mirror in the palm of her hand.

"Baby, you were terrific. Fan-tas-tic."

She snapped the compact shut and dropped it into her bag.

Rehearsing how she would exit Otto Öse's studio with dignity: Otto might be tidying up, or Otto might have poured a glass of rum, or two glasses of rum, in his scummy jam glasses, to celebrate the shoot, a ritual of his though he knew Norma Jeane didn't drink, and certainly wouldn't drink at this hour of the day. So he'd drink the second glass himself with a wink. She'd smile at him and wave—"Otto, thanks! I have to run!"—and walk out before he could protest. For he'd already given her the fifty dollars, safe in her wallet. She'd already signed the release.

But Otto called out to her, in his drawling voice, "Norma Jeane, hey, sweetheart—I'd like you to meet a friend of mine. An old comrade from the trenches. Cass."

Norma Jeane stepped out from behind the Chinese screen astonished to see a stranger beside Otto Öse! A boy with thick dark hair, sloe eyes. He was considerably shorter than Otto and compactly built, slender yet strong-looking, a dancer, perhaps, or a gymnast. He was smiling at Norma Jeane shyly. It was clear that he was attracted to her! The most beautiful boy Norma Jeane had ever seen outside the movies.

And those eyes.

THE LOVER

Because already we knew each other.

Because he'd gazed upon me, those eyes, haunting soulful beautiful eyes, from a wall of Gladys's long-ago apartment.

Because he would say, seeing me, *I knew you too. Fatherless like me. And your mother abandoned and debased like mine.*

Because he was a boy and not a man, though my age exactly.

Because in me he saw not the tramp, the slut, the joke who was "Marilyn Monroe" but the eager hopeful young girl who was Norma Jeane.

Because he, too, was doomed.

Because in his doom there was such poetry!

Because he would love me as Otto Öse would not, or could not.

Because he would love me as other men would not, or could not.

Because he would love me as a brother. As a twin.

With his soul.

THE AUDITION

All acting is aggression in the face of annihilation.

—From *The Actor's Handbook
and the Actor's Life*

How finally did it happen? It happened like this.

There was a film director who owed I. E. Shinn a favor. He'd gotten a tip from Shinn regarding a thoroughbred filly named Footloose running at the Casa Grande Stakes and the director played the filly to win (at 11 to 1) with money borrowed in secret from a wealthy producer's wife, and the director walked away from the racetrack with $16,500 which would help to pay off some of his debts, not all of his debts by any means because the director was an inveterate gambler and risk-taker, a genius in his craft some said, an irresponsible self-indulgent S.O.B. others said, a man not to be defined by ordinary standards of behavior, propriety, professional courtesy, decency, or even common sense: a "Hollywood original" who detested Hollywood but required Hollywood for the financial backing that made his idiosyncratic and expensive films possible.

And the leading man in the director's next film owed I. E. Shinn an even greater favor. In 1947, shortly after President Harry Truman signed the historic Executive Order 9835 requiring loyalty oaths and security programs for all federal employees, and "loyalty oaths" came to be demanded of employees by private businesses, the actor was one of a number of protesters in Hollywood, signing petitions and going on record as believing in such constitutional freedoms as freedom of speech and freedom of assembly.

Within a year he was under investigation as a subversive by the dread HUAC (House Un-American Activities Committee), exposing Communists and "Communist sympathizers" in the Hollywood film industry. It was revealed that the actor had been involved in contract negotiations between the left-leaning Screen Actors Guild and the major studios in 1945, demanding for members of the Guild a health and welfare program, better working conditions, a higher minimum wage, and royalty payments for reissues of films; the Actors Guild was charged with having been infiltrated by Communists, or their sympathizers, or dupes. Worse, the actor had been secretly denounced to HUAC by volunteer anticommunist informers as having consorted for years with known members of the American Communist Party including the screenwriters Dalton Trumbo and Ring Lardner, Jr., prominently blacklisted.

And so to escape the committee's subpoena and a hostile grilling in Washington, D.C., which would have resulted in ugly national publicity for the actor and the boycotting of his films by the American Legion and the Catholic Legion of Decency and other patriotic organizations (consider the fate of the once-adored Charlie Chaplin, now denounced as a "Red" and a "traitor") and inevitable blacklisting (no matter that the studios publicly denied the very existence of the blacklist), the actor was invited to meet privately with several key Republican California congressmen at the Bel Air home of a Hollywood entertainment lawyer who'd been put in contact with the actor by I. E. Shinn, the canny little agent. In this private meeting (in fact, a lavish dinner party complete with expensive French wines) the several congressmen questioned the actor informally and the actor impressed them with his soft-spoken masculine sincerity and patriotic ardor, for he was after all a World War II veteran, a G.I. who'd fought in Germany in the final grueling months of the war, and if he'd been attracted to Russian communism or socialism or whatever it was, please recall that Stalin, now a monster, was our ally at the time; Russia and the United States were not yet ideological enemies, the one a militant atheist state bent upon world domination, if not destruction, and the other the solitary hope of Christianity and democracy among the world's troubled nations. Please recall that only a few years ago it was understandable that a passionate young man like the actor might be drawn to radical politics in response to fascism. Sympathy for Russia had been promoted by newspapers and family magazines like *Life!*

The actor explained that he'd never actually been a member of the Communist Party, though he'd attended a few meetings, and he couldn't with any certainty "name names," which was the aim of HUAC. The Republican congressmen liked him and believed him and reported back to HUAC that he should be cleared, and no subpoena was issued after all. And if money was exchanged, it was cash, handed over discreetly from the actor's agent to the entertainment lawyer. Possibly the Republican congressmen received some of this payment too. The actor knew, or seemed to know, nothing about the transaction except of course that he'd been cleared and his name would be excised from the HUAC master list. And I. E. Shinn's role in the negotiations, as in similar negotiations in Hollywood in those years of unacknowledged "blacklists" and "clearances," would remain a mystery, like the man himself.

"Why not out of the goodness of my gnarly dwarf heart?"

So two key men involved in the upcoming Metro-Goldwyn-Mayer film were secretly indebted to I. E. Shinn. And each may have known of the other's indebtedness. And the shrewd little agent with the explosive laugh and the calm calculating eyes and the perpetual red carnation in his lapel bided his time like any gambler, knowing precisely when to call the director, the day before auditions for the single role in the film that was a possibility for his client "Marilyn Monroe." Shinn understood that the director, a Hollywood maverick, might be perversely impressed by the fact that the girl had been dropped by The Studio. So Shinn called and identified himself and the director remarked with good-natured irony, "This is about a girl, right?" and Shinn said with his usual abrasive dignity, "No. It's about an actress. A very special talent who would be ideal for the role of Louis Calhern's 'niece.' " The director groaned with a hangover headache, saying, "They're all special when we're fucking them." Shinn said, annoyed, "This girl is truly remarkable. She could be a major star if she's given the right role, and I believe that 'Angela' is the right role for her and so will you when you see her." The director said, "Like Hayworth? A gorgeous hick who can't act worth shit. A girl with bouncy breasts and a sulky lower lip and she's had electrolysis to improve her hairline and she's a bottle redhead or platinum blonde and she's going to be a star." Shinn said, "She will be. I'm giving you the chance to discover her." The director said, sighing, "OK, Is-aic. Send her over. Check with my assistant for the time."

Not telling Shinn he'd already decided on a girl for the role. It wasn't confirmed, he hadn't spoken with the girl's agent, but there was an indebtedness here, too, a sexual connection, and in any case the girl was a jet-haired beauty with exotic features, which was the type the screenplay indicated. The director could tell Shinn, if Shinn required telling, that his client just wasn't the type. And he'd pay back the favor he owed Shinn another time.

As the story goes, the next day promptly at four Shinn shows up with this girl—"Marilyn Monroe." A platinum blonde and gorgeous with an exquisite body in shimmering white rayon and so scared, the director sees, the poor kid can't speak except in a whisper. The director takes one look at "Marilyn Monroe" and his gut reaction is the girl can't act, she can't even fuck, but her mouth might be useful, and you could use her for decoration like the classy prow of a yacht or the silver hood ornament of a Rolls-Royce. Pale luminous skin like an expensive doll's and cobalt-blue eyes brimming with panic. And both her hands trembling, holding the heavy script. And her voice so breathy the director almost can't hear her speaking to him, like a schoolgirl nerved up, to declare she's read the script, the entire script, it's a strange disturbing story, like a novel by Dostoyevsky where you feel sympathy for criminals and don't want them to be punished. The girl says "Dost-ie-ev-sky," with an equal emphasis on each syllable. The director says, laughing, "Oh, you've read 'Dost-ie-ev-sky,' have you, honey?" and the girl blushes, knowing she's being mocked. And Shinn stands there, glowering, red-faced, spittle gleaming on his thick lips.

I didn't tag her as a hick. She looked pretty good. A sheltered girl out of Pasadena, upper middle class, lousy education, but somebody told her she could act. Catholic schoolgirl, almost. What a laugh! Shinn was in love with her, poor bastard. I don't know why I thought this was funny, I just did. You had the impression she towered over him but in fact he wasn't much shorter. Later I'd learn she was having an affair with Charlie Chaplin, Jr.! But right then, that day, it looked like she and Shinn were a couple. Typical Hollywood. Beauty and the beast, which is always funny unless you're the beast.

So the director instructs the blond "Marilyn Monroe" to begin her audition. There are six or eight people in the rehearsal room, all men. Folding chairs, blinds drawn against the bright sunshine. No carpet on the floor and the floor's strewn with butts and litter and the girl astonishes everyone by calmly lying down on the floor in her shimmering white rayon dress (neatly pressed with a narrow skirt, a cloth belt, and a boat-neck collar dipping to show just a portion of her creamy upper chest) before the director can figure out what she's doing or anyone can stop her. On the floor, on her back, arms outstretched, the girl earnestly explains to the director that the character's first scene begins with her asleep on a sofa so she has to lie down on the floor, that's how she's been rehearsing. *The first time you see Angela she's asleep.* That's *crucial.* You see her through the eyes of the older man, who's her "uncle," a married man, a lawyer. You don't see Angela except through his eyes, and later in the script you see Angela through the eyes of police officers. Only through men's eyes.

The director stares astonished at this platinum blonde lying on the floor at his feet. *Explaining the character to me! to me, the director!* She'd become as unself-conscious as a young willful child. An aggressive child. He forgets to light the Cuban cigar he's unwrapped and stuck between his teeth. There's absolute silence in the rehearsal room as "Marilyn Monroe" begins the scene by shutting her eyes, lying motionless in a mimicry of sleep, her breathing deep and slow and rhythmic (and her rib cage and breasts rising, falling, rising, falling), her smooth arms and her legs in nylons outstretched in the abandonment of sleep deep as hypnosis. What are the thoughts men think, gazing down upon the body of a beautiful sleeping girl? Eyes shut, lips just slightly parted. The opening of the scene lasts no more than a few seconds but it seems much longer. And the director is thinking, This girl is the first actress of the twenty or more he's auditioned for the role (including the black-haired actress he's probably going to cast) who has caught on to the significance of the scene's opening, the first who seems to have given the role any intelligent thought and who has actually read the entire script (or so she claims) and formed some sort of judgment on it. The girl opens her eyes, sits up slowly and blinking, wide-eyed, and says in a whisper, "Oh, I—must have been asleep." Is she acting, or has she actually been asleep? Everyone's uncomfortable. There is something strange here. The girl with seeming naïveté (or cunning) addresses the director and not the assistant who's reading Louis Calhern's lines, and in this way she makes the director, still with the unlit Cuban cigar clamped between his teeth, her "uncle" lover.

It was frank and intimate as her fingers on my balls. I'd come away thinking that had actually happened. It wasn't acting. She couldn't act. This was the real thing. Or was it?

Eleven years later the director would be working with "Marilyn Monroe" on the last film of her career, and he'd remember this audition and this moment. *It was all there, from the beginning. Her genius, you could call it. Her madness.*

By the end of the scene the director has regained some of his composure and managed to light his cigar. In fact, he isn't thinking that Shinn's young client is a genius. He's watching her with the masklike expression he's perfected as a person at whom others are always glancing, hoping to read his mind. But he doesn't know what he thinks right now. He won't consult his assistants; he isn't a man to take his cue from inferiors. So he tells the girl, "Thank you, Miss Monroe. Very good."

Is the audition over? The director sucks on his cigar, leafing through the script on his lap. It's a tense moment. Is it crueler to ask her to read another scene, or should he break off the audition now and explain to Shinn (who's been watching from the sidelines, tragic gargoyle face and eyes limpid with love) that "Marilyn Monroe" is certainly an unusual, arresting talent, very beautiful of course, but not quite right for the role, which calls for a black-haired exotic girl, not a classy blonde? Should he? Can he?—disappoint Shinn who's done him a good deed and made it possible for Sterling Hayden to escape the blacklist? Exactly what connection does Shinn have with HUAC and the strategies by which individuals can be "cleared" of subversion without testifying in Washington and risking their careers? You wouldn't want to cross I. E. Shinn, the director knows. He's thinking this, and brooding, used to respectful silence, when suddenly the girl says in that baby-breathy voice, "Oh, I can do better than this, let me try again. *Please.*"

He's so surprised at her audacity, the cigar almost falls from his mouth.

Did I let her try again? Sure. She was fascinating to watch. Like a mental patient, maybe. Not acting. No technique. She'd put herself to sleep and out would come this other personality that was her yet also not-her.

People like that, you can see why they're drawn to acting. Because the actor, in her role, always knows who she is. All losses are restored.

So, after the audition, as the story goes, the director informs I. E. Shinn he'll be telephoning soon. He shakes the agent's hand, which has a fierce grip but is chilled as if the blood has drained out of his fingers. He'd avoid shaking the girl's hand, not wanting contact with her, but she extends her hand to be shaken and he finds it soft, moist, warm, and a stronger grip than you'd expect. *A steely soul. She'll kill to get what she wants. But what does she want?* He thanks her again for the audition and assures her she'll be hearing from them soon.

What a relief when Shinn and "Marilyn" are gone! The director puffs vigorously on his cigar. He hasn't had a drink since his four-martini lunch and he's thirsty and feeling strangely resentful because he doesn't know what he feels. His assistants wait for him to speak. Or to make a sound, a joke. A gesture. He's been known to spit on the floor in playful disgust. He's been known to explode in a catalog of comic obscenity. He's an actor himself, he likes attention. But not annoying attention.

The assistant director clears his throat, edging near. What does the director think? The audition was pretty bad, wasn't it? Sexy blonde. Nice-looking girl. Like Lana Turner but too intense. Out of control, maybe. Not right for Angela. Or is she? No technique, can't act. Or perhaps Angela who's so confused doesn't know how to "act"?

Still the director hasn't spoken. Standing by a window, shoving the venetian blind aside. Sucking on his cigar. The assistant director comes to stand beside the director, though not exactly next to him. The director must've decided against Shinn's girl. Trying to think how not to disappoint Shinn too badly. Trying to think how maybe he could assure the agent that, next film, he'd find a role for beautiful "Marilyn." But, this film, it isn't going to work—is it? The director nudges his assistant as, a floor below, Shinn and the blonde leave the building and walk away to the curb. The director says, exhaling smoke in pain, "Sweet Jesus. Look at the ass on that little girl, will you?"

In this way, Norma Jeane's future was decided.

THE BIRTH

She would be born in the New Year of 1950.

In a season of clandestine radioactive explosions. Fierce hot winds rushing across the Nevada salt flats. The deserts of western Utah. Birds stricken in flight plummeting to earth like cartoon birds. Dying antelope, dying cougars, coyotes. Terror reflected in the eyes of jackrabbits. On Utah ranches bordering the government-restricted proving grounds of the Great Salt Lake Desert, dying cattle, horses, sheep. It was a time of "defensive nuclear testing." It was a time of ever-vigilant drama. Though the war had been over since August 1945, and it was now 1950 and a new decade.

It was a time, too, of flying saucers: "unidentified flying objects" sighted predominantly in the western American sky. Though these flat, swiftly moving objects would be seen in the Northeast as well. Myriad blinking lights, near-instantaneous appearances and disappearances. At any hour, day or night, though more likely night, you might glance up and see one. You might be blinded by flashing lights, fierce hot suction winds that took your breath away. An air of danger, yet of profound significance. As if the very sky was opening up and what was behind, hidden until now, would be revealed.

On the far side of the world, remote as the moon, the mysterious Soviets detonated their nuclear devices. They were Communist demons, bent upon the destruction of Christians. No truces were possible with them, as with any demons. It was only a matter of time—months? weeks? days?—until they attacked.

These are the days of vengeance Norma Jeane's lover intoned in his velvety tenor voice. *Yet: vengeance is mine, saith the Lord.*

He insisted that Norma Jeane meditate with him upon the photographs. They two were soulmates, brother and sister as well as lovers. They were twins, born in the same year, 1926, and under the same sign, Gemini. From Otto Öse he'd acquired these grainy reproductions of secret Air Force photographs of Hiroshima and Nagasaki after the atomic bombs were dropped on August 6 and August 9 of 1945. These were suppressed photos that would not be released to the media until 1952, and how Otto Öse had come into possession of them, Cass wasn't certain. The *ultimate pornography* Otto Öse said of these documents.

The devastation of cities. Burnt-out shells of buildings, vehicles. A hazy rubble wasteland through which human beings yet managed to stagger upright. There were close-ups in oddly rich, lurid colors of certain of these figures and their blank stricken faces and of the frozen hands of a clock recording 8:16 of a long-ago day and of human shadow silhouettes baked into walls. Quietly Cass Chaplin said, "None of us knew it then. The birth of our new civilization. This, and the death camps." Cass was drinking, sprawled naked on his bed, which was in fact a stranger's bed, for in their months of love he and Norma Jeane would dwell predominantly among the possessions of strangers, and he was running his sensitive fingertips over the photographs (which were only reproductions) like a blind man reading Braille. His voice trembled with both sorrow and satisfaction. His beautiful dark-brown eyes shone with feeling. "From now on, Norma, movie fantasies won't be powerful enough. Or the churches. God." Norma Jeane, distracted by the ugly photographs, didn't disagree. Rarely did she disagree aloud with her lover, who was magic to her, a twin self far deeper and more worthy than she herself might ever be. Charlie Chaplin's son! And Chaplin's soul gazing out of his glistening eyes as out of the eyes of the long-ago hero of *City Lights*. But she was thinking *No. People will need places to hide now. More than ever.*

ANGELA 1950

Who's the blonde? who's the blonde? the blonde?

The voices were men's voices. Most of the audience at the screening were men.

That blonde, Calhern's "niece"—who's she?

That good-looking blonde, the one in white—what's the name?

The sexy blonde—who the hell is she?

Not murmuring jeering voices in a mock fantasy but true voices. For the name "Marilyn Monroe" hadn't been listed among the major cast credits on M-G-M promotional material passed out at the screening. Her two brief scenes in the lengthy movie hadn't seemed important enough to warrant it. Nor did Norma Jeane expect it. She was grateful to be listed at all (as "Marilyn Monroe") among the credits at the end of the film.

It was not the real name of any real person. But it was the role I would play, and I hoped I would play it with pride.

But after the first public screening of *The Asphalt Jungle*, the question heard repeatedly was *Who's the blonde?*

I. E. Shinn was there to inform them: "Who's the blonde? My client 'Marilyn Monroe.'"

Norma Jeane was shaking with fear. Hiding in the powder room. In a locked toilet stall, where after several anxious minutes she'd managed to pee hardly a half cup of hot scalding liquid. And her legs in sheer nylons, and her white satin garter belt twisting and cutting into her belly. And her elegant white silk-and-chiffon cocktail dress with the spaghetti straps and low-cut bodice and body-clinging skirt bunched now clumsily about her hips, trailing onto the floor. An old childhood fear of staining her clothing, pee stains, bloodstains, sweat stains, gripped her. She was perspiring and she was shivering. In the screening room she'd had to pry her icy fingers loose from I. E. Shinn's strong steely fingers (the little agent was holding her tight, knowing she was nervous as a high-strung filly about to bolt) and flee after her second scene in which as "Angela" she'd cried, hidden her pretty face, betrayed her lover "Uncle Leon," and set in motion an action that would result in the older man's killing himself in a subsequent scene.

And I did feel guilt and shame. As if I'd truly been Angela taking revenge on the very man who loved me.

Where was Cass? Why hadn't he come to the screening? Norma Jeane was faint with love for him, need for him. Hadn't he promised to come and sit beside her and hold her hand, knowing how terrified she was of this evening, and yet he had not; and it was not the first time Cass Chaplin had promised Norma Jeane the gift of his elusive presence in a public place where eyes would move upon him excited in recognition—*Is it?* then in disappointment *No, of course not, it must be his son,* and then in quickened prurient interest *So that's Chaplin's son! And little Lita's!*—and then failed to show up. He would not apologize afterward or even explain himself, and Norma Jeane would find herself apologizing to him for her own hurt and anxiety. He'd told her that being Charlie Chaplin's son was a curse that others stupidly wished to believe must be a blessing—"Like it's a fairy tale, and I'm the King's son." He'd told her that the much-beloved Little Tramp was a vicious egoist who despised children, especially his own; he hadn't allowed his teenage wife to name their son for a full year after his birth, out of a superstitious dread of sharing his name with anyone, even his flesh-and-blood son! He'd told Norma Jeane that Chaplin divorced Little Lita after two years and disowned and disinherited him, Charlie Chaplin, Jr., because he wanted only the adulation of strangers, not the intimate love of a family. "As soon as I was born, I was posthumous. For if your father wishes you not to exist, you have no legitimate right to exist."

Norma Jeane could not protest this statement. She knew: yes, it was so.

Though thinking at the same time with childlike logic *Yet he would like me, I think. If ever we meet.* For Grandma Della had admired the Little Tramp, and Gladys too. And Norma Jeane had grown up with those eyes gazing upon her from out of what pockmarked wall of what forgotten "residence" of her madwoman mother. *His eyes. My soulmate. No matter our ages.*

Norma Jeane fumbled to adjust her clothing and left the safety of the toilet stall, grateful that the powder room was empty still. Like a guilty child she contemplated her flushed face in the mirror, not head-on but sidelong, dreading to see Norma Jeane's plain yearning face inside the beautiful cosmetic face of "Marilyn Monroe." Inside the carefully made-up eyes of "Marilyn Monroe," the staring hungry eyes of Norma Jeane. She seemed not to recall that Norma Jeane herself had been strikingly pretty; though her hair was dish-water blond, yet boys and men had stared after her in the street, and her photo in *Stars & Stripes* had set this all in motion. This ravishing blond "Marilyn Monroe" was the role she had to play, at least for the evening, at least in public, and she'd prepared elaborately for it, and I. E. Shinn had prepared elaborately for it, and she didn't intend to disappoint him. "I owe him everything. Mr. Shinn. What a good, kind, generous man he is." She'd spoken in this way to her lover Cass, who'd laughed and said reprovingly, "Norma, I. E. Shinn is an *agent*. A *flesh merchant*. Lose your looks, lose your youth and sex appeal, Shinn's *gone*."

Stung, Norma Jeane had an impulse to ask *And you, Cass? What about you?*

There was a mysterious dislike between Cass Chaplin and I. E. Shinn. Possibly, Cass Chaplin had once been a client of Mr. Shinn's. (Cass was a singer-dancer-choreographer with acting experience; he'd had numerous small roles in Hollywood films, including *Can't Stop Lovin' You* and *Stage Door Canteen*, though Norma Jeane couldn't remember him in these films, which she'd seen holding hands with Bucky Glazer a lifetime ago.) There would be a private dinner in a restaurant in Bel Air following the screening and Norma Jeane had invited Cass to the dinner as well, but I. E. Shinn intervened, saying this wasn't a good idea. "Why not?" Norma Jeane asked. "Because your friend has a reputation around town," Shinn said. "A reputation for what?" Norma Jeane demanded, though she supposed she knew. "Being 'left-wing'? A 'subversive'?" "Not only that," Shinn said, "though that's risky enough right now. You see what's happened to Chaplin, Sr.—he's been hounded out of the country, not for his beliefs but for his *attitude*. He's arrogant, and a fool. And Chaplin, Jr., is a drunk. He's a loser. A jinx. He's Chaplin's son but he hasn't Chaplin's talent." "Mr. Shinn," Norma Jeane protested, "that's unfair, and you know it. Charlie Chaplin was a great genius. Not every actor must be a genius." The gnomelike little man wasn't accustomed to being contradicted by his girl clients and especially not by Norma Jeane, who was so shy and malleable. Cass Chaplin must be corrupting her! Shinn's broad, bumpy forehead creased with worry and his eyes bulged and glared. "He owes money everywhere. He'll sign for a role and fail to show up. Or he shows up drunk. Or doped. He borrows cars and cracks them up and he leeches on to women—who should know a hell of a lot better—and men. I don't want you seen with him in public, Norma Jeane." "Then I won't go to the dinner myself!" Norma Jeane cried. "Oh, yes, you will. The studio expects 'Marilyn,' and 'Marilyn' will be there."

Shinn spoke loudly. He gripped her wrist and she quieted immediately.

Of course I. E. Shinn was right. She'd signed a contract with M-G-M. Not just to play the role of "Angela" but to fulfill publicity requirements too. "Marilyn" would be there.

In a fifty-seven-dollar dazzling-white silk-and-chiffon cocktail dress purchased for Norma Jeane by Mr. Shinn at Bullock's in Beverly Hills, a chic-sexy dress with a low-cut bodice and a slender fitted skirt that showed her figure to advantage. Fifty-seven dollars for a dress! Norma Jeane had a sudden girlish impulse to telephone Elsie Pirig. The dress was as glamorous as Angela's costume in the film, which perhaps it was meant to resemble. "Oh, Mr. Shinn! This is the most beautiful dress I've ever worn!" Norma Jeane pirouetted before a three-way mirror in the store's most fashionable salon, as her agent looked on, smoking a cigar. "Well. White suits you, dear." Shinn was pleased with Norma Jeane in the dress and pleased with the attention his client was drawing in the store. Beverly Hills matrons, rich and good-looking and expensively dressed, the wives of studio executives, were glancing in their direction wondering who the glamorous young starlet was with the redoubtable I. E. Shinn. "Yes. White suits you *very well*."

Norma Jeane was again taking voice lessons, acting lessons, dance lessons, now at M-G-M, and her public manner was more assured, however nervous she felt. Almost, she could hear piano music at a distance, beyond the hubbub of conversations, melodic dance music; if this were a movie, a musical, I. E. Shinn in his double-breasted sport coat with the red carnation in his lapel and the shiny pointy shoes would be Fred Astaire, leaping to his feet to take Norma Jeane in his arms and dance, dance, dance away with her as a startled audience of saleswomen and shoppers looked on.

After the cocktail dress, Shinn insisted upon buying two thirty-dollar suits for Norma Jeane, also at Bullock's. Both were stylish, with narrow pencil skirts and snug-fitting jackets. And he bought her several pairs of high-heeled leather shoes. Norma Jeane protested, but Shinn interrupted, saying, "Look. This is an investment in 'Marilyn Monroe.' Who, when *The Asphalt Jungle* is released, is going to be a hot property. I have faith in 'Marilyn' even if you don't." Was Mr. Shinn teasing or serious? He crinkled his Rumpelstiltskin face and winked at her. Norma Jeane said weakly, "I do have faith. It's just that—" "Just that—what?" "As Otto Öse explained to me, I'm photogenic. I guess. That means it's a trick, doesn't it? Of the camera lens or the optic nerve? I'm not really the way I look. I mean—" Shinn snorted in disgust. "Otto

Öse. That nihilist. That pornographer. I hope to Christ you've put Otto Öse well behind you." Quickly Norma Jeane said, "Oh, yes! Yes, I have." It was true: since the humiliation of the fifty-dollar nude photo session, she hadn't seen Otto Öse; when he'd called and left messages for her at her rooming house, she'd torn them into bits and never called back. She had not seen contact sheets for "Miss Golden Dreams" and seemed not to remember that she'd posed for a calendar. (She hadn't told I. E. Shinn, of course. She hadn't told anyone.) Since being cast in *The Asphalt Jungle* she'd concentrated solely on her acting and had no interest in modeling of any kind, however much she could have used the money. "Öse and Chaplin, Jr. Stay away from them and their kind." Shinn spoke vehemently. At such times, working his fleshy lips, he seemed a very old, even ancient man; all his playfulness vanished. "Their kind"—what did that mean? Norma Jeane winced to hear her lover casually dismissed, mysteriously linked with the cruel hawk-faced photographer, so lacking in Cass's tenderness and purity of heart. "But I l-love Cass," Norma Jeane whispered. "I hope he will marry me, someday soon." Shinn wasn't listening or didn't hear; he'd heaved himself to his feet, flourishing his crocodile-hide wallet, which was twice the size of an ordinary man's wallet, and giving instructions to a salesclerk. Norma Jeane now towered over him in her new russet-red leather high-heeled shoes and had to resist the impulse to slouch so she wouldn't be quite so tall. *Carry yourself like a princess,* a wise voice admonished her. *And soon you will be one.*

The shopping spree took place two days before the screening. Mr. Shinn drove Norma Jeane home to her bungalow-boardinghouse on Buena Vista and helped her carry her numerous packages inside. (Fortunately, Cass wasn't there, half dressed, sprawled on Norma Jeane's bed or sunning himself in a patch of winter sunshine on the tiny balcony to the rear. The small apartment smelled of him, an oily-rich scent, a scent of body heat and underarms and thick, always slightly damp raven-black hair, and if I. E. Shinn's hairy nostrils detected this odor, the agent was too tactful, or had too much pride, to give any indication.) Norma Jeane supposed she should offer Mr. Shinn a drink and not send him immediately away, but there was nothing in the kitchen except a bottle or two of Cass's (Cass favored whiskey, gin, brandy), and Norma Jeane was reluctant to touch these bottles. So she didn't offer Shinn a drink, or even invite him to sit down while she brewed coffee. No, no! She wanted the ugly little man gone so she could model her new clothes in the mirror, rehearsing Cass's arrival. *Look. Look at me. Am I beautiful for you?*

Norma Jeane thanked I. E. Shinn and walked him to the door. Seeing in the little man's yearning eyes that something more was required, in Marilyn's husky-breathy voice she said, "Thank you, Daddy."

Leaning down to kiss I. E. Shinn, light as a feather, on his astonished lips.

. . .

Norma Jeane dialed Cass's number from the powder room. It was a new number, for Cass was staying for several weeks in a new borrowed residence, on Montezuma Drive in the Hollywood Hills. "Cass, please answer. Darling, you know how I need you. Don't do this to me. *Please.*" The screening was over; Norma Jeane's fate was decided; from the theater foyer came a rising din of voices; it was not possible for Norma Jeane to hear the repeated query *Who's the blonde? who's the blonde? the blonde?* or even to imagine such a phenomenon. And I. E. Shinn proudly boasting *The blonde is my client, that's who she is: Miss Marilyn Monroe.*

Never would she have imagined that, following this legendary screening, immediately the studio would give "Marilyn Monroe" billing with the major cast of *The Asphalt Jungle*: Sterling Hayden, Louis Calhern, Jean Hagen, and Sam Jaffe in a film directed by John Huston.

Whispering into the receiver, "Cass, darling. *Please.*"

At the other end a telephone rang, rang.

Love at first sight.

Faint with love. Doomed!

Love enters through the eyes.

Norma he called her. He was the only one of her lovers ever to call her *Norma.*

Not "Norma Jeane." Not "Marilyn."

(Norma Shearer had been his idol when he'd been a boy. Norma Shearer in *Marie Antoinette.* The beautiful queen in all her finery, her absurd high-piled and bejeweled hair and layers of opulent fabric so stiff she could barely move, condemned to a cruel, barbaric, unjust death: to the guillotine!)

Cass she called him. *Cass my brother, my baby.* They were as gentle with each other as children who've been injured by rough play. Their kisses were slow and searching. They made love for long dreamy hours in silence, not knowing where they were, whose bed this was, when they'd begun, and when they would end, and where. Pressing their heated cheeks together desperate to ease together, to see through a single pair of eyes. *I love love love you! Oh, Cass.* Holding the beautiful tousle-haired boy tight in her arms like a prize wrested from other, greedy arms. Never fierce in love, she found herself fierce in love now.

Vowing *I will love you until death. And beyond.*

And Cass laughed at her and said *Norma. Until death is enough. One world at a time.*

She would not tell him about that long-ago time, his eyes, his beautiful eyes fixed on hers, out of the *City Lights* poster. How long ago she'd fallen in love with those eyes. Or were they the dark brooding-yet-playful eyes of the man in the framed photograph on Gladys's bedroom wall? *I love you. I will protect you. Never doubt me: I will come for you someday.* One of the great shocks of her life, which as Otto Öse predicted would not be a long life but which would be a snarled and dreamlike and riddlesome life of puzzle pieces fitted together by force, was that moment—and in the movies what ecstatic pulse-quickened music would signal that moment!—when she'd stepped out from behind the tattered Chinese screen in Otto Öse's studio knowing herself demeaned, debased, humiliated—and for only fifty dollars!—and there was Cass Chaplin smiling at her. *We know each other, Norma. We've always known each other. Have faith in me.*

A cinematic collapse of time. Days, weeks. Eventually months. Never would they live together (Cass found the idea of sharing an actual household made him anxious and asthmatic, mingling clothes in a closet for instance, things in bathrooms, in drawers, accumulating history together, couldn't breathe! couldn't swallow! Not that he was the Great Dictator's son incapable of maintaining a mature, responsible relationship with a woman, not that he was a cruel vindictive hedonist hypocrite like the Great Man, Cass was not, for this was in fact a physical symptom; Norma Jeane could observe it terrified at close quarters, eager to allow her lover to know *I'm not smothering you! I'm not that kind of woman*), but they spent every hour together (or almost, depending upon Cass's mysterious schedule of auditions and callbacks and long meditative walks in the rain as in the sun on the beach at Santa Monica) when Norma Jeane wasn't on the M-G-M set at Culver City.

It was my first true film. I plunged into it with all my strength. And that strength came from Cass. From a man loving me. For there was not just myself, just one. But two. I was strengthened by two.

You wanted to believe that. There was every reason to believe that. It might've been scripted, the words had that sound. Prepared words. Not-spontaneous words. Therefore words you could trust. Like reading the scripture when you have the key. When you have the secret wisdom. Like the jigsaw puzzle once it's completed, every piece in place and no piece lost. And how naturally they fitted together in a sweet fainting swoon, in a delirium of aching physical need, as if long ago they'd made love as children. As if there were no *maleness* and no *femaleness* between them. No need, for instance, for the embarrassing clumsiness of condoms. Ugly smelly demeaning condoms. "Rubbers," Bucky Glazer had called them. His blunt matter-of-fact way. And Frank Widdoes, hadn't he said "I'd use a rubber. Don't worry." But Norma Jeane, staring smiling through the windshield, had not heard and would not hear for it would not be repeated.

Such bluntness was not Norma Jeane's way. Hers was the way of romance. For her lover was beautiful as any girl and side by side in the mirror flushed and their eyes dilated by love they laughed and kissed and tousled each other's hair and you could not have said who was more beautiful and whose body more desirable. Cass Chaplin! She loved to walk with him and see women's eyes fasten upon him. (And men's eyes too! Oh, she saw.) They hated clothes between them and walked about naked when they could. It was Norma Jeane's Magic Friend in the Mirror come alive. Her lover was hardly an inch taller than she and he had a smooth-muscled torso with a patina of fine dark hairs covering his flat breasts hardly thicker than the down on Norma Jeane's forearms and she loved to stroke his torso, his shoulders, his supple lean muscled arms, thighs, legs, and she loved to brush his thick, damp, oily hair back from his forehead, and kiss kiss kiss his forehead, and his eyelids, and his mouth, sucking his tongue into her mouth, and his penis rose quick and eager and warm and quivering in her hand like a living creature. This was no cruel wicked dream of a bleeding cut between the legs; this was fate, not desperation. *Those eyes!*

Immediately you're in love it's as if you've always been in love.

A cinematic collapse of time.

Clive Pearce! There came the morning she realized.

At rehearsal she'd been awkward and wooden in reciting her lines. How clumsy she was, working with the renowned elder actor Louis Calhern, who seemed never to look directly at her! Did he despise her, as an inexperienced young actress? Or was he bemused by her? Where at her audition Norma Jeane had spoken Angela's lines with seeming spontaneity, naively lying on the floor, now on her feet she was paralyzed with fear at the enormity of the risk before her. *What if you fail. If you fail. You will fail. Then you must die.* If fired from the film she would be obliged to destroy herself, yet she was deeply in love with Cass Chaplin and hoped one day to have his child— "How can I leave *him*?" And there was her obligation to Gladys in the hospital at Norwalk. "How can I leave *her*? Mother has no one but me."

Her scenes with Calhern were exclusively interiors, rehearsed and shot on a sound stage at the M-G-M lot in Culver City. In the film, Angela and her "Uncle Leon" were alone together but in reality, on the set, they were surrounded by strangers. There was a curious comfort in shutting these others out. Cameramen, assistants. The great director himself. As at the orphanage she'd swung high, high on the swing, shutting out the rest of the world. In the clamorous dining room making her way to her table unseeing and unhearing. That was her secret strength, which no one could take from her. She believed her character Angela was herself, except stunted. Certainly she,

Norma Jeane, contained Angela. Yet Angela was too narrow to contain Norma Jeane. It was a matter of mastery! In the film story, Angela is undefined. Shrewdly Norma Jeane perceived the girl to be her Uncle Leon's fantasy. (And the fantasy of the moviemakers, who were male.) In the beautiful blank blond Angela, innocence and vanity are identical. There is no true motivation to her character except childlike self-interest. She initiates no scenes, no dramatic exchanges. She is purely reactive, not active. She speaks lines like an amateur actress, groping and improvising and taking her cues from "Uncle Leon." By herself, she does not exist. No woman in *The Asphalt Jungle* exists except by way of men. Angela is passive as a pool of water in which others see their reflections, but she does not herself "see." It's no accident that the first time Angela is seen, she lies asleep on a sofa in a twisted position and we see her through her elder lover's possessive eyes. *Oh! I must have fallen asleep.* Yet awake, eyes widened in perpetual wonder, Angela is a sleepwalker.

In rehearsals Calhern was nervous with Norma Jeane. He did despise her! His character was "Alonzo Emmerich," and he was fated to put a bullet through his brain. Angela was his hope of renewed youth and life: a futile hope. *He blames me. He can't touch me. There's rage, not love in his heart.*

She couldn't find the key to him. The key to the scenes between them. She knew that, if they failed to play well together, she would have to be replaced with another actress.

Obsessively she rehearsed her scenes. She had few lines, and most were in response to "Uncle Leon" and, later, to the police officers who interrogate her. She rehearsed with Cass when he was available, and when he was in the mood. He wanted her to succeed, he said. He knew what it meant to her. ("Success" meant relatively little to him, son of the most successful film actor of all time.) Yet quickly he became impatient with her. He shook her like a rag doll to wake her from her Angela trance. He teased her, trying to keep the anger out of his voice. "Norma, for Christ's sake. Your director will lead you step by step through your scenes, that's what movies are. Not real acting, like the theater; not where you're on your own. Why work so hard? Turn yourself inside out? You're sweating like a horse. Why does this matter so much?"

The question hovered between them. *Why does it matter so much? So much!*

Knowing it was absurd, what she could not explain to her lover—*Because I don't want to die, I'm in terror of dying. I can't leave you.* Because to fail in her acting career was to fail at the life she'd chosen to justify her wrongful birth. And even in her mildly deranged state she understood the illogic of such a statement.

She wiped at her eyes. She laughed. "*I* can't choose what matters to me, like you. I don't have that power."

Help me to have that power. Darling, teach me.

Norma Jeane's insomnia worsened. A roaring in her head in which murmurous mocking voices lifted, jeering laughter, indistinct and yet familiar. Were these her judges, or spirits of the damned awaiting her? She had only Angela to pit against them. She had only her work—her performance—her "art." *Why does it matter so much?* She was sleepless when she was alone in her tiny apartment in her Salvation Army brass bed or when Cass was with her, in that bed or in another. (Elusive Cass Chaplin! The beautiful boy had many friends in Hollywood, Beverly Hills, Hollywood Hills, Santa Monica, Bel Air, Venice and Venice Beach, Pasadena, Malibu, and everywhere in Los Angeles, and these friends, most of them unknown to Norma Jeane, had apartments, bungalows, houses, estates in which Cass was welcome at any time, night or day. He seemed to have no permanent address. His possessions, mainly clothes, and these clothes expensive gifts, were scattered among a dozen households and trundled about with him in a duffel bag and in a large battered leather suitcase with the scrolled gilt initials CC.)

Prowling the early-morning hours barefoot and shivering. If Cass was gone from her she missed him painfully but if he was with her, sleeping, she was jealous of his sleep, which she could not penetrate and in which he eluded her. At such times she remembered her lost friend Harriet and her baby, Irina, who'd been Norma Jeane's baby too. Harriet had told Norma Jeane that for a long time as a girl she'd been insomniac, too, then she'd gotten pregnant and fell asleep all the time and after her baby was born and her husband was gone from her she slept, slept as much as she could, and it was a peaceful dreamless sleep and one day maybe Norma Jeane would know this sleep if she was lucky. *If I become pregnant. If I have a baby. But not now. But when?* She could not imagine Angela pregnant. She could not imagine Angela beyond the script. She'd memorized Angela's lines to the point at which the lines ceased to have meaning, like foreign words repeated by rote. She'd begun to exhaust herself in her first week on the set. Never had she guessed that acting was so physically draining. Like lifting her own weight! She began to cry, unless she was laughing. Wiping her eyes with the palms of both hands.

And there was Cass, the beautiful naked boy, tousle-haired, approaching her where she stood on her tiny balcony, extending his opened palm on which lay two white capsules. "What are those?" Norma Jeane asked guardedly. "A potion, darling Norma, to help you sleep. To help us both sleep," Cass said, kissing the damp nape of her neck. "A magic potion?" Norma Jeane asked. Cass said, "There is no magic potion. But there is this potion."

Norma Jeane turned away, disapproving. It wasn't the first time that Cass had offered her sedatives. Barbiturates, they were called. Or whiskey, gin, rum. And she wanted badly to give in. She knew it would please her lover, who rarely slept without having drunk or taken pills or both. Mere exhaustion, Cass boasted, wasn't enough to slow him down. He was saying, his breath warm in Norma Jeane's ear and one of his arms gently around her, cradling her breasts, "There was a Greek philosopher who taught that, of all things, not to have been born is the sweetest state. But I believe sleep is the sweetest state. You're dead, yet alive. There's no sensation so exquisite."

Norma Jeane pushed her lover away, more forcibly than she intended. She didn't love Cass Chaplin at such times! She loved him but was fearful of him. He was the very devil tempting her. She knew how Dr. Mittelstadt would disapprove. The teachings of Christian Science. Her great-grandmother Mary Baker Eddy. "No, it isn't right. For me. An artificial sleep."

Cass laughed at her, but Norma Jeane refused the sleeping potion and that night remained awake and anxious as Cass peacefully slept and slept through the early morning when Norma Jeane prepared to leave for the studio, and through the long day at Culver City Norma Jeane was edgy, nerved up, and shrill, and faltered in the very lines she'd memorized, and she saw how John Huston regarded her, the man's assessing eyes; he was wondering if he who never made mistakes in casting had made a mistake with her, and on the next night she accepted both capsules from Cass, who gave them to her solemnly, placed on her tongue like communion wafers.

And how deeply, how peacefully Norma Jeane slept that night! Not in memory had she slept so profoundly. *An artificial sleep but a healthy sleep, isn't it?* A magic potion after all.

And next morning on the set, rehearsing with Louis Calhern, Norma Jeane suddenly realized: *Clive Pearce!*

She would attribute her insight to Cass's magic potion. A dreamless sleep but maybe not entirely. Maybe, in a dream, the elder man had appeared to her?

For it seemed clear to her now: Louis Calhern who was her "Uncle Leon" was in fact Mr. Pearce. In the role of Alonzo Emmerich, Mr. Pearce.

She'd been seeing the renowned Calhern as a stranger when in fact he was Mr. Pearce, returned to her, approximately the same age, approximately the same girth and body shape and wasn't Calhern's ravaged-handsome face the very face of Clive Pearce, years later? The furtive eyes, the twitchy mouth, yet the pride in his bearing, or a memory of pride; above all, the cultivated, slightly ironic voice. A light must have shone in Norma Jeane's eyes. An lelectric current must have run through her supple, eager girl's body. She was "Marilyn"—no, she was "Angela"—she was Norma Jeane playing

"Marilyn" playing "Angela"—like a Russian doll in which smaller dolls are contained by the largest doll which is the mother—now she understood who "Uncle Leon" was and immediately she became soft, seductive, as wide-eyed and trusting as a child. Calhern noticed at once. He was an actor skilled in technique and could imitate emotion as if signaling it; he was not a natural actor, yet he noticed the change in "Angela" at once. The director noticed at once. At the end of the day's rehearsal he would say, he who so rarely praised any of the cast and had said virtually nothing to Norma Jeane until now, "Something happened today, eh? What was it?" Norma Jeane, who was very happy, shook her head wordlessly and smiled as if she didn't know, for how could she explain, who could not have explained it to herself?

She could take direction, that was part of her genius. She could read my mind. Of course it might not have happened, it seemed to me accidental, as if I'd been sowing seeds on the ground and only one took hold.

Their single kiss. Norma Jeane and Clive Pearce. He'd never kissed her full on the mouth, as he'd wanted to. He'd touched her squirmy body and he'd tickled her and (she believed) he'd kissed her where she couldn't see but never full on the mouth and now she melted against him, yearning and yet child-like, virginal, for it was her soul that opened itself to the older man, not her tight girl's body. *Oh! oh I love you! never leave me* she would forgive Mr. Pearce for deceiving her, driving her to the orphans' home and abandoning her; yet now that Mr. Pearce was returned to her, as the patrician lawyer Alonzo Emmerich, who was "Uncle Leon," she immediately forgave him and after the remarkable breathless kiss she continued to lean into him, Angela's eyes misty and intense and her lips slightly parted, and Louis Calhern who was a veteran actor of decades stared at her in astonishment.

The girl wasn't acting. It was herself. She became the Angela my charac-ter wished. His desire.

From that hour onward, Norma Jeane would have no more anxiety as Angela.

On the set Norma Jeane was quiet and respectful and watchful and shrewd. Now she'd solved the puzzle of her own role, it fascinated her to see how others had solved, or were struggling with, theirs. For acting is the solv-ing of a succession of puzzles of which no single puzzle can explain the oth-ers. For the actor is a succession of selves held together by the promise that in acting all losses can be restored. It would be a curiosity that the young blond client of I. E. Shinn, "Marilyn Monroe," would so intensely watch others' scenes, rehearsals, and filming, showing up on the set even when she wasn't scheduled to work.

She slept her way up. Beginning with Z, then X. There was Shinn, of course. And Huston certainly. And the film's producers. And Widmark. And

Roy Baker. And Sol Siegel, and Howard Hawks. And anybody else you can name.

Norma Jeane believed that, in the presence of gifted actors, her pores might absorb wisdom. In the presence of a great director, she might learn how to "direct" herself. For Huston was a genius; from Huston she learned the essential film truth that it doesn't matter what goes into a scene, only what comes out. It doesn't matter who you are or who you are not, only what you project onto film. And the film will redeem you and outlive you. On the set, for instance, Jean Hagen, who played Sterling Hayden's lover, exuded personality and was much liked. Yet on the screen her character came off as overly emotional, jumpy, not seductive enough. Norma Jeane thought *I'd have played that role slower, deeper. She isn't mysterious enough.*

While the young blond Angela in her very shallowness exuded mystery. For you couldn't be sure if that shallowness wasn't instead an unfathomable depth. Is she manipulating the besotted old man with her innocence? Does she want her "uncle" destroyed? The unnerving blankness in her face was the reflecting pool in which others, including the audience, might gaze.

Norma Jeane felt a thrill of elation, excitement. She was an actress now! Never again would she doubt herself.

She surprised John Huston by asking if he would retake scenes with which he'd seemed satisfied. When he demanded to know why, Norma Jeane said, "Because I know I can do better." She was nervous, but she was determined. And she was smiling. "Marilyn" smiled all the time. "Marilyn" spoke in a low, husky-sexy voice. "Marilyn" nearly always got her way. Though Louis Calhern might have been satisfied with his own performance he readily agreed to further retakes, beguiled by "Marilyn." And it was so; each retake made her performance stronger.

On the final day of filming, John Huston commented wryly to her, "Well, Angela. Our little girl's all growed up, eh?"

Never again doubt. I am an actress. I know. I can be. I will be!

Yet as the date of the screening neared, Norma Jeane began to feel the encroachment of her old anxiety. For it was not enough to be satisfied with a performance and to have been praised by co-workers; there awaited still a vast world of strangers who would have their own opinions, and among these were Hollywood film professionals and critics who knew nothing of Norma Jeane Baker and cared no more for her than one might care for a solitary ant crossing a sidewalk upon which one might accidentally, unknowingly, tread. And goodbye, ant!

Norma Jeane confessed to Cass she didn't think she could bear to attend the screening. And especially not the party afterward. Cass shrugged, saying yes you will, it's expected of you. Norma Jeane persisted, saying what if she became sick to her stomach? What if she fainted? Cass shrugged again. It was impossible to gauge if he was happy for Norma Jeane or jealous, if he resented her working with a renowned director like Huston or whether he was genuinely excited for her. (What of Cass Chaplin's career? Norma Jeane didn't ask him how interviews, auditions, callbacks turned out. She knew he was sensitive and hot-tempered. As he wryly admitted, he was as easily insulted as the Great Dictator himself. Offered a small part as a dancer in an upcoming M-G-M musical he'd accepted the role and a few days later changed his mind when he learned that another young male dancer, a rival, had been offered a larger part.) Norma Jeane pushed herself into Cass's embrace and buried her face in his neck. He was more brother than lover now, a brother twin who could protect her from the world. How she wished she could hide in his arms! Forever and ever, in his arms.

"But you don't mean that, Norma," Cass said, stroking her hair with his fingers distractedly, snagging his nails in her hair—"you're an actress. You may even be a good actress. An actress wants to be seen. An actress wants to be loved. By multitudes of people, not just one lone man." Norma Jeane protested, "No, Cass darling, that isn't so! All I really want is *you*."

Cass laughed. Snagging his blunt bitten nails in her hair.

Yes, but she was serious. She would marry him, she would have his baby, she would live with him and for him forever afterward in Venice Beach, for instance. In a small stucco house overlooking a canal. Their baby, a boy with dark tousled hair and beautiful sloe eyes, would sleep in a cradle close beside their bed. And sometimes their baby would sleep between them, in their bed. A prince of a baby. The most beautiful baby you ever saw. Charlie Chaplin's grandson! Norma Jeane's voice cracked with excitement. "Grandma Della, you won't believe this. You won't! My husband is Charlie Chaplin's *son*. We're crazy about each other, it was love at first sight. My baby is Charlie Chaplin's *grandson*. Your *great-grandson*, Grandma!" The big-boned old woman stared at Norma Jeane in disbelief. Then her face broke into a smile. Then a grin. Then she laughed aloud. *Norma Jeane, you sure have surprised us all. Norma Jeane, sweetie, we're all so proud of you.*

And Gladys would accept a grandson as she'd never have wished to accept a granddaughter. It was just as well Irina had been taken from them.

When your number's up. It happens fast or not at all. Through a narrow slatted window of the bungalow on Montezuma Drive she saw the lithe naked figure moving across the carpet. It was Cass Chaplin, oblivious of her. He leaned over a piano keyboard and played several chords, faint fluid

cascading notes, beautiful as Debussy or Ravel, who were his favorite com-
posers, and with a pencil he seemed to be taking notes or inscribing music
in a notebook. For several days during Norma Jeane's final week of filming
in Culver City he'd retreated to this hideaway house off Olympic Boulevard
to work on a ballet composition and choreography. (The Spanish bungalow
overgrown with leprous palm trees and tangled vines was the property of a
blacklisted screenwriter currently in exile in Tangier.) Music was his first
love, Cass had told Norma Jeane, and he was eager to return to it. "Not acting. I'm not an actor. Because I don't want to inhabit other selves. I want to
inhabit music, which is pure." When he'd been in the vicinity of a piano,
Cass had played parts of his piano compositions for Norma Jeane, which
she'd thought very beautiful; he was always dancing for her, but only playfully and only for a few minutes. Now, standing on the leaf-littered front
walk of this house scarcely known to her, Norma Jeane gazed through the
slatted window at the wraithlike figure of her lover, a pulse beating in her
head. *I can't interrupt him. It's wrong to interrupt him.*

She thought *He would hate me for spying on him, I can't risk that.*

She withdrew to the far side of the walk and for forty mesmerized minutes listened to the striking of chords, the rising and fading piano notes
inside. A suspension of time she wished might go on and on, forever.

When your number's up.

Shinn in the guise of truth-telling. Dropping his gravelly voice to inform her
that contrary to what Chaplin junior wanted her to think, Chaplin senior
had settled a small fortune on his ex-wife and son. He'd been forced to by
lawyers. "Of course," Shinn said, smirking, "it's vanished now. Little Lita
spent it twenty-five years ago."

Norma Jeane stared at Shinn. Had Cass lied to her? Or had she misunderstood? She said, faltering, "It comes to the same thing, then. His father
disinherited and disowned him. He's *alone*."

Shinn snorted in derision. "No more alone than the rest of us."

"He's c-cursed by his father and it's a double curse because his father
is Charlie Chaplin. Why can't you be sympathetic, Mr. Shinn?"

"I am! I'm brimming with sympathy. Who gives more to charity? The
crippled-kids fund, the Red Cross? The Hollywood Ten defense? But I'm not
sympathetic with Cass Chaplin." Shinn tried to speak humorously, but his
enlarged nose with its deep hairy nostrils quivered with rage. "I've told you,
darlin', I don't want you to be seen in public with him."

"And in private?"

"In private, take precautions. Two of *him* is already more than enough."

Norma Jeane had to think for a moment before she understood.

"Mr. Shinn, that's cruel. Cruel and crude."

"That's I. E., eh? Cruel and crude."

Norma Jeane's eyes filled with tears. She was close to slapping Shinn. Yet she wanted to clutch at his hands and beg his forgiveness, for what would she do without him? No, she wanted to laugh in his face. His creased putty face. His hurt, furious eyes.

I love him, *not you. I could never love* you. *Force me to choose between the two of you and you'll regret it.*

Norma Jeane was trembling, as indignant as I. E. Shinn and beginning to be as forceful in her speech. Shinn relented. "Hey, look, darlin'. I mean only to be helpful. Practical. You know me: I. E. I'm thinking only of you, dear. Of your career and well-being."

"You're thinking of 'Marilyn.' *Her* career."

"Well, yes. 'Marilyn' is mine, my invention. Her career and well-being I care about, yes."

Norma Jeane murmured something Shinn couldn't hear. He asked her to repeat it and she said, sniffing, " 'M-marilyn' is only a career. She hasn't any 'well-being.' "

Shinn laughed, a startled explosive laugh. He'd risen from his swivel chair behind his desk and was pacing on the carpet, flexing his stubby fingers. Behind him a plate-glass window opened out onto hazy sunshine and a confusion of traffic on Sunset Boulevard. Norma Jeane, who'd been sitting in one of Shinn's notoriously low chairs, rose to her feet as well, though shakily. She'd come to Shinn's office direct from a dance class, and her calves and thighs ached as if they'd been pummeled with hammers. She whispered, "*He* knows I'm not 'Marilyn.' *He* calls me Norma. *He's* the only one who understands me."

"*I* understand you."

Norma Jeane stared at the carpet, biting a thumbnail.

"*I* invented you, *I* understand you. *I'm* the one who has your best interests at heart, believe me."

"You d-didn't invent me. I did it myself."

Shinn laughed. "Don't get metaphysical, eh? You're sounding like your ex-friend Otto Öse. And he's in trouble, y'know . . . on the new list drawn up by the Subversive Activities Control Board. So stay away from *him*."

Norma Jeane said, "I have n-nothing to do with Otto Öse. Not any longer. What is it, this Subversive Control Board?"

Shinn pressed a warning forefinger against his lips. It was a gesture he and others in Hollywood made frequently, both in private and in public. The gesture was meant to be broadly comical with a wriggling of eyebrows like Groucho, but of course it wasn't a joke; you saw the frightened eyes. "Never mind, sweetheart. The subject isn't Öse, and the subject isn't Chaplin junior. The subject is 'Marilyn.' *You*."

Norma Jeane was feeling ill. "But is Otto b-blacklisted too? Why?"

Shinn shrugged his misshapen shoulders as if to say *Who knows? Who cares?*

Norma Jeane cried softly, "Oh, why are people doing this! Informing on each other! Even Sterling Hayden. I heard—naming names to the Committee. And I admired him. All those poor people blacklisted and out of work and the Hollywood Ten in *prison!* Like this is Nazi Germany, not America. Charlie Chaplin was so brave not to cooperate and to leave the country! I admire him. I think Cass admires him too—but he won't admit it. And Otto Öse isn't a Communist, truly! I could be a witness for Otto, I could swear on a Bible. He always said that Communists are deluded. He isn't a Marxist. *I* could be a Marxist. If I understand what Marx says. It's like Christianity, isn't it? Oh, he was right, Karl Marx—'Religion is the opiate of the people.' Like drinking and the movies. And the Communists are for the people, aren't they? What's wrong with that?"

Shinn listened in astonishment to this outburst. He said loudly, "Norma Jeane, enough! More than enough."

"But, Mr. Shinn, it's so unfair!"

"D'you want to get us both listed? What if this office is wired? What if"—he gestured toward his outer office, where his secretary-receptionist had a desk—"there're hired spies listening? God damn, you're not that dumb a blonde, so *cease.*"

"But it's unfair—"

"So? Life is unfair. You've been reading Chekhov, eh? O'Neill? You know about Dachau, Auschwitz, eh? *Homo sapiens* the species that devours its own kind? Grow up."

"Mr. Shinn, I don't know how. I don't see g-grown-ups I admire or even understand." Norma Jeane spoke earnestly, as if this were the true subject of their discussion. She seemed to be pleading with him, wanting to clutch at his hands. "Sometimes I can't sleep at night I'm so confused. And Cass, he—"

Shinn said, " 'Marilyn' doesn't have to understand or think. Jesus, no. She has only to *be.* She's a knockout and she's got talent and nobody wants tortured metaphysical crap out of that luscious mouth. Trust me on this, sweetheart."

Norma Jeane gave a little cry, backing off. As if he'd hit her.

She would remember later, *maybe he had hit her.*

"M-maybe 'Marilyn' will die another time," she said. "Maybe nothing will come of the debut. The critics might hate me or not even notice me and it will be like *Scudda-Hoo! Scudda-Hay!* again and I'll be dropped by M-G-M like I was dropped by The Studio and maybe that would be the b-b-best thing for me *and* for Cass."

Norma Jeane fled. Shinn followed close behind her, puffing and panting. Through the outer office, where his secretary-receptionist stared at them, and into the corridor. He shouted after her, twitching his nostrils like an infuriated dog—"You think so, eh? Wait and see!"

Who's the blonde? That evening in January 1950. Avoiding her desperate eyes in the mirror as another time she dialed the number of the bungalow on Montezuma Drive and another time the phone rang at the other end with that hollow melancholy sound of a phone ringing in an empty house. Cass was angry with her, she knew. Not jealous (for why should he be jealous of *her*, he who was the son of the greatest film star of all time?) but angry. Disgusted. He knew Shinn disapproved of him and didn't want him invited to the dinner at Enrico's. It was nearly nine o'clock now, and the powder room was beginning to be crowded. Uplifted voices, perfume. Women were looking at her. Cutting their eyes at her. One of them smiled and put out her hand; her beringed fingers hooked around Norma Jeane's. "You're 'Angela,' dear? A wonderful debut."

The woman was a M-G-M executive's wife, a former minor actress of the thirties.

Norma Jeane could hardly speak. "Oh! Th-thank you."

"What a strange, disturbing film. It isn't what you expect, is it? I mean— the way it turns out. I'm not sure I understand it completely, do you? So many men killed! But John Huston is a genius!"

"Oh, yes."

"You must feel so privileged, working with him?"

Norma Jeane was still clutching at the woman's hand. She nodded eagerly, her eyes filling with tears of gratitude.

Other women kept their distance. Eyeing Norma Jeane's hair, bust, hips.

That poor child. They'd dressed her up like a big doll looking so glamorous and sexy and here she was trembling and hiding in the powder room sweating so you could smell her. I swear, she wouldn't let go of my hand! She'd have trotted after me like a puppy if I'd let her.

The screening was over at last. *The Asphalt Jungle* was a success. Or anyway that was what people were saying, repeating, amid handshakes, hugs and kisses, and tall glasses of champagne. And where was I. E. Shinn in his tux to intercede for his dazed client?

"*Hel*-lo, 'Angela' "

"H'lo"

"That was a dandy performance"

"Thank you"

"I mean it I'm serious that was a jim-dandy performance"

"Thank you"

"A humdinger of a performance"

"Thank you"

"You're a dandy-looking girl"

"Thank you"

"Somebody said this is your debut"

"Oh, yes"

"And your name is"

" 'M-marilyn Monroe' "

"Well, congratulations '*Marilyn Monroe*' "

"Thank you"

"I'm going to give you my card '*Marilyn Monroe*' "

"Thank you"

"I got a feeling we'll be meeting again '*Marilyn Monroe*' "

"Thank you"

She was happy. She'd never been happier. Not since the Dark Prince hauled her up onstage to share the blinding lights with him, lifting her high for all to admire and to applaud and kissing her forehead in blessing *I anoint you my Fair Princess my bride.* In her ear he whispered the secret admonition, *It's all right to be happy now. You have earned happiness. For a while.* In celebration of such happiness cameras flashed in the crowded foyer. There stood, smiling for photographers, blond-knockout Angela and her somewhat abashed-looking chain-smoking "Uncle Leon." There stood Angela and the male lead of the film, Sterling Hayden, with whom she hadn't had a single scene. And there stood Angela and the great director, who'd made her happiness possible. *Oh, how can I thank you I can never thank you enough.* Norma Jeane laughed giddily, seeing out of the corner of her eye Otto Öse hawk-faced and glowering behind an uplifted camera at the edge of the crowd; Otto Öse in his baggy black clothes like a scarecrow resentful of his servile role, he who should have been an artist, a maker of original arresting art, a maker of Jewish art, a maker of art radical and revolutionary since the unspeakable revelations of the gas ovens, the final solution, the atomic bombs. Norma Jeane wanted to scream at him *You see? I don't need you! Your sleazy girlie pix. Your nude calendars. I'm an actress, I don't need you or anyone. I hope they arrest you and take you away!* But when she looked more closely she saw that it wasn't Otto Öse after all.

What a smile on Shinn's face! He looked like a crocodile, a no-leg crocodile, careening around on its tail. The sweaty-sexy glisten of his oversize face. She giggled, imagining what it would be like making love with such a creature. Having to shut her eyes and shut down her brain. *Oh no, I can only marry for love.*

She'd never been happier than now. Shinn seized her by the hand, hauling her across the foyer. He'd invented her; she was his. Not true, but she would acquiesce. She would not rebel, not yet. Never happier than this magic night. For she was Cinderella, and the glass shoe *fit*. And she was better-looking and sexier and more exciting than the female lead, Jean Hagen, whom fewer photographers sought; it was embarrassing how they favored the unknown young knockout blonde who couldn't act her way out of a paper bag, some were saying, sneering behind their hands, but Jesus lookit the tits, lookit the ass, move over Lana Turner.

Happy, high on champagne as she hadn't been since her wedding night. Though he had not answered the phone. Though he knew how to punish her. Hurt and angry with her. He'd hidden himself away, deeply asleep in the luxurious borrowed bed in which only the previous night they'd made tender protracted love lying side by side and their eager bodies fitted together and their eager mouths pressed together and their eyeballs rolling back in their skulls at precisely the same moment—*Oh! oh oh! Darling I love you*— and she'd required no magic potion to sleep that night as she hadn't for a succession of nights since finishing her work on the movie and she was confident she would not ever require a sedative to help her sleep again for what a relief it was, what joy; these people liked her after all! these Hollywood people liked her! asking *Who's the blonde? Why isn't she listed with the cast?* and Mr. Z of The Studio would be astonished and chagrined, the cruel bastard how he'd exploited her as a young contract player and dumped her, and now the M-G-M executives would value her and in any case the producers of *The Asphalt Jungle* would list "Marilyn Monroe" with the cast subsequent to the screening; weeks and months of publicity would follow when the radiant-sexy blond beauty "Marilyn Monroe" would appear in dozens of newspapers and magazines and be awarded such timely honors as *Miss Model Blonde 1951, Screen World "New Face" 1951, PhotoLife Most Promising Starlet 1951, Miss Cheesecake 1952*, and *Miss A-Bomb 1952*, an award presented in Palm Springs by Frank Sinatra. And the radiant-sexy blond beauty would be everywhere on newsstands, on the covers not of *Sir!* and *Swank*, which she'd outgrown as she'd outgrown the subclass of photographers who worked for such magazines, but on the respectable glossy covers of *Look, Collier's*, and *Life* ("New Faces of 1952"). By which time "Marilyn Monroe" would be a contract player again at The Studio, her salary raised by the chastened Mr. Z to five hundred dollars a week.

"Five hundred! At Radio Plane they weren't even paying me fifty a week."

Never happier.

Except that evening in January 1950 when it began, when "Marilyn" was born. When she'd been sick with love for Cass Chaplin and he hadn't come to the screening or to Enrico's afterward and she was alone celebrating her happiness with a crowd of elegantly dressed strangers and with glasses of champagne, "Marilyn Monroe" resplendent in her wedding-white silk-and-chiffon cocktail dress from Bullock's so dramatically low-cut her breasts nearly sprang out of the straining fabric. That evening Shinn the wily agent introduced his incandescent client to B, J, P, and R, studio executives and producers whose names she didn't catch, and each of these smiling men clasped her hand, or hands, and congratulated her on her "debut."

And there came V, the popular handsome freckled former All-American football star from Kansas who'd made wartime movies for Paramount including the box-office hit *The Young Aces*, which had made even Bucky Glazer cry; Norma Jeane recalled clutching at her young husband's hand during the terrifying scenes of air combat, and there were such tender love scenes between V and gorgeous Maureen O'Hara, which she'd watched avid and wide-eyed imagining herself in O'Hara's place though angry at herself, too, how silly a fantasy for a happily married young wife, how childish and futile. And now there came to her, pushing through the crowd, six years later, V in person! V in civilian clothes, not his Air Force uniform! V so boyish and freckle-faced you'd have guessed he was twenty-nine, not thirty-nine, only his thinning hair suggesting he wasn't any longer the impetuous young pilot of *The Young Aces* who'd flown missions over Germany and who'd been shot down over enemy territory in one of the longest falling-spiraling shots in cinema history, so contrived that the screaming fainting audience falls with him in the burning plane until he manages, wounded, to parachute out as in a nightmare, and Norma Jeane stared seeing the man before her, six feet tall and stocky in the shoulders and torso, just perceptibly heavier about the jaws yet freckled still and the eyes warm and intense as she remembered them. For once you've seen a man close up in such intimacy you carry his image inside you like a dream. Once you've fantasized a love scene with a man in close-up you cherish the memory of his kisses in your heart.

"You! Oh, it's—you?" Norma Jeane spoke so softly she couldn't be heard above the conversational din and perhaps hadn't intended to be heard. How badly she wanted to take hold of V's big capable hands and tell him how she'd adored him, how she'd cried when he was wounded and taken prisoner and cried when he was reunited at last with his fiancée and cried going home to Verdugo Gardens and ol' Hirohito grinning atop the console radio—"My life as it was then, I don't know who I *was*." But she didn't grab his hands and she didn't speak of Verdugo Gardens. She had only to lift her face and smile at V as he leaned close to her (as if, already, these two were lovers) congratulating her on her film debut. What could Norma Jeane who was "Marilyn Monroe" murmur but *Thank you, oh thank you*—blushing like a high school girl.

V drew her into a relatively quiet corner of the restaurant to speak earnestly with her about the film, the subtleties of the screenplay and the characterizations and the remarkable ending; how did she like working with an exacting director like Huston?—"He makes you feel good for once about your craft, doesn't he? About the life people like us have chosen."

Puzzled, Norma Jeane said, "C-chosen? Did we? To be actors, you mean? Oh, I—I never thought of it that way."

V laughed, startled. Norma Jeane wondered had she said the wrong thing? *You never knew when she was serious. These things that sprang from her.*

V the war-ace box-office star of youthful middle age, reputed to be in private life a good decent man shabbily treated by his minor-actress wife who'd won custody of their children and a large divorce settlement after only a few years of marriage, and "Marilyn Monroe," the gorgeous young starlet. From a short distance, like a brooding proprietary father, I. E. Shinn observed.

Abruptly there came up to the attractive couple a near-bald middle-aged man with pouched turtle eyes and deep creases beside his mouth. In his unpressed gabardine suit he wasn't one of the M-G-M party but it was clear that some of the guests knew him, as V did, and looked aside embarrassed and frowning. "Excuse me? Excuse me? Will you sign, please?" V had turned away, but there stood Norma Jeane in her gay giddy mood, open-eyed, welcoming. The turtle-eyed man pushed uncomfortably close. He had a petition for her to sign that he thrust into her face, and Norma Jeane squinted, seeing it had been prepared by the National Committee to Preserve First Amendment Rights of which she'd heard, or believed she'd heard. In the dim light of the restaurant she could make out a large-print headline WE THE UNDERSIGNED PROTEST THE CRUEL AND UN-AMERICAN TREATMENT OF followed by double columns of printed names. The first name of the left-hand column was **Charlie Chaplin** and the first name of the right-hand column was **Paul Robeson**. Beneath the columns were many blanks but no more than a half-dozen signatures. The turtle-eyed man identified himself with a name Norma Jeane didn't recognize, saying he'd been a screenwriter for *The Story of G.I. Joe* and *The Young Aces* and many other films until he'd been blacklisted in 1949.

Norma Jeane, who'd been warned by her agent never to sign any of the petitions circulating in Hollywood, said vehemently, "Oh, yes, I will! I will." In her gay giddy mood, with V looking on, she was immediately incensed. She blinked away tears of hurt and indignation. She said, "Charlie Chaplin and Paul Robeson are great artists. I don't care if they're Communists or—whatever! It's t-terrible what this great country of America is doing to its g-greatest artists." She took a pen offered by the turtle-eyed man and would have signed at once except V, who'd been trying to draw her away from the turtle-eyed man, now said, "Marilyn, I don't think you should," and the turtle-eyed man said loudly, "You! Damn you! This is between the young lady and me." Norma Jeane said to both men, "But what's my name? 'Monroe'—? I've forgotten my name." She went to a nearby table, where to the surprise of people sitting there she tried to sign the unwieldy petition except she'd laid it atop silverware. She was laughing, though still indignant. "Oh, yes—'Marilyn Monroe.' " With a flourish she signed twice, as *Marilyn Monroe* and as *Mona Monroe*. She began to sign as *Norma Jeane Glazer* except I. E. Shinn, breathing flames through both nostrils, snatched the pen from her and crossed out the names.

"Marilyn! God *damn*! You are *drunk*."

"I am *not*! I'm the only sober person *here*."

That evening at Enrico's she met V. That evening she lost her lover Cass.

She fled Enrico's. She was sick of them all. Cass was right. *They're flesh merchants all of them.* Outside the restaurant as she tried to get into a taxi there was a small crowd gathered. "Who's she? The blonde." "Lana Turner?—no, too young." Norma Jeane laughed uneasily. In her low-cut white silk-and-chiffon. In her spike-heeled shoes. A pudgy smiling man in a plastic raincoat walked into her, intentionally it seemed. Another petition thrust into her face? No, it was an autograph book. "Sign, please!"

Norma Jeane murmured, "I c-can't. I'm nobody."

She had to escape! Another man came to her rescue, opening the rear door of the taxi and helping her climb inside. She had a fleeting frightened impression of a battered face like something shaped out of putty. The nose was flattened and broad at the tip like a trowel; the eyes were puffy, and both lids drooped; the eyebrows appeared to be singed; one ear was partly missing like something corroded. A rancid yeasty smell like Gladys at Norwalk.

That smell would stay with her through the long night until early next morning she'd cleanse herself in fury and desperation.

Maybe it's my own smell. Maybe it's beginning.

Shinn had insulted her. V had discreetly backed away. The turtle-eyed man had been ejected from Enrico's. Norma Jeane pressed her fingertips against her eyelids to erase them all. It was a habit of the orphanage. A strategy of the Time Traveler pulling the rod of his magic machine to propel him swiftly through time. So when she opened her eyes after fifteen or so minutes she was at the Spanish-style bungalow on Montezuma Drive. The borrowed house was near the foot of the mountain, not near the top like the millionaires' houses. Norma Jeane was shivering and excited and she hadn't eaten since noon that day, except for a few canapés hungrily and absentmindedly devoured at the reception. She'd left behind the white fox stole lent to her by the M-G-M wardrobe department but Mr. Shinn had the check claim ticket; he'd return it. Oh, but she hated him! She would quit as his client and if that meant she never got another Hollywood job, so be it. She'd brought her little white beaded purse but she hadn't more than five dollars in change; fortunately, this was enough for the taxi driver, who was asking was she sure this was the right address, it looked dark. "Maybe I should wait, miss? If you might want to go somewhere else?" Her immediate response was a curt "No. I don't want to go somewhere else" but a shrewder response followed—"All right, yes, why don't you wait. But only for a minute. Thank you." She had no difficulty making her way up the steep cracked sidewalk in her high-heeled shoes, which meant she wasn't drunk on champagne as that cruel dwarf-man had accused her.

Oh Cass I love you, I've been missing you so, it was a success I think. I was a success. I mean, it's a beginning. Just a minor role. But a beginning. I don't need to be ashamed of myself. That's all I ask, not to be ashamed. I don't expect happiness. My only happiness is from you. Cass—

The little bungalow overgrown with sickly palm trees and a leafless and flowerless vine did appear to be deserted but Norma Jeane peered through a front window and saw a dim light burning at the rear. The front door was locked. She had a key, but where was it?—not in her little white-beaded purse. Or maybe she hadn't a key. Calling softly, "Cass? Darling?" He was sleeping, she supposed. She hoped it wasn't a heavy drugged sleep from which she'd be unable to wake him.

The taxi idled on the gravel road; Norma Jeane pulled off her high-heeled sandals and made her way groping to the rear of the house. Cass never bothered to lock the back door. In the darkness she saw an empty wading pool littered with palm fronds. The first time she'd seen this shabby little pool she'd had a strange hallucinatory vision of little Irina wading in it, in aqua-bright water. Cass had seen her staring, white-faced, and asked what was wrong, but she hadn't told him. He knew about Norma Jeane's early marriage and divorce and he knew about Gladys who'd been a poet until her breakdown and he knew about Norma Jeane's father who was a prominent Hollywood producer who'd never publicly acknowledged his "illegitimate" daughter. But that was all he knew.

"Cass? It's Norma." Inside the house was an odor of whiskey. An overhead light burned in the kitchen but the narrow hall was darkened. Norma Jeane saw no light beneath the bedroom door, which was ajar. Softly she called again, "Cass? Are you sleeping? *I'm* sleepy!" Suddenly she felt like a big cuddly kitten. She pushed open the door. Light from the kitchen slanted inside. There was the bed, a luxurious double bed too large for the cramped room, and there was Cass in bed, naked except for a sheet covering him to the waist. Norma Jeane had a confused impression of dark furry-matted hair on his chest that she'd never seen before and his shoulders and torso were more muscular than she recalled and again she whispered, "Cass?" even as she realized there were two figures in the bed, two young men. The nearer, the stranger, remained lying on his back, the sheet now barely covering his hairy groin and his arms behind his head, while the other, Cass, shoved himself up on his elbow, smiling. Both young men were covered in sweat. Young beautiful male bodies gleaming. Quickly before Norma Jeane could escape Cass leapt naked from the bed, lithe as a dancer, grabbing her wrist, and with his other hand he tugged at his companion's thigh.

"Norma, darling! Don't run away. I want you to meet Eddy G—he's my twin too."

THE BROKEN ALTAR

A little Westwood secretary figuring to improve her mind.

A religious fanatic, maybe. Or the daughter of such. That type you get to recognize in southern California.

Mostly we paid her no attention. Prof Dietrich would inform us afterward that she'd never missed a single class until November. But she was so quiet in class, it was like she was invisible. Slipping into her seat early each week she'd lean forward over her book rereading the assignment so if you glanced in her direction you'd get the clear signal *Don't talk to me please, don't even look at me.* So it was easy not to notice her. She was serious and down-looking and prim without makeup and her skin pale and slightly shiny and her ash-blond hair rolled back and pinned up in the style women were wearing during the war if they worked in factories. It was a look of the forties and of another time. And sometimes she'd tie a scarf around her hair. She wore nondescript skirts and blouses and loose-fitting cardigans and flat-heeled shoes and stockings. No jewelry, no rings on either hands. And her fingernails plain. You'd figure her about twenty-one but younger than that in experience. Living at home with her parents in a little stucco bungalow. Or maybe her widowed mother. The two of them singing hymns, Sunday mornings, in some drab little church. A virgin for sure.

If you said hello to her or made a friendly remark in her direction the way some of us did, breezing into class and eager to talk and laugh and exchange news before class, she'd lift her eyes quick and startled-blue and shrink back in the same reflex. It was then you'd see, like a kick in the groin, that this little girl was good-looking, or might've been good-looking, if she'd known it. But she didn't know. She'd lower her eyes or turn away and rummage in her shoulder bag for a tissue. Mumble something polite and that was that. *Don't even look at me, please!*

So, who would? There were other girls in the class, and women, and they weren't shy.

Even her name was a nothing name. You'd hear it and forget it in the same moment. "Gladys Pirig"—Prof Dietrich read it off, first class meeting. Reading the roll in his deep sonorous voice and making marks beside our names, and he'd peer up at us over his glasses and make a twitchy gesture with his mouth meant to be a smile. Some of us knew Prof Dietrich from previous classes in night school and liked him, which was why we were enrolled for another, so we knew he was a good-natured generous and optimistic man but a tough grader even in the night school where we were all adults.

"Prof Dietrich" we called him, or just "Prof." We knew from the UCLA catalog he wasn't an actual professor only just an "adjunct instructor" but we called him "Prof" and he'd blush a little but not correct us. Like it was a game we played that we night school students were important enough to merit a professor and he wasn't going to disillusion us.

This class was Renaissance Poetry. UCLA Night School, fall 1951, Thursday evenings 7 to 9 P.M. Thirty-two of us were enrolled and it was surprising, and a testament to Prof Dietrich, that almost everybody showed up for most classes, even after the winter rainy season began. We were veterans on the G.I. bill and retired men and middle-aged housewives with no kids left at home and office workers and two young students from Westwood Theological Seminary, and a few of us were would-be poets. The dominant group in the class, apart from two or three outspoken vets, were a half-dozen schoolteachers, female, in their thirties and forties, taking extra courses to beef up their credentials. Most of us worked days. And long days they were. You had to love poetry, and you had to believe that poetry was worthy of your love, to spend two hours in a classroom at the end of a workday. Prof Dietrich was an excitable energetic teacher so you'd get caught up in his enthusiasm even if you didn't always understand what he was declaiming about. In the presence of such teachers, it's enough to know that they know.

Like the first class period after reading through our names, Prof Dietrich stood before us clasping his chunky, chafed-looking hands together and said,

"Poetry. Poetry is the transcendental language of mankind." He paused and we shivered, figuring whatever the hell that meant it was worth the tuition at least.

How Gladys Pirig took this, nobody would notice. Probably she wrote it down in her notebook, schoolgirl-style, as she had a habit of doing.

We began the semester reading Robert Herrick, Richard Lovelace, Andrew Marvell, Richard Crashaw, Henry Vaughan. We were gearing up, Prof Dietrich said, for Donne and Milton. In his booming dramatic voice like Lionel Barrymore's, reciting Richard Crashaw's "Upon the Infant Martyrs"—

"To see both blended in one flood;
The mother's milk, the children's blood,
Makes me doubt if Heaven will gather
Roses hence, or lilies rather."

And Henry Vaughan's "They Are All Gone into the World of Light"—

"They are all gone into the world of light!
    And I alone sit lingering here;
Their very memory is fair and bright,
    And my sad thoughts doth clear."

We'd analyze and discuss these knotty little poems. Always there was more than you'd expect. One line opened up another, and one word another, it was like a fairy-tale riddle leading you in, and further in, and still further. For some of us in the class it was a revelation. "Poetry! Poetry is compression," Prof Dietrich told us, seeing the bewilderment on some faces. His eyes shone inside the smudged wire-rimmed glasses that he'd take off and put back on and take off again a dozen times during the class period. "Poetry is the soul's shorthand. Morse code." His jokes were clumsy and corny but we all laughed, even Gladys Pirig, who had a squeaky little laugh that sounded more surprised than mirthful.

Prof Dietrich had a determinedly light tone. He meant to be funny, witty. Like he was carrying a burden of something else, something darker and snarled, and his jokes were a way of deflecting our attention from it, or maybe his own. He was about forty years old and going soft in the middle, a big-boned guy like a bear on its hind legs, about six feet three and weighing maybe two hundred twenty pounds. A linebacker but with this chiseled chipped-at sensitive face, quick to blush and acne-pitted, yet the women in the class considered him handsome in the battered Bogart style, his myopic eyes "sensitive." He wore mismatched coats and trousers and vests, and plaid neckties that bunched beneath his chin. From some remarks he'd made absentmindedly about London during the war you had the idea he'd been there, probably stationed there for some time, you had a quick glimpse of the man in a uniform but that was it, just a glimpse; he'd never talk about himself, not even after class. "Poetry is the way out of the self," Prof told us, "and poetry is the way back into the self. But poetry is not the self."

Nobody wrote better poetry, Prof Dietrich said, than the Renaissance poets, not even counting Shakespeare (Shakespeare was another course). He lectured us on the poetic forms, especially on the sonnets—English and Petrarchan, or Italian. He lectured us on "mutability"—"the vanity of human wishes"—"the fear of growing old and dying." This was a Renaissance theme so prevalent you could say it was "a cultural obsession, a pandemic neurosis." One of the theological students asked, "But why? When they believed in God?" and Prof Dietrich laughed and hitched up his trousers and said, "Well, maybe they did, and maybe they didn't. There's a profound difference between what people say they believe and what, in their guts, they truly believe. Poetry is the lancet that digs through dead tissue into the truth." Someone commented that, after all, people didn't live very long centuries ago; men were lucky to live to be forty and women died young in childbirth frequently, so it made sense, didn't it? "They worried about dying all the time. It could happen any time." One of the female teachers, a practiced talker, said argumentatively, "Oh, bosh! Probably 'mutability' was just a topic these male poets wrote about, like 'love.' They wanted to be poets and they had to write about *something*." We laughed. We disagreed. We began talking excitedly as we always did, starved for serious intellectual conversation in our lives, or what passed for intellectual conversation. We interrupted one another.

"Love poems, love lyrics, like in our own popular songs of today, and movies—they're the subjects, see? Like nothing else in life is important? But at the same time, maybe they're just—y'know, 'subjects.' Maybe none of it is real."

"Yes, but it was real once, wasn't it?"

"Who knows? What the hell is 'real'?"

"You're saying *love* isn't real? *Dying* isn't real? What?"

"Well, everything was real at one time! Otherwise how'd we even have the words for these things?"

During these free-for-alls over which Prof Dietrich presided like a gym teacher, pleased at so much activity but maybe a little worried things might get out of control, the blond Gladys Pirig would sit silent, staring at us. During Prof's lectures she took notes, but at these times she'd lay down her pen.

You could see she was listening hard. Tense and quivering and her backbone ramrod straight so *you could see she was a girl who made too much of things like every instant was a streetcar rattling past she needed to catch and was in terror she might miss.*

A little Westwood office worker, but she'd been encouraged by some teacher in high school to reach out for something better and maybe she'd written poetry and this teacher had praised her so she was writing poetry still, in secret and out of a dread it wasn't any good. Her pale lips moved silently. Even her feet were restless. Sometimes we'd notice her half-consciously rubbing her legs, her calves, as if her muscles ached, or flexing her feet as if they were cramping on her. (But nobody would've figured she was taking dance lessons, probably. You just wouldn't have figured Gladys Pirig for anything physical.)

Prof Dietrich wasn't the kind of bullying teacher to call on quiet or shy students but obviously he was aware of this neat well-groomed excruciatingly shy blond girl seated right in front of him, as he was alert and aware of all of us; and one evening he inquired who'd like to read aloud George Herbert's "The Altar" and he must've seen something quick and yearning in the girl's face, because instead of calling on one of us with our hands in the air he said in a kindly voice, "Gladys?" There was a moment's silence, a pause when you could almost hear the girl suck in her breath. Then she whispered, in the way of a child taking a dare, reckless, even smiling, "I'll t-try."

This poem. It was a religious poem you could figure, but printed in a peculiar way. A thick horizontal column of print at the top, a thinner vertical column, and a matching thick horizontal column at the bottom. It was a "metaphysical" poem (we'd been told) which meant it was a tough nut to crack but beautiful language you could let flow past like you'd listen to music. Gladys was nervous you could see but she turned a little in her desk to face us, propped up her book, took a deep breath, and began to read, and—well, it was wholly unexpected, not just Gladys's husky dramatic voice, which managed to be breathless and powerful simultaneously, spiritual and sexy as hell, but the mere fact that she was reading to us at all, that she hadn't refused or run out of the room when Prof made his request. On the page "The Altar" was a puzzle, but when that little blond girl read it, it suddenly made sense.

"A broken ALTAR, Lord, thy servant rears,
Made of a heart, and cemented with tears;
        Whose parts are as thy hand did frame;
        No workman's tool hath touched the same.
        A   HEART   alone
        Is   such   a   stone
        As   nothing   but
        Thy   power   doth   cut.
        Wherefore   each   part
        Of   my   hard   heart
        Meets   in   this   frame,
        To   praise   thy   Name;
        That, if I chance to hold my peace,
        These stones to praise thee may not cease.
        O let thy blessed SACRIFICE be mine
        And sanctify this ALTAR to be thine."

When Gladys finished, we burst into applause. All of us. Even the school-teachers you might've figured would be jealous of this performance. For there was Prof Dietrich gaping at this girl we figured for an office worker like he couldn't believe his ears. He was half sitting against the teacher's desk in his usual casual position, shoulders slouched and head bent over the text, and when Gladys finished he joined in the applause and said, "Young lady, you must be a poet! Are you?"

Now fiercely blushing, Gladys hunched her shoulders and mumbled something we couldn't hear.

Prof Dietrich persisted, half teasing in his teacherly kindly way, like this episode, too, was something almost a little out of his control and he needed to use just the right words. "Miss Pirig? You are a poet—of some rare sort!"

He asked Gladys why the poem was printed in such strange typography and Gladys again spoke inaudibly and Prof said, "Louder, please, Miss Pirig," and Gladys cleared her throat and said, only just audibly, "It's m-meant to be an altar, the way it looks?" but now her voice was hurried and lacking in timbre and it did seem she might be about to bolt from the room like a spooked animal. So Prof quickly said, "Thank you, Gladys. You are correct. Class, d'you see? 'The Altar' is an altar."

The damnedest thing! Once you saw it, you couldn't not see it. Like one of those Rorschach ink-blot tests.

"A Heart alone." The girl's voice intoning those words. "A Heart alone is such a stone." Through our lives we'd hear it, every one of us in the room that evening.

November 1951. A long time ago. Jesus! You don't want to think how few of us are still living, this hour.

Sure, we watched her after that. We talked to her more, or tried to. She wasn't anonymous anymore. Gladys Pirig—she was mysterious and sexy. Mysterious *is* sexy. That ash-blond hair, that husky breathy voice. Maybe a few of us tried to look her up in the L.A. phone directory, but no "Gladys Pirig" was listed. Prof called on her once or twice more and she stiffened without answering him but it was too late. And she was looking familiar to us. Not to everybody in the class but to a few. No matter she dressed herself more than ever in secretary clothes and her hair rolled and pinned like Irene Dunne and if you tried to strike up a conversation with her she'd back off like a scared rabbit. *What she seemed like, if you had to put a name to it, was a girl who'd been rough-handled by men.*

And there was the Thursday night one of us came to class early with a copy of *Hollywood Reporter* and passed it around and we stared in astonishment yet maybe not by this time entirely in surprise. "Marilyn Monroe. Jesus." "That's her? That little girl?" "She isn't a girl, and she isn't little. Look."

We looked.

Some of us wanted to keep our discovery a secret, but we had to show Prof, we had to see the look on Prof's face, and he stared and stared at the photo feature in *Hollywood Reporter*, both with his glasses on and his glasses off. For here was a luscious four-column photo of this dazzling blond Hollywood actress, not yet a star but you could see she'd be one soon, just about spilling out of a low-cut sequined dress and with her face so made up it looked like a painting: MARILYN MONROE, MISS MODEL BLOND 1951. Plus stills from *The Asphalt Jungle* and the release of *All About Eve*. Prof said hoarsely, "This starlet—Marilyn Monroe. This is *Gladys?*" We told him yes, we were sure. Once you made the connection it was obvious. Prof said, "But I saw *The Asphalt Jungle*. I remember that girl, and our Gladys isn't anything like her." One of the seminarians who'd been looking on said, "I just saw *All About Eve*, and she was in it! It's just a small role but I do remember her. I mean, I remember the blonde who must've been her." He laughed. We were all laughing, excited and thrilled. Some of us, we'd lived through moments of what you'd call surprise in the war, when what you'd been thinking was one way was revealed suddenly and forever as not that way at all, and your very existence of no more substance or significance than a strand of cobweb, and this moment was a little like that, the surprise of it, the irreversible revelation of it, except of course it was a happy moment, a giddy moment, like we'd all won the lottery and were celebrating. The seminarian was enjoying the attention we gave him, adding, " 'Marilyn Monroe' isn't anybody you'd be likely to forget."

Next class period, a dozen of us arrived early. We had copies of *Screen World, Modern Screen, PhotoLife*—"Most Promising Starlet 1951." Another copy of *Hollywood Reporter* with a photo of "Marilyn Monroe at a movie premiere, escorted by the handsome young actor Johnny Sands." We even had back issues of *Swank, Sir,* and *Peek.* There was a feature in *Look* from last fall—"Miss Blond Sensation: MARILYN MONROE." We were passing these around excited as kids when in walked Gladys Pirig in a khaki-colored raincoat and hat, a mousy little girl nobody'd have given a second glance to. And she saw us and the magazines and must've caught on at once. Our eyes! We'd meant to keep our secret but it was like a lit match held to dried sedge. One of the pushy guys went right up to her and said, "Hey. Your name isn't Gladys Pirig, is it? It's Marilyn Monroe." He was crude enough to hold up *Swank* with her on the cover in a flimsy red nightie and red high heels and her hair tousled and her shiny red lips pursed in a kiss.

"Gladys" looked at him as if he'd slapped her. Quickly she said, "N-no. That isn't me. I mean—I'm not her." There was panic and horror on her face. This was no Hollywood actress, just a frightened girl. She would've run out but some of us were blocking her way, not deliberately, it was just how we happened to be standing. And others coming into the room. The sharp-eyed schoolteacher contingent, who'd been hearing the rumor. And Prof Dietrich was early by at least five minutes. And this pushy guy was saying to her, "Marilyn, I think you're great. Can I have your autograph?" He wasn't kidding. He was holding out his Renaissance text for her to sign. Another guy, one of the veterans, was saying, "*I* think you're great. Don't let these crude assholes make you nervous." And another guy was saying, in mimicry of Angela from *The Asphalt Jungle,* " 'Uncle Leon, I ordered salt herring for your breakfast, I know how you like it,' " and she even laughed at this, a small squeaky laugh—"Well. You've got me there, I guess." And there came Prof Dietrich looking self-conscious but excited, too, his face flushed, and tonight he was wearing a decent-looking navy blue coat not missing a single button and pressed trousers and a bright plaid tie, and he said, awkwardly, "Um, Gladys—Miss Pirig—I've heard, I believe—we have a 'starlet' in our midst. Congratulations, Miss Monroe!" The girl was smiling, or trying to smile, and managed to say, "Th-thank you, Professor Dietrich." He told her he'd seen *The Asphalt Jungle* and thought the movie was "unusually thoughtful for Hollywood" and her performance was "excellent." You could see it made her uncomfortable to hear this from him. The big man's gleaming eyes, broad eager smile. "Gladys Pirig" had no intention of taking her seat as usual but wanted only to escape us.

Like the earth was shaking beneath her. Like she'd been deluded enough to think it would not, though this was southern California and what else could you expect?

She was backing toward the door, and we were crowding and jostling around her, talking in loud voices to get her attention, competing with one another for her attention, even the female schoolteachers, and her Renaissance textbook, which was a heavy, hefty book, slipped from her fingers and fell to the floor and one of us snatched it up and handed it to her but held on to it only just a little so she couldn't rush away and she said, practically begging, "L-leave me alone, please. I'm not the one you w-want." That look on her face! That look of hurt, pleading, terror, and female resignation in her beautiful face some of us would be deeply moved to see two years later in the climactic scene of *Niagara*, when the adultress Rose is about to be strangled by her maddened husband, that look on Monroe's face we would believe ourselves the first to have seen, one rainy Thursday evening in November 1951 as "Gladys Pirig" managed to slip away, abandoning her book to us, and we gaped after her, and Prof Dietrich called out in dismay— "Miss Monroe! Please. We won't make any more fuss, we promise."

But no. She'd left. A few of us followed her to the stairs. She bolted and ran. Down those stairs as fast as a boy might've run, or a terrified animal, and no looking back.

"Marilyn!" we cried after her. "Marilyn, come back!"

But she never returned.

RUMPELSTILTSKIN

What is this spell? How long will it last? Who has done this to me?

Not the Dark Prince or even her secret lover V had begged her to marry him, but the dwarf Rumpelstiltskin.

There were no lines provided for her. She dared not laugh. She protested in her soft, fading voice, "Oh, but you don't mean it, Mr. Shinn!"

He said, smiling—as a Hollywood wit once said of I. E. Shinn—like a nut-cracker might smile if it could smile, "Please. You know me by now, dear. I'm Isaac. Not Mr. Shinn. You know me, and you know my heart. Call me Mr. Shinn and I will dissolve into dust like Bela Lugosi as Count Dracula."

Norma Jeane said, wetting her lips, "Is-aac."

"That's the best your expensive acting coach has taught you? Try again."

Norma Jeane laughed. She wanted to hide her eyes from the agent's shiny glaring all-penetrating gaze. "Isaac. Is-aac?" It was more a pleading than a reply.

In fact, this was not the first time that the formidable Rumpelstiltskin had asked the Fair Princess to marry him, but she was in the habit of forgetting between proposals. Amnesia like morning mist obscured such episodes. They were intended to be romantic but a harsh jangling music interfered. As the Fair Princess she had so much to think about! Her life was being eaten up by a calendar of densely annotated days and hours.

The Beggar Maid in disguise as the Fair Princess. Under an enchantment so that at least in the eyes of commoners like herself she appeared shining and resplendent as a Fair Princess.

It was exhausting to play such a role but there was no other role for her ("with your looks, your talent") at the present time, as Mr. Shinn was patient to explain. In every decade there must be a Fair Princess exalted above the rest and the role demanded not just extraordinary physical gifts but an accompanying genius, as Mr. Shinn was yet more patient to explain. ("You don't believe that beauty is genius, sweetheart? One day, when you've lost both, you will.") Yet looking into any mirror, she saw not the Fair Princess whom the world saw and marveled over but her old Beggar Maid self. The blue startled eyes, the slightly parted, apprehensive lips. As vividly as if it had happened only last week she recalled being banished from the stage at Van Nuys High. She recalled the drama teacher's sarcasm and the murmurs and laughter in her wake. This humiliation seemed quite natural to her, a just assessment of her worth. Yet somehow she'd become the Fair Princess!

What is this spell? How long can it last? Who has done this to me?

She was being groomed for "stardom." It was a species of animal manufacture, like breeding.

Of course Rumpelstiltskin claimed credit, for he alone had the power to cast magic spells. Norma Jeane had come by degrees to believe that I. E. Shinn was indeed solely responsible: the dwarf magician who professed to adore her. (Otto Öse had long since departed from her life. Rarely did she think of him now. How strange, she'd once confused Otto Öse with the Dark Prince! But he was no prince. He was a pornographer, a pimp. He'd looked upon her naked, yearning body without tenderness. He'd betrayed her. Norma Jeane Baker was nothing to him, though he'd scavenged her out of a trash heap and saved her life. He'd disappeared from Hollywood sometime in March 1951 when served with a subpoena to testify before the California Joint Fact-Finding Committee on Un-American Activities.) These were the days when Shinn summoned Norma Jeane to his office on Sunset Boulevard, where he'd have spread out on a table an advance copy of a glossy magazine featuring "Marilyn Monroe" in poses she'd entirely forgotten—"Baby, look what your doppelgänger has been up to. Luscious, eh? This should make The Studio execs take notice." Often he telephoned her late at night to gloat over a planted item in a gossip column, the two of them laughing uproariously like people who've won a lottery with a ticket found on the street.

You don't deserve to win with such a ticket.

But then, who does?

This evening it was the same marriage proposal with a startling variant: Isaac Shinn would draw up a prenuptial contract with Norma Jeane Baker a.k.a. "Marilyn Monroe" leaving her virtually all his estate when he died, cutting out his children and other current heirs. I. E. Shinn, Inc., was worth millions—and she would inherit all! This he presented to her as a magician might, with an exaggerated flourish, a phantasmagoric sight to a credulous audience; yet Norma Jeane could only squirm in her seat and murmur, deeply embarrassed, "Oh, thank you, Mr. Shinn!—I mean, Isaac. But I couldn't do such a thing, you know. I just c-couldn't."

"And why not?"

"Oh, I—I couldn't be the one to, the one to—oh, you know, hurt your f-family. Your real family."

"And why not?"

In the face of such aggression, Norma Jeane suddenly laughed. Then blushed furiously. Then said, soberly, "I l-love you, but I—I'm not in love with you."

There. It was said. In the movie, it would have been said sadly but with eloquence. In Mr. Shinn's office, it was uttered in a rush of shamed speech. Shinn said, "Hell. I can love enough for us both, sweetheart. Try me." His tone was jocular but each knew he was deadly serious.

With unconscious cruelty Norma Jeane blurted out, "Oh, but—that still wouldn't be enough, Mr. Shinn."

"Touché!" Shinn clowned, clutching at his heart as if he were having a heart attack.

Norma Jeane winced. This wasn't funny! But so like Hollywood people, who played at the emotions they truly felt. Or maybe the emotions they truly felt could only be expressed in play? Everyone knew that I. E. Shinn had a cardiac condition.

I can't marry you just to keep you alive, can I?

Must I?

The Fair Princess was only a Beggar Maid. Rumpelstiltskin might clap his hands and she'd vanish.

During the course of this conversation, neither Norma Jeane nor Shinn would allude to Norma Jeane's secret lover V, whom she hoped to marry soon. Oh, soon!

It was true, Norma Jeane didn't love V with the abandon and desperation with which she'd loved Cass Chaplin. But maybe that was a good thing. She loved V with her saner emotions.

Once V's divorce was finally settled. Once his vicious ex-wife decided she'd sucked enough of his bone marrow.

Exactly what Shinn knew of Norma Jeane and V, Norma Jeane couldn't be sure. She'd confided in him as her agent and friend—to a degree. (She hadn't confided in him that she'd swallowed an almost-full bottle of Cass's barbiturates but got sick to her stomach and vomited them back up again, a slimy bilious paste, the morning after the night of Cass's betrayal.) Norma Jeane had the uneasy sense that, being I. E. Shinn, he might know more about V and herself than she herself knew, for he had spies reporting to him on his favored clients. Yet he would not speak of V as he'd spoken so disparagingly and insultingly of Charlie Chaplin, Jr., because he liked and admired him as a "good, decent Hollywood citizen, a guy who'd paid his dues." V had been a strong box-office attraction of the forties and was still a leading man in the fifties, in some quarters at least. V wasn't Tyrone Power and he wasn't Robert Taylor and he certainly wasn't Clark Gable or John Garfield, but he was a solid, reliable talent, a ruggedly handsome freckled-boy face known to millions of moviegoing Americans.

I love him. I mean to marry him.

He has said he adores me.

Shinn brought his pudgy dwarf fist down on his desktop, hard. "Your mind's drifting, Norma Jeane. *I'm* on."

"I'm s-sorry."

"I realize you don't 'l-love' me, sweetheart, in quite that way. But there are other ways." Shinn spoke delicately now, choosing his words with care. "So long as you respect me, as I think you do—"

"Oh, Mr. Shinn! Of course."

"And trust me—"

"Oh, yes!"

"And so long as you know that I have your best interests at heart—"

"Oh, yes."

"We would have a strong unshakable foundation for a marriage. Plus the prenuptial agreement."

Norma Jeane hesitated. She was like a dazed ewe being herded expertly toward the pen. Balking just at the entrance.

"But I—I can only marry for l-love. Not for money."

Shinn said sharply, "Norma Jeane! God damn, you haven't been listening. Didn't Huston teach you to listen to your co-actors? To *concentrate?* Your facial expression and your posture signal you're only just 'indicating'—you aren't *feeling*. In which case, how the hell d'you know what you honestly feel?" What a question! Shinn pulled such tactics often with his clients. He assumed the director's role, analyzing, assigning motives. You couldn't quarrel with him. His eyes were tawny coals. Norma Jeane felt a sensation of falling, vertigo.

Better to give in. Say yes. Whatever he wishes. The magic knowledge is his. He is your true father.

Norma Jeane had made inquiries into the private life of I. E. Shinn and knew he'd been married twice, the first time for sixteen years. He'd divorced his wife and shortly afterward married a young contract player at RKO, from whom he was divorced in 1944. He was fifty-one years old. He had two grown children from his first marriage. Norma Jeane had been relieved to hear that Shinn was known as a good decent father who'd had an amicable parting with their mother.

I could only marry a man who loves children. Who wants children.

Shinn was staring at Norma Jeane oddly. Had she spoken aloud? Made faces? Shinn said, "You're not religious, dear, are you? I'm certainly not. I may be a Jew, but—"

"Oh. You're a *Jew?*"

"Of course." Shinn laughed at the expression on the girl's face. Here was Angela, in the flesh! "What d'you think I am, Irish? A Hindu? A Mormon elder?"

Norma Jeane laughed, embarrassed. "Oh gosh, well, I—I knew you were J-jewish, but somehow I—" She paused, shaking her head. It was an amazing movie performance: the dumb blonde. And so adorable. "Until you said it? 'Jew.' "

Shinn laughed. "That's what 'Isaac' is, sweetheart. Right out of the Hebrew Bible."

Shinn had been holding Norma Jeane's hands. Impulsively, Norma Jeane lifted his hands to her mouth and covered them with kisses. In an ecstasy of self-abnegation she whispered, "I'm a Jew too. In my heart. My mother so admired the Jewish people. A superior race! And I think I am part Jewish too. I never told you, I guess?—Mary Baker Eddy was my great-grandmother. You've heard of Mrs. Eddy? She's famous! *Her* mother was a Jew. Jewess? They didn't practice the religion because they had a vision of Christ the Healer. But I am a descendant, Mr. Shinn. *The same blood beats in my veins.*"

These words of the young Princess were so remarkable, Rumpelstiltskin could think of no reply.

THE TRANSACTION

It wasn't me. Those many times. It was my destiny. Like a comet veering toward Earth, and the gravitational pull. You can't resist. You try, but you can't.

W summoned Norma Jeane to him at last. Now that she was "Marilyn." It had been years.

She knew why: The Studio was contemplating hiring her for a movie called *Don't Bother to Knock*. She'd auditioned, and she'd been told she was "terrific." Now she was waiting. I. E. Shinn was waiting. The summons came from W, the male lead.

Why had she been thinking obsessively of Debra Mae these past forty-eight hours? It made no sense. There is no "death" yet the dead stay dead. It was only harmful to think of them. *They would not wish our pity* Norma Jeane thought.

She'd wondered if Debra Mae had ever been summoned by W. Or by N, or D, or B. Z, she knew, had indeed summoned the dead girl. But Z had also summoned her, and *she wasn't dead*.

"Marilyn. Hel-lo."

He was staring frankly at her. Smiling his lopsided smile. Always it's a surprise to see in life the movie close-up. This was W of the cruel sexual wolf smile. You imagined sharp canine teeth. You imagined a hot panting breath that might scald. In fact, he was a handsome man with a lean face like a hatchet and squinting taunting eyes. *Hates women. But you can make him love YOU.* And she was looking so pretty and so soft: a bonbon. A cream puff. Something to lick vigorously with the tongue, not chew and gnaw. Maybe he'd have mercy? Or did she want mercy? Maybe not. W wasted no time circling her shivery-bare forearm with his fingers. Her skin was creamy-pale and his was much darker. Nicotine-stained fingers, and strong. The shock of it went through her. A stab in the pit of the belly. A moistening there. Men were the adversary, but you must make your adversary want you. And here was a man not-gentle as V, her secret lover, was gentle. Here was a man not a twin of Norma Jeane's as Cass Chaplin had been a twin.

"Long time no see, eh? Except in the funny papers."

In his films W was often a killer. You cheered him as a killer. For he was one who enjoyed killing. An overgrown, lanky boy with mischievous eyes and that sexy lopsided smile. That goofy high-pitched giggle. W's film debut was pushing a crippled woman in a wheelchair down a flight of stairs. His giggle as the chair careens down the stairs, careens and crashes, and the woman screams, the camera looking on in a pretense of horror. *Hell, you know you always wanted to push a crippled old dame down the stairs; how many times did you want to push your old bitch of a mother down the stairs and break her neck?*

They were in a ground-floor flat in an apartment building off La Brea, near Slauson. Not a part of L.A. that Norma Jeane knew. In her hurt and shame she would not recall it clearly afterward. How many flats, bungalows, hotel suites, "cabanas," and weekend estates in Malibu she would not recall clearly afterward in these early years of what she presumed would be her career, or in any case her life. Men ruled Hollywood, and men must be placated. This was not a profound truth. This was a banal and thus a reliable truth. Like *no evil, no sin, and no death. No pain.* The flat, its windows shadowed by spiky palm trees, was sparsely furnished, like a dream in which the edges aren't filled in. A borrowed flat. A shared flat. No carpets on the scarred wooden floors. A few scattered chairs, a lone telephone on a windowsill littered with insect corpses. A lone page from *Variety* with a headline vaguely glimpsed containing the words "Red Skelton," unless it was "Dead Skeleton." In a shadowy rear room, a bed. A new-looking satiny mattress and a loose sheet drawn over it in what appeared to be haste but might as easily have been dreaminess, contemplation. What solace we take in the mind's frantic scurrying to assign meaning and motive. The world is, she was coming to see, a gigantic metaphysical poem whose invisible interior shape is identical with its visible shape and of the exact same size. Norma Jeane in her spike-heeled shoes and flowery summer dress like a cover of *Family Circle* was thinking possibly the sheet was clean but probably (you had to be realistic at the age of twenty-six if you'd been married at the age of sixteen) not. In the tiny smelly bathroom there would be towels, possibly clean but probably not. In the wicker wastebasket, coiled together and stiffened like slug fossils, you knew what you'd see, so why look?

She laughed now, turning with charming awkwardness—"Oh! *What*—?" so W could steady her, comfort her as in a gesture of masculine protectiveness. "Nothing, baby. Just—y'know—bugs." In the corner of her eye a scurrying of roaches shiny as pieces of black plastic. Only roaches (and she had plenty of her own, at home), yet her heart quickened in alarm.

W snapped his fingers in her face. "Daydreamin', honey?"

Norma Jeane laughed, startled. Her first reflex was always to laugh and to smile. At least it was her new sexy-husky laugh, not the ridiculous squeak. "Oh—no no no *no*"—blundering on, improvising as in acting class—"just I was thinking, there aren't rattlesnakes here. That's something to be always grateful for, there aren't rattlesnakes actually in a room with you? Or waking up in bed?" This was more a breathless inquiry than a statement. In W's presence as in the presence of any man of power you didn't make statements except in the form of inquiries. This was only good manners, female tact. Her reward was, W laughed. A hearty belly laugh. "You're a scream, Marilyn. Or—what, Norma? Which?" There was an excited sexual tension between them. His taunting eyes on her breasts, her belly, her legs, slender bare ankles in the sling-back high heels. His taunting eyes on her mouth. W liked her sense of humor, she could see. Often men were surprised by Norma Jeane's odd sense of humor, not expecting it from "Marilyn," who was a sweet dumb blonde with the intelligence of a mildly precocious eleven-year-old. For this was a sense of humor like their own. Mordant and dissonant, like biting into a cream puff and discovering ground glass.

W was telling a rattlesnake story, with gusto. In rattlesnake season, everyone had a rattlesnake story. Men competed with one another. Women usually just listened. But women were essential as listeners. Norma Jeane was no longer thinking of Debra Mae, she was plagued now by thinking of a rattlesnake nudging its beautiful cudgel-shaped head, flicking tongue, and venomous jaws up into what's called the vagina, her vagina, which was only just an empty cut, a nothingness, and the womb an empty balloon requiring blowing up to fulfill its destiny. She made an effort to listen to W, who would be her leading man if she was hired. If she was hired. Trying to shape her beautiful-doll face into an expression that would make this asshole think she was listening to him and not again drifting off.

I want to play Nell. I am Nell. You can't keep me from her. I will steal the movie out from beneath your eyes.

W was asking in a drawl did she remember how they'd met at Schwab's? Norma Jeane said sweetly of course she remembered. How could she not?— "But was this g-girlfriend of mine Debra Mae with me that morning? Or some other morning?" The words slipped out. Norma Jeane couldn't reclaim them. W shrugged. "Who? Naw." He was standing so close now she could smell him. A frank perspiration odor. And tobacco. "So, you think we could work together? Eh?" and Norma Jeane said, "Oh yes, I th-think we could. I do." "Saw you in *The Asphalt Jungle* and what's the other one? *Eve*. Yeah, I was impressed." Norma Jeane was smiling so hard, her jaw began to shake. There was the long look between them. No movie music, only traffic outside and the scurrying of roaches like miniature muffled laughter. Unless she was imagining this?—but she knew. You always know. That look so eloquently saying *I want to fuck you. You're not a cock tease, are you?* W would be the only box-office name in the film. At least, the only proven box-office name. W had the right to choose his co-stars. Norma Jeane would hear from the producer D, if W liked her OK. He'd pass her on to D in that case. Or maybe not? Of course there was the director N, but he was in the hire of D, so possibly N wouldn't be a factor. There was the studio executive B. What you heard of B made you wish not to hear more. *No evil, no sin, and no death. No ugliness except as our ignorant eyes betray us.*

What if Mr. Shinn knew of this summons of W? (Was it possible I. E. Shinn did know?) Norma Jeane was so ashamed of herself, she'd had to decline his marriage proposal after having seemed to accept it. She was crazy! Since that terrible day Isaac Shinn was brusque and businesslike and communicated with Norma Jeane mainly through an assistant and on the phone. Never did he take her to dinner at Chasen's or the Brown Derby now. Never did he, with some sweet lame excuse, "drop by" her place on Ventura. Oh, God, he'd wept as she'd never seen a grown man weep. His heart broken. You can only break a man's heart once. She had not meant to deceive him, she'd been confused with his talk of being a Jew. The sick sensation washed over her, seeing I. E. Shinn reduced to tears. *This is what love does to you. Even to a man. Even to a Jew.*

Still, he'd sent her the script of *Don't Bother to Knock*. He still wanted "Marilyn Monroe" as his client. He told her the best thing about the script was the title. The script was contrived and melodramatic and there were excruciatingly awful "comic" interludes but if she landed the role of Nell it would be "Marilyn's" first starring role. She'd be playing opposite Richard Widmark. Widmark! A serious dramatic role, not the usual dumb-blonde crap. "You'd play a psychotic baby-sitter," Shinn said. "A *what?*

Who—?" Norma Jeane asked. "A schizzy baby-sitter who almost shoves a little girl out a window," Shinn said, laughing. "She ties the brat up and gags her. It's risky stuff. There's no actual love interest with Widmark, his character's a dud, but you get to kiss, once. There's some sexy stuff and Widmark will be good. This Nell-the-baby-sitter tries to seduce him, confusing him with a fiancé who's dead, a pilot shot down in the Pacific, in the war. A tearjerker. It's phony as hell but maybe nobody will notice. In the end, Nell threatens to slash her throat with a razor blade. She's taken away by the cops to a loony bin. Widmark's with another woman. But you'd have more scenes than anyone else in the movie and an opportunity for once to *act*."

Shinn was trying to be enthusiastic but his telephone voice didn't sound authentic. It was a reasonable voice, a sane voice. A croaky-froggy middle-aged voice. A voice buttoned to the neck in a cardigan sweater. A bifocal voice. What had happened to fierce Rumpelstiltskin? Had Norma Jeane imagined his magic? And what of the Fair Princess, his creation, if Rumpelstiltskin was losing his power?

He knew me: the Beggar Maid. They all knew me.

Saying pleasantly, "You're free to leave at any time."

"Sweetheart. We got the part."

Three days later, here was I. E. Shinn on the phone, gloating.

Norma Jeane gripped the receiver tight. She hadn't been feeling well. She'd been reading books Cass had left for her, *The Actor's Handbook and the Actor's Life*, filled with his annotations, *The Diary of Nijinski*. When she tried to speak to Shinn, her voice failed.

Shinn said, annoyed, "You awake, kid? The baby-sitter. I'm telling you you got the female lead. Widmark asked for you. We got the part!"

One of the books slipped to the floor. Her neatly sharpened pencil rolled across the carpet.

Norma Jeane tried to clear her throat. Whatever it was.

Hoarsely she whispered, "That's g-good news."

"Good news? It's terrific news." Shinn said accusingly, "Is somebody there with you? You don't sound very happy, Norma Jeane."

Nobody was in the rented flat with her. V hadn't called in several days.

"I am. I am happy." Norma Jeane began to cough.

Shinn talked excitedly through her coughing. You'd think he had forgotten his heartbreak. His mortification. You wouldn't think this was a man now fifty-two years old and soon to die. Norma Jeane succeeded in clearing her throat and spitting a clot of greenish phlegm into a tissue. A similar clotty moisture stung her eyes. For days it had packed her sinuses, worked its way into the crevices of her brain, hardened between her teeth. Shinn was complaining. "You don't sound happy, Norma Jeane. I'd like to know why the hell *not*. I bust my ass over at The Studio talking you up with D and you're 'Uh-huh, I'm *hap-py*' "—mimicking what Norma Jeane presumed he believed to be her voice, a nasal, whiny baby voice. He paused, breathing hard.

Norma Jeane squinted along the telephone line and saw him, jewel-like glaring eyes, the prominent nose with flaring, hairy nostrils, the hurt mouth like something mashed. A mouth she'd been unable to kiss. He'd moved to kiss her and she'd flinched and turned away with a cry. *I'm sorry! I just can't! I can't love you! Forgive me.*

"Look, 'Nell' will be dynamite. OK, the part doesn't make much sense and it's a lousy ending, but it's your first starring role. It's a serious film. Now 'Marilyn's' really on her way. You doubt me, eh? Your only friend, Isaac?"

"Oh, no! No." Norma Jeane spat again into the tissue and quickly crumpled it in her fist without looking at it. "Mr. Shinn, I would never d-doubt *you*."

NELL 1952

Transformation—that is what the actor's nature, consciously or subconsciously, longs for.

—Michael Chekhov,
To the Actor

I

I knew her. I was her. Not her lover but her father was gone from her. They told her he was lost in the war. They lied: it was only to her he was lost.

2

Frank Widdoes.

Culver City Homicide Detective Frank Widdoes!

At the first rehearsal of *Don't Bother to Knock* she realized who "Jed Towers" was. Not the famous actor (for whom she felt no emotion, not even contempt) but her lost lover Frank Widdoes, whom she hadn't seen in eleven years. In "Jed Towers" she perceived the detective's cruel-guilty-yearning eyes. This man was miscast in the film as a gruff-guy-good-at-heart. It was a role for V, not for W, with his lopsided grin and taunting eyes. In fact, W was a thug, a killer. A sexual predator. Yet at his touch Nell melted. You had to employ such a corny term—"melted." That mad shining certainty in her widened eyes. In the very pertness of her little-woman's body. (Norma Jeane insisted upon wearing Nell's bra jacked up tight. Her breasts constrained beneath the prim fabric. Soon it would be Marilyn's signature to go without underwear but, as Nell, underwear was required. "The bra straps should show through the cloth, when I'm seen from the back. She's trying to hang on to her sanity. She's trying *so hard*.")

I love you, I will do anything for you. There is no me only YOU.

She would kiss "Jed Towers." Passionately, hungrily. She would move into the man's arms with such intensity, Richard Widmark would be astonished. And a little frightened of her. Is this acting? Is Marilyn Monroe playing Nell or is Marilyn Monroe so hungry and eager for *him*? But what after all is "acting"? Norma Jeane had never kissed Frank Widdoes. Not as he'd wanted her to kiss him. She knew, and she'd denied him. She'd been frightened of him. An adult man possesses the power to enter your soul. Her boyfriends were boys only. A boy has no power. The power to hurt, maybe, but not the power to enter your soul. "Norma Jeane. Hey. C'mon." She'd had no choice but to climb into his car, her long curly dark-blond hair swinging about her face. What could Widmark know of Widdoes? Not a thing! Hadn't a clue. He'd made her kneel before him but she hadn't loved *him*. His swagger, his sexual arrogance, his penis of which he was so proud she hadn't loved; it wasn't real to her. What was real to her was Frank Widdoes stroking her hair. Murmuring her name. Her name magical-sounding in her own ears, in his voice. In itself "Norma Jeane" was not a magical name but in Frank Widdoes's deep yearning voice it was magical, and she knew she was beautiful, and she was desired. *To be desired is to be beautiful.* Because he'd hidden her, called her name, she'd climbed into his car. An unmarked police car. He was an officer of the law. Of the state. In the hire of the state he could kill. She'd seen him pistol-whip a boy, bring him to his knees and to the blood-splattered pavement. He carried a revolver in a holster strapped around his left shoulder and one rainy-smoggy afternoon by the railroad embankment where the body had been found he took her hand, her soft small hand, and closed her fingers around the butt of the revolver, warm from his body. Oh, she'd loved him! Why hadn't she kissed him? Why hadn't she let him undress her, kiss her as he wanted to, make love to her with his mouth, his hands, his body? He had "protection" in his wallet, in an aluminum foil wrapper. "Norma Jeane? I promise. I won't hurt you."

Instead, she'd let him brush her hair.

For here was her true father. He would hurt others for her sake, but never her.

She'd lost Frank Widdoes. He had disappeared from her life with the Pirigs, Mr. Haring, her long curly dark-blond hair and slightly crooked front teeth. Yet there was the movie character "Jed Powers" staring at her. Richard Widmark was the actor's name.

Seeing not Widmark—who meant no more to me by that time than a

*movie poster of the famous actor—but Frank Widdoes, who had entered my
soul.* What passion in Nell! Her skin heated, and her body primed for love!
She's behaved recklessly, signaling to this stranger with a flurry of venetian
blinds. She's a baby-sitter in a big-city hotel. She's stepped into a fantasy.
Glamorous borrowed clothes, borrowed perfume, jewelry, and makeup, that
have transformed mousy Nell into a seductive blond beauty ready to take on
"Jed Powers" with her young eager body. *Every action requires justification.
You must locate a reason for everything you do onstage.* Nell has only just
been discharged from a mental hospital. She's tried to commit suicide. Her
scarred wrists. She's terrified as Gladys was terrified at the prospect of leaving Norwalk. Gladys's hands taut as claws. Gladys's thin body stiffening
when Norma Jeane pleaded *Maybe you can come stay with me, some weekend? There's Thanksgiving. Oh, Mother!*

The stranger arrives, knocking at Nell's door. His taunting eyes move
upon her; his appraisal is unmistakably sexual. He has brought a bottle of
rye, he's excited and nervous too. Her eyelids quiver as if he's stroked her
belly; her childish voice drops—"You like the way I look?" Later they kiss.
Nell moves into the kiss like a hungry sinewy snake. "Jed Powers" is taken
by surprise.

Widmark was taken by surprise. Never would he know who was
"Marilyn," who was "Nell." It wasn't Widmark's style of acting. He was a
skilled technical actor. He followed a director's direction. Often his mind
was elsewhere. There was something humiliating about being an actor, if you
were a man. Any actor is a kind of female. The makeup, the wardrobe fit-
tings. The emphasis on looks, attractiveness. Who the hell cares what a man
looks like? What kind of man wears eye makeup, lipstick, rouge? But he'd
expected to walk away with the movie. A crappy melodrama that might've
been a stage play it was so talky and static, mostly a single set. "Richard Widmark" was the sole box-office name in the cast and he took it for granted
he'd dominate the movie. Swagger through *Don't Bother to Knock* as the
love interest of two good-looking young women who never meet. (The other
was Anne Bancroft, in her Hollywood debut.) But every fucking scene with
"Nell" was a grapple. He'd swear that girl wasn't acting. She was so deep
into her movie character you couldn't communicate with her; it was like trying to speak with a sleepwalker. Eyes wide open and seemingly seeing, but
she's seeing a dream. Of course, the baby-sitter Nell was a kind of sleepwalker; the script defined her that way. And, seeing "Jed Powers," she
doesn't see him, she sees her dead fiancé; she's trapped in delusion. The script
failed to explore the psychological significance of the issue it raised as melodrama: where does dreaming end and madness begin? Is all "love" based
upon delusion?

Afterward Widmark would tell the story of how the cunning little bitch

Marilyn Monroe stole every scene they were in together! every scene! It wasn't evident at the time, only when they saw the day's rushes. And even then it wasn't as clear as it would be at screenings when they saw the movie in its entirety. In fact, every scene Marilyn Monroe was in, she managed to steal. And when "Nell" wasn't on camera, the movie died. Widmark hated "Jed Powers"—all talk. He didn't get to kill anybody or even to punch, kick, maul; it was the psycho baby-sitter blonde who had the juicy action scenes, tying and gagging the bratty little girl, almost shoving her out a high window. (At the screening even among Hollywood veterans half the audience was gasping and pleading "No! no!") The hell of it was, on the set Marilyn Monroe appeared scared stiff. A poker up her ass. "What a dummy. That beautiful face and fig- ure, and you wanted to steer clear of her, like what she had was contagious. In those 'love' scenes with her it was like my guts were being sucked out of me, and frankly I don't have guts to spare. Either she can't act at all or she's act- ing all the time. *Her entire life's an act, like breathing.*"

What really pissed Widmark off, Nell had to do every fucking scene over and over. This breathy stubborn voice—"Please. I can do better, I know." So we'd redo what we'd already done and the director had said was good. Sure, possibly it was improved next time, and improved a little more the next time, but so what? Was that crappy little melodrama worth it?

Maybe she was fighting for her life, but he wasn't.

3

So strange. There was a morning she realized. Only "Marilyn Monroe" was known here, not Norma Jeane.

4

I did want to kill the child! She was growing too tall, she wasn't a child any longer. She was losing what had made her special.

Saying to the director, "Her motive for wanting to kill the child is: the child is her. The child is Nell. She wants to kill herself. She doesn't want to grow up, and if you don't grow up you must die. I wish you'd let me add lines of my own! I know I could do better. Nell is a poet, you see. Nell has taken a night-school course in poetry and she has written poetry about love and death. Losing her love to death. She was hospitalized and now she's out but still she's behind bars, her mind has imprisoned her. Why are you look- ing at me like that? It's the clearest thing. It's obvious. Let me play Nell my way, I *know*."

5

Nijinski, too, was a child abandoned by his father. His handsome dancer-father. Abandoned, and a prodigy. Dance, dance! His debut at the age of eight, his collapse twenty years later. What can you do but dance, dance? Dance! You dance on fiery coals and the audience applauds, for when you cease dancing the fiery coals devour you. *I am God, I am death, I am love, I am God and death and love. I am your brother.*

6

Calm as a wind-up doll. Yet invisibly she was tense, quivering. Her skin was clammy-pale (Nell's skin was clammy-pale) yet heated to the touch. *When we kissed I sucked his soul into me like a tongue. I laughed, the man was so frightened of me!* She was not mad (Nell was mad in her place) yet she saw with the piercing eyes of madness. Of course she was not Nell but the young capable actress who "played" Nell as one might "play" the piano. Yet she contained Nell. An actor is greater than the parts he contains, so Norma Jeane was greater than Nell because she contained Nell. Nell was the germ of madness in the brain. Nell promised in a whisper, "I will be any way you want me to be." At the end she whispered, as she was taken away, "People who love each other . . ." Nell the Beggar Maid. Nell with no last name. She dared to transform herself into a princess by appropriating a rich woman's possessions: an elegant black cocktail dress, diamond earrings, perfume, and lipstick. But the Beggar Maid was unmasked and humiliated. Even her attempt to kill herself was thwarted. In a public place, the foyer of a hotel. Strangers gawking at her. *Never so happy as when I brought the edge of the razor against my throat.* And there was Mother's voice urging *Cut! Don't be a coward like me!* But Norma Jeane replied calmly *No. I am an actress. This is my craft. I do what I do to simulate, not to be. For while I contain Nell, Nell does not contain me.*

It was a time of self-discipline. She starved herself and drank ice water. She ran the early-morning streets of West Hollywood as far as Laurel Canyon Drive until her healthy young body thrummed with energy. She had no need of sleep. She took no magic potions to help her sleep. Through the nights alternating between her vigorous actor's warm-up exercises and reading books, most of them secondhand or borrowed. Nijinski fascinated her. There was such beauty and certitude in his madness. It began to seem to her that she'd known Nijinski years ago. Several of his dream experiences were her own.

She contained Nell, but certainly Norma Jeane wasn't Nell. For Nell was an immature woman, emotionally stunted. She could not live without a lover to keep her from madness and self-destruction. She had to be defeated, banished. Why didn't Nell take her revenge? Norma Jeane was tempted to shove the fretful child actress out the window in their suspenseful scene. As Mother had been tempted to drop her girl baby onto the floor. Screaming at the nurse *It slipped from my hands! I'm not to blame*. Norma Jeane halted production, asking the director, N, please could she rewrite part of a scene? Just a few lines? "I know what Nell would say. These aren't Nell's words." But N refused her. N was perplexed by her. What if every actress wanted to rewrite her lines? "I'm not every actress," Norma Jeane protested. She didn't tell N that she was a poet and she deserved words of her own. She was furious with the injustice of Nell's fate. For madness must be punished in a world in which mere sanity is prized. The revenge of the ordinary upon the gifted.

Even I. E. Shinn was beginning to take note of the changes in his client. He'd visited the set of *Don't Bother to Knock* several times. The look on Rumpelstiltskin's face! Norma Jeane had been so deep into Nell she'd hardly been aware of him, as of other observers. Between takes she hurried away to hide. She wasn't "sociable." She missed interviews. The other actors didn't know what to make of her. Bancroft was in awe of her intensity but wary of her. Yes, it might be contagious! Widmark was sexually attracted to her but had come to dislike and distrust her. Mr. Shinn cautioned her not to "wear herself out"—not to be "so intense." She wanted to laugh in his face. She was moving beyond Rumpelstiltskin now. Let him cast his spells. As if "Marilyn" was his invention. His!

It was a time of self-discipline. She would recall it, this season of Nell, as the true birth of her life as an actress. When she first realized what acting might be: a vocation, a destiny. Her "career" was vulgar publicity arranged by The Studio. It had nothing to do with this rapt inner life. Alone, she lived and relived Nell's scenes. She'd memorized Nell's words. She was groping to find a body for Nell, a speech rhythm. In the night, too restless to sleep after the intensity of the workday, she was reading Michael Chekhov's *To the Actor* and she was reading Constantin Stanislavski's *An Actor Prepares* and she was reading a book urged upon her by a drama tutor, Mabel Todd's *The Thinking Body*.

The body is unstable,
that is why it has survived.

This seemed to her poetry, a paradox that is truth. She knew her acting was sheerly gut instinct and perhaps she was not acting at all and this expenditure of spirit would burn her out by the age of thirty. So Mr. Shinn warned. Norma Jeane was like a young athlete eager to push to the limit and beyond, trading her youth for the applause of the crowd. That had happened to the prodigy Nijinski. Genius has no need of technique. But "technique" is sanity. Her teachers told her she lacked "technique." But what is "technique" but the absence of passion? Nell was not accessible by way of "technique." Nell was accessible only by plunging into the soul. Nell was fiery and doomed. Nell must be defeated, her sexuality denied. Oh, what was Nell's secret? Norma Jeane came near yet couldn't penetrate it. She could "be" Nell only to a point. She spoke with N, who had no idea what she was talking about. She spoke with V, saying she'd never realized, acting might be so lonely.

V said, "Acting is the loneliest profession I know."

7

Never did I exploit her, I did not. I did not steal from her. This was her gift to me. I swear!

It was an urgent morning when in a borrowed Buick convertible Norma Jeane drove to Norwalk State Hospital. It was a free morning. She was free of Nell for the day. No scenes of Nell's were being rehearsed or filmed that morning. As usual, Norma Jeane brought Gladys presents: a slender book of poems by Louise Bogan, a small wicker basket of plums and pears. Though she had reason to believe that Gladys rarely read the poetry books given to her and was mistrustful of food gifts. "But who would poison her? Who but herself?" Norma Jeane would leave money for Gladys as usual. She was embarrassed she hadn't visited Gladys since Easter and it was September now. She'd sent her mother a money order for twenty-five dollars but hadn't yet told her the good news about *Don't Bother to Knock*. Norma Jeane hadn't told Gladys good news of her life and career for some time, reasoning *Maybe it isn't true exactly? Maybe it's a dream? They will take it all away?*

For the visit to the hospital Norma Jeane wore stylish white nylon slacks, a black silk blouse, a diaphanous black scarf looped around her gleaming platinum-blond hair, and shiny black pumps with a high-medium heel. She was gracious, soft-voiced. She was not anxious, edgy, watchful; she was not Nell, she'd left Nell behind; Nell would be terrified of entering a mental hospital, Nell would be paralyzed at the gate and incapable of entering. "How clear it is, *I am not Nell*."

Telling herself *It's only a role. A part in a movie. The very concept of*

*"part" means "part of a whole." Nell is not real, and Nell is not you. Nell
is not your life. Nor even your career.*

Nell is sick, and you are well.

Nell is but the "part," and you are the actress.

This was true. This was true!

Now this morning she was the Fair Princess visiting her mother at Norwalk. Her "mentally disturbed" mother, whom she loved and had not forsaken. Her mother, Gladys Mortensen, whom she would never forsake, as
so many daughters, sons, sisters, and brothers had forsaken family members
committed to Norwalk.

Now she was the Fair Princess, whom others observe with hope and
excited admiration, measuring the distance between themselves and her and
wanting that distance to be exact.

Now she was the Fair Princess admonished by The Studio as by the Preene
Agency to appear in public perfectly groomed and costumed, not a hair out
of place, for never are you unobserved at such times, the eyes and ears of the
world are turned upon you.

Immediately she was aware of the receptionist and the nurses observing
her with smiling interest. As if an upright flame had entered the dreary hospital. And there came Dr. K, who'd never before appeared so quickly. And
a colleague, Dr. S, whom Norma Jeane had never seen before. Smiles, handshakes! All were eager to see Gladys Mortensen's film-actress daughter.
None of these people had seen *The Asphalt Jungle* or *All About Eve* but
they'd seen or believed they'd seen photographs of the glamorous starlet
"Marilyn Monroe" in newspapers and magazines. Even those who knew no
more of "Marilyn Monroe" than of Norma Jeane Baker were determined to
catch a glimpse of her as she was led through a labyrinth of corridors to distant Wing C. ("C" for "Chronic Cases"?)

*She is pretty, isn't she? So glamorous! And that hair! Of course it's fake.
Look at poor Gladys, her hair. But they resemble each other, don't they?
Daughter, mother. It's obvious.*

Yet Gladys seemed scarcely to recognize Norma Jeane. It was her sly-
stubborn habit to withhold a quick recognition. Sitting on a sagging sofa in
a corner of the dim-lit and smelly lounge like a sack of laundry. Maybe this
was a lonely mother waiting for her daughter's visit, but maybe not. Norma
Jeane felt a stab of disappointment and hurt: Gladys was wearing a shapeless gray cotton dress very like the one she'd worn on Easter Sunday, though
Norma Jeane had told her they'd be going out for brunch. Today, too, they
were going out, into the town of Norwalk. Had Gladys forgotten? Her hair
looked as if it hadn't been combed in days. It was limp, greasy, and a strange
graying-brown metallic hue. Gladys's eyes were sunken yet watchful; beau-

tiful eyes still, though smaller than Norma Jeane recalled. As Gladys's mouth was smaller, bracketed by severe knife creases.

"Oh, M-mother! Here you are." It was an inane unscripted remark. Norma Jeane kissed Gladys's cheek, instinctively holding her breath against the stale yeasty body odor. Gladys lifted her mask face to Norma Jeane and said dryly, "Do we know each other, miss? You *smell*." Norma Jeane laughed, blushing. (There were hospital workers within earshot. Pointedly lingering at the doorway. Greedily absorbing what they could see and hear of "Marilyn Monroe's" visit to her mother.) This was a joke, of course: Gladys disliked the chemical smell of Norma Jeane's bleached hair mixed with the scent of the rich Chanel perfume that V had given her. Embarrassed, Norma Jeane murmured an apology and Gladys shrugged forgiveness, or indifference. She seemed to be waking slowly from a trance. *How like Nell. Yet I did not steal from her, I swear.*

Now came the brief ritual of gift giving. Norma Jeane sat beside Gladys on the sagging sofa and handed over the poetry book and the fruit basket, speaking of these objects as if they were significant items and not props, stage business, something to do with her hands. Gladys grunted thanks. She seemed to enjoy receiving presents if in fact she had little use for them and very likely gave them away as soon as Norma Jeane was gone, or took no care to prevent their being stolen from her by her fellow inmates. *I did not steal from this woman. I swear!* Norma Jeane would do most of the talking, as usual. She was thinking that she must not allow Gladys to know of Nell; Gladys must know nothing of the lurid melodrama *Don't Bother to Knock*, with its portrayal of a mentally disturbed young woman who abuses and comes close to killing a little girl. Such a movie would be strictly off-limits for Gladys Mortensen, as for any Norwalk patient. Still, Norma Jeane couldn't resist mentioning to Gladys that she'd been working lately as an actress—"serious, demanding work"; she was still under contract to The Studio; there'd been a feature on her as one of a new crop of Hollywood starlets in *Esquire*. Gladys listened to this in her usual somnambulist way, but when Norma Jeane flipped open the magazine and showed her the glamorous-gorgeous full-page photo of "Marilyn Monroe" in a low-cut white-sequined dress, smiling joyously into the camera, Gladys blinked and stared.

Norma Jeane said apologetically, "That dress! The Studio provided it. *I* don't own it." Gladys scowled. "You don't own a dress you're wearing? Is it clean? A clean dress?" Norma Jeane laughed uneasily. "This doesn't look much like me, I know. They say Marilyn is photogenic." Gladys said, "Huh! Does your father know?" Norma Jeane said, "My f-father? Know what?" "About this 'Marilyn.'" Norma Jeane said, "He wouldn't know my professional name, I guess. How could he?" But Gladys had become animated. She was staring with pride, maternal pride, wakened from her trance of years and contemplating the splendid display, like ripened fruits, of six beautiful young starlets, any one of whom might be her daughter. Norma Jeane felt a sting as if she'd been rebuked. *She would use me to reach him. That's my value to her. She loves him, not me.*

Norma Jeane said, cleverly, "If you told me Father's name, I could send him this magazine. Gosh, I could—call him sometime. If he's still living? In Hollywood?" Norma Jeane hesitated to tell her mother that she'd been inquiring after her elusive father for years, and well-intentioned people, usually men, had provided names; but none had come to anything. *They're humoring me. I know. But I can't give up!* (Clark Gable she'd flirted nervously with, drunk on champagne at an opening. Joking with the famous man that they might be related and he'd been mystified, not knowing what on earth this gorgeous young blonde was getting at.) Norma Jeane repeated, "If you told me Father's name. If—" But Gladys was losing her enthusiasm. She let the magazine fall shut. She said, in a flat dead voice, "No."

Norma Jeane combed her mother's hair, primped her up a bit, and impulsively looped about her mother's creased neck the diaphanous black scarf, which was also a gift from V, and led her hand in hand out of the hospital. Norma Jeane had made the required arrangements; Gladys Mortensen was a patient with such privileges. It was a long tracking shot, with a buoyant mood music beneath. In their wake, uniformed hospital staff, even the courteous Dr. X, observed smilingly. The receptionist told Gladys, "How pretty you look today, Mrs. Mortensen!" In the floating black scarf Gladys Mortensen had become a woman of dignity. She gave no sign she'd even heard this remark.

Norma Jeane took Gladys into Norwalk, to a beauty salon, where Gladys's straggly hair was shampooed, styled, and set. Gladys was unresisting if not very cooperative. Next, Norma Jeane took Gladys to an early lunch at a tearoom. There were only women customers, and not many of these. They frankly stared at the striking young blonde with the frail middle-aged woman who might have been—must have been?—her mother. At least, Gladys's hair now looked presentable, and the scarf hid the stained and rumpled bosom of her dress. Outside the undersea atmosphere of the mental hospital, Gladys might look virtually normal. Norma Jeane ordered for them both. Norma Jeane helped her mother pour tea into her cup. Norma Jeane said mischievously, "Isn't it a relief to be *out!* Out of that awful place! We could just drive and drive, couldn't we, Mother? Just—drive! You're my mother, it would be perfectly legal. Up the coast to San Francisco. To Portland, Oregon. To—Alaska!" How many times Norma Jeane had suggested to Gladys that Gladys spend a few days with her in her Hollywood apartment; a quiet weekend—"Just us two."

Now that Norma Jeane was working twelve-hour days on the set, this wasn't a very likely possibility; still there was the idea, the perennial offer. Gladys shrugged and grunted, bemused. Gladys chewed her food. Gladys sipped tea without seeming to mind that the steaming liquid burnt her lips. Norma Jeane said flirtatiously, "You need to get out more, Mother. There's nothing wrong with you really. 'Nerves'—we all have 'nerves.' There's a full-time doctor at The Studio who's hired just to prescribe nerve pills for actors. *I* refuse. *I* would rather be nervous, I think." Norma Jeane heard her provocative girlish voice. The voice she'd cultivated for Nell. Why was she saying such things? It was fascinating to listen. "Sometimes I think, Mother, you don't want to get well. You're hiding in that awful place. And it *smells*." Gladys's mask face stiffened. The deep-set eyes seemed to recede. Her hand shook holding the cup, tea spilled onto the black scarf unnoticed. Norma Jeane continued to speak in a lowered girlish voice. They might've been co-conspirators, mother and daughter! They might've been planning an escape. Norma Jeane was not Nell but this was Nell's voice, and her eyes were narrowed and glowing like Nell's in those ecstatic scenes in which "Jed Powers" was overpowered by her, as "Widmark" was overpowered by "Marilyn Monroe." Gladys had never met Nell. Never would Gladys meet Nell. It would be cruel, like looking into a distorting mirror: a mirror that made of the aging woman a girl again, radiant in beauty. Norma Jeane contained Nell as any skilled actress contains a role, but certainly Norma Jeane was not Nell for *Nell did not exist*. They had taken her lover from her, and they had taken her father from her, and they were claiming she was mad, and because of this *Nell did not exist*.

"That's the puzzle I can't comprehend, Mother, of all the puzzles," Norma Jeane said thoughtfully. "That some of us 'exist'—and most don't. There was an ancient Greek philosopher who said that the sweetest thing of all would be not to exist, but I don't agree with that, do you? Because then we would lack knowledge. We've managed to be born and that must mean something. And before we were born, where were we? I have an actress friend named Nell, she's under contract as I am at The Studio, and she has told me she lies awake at night, through the night, tormenting herself with such questions. What does it mean to be born? After we die, will it be the same thing as it was before we were born? Or a different kind of nothingness? Because there might be knowledge then. Memory." Gladys shifted uneasily in her straight-backed chair and made no reply.

Gladys, sucking in her bloodless lips.

Gladys, keeper of secrets.

It was then that Norma Jeane saw Gladys's chafed hands. It was then that Norma Jeane recalled having seen, back in the visitors' lounge, her mother's hands clasped on her knees and later buried in her lap. Her mother's hands shut into fists. Or opened, and the thin fingers restlessly stroking one another. Broken and bitten, blood-edged fingernails digging at one another. At times, Gladys's hands seemed almost to be wrestling each other for dominance. Even when Gladys professed a sleepwalker's indifference to what was being said to her, there in her lap was evidence of her alertness, her agitation. *The hands are her secret. She has given up her secret!*

There was the Fair Princess returning her mother to Norwalk State Psychiatric Hospital, Wing C, for safekeeping. There was the Fair Princess wiping tears from her eyes as she kissed her mother goodbye. Gently the Fair Princess unwound the diaphanous black scarf from around the aging woman and looped it about her own unlined, lovely neck. "Mother, forgive me! I love you."

8

She had not intended it. She would not have exploited her mother. Perhaps she was unconscious of it, in fact. *The hands! Nell's restless seeking hands. Hands of madness.* In *Don't Bother to Knock*, there was Norma Jeane as Nell with Gladys Mortensen's hands and mesmerized stare. Gladys Mortensen's soul, in Norma Jeane's young body.

Cass Chaplin and his friend Eddy G saw the movie in a classy Brentwood movie house a short drive from the place they were house-sitting for a Paramount exec's ex who'd long had a crush on Eddy G. Norma Jeane was so fantastic, this sick-crazy-sexy blonde—with bra straps showing!—they returned for a second visit, this time liking Norma Jeane even more. Inevitable as death is THE END. Cass nudges Eddy. "Know what? I'm still in love with Norma." And Eddy G says, shaking his head like he's trying to clear it, "Know what? *I'm* in love with Norma."

THE DEATH OF RUMPELSTILTSKIN

One day he was screaming at her over the phone, the next day he was dead.

One day she was stricken with shame, the next day stricken with grief and remorse.

I didn't love him enough. I betrayed him.

He was punished in my place, God forgive me!

What a scandal! The "Golden Dreams" nude pinup of Norma Jeane taken by Otto Öse years ago had been belatedly, sensationally, identified on the front page of the tabloid *Hollywood Tatler*:

NUDE CALENDAR PIX
MARILYN MONROE?
Denial by the Studio
"We Had No Knowledge" Claim Execs

Immediately the lurid little tale was taken up by *Variety*, the *L.A. Times*, *Hollywood Reporter*, and the national news services. The nude pinup itself was reprinted with strategic parts of the girl model's voluptuous body blacked out or draped suggestively in what looked like opaque black lace. ("Oh, what have they done to me? This is true pornography.") The pinup would become a hot subject for gossip columnists, radio personalities programs, even newspaper editorials. Nude photographs of contract actresses were outlawed by the studios; "pornography" was forbidden. The studios were desperate to keep their merchandise "pure." Hadn't Norma Jeane signed a contract stipulating that behavior *contrary to the morals* of the Hollywood community would result in suspension of her contract or even termination? A sharp-eyed reporter for the *Tatler* (with a personal taste for young-girl nudes) had come upon the photo on an old calendar and examined the girl's face and had a hunch that the model was the rising young blond actress Marilyn Monroe; he'd investigated and learned that the model had identified herself in a 1949 contract as "Mona Monroe." What a scoop! What a scandal! What an embarrassment for The Studio! "Miss Golden Dreams" had appeared in a 1950 glossy girlie calendar called *Beauties for All Seasons* published by Ace Hollywood Calendars, the kind of calendar to be found in gas stations, taverns, factories, police precincts, and firehouses, men's clubs and barracks and dormitories. "Miss Golden Dreams" with her eager, vulnerable smile and smooth bared armpit and beautiful breasts, belly, thighs, and legs, and her honey-blond hair tumbling down her back had inhabited how many thousands or tens of thousands of masculine dreams of no more harmful significance than any fleeting image that triggers orgasm and is forgotten upon waking. The girl was one of twelve nude beauties of whom none was identified in the calendar itself. She did not in fact very closely resemble the myriad publicity photos of "Marilyn Monroe" that had begun to appear in the media in 1950, arranged by The Studio for distribution as any manufacturer might send out mass-market logos, eye-catching advertisements for consumer goods. "Miss Golden Dreams" might have been a younger sister of "Marilyn Monroe": less glamorous, less stylized, her hair seemingly natural, little eye makeup and no conspicuous black beauty mole on her left cheek. How had the reporter recognized her? Had someone given him a tip?

Norma Jeane had been shown neither the contact sheets nor any prints of the now-notorious photo for which Otto Öse had given her, in cash, fifty dollars. If asked, Norma Jeane might have claimed she'd forgotten the photo session entirely as she'd forgotten, or almost forgotten, the predatory Otto Öse.

No one seemed to know where Öse had gone. Some months ago, during a break in the filming of *Don't Bother to Knock*, Norma Jeane had gone on an impulse to Otto's old studio, thinking—well, he might need her? He might miss her? He might need money? (She had a little money now. Her anxiety with each paycheck was she'd spend it quickly and have little to show for it.) But Otto Öse's shabby old studio was gone and in its place was a palmist's shop.

There was a cruel rumor that Otto Öse had died of malnutrition and an overdose of heroin in a filthy hotel in San Diego. Or Otto had returned in defeat to his birthplace in Nebraska. Sick, broken, dying. Suffocated by the sludge sea of fate. The brainless tide of Will. He'd pitted his frail human vessel—the "idea" of his individuality—against this ravenous Will, and he'd lost. In his copy of Schopenhauer's *World as Will and Idea* which he'd lent her to read, Norma Jeane had come upon *The suicide wills life, and is only dissatisfied with the conditions under which it has presented itself.* "I hope he's dead. He betrayed me. He never loved me." Norma Jeane wept bitterly. Why had Otto Öse pursued her with his camera? Why hadn't he let her hide from him at Radio Plane? She'd been a girl, a girl wife, hardly more than a child; he'd exposed her to the world of men. Men's eyes. The hawk plunging its beak into the songbird's breast. But why? If Otto Öse hadn't come along and ruined her life, Norma Jeane and Bucky would still be married. They would have several children by now. Two sons, a daughter! They would be happy! And Mrs. Glazer, a loving grandmother. So happy! For hadn't Bucky whispered to her at the very hour of his departure for Australia—"As many kids as you want, Norma Jeane. You're the boss."

The tacky little scandal! Vulgar and shameful set beside headlines of U.S. casualties in Korea, front-page photos of "atom bomb spies" Julius and Ethel Rosenberg sentenced to death in the electric chair, reports of hydrogen bomb tests in the Soviet Union. I. E. Shinn had only just telephoned Norma Jeane to congratulate her on more good reviews of *Don't Bother to Knock*. You had to realize the agent hadn't expected such a response, for most of the reviews, he said, were serious, intelligent, respectful—"As for the others, the assholes, the hell with them. What do they know?" Norma Jeane shuddered. She wanted to hang up the phone quickly. She'd felt since the premiere like a bird on a wire, vulnerable to stones, bullets. A hummingbird observed through a rifle scope. Shinn meant well as V meant well, and other friends, defending her against critics of whom she knew nothing and would not know.

Shinn was now reading her excerpts of reviews from newspapers across the country in his rapid-fire Walter Winchell voice, and Norma Jeane tried to listen through a roaring in her ears. " 'Marilyn Monroe, a rising new Hollywood talent, proves herself a strong, dynamic film presence in this darkly disturbing thriller also starring Richard Widmark. Her portrayal of a mentally unbalanced young baby-sitter is so chillingly convincing you would be led to believe'—"

Norma Jeane clutched at the phone receiver. She tried to feel a thrill of happiness. Of satisfaction. Oh, yes, she *was* happy . . . wasn't she? She knew she'd acted capably, and perhaps more than capably. Next time she would be better. Except the thought was troubling her: what if Gladys were to see *Don't Bother to Knock*? What if Gladys saw how Norma Jeane had appropriated her talon hands, her dreamy not-there mannerisms? Norma Jeane interrupted Shinn to exclaim, "Oh, Mr. Shinn! Don't be mad at me. I know this is s-silly, but I have such a strong feeling, it's like an actual memory, that I was n-naked in the movie?" She laughed uneasily "I wasn't, was I? I can't remember." Somehow it had come to her in a flash that she'd had to remove her clothes in one of the scenes. Nell had had to remove the rich woman's cocktail dress because it wasn't hers. Shinn exploded. "Norma Jeane, stop! You're being ridiculous." Norma Jeane said, apologetically, "Oh, I know it's silly. It's just a—a thought. At the premiere I shut my eyes a lot. I couldn't believe that girl was me. And already, you know, as time passes—time is like this fast river that runs through us—already it *isn't*. But everybody in the audience would think it was me: 'Nell.' And afterward at the party: 'Marilyn.' "

Shinn said, "Are you on painkillers? Is it your period?" Norma Jeane said, "N-no, it is not. That's no business of yours! I'm not on painkillers, I am not." The remainder of that precious conversation with I. E. Shinn! The last time he would speak to her with kindness, with love. He'd talked to her of business. The Studio was considering her for a new film opposite Joseph Cotten, *Niagara* it was titled, and set at Niagara Falls; Norma Jeane would be playing a scheming, sexy adulteress and would-be murderess named Rose. "Sweetheart, 'Rose' is going to be terrific, I promise you. This film is a whole lot classier than *Don't Bother*, which privately I think, and don't quote me, is a stagy piece of crap except for you. Now, if I can get a better deal with those bastards—"

Hours later, Shinn called back. He was screaming at Norma Jeane even as she lifted the receiver. "—never told me you did such a thing! When was this, 1949? When in 1949? You were under contract then, weren't you? You fool! You dope! The Studio is probably going to suspend you, and at the worst possible time! 'Miss Golden Dreams'! What was it, soft-core porn? That fucker Otto Öse? May he rot in hell!" Shinn paused to draw breath, snorting like a dragon. Norma Jeane would halfway think, afterward, that Rumpelstiltskin had been right in the room with her. She stood stunned, clutching the receiver. What was this man talking about? Why was he so angry? "Miss Golden Dreams"—what did that mean? Otto Öse? Was Otto dead? Shinn said, " 'Marilyn' was mine, you dumb broad. 'Marilyn' was beautiful, and she was mine; *you had no right to despoil her.*"

I. E. Shinn's last words to Norma Jeane. And never would she see him again except in his casket.

. . .

"It's like I'm a C-commie, I guess? All the papers after me."

Norma Jeane tried to joke. Why was it so important? Why wasn't it funny? Everybody so angry at her! Hating her! Like she was a criminal, a pervert! She'd explained that she had posed nude only once in her entire life and she'd done it then only for money—"Because I was desperate. Fifty dollars! *You'd* be desperate too."

When we showed her the calendar she didn't recognize herself. She didn't seem to be pretending. She was smiling, sweating. She leafed through the calendar looking for "Miss Golden Dreams" until one of us pointed it out to her and she stared and stared and this panicked look came into her face. And then it was like she was pretending to recognize herself, to remember. And she couldn't.

Already she was missing I. E. Shinn! In terror he would fire her as his client. He hadn't been allowed to come to The Studio with her for the emergency meeting in Mr. Z's office. All afternoon she would be hidden away with these angry disgusted men. They never once laughed at her jokes! She'd become accustomed to men laughing uproariously at her mildest witticisms. "Marilyn Monroe" would be an inspired comedienne. But not quite yet. Not with these men.

There was bat-faced Mr. Z, who could barely bring himself to look at her. There was corkscrew-curly Mr. S, who stared at her as if he'd never seen a female so degraded, so despicable, and could not tear his eyes away. There was Mr. D, who was a co-producer of *Don't Bother to Knock* and had summoned Norma Jeane to him the evening following her meeting with W. There was grim-faced Mr. F, who was head of public relations at The Studio and clearly distressed. There were Mr. A and Mr. T, attorneys. From time to time there were others, all men. In her dazed state Norma Jeane wouldn't recall clearly afterward. Mr. Shinn screaming at her! Other voices, on the phone, screaming at her! And what did she do? She rushed into the bathroom of her apartment and fumbled open the medicine cabinet and took up a razor blade as Nell had taken up a razor blade, but her fingers shook, and already the phone was ringing again, and the flimsy razor blade slipped from her fingers.

She'd known she must medicate herself to get through the crisis. It was her first instinct, as at another time in her life her first instinct might have been prayer. *Nude photo. "Marilyn Monroe." Found out. Hollywood Tatler. Wire services. Studio furious. Scandal. Catholic Legion of Decency, Christian Family Entertainment Guide. Threats of censor, boycott.* Quickly she'd taken two codeine painkillers of the kind prescribed for her by a studio physician for menstrual cramps and migraine, and when these didn't take immediate effect she panicked and swallowed a third.

Now through a telescope she could observe the blinking blond woman surrounded by furious men. The blond woman was smiling the way you'd smile on a tilting surface to indicate that you weren't aware of the tilting. Telling herself that the situation was grave. In a Marx Brothers movie it would be comedy. *Dumb broad. Sad, sick cow.* The Studio meant to market the blond woman's body but only on its own strict terms. Downstairs there was a milling gang of reporters and photographers. Radio and TV crews. They'd been notified that Marilyn Monroe and a Studio spokesman would soon be issuing a statement regarding the nude calendar photo. But wasn't this ridiculous? Norma Jeane protested, "It's like I'm General Ridgway making some pronouncement in Korea. This is only a silly *picture.*"

The men continued to stare at her. There was Mr. Z, who had not exchanged a word with Norma Jeane since she'd come to see his aviary nearly five years ago. How young she'd been then! Since that occasion, Mr. Z had been promoted to head of productions. Mr. Z, who'd hoped to destroy Marilyn Monroe's career to punish her for being a tramp and for having bled on his beautiful white fur carpet. *Unless that never happened? But why would I remember it so clearly?* Never would Mr. Z forgive Marilyn though she was under contract at his studio; never could Mr. Z rid himself of Marilyn because he feared she would be hired by a competitor. He was a raging father, she a repentant and yet provocative daughter.

Norma Jeane was pleading, "Why's it so important? A nude photo? Of just *me?* Did you ever see those photos of the Nazi death camps? Or of Hiroshima, Nagasaki? Piles of corpses like lumber? Little children and babies too." Norma Jeane shuddered. Her words were upsetting her more than she'd intended. This was all unscripted, and she was getting unmoored. "*That's* something to be upset about. *That's* pornography. Not some sad dumb broad desperate for fifty dollars."

Which was why we never trusted her. She couldn't follow a script. Anything might come from that mouth.

Next morning the phone she'd purposefully left off the hook was ringing her out of sleep. She would swear she'd heard vibrations! Her heart leapt, thinking this would be Mr. Shinn, forgiving her. Wouldn't he have to forgive her, since The Studio had? Since The Studio decided not to fire her? At the press conference, she'd performed brilliantly as "Marilyn Monroe." Telling the reporters just the truth. *I was so poor in 1949, I was desperate for just fifty dollars, I never posed for nude photos before or since and I'm sorry now but I'm not ashamed. I never do anything I'm ashamed of, that's my Christian upbringing.*

Norma Jeane fumbled to replace the receiver seeing it was almost 10 A.M.

and immediately the phone rang and eagerly she lifted the receiver. "H-hello? Is-aac?" but it wasn't Mr. Shinn, instead it was Mr. Shinn's assistant, Betty (who Norma Jeane had reason to believe was an F.B.I. spy? though she couldn't have explained why this might be so, nor did it seem probable, given Betty's steadfast devotion to her boss)—"Oh, Norma Jeane! Are you sitting down?" Betty's voice was cracked and choked. Norma Jeane was sprawled naked in her smelly bed almost calmly gripping the phone receiver, thinking *Mr. Shinn is dead. His heart. I have killed him.*

Sometime later that morning Norma Jeane swallowed the remainder of the powerful codeine tablets, approximately fifteen pills. Washed down with slightly rancid buttermilk. Naked and shivering she lay down on the bedroom floor to die staring at the finely cracked, shadowy ceiling *Now Baby is lost to us, to both of us forever*. Would it have been a baby with a twisted spine? It would have been a baby with beautiful eyes and a beautiful soul. Within a few minutes she vomited everything up, a slimy-chalky bilious paste that would harden like concrete between her teeth though she brushed, brushed, brushed until her tender gums bled.

THE RESCUE

April 1953 when the Gemini entered Norma Jeane's life. *If I'd known they were watching over me, I would have been stronger.*

Things happened. And would continue to happen. A dump truck loaded with all the glittering tinselly Christmas gifts she'd never gotten at the Los Angeles County Orphans Home pulled up and unloaded its riches on top of her. "Oh!—is this happening to *me?* What is this that is happening to *me?*" A life that had been inward and brooding as a lonely child practicing scales on a piano was now outward and festive as a musical-comedy score turned up so high you can't hear the lyrics, only the music. The din.

"It scares me, y'know?—because I am not her. Absolutely *I am not Rose.*"

"I mean, I am not a slut. I'd love a man like Joseph Cotten, I would! He's been injured in his mind, in the War. Maybe in his body too. He's—what you call 'impotent,' I guess? It isn't clear. There's this one scene we're kind of—loving. Rose is manipulating him but he doesn't know it; he's laughing, he's crazy about her, you can tell. This scene, I'll play straight. Like Rose would play it with him. I mean—she's acting, but I'll play her like she isn't acting. One thing, I'd be scared as hell to mock a man to his face, a man who, y'know, can't—isn't—*a man*. In that way."

The Studio ("after I sucked all their cocks one by one around the table") forgave her for the nude photo scandal and raised her salary to $1,000 a week plus incidental expenses. Immediately, Norma Jeane made arrangements to transfer Gladys Mortensen from Norwalk to a much smaller private mental hospital in Lakewood.

Her new agent (who'd taken over I. E. Shinn, Inc.) advised her: "Keep it quiet, honey, OK? Nobody need know 'Marilyn Monroe' has a mental-patient mother too."

In Monterey, in the resort hotel to which they'd come off-season. The suite overlooking the Pacific, the cliffs. Giant boulders like madness rolling around in the brain. Blinding-glaring sunset. So V says, "Now we know what hell looks like, at least. I mean, at least what hell looks like." Norma Jeane, bright and perky as "Marilyn," quips, "Oh, hey! It's what hell *feels* like. That's the thing." And V laughs, sipping his drink. What's he murmur? Norma Jeane can't quite hear—"And that too."

The lovers have come to the resort hotel in Monterey to celebrate "Marilyn's" new contract at The Studio. Star billing in *Niagara*, her name over the title. More important, V's child-custody settlement. And there is V's recent starring role on Philco Playhouse, for which he's received good reviews nationwide. So V says, "Hell, it's only TV. Don't be condescending." Norma Jeane says in her serious-throaty "Marilyn" voice, "Only TV? TV is the future of America, I'd say." V shudders. "Jesus, I hope not. That tacky little black-and-white box." Norma Jeane says, "Movies started out, they were a tacky little black-and-white box too. You wait, darling." "Nope. Darling can't wait. Darling ain't that young anymore." Norma Jeane protests, "Oh, hey—whaaat? You *are!* You're the youngest guy I know." V finishes his drink. Smiles into the glass. His broad boyish-freckled face looks like papier-mâché. "*You're* young, baby. Me, maybe I've had my career."

They would return to Hollywood, to their separate places, noon Sunday.

These invented scenes. Improvised after the fact. They would plague her through the remainder of her life.

Nine years five months of that life.

And the minutes rapidly ticking.

Could there be an hourglass of time in which time runs in the opposite direction? Had Einstein discovered that time might run backward, if a ray of light could be reversed?

"But why not? You have to wonder."

Einstein dreamt with his eyes open. "Thought experiments." That was no different really from an actor improvising as Norma Jeane did, after the fact. Which was why "Marilyn Monroe" would be increasingly late for appointments. Not that Norma Jeane Baker was paralyzed with shyness, indecision, self-doubt staring at her luminous beautiful-doll face in whatever mirror of desperation and hope; no, it was the invented improvised scenes that held her.

See, if there'd been a director and he'd said, OK, let's run through this again, you would, wouldn't you? Again and again—however many times required to get it perfect.

When there is no director you must be your own director. No script to guide you?—you must compose your own script.

In that way, so simple and clear a way, seeming to know what is the true meaning of a scene that eluded you in the living of it. The true meaning of a life that eluded you in the dense thicket of living it.

In all this external search, says Constantin Stanislavski, *an actor must never lose his own identity.*

"Never would I be a tramp like Rose! I mean . . . I respect men, I'm crazy about men. I love men. The way they look, talk . . . smell. A man in a long-sleeved white shirt, y'know?—a formal shirt?—with cuffs and cuff links. That drives me crazy. I could never mock any man. Especially a veteran like Rose's husband! A 'disabled' person mentally. That's the meanest, cruelest. . . . Yeah, I'm kind of worried what the public's gonna think? 'Marilyn Monroe's such a slut, and she's just played a psychotic baby-sitter? This Rose is not only unfaithful to her husband but mocking him to his face and *conspiring to kill him?* Oh, gee."

These invented scenes, improvisations. Soon she'd be so plagued by them, she could not recall a time when her mind had been freer.

"It's just so simple. You want to get it *right.*"

Deserve to live? *You?* What a sad, sick cow. What a slut. She wouldn't ask V for his advice. She wouldn't wish to show her lover such weakness. Yet she had to wonder: Had Nell something to do with this? Nell and Gladys. For Gladys-was-Nell. In disguise. Norma Jeane had appropriated Gladys's hands, not guessing that Gladys had taken her over as a demon may inhabit a body. (If you believe in such superstitions. Norma Jeane did not.) That morning driving to Norwalk, she'd stepped into a contagious atmosphere. It's said that hospitals are swarming with (invisible) germs, why not mental hospitals? They'd be worse. More lethal. Norma Jeane was reading Sigmund

Freud, *The Interpretation of Dreams*, the book's pages blotched and peeling from chemical bleach, from the hairdresser's. How everything is determined from infancy. Yet you have to figure what about actual germs? viruses? cancer? cardiac failure? these are *real*.

Maybe, once she was settled at Lakewood, Gladys would forgive her?

At a Bel Air party, on the terrace above the shrieking peacocks. So dark (only just flickering candle flames) you couldn't see faces until they loomed up close. This one, a Robert Mitchum rubber mask. The sleepy-droopy eyes, the sly downturned smile. That drawl like the two of you are in bed together and it's a humdinger of a close-up. And he's tall, not some runt. Norma Jeane is transfixed, seeing a movie idol face-to-face and the man's warm boozy breath in her ear, and this once she's grateful that V has drifted off from her. Robert Mitchum! Eyeing *her*. In Hollywood, Mitchum's got the kind of reputation that would get another actor suspended from his studio. How he's escaped the attention of HUAC, nobody knows. Over the peacocks' manic screams there's this conversation Norma Jeane will play and replay to herself like a record.

MITCHUM: H'lo there, Norma Jeane. Don't be bashful, honey—I knew you before "Marilyn."

NORMA JEANE: What?

MITCHUM: A long time before "Marilyn." Over in the Valley.

NORMA JEANE: You're Robert M-mitchum?

MITCHUM: Call me Bob, honey.

NORMA JEANE: You're saying you know me?

MITCHUM: I'm saying I knew "Norma Jeane Glazer" a long time before "Marilyn." Back in 'forty-four, 'forty-five. See, I worked at Lockheed on the assembly line with Bucky.

NORMA JEANE: B-bucky? You knew Bucky?

MITCHUM: Naw, I didn't *know* Bucky. I just worked with Bucky. I didn't approve of Bucky.

NORMA JEANE: Didn't approve—? Why?

MITCHUM: Because that half-ass sonbitch brought in these photos of his pretty teenage wife he'd pass around to the guys, bragging on them, till I gave him what for.

NORMA JEANE: I don't understand. What?

MITCHUM: Hell, it was a long time ago. He's out of the picture, I guess?

NORMA JEANE: Snapshots? What snapshots?

MITCHUM: Go for broke, "Marilyn." The Studio gives you shit, do like Bob Mitchum and give 'em worse shit right back. And good luck.

NORMA JEANE: Wait! Mr. Mitchum—Bob—

V was watching now. V making his careful way back. V in an open shirt, a single button of his pale linen sport coat buttoned. V the All-American freckle-faced boy pushed to the limit of his endurance by the Nazi enemy, ripping a bayonet out of the hands of a German and stabbing it into his guts and the All-American audience cheering like it's a touchdown at the high school. V took hold of Norma Jeane's bare shoulder and inquired what Robert Mitchum was saying to her, she looked so intrigued, practically falling into the bastard's arms, and Norma Jeane said Mitchum had once been a friend of her ex-husband's. "A long time ago, I guess. They were boys together over in the Valley."

It was that party, the mega-millionaire Texas oilman with the eye patch wanting to invest in The Studio, the amazing bird and animal menagerie outdoors amid tall candles on posts, and a trick translucent paper moon above the palm trees lighted from within so guests thought there were *two moons in the sky!*—that party, the Gemini (who'd come uninvited but driving a borrowed Rolls) were watching over Norma Jeane from a distance. They'd seen Mitchum but hadn't heard his words. They'd seen V and hadn't heard.

"Just I feel, sometimes—my skin isn't there? A layer's missing? Everything can hurt. Like sunburn. Since Mr. Shinn died. I miss him so. He was the only one who believed in 'Marilyn Monroe.' The studio bosses didn't, for sure. 'That tramp' they called her. *I* never did, much. There's so many blondes. . . . After Mr. Shinn died, I wanted to die too. I caused him to die, I broke his heart. But I knew I had to live. 'Marilyn' was his invention, he claimed— maybe that was so. I would have to live for 'Marilyn.' Not that I'm religious, exactly. I used to be. Now, I don't know what I *am*. I don't truly believe anybody knows what he or she believes; it's just what they tell you, what they think they should say. Like these loyalty oaths we have to sign. Everybody has to sign. A Communist would lie, right? So what's the point? But, see— I figure there's a certain obligation. A responsibility? This story of H. G. Wells, *The Time Machine*? The Time Traveler travels into the future on this machine he can't completely control, travels far into the future, and there's this vision: the future is already there, ahead of us. In the stars. I don't mean superstitious stuff like—is it astrology? Palm reading? Trying to predict the future, and always such petty things! *I* could see in the future, I'd ask what's the cure for cancer? Or for mental illness? I mean, the future is ahead of us like a highway not yet traveled, maybe not yet paved. You owe it to whomever would be your descendants, the offspring of your children, to remain alive. To assure the children are born. Does that make sense? I believe that. There's a baby-dream of mine . . . so beautiful. Well, I won't talk about it, it's private. Only I wish, in the dream, there'd be a hint who's the father!"

April 1953. There was Norma Jeane in retreat, hidden away in a powder room crying. Loud music outside, screams of laughter. She was so hurt! Insulted. The Texas oilman touching her to see if she was "real." Wanting to dance the boogie with her. He hadn't the right. Not that kind of dancing. What if V had seen? And bat-faced Mr. Z and cruel leering Mr. D looking on. *I am not your whore for hire. I am an actress!* Times like these, Norma Jeane missed Mr. Shinn *so*. For V loved her but didn't seem to like her much. That was the plain truth. Also, it seemed lately he was jealous of her: her career! V, who'd been famous when Norma Jeane was in high school, mooning up at his freckled-boyish face on the screen. And maybe V didn't love her either. Maybe V only liked to fuck her.

It required ten minutes to repair the damage done to her mascara alone. Ten minutes to coax pretty bouncy life-of-the-party blond Marilyn back. "Oh, just in time!"

An elegy for I. E. Shinn.

> In the caverns of the sky
> The spirits of the departed lie.
>
> But this *is* a lie.
> It's only just—we don't want them to die!

The only poem Norma Jeane had written in a long time. And it was a lousy poem.

Sometimes in bed in the arms of the very man she's in despair of losing. Her mind jumps like a flea on a griddle! She's sighing, moaning, groaning as she draws her fingers through his curly still-thick hair. Entwined happy as an eel in his freckled fatty-muscled arms. (There's a tiny American-flag tattoo on his left bicep. So kissable!) And he rolls on top of her, kissing her wildly, penetrating her as best he can and if his erection holds (you hold your breath hope-hope-hoping!) he makes love to her in gasping lurching pumplike motions; as he approaches the end it shifts gear to become a quirky-jumpy-whimpery-quivery motion, every man has his unique style of lovemaking in contrast to every man you're required to suck off where it's always the same, skinny cock or fat cock, short cock or long cock, smooth cock or ropey-veined cock, lard-colored cock or blood-sausage-red cock, soapy-clean cock or mucus-crusted cock, tepid cock or steaming cock, smooth cock or wrinkled cock, youthful cock or decrepit cock, always the same cock, and it's repulsive. When Norma Jeane loves a man as Norma Jeane loves V she gives an Oscar performance. True, she's always had a difficult time feeling physical sensation with V that's genuine. As she'd had a difficult time feeling much with Bucky Glazer snorting and puffing *giddy-ap horsey!* and coming all over her belly like a nasty sneeze, if he remembered to yank out in time. Oh, she wants so much to please V! Seeming to know beforehand, as *Screen Romance, PhotoLife, Modern Screen* reveal in their coverage of the stars, it's only love that matters, true love, not "just a career." Well, Norma Jeane knows this already. It's only just common sense. With V she simulates in her mind what it might feel like, sexual pleasure; a slow and then a quicksilver rising to orgasm; recalling those long languorous times with Cass Chaplin, in a stupor of pleasure not knowing if it was night or day, morning or late afternoon, Cass never wore a watch and rarely wore clothes, indoors damp-eyed and unpredictable as a wild creature, and when they made love every part of their sweaty bodies stuck together, even their eyelashes!—finger- and toenails! Oh, but Norma Jeane loves V more than she ever loved Cass. She believes this. V is a real man, an adult citizen. V has been a husband. So with V, who's a proud man like all men she's ever known, Norma Jeane wants him to feel like the King of the World. Wants him to feel she's feeling something special. The few porn films she's seen, she always feels ashamed thinking the girls could try harder to make it seem like it mattered.

Sometimes she has an actual climax. Or something in the pit of her belly. A squirmy squealing sensation rising to a shocked and disbelieving crisis, then out like a switched-off light. Is that an orgasm? Sort of, she's forgotten. But murmuring, "Oh, darling, I love you. Love love love *you*." And this is true! Enraptured thinking how once, as a girl-wife, she'd clutched her husband's hand in a movie house in Mission Hills watching this man, her lover, as a brash boy pilot in *The Young Aces*: the way he'd parachuted down, down, down to the earth amid smoke and gunfire and nearly unbearably suspenseful movie music, and could Norma Jeane have ever guessed she'd one day be making love with that very man, what astonishment!

"Of course, it isn't the same man, I guess. It never is."

Behind the blinding klieg lights and hidden in the strategic shadows beyond, the Sharpshooter. Nimble as a lizard squatting on a garden wall in zip-up night-colored rubber surfer's suit. It's a matter of conjecture even among those in the know: is there a single Sharpshooter in southern California or are there a number of Sharpshooters? It makes sense (common sense!) that there would be a number of Sharpshooters assigned to specific districts of the United States, with a concentration on notorious Jew-saturated regions like New York City, Chicago, and L.A./Hollywood. In the sensitive night scope of his high-powered rifle the Sharpshooter calmly observes the oil mega-millionaire's guests. It's an early, innocent era of surveillance, he can't pick up their words, even their shouted words, amid so much hilarity. Does he hesitate, seeing the quasi-familiar faces of the stars among the others? Always, seeing a "star" face, you feel a slight recoil, a stab of disappointment, as of a wish too readily granted. Yet how many beautiful faces! And powerful men's faces, blunt craggy pushed-out brows, skulls oversize and rounded as bowling balls, glistening insect eyes. Black tie, tuxedos. Starched frilled shirts. These are elegant glittery folks. Yet the Sharpshooter, a practiced professional, is swayed by neither beauty nor power. The Sharpshooter is in the hire of the United States, and beyond the United States in the hire of Justice, Decency, Morality. You could say *in the hire of God.*

This is the balmy-breezy eve of Palm Sunday, the Sunday before Easter. At the oil mega-millionaire's French Normandy estate in the hills of prestigious Bel Air. Norma Jeane is thinking *Why am I here among strangers?* even as she's thinking *One day I will live in a mansion like this, I promise!* She's uneasy, sensing herself being observed. Eyes drift onto "Marilyn Monroe" as moths are attracted to light. She's wearing a low-cut lipstick-red dress that reveals a good deal of her breasts and clings to her hips and narrow waist. A sculpted doll, yet she's moving. She's animated and smiling and clearly very very happy to be among such exalted company! And that fine-spun cotton-candy platinum hair. And those translucent blue eyes. The Sharpshooter is thinking he has seen this one before, didn't this juicy blonde sign a petition defending Commies and Commie-symps, defending those traitors Charlie Chaplin and Paul Robeson (who's a nigger in addition to being a traitor, and an uppity nigger at that); this girl's name is on file, however many names and aliases she has, the State can track her. The State knows her. The Sharpshooter lingers on "Marilyn Monroe," fixing her squarely in his rifle scope.

Evil can take any form. Absolutely any form. Even a child form. The force of evil in the twentieth century. Must be identified and eradicated like any source of plague.

And beside the rising starlet "Marilyn Monroe" there's V, the veteran actor, war-hero patriot of *The Young Aces* and *Victory Over Tokyo,* films the Sharpshooter thrilled to in his youth. Are these two an item?

If I was a true tramp like Rose I'd want all these men. Wouldn't I?

. . .

Partly the party was in celebration of the Hollywood Heroes.

Norma Jeane hadn't known beforehand. She hadn't known that Mr. Z, Mr. D, Mr. S, and others would be there. Smiling at her with angry hyena teeth.

Hollywood Heroes: The patriots who'd saved the studios from the wrath of America and financial ruin.

These were the "friendly" witnesses who'd testified in Washington before the House Un-American Activities Committee, righteously denouncing Communists and Communist sympathizers and "troublemakers" in the unions. Hollywood was being unionized, it was Commies who were to blame. There was handsome leading man Robert Taylor. There was dapper little Adolphe Menjou. There was suave-talking, perpetually smiling Ronald Reagan. And homely-handsome Humphrey Bogart, who'd initially opposed the investigations and then abruptly recanted.

Why? Because Bogie knows what's good for him like the rest of us. Ratting on your friends, that's the test of a true patriot. Ratting on your enemies anybody can do.

Norma Jeane shuddered. She whispered to V, "Maybe we should leave? I'm afraid of some people here."

"Afraid? Why? Your past catching up with you?"

Norma Jeane laughed, leaning against V. Men were such jokers!

"I t-told you, darling: I don't have any past. 'Marilyn' was born yesterday."

What a shrieking! Like babies bayoneted.

They were gorgeous iridescent green-and-blue peacocks strutting and shaking their heads in twitchy motions like Morse code. The party guests clucked and cooed at them. Clapped their hands to startle them. Strange to Norma Jeane that the peacocks' widespread peacock tails weren't erect but were dragged ingloriously behind the birds on the ground. "It's like they're a burden to them, I guess? Such big beautiful heavy tails to carry around." All evening Norma Jeane had been hearing herself utter flat, banal words for lack of a script. When isolated words came to her like *valediction, ecstasy, altar*, she could not speak them, for what did they mean in the context of the Texas oil mega-millionaire's estate? Norma Jeane had no idea. And V would scarcely have heard her above the din.

They were walking along a serpentine path beside an artificial mountain brook. On the other side of the brook were more peacocks, as well as graceful upright birds with lewd neon-pink plumage—"Flamingos?" Norma Jeane had never seen flamingos close up. "Such beautiful birds! They're all alive, I guess?" The oil mega-millionaire was a famed amateur collector of exotic fowl and beasts. Guarding the front gate of his estate were stuffed elephants, with curving ivory tusks. Their eyes were light reflectors. So lifelike! Atop the roofs of the French Normandy château were stuffed African vultures, rows of them like ominous furled black umbrellas. Here beside the brook was a South American spotted puma in a cage, and inside a large wire enclosure were howler monkeys, spider monkeys, and bright-feathered parrots and cockatoos. Party guests were admiring a giant boa constrictor in a tubular glass cage, looking like a long fat banana. Norma Jeane cried, "Ohhh!—I wouldn't want that guy to hug me, no thanks."

It was a cue for V to playfully hug Norma Jeane around the rib cage. But V, staring at the enormous snake, missed his cue.

"Oh, what's that?—such a big, strange pig!"

V squinted at a plaque embedded in a palm tree. "A tapir."

"A what?"

"Tapir. 'Nocturnal ungulate of tropical America.' "

"Nocturnal *what?*"

"Ungulate."

"Goodness! What's a tropical ungulate doing *here?*"

Blond Norma Jeane spoke in exclamations to hide her growing anxiety. Was she being watched? By hidden eyes? Behind the restless klieg lights scanning the crowd? At times, raked by the lights? V's handsome face appeared bleached out, a fine-wrinkled parchment mask. His eyes were just sockets. What was the purpose in being here? A sweat droplet, coarsened by talcum powder, inched downward between Norma Jeane's big beautiful breasts in the snug red dress.

Always there is a script. But not always known to you.

At last they moved upon her.

She'd been waiting, and she knew.

Like hyenas circling. Grinning.

George Raft! A low suggestive voice. "*Hel*-lo, 'Marilyn.' "

Bat-faced Mr. Z, head of production at The Studio. " 'Marilyn,' hel-*lo.*"

Mr. S and Mr. D and Mr. T. And others Norma Jeane could not have identified. And the Texas oil mega-millionaire who was a principal investor in *Niagara.* Their gargoyle faces shot with shadow as in an old German Expressionist silent film. As V looked on from a short distance the men touched Norma Jeane, drew their sausage fingers over her, bare shoulders, bare arms, breasts, hips, and belly, they leaned close and laughed softly together, with a wink in V's direction. *We've had this one. This one, we've all had.* When Norma Jeane pushed free of them and turned to V, he was gone.

She hurried after him. They'd been about to leave the party; it wasn't yet midnight. "Wait! Oh, please—" In her panic she'd forgotten her lover's name. She caught up with him, clutched at his arm; he threw her off, cursing. He might have muttered over his shoulder, "Good night!" or "Goodbye!" Norma Jeane pleaded, "I—wasn't with any of them. Not really." Her voice faltered. What a poor actress she was. Tears streaking her mascara again. It was too arduous a task to be beautiful and a woman! Suddenly Norma Jeane felt someone take her hand and turned, startled, to see—Cass Chaplin? She felt someone grip her other hand, strong fingers twining through hers, and turned to see—Cass's lover Eddy G? The handsome black-clad young men had moved up swiftly and noiselessly as pumas behind Norma Jeane as she stood at the edge of the terrace swaying in her high heels, dazed with hurt and humiliation. In his smooth boy's voice, Cass murmured in her ear, "You don't belong with people who don't love you, Norma. Come with us."

THAT NIGHT . . .

That night, the first of their nights!

That night, the first night of Norma Jeane's new life!

That night, in the borrowed black 1950 Rolls-Royce they drove to the ocean above Santa Monica. The wide white wind-ravaged beach, deserted at this hour. A bright pearly moon, wisps of cloud blown across the sky. Shouting, singing! It was too cold to strip and swim, even to wade in the crashing surf, but there they were, running along the beach at the edge of the water laughing and shrieking like deranged children, arms around one another's waists. How clumsy they were, yet how graceful, three beautiful young people in the prime of their reckless youth, two young men in black and a blond girl in a red cocktail dress—three of them in love? Can three be in love as fatally as two? Norma Jeane kicked off her shoes and ran until her stockings were in tatters, and still she ran, clutching at the men, shoving at them, for they wanted to stop and kiss, and more than kiss, they were excited, aroused as healthy young animals, and Norma Jeane teased them, eluding them, for how fast she could run, in bare feet, what a tomboy this gorgeous blonde, screaming with laughter in a delirium of happiness. She'd forgotten the party in Bel Air. She'd forgotten her lover walking away, out of her life, his stiff adamant back. She'd forgotten a fraction of a second's devastating judgment *You never deserved to live, this is proof.*

In her excitement she might have been thinking these young princes had come for her at the Home, they'd freed her from her place of confinement to which wicked stepparents had brought her and abandoned her. Almost, she couldn't have identified these men. Yet of course she knew: Cass Chaplin and Eddy G. Robinson, Jr., despised sons of famous fathers, outcast princes. They were penniless yet dressed expensively. They had no homes yet lived in style. They were rumored to be excessive drinkers, they took dangerous drugs—yet look at them: perfect specimens of young American manhood. Cass Chaplin, Eddy G—they'd come for her! They loved her! *Her* whom other men despised, used, and discarded like tissue. As the men would tell and retell the tale, it would come quickly to seem that they'd crashed the Texan's party exclusively for her.

What I couldn't know, they would make my life possible. They would make Rose possible, and beyond.

One of them wrestled her to the cold damp sand, hard-packed as dirt. She was fighting, laughing, her red dress torn, her garter belt and black lace panties twisted. The wind in her hair, making her eyes tear so almost she couldn't see. Full on her startled lips Cass Chaplin began to kiss her, gently, then with increasing pressure, and with his tongue as he hadn't kissed her in so long. Norma Jeane grabbed at him desperately, arms around his head, Eddy G sank to his knees beside them and fumbled with the panties, finally ripping them off. He stroked her with skillful fingers and then with his skillful tongue he kissed her between the legs, rubbing, nudging, poking, in a rhythm like a giant pulse, Norma Jeane's legs twined about his head and shoulders desperately, she was beginning to buck her hips, beginning to come, so Eddy quick and deft as if he'd practiced such a maneuver many times shifted his position to crouch over her, as Cass was now crouching over her head, and both men penetrated her, Cass's slender penis in her mouth, Eddy's thicker penis in her vagina, pumping into her swiftly and unerringly until Norma Jeane began to scream as she'd never screamed in her life, screaming for her life, clutching her lovers in such a paroxysm of emotion they would laugh ruefully over it later.

Cass would display three-inch scratches on his buttocks, mild bruises, welts. In a parody of a Muscle Beach bodybuilder, strutting naked for them to admire, Eddy would display plum-colored bruises on his buttocks and thighs.

"It must've been, Norma, you were waiting for us?"

"It must've been, Norma, you were starved for us?"

Yes.

ROSE 1953

1

"I was born to play Rose. *I was born Rose.*"

2

This season of new beginnings. Now she was Rose Loomis in *Niagara*, the most talked-of film in production at The Studio; and now she was Norma, Cass Chaplin's and Eddy G's girl lover.

What wasn't possible, now!

And Gladys in a private hospital. *Just to know I've done the right thing. I don't love her, I guess. Oh, I love her!*

She'd been wakened from her lethargy as by a tremor of the earth. This fragile crust of southern California earth. She'd never felt so *alive*. Not since her happy days at Van Nuys High when she'd been a star of the girls' track team and ran to cheers and praise and a silver medal. *Just to know I'm wanted. Somebody needs me.* When she wasn't with Cass and Eddy G, she was thinking dreamily of Cass and Eddy G; when she wasn't making love with Cass and Eddy G, she was recalling the last time they'd made love, which might've been only a few hours ago, her body still suffused with the heat and wonder of sexual pleasure. *Like a shock treatment to the brain.*

Sometimes the beautiful boys Cass Chaplin and Eddy G dropped by The Studio to visit Norma Jeane on the set. Bringing "Rose" a long-stemmed red rose. If Norma Jeane had a break, and if circumstances allowed, the three of them might withdraw to her dressing room to spend some private time together. (And if circumstances weren't always ideal, what's the difference?)

She'd have this glazed look like she'd just been fucked. And a smell coming off her you couldn't mistake. That was Rose!

3

So much energy now that V was out of her life.

Now that a cruel false hope was out of her life.

"All I want is to know what's real. What's true. I will never be lied to again, ever."

It was not good timing but symptomatic of her life as her life was becoming, ever more accelerating and turning back upon itself, appointments and telephone calls and interviews and meetings, and often "Marilyn Monroe" failed to appear or appeared hours late, breathless and apologetic; yet the week before beginning work on *Niagara*, Norma Jeane allowed herself to be talked into moving into a new apartment, airier than the old, slightly larger, in a handsome Spanish-style building near Beverly Boulevard. A distinct step up from her previous neighborhood. Though Norma Jeane couldn't really afford a more expensive apartment (where did her salary *go?* some weeks even her check for the Lakewood Home was delayed), and had to borrow money for the lease and for new furnishings, yet she'd moved at the insistence of her lovers. Eddy G said, " 'Marilyn' is going to be a star. 'Marilyn' deserves better than this." Cass sniffed in contempt. "This place! Know what it smells of? Old dreary love. Stale paste on sheets. Nothing more rancid than old dreary stale-paste love." When he and Eddy G stayed the night in the old apartment with Norma Jeane, the three of them curled together like puppies in Norma Jeane's Salvation Army brass bed, the men had insisted on opening all the windows to let in fresh air, and they'd refused to draw the blinds. Let all the world gape at them, what did they care? Both Cass and Eddy G had been child actors, accustomed to being watched and paying little heed to who was watching. Both boasted they'd performed in porn films as teenagers. "Just for the hell of it," Cass said, "not for the cash." Eddy G said, with a wink at Norma Jeane, "*I* didn't sneer at the cash. I never do." Norma

Jeane didn't know whether to believe such tales. The young men were shameless liars, yet most of their lies were laced with truth, as a sweet dessert might be laced with cyanide; they dared you to disbelieve and they dared you to believe. (What tales they told of their famous/infamous fathers. Like brother rivals they competed with each other to shock Norma Jeane: which man was the more monstrous, the woebegone Little Tramp or the tough-guy Little Caesar?) But it was so, the beautiful young men drifted about Norma Jeane's apartment naked, innocent, and oblivious as spoiled children. Cass declared it wasn't personal slovenliness but principle: "The human body is meant to be seen, admired, and desired, not hidden away like an ugly festering wound." Eddy G, the vainer of the two, as he was slightly younger and less mature, said, "Well. There's plenty of bodies that are ugly festering wounds and should be hidden. But not yours, Cassie, and not mine; and for sure not our girl Norma's."

It was like Norma Jeane's Magic Friend of childhood. Her Magic Friend in the Mirror, who was so much more beautiful when naked, and Norma Jeane's secret.

One night she told Cass and Eddy G about her Magic Friend. Eddy G laughed and said, "Just like me! I'd set up a mirror to watch myself on the toilet, even. Anything I did in the mirror, I could hear waves and waves of applause." Cass said, "In our household, which was essentially under an evil spell, my father 'Chaplin' was all the magic. A great man draws magic into himself, like reverse lightning. There's nothing to spare for anyone else."

Norma Jeane's new apartment was on top, the eighth floor of the building. Where it was less likely they'd be observed. But when Norma Jeane spent the night with Cass and Eddy G elsewhere, in one or another of their borrowed residences, who knew who might be watching from outside? Only when a house was surrounded by dense foliage or protected by a high fence did Norma Jeane feel entirely safe. Her lovers teased her for being a prude—
" 'Miss Golden Dreams,' of all people." Norma Jeane protested. "What scares me is somebody taking pictures. Just looking with their eyes, I wouldn't mind that."

The eyes and ears of the world. One day that will be your sole place of refuge, but not just yet.

4

Around this time, too, Norma Jeane acquired a new car: a 1951 lime-green Cadillac sedan convertible with a broad grinning chrome grille and flaring tail fins. Whitewall tires, a six-foot radio antenna, genuine palomino-hide seat covers front and rear. It was bought through a friend of a friend of Eddy G's, a bargain at seven hundred dollars. Yet Norma Jeane saw this vehicle, parked on the street like a nightmare tropical drink in glass-and-metal mutation, with the coolly appraising eyes of Warren Pirig. "Why's it priced so low?" Eddy G said, "Why? 'Cause my friend Beau has been admiring 'Marilyn Monroe' from afar. Says he fell for you hard in *The Asphalt Jungle* but first laid eyes on you as 'Miss Paper Products'—something like that? You were this dazzling blonde he says in a paper swimsuit and high heels and the swimsuit caught fire? Remember any of that?" Norma Jeane laughed at this but persisted in her questions. (Norma had such prole-bulldog ways sometimes! Right out of *Grapes of Wrath*.) "Where's your friend Beau this minute? Why can't I meet him?" Eddy G shrugged and said with charming evasiveness, "Where's Beau? This minute? Where Beau don't feel the social embarrassment of a lack of wheels. Where Beau is, you could say, ensconced."

Norma Jeane had further questions, but Eddy G shut her mouth by pressing his own against it, hard. They were alone in Norma Jeane's new, barely furnished apartment. It was rare for Norma Jeane to be alone with only one of her lovers! Rare for her even to glimpse Eddy G without Cass, or Cass without Eddy G. At such a time the absence of the other was palpable as any presence, maybe more so, for you kept waiting uneasily for the absent man to enter the room. It was like hearing footsteps ascending a stairs—and never coming to the top. It was like hearing that faint tinkling ring that sometimes precedes a phone's ringing, if no ringing actually follows. Eddy G grabbed Norma Jeane around the rib cage and shut her in his embrace so hard she could scarcely breathe. Eddy G's snake tongue in Norma Jeane's mouth, so Norma Jeane's protesting tongue was silenced.

It wasn't right to make love without Cass, was it?—how could they even touch each other without Cass?

Eddy G seemed angry. Such authority in anger! Eddy G, who'd sabotaged his acting career by mocking his lines at auditions, arriving late or drunk if hired, or both late and drunk on the set, or failing to arrive at all—Eddy G swooping down upon Norma Jeane like an avenging angel. Bright brown eyes and dark quilled hair and pasty pallor beautiful to her. Eddy G deftly pushed Norma Jeane to the floor, no matter it was a hardwood floor, there was a doglike urgency in his need to copulate, and to copulate at once; he spread her knees and her thighs and penetrated her, and Norma Jeane felt a stab of shame, of hurt, of regret, it was Cass Chaplin she loved, it was Cass Chaplin she wanted to marry, Cass Chaplin who was destined to be the father of her baby; yes, but she loved Eddy G, too, Eddy G, standing six feet tall and yet compactly built like his famous father, tight-muscled, his spoiled boy's face pale and pettish and almost pretty, and his lips fleshy, pouty, made for sucking. Without knowing what she did, Norma Jeane clutched at Eddy G. Her arms, her legs, her tender chafed thighs. Chafed from so much lovemaking. Starved for love and lovemaking. And like a warm sweet balloon the sensation, opening up, and up inside her, astonishing her who felt always so tight inside herself, a snarled convolution of thoughts-gone-wrong, thoughts-forbidden-to-be-uttered, there in the pit of her belly in those secret places for which available words like *vagina, womb, uterus* were inadequate and yet such a word as *cunt* had only a cartoon meaning, coined by the enemy. The balloon opened, and opened. Norma Jeane's spine was a bow, curving tight, tighter. Writhing on the hardwood floor, head turning from side to side and eyes struck blind.

This is what Rose loves. Rose loves to fuck and to be fucked. If the man knows how.

Norma Jeane screamed and would have torn off a chunk of Eddy G's lower lip except, feeling her muscles begin to contract, knowing she was about to come and how powerful this starved girl's orgasms were, canny Eddy G lifted his head so those teeth couldn't catch him.

She wasn't a perfect fuck by any means. Basically I guess she never knew how. Or how to give a blow job, either: you'd just fuck her mouth, and it was a luscious mouth so that was OK but it was something you did for yourself, like jerking off. Which is weird considering who she was, or would become: the number-one sex symbol of the twentieth century! The thing you'd hear about her in those years was mostly she'd only just lie there and let it be done to her like a corpse practically with her hands clasped together on her chest. But with Cass and me it was the exact opposite; she'd get so excited, so crazed, there wasn't any rhythm to it, she'd never masturbated as a kid she told us (we had to teach her!) so maybe that was why, her body was this gorgeous thing she'd stare at in the mirror but it wasn't her exactly, and she didn't know how to operate it worth shit. Funny! Norma Jeane having an orgasm was like stampeding for an exit. Everybody screaming and trying to push out the door at the same time.

When the two of them woke an hour later, prodded out of a stuporous sleep by Cass's foot, whatever Norma Jeane had meant to ask Eddy G about the lime-green Caddy, whatever had seemed so crucial for her to ask, had long been forgotten.

Cass smiled down at them. He sighed. "You two! So peaceful. It's like that sculpture of *Laocoön*, if the serpents and the boys had fucked instead of the serpents squeezing the boys to death? And they all fell asleep afterward, twined together? And that way, and not the other, became immortal?"

Beneath the soiled palomino hide covering the rear seat of her new car, Norma Jeane was to discover a scattering of small dark stains like sticky raindrops. Blood? Beneath a soiled plastic mat on the car's floor, Norma Jeane was to discover a manila envelope containing perhaps four ounces of a white fine-grain powder. Opium?

She licked a few grains with her tongue. No taste.

When she showed the packet to Eddy G, he quickly took it from her. Winked at her and said, "Thanks, Norma! Our secret."

5

"Rose had a baby, I think. And the baby died."

She was stubborn yet smiling. Unconsciously (consciously?) stroking her breasts from beneath, as she spoke. Sometimes she'd even palm herself, slowly, thoughtfully, as if the circling self-caressing gesture was part of thinking, her hand against the pit of her belly, her groin all but outlined in the tight-fitting costumes.

Like she was making love to herself right in front of you. Like a small child might do, or an animal rubbing itself.

On the *Niagara* set, as in Hollywood generally, there were competing theories. The first was that the female lead "Marilyn Monroe" could not act and did not need to act because in sluttish "Rose Loomis" she was only playing herself and that was why the studio bosses had cast her (for it was well known through Hollywood that the bosses, from Mr. Z down, despised Marilyn Monroe as a common tramp hardly better than a hooker or porn-film performer); the second was a more radical theory, advanced by her directors and certain of her fellow actors, that she was a born actress, a natural, in that way a kind of genius, however "genius" is defined, and what was "acting" to her had to be discovered the way a drowning woman flailing her arms, kicking her legs, might discover through desperation how to swim. Swimming "came to her" naturally!

The actor uses his face, his voice, and his body in his craft. He has no other tools. His craft is himself.

Within the first week of filming, the director, H, began to call Norma Jeane "Rose" as if he'd forgotten her professional name. This was flattering to her, amusing. It did not seem to her immediately insulting. Both H and her co-star, Joseph Cotten, a gentleman actor uncertain in his role, a leading man of the generation of Norma Jeane's former lover, V, and resembling V in numerous ways, behaved as if they were in love with "Rose" or were so fascinated by her they could look nowhere else but at her; or were they revulsed by her, her flagrant female body and flaunted sexuality, feared and loathed her, and so could look nowhere else? The actor who played Rose's lover, and who got to kiss her in protracted love scenes, was so sexually aroused by her Norma Jeane had to laugh at him; if she hadn't belonged to the Gemini (as Cass and Eddy G playfully called themselves), she'd have invited him to come home with her. Or to make love with her in her dressing room, why not? It was maddening how "Rose" absorbed most of the light in any scene no matter how meticulously it was lighted. Maddening how without seeming effort she absorbed most of the life of any scene no matter how the other actors expended their actorly selves. In the daily rushes they were revealed as two-dimensional cartoon figures while "Rose Loomis" was a living person. Her pale luminous skin that gave the suggestion of being hot, her uncanny eyes of the translucent blue of a churned winter ocean slivered with ice, her languid somnambulist movements. When she began to stroke her breasts on camera it was difficult for the mesmerized H to stop the scene; though such scenes would never pass the censor and would have to be cut. In a crucial scene, laughing at her desperate husband, mocking him for his impotence by suggesting she'd have sex with the next man she met, Rose rubbed the palm of her hand against her groin in an unmistakable gesture.

Why? It was obvious why. He couldn't give her what she wanted, she'd give it to herself.

But this was strange. It was much-repeated, and advanced as strange. How on the set of *Don't Bother to Knock* not a year before, the young blond actress Marilyn Monroe had had a reputation for being prudish, stiff, painfully shy, shrinking from physical contact and even eye contact; she'd hidden in her dressing room until summoned and was even then reluctant to appear, panicky-eyed like her screen character and not "acting." Yet on the more open, more frequently visited and reported-on set of *Niagara*, the same young blond actress betrayed no more self-consciousness than a baboon. She would have walked out nude for her shower scene except a wardrobe girl intercepted her with a terry-cloth robe; she would have tossed away the bath towel she wrapped herself in after the shower, except the same wardrobe girl intercepted her with the same terry-cloth robe. It was the actress's decision to strip naked for bed scenes where another actress, even a screen siren like Rita Hayworth or Susan Hayward, would have worn flesh-colored undergarments that would be undetected beneath the white sheet. It was the actress's spontaneous decision to raise her knees beneath the sheet and spread her legs, her manner bawdy and suggestive and anything but "feminine." Here's a woman who promises not to be meek and passive in bed! During filming, the sheet often slipped to reveal a nipple or an entire pearly breast. H had no choice but to stop the scene, mesmerized as he was. "Rose! We'll never get this past the censor." H was the watchful father, his was the moral responsibility. Rose was the wayward sexually wanton daughter.

That damned woman. So beautiful you couldn't take your eyes off her. When Cotten finally strangled her, some of us burst into spontaneous applause.

Part of *Niagara* was filmed in Hollywood on The Studio's lot; part was filmed on location at Niagara Falls, New York. It was on location that the character of "Rose Loomis" became even more forceful and unpredictable. The actress demanded stronger lines for her. She objected to her "clichéd" speeches. She pleaded to be allowed to write dialogue of her own; when refused, she insisted upon miming parts of scenes, not speaking them. Norma Jeane believed that "Rose Loomis" was an underwritten, unconvincing role that was a clumsy steal from Lana Turner's seductress-waitress-murderess in *The Postman Always Rings Twice*. She believed the studio bosses had set her up for humiliation. But she would show them, the bastards.

She insisted that scenes be repeated and repeated. A half-dozen times. A dozen times. "To make it perfect."

Anything less than perfect threw her into a panic.

One day while preparing to film the long teasing tracking scene in which "Rose Loomis" walks—briskly yet seductively—away from the camera, Norma Jeane suddenly turned to H and his assistant and said, not in her character's voice but in a normal, matter-of-fact tone, "It came to me last night. Rose had a baby, I think. And the baby died. I didn't realize it consciously but that's why I play Rose this way. She has to be more than the script says; she's a woman with a secret. I can remember how it happened."

H asked doubtfully, "What? How what happened?"

He was stymied, as he'd been by "Rose Loomis" for weeks. Or by "Marilyn Monroe." Or—whoever she was! Not knowing if he should take this woman seriously or dismiss her as a joke.

She said, as if he hadn't interrupted, "This baby. Rose shut it in a bureau drawer, and it suffocated. Not here, of course. Not in a motel room. Somewhere in the west. Where she was living before she married this husband. She was in bed with a man and didn't hear the baby crying inside the drawer, and when they were finished they never knew the baby was dead." Her eyes were narrowed, peering beyond the garishly lit set as into the shadowy regions of the past. "Later, Rose took the baby out of the drawer and wrapped it in a towel and buried it in a secret place. No one ever knew."

H laughed uneasily. "So how the hell do *you* know?"

A dizzy blonde he'd want to call her. That was the quickest strategy of dismissal. Was he worried she'd undermine his authority as director, the way "Rose Loomis" undermined the authority and the manhood of her husband?

"Hey, I know!" Norma Jeane said, surprised that H might doubt her. "I used to know Rose."

6

A giant woman! And that woman was her.

In Niagara Falls she began to dream as she'd never dreamt in California. These were waking dreams vivid as cinematic flashes. A giant woman, a laughing yellow-haired woman. Not Norma Jeane and not "Marilyn" or "Rose"—"but it's me. I'm inside her."

Instead of a shameful bleeding gash between her legs there was a protuberance like an enlarged swollen pudendum. This organ pulsed with hunger and with desire. Sometimes Norma Jeane merely brushed her hand against it, or dreamt of brushing her hand against it, and in that instant, like a match flaring up, she came to climax and woke moaning in her bed.

7

The Slut. Rose is taunting her husband because he's no good to her, he's not a man. She wants him dead and gone. Because he's not a man, and a woman needs a man. If a man isn't a husband to her, she has a right to get rid of him. In the movie the plan is for Rose's lover to push him into the Niagara River so he'll be swept over the Falls. It's a nasty truth for 1953: a woman might be a man's wife yet not belong to him. Not her body and not her soul. A woman might be a man's wife and not love him, and who she wants to make love with is her own choice. Her life's her own even to throw away.

I loved Rose. Maybe I was the only woman in the audience but I'd guess not, the movie was such a smash, long lines waiting to get in like a kids' Saturday matinee. Rose was so beautiful and sexy, you wanted her to get her way. Maybe all women should get their way. We're sick of being sympathetic and understanding. We're sick of forgiving. We're sick of being good!

8

"Like a message might come at any time. Whether I understood or not."

That was always Norma Jeane's faith as a reader of books.

You opened a book at random and leafed through the pages and began to read. Seeking an omen, a truth to change your life.

She'd packed a suitcase with books, to take with her on location. She'd begged Cass Chaplin and Eddy G to accompany her, and when they declined she extracted from them the promise they'd fly east to visit her, though knowing at the time neither would come, the habit of Hollywood was so deep in them.

"Call us, Norma. Keep in touch. *You* promise."

There were days when the filming of *Niagara* went well, and there were days when the filming of *Niagara* didn't go well, and usually on these days "Rose Loomis" was to blame or was in any case blamed.

She was an obsessive-compulsive. She couldn't do anything once. Terror of failure was her secret.

Those nights, Norma Jeane declined to eat dinner with the others. She'd had enough of them, and they'd had enough of her. She herself had had enough of "Rose Loomis." She took a lengthy bath and sprawled naked across the double bed in her suite in the Starlite Motel. She never watched TV, and she never listened to the radio. She was still reading the disjointed and radiantly mad diary of Nijinski, which inspired her to poetry in imitation of Nijinsky's dreamy incantatory lines.

I want to tell you that I love you you
I want to tell you that I love you you
I want to tell you that I love I love I love.
I love but you do not. You do not love love.
I am life, but you are death.
I am death, but you are not life.

Norma Jeane wrote frantically. What did these lines mean? She could not have said if she was addressing Cass Chaplin and Eddy G, or whether she was addressing Gladys, or her absent father. Now she was thousands of miles from California for the first time in her life, she saw vividly and painfully. *I need you to love me. I can't bear it that you don't love me.*

There were two or three days, when her period came late, when Norma Jeane convinced herself she was pregnant. Pregnant! Her nipples ached, and her breasts felt swollen; her belly seemed rounded to her, the skin glistening white, and the partly shaved, sparse bleached pubic hair stiff as if with static electricity. This had nothing to do with "Rose," who'd let a helpless infant suffocate in a drawer and who would abort any pregnancy that interfered with her desire. You could just imagine Rose climbing onto an examining table and spreading her legs and telling the abortionist to "make it quick, I'm not sentimental."

Making love, those careless boys Cass Chaplin and Eddy G never used condoms. Unless, as they said, they were pretty sure a partner was "sick."

Twined in the young men's supple downy arms, in a stupor of erotic pleasure as an infant sated at the breast, and with no more thought of the future
than an infant, Norma Jeane drifted into sleep and in her dreams lay in her
lovers' arms, in utter bliss. *If it happens, it was meant to be.* With one part
of her mind she wanted to have a baby—it would be both Cass's and Eddy
G's baby—and with another, more lucid, part of her mind she knew this
would be a mistake.

As Gladys had made a mistake, having another daughter.

She rehearsed telephoning Cass and Eddy G. "Guess what? Good news!
Cass, Eddy—you're going to be *fathers*."

Silence! The looks on their faces!—Norma Jeane laughed, seeing the men
as clearly as if they were in the room with her.

Of course, she wasn't pregnant.

As in a malevolent fairy tale where you never get your true wish, but only
false wishes, it isn't so easy to get pregnant if it's pregnancy you want.

So, midway in the scene in which "Rose Loomis" is taken to the morgue
to identify her drowned husband but is shown her drowned lover instead
and faints dead away, Norma Jeane began to bleed. It was a cruel trick!
"Rose Loomis" in a skirt so tight she can barely walk in high heels, a belt
cinching her narrow waist. "Rose Loomis," who wears the scantiest lace
underwear, quickly soaking up blood. Her fainting spell is genuine, almost.
She would have to be helped to a waiting car.

Norma Jeane was to be bedridden for three miserable days. She bled brackish clotted ill-smelling blood, her head raged with a blinding migraine. This
was "Rose's" punishment! The attending studio physician supplied her with
a generous quantity of codeine painkillers—"Just don't drink, promise?"
There was a notorious laxness among the studio-employed physicians of
Hollywood, an indifference to a patient's future beyond the film project at
hand. While Norma Jeane was in bed, filming on *Niagara* had to be done
around her. Word came back to her that, without "Rose," the daily rushes
were flat, dull, disappointing. It struck Norma Jeane for the first time that
she was crucial to this film, and not Joseph Cotten, and certainly not Jean
Peters. For the first time, too, she wondered what these other leading actors
were being paid.

In the Starlite Motel, Norma Jeane was reading Nijinsky, and she was
reading Stanislavski's *My Life in Art*, which Cass Chaplin had given her on
the eve of her departure. A precious hardcover book, with Cass's handwritten annotations. She was reading *The Actor's Handbook and the Actor's
Life* and she was reading in Freud's *Interpretation of Dreams*, which made
her sleepy, it was so dogmatic and dull, a voice droning like a metronome.
Yet wasn't Freud a great genius? Wasn't he like Einstein, Darwin? Otto Öse
had alluded favorably to Freud, and so had I. E. Shinn. Half of upscale

Hollywood was "in therapy." Freud believed that dreams were the "royal road to the unconscious" and Norma Jeane would have liked to travel that road, to seize control of her wayward emotions. *So I could free myself not of love but of the requirement of love. So that I could free myself of wishing to die if I am not loved.* She was reading Tolstoy's *The Death of Ivan Ilyich*, which was not a story "Rose Loomis" would have had the patience or the temperament to read. *So that I could look upon death. Not Rose, but me.*

The story would be told of how H himself had to come fetch Marilyn Monroe, exasperated and anxious when she'd failed to appear on the set after several summonses. Discovering her costumed in her skintight dress and glaring makeup for Rose's climactic strangulation scene at the hands of her avenging husband. She stared at H in the mirror as if for an instant not recognizing him. As if for an instant H himself might have been Death. That loopy stricken smile. And breathy giggle! For she'd been crying over the terrible death of Ivan Ilyich, was that it? Crying over the death of a fictitious nineteenth-century Russian civil servant who hadn't even been a particularly good or worthy man. An inky mascara trail on one rouged cheek and quickly, guiltily, she said, "I'm coming! Rose is ready to d-die."

9

Yet she died in terror. That's a fitting punishment. Except the bitch should've suffered a little more. And we should've seen it close up, camera right in her face. Not looking down from above. That cross-hatching of light making the death beautiful like a painting. Rose fallen and dead. A body sprawled inert. So suddenly Rose isn't Rose but only the female body, dead.

IO

"Why won't you answer? Where are you?"

Alone in the Starlite Motel in Niagara Falls, Norma Jeane so badly missed Cass Chaplin and Eddy G, who were rarely at any of the numbers they'd given her when she called, mystery residences in which the phones rang, rang, and rang or were answered by uncomprehending Hispanic or Filipino maids. So badly missed them that she did finally "make love" to herself as they'd taught her, envisioning Cass and Eddy G, both her lovers simultaneously conjoined in a single accelerated and panicked stroking of fingers that brought her to a climax so explosive, so frightening, she seemed to lose consciousness, waking a few seconds later, still dazed, a trail of saliva on her chin and her heart pounding at a dangerous clip. *If I was Rose I'd love how this feels. But I'm not Rose I guess.* She began to cry with the hopelessness of it, the shame. So badly missed her lovers, she'd come almost to doubt they existed. Or, if existing, that they adored their Norma as they claimed.

Norma Jeane wouldn't have been devastated, she told herself, if Cass and Eddy G were involved together, or singly, with other men. (She guessed that was a way of life for male homosexuals: quick, casual sex. She tried not to think about it.) But yes, yes, Norma Jeane would have been devastated if they took on another girl lover in her absence.

Her strength was, she was the Female. There were two Males, and she was the Female. "A magical and indissoluble triumvirate" in Cass's exalted words. Oh, they did adore her! They loved her. She was certain. They were radiant with pride and possession appearing with her in public. The Studio invention "Marilyn Monroe" was on the verge of Fame, and canny Hollywood-born Cass and Eddy G knew what this could mean even if their girl seemed not to know. ("Oh!—that isn't going to happen, don't be silly. Like Jean Harlow? Joan Crawford? I'm not that important. I know what I am. How hard I work. How scared I am. It's just a trick of the cameras, that I look the way I do sometimes.") Even when Cass and Eddy G laughed at her, she understood that they loved her. For they laughed at her as you'd laugh at a younger, silly sister.

Yet sometimes, well—sometimes their laughter was a little cruel. Norma Jeane tried not to recall those times. When the boys ganged up on her, you could say. Making love to her so it hurt. In *that way* she didn't like, it hurt, and it hurt for a long time afterward so she could hardly sit, and had to sleep lying on her stomach and take painkillers, or one of Cass's magic-potion pills, and why they liked it *that way* she couldn't comprehend.

"It just isn't natural, is it? I mean—it can't be."

Laugh, laugh at little Norma blinking tears from those lustrous baby-blue eyes.

Sometimes it was Norma Jeane's feelings they hurt, referring to her repeatedly as *she* even when she was present. *She, she, she!* Sometimes they referred to her slyly, mysteriously, as *Fish*.

As in "Hey, Fish, lend us a twenty?"

As in "Hey, li'l Fishie, lend me a fifty?"

(Norma Jeane recalled that she'd once or twice overheard Otto Öse on the phone referring to her, or to another of his girl models, as "fish." But when she asked Cass what the term meant, he shrugged and drifted out of the room. She asked Eddy G, who told her bluntly, for in their triumvirate of personalities Eddy G was Cass Chaplin's younger, brasher brother. "Fish? Why, you're 'fish,' Norma. You can't help it." "But why? What does 'fish' mean?" Norma Jeane persisted, smiling. Eddy G smiled, too, saying pleasantly, " 'Fish' only just means female. The sticky scales, the classic stink. A fish is slimy, y' see? A fish is a kind of female no matter if it's actually a male, specially when you see a fish gutted and laid out, get my meaning? It's nothing personal.")

Yet Norma Jeane's strength was Female. As "Marilyn Monroe"—"Rose Loomis"—was Female.

They can't have babies without us. They can't have sons.

The world would end without us! Females.

She was dialing one of the Hollywood numbers another time.

How many times that evening. That night. And what time was it in Los Angeles? Three hours ahead or three hours behind? She never could get it straight.

"It's one A.M. here, that means it's ten P.M. there? Or—eleven?"

Eagerly she was dialing the number of her own new, still barely furnished apartment near Beverly Boulevard. This time, the phone was answered.

"Hello?" The voice was female, and sounded young.

THE GEMINI

The Greeting. There they were, awaiting their beloved at the gate! Continental Airlines, Los Angeles International Airport. In new stylish clothes—blazers, vests, ascots, silk shirts with prominent cuff links—and matching fedoras. A smoldering dark-eyed young man with thick black hair and Chaplinesque woeful-lover gaze and black mustache. Beside him, slightly taller, a compactly built young man with Edward G. Robinson's pugnacious yet somewhat effeminate features, fleshy-pouty lips, and passionate eyes. The one who resembled Chaplin was carrying a half-dozen long-stemmed white roses and the one who resembled Robinson was carrying a half-dozen long-stemmed red roses. When a young blond woman in dark glasses appeared amid a line of passengers disembarking from the plane, in a white sharkskin suit wrinkled from the cross-country flight, her cotton-candy hair nearly hidden by a slope-brimmed straw hat, the dapper young men stared at her blankly.

"What's wrong? Don't you kn-know me?"

Norma Jeane gave to the tense moment a musical-comedy deftness. That was her gift, a knack for desperate improvisation. She laughed gaily and smiled her million-dollar smile. She waved a hand in the young men's faces to wake them.

"*Nor*-ma!"

The other passengers stared as the young men rushed to embrace Norma Jeane. Eddy G hugged her so hard he lifted her grunting in the crook of his right arm, all but crushing her ribs. Then Cass with a dancer's stealthy grace embraced her and kissed her full on the mouth, wet and hungry.

But who were they? Actors? Fashion models? Each looked teasingly familiar, like somebody else.

"Oh, *Cass*."

Norma Jeane wept, burying her face in the white roses.

But Eddy G intervened, stepping back to her and also kissing her wetly on the mouth. "My turn." Norma Jeane was too startled to kiss him back or even to shut her eyes. She was having a hard time catching her breath. So many roses thrust at her. And some had fallen to the ground. The plane landing had frightened her, a bumpy landing in sulfurous swirling smog, and this greeting had frightened her even more. Cass was deeply moved, gazing into her eyes. "Norma, it's just you're so—beautiful. I guess—"

Eddy G flashed his fleet boyish grin. As he made friends howl with laughter doing his Little Caesar imitation, so now he mimicked his famous father without seeming to know what he did, sneering, speaking out of the corner of his mouth. It was Eddy G's style to react quickly to avoid embarrassment. "Yeah! Kind of, it's easy to forget. How beautiful 'Marilyn' is."

The young men laughed. Norma Jeane joined in, uncertainly.

What changes in Cass and Eddy G! Almost, Norma Jeane might not have recognized *them*.

Not just the stylish clothes. (Did they have a new friend, a new generous "benefactor"? One of their "older lovelorn-male types" it was impossible for them to resist?) Cass had let his hair grow thicker and curlier and was sprouting a silky-black mustache so like the Little Tramp's you had to look closely to determine this couldn't be the original. Eddy G was edgy and excited (his current drug of choice was Dexamyl, superior to Benzedrine in all ways and guaranteed *nonaddictive*); his dark eyes shone, though his eyelids were puffy and capillaries had burst in his left eyeball in a delicate lacework of blood.

"*Nor*-ma. Welcome back to L.A."

"God, we missed you. Don't ever leave us again, promise?"

Norma Jeane struggled to carry the thorny roses, as Cass and Eddy G strode beside her, talking and laughing excitedly. Plans for that evening. Plans for tomorrow evening. Advance buzz on *Niagara*—"Walter Winchell predicts it's gonna be a bombshell." Walking three abreast through the crowded terminal, gaudy and self-displaying as peacocks. Norma Jeane was trying not to notice the eyes of strangers fixing avidly and curiously upon them. Strangers pausing to turn and look after them.

Norma Jeane had left keys to her car with Cass and Eddy G, and they'd driven the lime-green Caddy out to the airport. She noticed a long deep scrape on the right rear fender. Serrated dents in the chrome grille. She laughed and said nothing.

Eddy G drove. Norma Jeane sat between her lovers in the crowded front seat. The convertible top was down. Sulfur-tinged air whipped at Norma Jeane's eyes. As Eddy G sped through traffic he took Norma Jeane's hand to press against his swelling groin. Cass took Norma Jeane's other hand to press against his swelling groin.

But they don't know me really. They didn't recognize me.

The Vow. Somehow it happened: the Château Mouton-Rothschild 1931 slipped through his fingers, he who was responsible for acquiring the bottle from a friend of a friend of a friend whose cavernous wine cellar up on Laurel Canyon Drive could accommodate such mysterious losses, and God damn the bottle was two-thirds full. Glass shattered. Slivers flew across the hardwood floor like demonic thoughts. The tarty-sharp stink of the expensive wine would prevail for months. "Oh, God! Forgive me." Whoever it was, forgiven. Dreamy-sticky kisses. Those lovelorn woebegone eyes. You laughed at such eyes, such beauty. Lost in rapture that went on and on. They were young enough, and the Dexamyl helped, to make love forever. Making love was the sweetest high. Other highs were interior, in the brain, but making love was shared, wasn't it? Or usually.

"Oh!—it hurts. I'm sorry. I c-can't help it, I guess!"

There were no blinds on these windows. The windows wide open to the sky. You could determine through shut eyelids if it was a clear southern California day or a not-clear day, if it was dawn or twilight, deep starry night or deep murky night, or "the great noontide" as Cass intoned, quoting Zarathustra, his early adolescent love. ("But who is Zarathustra?" Norma Jeane asked Eddy G. "Is this somebody we should know?" Eddy G said, shrugging, "Sure. I guess so. I mean—eventually you know everybody here. Sometimes the names change but if you've met, you've met.") In *Hollywood Tatler*, in *Hollywood Reporter*, in *L.A. Confidential* and *Hollywood Confidential*, tabloid photos of these glamorous young people. In gossip columns.

YOUNG MEN-ABOUT-TOWN CHARLIE CHAPLIN JR AND EDWARD G. ROBINSON JR AND BLOND SEXPOT MARILYN MONROE: A THREESOME?

Vulgar, said Cass. Exploitative, said Eddy G. "Marilyn" is a serious actress, said Cass. He hated this one of himself looking like a complete asshole, his mouth open like he's panting, said Eddy G. Yet they tore out the most lurid photos and taped them to the walls. The week they made the cover of *Hollywood Confidential*, a photo taken of the three of them playfully dancing together in a bar on the Strip, Cass and Eddy G bought a dozen copies of the magazine to tear off the covers and tape them to Norma Jeane's bedroom door. Norma Jeane laughed at them, they were so vain. In turn, they were merciless in teasing her—"Is this the sexpot? Or this?" Grabbing at her buttocks and at her vagina. Norma Jeane squealed and pushed their hands away. Just the touch of them, their quick hard fingers, the heat in their faces, made her melt. Oh it was a cliché but it was *so*.

It was Norma Jeane who cheered the boys up when they needed cheering, which was a frequent phenomenon after their long antic nights and manic days. After Eddy G's car crash, in a borrowed Jaguar. After Cass's blood-platelet count dropped to an alarming low and he had to be hospitalized for three hellish days. After Eddy G, cast as Horatio in a local production of *Hamlet* and much praised by the L.A. press, woke one afternoon to his mind "struck blank—like somebody'd hosed it down" and could not make that evening's performance or any performance following. After Cass, cast in a M-G-M musical in a chorus-boy role, broke his ankle during the first week of rehearsals—"Don't hand me any Freudian bullshit, this was an *accident*." Norma Jeane nursed them, and Norma Jeane listened to them. Sometimes not hearing what they said. Their aggrieved insulting words. For perhaps it matters less what people say than that they speak to you in earnest and with-out subterfuge, clutching your hand, gazing into your eyes. "Oh, Norma. I guess I do love you." Eddy G, his spoiled-boy face suddenly crinkling like an infant's on the verge of tears. "I'm jealous of you and Cass. I'm jealous of you and anybody who looks at you. If I could love any w-woman, it would be you." And there was dreamy-eyed Cass, Norma Jeane's first true love. *Those eyes. The most beautiful eyes of any man.* She'd first glimpsed them when she was a child, a long-ago lost Norma Jeane struck with wonder by all that she encountered to which she could have given no name in her mother's glamorous and mysterious life. "Norma? When you say you love me, when you look at me, even—who do you see, truly? Do you see *him*?"

"No. Oh, no! I see only you."

How eloquent they were, how brilliantly articulate and funny and inspired, Cass Chaplin and Eddy G talking of their famous/infamous fathers. "Cronus fathers" Cass called them, white-faced with hatred. "Gobbling up their young." ("But who is Cronus?" Norma Jeane asked Eddy G, not want-ing Cass to know how uneducated she was, and Eddy G told her vaguely, "It's some ancient king, I think. Or maybe, wait—it's Greek for Jehovah. Yeah, Greek for God. I'm pretty sure.") In Hollywood there were numerous children of celebrities, and a cruel enchantment hovered over most of them. Cass and Eddy G seemed to know them all. They were the bearers of glamorous names ("Flynn," "Garfield," "Barrymore," "Swanson," "Talmadge") that weighed upon them like physical infirmities. They appeared stunted and immature, though their eyes were old. Already as young children they were versed in irony. Rarely were they surprised by acts of cruelty, including their own, but they could be moved to helpless tears by simple acts of kindness, generosity. "But don't be nice to us," Cass warned. Eddy agreed vehemently. "Yeah! Like feeding a cobra. *I'd* use a ten-foot stick on me, myself." Norma Jeane pointed out, "But at least you two *have* fathers. You know who you *are*." "That's exactly the trouble," Cass said irritably. "We knew who we were before we were born." Eddy G said, "Cass and me, it's a double curse— we're *juniors*. Of men who never wanted us born." Norma Jeane said, "How do you know they never wanted you to be born? You can't trust your mothers to tell you the absolute truth. When love goes wrong and a couple gets divorced—" Both Cass and Eddy G snorted with derision. "Love! Are you serious? Fucking bullshit 'love' little Fishie is telling us."

Norma Jeane said, hurt, "I don't like that name—Fish. I resent that." "*We* resent you telling us what we should be feeling," Cass said heatedly. "You never knew your father, so you're free. You can invent yourself. And you're doing a terrific job of it—'Marilyn Monroe.' " Eddy G said, excited, "Right! You're free." He seized Norma Jeane's hand in his impulsive boyish way and nearly cracked her fingers. "You don't bear the name of the fucker who fucked you into existence. Your name is so totally phony: 'Marilyn Monroe.' I love it. Like you gave birth to yourself." They were addressing her but ignoring her; yet Norma Jeane understood that, without her presence, they wouldn't have been talking so seriously, just drinking or smoking dope. Cass declared loudly, "If I could give birth to myself, I'd be reborn. I'd be redeemed. The children of 'the great' can't ever surprise themselves because everything we might do has already been done, better than we can do it." He spoke not with bitterness but with an air of lofty resignation, like an actor reciting Shakespeare. "Right!" said Eddy G. "Any talent we might have, the old man has it better." He laughed and nudged Cass in the ribs. "Of course, my old man is practically shit next to yours. Two-bit gangster flicks. Anybody can imitate him sneering. But Charlie Chaplin. There was a time, practically, that guy was king out here. And he sure made a bundle." Cass said, "I've asked you not to talk about my father, God damn you. You know shit, about him and about me." "Oh, fuck yourself, Cassie, what's the big deal? I'm the kid my old man screamed at, when I cried and wet my pants; he's yelling at my mother and I rushed him—I was five years old and already nuts—and he kicks me halfway across the room. My mother swore to it in divorce court, and there's hospital X-rays to corroborate her testimony." "*I* had to testify in divorce court. My mother was too sick-drunk." "*Your* mother? What about *my* mother?" "At least your mother isn't crazy." "Are you serious? You don't know shit about my mother."

So they quarreled, hotly, peevishly, like brothers; Norma Jeane tried to reason with them, like June Allyson in one of those talky forties movies where reason might prevail, if you were also pretty and incensed. "Cass, Eddy! I don't understand you. Either of you. Eddy, you're an excellent actor, I've seen you. You're inspired by serious roles, poetic language: Shakespeare, Chekhov. Not movies but the stage. *That's* the true test of acting. Only you give up too soon. You want too much from yourself, and you give up. And you, Cass—you're a wonderful dancer." Norma Jeane was speaking more and more rapidly as the men stared at her in silent contempt. Their faces were as empty of expression as those of tombstone effigies. "You're like music in motion, Cass! Like Fred Astaire. And the dances you've composed are beautiful. Both of you are—"

Norma Jeane was appalled by the hollowness of her words, though she knew them to be legitimate. She wasn't exaggerating! In certain quarters, the sons of Charlie Chaplin and Edward G. Robinson were known to be "gifted"—but "damned." For merely "gifted" is of no use without other qualities of character: courage, ambition, perseverance, faith in yourself. Fatally, both young men lacked these qualities. Eddy G said, sneering, "So I have a knack for acting? What's 'acting,' baby? It's shit. They're all shits. My old man and his old man, the fucking Barrymores, fucking Garbo. It's faces, that's all. Asshole audiences look at these faces and some kind of shit magic occurs. You got the right bone structure, anybody can act." Cass intervened. "Hey, Eddy. *That's* shit." "Like hell it's shit!" Eddy G said fiercely. "Anybody can act. It's a fraud. It's a joke. You get up there, a director coaches you, you say the lines. Anybody can do it." Cass said, "Sure. Anybody can do anything. But not well." Eddy G turned with sudden cruelty to Norma Jeane. "Tell him, baby. You're an 'actress.' It's a crock, right? Without your sweet ass and tits, you'd be nothing and you know it."

Not that night but another. This night. Welcoming Norma Jeane home from Niagara Falls. To what had been her "new" apartment now ravaged and ill-smelling well before the Château Mouton-Rothschild smashed on the living room floor and was too much trouble to mop up. But there was a bottle of French champagne, and this time Cass insisted upon opening the bottle. He filled their glasses to the brim; champagne bubbled over their fingers. A ticklish sensation! Cass and Eddy G gallantly lifted their glasses in homage—"Our Norma back with us. Where she belongs." "Our 'Marilyn,' who's so gorgeous." "And who can *act.*" "Oh, yeah! Like she can *fuck.*" The men laughed, though not meanly. Norma Jeane drank and laughed with them. From their not-so-veiled allusions she understood that, sexually, she wasn't much. Maybe most men preferred other men, or would if they had the option; obviously a man knows what another man wants, and Norma Jeane hadn't a clue. So she laughed and drank. It was wiser to laugh than to cry. Wiser to laugh than to think. Wiser to laugh than not to laugh. Men loved her when she laughed, even Cass and Eddy G, who saw her up close, without makeup. Champagne was her favorite drink. Wine gave her a headache but champagne aerated her brain, lifted her heart. She was so sad sometimes! Though she'd put her guts into "Rose Loomis" and she seemed to know (without vanity, without elation) that *Niagara* would be a hit because of her, and her career would be launched if she wished it, yet she felt so sad sometimes. . . . Well, champagne was her wedding drink. She told Cass and Eddy G about that wedding, and they listened and laughed. They were haters-of-marriage, haters-of-weddings; this was delicious to them. The borrowed twice-soiled wedding garments. The pain she'd endured during her first "intercourse." Her eager young husband heaving, pumping, sweating, groaning, snorting, and gasping. Through their brief marriage, the slippery-medicinal odor of condoms. And ol' Hirohito grinning atop the radio console—"Sometimes the only person I had to talk to all day." And Norma Jeane was all the time having her period, it seemed. Poor Bucky Glazer! He'd deserved a better wife than Norma Jeane. She hoped, now that he was remarried, he'd found a woman who didn't have practically a miscarriage every time she had her period.

Why am I saying these terrible things?
Anything to make men laugh.

Cass led them outside onto the balcony. When had the sun disappeared? It was a vivid damp night, but which night? The city of Los Angeles sprawled below. To the north were hills, more sparsely lit. Part of the sky was cobbled in cloud and part was open, a gigantic crevice into which you might stare and stare. Norma Jeane had read that the universe was billions of years old and all that astrophysicists knew was that its age was forever being readjusted, moved back into "deep time." Yet it had begun in a single nanosecond's explosion out of—what? A particle so small it could not have been seen by the human eye. Yet, looking at the sky, you "saw" beauty in the stars. You "saw" constellations with human and animal figures in them, as if the stars, scattered through time and space, were on a single flat surface, like comics. Cass said, "There's Gemini. See? Both Norma and I are Geminis. The 'fated' twins."

"Oh, where?"

He pointed. Norma Jeane wasn't sure that she saw, or even what she was supposed to be seeing. The sky was an immense jigsaw puzzle and she was missing too many pieces. Eddy G said impatiently, "I don't see it. Where?"

"*They*. The twins are *they*."

"What twins? This is so weird."

Months ago, Eddy G had told Norma Jeane and Cass that he, too, was a Gemini, born in June. He'd been eager to be identical with them. Now he seemed to have forgotten. Cass tried to point out the elusive constellation another time, and this time Norma Jeane and Eddy G saw, or believed they saw. Eddy said, "Stars! They're overrated. They're so far away, it's hard to take them seriously. And their light is extinct by the time it reaches Earth."

"Not their light," Cass corrected. "The stars themselves."

"Stars are light. That's all they are."

"No. Stars have substance, originally. 'Light' can't be generated out of nothing."

There was friction between the men. Eddy G wasn't one to be corrected. Norma Jeane said, "And that's true for human 'stars' too. They must be something, not just nothing. There must be substance to them."

Poor blundering Norma Jeane! Here was an allusion, however indirect and well intentioned, to her lovers' monster fathers. Cass said with savage satisfaction, "The fact of a star is, it burns out. Celestial stars or human."

Eddy G giggled. "I'll drink to that, baby."

Eddy G had brought the champagne bottle outside with them, resting it precariously on the narrow railing. He refilled their glasses. In the fresher air he seemed to have revived, which was typical of Eddy G in those days. "What the fuck is 'Gemini,' Cass? You said twins?"

"Yes and no. The principle of the Gemini is that they aren't two, essentially. They're identical twins with a strange relationship to death." He paused. Like any actor, he knew when to pause.

Of the two men, Cass Chaplin was by far the better educated: he'd been sent by his distraught mother to a Jesuit boarding school, where he'd studied medieval theology, Latin, and Greek. He'd dropped out before graduation, or had possibly been expelled, or he'd had one of his several breakdowns. At the time of their first love affair, when Norma Jeane had loved him so passionately, she'd examined all his possessions she could get her hands on, without his knowing; she'd discovered in one of his shabby duffel bags a voluminous looseleaf journal titled GEMINI: MY LIFE IN (P)ART. It was filled with musical compositions, poetry, strikingly realistic drawings of human faces and figures. There were erotic studies of nudes, both female and male, making love to themselves, faces contorted with anguish or shame. *But this is myself!* Norma Jeane had thought. Since Charlie Chaplin, Sr., had been publicly interrogated by the House Un-American Activities Committee a few years before and pilloried in the daily press as a "Commie traitor," and had fled into exile in Switzerland, it seemed to Norma Jeane that Cass had become more scattered in his energies; he was overly excitable and then depressed for days; he was as insomniac as she and required Nembutal to sleep; he was drinking more. (At least, unlike Eddy G, he wasn't smoking the latest Hollywood rage, hashish.) It was months since he'd auditioned for any role. He wrote music and tore it up. Norma Jeane wasn't supposed to know, but several mean-spirited acquaintances including her agent had taken pains to inform her that Cass Chaplin had been arrested and held overnight by Westwood police for public drunkenness and disturbing the peace. Making love with her, he was sometimes impotent; at these times, as Cass said, Eddy G would have to serve for them both.

Which Eddy G, inexhaustible or seeming so, his cock a perpetual source of wonderment to his friends, was happy to do.

Cass was saying, "The Gemini were twin brothers named Castor and Pollux. They were warriors and one of them, Castor, was killed. Pollux missed his brother so badly, he begged Jupiter, the king of the gods, to be permitted to give his own life as a ransom for his brother. Jupiter was moved to pity—sometimes, if you efface yourself enough and get them in the right mood, the old-bastard gods come through—and allowed Castor and Pollux both to live, but not at the same time. Castor lived one day in the heavens, while Pollux was in Hades, or hell; then Pollux lived one day in the heavens, while Castor was in hell. They alternated life and death but they didn't see each other."

Eddy G snorted in derision. "Jesus, what crap! It's not only loony, it's banal as hell. *It happens all the time.*"

Cass continued, speaking to Norma Jeane. "Then Jupiter took pity on them again. He rewarded their love for each other by placing them up there in the stars together. See? The Gemini. Forever."

Norma Jeane hadn't yet seen the star pattern, really. But she raised her eyes upward, smiling. It was enough to know that the Gemini were there, wasn't it? Did she have to *see?* "So the Gemini are twins in the sky, and they're immortal! I always wondered—"

Eddy G cut in. "And what's it got to do with death? Or with *us?* I sure feel goddam human and mortal. I don't feel like any fucking star in the sky."

The champagne bottle fell to the balcony floor and broke. It didn't shatter as badly as the wine bottle and there wasn't much liquid left. "*Je*-sus! Not again." But Cass was laughing, and Eddy G was laughing. In the wink of an eye they were Abbott and Costello. Eddy G scooped up some of the broken pieces of glass and brayed, his expression drunken-beatific, "Blood vow! Let's make a blood vow! We're the Gemini, the three of us. Like twins but there's *three.*"

Cass said excitedly, his words slurred, "That's a—what-d'you-call-it—triangle. A triangle can't be divided in two, like two can be."

Eddy G said, "Never forget one another, OK? The three of us? Always love one another like right now."

Cass said, panting, "And die for each other, if needed!"

Before Norma Jeane could stop him, Eddy G raked a piece of glass across the inside of his forearm. Blood immediately sprang out. Cass took the glass from him and raked it across the inside of his forearm; even more blood sprang out. Norma Jeane, deeply moved, unhesitatingly took the glass from Cass and with shaky fingers drew it across her forearm. The pain was swift and sharp and potent.

"Always love one another!"

" 'The Gemini'—always!"

" 'In sickness and in health—' "

" 'For richer or poorer—' "

" 'Till death do we part.' "

They pressed their bleeding arms together like drunken children. They were breathless, laughing. The sweetest act of love Norma Jeane had ever known! Deep in his throat, mock-gangster-style, Eddy G growled, "Till death? Hell, beyond death! *Beyond death do we part.*" They stumbled together, kissing. Their hands pulled at one another's already disheveled and stained clothing. They were on their knees and would have made clumsy love there on the balcony except a glass shard pierced Cass's thigh—"*Je*-sus!" They stumbled back inside the apartment, arms around one another, and fell together, as yearning and crazed for affection as puppies, onto Norma Jeane's long-unmade bed, where in a delirium of passion they would make love intermittently through the night.

That night I believed Baby must be conceived. But it was not so.

The Survivor. The premiere of *Niagara*! For some, a historic night. Even before the lights went down, everybody knew. Cass and I couldn't sit with Norma; she was with The Studio bosses up front. They hated her guts, and she hated theirs. But that's how things were in Hollywood in those days. They'd got her under contract for $1,000 a week. She'd signed when she was desperate and would be fighting them for years. In the end, the bosses won. The night of *Niagara*, this cruel bastard Z is seated beside Norma but getting up to meet people, shake hands, he's blinking like he doesn't get it, he wants to get it but he can't. A man convinced he's got a sow's ear, and people are acting like he's got a silk purse instead! Can't figure it out. All through the career of "Marilyn Monroe," which would make millions for The Studio and hardly a fraction of that for her, these guys can't figure it out. That night, there was "Marilyn" in a red-sequin dress with bare shoulders, mostly bare breasts, a costume they'd sewn her into, entering the theater and walking down the aisle in these mincing baby steps; she's being gaped and gawked at like a freak. Five hours was the minimum the makeup people spent on her for these occasions. Like preparing a cadaver, Norma said. And I can see she's looking around for Cass and me (up in the balcony) and can't find us. And she's this lost little girl in a whore costume. And anyway gorgeous. I poked Cass and said, "That's our Norma." It was like we could've bawled.

The lights go down, and *Niagara* begins, with a scene at the Falls. And a man looking small and powerless beside all that rushing, roaring water. Then switch to Norma—I mean "Rose." In bed. Where else? Naked under just a sheet. She's awake, but pretending she's asleep. Through the movie this "Rose Loomis" does one thing and pretends another and the audience is in on it but not her dumb-fuck husband. The guy is some kind of war-combat psycho, a pathetic case, but the audience doesn't give a shit about him. Everybody's always waiting for "Rose" to come back on-screen. She's just luscious and over-the-top evil. She's way beyond Lana Turner. You'd swear, remembering *Niagara*, there was at least one complete nude scene. In 1953? You just can't take your eyes off her. Cass and me, we'd see *Niagara* a dozen times. . . . It's because Rose is *us*. In our souls. She's cruel in ways we are. She's without any morality, like an infant. She's always looking at herself in the mirror just like we'd look if we looked like her. She's stroking herself, she's in love with herself. Like all of us! But it's supposed to be *bad*. In those bed scenes, you'd wonder how they got past the censor. She's got her knees spread, and you swear you can see her blond cunt through the sheet. You're just mesmerized, staring. And her face, that's a special kind of cunt. The wet red mouth, the tongue. When Rose dies, the movie dies. But her dying is so beautiful, I almost came in my pants. And this is a girl, this is Norma, who truly can't fuck worth shit, you had to do ninety-five percent of the work, and she's going 'Oh-oh-*oh!*' like it's acting class and this is some line she's memorized. But in the movies, "Marilyn" *knew*. It was like only the camera knew how to make love to her the way she needed, and we were voyeurs just hypnotized watching.

About midway in the movie, when Rose is mocking and laughing at her husband for not being able to get it up, Cassie says to me, "This isn't Norma. This is not our little Fishie." And the hell of it was, it wasn't. This Rose was a total stranger. This was nobody we'd laid eyes on before. Out here, people thought "Marilyn Monroe" was just playing herself. Every movie she made, no matter that it was different from the others, they'd find a way to dismiss it—"That broad can't act. She's just playing herself." But she was a born actress. She was a genius, if you believe in genius. Because Norma didn't have a clue who she was, and she had to fill this emptiness in her. Each time she went out, she had to invent her soul. Other people, we're just as empty; maybe in fact everybody's soul is empty, but Norma was the one to know it.

That was Norma Jeane Baker when we knew her. When we were "the Gemini." Before she betrayed us—or maybe we betrayed her. A long time ago, when we were young.

Happiness! Not the morning after *Niagara* opened but a few mornings later. And Norma Jeane, who'd been sleeping badly for months, woke after a night of deep restful sleep. A night without Cass's magic tablets. She'd had astonishing dreams. Skyrocket dreams! Rose was dead but Norma Jeane in these dreams was alive. "The promise was, I would always be alive." And she was a healthy alive woman, tall and strong and as quick-moving in her body as an athlete. Not a bleeding-draining cut of humiliation between her legs but the curious poking-out sexual organ. "What is this? What am I? I'm so *happy.*" In the dream she had permission to laugh. To run along the beach barefoot and laughing. (Was this Venice Beach? But not Venice Beach now. Venice Beach of long ago.) Grandma Della was there, wind whipping her hair. What a loud belly laugh Grandma Della had, Norma Jeane had almost forgotten. The thing between Norma Jeane's legs, maybe Grandma Della had one too? It wasn't a man's cock, nor was it a woman's vagina exactly. It was just—"What I *am*. Norma Jeane."

She woke laughing. It was early: 6:20 A.M. It had been a night she'd slept alone. Solitary in her bed and she'd missed the men until falling asleep, where she hadn't missed them at all. Cass and Eddy G hadn't come home from— where? A house party out in Malibu, or maybe Pacific Palisades. Norma Jeane hadn't been invited. Or maybe she'd been invited and said no. No no no! She wanted to sleep, and she wanted to sleep without magic tablets, and she'd slept, now waking early and a strange passionate strength suffusing her body. So happy! She splashed her face with cold water and did acting-class warm-up exercises. Then dancer's warm-up exercises. How like a foal her body felt, yearning to run! She put on pedal pushers, leg warmers, a baggy sweatshirt. Tied her hair into two stiff, short braids. (Hadn't Aunt Elsie braided her hair for one of Norma Jeane's races at Van Nuys? To keep her long curly-kinky hair from getting in her face.) And out she went to run.

The narrow palm-lined streets were almost deserted, though on Beverly Boulevard traffic was beginning. Since the opening of *Niagara* her agent telephoned her constantly. The Studio telephoned her constantly. Interviews, photo sessions, more publicity. There were movie posters of "Rose Loomis"

everywhere in America. There were the current co
Inside Hollywood. Reviews were read excitedly to
the name "Marilyn Monroe," so repeated, came to
of a preposterous stranger, a name to which oth
accrued, and these words, too, the invention of stra

A bombshell of a performance. A raw disturb
frankly sexy no-holds-barred female like no other since Jean Harlow. The
elemental power of nature. A serpentine performance. You hate Marilyn
Monroe—but you admire her. Dazzling, brilliant! Sexy, seductive! Move
over, Lana Turner! Shocking near-nudity. Compelling. Repulsive. More las-
civious than Hedy Lamarr. Theda Bara. If Niagara Falls is one of the seven
wonders of the world, Marilyn Monroe is the eighth.

Listening to this, Norma Jeane became restless. Paced about holding the
receiver loosely against her ear. She laughed nervously. She lifted a ten-pound
dumbbell with her free hand. Stared into a mirror, out of which stared back
at her, timid and uncomprehending, the girl in the long beautiful beveled
mirror at Mayer's Pharmacy. Or suddenly she bent, swayed, touched her toes
rapidly ten times in a row. Twenty times. These words of praise! And the
name "Marilyn Monroe" like a litany. Norma Jeane was uneasy, knowing
these words recited in triumph by her agent and by studio people might be
any words.

These words of strangers possessing the power to determine her life. How
like the wind they were, ceaselessly blowing. The Santa Ana wind. Yet there
must come a time when even the wind would stop blowing, and these words
would vanish, and—then? Norma Jeane told her agent, "But there isn't anyone there. 'Marilyn Monroe.' Don't they know? It was 'Rose Loomis' and
she was just—on the screen. And she's d-dead. And it's over." It was her
agent's habit to laugh at Norma Jeane's naïveté as if she meant to be witty.
He said reprovingly, "Marilyn. My dear. It is *not over.*"

For forty rapturous minutes she ran. When, panting, her face gleaming
with sweat, she turned into the front walk of her apartment building, there
were two young men making their way unsteadily to the front entrance.
"Cass! Eddy G!" They were disheveled and unshaven and pasty-skinned.
Cass's expensive dove-gray silk shirt was unbuttoned to the waist and stained
with a urine-colored liquid. Eddy G's hair lifted in snaky-manic tufts. There
was a fresh scratch beside his ear, curved like a red hook in the flesh. The
men stared appalled at Norma Jeane in her UCLA sweatshirt, pedal pushers
and sneakers, and braided hair, the healthy sweat sheen on her face. Eddy G
whimpered, "Norma! Are you *up?* This hour?" Cass winced as if his head
was pounding. Reproachfully he said, "Jesus! *You're* happy." Norma Jeane
laughed, she loved them so. She hugged them, and kissed their scratchy

nd ignored their reeking smells. She said, "Oh, I am! I *am* happy!
art could burst almost, I'm so happy. Know why? Because now there's
se, people can see it isn't *me*. People in Hollywood. They can say, 'She
created Rose, look how different she is. *She's* an actress!' "

Pregnant! Under the name "Gladys Pirig" she'd been seeing a gynecologist-
obstetrician in a part of Los Angeles as remote from Hollywood as if it were
in another city. When he told her, yes, she was pregnant, she began to cry.
"Oh, I knew. I guess I knew. I've been feeling so swollen. And so *happy*."
The doctor, mishearing, seeing only this young blond woman's tears, reached
for her hand, which was ringless. "My dear. You're healthy. It will be all
right." Norma Jeane drew away, offended. "I'm happy, I said! I *want* to have
this baby. My husband and I have been t-trying for years."

Immediately she called Cass Chaplin and Eddy G. She would spend most
of the afternoon trying to track these two down. She was so excited she
forgot a luncheon appointment with a producer, and she forgot an interview scheduled with a New York journalist and appointments at The Studio. She would postpone her next film, which was to be a musical. She
could make money being photographed for magazines for a while. How
many months before she showed? Three? Four? There was *Sir!* pleading
for a cover photo, and now their fee was a cool $1,000. There was *Swank*,
and there was *Esquire*. There was a new magazine, *Playboy*; the editor
wanted "Marilyn Monroe" for the first cover. After that, she would let her
hair grow out to its natural color. "If they keep bleaching it like this, it
will be ruined." The wild thought came to her: she would call Mrs. Glazer!
Oh, she missed Bucky's mother! It was Mrs. Glazer she'd adored, not
Bucky. And Elsie Pirig. "Aunt Elsie, guess what? I'm pregnant." Though
that woman had betrayed her, still Norma Jeane missed her and forgave
her. "Once you have a baby you're a woman forever. That makes you one
of them, they can't deny you." Thoughts were flying swift as bats in her
head. She couldn't sort them out. Almost, she might have believed they
weren't her thoughts. And wasn't there someone she was forgetting? Someone she should telephone?

"But who? I can almost see her face."

The Celebration. That night she met Cass and Eddy G at their neighborhood
Italian restaurant on Beverly Boulevard. A place where "Marilyn" was rarely
recognized. And in her ragtag clothes, hair hidden beneath a scarf, no
makeup, and practically no eyebrows, Norma Jeane was safe. Eddy G said,
sliding into the booth beside her, kissing her cheek with widened eyes, "Hey,
Norma, what's it? You look—" And Cass said, sliding into the booth across
from her, grinning and in dread, "—fraught." Norma Jeane had been plan-

ning to whisper into their ears, each in turn, *Guess what! Good news! You're going to be a father.* Instead, she burst into tears. She took their limp stunned hands in hers and kissed the hands in turn, wordless, and the men were frightened of her, exchanging a glance between themselves. Cass would say afterward, sure he'd known, he'd known Norma must be pregnant, she hadn't had a period recently, and her periods were so painful, such a massive physical assault upon the poor girl, and a trial to any lover; of course he'd known, or must have known. Eddy G would profess absolute shock. And yet—surprise? How could he be surprised? With all their lovemaking, and his inexhaustible flaring-up cock in particular? For sure, *he* was the father. It wasn't a distinction he maybe wished for, not one hundred percent, though there was a thrill of pride in it, he couldn't deny. A baby of Edward G. Robinson, Jr.'s, with one of the most beautiful women in Hollywood! Both men knew how Norma yearned for a baby; this was one of Norma's endearing traits for as long as they'd known her, how naive, how sweet, what faith she had in the redeeming power of "being a mother," though her own mother was a certified nut who'd abandoned her and (the rumor circulated through Hollywood) had once tried to kill her. Both men knew how Norma yearned to be what she believed to be *normal.* And if a baby didn't make you normal, what would?

So that evening when Norma began to cry and kissed their hands, wetting their hands with her tears, Cass said quickly, with as much sympathy as he could manage, "Oh, Norma. You think you *are?*" And Eddy G said, voice cracking like a teenager's, "This is what I think it is? Ohhhh, man." Both were grinning. Panic clutched at their hearts. They were not yet thirty, and still boys. So long had they been out-of-work actors, even simulating emotions came clumsily to them. In their exchanged glance was the knowledge that, with this kooky girl, there would be no abortion, no easy way out. Not just that Norma wanted a baby, she'd many times spoken with horror of abortion. In her sweet dumb heart she was a Christian Scientist. She believed much of that crap, or wanted to believe. So there would be no abortion; it was pointless to bring up the subject. If her Gemini lovers had been planning that "Marilyn Monroe" would be making serious money soon, this was an upset in their plans. In their fantasy travels, a definite roadblock. But, if they played their cards right, only just temporary.

Norma Jeane fixed her beautiful anxious glistening eyes on theirs.

"Are you h-happy for me? I mean—us? The Gemini?"

What could they say but *yes.*

The Stuffed Tiger. An episode you'd think must be a dream. Yet it was real. It was real, and shared by the Gemini. Though drunk on red wine (she'd had only two or three glasses while the men finished off two bottles), Norma

Jeane wouldn't recall it clearly afterward. She, Cass, and Eddy G had been celebrating the news, giddy and excited and tearful, and around midnight they'd left the restaurant, and up the street and around a corner they passed a darkened toy shop, a small shop they must have passed many times before without noticing, unless Norma Jeane had paused to gaze wistfully into the front window now and then at the exquisite handmade stuffed animals, a big family of dolls, carved alphabet blocks, toy trains, trucks, automobiles, but neither Cass nor Eddy G had ever seen the toy shop before, they'd have sworn, and what a coincidence, Cass declared, that night of all nights—"It's the *movies*. The kind of thing that happens only in the *movies*." Drinking didn't dull Cass's senses but made him sharper, more lucid; of that, he was convinced. Eddy G said, growling out of the corner of his mouth, "The *movies!* Everything we live, the fuckers have got to it first!" Norma Jeane, who rarely drank and vowed not to drink again during her pregnancy, swayed, leaning against the window. Her breath steamed the glass into an exclamatory O. Was it possible she was actually seeing what she saw? "Oh!—that little tiger. I had one like him once. A long time ago when I was a girl." (Was this so? The little stuffed tiger toy, Norma Jeane's lost Christmas present at the orphanage? Or was this tiger larger, fuzzier, more expensive? And there was the tiger Norma Jeane had sewn for little Irina out of dime-store materials.) With the swift brutal agility for which Edward G. Robinson's son was known in the Hollywood demimonde, Eddy G swung his fist against the window and smashed it, and after the broken glass rained down, and Norma Jeane and Cass stood staring in astonishment, calmly he reached inside for the toy.

"Baby's first plaything. Cute!"

The Guilty Reparation. Late next morning, stricken with guilt and feeling headachy and hung over and slightly nauseated, Norma Jeane returned to the toy shop. "Maybe it was a dream? It didn't seem real." In her shoulder bag was the little stuffed tiger. She hadn't been wanting to think that the store window had truly been broken as a consequence of her impulsive remark. But there was no mistaking the fact that Eddy G had handed her the toy, and she'd slept with it under her pillow that night, and it was in her shoulder bag right now. "But what can I do? I can't just give it back."

There was the toy shop! HENRI'S TOYS. In smaller letters, *Handmade Toys My Specialty*. It was almost a miniature store, the facade measuring no more than twelve feet across. And how wounded it looked, a section of its display window broken and awkwardly replaced with plywood. Norma Jeane peered through the glass and saw with dread that, yes, the store was open. Henri was inside, at the counter. Shyly she pushed the door open and a bell tinkled overhead. Henri glanced up at her with mournful eyes. The shop was dimly lighted like the interior room of a castle. The air smelled of a long-ago time. Nearby on Beverly Boulevard there was a heavy midday traffic but in HENRI'S TOYS there was a restful, soothing calm.

"Yes, miss? Can I help you?" It was a tenor voice, melancholy yet unaccusing. *He won't blame me. He isn't one to judge.*

Norma Jeane said, with childlike emotion, stammering, "I—I—I'm so sorry, Mr. Henri! It looks like somebody broke your window? Was it a robbery? Was it just last night? I live right around here and I—hadn't seen the window broken before."

Mournful-eyed Henri, a man of no age Norma Jeane might have guessed, except he wasn't young, smiled a bitter little smile. "Yes, miss. It was last night. I have no burglar alarm. Always I've thought, who would steal *toys*?"

Norma Jeane clutched her shoulder bag, trembling. She said, "I h-hope they didn't take much?"

Henri said with muted anger, "I'm afraid, yes, they did."

"I'm so sorry."

"As many toys as they could carry, and the most expensive. A hand-carved train, a life-size doll. A hand-painted doll with human hair."

"Oh!—I'm *so sorry*."

"And smaller items, stuffed animals my sister sews. My sister who is blind." Henri spoke with quiet vehemence, stealing a glance at Norma Jeane as one might steal a glance at the audience behind a row of lights.

"Oh? Blind? You have a—blind sister?"

"Yes, and she's a gifted seamstress, sewing animals purely by touch."

"And these were stolen, too?"

"Five of them. Plus the other items. And the window smashed. I've explained it all to the police. Not that they will ever apprehend the thieves, I don't expect it. The cowards!"

Norma Jeane wasn't sure if Henri meant the thieves or the police. She said hesitantly, "But you have insurance?"

Henri said indignantly, "Well. I should hope, miss, that I do have insurance. I'm not a complete fool."

"That's g-good, then."

"Yes. It's good. But it doesn't alleviate the shock to my nerves, and my sister's, and it doesn't restore my faith in human nature."

Norma Jeane removed the little striped tiger from her shoulder bag. Trying not to notice how Henri stared at her, she said quickly, "This—I found it in an alley behind my building. I live just around the corner. I guess it's yours?"

"Why, yes—"

Henri was staring at her, blinking. His parchment-pale face darkened just perceptibly with blood.

"I f-found it. On the ground. I thought it m-must belong to you. But I'd like to buy it? I mean—if it isn't too expensive?"

Henri stared at Norma Jeane for a long wordless moment. She could not fathom what he was thinking any more than, she guessed, he could fathom what she must be thinking.

"The striped tiger?" he said. "It's one of my sister's specialties."

"It's soiled, a little. That's why I'd like to buy it. I mean"—Norma Jeane laughed nervously—"you probably couldn't sell it now. And it's so beautiful."

She was holding out the little striped tiger in both her hands, for Henri to see. Norma Jeane was standing in front of the counter, only a foot or so from him, but he made no motion to take it from her. He worked his mouth, considering. He was shorter than Norma Jeane by several inches, a carved-looking little man with large black-button eyes, jutting ears and elbows. "Miss, you're a good person. You have a good heart. I'll let you have the tiger for—" Henri paused, smiling, a more genuine smile now, seeing Norma Jeane perhaps as younger than she was, in her early twenties, a student actor or dancer, a pretty but unexceptional girl with a round boneless innocent face, her skin pasty without makeup. In flat-heeled shoes she looked both busty and boyish. So lacking in self-confidence and presence, she would never succeed in show business. "—ten dollars. Marked down from fifteen."

The little price tag on the tiger, which Henri seemed to have forgotten, indicated, in pencil, $8.98.

Quickly, relieved, Norma Jeane smiled and took out her wallet. "No, Mr. Henri! Thank you. But the toy is for my first baby, and I want to pay the full price."

THE VISION

Always, Norma Jeane would remember.

They'd gone for one of their nighttime drives. A romantic southern-California late-summer nighttime drive. In the lime-green Caddy with its broad grinning chrome grille and fluted fins. Like the prow of a boat the chrome grille and front fenders crested the waves of a shadowy light-splotched sea. Cass Chaplin, Eddy G, and their Norma. So much in love! Pregnancy made Norma even more beautiful; her lovely skin glowed, her eyes were bright, clear, lucid, and intelligent. Pregnancy made the beautiful young men more beautiful too. More mysterious, secretive. For no one would know of their secret until they wished to disclose it. Until Norma wished to disclose it. All three were inclined to be dreamy and dazed, contemplating the impending birth. Laughing aloud, catching one another's eyes. Was it real? Yes, it was real. It was real real *real*. "Not the movies," Cass cautioned them, "but real life." Eddy G had joined AA, and Cass was considering. It was a grave step, to surrender drinking! But if he still had his drugs? Or would that be cheating? Eddy G wisely reckoned that, if there was ever any right time for him to go on the wagon, as his old man had done, not once but many times, well, it was now. With dull amazement he said, "I'm not getting any younger. Or any healthier."

Norma Jeane's doctor had calculated she was five weeks pregnant; the baby would be born in mid-April. He told her she was in excellent health. Her only ailment was her heavy menstrual flow and its attendant pain, but she would not be menstruating now. What a blessing! "Just that is worth it. No wonder I'm so happy." She was sleeping reasonably soundly and without barbiturates. She was exercising. She was eating a half-dozen small meals a day, a preponderance of grains and fruits, hungrily, with only occasional nausea. She could not eat red meat and she abhorred fat. "Little Momma" they called her teasingly, no more "Little Fishie" (at least to Norma's face). Truly they were in awe of her! They did adore her. The female point of the indissoluble triangle. She'd been fearful, yes certainly it had passed through her head that both her young lovers might abandon her, yet they had not, and seemingly would not. For never had the men been truly in love with any of the numerous girls and young women they'd impregnated, or were led to believe they'd impregnated; never had any girl or young woman of their intimate acquaintance declined the possibility of an abortion. Norma was different; Norma was like no other.

Maybe we were afraid of her, too. We were starting to understand we didn't know her.

Cass was driving, swinging the Caddy along near-deserted streets by moonlight. Norma Jeane, cuddling between her handsome young lovers, had never felt so content. Never so happy. She'd taken Cass's hand, and Eddy G's hand, and was pressing their moist palms, with her own, against her belly where Baby was growing. "One day soon, we'll feel his heartbeat. Just wait!" They'd been cruising north on La Cienega. Past Olympic Boulevard, past Wilshire. At Beverly, Norma Jeane supposed Cass would turn east to bring them home. But instead he continued north, to Sunset Boulevard. The car radio was playing romantic music of the forties. "I Can Dream, Can't I?" "I'll Be Loving You Always." A five-minute news break, the top story, about another girl found sexually abused, murdered, a naked body, "an aspiring actress-model" from Venice missing for several days and at last found wrapped in a tarpaulin on the beach beyond the Santa Monica pier. Norma Jeane listened, transfixed. Eddy G deftly changed the station. This was not new news: the story had broken the previous day. The girl was no one Norma Jeane knew. No name she'd ever heard before. Eddy G found another pop station where Perry Como was singing "The Object of My Affection." He whistled along with it, huddling against Norma Jeane's body, which seemed to him so restful now, so consoling and *warm*.

Strange: Norma Jeane had never told Cass and Eddy G about HENRI'S TOYS. Though the Gemini had vowed to share all things and to have no secrets from one another.

"Cass, where are you taking us? I want to go home. Baby's so *sleepy*."

"This is a vision for Baby to see. Just wait."

There seemed to be some understanding between him and Eddy G. Norma Jeane was starting to feel uneasy. And so sleepy. Like Baby was sucking her down into him, into his quiet lightless space that predated all time. *Before the universe began. I was. And you with me.*

They were at Sunset and turning east. This part of the city Norma Jeane dreaded from years ago, her trolley rides to The Studio for classes and for auditions and on the morning she was informed her contract had been terminated. Always on Sunset Boulevard there was traffic. A steady stream of cars like vessels borne upon the River Styx. (How did you pronounce "Styx"? Just—"sticks"? Norma Jeane would ask Cass, sometime.) And now began the succession of brightly illuminated billboards passing overhead. Movies! Movie-star faces! And there, most spectacular of all, the towering billboard for *Niagara*, across whose width of perhaps thirty feet stretched the platinum-blond female lead, her voluptuous body, beautiful taunting face, and suggestive red-glistening parted lips so riveting it had become an L.A. joke how traffic slowed and some vehicles came to a stop altogether.

Norma Jeane had seen *Niagara* posters, of course. Yet she'd avoided seeing this infamous billboard.

Eddy G said, in a thrilled voice, "Norma! You can look or not, but—"

Cass cut in: "—there she is. 'Marilyn.' "

"Marilyn"

1949–1953

"FAMOUS"

You must construct a circle mentally, a circle of light
and attention. You must not allow your concentration
to go beyond it. If your control begins to lessen you
must withdraw quickly to a smaller circle.

—Stanislavski,
An Actor Prepares

This new year of wonders 1953. Never could Norma Jeane have believed. The year "Marilyn Monroe" became a *star* and the year Norma Jeane became *pregnant*.

"I'm so happy! All my dreams have come true."

Breaking upon her like the harsh stinging surf on the beach at Santa Monica when she'd been a child. She remembered vividly as if it had been yesterday. But now soon she would be a mother herself, and her soul healed. Now soon she would silence that metronome voice.

Wherever you are, I'm there. Even before you get to the place where you are going. I'm already there, waiting.

"I can't take the role. I'm sorry. . . . Yes, I know it's 'once-in-a-lifetime.' But so is everything."

The role of Lorelei Lee in Anita Loos's musical comedy *Gentlemen Prefer Blondes*. A long-running Broadway musical The Studio had purchased for Marilyn Monroe, who since *Niagara* was now their highest-grossing actress. "And you're turning it down?" her agent asked incredulously. "Marilyn. I don't believe you."

Marilyn. I don't believe you. Norma Jeane shaped the prissy words in silence. Too bad she was alone, neither Cass nor Eddy G to laugh with her. She didn't reply. Her agent was speaking rapidly. Here was a man who knew her only as Marilyn. And he feared and disliked her. He didn't love her as I. E. Shinn had loved her. "Rin Tin Tin" she called him behind his back, for he was an eager bristling barking kind of man, an old-young man, fiercely ambitious and clever without being intelligent; Rin Tin Tin was slavish to people in power and bossy and imperial with others, the young women in his office, clerks and waiters and taxi drivers. How had it happened that the formidable I. E. Shinn was gone, and in his place—Rin Tin Tin? *How can I trust you? You don't love me.*

Now Marilyn Monroe had become what was called "famous," Norma Jeane could trust no one who hadn't known her previously and who hadn't loved her then. Cass Chaplin had warned her they'd be swarming over her like lice. Cass had said, "My father's favorite saying is, 'When you've got millions of dollars, you've got millions of friends.' " Norma Jeane would never have millions of dollars but "fame" was perceived as a kind of fortune, to be spent at whim. "Fame" was wildfire no one could control, even the studio bosses who were taking credit for it. Bouquets of flowers from these men! Invitations to lunch, dinner. Parties at their lavish Beverly Hills homes. *Yet still they think I'm a tramp.*

At the party following the *Niagara* premiere, Norma Jeane, who certainly wasn't Rose but who'd had several glasses of champagne, had said in Rose's mocking undertone to the bat-faced Z, Do you remember that day in September 1947? I was just a girl. I was so scared! I hadn't yet been given my Studio name. You invited me to your office apartment to see your collection of stuffed dead birds—your "aviary." Do you remember hurting me, Mr. Z? Do you remember making me bleed, Mr. Z? On my hands and knees, Mr. Z? Do you remember screaming at me, Mr. Z? Years ago. And then you dropped my contract, Mr. Z? Do you remember?

Z stared at Norma Jeane and shook his puzzled head, no. He licked his lips; his dentures shone uneasily. Though his face was a bat's face, the oddly granular texture of his skin, especially his chafed-looking scalp, was a lizard's. Now shaking his head no, no. The cruel yellow-tinged eyes opaque.

You don't? You don't remember?

I'm afraid I do not, Miss Monroe.

The blood on your white fur rug, you don't remember?

I'm afraid I do not, Miss Monroe. I have no white fur rug.

Did you kill Debra Mae, too? Did you cut up her body, afterward?

But Z had already turned away. Another powerful lizard man had drawn his attention. He hadn't heard Norma Jeane's words in the fierce furious voice of Rose Loomis. And the celebration was too festive. Voices, laughter, a Negro jazz combo. Now was hardly the time for a settling of accounts with the enemy. For others were crowding near, eager to congratulate Marilyn Monroe on her success. *Niagara* was a B-feature, low-budget and swiftly filmed, and it would make lots of money on its investment, so now it was a good idea for Norma Jeane to swallow her bitterness and smile, smile, smile prettily as Marilyn.

Though wanting so badly to clutch at Z's tuxedo sleeve and confront him. Except a sober warning voice intervened.

No! Don't. That is a thing Gladys would do. At such a time, before witnesses. But you who are Marilyn Monroe will not do such a thing because you are not sick like me.

In this way the dangerous moment passed. Norma Jeane began to breathe more calmly. She would recall afterward her surprise and relief that Gladys had given her such good advice. Surely, this was a turning point in both their lives! *To know that she wished me well and not ill. To know she was happy for me.*

There was Rin Tin Tin at her side. Bristling-proud as if he'd invented her.

Rin Tin Tin was taller than Rumpelstiltskin by several inches, and not deformed in the upper back, and his sleek oiled head was an ordinary man's head, not overlarge or subtly misshapen. His eyes were the eyes of an ordinary avaricious man; there was even a wayward streak of kindness in him sudden as a sneeze, a quick boyish-hopeful smile. Yet still that underlying fear and distrust of his blond actress client who'd become, overnight it seemed, famous. Like all business associates of suddenly successful actors, Rin Tin Tin worried that his client would be stolen from him by someone like himself only more so. Norma Jeane missed Mr. Shinn! At such public occasions, his absence swept upon her like a whiff of scraped plates, dumped garbage from a kitchen behind the scenes. It did not seem possible that I. E. Shinn was gone and these other dwarfs continued to exist. And Norma Jeane continued to exist. If Isaac were here, he would see that Norma Jeane was becoming uneasy, made anxious by having to smile at strangers; she was drinking too much, out of nerves, and these effusive compliments and congratulations only confused her, who needed to be admonished for having failed to do the very best work of which she was capable.

Fear your admirers! Talk of your art only with those who can tell you the truth. So the great Stanislavski warned.

Now she was surrounded by admirers. Or such was the pretense.

Mr. Shinn would have stood with Norma Jeane in a corner, shrewd canny Rumpelstiltskin making her laugh with his wicked sarcasm and droll asides. *He* would be shocked to hear of her pregnancy—furious at first, for if there was anyone he disliked more than Cass Chaplin, it was Eddy G. Robinson, Jr.;

he knew nothing of how the Gemini had saved Norma Jeane's life—yet within a few days, Norma Jeane was certain, he'd have been happy for her. *What the Fair Princess wants, that shall the Fair Princess be granted.*

"—on the line? Marilyn?"

Norma Jeane was wakened from her trance by an annoying little radio voice. No, a telephone voice. She'd been half lying on a sofa and the telephone receiver had fallen beside her. Both her warm moist palms were pressed against the pit of her belly, where Baby slept his secret wordless sleep.

Norma Jeane lifted the receiver, confused. "Y-yes? What?"

It was Rin Tin Tin. She'd forgotten him. When had he called? This was so embarrassing! Rin Tin Tin asking was something wrong and calling her *Marilyn* as if he had the right. "No. Nothing is wrong. What did you want?"

"Will you listen, please? You've never done musical comedy before, and this is a fantastic opportunity. The deal is—"

"Musical comedy? I can't sing, and I can't dance."

Rin Tin Tin barked with laughter. Wasn't his client fun-ny! The next Carole Lombard.

He said, "You've been taking lessons, and everybody at The Studio I've spoken with says you're"—he paused, searching for the right, plausible term—"very promising. A natural talent."

It was true: a childlike joyous energy seemed to suffuse her, when she wasn't herself but *in music*. Dancing, singing! And now she had something truly to be happy about. "I'm sorry. I can't. Not now."

There was a sharp intake of incensed doggy breath. Panting.

"Not now? Why not *now*? Marilyn Monroe is the newest box-office star *now*."

"My private life."

"Marilyn, what? I didn't quite hear."

"My p-private life. I have my own life! I'm not just—a thing in the movies."

Rin Tin Tin chose not to hear this. That had been a trick of Rumpelstiltskin's too. He said eagerly, as if this were news just handed to him in a telegram, "Z has purchased *Gentlemen Prefer Blondes* for you. He doesn't want Carol Channing from the Broadway production, though she made the musical a hit. He wants it as a showcase for you, Marilyn."

A showcase! For what?

Casually Norma Jeane said, stroking her belly as Rose might have done, the tight rounded just-perceptible swelling that was Baby, "How much would I get?"

Rin Tin Tin paused. "Your contract salary. Fifteen hundred a week."

"How many weeks?"

"They estimate about twelve."

"And how much would Jane Russell get?"

Again Rin Tin Tin paused. He must have been surprised that Norma Jeane, who seemed so vague and distant and distracted, so uninterested in Hollywood trade gossip, claiming not even to read most of the publicity explosion about Marilyn Monroe, would know not only that Jane Russell was to co-star in the film but that a query about Jane Russell's salary would be painful to her agent.

Evasively he said, "The deal is pending. Russell has to be lent by another studio."

"Yes, but how much?"

"The figures aren't finalized."

"How *much*?"

"They're asking one hundred thousand."

"One hundred thousand!" Norma Jeane felt a stab of hurt in the pit of her belly. Baby, too, was insulted. But Baby's sleep would not be disturbed. For Norma Jeane felt mostly relief. She said, laughing, "If the film takes twelve weeks to make, then my salary would be eighteen thousand dollars. And Jane gets a hundred thousand? 'Marilyn Monroe' has to have pride, doesn't she? That's an insult. Jane Russell and I went to high school together in Van Nuys. She was a year older and got more roles in school plays than I did, but we were always friends. She would be embarrassed for me!" Norma Jeane paused. She'd been speaking rapidly; though she wasn't upset, her voice sounded angry. "I—I'm going to hang up now. Goodbye."

"Marilyn, wait—"

"Fuck Marilyn. *She isn't here.*"

There was the morning an emergency call came from Lakewood. Gladys Mortensen was missing!

During the night she'd slipped away from her room, and from the hospital, and (they'd come to the reluctant conclusion now that they'd searched thoroughly) from the hospital grounds. Could Norma Jeane come as quickly as possible? "Oh yes. Oh *yes.*"

She would tell no one. Not her agent, not Cass Chaplin, not Eddy G. *Hoping to shield them. This heartbreak that is my own, only.* And she feared the obvious lack of interest in her lovers' eyes whenever she alluded, however elliptically, to her sick mother. ("We all have sick mothers," Cass remarked lightly. "I'll spare you mine if you spare me yours. Deal?")

Norma Jeane threw on clothes, one of Eddy G's straw fedoras, a pair of dark-tinted sunglasses. She contemplated, but finally didn't take, a mineral-blue Benzedrine tablet from Cass's stash in the bathroom. She was sleeping as many as six hours a night, a deep restful sleep, for pregnancy agreed with her as her doctor assured her, beaming like a father-to-be so that Norma Jeane had begun to worry he'd recognized her. What if he took photos of her while she was anesthetized, delivering her baby?

She drove to Lakewood in morning traffic. Anxious about Gladys, for what if Gladys had injured herself? *Somehow she knows about the baby. Is it possible?* She knew she must guard against attributing omniscient thoughts to Gladys; she wasn't a little girl any longer, and Gladys wasn't her powerful all-knowing mother. *Yet somehow she might know. And that's why she has run away.* Driving to Lakewood, Norma Jeane passed one, two, three movie houses in which *Niagara* was playing. Stretched across the top of the marquee of each theater was MARILYN MONROE, her skin creamy and luminous, MARILYN MONROE in a low-cut red dress that barely contained her swelling breasts. MARILYN MONROE was smiling provocatively with glossy-sexy pursed lips at which Norma Jeane glanced shyly.

The Fair Princess! Never before had Norma Jeane quite realized how the Fair Princess both mocked her admirers and enhanced them. She was so beautiful, and they were so ordinary. She was the source of emotion, and they were in thrall to emotion. Who was the Dark Prince worthy of *her*?

Yes, I'm proud! I admit it. I worked hard, and I'm going to work harder.

That woman in the poster isn't me. But she's the work I created. I deserve my happiness.

I deserve my baby. This is my time!

When Norma Jeane arrived at the private hospital at Lakewood, by magic it seemed Gladys had been returned. She'd been found sleeping in a pew in a Catholic church less than three miles away, on busy Bellflower Boulevard. Confused and disoriented, but unresisting, she'd been brought back to the hospital by Lakewood police. When Norma Jeane saw Gladys she burst into tears and embraced her mother, who smelled of wetted ashes, damp clothing, urine.

"But Mother isn't even Catholic. Why on earth would she go *there?*"

The director of the Lakewood Home apologized profusely to Norma Jeane. Carefully he called her "Miss Baker." (It was strictly confidential that Gladys Mortensen was the mother of a certain film actress. "Don't betray me!" Norma Jeane had begged.) He insisted that patients were checked in their rooms every evening at 9 P.M.; windows and doors were checked; there were security guards at all times. Quickly Norma Jeane said, "Oh, I'm not angry. I'm just so grateful that Mother is safe."

Norma Jeane spent the remainder of the day at Lakewood. It was a blessed day after all! She pondered how to tell Gladys her news. A mother is not always prepared to hear happy news from a daughter for a mother is most herself when mothering a daughter. Yet now Norma Jeane was mothering Gladys, who seemed so frail and tentative in her movements, blinking and squinting at Norma Jeane as if uncertain who she was. Several times she said, worriedly rather than accusingly, "Your hair is so *white*. Are you old like me?"

Norma Jeane helped bathe her mother, washed Gladys's matted hair herself, and carefully combed it out. She spoke brightly to Gladys, hummed and sang as if to a small child. "Everyone was so worried about you, Mother. You won't ever run away again, will you?" Sometime in the early hours of the morning, Gladys had managed to unlock not one but several doors (unless just possibly these doors hadn't been adequately locked, despite the protestations of the staff) and make her way undetected across the front lawn of the Home; once on the street, she'd managed to make her way undetected two and a half miles to St. Elizabeth's Church, where she was found the next morning when parishioners entered the church for seven o'clock mass. She was wearing a beltless beige cotton dress with a drooping hemline and no underwear beneath. She'd had on corduroy bedroom slippers when she left the hospital but seemed to have lost them during her journey; her bony feet were covered in shallow cuts. Tenderly Norma Jeane washed her mother's feet and applied iodine to the cuts. "Mother, where were you going? You could have asked me, you know. If you wanted to go somewhere. Like to a church."

Gladys shrugged. "I knew where I was going."

"You could have been injured. Hit by a car, or—lost."

"I was never lost. I knew where I was going."

"But where?"

"Home."

The word hovered in the air, strange and wonderful as a neon insect. Norma Jeane, shaken, had no idea how to reply. She saw that Gladys was smiling. A woman with a secret. Long ago in another lifetime she'd been a poet. She'd been a beautiful young woman to whom men, including powerful Hollywood men like Norma Jeane's father, had been attracted. Before Norma Jeane's arrival at the hospital, Gladys had been given a drug to "quiet her nerves." She showed little sign now of agitation or even of embarrassment for having caused so much commotion. Sleeping on the hard wooden pew, she'd wet her clothes but hadn't been embarrassed about that either. *She's a child. A cruel child. She's taken Norma Jeane's place.*

Gladys's once-beautiful eyes were shadowed and as without luster as stones, and her skin had a grainy, greenish cast; yet oddly, for all that she'd been wandering in the night barefoot, she didn't look much older than Norma Jeane recalled. It was as if a spell had been cast upon her years ago:

others around her would age but not Gladys. Norma Jeane said, gently reproving, "Any time you want, Mother, you can come home with me. You know that." There was a pause. Gladys sniffed and wiped at her nose. Norma Jeane imagined she could hear the woman's derisive laughter. *Home! With you? Where?* Norma Jeane said, "You're not old. You shouldn't call yourself old. You're only fifty-three." Slyly Norma Jeane said, "How'd you like to be a grandmother?"

There. It was said. *Grandmother!*

Gladys yawned. A craterous yawn. Norma Jeane was disappointed. Should she repeat her question?

Norma Jeane had helped her mother into bed, where she lay in a clean cotton nightgown amid clean cotton sheets. The sour, sad odor of urine was gone from Gladys's person but remained, faint as an echo, in the room. Gladys's private room, for which "Miss Baker" paid a hefty sum each month, was the size of a large closet, with a single dormer window overlooking a parking lot. There was a bedside table, a lamp, a single vinyl chair, a narrow hospital bed. On the aluminum bureau amid toiletries and items of clothing were several stacks of books, gifts from Norma Jeane over the years. Most of these were volumes of poetry, pretty, slender books with the look of having rarely been opened. Comfortably settled in bed, Gladys looked as if she were about to drift into sleep. Her metallic-brown hair had dried in snaky tufts. Her eyelids drooped and her bloodless lips hung slack. Norma Jeane saw with a pang of loss that her mother's ropy-veined hands, Nell's hands, once so fretful, so alive with an angry volition of their own, were now limp. Norma Jeane took these hands in hers. "Oh, Mother, your fingers are so *cold*. I'll have to warm them."

But Gladys's fingers resisted warming. Instead, Norma Jeane began to shiver.

Norma Jeane tried to explain why she hadn't brought a present for Gladys today. Why they wouldn't be going into town, to take Gladys to a hairdresser and to a nice tearoom for lunch. She tried to explain why she couldn't leave much spending money for Gladys—"I have eighteen dollars in my wallet! It's so embarrassing. My contract pays me fifteen hundred dollars a week but there are so many expenses. . . ." It was true: often Norma Jeane was forced to borrow money, fifty dollars, one hundred dollars, two hundred dollars from friends or friends of friends. There were men eager to lend Marilyn Monroe sums of money. And no I.O.U.s. Gifts of jewelry—and Norma Jeane had no use for jewelry, much. Cass Chaplin and Eddy G, practical-minded young men, weren't offended. As fathers-to-be, they had to think of the future, and you can't think of the future without thinking about money. Each had been disinherited by his famous father, so it seemed only logical that other older men, fathers of another kind, should support them. They were always trying to convince Norma Jeane that this was true for her, too. She too had been cheated of her inheritance. It was their idea that the three of them should move into the Hollywood Hills for the duration of Norma Jeane's pregnancy. If they couldn't locate a suitable house for no rent, they would have to have money for rent. It was their idea also that each of them insure himself for $100,000—unless maybe $200,000—naming the other two as beneficiaries. "Just in case. You can't be too prepared. With a baby on the way. Of course, nothing's gonna happen to the Gemini!" Norma Jeane hadn't known how to reply to this suggestion. Insure herself? The prospect frightened her, for it indicated so clearly that one day she must die.

But not "Marilyn." *She* was on film and in photos. Everywhere.

Suddenly Gladys opened her eyes wide, trying to bring them into focus. Norma Jeane had the uneasy feeling that her reaction wasn't to Norma Jeane's words. Excitedly she said, "What year is this? What time did we travel to?"

Norma Jeane said soothingly, "Mother, it's May 1953. This is Norma Jeane, here to take care of you."

Gladys squinted suspiciously at her. "But your hair is so *white*."

Gladys shut her eyes. Kneading Gladys's limp fingers, Norma Jeane tried to think how to tell her mother the good news without upsetting her. *A baby. Already almost six weeks old. Aren't you happy for me?* Somehow it seemed to her that Gladys already knew. That was why Gladys was so elusive, determined to escape into sleep.

Norma Jeane said tentatively, "When you h-had me, Mother, you weren't married I guess? You didn't have a man supporting you. Yet you had a baby. That was so brave, Mother! Another girl would have—well, you know. Gotten rid of it. Of *me*." Norma Jeane laughed a startled squeaking laugh. "Then I wouldn't be here, at all. There wouldn't be any 'Marilyn.' And she's getting so famous now, fan letters! telegrams! flowers from strangers! It's so . . . strange."

Gladys refused to open her eyes. Her face was softening like melting wax. Saliva glinted at one corner of her mouth. Norma Jeane spoke without knowing what she said. With a part of her mind she seemed to know how implausible it was, preposterous, her plan to have a baby. A baby, and no husband? If only she'd married Mr. Shinn. If only V had loved her a little more, he might have married her. It would be the end of her career. Absolutely the end of her career. Even if, in haste, she married one of the Gemini, the scandal would destroy her. Marilyn Monroe, newly famous, a balloon inflated by the media, would be gleefully destroyed by the media.

"But you were brave. You did the right thing. You had your baby. You had . . . *me*."

But Gladys's eyes were closed. Her bloodless lips hung slack. She'd slipped into sleep as if into a dark mysterious water where Norma Jeane couldn't follow. Though she heard the lapping of waves close beside the bed.

From the Lakewood Home, Norma Jeane made a single telephone call to a number in Hollywood. The phone rang and rang at the other end. "Help me, please! I need help so badly."

Norma Jeane would have liked to leave the Lakewood Home immediately, for she'd been crying and the skin around her eyes felt raw and reddened. She was Nell, disoriented and panicky but compelled by the presence of others to behave *as if normal*. Yet the director insisted upon speaking with her in private. He was a middle-aged man with an oyster-round face, magnified-looking eyeglasses with chunky black plastic frames. By the excitement in his voice Norma Jeane understood that he was seeing not her, the daughter of the mental patient Gladys Mortensen, but a film actress. Maybe a "blond sexpot film actress." Would he dare to ask for her autograph? At such a time? She'd scream profanities at him if he did. She'd burst into tears. She couldn't bear it!

Dr. Bender was discussing Gladys Mortensen. How well, "generally," Gladys Mortensen had been doing since entering Lakewood. Yet how, sometimes, like many patients in her condition, she "lapsed"—"relapsed"—and behaved in unexpected and dangerous ways. Paranoid schizophrenia, Dr. Bender explained, with the air of a kindly, solicitous recording device, is a mystery illness. "Always, it has reminded me of multiple sclerosis. As mystery illnesses no one truly understands. A syndrome of symptoms." Some theorists believe that paranoid schizophrenia can be explained by the patient's interaction, or thwarted interaction, with her environment and with other people; some theorists, Freudians, believe it can be explained by the patient's childhood; some theorists believe it has a purely organic biochemical origin. Norma Jeane nodded to show she was listening. She smiled. Even at such a time, exhausted and depressed and the baby in her womb aching, beginning to recall the numerous appointments she'd missed that day at The Studio, totally forgotten, hadn't called to postpone or explain, she knew she must *smile*. Smiles were expected of all women and especially of *her*.

Norma Jeane said sadly, "I don't ask any longer when my mother will be discharged. I guess she never will be. Just so long as she's safe and h-happy, I guess that's the most we can expect?"

Gravely Dr. Bender replied, "At Lakewood, we never give up on a patient. Never! But, yes—we are realists too."

"Is it inherited?"

"Excuse me?"

"My mother's illness? Are you born with it, in your blood?"

"In your *blood?*" Dr. Bender repeated these words as if he'd never heard anything quite like them before. Evasively he said, "There has been noticed, in some families, a certain tendency, yes, but in others absolutely *not.*"

Norma Jeane said hopefully, "My f-father was a very normal man. In all ways. I don't know him, except from photos. I've only heard of him. He d-died in Spain, in 1936. I mean, he was killed. In the war."

As Norma Jeane rose to leave, Dr. Bender did ask her for an autograph, with apologies, quickly explaining that he wasn't the kind of person who did such things, but would Norma Jeane mind terribly?—"It's for my thirteen-year-old Sasha. She wants to be a movie star, she thinks, too!"

Norma Jeane felt her mouth smile graciously, as it had been trained. Though she could feel a migraine beginning. Since becoming pregnant, and no menstrual periods, she'd been spared blinding headaches as she'd been spared paralyzing cramps, but now she felt a migraine coming on and wondered in panic how she would transport herself and Baby back home. Yet graciously she signed the cover of *Photoplay* in the airy sweeping script The Studio had devised for "Marilyn." (Her own signature, "Norma Jeane Baker," was a tiny backhand.) The *Photoplay* cover portrayed Marilyn as Rose, voluptuous, sexy, her head tilted back, eyes narrowed and dreamy, and lips provocatively pursed. Her swelling breasts nearly spilled out of an electric-blue silk halter dress Norma Jeane could have sworn she'd never worn. In fact, she'd forgotten this cover. She'd forgotten the photo shoot. Maybe it had never happened?

Yet there, *Photoplay* for April 1953, was proof.

To My Baby

In you,
the world is born anew.

Before you—
there was none.

THE MAGI

They were Hedda Hopper, P. Pukham ("Hollywood After Dark"),
G. Belcher, Max-the-Man Mercer, Dorothy Kilgallen, H. Salop, "Keyhole,"
Skid Skolsky (who dredged for hot Hollywood gossip from his perch on
the mezzanine at Schwab's Drugstore), Gloria Grahame, V. Venell, "Buck"
Holster, Smilin Jack, Lex Aise, Cramme, Pease, Coker, Crudloe, Gagge,
Gargoie, Scudd, Sly Goldblatt, Pett, Trott, Leviticus, *BUZZ YARD*,
M. Mudd, Wall Reese, Walter Winchell, Louella Parsons, and HOLLYWOOD
ROVING EYE among others. Their columns of excited newsprint appeared in
*L.A. Times, L.A. Beacon, L.A. Confidential, Variety, Hollywood Reporter,
Hollywood Tatler, Hollywood Confidential, Hollywood Diary, Photoplay,
PhotoLife, Screen World, Screen Romance, Screen Secrets, Modern Screen,
Screenland, Screen Album, Movie Stories, Movieland, New York Post, Film-
land Tell-All, Scoop!*, and other publications. They were syndicated by the
United Press and the American Press. It was their tireless task to spread the
word. To shake the sheets and fan the flames. They ran ahead, loosing skeins
of gasoline in the underbrush, to hasten the rush of the flames. They bla-
zoned, they heralded, they beat the drums. They blew bugles, trumpets, and
tubas from the ramparts. They rang the bells, and they sounded the alarms.
Together and individually, in a chorus and in arias, they proclaimed,

acclaimed, broadcast, and forecast. They ballyhooed. They disclosed, and they exposed. They praised, dispraised, promulgated, and disseminated. They were volcanoes of words. They were tidal waves of words. They pitched, they advanced, they plugged, and they slugged. They spotlighted. They limelighted. They hawked. They puffed, blurbed, fanfared, hoopla'd, ventilated, and hyperventilated. They predicted, and they contradicted. The "meteoric" rise of, the "tragic" descent of. They were astronomers plotting the trajectories of stars. Ceaselessly they scoured the night sky. They were there at the birth of the star and they were there at the death. They rhapsodized the flesh and they picked at the bones. Greedily they licked the beautiful skin and greedily they sucked the delicious marrow. In boldface in the fifties proclaiming MARILYN MONROE MARILYN MONROE MARILYN MONROE. *Photoplay* Gold Medal Best New Star 1953. *Playboy* Sweetheart of the Month November 1953. *Screen World* Miss Blond Bombshell 1953. In glossy magazines *Life, Collier's, Saturday Evening Post, Esquire.* In posters with a crippled child in a wheelchair gazing up at her erect blond beauty: REMEMBER TO GIVE GENEROUSLY TO THE MARCH OF DIMES. MARILYN MONROE.

To Cass she'd say, laughing anxiously, "Oh—she's pretty, I guess. This photo. This dress. Gosh! But it isn't me, is it? What about when people f-find out?"

The strange shiny opacity of her blue doll-baby eyes he'd be capable of decoding only in retrospect, and then without absolute certainty. For he hadn't been listening closely. With Norma, you rarely did. She talked to herself, her thoughts crowded her brain and spilled over. The way she clenched her hands, flexed her fingers, touched her lips unconsciously as if to check— what? That she had lips? That her lips were young, fleshy, firm? And Cass had his own broody thoughts. Saying, distractedly, stroking Norma's hand, which typically Norma turned over to grasp at his hand, her surprisingly strong fingers clutching at his, "Hell, baby: *we* found out and we love you anyway. Right?"

He figured it had to do with her being pregnant, and scared.

"CAN'T GET ENOUGH
OF POLISH SAUSAGE"

Her lovers! From out of the voluminous F.B.I. file labeled MARILYN MONROE A.K.A. NORMA JEANE BAKER.

These were Z, D, S, and T, among a half dozen others at The Studio. These were the Commie photographer Otto Öse, the Commie screenwriter Dalton Trumbo, the Commie actor Robert Mitchum. These were Howard Hughes, George Raft, I. E. Shinn, Ben Hecht, John Huston, Louis Calhern, Pat O'Brien, Mickey Rooney, Richard Widmark, Ricardo Montalban, George Sanders, Eddie Fisher, Paul Robeson, Charlie Chaplin (senior) and Charlie Chaplin (junior), Stewart Granger, Joseph Mankiewicz, Roy Baker, Howard Hawks, Joseph Cotten, Elisha Cook, Jr., Sterling Hayden, Humphrey Bogart, Hoagy Carmichael, Robert Taylor, Tyrone Power, Fred Allen, Hopalong Cassidy, Tom Mix, Otto Preminger, Cary Grant, Clark Gable, Skid Skolsky, Samuel Goldwyn, Edward G. Robinson (senior), Edward G. Robinson (junior), Van Heflin, Van Johnson, Tonto, Johnny "Tarzan" Weissmuller, Gene Autry, Bela Lugosi, Boris Karloff, Lon Chaney, Fred Astaire, Leviticus, Roy Rogers and Trigger, Groucho Marx, Harpo Marx, Chico Marx, Bud Abbott and Lou Costello, John Wayne, Charles Coburn, Rory Calhoun, Clifton Webb, Ronald Reagan, James Mason, Monty Woolley, W. C. Fields, Red Skelton, Jimmy Durante, Errol Flynn, Keenan

Wynn, Walter Pidgeon, Fredric March, Mae West, Gloria Swanson, Joan Crawford, Shelley Winters, Ava Gardner, *BUZZ YARD*, Lassie, Jimmy Stewart, Dana Andrews, Frank Sinatra, Peter Lawford, Cecil B. DeMille, and numerous others. And this was just up to 1953 when she was twenty-seven years old! The most scandalous were yet to come.

THE EX-ATHLETE:
THE SIGHTING

"I want to date her."

The Ex-Athlete was nearing forty. It had been years since he'd swung his final bat in major league baseball, hit his final home run, smiled shyly as seventy-five thousand fans erupted in a frenzy of adulation. In his time he'd broken baseball records dating back to 1922. He was compared favorably to Babe Ruth. He'd become an American legend. An American icon. He'd married, begat children, and had been divorced by his wife on grounds of "cruelty." Well, he had a temper! Can't blame a normal red-blooded man for having a temper. Also, he was "Italian, and jealous." He was "Italian, and never forgot a slight, and never forgave an enemy." He had an Italian nose, swarthy Italian good looks. In public he was well-groomed. In public he was quiet, well-mannered. He had a reputation for shyness. He had a reputation for gallantry. He favored sports shirts for casual wear, tailor-made dark suits for evening wear. He'd been born in San Francisco into a family of fishermen. He was Catholic. He was a man's man. By temperament he was a family man. But where was his family? He dated "models." He dated "starlets." His name was sometimes in boldface, in gossip columns. By the time he'd retired from baseball he was earning $100,000 a year. He'd given money to his parents, he'd bought property and made investments. He was known to have "ties" with certain Italian businessmen in San Francisco, Los

Angeles, and Las Vegas. Unsurprisingly, he favored Italian restaurants: veal scampi, pasta, an occasional risotto. But it had to be a scrupulously prepared risotto. He was a big tipper, usually. He went dead-white in the face if served badly. You wouldn't want to insult this man, willfully or otherwise. He was a man to call the shots. Women referred to him slyly as the "Yankee slugger." He drank. He smoked. He brooded. He was addicted to sports. He had many men friends, some of them ex-athletes like himself and all of them addicted to sports. Yet he was lonely. He wanted a "normal life." He watched baseball, football, boxing on TV. When he attended baseball games he was always singled out for attention and applause. The crowd loved the way he rose to his feet—bashful smile, wave of the hand—and sat down quickly, his face flushed. He met his friends in restaurants and nightclubs. Often they were boisterous, picky about food and service, the last ones to leave the premises. But they were great tippers. In public places the Ex-Athlete enjoyed signing autographs, but he did not like to be crowded or jostled. He liked a good-looking woman at his side. Smiling, beaming. Often there were photographers. He liked a woman to cling to his arm but not to cling to *him*. He disliked women who "tried to be men." He was filled with indignation and revulsion at the thought of "unnatural" women who didn't want to have children. He disapproved of abortion. He may have practiced birth control, though the Church forbade any method except rhythm. He disapproved of Communists and Communist sympathizers, "Reds" and "pinkos." He had not read a book, perhaps had not opened a book, since high school in San Francisco. His grades there had been average. By the age of nineteen he'd become a pro ballplayer. He enjoyed movies, especially comedies and war movies. He was a big man, restless if forced to sit for too long. He attended church only sporadically but never failed to do his Easter duty. When kneeling for Holy Communion, he shut his eyes as he'd been taught as a boy. He did not chew the wafer, he allowed the wafer to melt on his tongue as he'd been taught as a boy. He would no more have taken communion without confessing his sins than he would have stood up in the midst of mass and screamed profanities and obscenities at the priest. He believed in God, but he believed in free will. By chance he saw "Marilyn Monroe" in a publicity photo in the *L.A. Times*. The blond Hollywood actress was posing prettily between two baseball players. *Start of a new season. Batter up!*

The Ex-Athlete stared at this photo for a long time. A hardball, a bat, a dazzlingly pretty radiantly smiling girl with the sweetest face, a sculpted body like the Venus de Milo, and that cotton-candy hair. Here was an angel, an angel with breasts and hips. The Ex-Athlete immediately telephoned a friend in Hollywood, owner of a well-known Beverly Hills restaurant. "This blonde, Marilyn Monroe."

The friend said, "So? What about her?"

"I'd like to date her."

"*Her?*" the friend laughed. "That broad's a tramp. She's been a tramp from the get-go. She's a bottle-blonde. A cow. She don't wear underwear. She pals around with Jews and lives with two faggot junkies. She's sucked every cock in town and more from out of town. She's spent weekends in Vegas servicing the guys. Never leaves the suite. Can't get enough of Polish sausage."

There was silence. The friend in Hollywood thought the Ex-Athlete had quietly hung up, for that was his way sometimes. Instead, the Ex-Athlete said, "I want to date her. Make the arrangements."

THE CYPRESSES

It was Baby's sixth week. It was Norma Jeane's birthday week.

Twenty-seven! Almost too old for a first baby, they say.

It was a time of sudden revelations.

"Heyyyy, know what? This thought came to me."

The Gemini, the beautiful threesome, were en route to a villa-for-rent. The Cypresses, in the Hollywood Hills. Top of Laurel Canyon Drive. This was the sixth or seventh "villa" the Gemini had been shown since the start of their "epic search." (These were Cass's words. Cass was their master of words.) They were seeking the ideal environment for Norma Jeane's pregnancy and, after his birth, for Baby's early months. "We are the products of our time and place," Cass said. "We are not pure spirit. Of the earth we are born, and precious metals from the distant stars. We must rise above the smog-bound City of Angels as above history—hey, you two listening?" (*Yes, yes!* Norma Jeane, starry-eyed in love, was always listening; Eddy G, he'd shrug and nod: sure.) "In each birth, the world begins anew. In this birth, we'll assure it! The future of civilization may rest in a single birth. The Messiah. You can say the odds are against the Messiah but so what? Toss the dice."

When Cass Chaplin spoke so eloquently, with such passion, who were Norma Jeane and Eddy G to *doubt*?

Norma Jeane was the Beggar Maid beloved by two ardent princes. One gave her books to read, books that "meant much" to him, the other gave her flowers, solitary flowers, flowers with a look of having been picked with inspired haste, their stems broken off short, beautiful delicate petals just past their bloom, leaves stippled with black spots.

"Beautiful Norma, we adore you."

So happy. And never so healthy in my body, so I came to see that worship of God is but the spirit of Divine Health (or Healing).

There is no Devil. The Devil is a sickness of mind.

That day, Eddy G was driving them up into the Hollywood Hills above the smog-bound wicked city. The sky overhead was a fair fading blue. The air was stirred by a warm dry wind. Gravel crunched beneath the wheels of the lime-green Caddy driven with the usual skill and that air of just-restrained mayhem typical of Eddy G, who, when cast in films, was the good-looking-young-brash-guy-who-dies, usually violently. Norma Jeane sat beside Eddy G, and beside Norma Jeane was Cass Chaplin. (Poor Cass! "Not myself this morning, but who the hell I *am* I don't know.") Norma Jeane in the prime of her young beauty sat smiling between her Gemini lovers, the palm of her right hand cupped protectively against her belly. Her warm moist hand, her beginning-to-swell belly.

Baby's sixth week. Was it possible!

The Gemini, the beautiful threesome, on this fair fine morning in southern California driving up Laurel Canyon Drive to meet the real estate agent who'd taken their epic search as her own, who meant to close a deal with them soon. They called the woman, behind her back, "Theda Bara," for she'd made herself up in that dopey-sexy style of a bygone era; you felt sorry for her (well, Norma Jeane did), yet almost you wanted to laugh in her face (Cass and Eddy G). And suddenly, so spontaneously you'd swear he had only just this instant thought of such a thing, Eddy G cried, thumping the steering wheel, "Heyyyy, know what? This thought came to me." Norma Jeane asked what thought? and Cass grunted something unintelligible (oh, God, Cass's guts were churning with such fury Norma Jeane could almost feel it; she'd been made to feel subtly guilty by his telling her he had "sympathetic morning sickness," exacerbated by the fact that she had virtually no morning sickness herself). Eddy G went on, excited. "It's like a revelation, y'know? What we must do, the three of us, before Norma has the baby, is draw up our wills and insurance policies so something happens to one of us, the other two and Baby collect." Eddy G paused. His air of boyish enthusiasm, his unscripted energy. "I know a lawyer. I mean, one to trust. Y'see? Whaddya think? You two listening? So Baby will be better protected."

There was a beat. Norma Jeane was in a dreamy state. Awash in dreams of the previous night. Strange vivid hallucinatory dreams! A flotilla of dreams, pregnancy dreams she'd described to Cass, saying she'd never had such dreams before, oh, never! Her insomnia had vanished as if it had never plagued her. Never was she tempted to take pills from the household supply. Rarely was she tempted to drink. Drifting into sleep almost as soon as her head hit the pillow, though the beautiful boys fondled and sucked and bit and poked her, laughing and tussling each other like kids across, or on top of, her comatose female body. The Sleeping Princess they called her. Her breasts they swore were filling up with cream. Mmmm! Yet the river of night bore her innocently aloft, the river nourished her.

Never so healthy, Mother! Why didn't you tell me having a baby would be like this!

Cass said, clearing his throat, a little edgy, like an actor not up for his scene, "Hey. Terrific idea, Eddy. Yeah! I worry about the kid sometimes. This San Andreas Fault." He turned to Norma Jeane to inquire gently, "How's it sound to you, Little Momma?"

Again, a beat. Norma Jeane seemed not to be responding to this dialogue as the male Gemini wished. She would recall afterward it was so strange: as in a shoot, you can see how your co-actor is willing you to behave in a certain way, as a bridge to his next bit of dialogue, but just possibly you're holding back, some instinct in your actor's soul urges you to hold back, to resist, not to go along with it.

"Norma? What's your take on this?"

Eddy G gunned the Caddy's motor. They were flying up the narrow canyon drive. He's angry, Norma Jeane thought. Eddy G fiddled with the dashboard radio, a dangerous habit of his while driving. "The Song from Moulin Rouge" came blaring.

Laurel Canyon Drive was long, curvy. Norma Jeane was determined not to recall the L.A.P.D. roadblock. And Gladys in her nightgown.

I was just a girl then. Now look at me!

Cass was pressing his hand over Norma Jeane's hand, which was pressed against her belly. Against Baby. Of the two men, Cass was the more affectionate when in the mood; Cass was a master of romance, not in the comic style of Chaplin senior but in the solemn Valentino style no female can resist. Eddy G, since the onset of the pregnancy, was likely to tease and banter nervously and shrank from touching Norma Jeane.

"The crucial thing is, darling, the baby should be protected. From the vicissitudes of fate. What if there's another Depression? Could be! Nobody was prepared for the first. What if the movies go belly-up? Could be! Everybody in the U.S. is gonna own a TV soon. 'No one who shares a delusion ever recognizes it as such,' says Freud. In southern California, delusion is the very air we breathe. So financially I think it might be a good idea for us to prepare for Baby's future."

Norma Jeane stirred uneasily. It was her turn to speak. This was acting class; she'd been thrown into a scripted scene to improvise. One of those exercises, you're sent out of the room, then called back in to play the scene out with two or more actors who've memorized a script.

Cass was nuzzling his cheek against Norma Jeane's. The smell of his breath was morning staleness mixed with sweetish staleness like rotted wisteria. "Not that anything is gonna happen to *us*, Little Momma. We're our own lucky stars."

Now she remembered! That dream where she'd been trying so hard to nurse Baby but his lips would not suck. Do a newborn baby's lips suck automatically? reflexively? It must be instinct, nature, like a bird building its nest, bees building a hive. But how strange to her that in her dreams Baby had no face (yet!) only just a halo of shimmering light. Norma Jeane said, "Oh, gosh, did you ever *think*? What people mean by God is maybe just *instinct*? How you know what to do in a new circumstance without knowing why you know? Like animals tossed into water, they already know how to swim? Even newborns?"

The male Gemini stared ahead at the rushing canyon road.

There was Theda Bara awaiting them. At the flung-open gate of The Cypresses. Forcing a smile with dark-lipsticked bee-stung lips and waving gay as a flapper. Her sexy seductiveness was of a bygone era; she was somewhere between the ages of thirty-five and forty-five, if not older. A clay-colored skin, tight and polished about the eyes. Norma Jeane felt sorry for her, and impatient with her. *Grow up. Give up!*

Eddy G shouted, sincere-sounding, "Hey, sorry! We late?" He was such a hulking-handsome boy, even if unshaven in wrinkled khakis and smelling of what deodorant ads called B.O., you'd forgive him anything, almost. And Cass Chaplin, with his sulky boy-doll face and unkempt Little Tramp hair women yearned to run their fingers through. And the shy quiet distracted blonde, whom the realtor had recognized immediately as Marilyn Monroe, the newest Hollywood sensation, but whose privacy she certainly intended to respect. The notorious threesome! Of course they were late, more than an hour late, the Gemini were always late. The miracle was if the trio ever turned up anywhere anytime at all.

Theda Bara, in exaggerated eye makeup, rust-colored sharkskin suit, and crocodile high heels, shook hands eagerly with her clients. How quick she was to placate these glamorous young Hollywood people. "You're not late at all! Don't give it a second thought. I love it up here in the Hills. The Cypresses is my favorite property right now, for the view alone. On a clear day it's breathtaking. If it wasn't for that mist or fog or whatever it is we could see all the way to Santa Monica and the ocean." She paused, smiling harder. "I hope you young people won't judge The Cypresses too quickly? It's a unique house."

Cass whistled. "I can see that, ma'am."

"*I* can see that, ma'am, and I'm totally wasted," Eddy G said. This was meant as a joke, for Eddy G was never *totally wasted* so early in the day.

The young blond woman who'd previously introduced herself to the realtor as "Norma Jeane Baker" now stared at the French Normandy mansion through dark glasses, rapt and solemn as a little girl. She appeared to be wearing little makeup but her skin was luminous. Her platinum-blond hair was all but hidden by a crimson turban of the kind worn by Betty Grable in the forties. Her breasts were covered by a loose-fitting white silk tunic. She wore white silk slacks wrinkled at the crotch, and she was barefoot in flat-heeled straw sandals. In a breathy, wondering voice she said, "Oh!—it's beautiful. Like in a fairy tale, but which one?"

Theda Bara smiled uncertainly. She decided this wasn't a query that merited a reply.

She'd begin, she told them, with a tour of the grounds. "So we can get our bearings." Briskly she led them over cobblestones, across flagstone terraces, past a kidney-shaped swimming pool upon whose shivering aqua water floated desiccated palm fronds, the bodies of dead insects, and several small birds. "The pool is cleaned every Monday morning," she said apologetically. "I'm sure it was cleaned this week." Norma Jeane seemed to see shadows flitting across the bottom of the pool as of ghost swimmers; she didn't want to look too closely. Eddy G clambered up onto the diving board and flexed his knees as if about to dive in. Cass drawled to the women, "*Don't* dare him, please. Don't even look at him. I don't intend to drown trying to rescue him." "Fuck you, Jew-boy," Eddy G said. He was laughing but he sounded genuinely incensed.

Quickly, Theda Bara continued the tour.

Norma Jeane whispered to Eddy G, "That's rude. What if she's Jewish?"

"She knows I'm just joking. Even if you don't."

So high above the city, there was a persistent wind. How it would be to live here during Santa Ana season, Norma Jeane dreaded to think. Maybe it wouldn't be a good atmosphere for a pregnant woman or for an infant. Yet Cass and Eddy G, who'd both lived in elegant homes as young children, wanted a house in the hills, something "exotic," "special." Money didn't appear to be a concern of theirs, but from where, exactly, would the rental money come? And you'd need to hire servants for a house like this. Norma Jeane wouldn't be receiving any bonuses from *Niagara*, although it was a box-office hit; she was a Studio contract player and she'd been paid. Cass and Eddy G knew this! Now she was pregnant, she couldn't make another movie for a year. Or more. (And maybe her career was over.) But when she inquired how much The Cypresses rented for a month, the men told her it was reasonable enough, not to worry. "We can swing it. We three."

Norma Jeane was examining another zigzag crack, this one in a stucco wall decorated with exquisite Mexican mosaics. It was crawling with tiny black ants.

The Cypresses was so named because Italian cypresses had been planted around the house instead of palm trees. A few of these had retained their graceful sculpted shapes but most had become stunted from the continual wind, disfigured like tortured creatures. You could almost see them writhing. Dwarves, elves, evil fairies. But Rumpelstiltskin hadn't been evil, he'd been Norma Jeane's only friend. He'd loved her without qualification. If only she'd married Mr. Shinn!—and he hadn't died. She would be having I. E. Shinn's baby now, she'd have a big beautiful house of her own, and all of Hollywood would respect her, even the bosses at The Studio. (But Isaac had betrayed her, for all his talk of love. He hadn't left her anything in his will. Not a penny! He'd signed her to a seven-film contract at The Studio that made her virtually a slave.)

Theda Bara was ushering them into the house. Into the baronial front foyer. It was like a museum: a marble floor, brass and crystal chandeliers, silk wallpaper, mirrored panels, and a sweeping staircase. The living room was sunken and so large that Norma Jeane had to squint to see the farthest walls. Here, furniture was shrouded in white and the parquet floor was bare. Above a gigantic stone fireplace were crossed swords. Close by was a suit of medieval-looking armor. Cass whistled. "D. W. Griffith. One of his weird epics." Oval mirrors framed in gold filigree reflected oval mirrors framed in gold filigree in an infinite regress that made Norma Jeane's heart flutter.

There is madness here. Don't enter!

But it was too late, she couldn't turn back. Cass and Eddy G would be furious with her.

The property's current owner was the Bank of Southern California. No one had lived in The Cypresses for several years except short-term renters. The previous owner had been a film beauty of the thirties, a minor actress who'd outlived her wealthy producer husband by decades. This woman, a local legend, had had no children of her own but had adopted a number of orphaned children, some of them Mexican-born. One or two of these children had died "of natural causes" and others had disappeared or had run away. The woman had brought into her household a shifting number of "relatives" and "assistants," who had in turn stolen from her and abused her. There were lurid tales told of the woman's drinking, drug addiction, suicide attempts. Yet she'd given large sums of money to local charities, including the Sisters of Perpetual Mercy, an extreme Catholic order devoted to continual fasting, prayer, and silence. Norma Jeane had not wanted to hear the worst of these tales. She knew how misleading such tales could be. "Even beginning with the truth, what people say shifts into lies." Norma Jeane's heart pounded with the injustice of it, cruel things whispered of the woman who'd lived alone in this house at the end, found dead in her bedroom by a housekeeper. The coroner had ruled "misadventure" through malnutrition, barbiturates, and alcohol. Norma Jeane whispered, "It isn't fair. Those vultures!"

Ahead, Theda Bara in her spike high heels was talking and laughing with the men. Allowing herself to think they might actually rent The Cypresses. She said to Norma Jeane, "It's a fantasy house, isn't it, dear? So original and inventive. Your friends were telling me, the three of you are going into seclusion? This is the ideal place, I promise you."

The downstairs tour was taking a long time. Norma Jeane was beginning to feel fatigued. This house! Delusions of grandeur! Eight bedrooms, ten bathrooms, several living rooms, an enormous dining room with crystal chandeliers that quivered and vibrated as if the ceiling were shifting, a breakfast room large enough to seat two dozen guests. Always you were descending little flights of steps or ascending others. In a sunken area overlooking the swimming pool was a lounge with a long curving bar, leather booths, a dance floor, and a jukebox. Norma Jeane made straight for the jukebox, which was not only darkened and unplugged but empty of records. "Damn! Nothing's so sad as a jukebox not plugged *in*." She turned sulky, sullen. She'd have liked to play a record and dance. Jitterbug! She hadn't jitterbugged in years. And the hula: she'd loved to do the hula, and she'd been a terrific hula dancer, aged fourteen. Now she was twenty-seven and pregnant and exercise was good for her; why shouldn't she dance? If "Marilyn" did *Gentlemen Prefer Blondes*—which she wasn't going to do—she'd be dancing as a showgirl, in glamorous expensive costumes, in elaborately choreographed musical numbers like Ginger Rogers with Fred Astaire, fancy-phony stuff, not the kind of dancing Norma Jeane truly loved.

"First thing we'll do, Norma: plug the jukebox *in*," Eddy G promised.

Had it been decided somehow? without her agreeing?

Still Theda Bara led them on. Talking and laughing flirtatiously with the men. Who in stylish but wrinkled and not-clean clothes looked like exactly who they were: cast-off sons of Hollywood royalty. Norma Jeane was left to follow behind, gnawing at her lower lip. Oh, she distrusted her lovers! Baby too distrusted them.

An actor is instinct.

But for instinct there is no actor.

Norma Jeane was trying to remember a vivid disturbing dream she'd had just before waking that morning. She'd been holding Baby against her swollen aching breasts wanting to nurse him but someone appeared and yanked at him. . . . Norma Jeane had cried *no! no!* and still the hands tugged at Baby and she'd been able to escape only by forcing herself awake.

"Norma Jeane," the woman realtor said politely, "is something wrong? I thought I'd take you through here. . . ." Norma Jeane was shielding her eyes from so many damned mirrors! There were oval mirrors, rectangular mirrors, tall vertical mirrors, mirror panels on nearly every wall in this house. One of the downstairs bathrooms was floor-to-ceiling mirrors edged with zinc! Every room you stepped into, there was your reflection stepping in and your face looming like a balloon, eyes snatching at eyes. This is what the girl in Mayer's mirror has come to! In the crimson turban and dark glasses Norma Jeane looked like a busty-leggy girl extra in *Road to Rio*, one Bob Hope would leer at. Norma Jeane was thinking that the point of her Magic Friend was she'd been secret. If you live with your Magic Friend continuously, the specialness is lost.

Cass might have read her thoughts; he said they'd take most of the mirrors down if that was what Norma Jeane wanted. "The Gemini can live without mirrors because we 'mirror' each other, right?"

"Cass, I don't know. I want to go home."

She loved him, and she didn't trust him. She didn't trust either of the men she loved. One of them was Baby's father, or was it possible both had fathered Baby? Today wasn't the first time they'd brought up the subject of insurance policies, and now they were suggesting wills too. Did they expect her to die, in childbirth maybe? Were they hoping for her to die? (But they loved her. She knew!) If only she had Mr. Shinn to consult. Maybe: the Ex-Athlete who wanted to "date" her?

The night before, Norma Jeane had told Cass about the famous ex-baseball player wanting to meet her, and Cass seemed more impressed than Norma Jeane herself had been, saying the Ex-Athlete was a hero to many Americans as much or maybe more than any movie star, so maybe Norma Jeane should meet him. Norma Jeane protested, saying she didn't know the first thing about baseball and didn't care about it and anyway she was pregnant—"He wants to 'date' me, he says! We know what that means." "You can play hard to get. Hard to get into. Great role for Marilyn." "He's famous. He must be rich." "Marilyn's famous. She's not rich." "Oh, but I'm not—famous like him. *He* had a long career before he retired. Everyone loves him." "So why not you?" Norma Jeane had glanced anxiously at Cass to see if he was jealous, but he didn't seem to be. Yet Cass, unlike Eddy G, was hard to read.

Norma Jeane hadn't told Cass that she'd turned down the famous Ex-Athlete. Not in person, for the man hadn't called her personally, but through a third party who'd contacted her agent. What nerve! As if "Marilyn Monroe" was merchandise. You saw the billboard, you made a call and an offer. What was Marilyn's price?

On the second floor of The Cypresses, in the older, French Normandy section of the house, the undulating brass and crystal chandeliers were more evident. A sickly, sinister golden light rayed through windows as if from a source other than the sun. There was an odor of stopped-up drains, insecticide, and stale perfume. And the incessant wind. . . . Norma Jeane imagined she could hear voices, children's muffled laughter. It had to be the wind, rattling windowpanes or chandeliers. She noticed Cass glancing irritably about; he must have been hearing this sound too. He'd been sick that morning, with a hangover, an alarming *not-thereness* in his eyes when Norma Jeane stole a glance at him. While Theda Bara was explaining the house's complicated intercom system, Cass stood rubbing his eyes and working his mouth as if something was caught inside he couldn't swallow. Norma Jeane tried to slip an arm around him but he nudged her aside, embarrassed. "*I'm* not your baby. Lay off."

Why did we come to this terrible place? It was not a vision we sought.

Theda Bara spent some time describing the property's complicated burglar alarm, floodlight, and surveillance system. Evidently it had cost nearly a million dollars to install. The previous owner, she said, had had an "extreme fear" of someone breaking into the house and murdering her.

"Just like my mother," Eddy G said morosely. "That's the first symptom. But it isn't the last."

Norma Jeane tried to lighten the mood. "Why'd anybody want to murder *me*? I always ask. Because, y'know—who's that important?"

Theda Bara said with a cool smile, "Lots of people in this part of the world are important enough to murder. And even more are wealthy."

Norma Jeane felt this as a rebuff, though she didn't understand it. She wondered, with a smile: What would the famous Ex-Athlete think if he knew she was pregnant? And in love with not one handsome sexy young man but two?

Maybe I was a tramp. Gee, there was plenty of proof!

It was then the strange things began. While Eddy G was asking the realtor questions. Norma Jeane wasn't listening much, and Cass had all but dropped out, ashy-skinned, itchy. Working his mouth as if trying to swallow. The air was so dry, it was like sand accumulated in your mouth. Norma Jeane wanted to hold Cass in her arms, kiss and comfort him. In a corner of her eye suddenly there was a scuttling-scurrying movement. A shadow in flight. Across one of the mirrors? Neither Theda Bara nor Eddy G noticed, but Cass turned to stare in terror. Yet there seemed to be nothing. When Theda Bara showed them still another bedroom, behind a brocaded drape there seemed to be something moving, agitated. "Oh!—look." Norma Jeane spoke without thinking. Theda Bara said uncertainly, "It's—nothing, I'm sure." Bravely the realtor would have strode over to see, but Cass held her back. "No. Fuck it; just shut the *door*."

They left, and the door was shut.

Norma Jeane and Eddy G exchanged a worried glance. What was wrong with Cass? Of the threesome, Cass Chaplin had to be the one in control.

Norma Jeane had been hearing muffled soprano voices, children's cries and laughter, yet of course it was the wind, only the wind, only her fevered imagination, and when Theda Bara led them into the nursery Norma Jeane saw with relief that it was empty; except for the murmurous wind, it was silent. *Why am I so silly? Nobody would have killed a child here.* "What a b-beautiful room!" Norma Jeane felt she must say. But the nursery wasn't beautiful, only just large. And long. Most of the outer wall was foggy plate glass, looking into empty space as into eternity; the other walls had been painted flamingo pink and decorated with cartoon figures the size of human adults. These were both quaint old-fashioned Mother Goose creatures and American-cartoon creatures: Mickey Mouse, Donald Duck, Bugs Bunny, Goofy. The flat blank eyes. The happy-human grins. The white-gloved hands instead of animal paws. But why so *large*? Norma Jeane stood eye-to-eye with Goofy, and it was Norma Jeane who backed down. She said, making a joke of it, "This character a sweater girl isn't going to impress."

As sometimes at parties, smashed out of his mind as his drinker-druggie friends fondly described him, Cass Chaplin began to expostulate—on Thomistic philosophy, or geological fault lines in Los Angeles County, or the "secret lynching heart" of America that wasn't, in Cass's view, imported to the New World from the Old but had in fact awaited the American Puritans when they came to settle here in the wilderness—now, abruptly, like a sleepwalker awaking from a trance, Cass began to speak of animal figures in children's books and in movies. "Jesus! It would be terrifying if animals could talk. If in fact they were ourselves. Yet in the children's world that's always the case. Why?"

Norma Jeane surprised him by saying, "That's because animals are human! They can't talk the way we do but they communicate, sure they do. They have emotions like us—pain, hope, fear, love. A mother animal—"

Eddy G interrupted. "Not cartoon animals, sweetheart. They never have litters."

Cass said, with surprising rancor, "Our Norma loves animals. That's because she doesn't know any. She imagines they would love her back without qualification."

Norma Jeane said, hurt, "Hey, don't talk about me like I'm not here. And don't condescend to me."

The men laughed. Possibly they were proud of her, flaring up like this, even removing her sunglasses like Bette Davis or Joan Crawford in a melodrama, confronting her betrayers. "Norma says 'Don't condescend.' " "Even Fishie has her pride." "*Especially* Fishie has her pride." Theda Bara was looking from one to the other to the third, her bee-stung lips parted in amazement. What was going on here? Who were these reckless young people?

Deliberate as a stab in the heart. A stab in the belly.

She. Norma Jeane was *she.* Never could she be anything except *she.* The third point of Gemini. That distant third point of the eternal triangle which Cass had described as Death. Norma Jeane was made to realize that it would never make any difference to the men—how much she loved them, how she would sacrifice for them, how celebrated she would be by strangers, and how talented an actress—always she was *she.* She was their Fishie, she was Fish.

The men's laughter subsided. Except for the wind it was very quiet.

They would have left the ghastly pink nursery, Theda Bara was clearing her throat to say a few final upbeat words, when there came a sudden slithering sound. Close by their feet, partly hidden by a playpen, there was a rushing shadow. "Rattlesnake!" the realtor cried.

Panicked, Eddy G climbed onto a table. It was a plastic-topped picnic table on a little island of fake grass and miniature palm trees. He grabbed Norma Jeane's arm and lifted her up beside him, and he helped Theda Bara and poor trembling Cass, who'd gone dead-white in the face, four adults panting and cringing.

"The snake! It's the same one," Cass said. His ravaged boy-doll face was covered in sweat and his eyes were dilated. 'It's my fault. I'm to blame. I shouldn't have brought us here."

Norma Jeane said, meaning to be practical because Cass was making no sense, "Would a rattlesnake really *attack*? A human being? They're supposed to be more scared of us."

Theda Bara was moaning "Oh oh *oh*" as if about to faint; Eddy G had to hold her up. "Ma'am, it's gonna be all right. I don't actually see the fucker. Anybody see the fucker?"

Norma Jeane said, "*I* never did see any snake. But I heard him, I think."

Cass said, hunched and trembling, "It's my fault. These things. I started seeing them in bathrooms, in toilets, and I can't stop. It's only because of me they're here."

It seemed to be so; there was no snake in the nursery. Norma Jeane and Eddy G helped comfort Theda Bara, who'd had a terrible fright and wanted now only to leave The Cypresses, and Cass, who'd drifted into a kind of fugue state, like a man in shock, his eyes open and dilated and unfocused. He spoke incoherently, repentantly. It was his fault, he brought these things with him everywhere, they would kill him finally, and there was nothing to be done. Norma Jeane wanted to take Cass into a bathroom and wash his face in cold water but Eddy G advised no, there wouldn't be any water, and if there was it'd be rust water and warm as blood—"That'd spook him all the more. Let's just get him home."

Norma Jeane asked, "Did you know about this, Eddy? These 'things' of his?"

Evasively Eddy G said, "I wasn't sure whose they were, y'know? His or mine."

Driving back into the city, a sobered Eddy G at the wheel and Norma Jeane beside him shaken and scared, pressing the palms of both hands against Baby to comfort him, and Cass, his shirt torn open so he could breathe, lying shivering and whimpering in the back seat. Norma Jeane said in an undertone to Eddy G, "Oh, God. We should take him to a doctor. It's d.t.'s, isn't it? The Cedars of Lebanon. The emergency room." Eddy G shook his head. Norma Jeane said, pleading, "We can't just pretend he isn't sick, like there's nothing wrong with him." Eddy G said, "Why not?"

Once they were off curvy Laurel Canyon Drive and on the Boulevard, and back on Sunset, Cass surprised them by sitting up, sighing and blowing his cheeks, and laughing, embarrassed. "Jesus. Sorry. I don't remember what all that was but don't fill me in, OK?" He squeezed the nape of Eddy G's neck, and he squeezed the nape of Norma Jeane's neck. His touch was icy but comforting. Both Eddy G and Norma Jeane shivered with a weird quick kind of desire. "What I think it is, y'know?—sympathetic pregnancy. Norma's so healthy and sane about this, one of the Gemini's gotta crack up? I don't mind, for the duration, it's *me*."

This was so convincing, and so like a strange kind of poem, what could you do but believe?

That dream. The beautiful blond woman crouched before her, impatiently tugging at her hands. The blond woman so beautiful you couldn't see her face. You shrank from seeing her face. She'd stepped out of a mirror. Her legs were scissors, her eyes were fire. Her hair lifted in pale undulating tendrils. *Give it to me! You sad, sick cow.* She was trying to yank the crying infant from Norma Jeane's weakening hands. *No. This isn't the right time. This is my time. You can't deny me!*

"Where Do You
Go When You
Disappear?"

Life and dreams are leaves of the same book.

—Arthur Schopenhauer

There came the morning when she knew what she would do.

It was a morning after The Cypresses, and it was a morning after Lakewood.

A morning after a long night of turbulent dreams like boulders rolling over her soft helpless body.

She called Z, to whom she hadn't spoken since the night of the premiere. She told him what the situation was. She began to cry. Maybe the crying had been rehearsed, Z would think, but possibly not. Z listened in silence. She might've figured this was a shocked silence but in fact it was a practical silence, Z having been in this position, heard these words, a well-worn script by an anonymous screenwriter, many times. "What I'll do, Marilyn, is turn you over to Yvet." The name was pronounced "Ee-vay." It was not a name Norma Jeane had ever encountered before. "You know Yvet. She'll help you."

Yvet was Z's secretary-assistant. Norma Jeane remembered her from the shameful morning of the Aviary. How many years ago! Before, even, Norma Jeane had been *named*. In a time of innocence so distant to her now she could not recall the girl she'd been and even the stark stuffed birds of the Aviary seemed to her but provisional, not that she hadn't seen them, witnessed them, heard their cries of pain and terror, but rather that the experience had happened to someone else, or had happened in a movie that Cass Chaplin might identify: something by D. W. Griffith?

Yvet averting her eyes, that gaze of pity and contempt. *There's a powder room just outside.*

Yvet came on the line, and the woman was sympathetic and matter-of-fact and older-sounding than Norma Jeane would have guessed. Calling her "Marilyn." Well, why not? At The Studio, she was Marilyn. In film credits, she was Marilyn. In the world so shimmering-vast it might be eternity, she was Marilyn. Yvet was saying, "Marilyn? I'll make the arrangements. And I'll accompany you. Plan for tomorrow morning, eight A.M. I'll pick you up at home. We'll just be driving a few miles outside Wilshire. It's a clinic, it's nothing back-street or dangerous. He's a revered physician. He's got a nurse. You won't have to stay long. But, if you want to, you can stay all day. Sleeping, resting. They'll dope you up. You won't feel, well—you won't feel *nothing*, sure you'll feel *something*. When the drug wears off. But it's just physical, and it goes away, and then you'll feel just fine. Trust me. You're still on the line, Marilyn?"

"Y-yes."

"I'll be there to pick you up, tomorrow morning, eight A.M. Unless you hear otherwise."

She didn't hear otherwise.

THE EX-ATHLETE AND
THE BLOND ACTRESS:
THE DATE

**When you believe you are acting, you will suddenly
discover your truest self.**

—From *The Paradox of Acting*

The Ex-Athlete took the Blond Actress on their first date to Villars Steakhouse in Beverly Hills.

They dined there from 8:10 P.M. until 11 P.M.

A shimmering luminous light hovered about their table.

The glamorous couple was observed through mirrors by discreet diners
who, at Villars, one of the most exclusive restaurants in Beverly Hills, would
not have wished to stare. It was perceived that the Ex-Athlete, known for his
taciturnity as well as for his remarkable baseball skills, spoke relatively
little at the start but communicated with looks. His gaze was smoldering: Ital-
ian-dark. His horsey-handsome face was clean-shaven, youthful for his age.
His near-black hair, receding at the temples, was perceived through mirrors
to be thick, untouched by gray. Like a lawyer or a banker he wore a navy blue
pin-striped suit, starched white shirt, and highly polished black leather shoes.
His necktie was a rich royal blue silk embossed with miniature figures of baseball bats in eggshell-white. When the Ex-Athlete addressed a waiter, giving orders for his companion and himself, he was heard to speak in an oddly
measured voice. *She will have* . . . *and I will have*. . . . *She will have* . . . *and I
will have*. . . . *She will have* and *I will have*. . . . The Blond Actress was very
beautiful but nervous. Like an ingenue in her first stage performance. At times

during the evening her agitation was such, her mirrored reflection became blurred as if by mist or steam, and we couldn't see her. Sometimes she vanished altogether! At other times, when she laughed, her red-glossy mouth glared, and that was all we could see. *Mouth like a cunt. That's her secret. She's too dumb to know?* To some observers at Villars, the Blond Actress looked "exactly like" her photographs; to others, the Blond Actress looked "nothing like" her photographs. The Blond Actress was wearing, and this must've been a calculated surprise, not her trademark plunging-neckline stark red or stark white or stark black but a pastel pink silk-and-wool cocktail dress with a girlish pleated skirt and a pearl-beaded bodice and a high tight neckline at which she tugged unconsciously with manicured fingernails. Above her left breast was pinned a creamy-white gardenia like a prom corsage which frequently, with a shy little smile at the Ex-Athlete, she sniffed.

So sweet! Thank you so much! Gardenias are my favorite flower.

The Ex-Athlete's face darkened pleasurably with blood. He seemed about to speak but did not. He smiled, he frowned. There was a mild tic in his left eye. Light emanating from the couple's table was dappled and undulating like reflected water. The Ex-Athlete was thrilled by the Blond Actress's beauty, or intimidated by it. In the eyes of some observers, the Ex-Athlete was already resentful of the Blond Actress's beauty, and from time to time glanced irritably about the candlelit murmurous restaurant as if he sensed us watching, though at such moments all our eyes were averted.

Except: the Sharpshooter in civilian clothes, lounging at the rear of the restaurant in a shadowy alcove between the bright bustling kitchen and the manager's office, never once averted his eyes or slackened in his interest. For to the Sharpshooter this was hardly a mere diversion but a crucial episode in a narrative to which he, as a mere agent, in the hire of an Agency, could neither give a name nor would wish to.

The Ex-Athlete was only just falling in love! All that lay in the future.

No. The future is now. All that's to come springs out of NOW.

This was a fact. Several times, shyly yet boldly, with the air of a man stealing a base, the Ex-Athlete let his hand fall onto the Blond Actress's.

An electric ripple through the candlelit murmurous interior.

It was observed that the Ex-Athlete's hand was "twice as large" as the Blond Actress's hand.

It was observed that the Ex-Athlete wore no rings, nor did the Blond Actress wear any rings.

It was observed that the Ex-Athlete's hand was darkly tanned and the Blond Actress's hand was feminine-pale and "lotion soft."

The Ex-Athlete began to relax to a degree. He was drinking scotch, and at dinner he was drinking red wine. The Ex-Athlete was encouraged by the Blond Actress to talk of himself. He told a sequence of baseball anecdotes, which perhaps he'd told before. But each telling of a fond familiar anecdote to a different audience is in fact a different anecdote; in the telling, we become different people. The Blond Actress appeared to be thrilled. She was listening attentively, only sipping at her drink, a fizzy fruity prom-girl drink in a tall frosted glass with a straw; she was leaning her elbows on the edge of the table, aiming her magnificent body at the Ex-Athlete. Often, she widened her blue-blue eyes.

Don't laugh, I used to love softball! In high school sometimes I played with the boys when they'd let me.

What was your position?

I guess—batter? When they let me.

The Ex-Athlete had two distinct laughs, a quiet restrained chuckle and an explosive belly laugh. The first was accompanied by a wincing look; the other, taking him by surprise, was sheer hilarity. The Blond Actress was delighted with this outburst of laughter from one so darkly taciturn. *Oh!— my daddy used to laugh just like that. Daddy brought the gift of laughter into every life he touched.*

The Ex-Athlete did not inquire after "Daddy." Enough to know, with an expression of sympathy and regret and an inner feeling of satisfaction, that the Blond Actress's father was dead and out of the way.

As the Blond Actress often faded from view, or rather was obscured from our sight by an aura of shimmering light, so too her laughter was uncertainly perceived. To some attentive observers it was "high-pitched like tinkling glass, pretty but nervous." To others it was "sharp, like fingernails scraping on a blackboard." Yet to others it was a "choked sad little squeak like a mouse being murdered." While to others it was "throaty, husky, a sexual moan."

Graceful in his baseball uniform, the Ex-Athlete was awkward in civilian clothes. By midevening he'd unbuttoned his coat. The expensive custom-tailored pin-striped suit fitted him tightly about the shoulders; maybe since retirement he'd gained ten to fifteen pounds in the torso and around the waist? The Blond Actress was perceived to be awkward too. Where in her films "Marilyn Monroe" was a fluid magical presence on the screen, like music, inimitable and unmistakable, in what's called "real life" (if an evening at Villars Steakhouse in the company of the most famous ex-baseball player of the era might be designated "real life") she was a girl child squeezed into the body of a fully mature female. The weight of her large breasts tugged her forward so that she was continually forced to lean back; the strain on her upper spine must have been considerable. And was she wearing a bra? *It sure looked like she wasn't.*

Or panties either. But a garter belt, and sheer stockings with sexy dark seams.

The Ex-Athlete "wolfed" his food. The Blond Actress "picked at" hers.

The Ex-Athlete had a twelve-ounce sirloin steak with sautéed onions, oven-roasted potatoes, and green beans. Except for the green beans he cleaned his plate. He ate much of a loaf of crusty French bread smeared with butter. For dessert, chocolate pecan pie with ice cream. The Blond Actress had fillet of sole in a light wine sauce, new potatoes, and asparagus. For dessert, poached pear. Often she raised her fork to her lips, then lowered it, as she listened with tremulous attention to the Ex-Athlete recounting one of his anecdotes.

In *The Paradox of Acting* she'd read:

All actors are whores.
They want only one thing: to seduce you.

She thought *If I am a whore, that explains me!*

Eagerly the Blond Actress smiled at the Ex-Athlete's anecdotes. She laughed as frequently as the occasion merited. By degrees, the Ex-Athlete shifted his chair closer to hers. His yearning body closer to hers. Midway in his enormous juicy steak he excused himself to use the men's room. He returned and shifted his chair closer to his companion's. It was noted, as the Ex-Athlete passed through the candlelit interior of the restaurant, that he smelled of a strong cologne, of whisky and tobacco. His hair smelled of an oily lotion. His breath smelled of meat. He was a cigar aficionado: Cuban cigars. There was one in its cellophane wrapper in his coat pocket. His gold cuff links were in the shape of baseballs and, like the silk necktie, were a gift from an admirer. When you're a sports celebrity, all the world is an admirer. Yet this evening, the Ex-Athlete was slightly off his stride. He smiled strangely, and he frowned. His forehead creased with emotion. Blood throbbed in both his temples. He was standing at the batter's plate forced to stare into a wicked sun. It was scaring the shit out of him, falling in love with this "Marilyn Monroe." So fast! And the memory of an ugly divorce still clattering in his head like bowling pins struck by a vicious ball.

The Ex-Athlete was a gentleman with women who deserved it. Like all Italian men. With women who'd demonstrated they didn't deserve it, like his bitch of an ex-wife, you couldn't blame him for losing control sometimes.

With a bitter twist of his mouth, the Ex-Athlete spoke quickly of his early brief marriage, his divorce, his ten-year-old son. Immediately the Blond Actress inquired after the son, whom clearly the Ex-Athlete adored in that sentimental, furious way of divorced dads who have been denied custody of their children and can see them only at court-appointed times.

Shrewdly, the Blond Actress made no inquiry after the ex-wife. Thinking *If he hates her he'll hate the next woman. Am I the next woman?*

The aura of light glowed, pulsed, nearly obscured the couple.

The Ex-Athlete asked the Blond Actress how she'd gotten her start.

The Blond Actress seemed puzzled. *What start?*

In movies. Acting.

The Blond Actress tried to smile. Strange and unnerving, she'd become in that instant an actress with no script.

I don't know. I guess—I was "discovered."

Discovered how?

She smiled a wincing sort of smile. A companion more sensitive than the Ex-Athlete would not have pursued this line of questioning.

The Blond Actress said, slowly at first, haltingly, then with more certainty, *I acted in high school. I was Emily in "Our Town" and a talent scout saw me. We had a wonderful drama coach at Van Nuys; he gave me faith in myself. He taught me to believe in myself.* Before the Ex-Athlete could ask another question, she said, in a breathy-fluttery way, that she was in rehearsal now for her first musical comedy, a big-budget studio production of *Gentlemen Prefer Blondes.* Oh, she was frightened!—the eyes of the world would be upon her. She was being trained carefully, dancing, singing. She was in the hands of a brilliant choreographer. She was thrilled to be involved in such a glamorous production. *I've always loved music. Dancing. Lifting people's hearts? Just wanting to make people feel happy about life, and want to live. Sometimes I think God made me a pretty girl and not, oh— a scientist?—a philosopher?—for that reason alone.*

The Ex-Athlete was staring at the Blond Actress. If there was a script between them, the Ex-Athlete had no lines. It would have been only a slight exaggeration to say he was struck dumb.

Now the Blond Actress ruefully complained, with a pouty pursing of her lips, of her tender aching feet and leg muscles, what with dance re-hearsals six days a week from ten in the morning till six in the evening. In an impulsive childlike gesture she stretched out a shapely leg and hitched her skirt up to the knee, caressing the calf. *It keeps cramping on me. Oh!*

Every eye in Villars noted how the Ex-Athlete's hand moved like a wounded animal, blundering, to touch with just the fingertips the Blond Actress's leg. How the Ex-Athlete murmured in tender confusion *It's a pulled tendon maybe. You need a massage.*

Like touching a hot stove, that skin of hers! Through the sheer nylon stocking.

With shaky fingers the Ex-Athlete lit a cigar. A white-clad waiter appeared to haul away their dirtied plates. The Ex-Athlete, emboldened by alcohol, began to speak of being retired *from the game*. What it meant to him. In his late thirties. Attentive as before, the Blond Actress listened. She was more at ease listening than speaking; when you listen, you don't need to improvise. She sat leaning forward on her elbows, her breasts predominant in the pearl-beaded pink bodice, rising and falling with the urgency of her breath, both her legs primly returned beneath the table.

The Ex-Athlete, exhaling smoke, told of his love of baseball ever since he was a boy; how baseball had been his salvation, a kind of religion to him, his team a close-knit family and the fans, too. The fans! The fans were fickle but wonderful. And how baseball had returned his own family to him, the respect of his father and his older brothers. Because he had not had this respect before he'd excelled in baseball. He hadn't been truly *a man*, in their eyes or in his own. They were commercial fishermen in San Francisco and he'd been no good at fishing and he'd hated the boat, the ocean, the dying struggling fish; luckily for him he'd been good at sports and baseball was his ticket up and out. He was one of the winners of the great American lottery, and he knew it, and he was grateful; he never took it for granted. And now—well, he was retired. He was outside the sport but still it was his life, always it would be his life, his identity. He had plenty to do, public appearances and endorsing products and radio and TV and advisory boards, but hell, he was lonely, had to admit he was lonely, lots of friends—and terrific friends they were, in New York especially—but he was lonely in his heart, had to admit it. Almost forty years old and he needed to settle down. This time permanently.

The Blond Actress brushed tears from her eyes. It was the effect of these heartfelt words and of the pungent cigar smoke wafting in her direction. Lightly she touched the Ex-Athlete's wrist. His wrist and the back of his hand were covered in coarse dark hairs that, contrasting with his dazzling-white shirt cuffs and the gold links, made her shiver. Saying, as if this was an adequate response to all he'd confided in her and not knowing what else to say, *Oh but!—you're in the papers so much! You don't seem retired.*

The Ex-Athlete laughed. He was flattered but amused.

Hey, I'm not in the papers as much as you, Marilyn.

That wincing smile again, the Blond Actress ducking her head and unconsciously plucking at the tight neck of her dress.

Oh, who?—me? That's just studio publicity. Oh, I hate it! And signing these phony pictures of me—"Love, Marilyn." All the letters "Marilyn" gets. A thousand a week—or maybe more? Anyway, it's just for a while till I get some money saved and can do some serious roles like, oh—on the stage? In a real theater? I could work with a real drama coach. I could belong to a repertory theater. I could do Our Town *again and I could do Irina in* The Three Sisters—*or Masha? When I was Rose in* Niagara, *y'know what I was thinking? Please don't laugh at me, I was thinking I could do Lady Macbeth someday—*

The Blond Actress broke off, seeing the Ex-Athlete wasn't laughing at her but wasn't taking much of this in. His gaze was soft-shimmering and intimate, as if they were lying side by side on pillows. He was sucking on his Cuban cigar.

Contritely the Blond Actress concluded *Anyway, it won't last forever, what I'm doing. But you, a champion athlete everybody loves—you will last forever.*

The Ex-Athlete pondered this. He seemed deeply moved yet uncertain how to respond. He shrugged his muscled shoulders. *OK* he said. *Yeah, I guess.*

It was an improvised scene in acting class. You understood instinctively that it needed something more, a dramatic turn, a kind of closure. The Blond Actress said, with a passionate intake of breath, *Oh, but mostly I w-want— to settle down, like you. Like any girl. And have a family. Oh, I love children so! I'm crazy about babies.*

It was then, out of nowhere as out of a trapdoor opening in a silent film, the individual identified as M. Classen, forty-three, rancher, of Eagle Bluffs, Utah, approached the couple's table. All observers stared. The Sharpshooter at the rear of the restaurant stared, senses acute as a whetted straight razor. What was this? Who was this? Looming over the Ex-Athlete and the Blond Actress, who in their total surprise simply blinked up at him, M. Classen had opened his wallet to show them a color snapshot of his eleven-year-old son Ike, a smiling freckled boy with chestnut hair who'd been a "natural-born ballplayer" until eighteen months ago he'd begun to lose weight, and bruised easily, and was always tired, and they took him to a doctor in Salt Lake City and he was diagnosed with leukemia—"That's blood cancer. From the U.S. Government nuclear testing! We know it! Everybody knows it! The way our sheep and cattle are poisoned too. At the edge of my property there's a testing range—OFF LIMITS BY ORDER OF U.S. GOVERNMENT. I own six thousand acres, I have my rights. The U.S. Government won't pay for Ike's blood transfusions; the bastards refuse even to acknowledge they got any responsibility. I'm no Commie! I'm one hundred percent American! I served in the U.S. Army in the last war! Please if you two could put in a word for me with the U.S. Government—" As suddenly as M. Classen appeared, he was hurried away. No sooner had the improbable scene come into lurid focus in the luminous aura surrounding the couple's table than it had ended. Shortly afterward the flush-faced maître d' returned to apologize profusely.

Unexpectedly, the Blond Actress hid her face, crying. Tears sparkling like jewels ran down her cheeks. The Ex-Athlete stared at her, stricken and confused. We could see how he wanted to seize the Blond Actress's hands in his and comfort her, but shyness restrained him. (And the stares of myriad strangers! Most of us had ceased troubling to watch through mirrors and were now watching quite openly the drama at the celebrity couple's table.) The Ex-Athlete's horsey-handsome face darkened with blood. He was help-less and angry. As the bumbling maître d' continued to apologize, the Ex-Athlete cut him off with a muttered obscenity.

No! Oh, p-please! It's nobody's fault. The Blond Actress pleaded with the Ex-Athlete, still crying, a tissue held to her eyes, and excused herself to use the ladies' room. What a scene: as she made her urgent yet sleepwalking way through the restaurant, escorted by the shaken maître d', the floating plat-inum-blond hair, the soft-sculpted female shape inside the clinging jersey dress with a multitude of shivery pleats, every eye in the restaurant fixed upon her rear, the remarkable movements of her lower body, as in a long tracking scene in which the camera follows, at a discreet distance, the yearn-ing eye of an invisible and anonymous voyeur. It seemed to all who stared, including even the experienced Sharpshooter, to whom movie stars and champion athletes were of no more intrinsic significance than bull's-eyes at target ranges, that the mysterious aura hovering about the couple's table now followed the Blond Actress until, nearly running into the ladies' room, she disappeared from our scrutiny.

There, the Blond Actress dabbed at her tearful eyes with a tissue and repaired the damage done to her mascara. Her face burned as if she'd been slapped. Such an awkward scene! When you aren't prepared to cry, crying *hurts*. And this collar cutting into her throat like a man's squeezing fingers *like Cass's fingers if ever he could get hold of her*. She was sniffing, and she was excited, and she became aware of the powder room attendant observing her, roused from the trance of such attendants by the Blond Actress's emotional state. The attendant was a few years older than the Blond Actress, with an olive-dark skin. With a slight speech impediment she asked, "Miss? You are all right?" The Blond Actress assured her yes, yes! In her agitated state the Blond Actress didn't care to be closely observed. She fumbled for her white beaded purse. She needed another tissue, which the attendant discreetly handed her. "Thank you!" The powder room interior was a fair flattering pink threaded with gold. Lighting was recessed and gentle. Through the mirror the Blond Actress saw the attendant's eyes upon her, that low-browed face, black hair skinned back and fastened at the nape of her neck, skimpy eyebrows and a receding chin and a small pursed smile. *You're beautiful and I'm homely and I hate you.* But no, the young woman seemed genuinely concerned. "Miss? Please, is there anything I can do?" The Blond Actress was staring at the attendant in the mirror. Was this young woman someone she should know? The Blond Actress had had too much to drink, champagne went immediately to her head and made her want to cry, or laugh; champagne had too many associations yet she couldn't resist drinking it, or red wine either, and the proximity of the Ex-Athlete all evening was even more disorienting, for here was a man whose celebrity eclipsed hers and could shelter her from hers. Here was a man who was a gentleman, and did anything else truly matter?

It was then that the Blond Actress realized she knew the olive-skinned attendant. Jewell! One of Norma Jeane's sister orphans at the Home, fifteen years ago. Jewell with her funny way of talking the crueler boys mocked. And Fleece, whom Jewell adored, sometimes mocked. Jewell was staring at the Blond Actress through the mirror *You belong here with me, this is your rightful place.* The Blond Actress was about to exclaim, with a smile, Oh, is it—Jewell? Don't we know each other?

Except a voice cautioned *No. Better not.*

Another woman entered the powder room, glamorously dressed. Quickly the Blond Actress went into one of the toilet stalls. To cover the tinkling sound of her pee, which since the Operation (as she thought of it) was hot, stinging, painful, she flushed the toilet once, and another time. So embarrassing! She wondered if Jewell recognized her; if in recognizing "Marilyn Monroe," Jewell recognized *her.* For the one was inside the other, playing the role invented for her.

Cass said to her over the phone, after he'd learned of the abortion, *Don't be blaming her! It's all you.*

When the Blond Actress returned to the sinks to wash her hands, the other woman had stepped into one of the stalls, thank God. Since there was no towel dispenser, the Blond Actress had to wait for the attendant to give her a hand towel; she thanked the young woman and dropped a fifty-cent coin into a bowl of coins and bills on a shelf. When she turned to leave, still the attendant said sharply, "Excuse me, miss?" The Blond Actress smiled at her, perplexed. Had she forgotten something? But she was clutching her beaded little purse. "Yes? What?" The attendant smiled strangely. She was holding out something to the Blond Actress in one of the hand towels. The Blond Actress squinted into it and saw a red mangled glob of flesh, about the size of a pear. It glistened with fresh blood. It appeared to be motionless. It had no lower body, only a miniature human torso; no face, but rudimentary eyes, a nose, and a tiny anguished crack of a mouth.

"Miss Monroe? You forgot this."

The Ex-Athlete had taken out his shiny new leather wallet and slapped it down on the table. Veins at his temples were pounding ominously. A beautiful woman crying, if her tears weren't in reproach of him, just melted his heart.

"Für Elise"

Always you must play yourself. But it will be an infinite variety.

—Stanislavski,
An Actor Prepares

It could not have been chance. For in that place in which she would dwell intermittently for the remainder of her blond life, there is no chance. *There I discovered all is necessity, like the barbs of quills that anchor flesh even as they lacerate it.*

"Für Elise"—that beautiful haunting melody.

"Für Elise"—that she'd once played, or tried to play. On Gladys's gleaming white piano that had once belonged to Fredric March. In the days of Highland Avenue, Hollywood. Gladys had sacrificed to make sure Norma Jeane had piano lessons and voice lessons, knowing someday Norma Jeane would be a performer. *Always, she'd had faith in me. And I knew so little.* There was her piano teacher Mr. Pearce whom she'd adored and feared lifting and firmly guiding her fingers along the keyboard.

"Norma Jeane. Don't be silly. *Try.*"

She was alone when she heard the music. Dreamily ascending an escalator in Bullock's, Beverly Hills. It must have been a Monday: no rehearsals at The Studio. She wasn't in disguise as Lorelei Lee ("The Role for Which Marilyn Monroe Was Born!") but as a Beverly Hills woman shopper. No one recognized her, she was certain. She'd come to Bullock's to buy presents for her makeup man, Whitey, who was such a character and made her laugh; and for Yvet, Mr. Z's assistant, who'd been so kind to her and so patient with her and would keep her secret for her; and a pretty nightgown for Gladys that she'd have delivered to the Lakewood Home with a card *Love, Your Daughter Norma Jeane*. She was wearing sunglasses so darkly tinted she had difficulty seeing price tags, and a sand-colored linen jacket that fitted her loosely, and linen slacks. Sailcloth cork-soled shoes to comfort her hurt, aching feet. Over her floating filmy-blond hair still slightly matted from sleep she'd tied an aqua scarf, very likely a gift to her or an appropriation by her. For in this phase of her life people were always pressing things upon her, items of clothing, even jewelry and heirlooms, if out of politeness or her habitual need to say something to forestall intimate questions she expressed the mildest admiration of these things.

Marilyn, try it on! Why, it's lovely on you! Please keep it, I insist.

On the escalator to the second floor of Bullock's, she began to hear the piano music without knowing what it was. For her own head was filled like a manic jukebox with quick-tempo musical-comedy sound, stridently syncopated dance music. Boisterous, vulgar. But this was classical music wafting downward from a higher floor. Not a tape or a recording, she was sure, but live music: a live pianist? He was playing Beethoven's "Für Elise"! Piercing her heart like a sliver of the purest glass.

"Für Elise," which Clive Pearce had played for Norma Jeane slowly, gently, sadly on the magical white piano before taking her away to the orphanage.

Her Uncle Clive. "One last time, my dear. Will you forgive me?"

She would! She did.

A hundred, a thousand times she forgave them all.

Actually, Marilyn Monroe is nothing like her pictures. She's younger-looking, pretty, and sweet-faced. Not a beauty. We saw her at Bullock's the other day, shopping. She looked like everyone else. Almost.

Like one under enchantment she followed the strains of "Für Elise" to the topmost fifth floor. She was so filled with emotion she couldn't have said why she was here, in this store; in fact, she hated shopping; being in public made her anxious; even if she was in disguise there was the possibility of shrewd, knowing eyes piercing that disguise for *this was a time of informants, witnesses.* (Even V, who'd been so popular a wartime star and who was one-hundred-percent patriotic, had recently been interrogated by a California state committee investigating Communists and subversives in the entertainment industry. Oh, if V gave them her name! Had she ever said anything to him in defense of communism? But V wouldn't betray her, would he? After what they'd meant to each other?) Yet the piano music drew her, she couldn't resist. Her eyes were welling with tears. She was so happy! In her life and in her career things were going well and she would think of the future and not the past and they'd given her the large dressing room at The Studio that had once belonged to Marlene Dietrich and of this alone she couldn't allow herself to think for such thoughts made her excitable and anxious. For she'd become insomniac again. Unless she worked, worked, worked, exercised and danced, and read and wrote in her journal until she was exhausted.

But they forbid her to try on clothes at Bullock's. All the good shops. Because she has stained things. She doesn't wear underwear. She isn't clean. She's a Benzedrine junkie, she sweats.

Bullock's fifth floor was its prestige floor. Expensive designer clothes, Fur Salon. Plush dusty-rose carpeting. Even the lighting was ethereal. On this floor, Norma Jeane had modeled clothes for Mr. Shinn and he'd bought her a white cocktail dress for the opening of *The Asphalt Jungle*. How easy her life had been, as Angela! There was no pressure upon "Marilyn Monroe" then; "Marilyn Monroe" had scarcely existed three years ago. I. E. Shinn alone had had faith in her. "My Is-aac. My Jew." Yet she'd betrayed him. She'd caused him to die of a broken heart. There were people in Hollywood, Mr. Shinn's close relatives, who despised her as a conniving whore and yet— what had she done? How was she to blame? "I didn't marry him and accept his money. I can only marry for love."

She'd loved Cass Chaplin and Eddy G, yet in a fevered hour she'd moved out of the apartment she shared with them. The Gemini. There was no future with the Gemini; she'd had to escape. She'd had time to take only essential clothes, her special books. She'd left everything else behind, including even the little striped tiger toy. Yvet had overseen that move, too. And leasing for Norma Jeane another apartment, on Fountain Avenue. (Yvet was acting under Z's direction, of course. For now Z, head of production at The Studio, was a zealous co-conspirator in her life, cordial and sympathetic with her, his million-dollar investment.) And now, too, the Ex-Athlete was claiming he loved her, he'd never loved any woman as he loved her, he wanted to marry her. On their second date already, before even they'd become lovers. Was it possible? A man so famous, so kind and generous and a gentleman, wanted to marry *her*? She'd wanted to confess to him what a bad wife she'd been to poor Bucky Glazer. Yet in her weakness and in her fear that he'd cease to love her she'd heard her girl's voice saying she loved him too and yes she would marry him someday.

Was she going to disappoint this good man, too? Break his heart?

I guess I am a tramp. . . . I don't want to be!

Slowly and cautiously Norma Jeane had been approaching the pianist from the rear. She didn't want to distract him. He was seated at an elegant Steinway grand near the down escalator, an older gentleman in white tie and tails, fingers moving unerringly along the gleaming keyboard. There was no sheet music before him; he played by memory. "It's him! Mr. Pearce!" Of course, Clive Pearce had aged considerably. It had been eighteen years. He was thinner and his hair had turned completely silver; the flesh about his intelligent eyes was crepy and discolored, his once-handsome face a ruin of creases and sagging jowls. Yet how beautifully he was playing piano for mostly indifferent, affluent women shoppers, the haunting sweetness of "Für Elise" ignored amid the chatter of sales clerks and customers. Norma Jeane wanted to shout at these others, How can you be so rude? Here is an artist. *Listen.* But no one on the floor was listening to Clive Pearce at the piano except his former student Norma Jeane, now grown up. She was biting her lip, wiping at her eyes behind the dark-tinted lenses.

Marilyn sure likes piano music! We watched her listening to some old guy playing piano upstairs at Bullock's, maybe she was faking but I don't think so. There were tears in her eyes. You could see she wasn't wearing a bra, her nipples all but poked through this flimsy white fabric.

In Norma Jeane's new, mostly unfurnished apartment on Fountain Avenue she'd placed beside her bed a Pantheon of Great Men whose likenesses she'd clipped from books or magazines. Prominent among these was an artist's interpretation of Beethoven: with powerful forehead, fierce expression, and unruly hair. Beethoven, the musical genius. For whom "Für Elise" was but a bagatelle, a trifle.

Also in the Pantheon were Socrates, Shakespeare, Abraham Lincoln, Vaslav Nijinski, Clark Gable, Albert Schweitzer, and the American playwright who'd recently been awarded a Pulitzer Prize for drama.

After "Für Elise," the pianist played several Chopin preludes, then Hoagy Carmichael's dreamy "Stardust." This, too, could not be mere chance, for the only beautiful song in *Gentlemen Prefer Blondes* was Mr. Carmichael's "When Love Goes Wrong, Nothing Goes Right," which Lorelei Lee sings. Norma Jeane listened reverently. She would miss several appointments that afternoon, including a crucial meeting with her costume designer, and she'd promised the Ex-Athlete, who was in New York, she'd be at home at 4 P.M. to take his call. She was trying to remember if she'd seen Clive Pearce in any films recently. For all the man's talent, he'd dropped off the edge; his contract at The Studio must have been terminated long ago. He was reduced to such engagements! Playing piano in a store. She would help him, if she could. A walk-on in *Gentlemen Prefer Blondes*, or maybe he could play piano? "It's the least I could do. I owe that man so much."

It was the pianist's break. Norma Jeane, clapping enthusiastically, came forward to introduce herself. "Mr. Pearce? Do you remember me? Norma Jeane."

Clive Pearce, rising from the piano bench, stared at her for a long astonished moment.

"Marilyn Monroe? Are you—?"

"I—I am, now. But I was—Norma Jeane. Do you remember? Highland Avenue? Gladys Mortensen? We lived in the same building?"

One of Mr. Pearce's eyelids drooped. There was a network of fine, nearly invisible veins in his sagging cheeks. But he was smiling broadly, blinking as if a blinding light were shining into his face. "Marilyn Monroe. I'm honored."

In his formal attire, white tie and tails and shiny black shoes, Clive Pearce looked like a mannequin come only partway to life. Norma Jeane had reached out warmly to shake hands, as she'd grown confident of doing, for now she was one whose hands people loved to shake and to caress lingeringly, and Mr. Pearce seized both her hands in his, gazing at her in wonderment.

"You *are* Clive Pearce, aren't you?"

"Why, yes. I am. How do you know me?"

"I'm actually Norma Jeane Baker. I should say, Norma Jeane Mortensen. You knew my mother Gladys, Gladys Mortensen?—you were a friend of hers, on Highland Avenue? Around 1935, this was."

Clive Pearce laughed. His breath smelled of copper pennies held too long in a moist hand. "That long ago! Why, you weren't born yet, Miss Monroe."

"I certainly was, Mr. Pearce. I was nine years old. You were my piano teacher." Norma Jeane was trying not to plead. Half consciously she was aware of a small gathering of strangers watching at a discreet distance. "Please, don't you remember me? I was just a little g-girl. You taught me to play 'Für Elise.' "

"A little girl, playing 'Für Elise'? My dear, I doubt it."

Mr. Pearce looked like one who suspects his leg is being pulled.

"My mother was—is—Gladys Mortensen? Don't you remember *her?*"

"Gladys—?"

"You were lovers, I thought. I mean, you loved my m-mother—she was so beautiful, and—"

The silver-haired old gentleman smiled at Norma Jeane and all but winked. *Your mother? A woman? No.* "My dear, you may be confusing me with someone else. One Brit is like another in Tinsel Town."

"We lived in the same apartment building, Mr. Pearce. Eight twenty-eight Highland Avenue, Hollywood. A five-minute walk to the Hollywood Bowl."

"The Hollywood Bowl! Yes, I think I remember the building, a dreadful run-down place teeming with cockroaches. I was only there a short time, thank God."

"My mother wasn't well, she had to be taken away and hospitalized? You were my Uncle Clive. You and Auntie Jessie drove me to the or-or-or-phanage?"

Now Mr. Pearce did become alarmed. His expression was fastidious and grim. "Auntie Jessie? Is some woman claiming she was my *wife*?"

"Oh, no. That was just what I called you. I mean—you wanted me to call you, you and her, but I c-couldn't. Don't you really remember?" Norma Jeane was frankly pleading now. Standing close to the elderly man, who was inches shorter than she recalled, so that the circle of onlookers couldn't hear quite them so well. "You taught me piano on an ivory-colored spinet Steinway, my mother had gotten it from Fredric March—"

At this, Clive Pearce snapped his fingers.

"The spinet! Of course. My dear, I have that piano in my possession."

"You have my m-mother's piano?"

"It's my piano, my dear."

"But—how did you get it?"

"How did I get it? Why, let me think." Clive Pearce frowned and tugged at his lips. His vision narrowed with the effort of remembering. "I believe our landlord took possession of some of your mother's belongings, in default of the money she owed him. Yes, I think that was it. The piano had been slightly damaged in the fire—I seem to recall a fire—and I offered to buy it. I had it repaired and I've had it ever since. A lovely little piano I couldn't bear to part with, ever."

"Not even for a—high price?"

Pursing his lips, Clive Pearce considered this. Smiling then in the way Norma Jeane remembered, the way that had made her shiver, puckish sly not-to-be-trusted Uncle Clive.

"My dear beautiful Marilyn, perhaps I could make a special concession for *you*."

In this magical way Clive Pearce was hired as an extra in *Gentleman Prefer Blondes*, playing piano in the background of a scene set in the luxurious lounge of a transatlantic steamer, and the Steinway spinet once belonging to Fredric March was purchased by Norma Jeane for sixteen hundred dollars, borrowed from the Ex-Athlete.

THE SCREAM.
THE SONG.

You are going to imagine that in the same space you
occupy with your own, real body there exists another
body—the imaginary body of your character, which
you have created in your mind.

—Michael Chekhov,
To the Actor

Not the sleek black Studio car fit for royalty but an ugly humpbacked Nash
of that melancholy hue of dishwater when the soap bubbles have burst and
the chauffeur in uniform and visored cap was a swarthy-skinned creature
part frog and part human, with enormous glassy-shiny eyes from which
she shrank. "Oh, don't look at me! This isn't me." She'd swallowed sand,
her mouth was dry. Or had they stuffed cotton batting into her mouth to
stifle her screams? Trying to explain this to the lipstick-smiling woman with
black-net-gloved hands pushing her into the rear of the Nash that she'd
changed her mind but the woman refused to listen. And the woman's hands
so strong, deft, and practiced. "No. Please. I w-want to go back. This is
a—" A girl's terrified breathy voice. Miss Golden Dreams? The Frog
Chauffeur drove his humped vehicle with commendable swiftness and skill
through the glaring streets of the City of Sand. It was not night, yet so
blinding was the sun you could see no more clearly than if it were night.
"Oh, hey!—I changed my mind, see? My m-mind is my own, to change.
It is!" There were grains of sand not only in her mouth but in her eyes.
The woman with the gloved hands made a face that might be described as
a smile-frown. There was a jolting stop. Norma Jeane was made to realize
that they had traveled through Time. *Any role for the actor is a journey in*

Time. It is your former self from which you depart forever. A sudden curb! A flight of concrete steps! A corridor and a pungent medical-chemical smell like the smell of Bucky Glazer's big-boy hands. Yet the surprise of (as in a movie in which a door is unexpectedly opened, with a surge of movie music) an elegantly furnished interior room. A *waiting room.* The walls were polished wood paneling, the wall hangings were Norman Rockwell reproductions from *The Saturday Evening Post.* There were "modern" chairs with tubular legs. A broad shiny desk and—a human skull? The skull was yellowed, finely cracked as if glazed, unnervingly hollow at the crown (the result of an autopsy? did they saw a circle of bone out of your skull?) and filled with pens, pencils, and the doctor's expensive pipes. This was Doctor's official day off. Doctor would be playing golf later this morning at the Wilshire Country Club with his friend Bing Crosby. Now there were bright lights, she was confusing as *bright lies.* At dawn she'd crawled from her sweaty bed to swallow down one, or two, or three codeine tablets. "Please won't you listen, please I've changed my mind." Yet it was not her mind to change. She told herself to cheer herself. *This light is sterilizing. The danger of germs and infection will be minimal.* (Such curious-comical thoughts often passed fleetingly through her mind on the set. The exaggeration of lights, the intensity of the camera's glassy staring eye, the knowledge that, as filming begins, as your film self emerges, effortless as the wink of an eye; for this duration of time you and your Magic Friend are one, in utter safety and bliss.) Still she was trying to explain she'd made a mistake, she didn't want the Operation; yes, but she was in "good hands"; Mr. Z had promised. A million-dollar investment cannot be risked. It was certain, she was at no risk. If she was "Marilyn Monroe," she would never be at risk if The Studio could prevent it. To assure her, Yvet was humming *These are good hands for curing your blues, these are good hands for shining your shoes. Good hands from mornin' till night.* Seeing they would not listen to her pleas, she next said, in her little-girl sexy comic-breathy Lorelei Lee voice:

Oh say!—know what, you all?—I kinda expect you all to start singing, and dancing?

Doctor did not smile at this remark, but Doctor did smile. He had a mushroom face, a fattish nose with hairs. He called her "My dear" perhaps to assure her he didn't know her name and would never utter her name. So there was that relief, Doctor didn't recognize his famous patient. None of them knew *her.* She was shivering naked, under a flimsy smock. Bucky had never allowed her to see any corpse, yet somehow she'd seen and she knew. The grayish skin, the eyes sunken in their sockets. You poke in the spongy skin with a forefinger and it doesn't spring back. She was cringing and biting her lip to keep from laughing hysterically, and they lifted her onto the table where tissue paper rustled and crinkled beneath her and she was leaking pee, so frightened, and they wiped it away wordless and positioned her feet in the stirrups. Her bare feet! The soles of the feet are so vulnerable! "Please don't look at me? Don't take any pictures?" Aunt Elsie had advised *Just stay out of their way, it's that simple.* That was how Norma Jeane made love, mostly: she lay very still, smiling happily in anticipation, sweet and unassertive and hopeful, and opened herself to her lover, made a gift of herself to her lover; isn't that what men want, truly? The surprise was, Ex-Athlete was a tender though vigorous lover, an older-man lover, like V, panting and sweating and grateful, and never would the Ex-Athlete who was a gentleman laugh at her, tease her as the Gemini had, unforgivably.

"Headline for the *Tatler*: LURID EXPOSÉ: SEX SYMBOL MARILYN QUERIES 'IS FUCK A VERB???' " Laugh, laugh.

Well, she'd laughed too. And Doctor was tickling her with his rubber fingers. Poky fingers, prodding inside her. Like Uncle Pearce up and down her sides, into the crack of her little ass like a naughty mouse. But out again so fast you didn't know little Mousie was there. The codeine had numbed her, she was in that state where you feel pain at a distance. Like hearing screams in the room next door. Doctor saying, Don't struggle, please. There will be a minimum of pain. This injection will put you into a light twilight sleep. We don't wish to restrain you. "Wait. No. There's some mistake. I—" She shoved the hands away. These were rubber hands. She couldn't see any faces. Overhead the light was blinding. It was possible she'd traveled far into the future and the sun had expanded to fill the entire sky. "No! This isn't me!" She'd managed to slip from the table, thank God. They shouted after her but she was gone. Running barefoot, panting. Oh, she could escape! It wasn't too late. She ran along the corridor. She could smell smoke. Still, it wasn't too late. Up a flight of stairs, the door was unlocked so she pushed it open. There, the familiar faces of Mary Pickford, Lew Ayres, Charlie Chaplin. Oh, the Little Tramp! Charlie was her true daddy. Those eyes! In the next room there was a muffled sound. Yes, Gladys's bedroom. A forbidden place sometimes but now Gladys was gone. She ran inside, and there was the bureau. And there, the drawer she must open. She tugged, tugged, tugged at that drawer. Was it stuck? Was she strong enough to open it? At last she got it open, and the baby was flailing its tiny hands and feet, gasping for air. Sputtering and drawing breath to cry. Just as the cold steel speculum entered her body between her legs. Just as they scooped her out as you'd scoop out a fish's guts. Her insides were running down the sides of the scoop. She tossed her head from side to side screaming until the tendons in her throat seized.

The baby screamed. Once.

"Miss Monroe? Please. It's time."

Well, more than time. They'd been calling her for how long? Knocking cautiously at her dressing-room door. Forty minutes she'd been sitting there in perfect hair, perfect cosmetic mask, in a staring trance in her gorgeous hot-pink silk gown, gloves to her elbows, and the tops of her remarkable breasts displayed, and the glittery costume jewelry screwed to her ears and around her lovely neck. And the glossy cunt-mouth perfection. Time to perform "Diamonds Are a Girl's Best Friend."

Monroe was flawless. A real professional. Once every word, every syllable, every note, and every beat was memorized, she was clockwork. She wasn't a "character"—a "role." She must've had the ability to see herself already on film, like an animation. This animation she could control from inside herself. She was controlling how the animation would be perceived by strangers, in a darkened theater.

That was all Marilyn Monroe was, on film: the animated image strangers would one day see and adore.

Once I was sent to fetch her, I knocked on the door and bent my ear to the door, and I swear I heard a baby scream inside. Not loud, not like there was any baby in that room, but for sure I heard a baby scream. Just once.

THE EX-ATHLETE AND
THE BLOND ACTRESS:
THE PROPOSAL

I

There would be those observers, considering the doomed marriage in retrospect, as one might anatomize a corpse, who wondered if it was a proposal at all and not rather a coercive statement of fact.

The Ex-Athlete saying quietly to the Blond Actress *We love each other, it's time we were married.*

And there was a pause. And in her dread of silence the Blond Actress whispered *Oh, yes! Yes, darling!* And in confusion adding with a nervous squeaky laugh *I g-guess!*

(Did the Ex-Athlete hear these last mumbled words? Evidence suggests *no*. Did the Ex-Athlete hear any words mumbled or otherwise from the Blond Actress's lips that challenged his pride? Evidence suggests *no*.)

And then they were kissing. And finishing the bottle of champagne. And then they were making love another time, tenderly and with childlike hope. (In the aptly named Imperial Suite of the Beverly Wilshire where The Studio was putting up Marilyn Monroe for the night following a gala party for five hundred guests at the hotel in celebration of the premiere of *Gentlemen Prefer Blondes*. Oh, what a night!) And the Blond Actress was crying, suddenly.

And the Ex-Athlete was deeply moved and did what lovers do in sappy romances or in forties films: he kissed away his beloved's tears.

Saying *I just love you so much*.

Saying *I just want to protect you from these jackals*.

Saying with boyish aggression, raising himself above her on his elbows, peering down at her as one might survey a treacherous landscape in the benign delusion that traversing it would not only be possible but an adventure, *I just want to take you away from here. I want you to be happy*.

2

At crucial moments the film careens out of focus. This is the single print in existence; you can imagine its value to collectors. Of course, the sound track is poor. Those among us who can read lips (it's a handy skill, for a fan) are at an obvious advantage yet not much of an advantage since the Ex-Athlete wasn't just a reticent man but, when he spoke, moved his lips oddly as if speech were an embarrassment, like his own abrupt and ungovernable emotion; and the Blond Actress when not purposefully enunciating for the camera (with which she could "communicate" as with no living person) had an exasperating tendency to mumble and swallow her words.

Marilyn we want to shout at her. Look up at us. Smile. A real smile. Be happy. You're *you*.

When the Ex-Athlete spoke of "jackals" and wanting to take the Blond Actress "away from here," he was alluding to The Studio (he knew how the executives were exploiting her, how little they paid her in exchange for how many millions of dollars she was earning for them) and to all of Hollywood and possibly to the vast world beyond, which, his instinct told him, despite his own celebrity did not wish her well. (Or either of them well. For hadn't baseball fans booed the Ex-Athlete when, limping with a bone spur, he'd failed to live up to their expectations?) His sweeping masculine disgust perhaps took in, as well, the die-hard ragtag band of a dozen or more fans at that very moment on rain-washed Wilshire Boulevard across from the hotel (for they'd been driven away by doormen from the hotel's grand front entrance) with oversized plastic-covered autograph books and cheap Kodak cameras, tirelessly waiting for the celebrity couple to emerge; unless it was enough for these worshipers to bask in the knowledge that, though invisible to them and in every way inaccessible to them, the swarthy handsome Ex-Athlete and the beautiful Blond Actress might at that very moment be coupling like Shiva and Shakti, unmaking and making the Universe?

This much is clear. After the Ex-Athlete says passionately *I want you to be happy*, the Blond Actress smiles in confusion and says something, but her words are lost in static. An indefatigable lip-reader, having studied this footage repeatedly, has speculated that the Blond Actress says *Oh!—but I am happy, I've been happy all my l-life*. Then like an exploding nova the Ex-Athlete and the Blond Actress in their desperate embrace amid the tangled silken bedsheets of the pharaoh-sized bed sizzle and flame into bodiless light—as the very film melts.

It's a fact of history. Appropriate if ironic. We've learned to live with it as with any irremediable fact of history. Our instinct is to immediately rewind the film and replay the footage, hoping this time it will turn out differently and we'll hear more clearly the Blond Actress's stammered words. . . .

But no, never will we hear.

3

At the clamorous premiere of *Gentlemen Prefer Blondes* at the refurbished Grauman's Egyptian Theatre on Hollywood Boulevard amid klieg lights and camera flashes and whistles and hoots and applause there had come, stealthy as a lioness, Mr. Z's trusted Yvet to murmur mysteriously into the Blond Actress's ear, "Marilyn. I've just learned. Be sure to go alone to your hotel suite tonight. Someone special will be waiting for you there."

The Blond Actress cupped a hand to her diamond-laden ear.

"Someone s-special? Oh. Oh!"

That glass sliver in the heart. Amid a fluttery-delicious Benzedrine rush, virtually every remark made to you is freighted with destiny, a sweet-painful stab in the heart. And Benzedrine and champagne, what a combination! The Blond Actress was only just discovering what everybody else in Hollywood knew.

"Is it—my f-father?"

"Who?"

Deafening music from the sound track—"A Little Girl From Little Rock." The clamoring crowd and an announcer's amplified voice and Yvet didn't hear, nor did the Blond Actress exactly mean her to hear. (Reasoning with Benzedrine logic if the mystery visitor was indeed the father of Norma Jeane Baker/Marilyn Monroe he'd have hidden his identity from strangers; his identity would be revealed solely, and privately, to *her*.) Yvet in svelte black velvet and a single strand of pearls, pewter hair, and bemused pewter eyes boring into the Blond Actress's soul. *I know you. I've seen your bloody cunt. Your insides scooped out like a fish's. I'm the one who knows.* Yvet pressed her forefinger against her lips. It's a secret! Can't tell. The Blond Actress—

who hadn't realized she was gripping the older woman's wrist like a scared euphoric teenage girl—decided not to be insulted by this warning but to express, as Lorelei Lee herself might have, simple gratitude. "Thank you!"

So I wouldn't bring a man back with me. Get drunk, pick somebody up. That's how they think of Marilyn.

The Ex-Athlete, to the extreme disappointment of The Studio's PR staff, was not accompanying the Blond Actress to the premiere. She would be escorted in her dazzling blond finery by Studio executives, her mentors Mr. Z and Mr. D. The Ex-Athlete was far away on the East Coast being honored in the Baseball Hall of Fame. Or was he in Key West marlin fishing with Papa Hemingway, one of the Slugger's biggest fans? Or was he in New York City, his favorite city, where you could be almost anonymous, dining with Walter Winchell in Sardi's, or dining with Frank Sinatra in the Stork Club, or at Jack Dempsey's Restaurant on Times Square at the ex-heavyweight champion's table, drinking and smoking cigars and signing autographs beside the legendary Dempsey himself.

"Know what 'celebrity' is, kid? Being paid to bullshit the rest of your natural life."

As soon as Dempsey won the heavyweight title in 1919, he'd lost his hunger for boxing. For the ring. For fans. Even for winning: "Winning's for chumps." The Ex-Athlete admired like hell his fellow ex-champ in a sport more masculine and more dangerous and therefore more profound than baseball, this Dempsey in battered elephant skin, overweight, winking, and laughing—*Hey, I made it. The great Dempsey!*

The Blond Actress wasn't jealous of the Ex-Athlete's boyish brotherly need for macho men. The Blond Actress could share in that need herself.

How many arduous-tedious hours had been required to prepare the Blond Actress for this festive evening! She'd arrived at The Studio at 2 P.M., already an hour late, in slacks, jacket, sailcloth flat-heeled shoes. She'd arrived at The Studio wearing no makeup except lipstick. No eyebrows! She hadn't yet swallowed her prescription Benzedrine so she was in a clear and acerbic mood. Her platinum-blond hair tied back into a ponytail, she looked possibly sixteen, a pretty but unextraordinary southern California high school cheerleader with an unusually well-developed bust. "Why the hell can't I just be myself?" she complained. "For once." She liked to entertain the Studio help. She liked their laughter and liked their liking her. *Marilyn's one of us. She's great.* There was perceived in her at times a frantic need to win the affection of hairdressers, makeup artists, wardrobe women, cameramen, lighting technicians, the army of Studio employees with only first names like "Dee-Dee," "Tracy," "Whitey," "Fats." *What's Marilyn Monroe really like?—terrific!* She gave them gifts. Some of these were gifts pressed upon her, others were purchased new. She gave them complimentary tickets. She remembered to ask them about their mothers' illnesses, their impacted wisdom teeth, their cocker spaniel puppies, their tumultuous love lives that seemed to her so much more absorbing than her own.

Don't let me hear you say anything against Marilyn, I'll shove your fucking teeth down your fucking throat. She's the only one of them who's human.

The day of the *Blondes* premiere, a half-dozen expert hands laid into the Blond Actress as chicken pluckers might lay into poultry carcasses. Her hair was shampooed and given a permanent and its shadowy roots bleached with peroxide so powerful they had to turn a fan on the Blond Actress to save her from asphyxiation and her hair was then rinsed another time and set on enormous pink plastic rollers and a roaring dryer lowered onto her head like a machine devised to administer electric shock. Her face and throat were steamed, chilled, and creamed. Her body was bathed and oiled, its unsightly hairs removed; she was powdered, perfumed, painted, and set to dry. Her fingernails and toenails were painted a brilliant crimson to match her neon mouth. Whitey the makeup man had labored for more than an hour when he saw to his chagrin a subtle asymmetry in the Blond Actress's darkened eyebrows and removed them entirely and redid them. The beauty mark was relocated by a tenth of a fraction of an inch, then prudently restored to its original position. False eyelashes were glued into place. In exasperation the priestly Whitey intoned, "Miss Monroe, please look *up*. Please don't *flinch*. Have I ever *stabbed you in the eye?*" The eyeliner pencil moved dangerously close to the Blond Actress's eye but did not in fact go in. By this time the Blond Actress had taken a Nembutal tablet to steady her nerves for she'd been feeling not anxious about the premiere that evening (there'd been numerous screenings of *Blondes*, sneak previews, and early reviews proclaiming the movie a surefire hit and Marilyn Monroe a perfect Lorelei Lee) but strangely angry and impatient. And maybe she missed the Ex-Athlete? She worried that he was staying away from the premiere because he resented so much attention lavished on her.

When the Ex-Athlete was gone from her, the Blond Actress keenly felt his absence. When the Ex-Athlete was with her, the Blond Actress often had little to say to him, and he to her.

"But maybe that's how marriage should be? Two souls. Still."

The Ex-Athlete was glowing-proud to be seen with the Blond Actress on his arm in public places. He was nearly forty; she was much younger and looked younger still. After such excursions, the Ex-Athlete was primed to make love with the vigor of a man half his age. Yet the Ex-Athlete was roused to anger if other men stared at the Blond Actress too pointedly. Or if vulgar remarks were made in his hearing. He didn't generally approve of the Blond Actress's public performances, her Marilyn self. He wanted her to dress provocatively for him, yet not for others. He'd been shocked and disgusted by *Niagara*, both the film and the lascivious and ubiquitous billboards. Didn't she have any contractual control over the way they marketed her? Didn't she care that she was being advertised like meat? When "Miss Golden Dreams" was resurrected to run as the centerfold in the first issue of *Playboy*, the Ex-Athlete had been infuriated. The Blond Actress tried to explain that the nude photo wasn't hers to control; it had been purchased from the calendar company without her permission and without payment to her. The Ex-Athlete fumed he could kill the bastards, every last one of them.

In the mirror, she stared eye to eye. "And maybe that's how marriage should be, too? A man who cares about me. Who'd never exploit me."

Before leaving for the theater, the Blond Actress swallowed one, maybe two, Benzedrines to counteract the effect of the Nembutal. Her heart felt like it was *slowing*. Oh, what a powerful need she had, she had such a powerful need to curl up on the floor and *sleep*. On this the happiest most triumphant evening of her life wanting nothing more than *to sleep, sleep, sleep like death*.

The Benzedrine would change that. Oh, yes! You could count on bennies to quicken the heartbeat and bring a delirious fizz to the blood and the brain. That sweet-hot rush hitting the brain like a lightning bolt out of the sky. But there was no danger here, for the Blond Actress's drugs were exclusively legal. Never would the Blond Actress succumb to the shabby fates of Jeanne Eagels, Norma Talmadge, Aimee Semple McPherson. Never would she deviate from *doctor's orders*. The Blond Actress was an intelligent, shrewd young woman, hardly a typical Hollywood actress. Those who knew her well knew her as Norma Jeane Baker, an L.A.-born girl who'd clawed her way up from the gutter. The Studio physician Doc Bob provided her with only appropriate drugs. She knew she could trust him, for The Studio would not risk its million-dollar investment. Benzedrine, sparingly: to "lighten a dark mood," to "provide quick and valuable energy" sorely needed by an exhausted actress. Nembutal, sparingly: to "calm the nerves," to provide a "restorative, dreamless sleep" sorely needed by an exhausted, insomniac actress. The Blond Actress worriedly asked Doc Bob if these drugs were addictive and Doc Bob laid a paternal hand on her dimpled knee and said, "Dear girl! Life is addictive. Yet we must live."

4

Five hours and forty arduous-tedious minutes were required to replicate the Blond Actress as Lorelei Lee of *Gentlemen Prefer Blondes*. But those cheering crowds along Hollywood Boulevard! Chants of *"Marilyn! Marilyn!"* You had to accept it was worth the effort, didn't you?

She'd been stitched into her gown. This feat alone had required more than an hour. It was the Lorelei Lee hot-pink silk strapless, cut low to reveal the tops of her creamy breasts, and it fitted her like a straitjacket. Small measured breaths, she was cautioned. On her arms, gloves to her elbows tight as tourniquets. In her tender ears, around her powdered neck, and on her arms were glittering diamonds (in fact, zircons, property of The Studio) and, on her platinum cotton-candy head, the "diamond" tiara she'd worn briefly in the film. A white fox stole from The Studio over her bare shoulders, and on her already hurting feet spike-heeled hot-pink satin slippers so tight and teetering the Blond Actress could walk only in mincing baby steps, smiling, leaning on the tuxedo arms of Mr. Z and Mr. D, dignified as funeral directors. Traffic along Hollywood Boulevard had been rerouted for blocks and thousands of spectators—tens of thousands? hundreds of thousands?—were seated in bleachers across the Boulevard and pressing up raucously behind police barricades. As the convoy of Studio limousines passed, the decapitated heads of fresh-budded red roses were tossed. A crazed chanting of the crowds—*"Marilyn! Marilyn!"*—you had to accept this was worth any effort, didn't you?

Spotlights blinded her, whoops and whistles and microphones shoved into her face. *"Marilyn!* Tell our radio audience: Are you lonely tonight? When're you two gonna get married?"

Wittily the Blond Actress said, "When I make up my mind, you'll be the first to know." A wink. "Before he does."

Laughter, cheers, whistles, and applause! A flurry of red rosebuds like deranged little birds.

With her glamorous brunette co-star Jane Russell, there was the Blond Actress blowing kisses and waving into spotlights, her eyes animated now and her rouged cheeks glowing. Oh, she was happy! *She was happy!* ☆GEMINI☆ (the film) preserves that happiness forever. If Cass Chaplin and Eddy G were out there anywhere in that crowd, staring at the Blond Actress—hating her, their Norma, their Little Momma, their pet Fishie; how the bitch had betrayed them; how she'd cheated them of the fatherhood they'd believed to be at the outset preposterous if not monstrous but had come to accept, in time, as an extraordinary if ungovernable destiny—even the beautiful boys of the Gemini couldn't deny the happiness of the Blond Actress, she-who-was-so-shy, confronting her first large crowd. *Fans!* The Benzedrine rush in its purest form. Hollywood loved it (or so it was said) that on the set of *Blondes,* the brunette Jane Russell and the blond Marilyn Monroe hadn't been rivals but friends. The girls had gone to the same high school! "What an amazing coincidence. Somehow you have to think. Only in America." In the presence of Jane Russell, the Blond Actress was inclined to be witty-sardonic, a bit naughty, while Jane, a devout Christian, was inclined to be naive and easily shocked. Just the reversal of the film. As the two lavishly dressed glamour girls stood on the platform beaming and waving at the crowd, both stitched into straitjacket low-cut gowns, both breathing in small measured gasps, the Blond Actress said out of the corner of her lipstick mouth, "Jane! Us two could cause a riot, guess how?" Jane giggled. "Strip?" The Blond Actress gave her a sidelong flirty look and jagged her, lightly, just below her enormous jutting breast. "No, baby. *Kiss.*"

The look on Jane Russell's face!

Such delicious moments, unknown to biographers and Hollywood historians, ☆GEMINI☆ (the film) preserves.

5

"Am I dead? What's all this?"

Floral displays crammed into her dressing room, which already she'd outgrown. Piles of telegrams and letters. Amateurishly wrapped gifts from "fans." These were the faceless, anonymous, devoted individuals who bought movie tickets across the vast North American continent, who made The Studio possible, and the Blond Actress. At first the Blond Actress had been flattered, of course, in the early giddy weeks of fame. She'd read and wept over her fan mail. Oh, some of these heartfelt, sincere letters! Aching-heart letters! Letters of the kind Norma Jeane might herself have written, as a star-struck young adolescent. There were letters from the handicapped, and from mysteriously ill and incapacitated long-term patients at V.A. hospitals, and from the elderly or the elderly-seeming, and from those who signed themselves like poets: "Wounded at Heart," "Devoted to Marilyn Forever," "Faithful Forever to *La Belle Dame Sans Merci.*" These, with the help of her assistants, the Blond Actress answered personally. "It's the least I can do. These poor, pathetic people—writing to Marilyn as you'd write to the Virgin Mary." (Already, even before the success of *Gentlemen Prefer Blondes*, "Marilyn Monroe" was receiving as much fan mail as Betty Grable at the height of her career, and far more than the aging Grable received now.) All this attention was exciting but disturbing. All this attention entailed responsibility. The Blond Actress told herself gravely *This is why I am an actress, to touch such hearts.* She signed hundreds of glossy photos of blond Studio images of Marilyn (as a bebop sweater girl with her hair in braids, as a sultry glamour girl with Veronica Lake hair, as sexy-lethal Rose suggestively stroking her bare shoulder, as the baby-faced showgirl Lorelei Lee) with the fixed-smiling diligence of the girl who'd put in exhausting uncomplaining eight-hour shifts at Radio Plane. For wasn't this, too, a kind of patriotism? Didn't this, too, require sacrifice? Since childhood, her first movies at Grauman's Theatre, in thrall to the Fair Princess and the Dark Prince, she'd understood that movies are the American religion. Oh, she wasn't the Virgin Mary! She didn't believe in the Virgin Mary. But she could believe in Marilyn— sort of. Out of kindness to her fans. Sometimes she imprinted a lipstick kiss on her photo and in the swooping signature she'd learned to replicate she signed,

until her wrist ached and her vision swam. Tasting panic, then realizing *The hunger of strangers is boundless and can never be appeased.*

By the very end of the Year of Wonders 1953, the Blond Actress had become skeptical. To be skeptical is to be melancholy. To be melancholy is to be publicly funny. Like a stand-up comedian the Blond Actress developed a comic routine to make her assistants laugh. "These flowers! Am I a corpse, this is a funeral home? A corpse needs a makeup man! Whitey!" The more they laughed, the more the Blond Actress clowned. She called "White-eey" in the drawn-out wail of Lou Costello's "Ab-*bott!*" She complained, flailing her arms in stage distress, "I'm a slave to this Marilyn Monroe. I signed up for a luxury cruise like Lorelei Lee, I'm in fucking steerage *paddling.*" In her comic turns, the Blond Actress spoke as nowhere else: a wonderful demonic flame touched her; she could be profane, and she could be vulgar; the studio assistants were sometimes scandalized, but they laughed, laughed until tears ran down their faces. Whitey said, reproachful as an elder uncle, "Now, Miss Monroe. You don't mean a word of what you say. If you weren't Marilyn, who'd you be?" Dee-Dee said, wiping her eyes, "Miss Monroe! You're cruel. Any one of us, anybody in the whole world, would give their right arms to be *you.* And you know it."

Crestfallen, the Blond Actress stammered, "Oh!—I d-do?"

She'd shift from one mood to another so fast! You couldn't figure it. Like a butterfly or a hummingbird.

It wasn't drugs! Anyway, not at first.

Some of the letters addressed to Marilyn Monroe weren't so loving. You'd have to call them aggressive, even a bit nasty, alluding to the actress's physicality. Some of them were from mentally disturbed persons. These, her assistants screened. Yet if she knew that letters were being kept from her, these were the very letters she wanted to see. "Maybe they have something to tell me? I'd be better off knowing?" "No, Miss Monroe," Dee-Dee wisely said, "letters like that aren't about you. They're about somebody thinking he's you." Yet there was something gratifyingly *real* about being called a bitch, a whore, a blond tramp. Where so much was a dreamy haze, anything promising to be *real* was bracing. Yet, fairly quickly, even hate mail became predictable and formulaic. As Dee-Dee saw, the Blond Actress's detractors were venting their hatred on an imaginary being. "Like movie critics. Some of them love Marilyn, and some of them hate Marilyn. What's that got to do with *me?*" The Blond Actress told no one, except the Ex-Athlete, after he'd become her lover and (she liked to think) her best friend, for the Ex-Athlete understood: what kept her searching through mounds of mail from strangers was the hope of seeking familiar names: names out of the past, names to link her with her past. Of course, some did write to her, mainly women, grown-up girls she'd once gone to high school with, or junior high on El Centro Avenue, even the Highland Elementary School ("You were always so well dressed, we knew your mother was in the movies and youd be an actress too someday"); old neighbors from Verdugo Gardens (though not the long-lost Harriet); women who claimed to have double-dated with Norma Jeane and Bucky Glazer before they were married, whose names the Blond Actress couldn't recall ("You were Norma Jeane then I believe. You and Bucky Glazer were the most devoted couple, we were all surprise youd gotten divorced. I guess it was the War???"). Elsie Pirig wrote, not once but several times:

Dear Norma Jeane, I hope you remember me? I hope you are not
angry with me? But I think you must be for I have never heard from
you in years and years and you know where I live, and my telephone
is unchanged.

The Blond Actress tore this letter into shreds. She hadn't known how much she hated her Aunt Elsie. When a second letter came, and a third, the Blond Actress crumpled them, in triumph, and threw them on the floor. Dee-Dee said, mystified, "Why, Miss Monroe. Who's that from, you're so upset?" The Blond Actress was touching her mouth in that unconscious way of hers, as if, observers said, she was checking to see that she had lips. She was blinking back tears. "My foster mother. When I was a girl. An orphan. She tried to destroy my life because she was jealous of me. She married me off at fifteen to get me out of the house. Because her h-husband was in love with me and she was j-j-jealous." "Oh, Miss Monroe! That's a sad story." "It was. But not now."

Warren Pirig never wrote, of course. Nor Detective Frank Widdoes. Of the numerous guys she'd dated in Van Nuys, she heard only from Joe Santos, Bud Skokie, and someone named Martin Fulmer she didn't remember. Mr. Haring never wrote. Her English teacher she'd adored, and who had seemed to like her. "I suppose he's disgusted with me. So far from what he taught me."

For a year or two after Norma Jeane left the Home she'd corresponded with Dr. Mittelstadt. The older woman had sent her Christian Science publications, birthday gifts. Then somehow they ceased to write. Norma Jeane guessed it was her fault, after she'd gotten married—"But why doesn't she write to me now? Even if she doesn't see movies she'd see Marilyn. Wouldn't she recognize me? Is she mad at me too? Disgusted? Oh, I hate her!—she's another one who left me on my own."

She was hurt, too, that Mrs. Glazer never wrote.

Of course, there wasn't a day when she stepped into her dressing room to confront her fan mail that she didn't think *Maybe my father has written! I know he's aware of me. My career.*

It wasn't clear how Norma Jeane's father knew of her career. Or how Norma Jeane could have known that this was so.

But weeks passed, and months, in this Year of Wonders. And Norma Jeane's father never wrote. Though Marilyn Monroe was becoming so famous, you couldn't avoid seeing her picture and her name everywhere and anywhere. Newspapers, gossip columns, movie billboards, movie marquees. Advance publicity for *Gentlemen Prefer Blondes*! A gigantic billboard on Sunset Boulevard! After the nude photo "Miss Golden Dreams 1949" appeared in the first issue of *Playboy*, as the centerfold of this brand-new bold and raunchy magazine for men, an avalanche of mail followed and yet more media attention. The Blond Actress protested to reporters, quite sincerely, that she had not given permission for "Miss Golden Dreams" to be reprinted in *Playboy* or anywhere else, but what could she do? She didn't own the negative. She'd signed away her rights. And all for fifty dollars, when she'd been desperately poor, in 1949. The gossip columnist Leviticus, known for his cruel wit and scandalous revelations in *Hollywood Confidential*, surprised readers with an entire column devoted to an open letter that began:

Dear "Miss Golden Dreams 1949,"

You are indeed "Sweetheart of the Month." Or any month.

You are indeed a victim of our culture's mercenary exploitation of feminine innocence.

You are one of the lucky ones: you will go on to flourish in a movie career. Good for you!

Yet, know: you are more beautiful and desirable even than "Miss Marilyn Monroe"—and that is saying a mouthful!

The Blond Actress was so deeply moved by the tender gallantry of Leviticus, she impulsively sent him a personally inscribed print of the controversial nude photo, signed, *Your friend forever, Mona/Marilyn Monroe*.
The Studio had printed up copies of "Miss Golden Dreams" for such purposes. "Why not? It was me, after all. Let those calendar people sue."
One day, a week before the premiere of *Gentlemen Prefer Blondes*, Dee-Dee handed over a fan letter to the Blond Actress with an odd stricken expression. "Miss Monroe? This is a confidential letter I guess."
The Blond Actress, sensing what the (typewritten) letter might be, eagerly took it up, and read:

Dear Norma Jeane,

This is possibly the hardest letter I have ever penned.

Truly I do not know why I am contacting you now. After so many years.

It is not that "Marilyn Monroe" is who she is. For I have my own life entirely. My career [from which I am newly & comfortably retired] & my family.

I am your father, Norma Jeane.

I will perhaps explain the circumstances of my relationship with you when we can meet face to face. ~~Until then~~

My beloved wife of many years who is ill does not know I am writing this. It would upset her greatly ~~and so~~

I have not seen a film of "Marilyn Monroe" & will not probably. I should explain that I do not see movies. I am a radio man by taste & prefer to "imagine." My brief stint at The Studio as a would be "leading man" opened my eyes to the crassness & stupidity of that world. No thank you!

To be frank, Norma Jeane, I would not see your movies because I do not approve of such ranchiness in Hollywood. I am a well educated & democratic man I believe. I am 100% for Senator Joe McCarthy in his crusade against the Communists. I am 100% Christian, as is my wife on both sides of her family.

There is no justification warranted, that Hollywood which is known to be a hive of Jews should be tolerated in so long harboring such traitorous individuals as one "Charlie Chaplin" whose films I am ashamed to admit, I once paid to see. ~~And there are~~

You will wonder why I am contacting you, Norma Jeane, after more than 27 years. To speak the truth, I have suffered a heart attack & have contemplated my life with gravity & I have not been proud of my behavior in all cases. ~~My wife does not know of~~

Your birthday is June 1, I believe, & mine is June 8 so we are under the sign of Gemini. As a Christian I do not take such old pagan tales seriously but there is perhaps an inclination in the temperament linking such people as us. I do not claim to know much about it as I do not read women's magazines.

I have before me an interview with "Marilyn Monroe" in the new "Pageant." Reading it my eyes began to fill with tears. You have told the interviewer that your mother is hospitalized & you do not know your father but "await him with every passing hour." My poor Daughter, I did not know. I have known of you at a distance. Your demanding mother kept us apart. Years passed & it became too much distance to surmount. I did send your mother checks & money orders for your support. I did not expect, nor did I receive, thanks from that quarter. Oh no!!!

I know that your mother is a sick woman. Yet before she was sick, Norma Jeane, she was evil in her heart.

She expelled me from your life. Her cruelty was [I know full well] she led you to believe that I expelled her.

I have go on too long. Forgive an aging man. Though I am not sick, but am making a full recovery my doctor says. He is surprised he said ~~considering the extent of~~

I will hope to contact you again soon, Norma Jeane, in person. Look for me, my precious Daughter, upon a special occasion in your life when both Daughter & Father can celebrate our long denied love.

                                        Your tearful Father

There was no return address. But the postmark was Los Angeles.

In triumph the Blond Actress whispered, "It's him." She laid the amateurishly typed sheets of stationery on the table before her and compulsively smoothed out the creases. For several strained minutes, Dee-Dee covertly observed, she continued this gesture, and read the letter another time, and said again, not to Dee-Dee but as if speaking aloud, "Oh, it's him. I knew. I never doubted. Right here, close by. All those years. Watching over me. I felt it. I knew."

Such happiness in that beautiful face—Dee-Dee would afterward marvel—*almost you couldn't recognize her.*

6

After Yvet whispered into the Blond Actress's ear their shared secret, the evening of the premiere passed in a careening haze warmed by Benzedrine and champagne, a buoyant Technicolor landscape glimpsed from, for instance, a roller coaster. *Be sure to go alone to your suite tonight. Someone special will be waiting.* Despite her father's remark that he was a "radio man" and scorned Hollywood, the Blond Actress was convinced he must be attending the premiere of *Gentlemen Prefer Blondes*; he had studio connections and could acquire a complimentary ticket. "If only he'd told me his name, I would have invited him to sit with me." He was somewhere in this crowd of affluent invited guests. Oh, she knew! She knew. An older man, obviously; yet not terribly old, not much beyond sixty. Sixty wasn't old, for a man! Look at the notorious Mr. Z. He would be a handsome white-haired gentleman, dignified and alone. Uncomfortable in his tux, for such pretentious occasions were distasteful to him. Yet he'd come, for her: this was indeed a "special occasion" in his daughter's life.

As the Blond Actress was scrutinized on all sides, she who'd been strategically stitched into her strapless evening gown of hot-pink silk revealing every sweet swelling curve and voluptuous jutting of her supreme mammalian body, so she smiled radiant as a high-wattage lightbulb and squinted into the crowd seeking *him*. If their eyes locked, she would know! Probably his eyes mirrored hers. She more resembled her father than she resembled her mother. She always had. Oh, she hoped he wouldn't be ashamed of his daughter, primped and painted and displayed like a big animated doll. "The Studio's gorgeous replacement for Betty Grable. Just in time." She hoped he wouldn't change his mind and retreat in disgust. Hadn't he said he had seen none of her films and probably would not—"He disapproves of 'ranchiness.' " The Blond Actress, swallowing a mouthful of champagne, laughed wildly, and fizzy liquid drained from her nostrils. "Oh, 'ranchy'—I wish I had Cass, to tell." Cass was the only individual in Hollywood the Blond Actress might have confided in. He knew of Norma Jeane's "sordid tabloid past" as he'd called it. At least as much as she'd wanted him to know.

When the Blond Actress made her decision to break with the Gemini, to have the Operation, and to sign on for Lorelei Lee in *Gentlemen Prefer Blondes*, despite the modest salary she'd receive (a little more than one-tenth of Jane Russell's), her agent sent her a dozen red roses and his congratulations:

MARILYN. HOW PROUD ISAAC WOULD BE OF YOU.

Well, that was so. In fact, everyone was proud of her. These veteran Hollywood people, studio executives, producers, moneymen and their sharp-eyed wives—smiling at the Blond Actress as if, at last, she was one of their own.

During the showing of *Gentlemen Prefer Blondes*, which the Blond Actress had seen in its entirety several times and which she'd seen, piecemeal, many more times (for even as "Lorelei Lee" she'd been a perfectionist on the set, as exasperating to her co-stars as to her director), the Blond Actress found it difficult to concentrate. Oh, the warm rushing fizzing of her blood! The happiness pounding in her heart! *Someone special will be waiting for you.* She was grateful that the Ex-Athlete wasn't beside her; or V (who'd come to the premiere with a new female companion, Arlene Dahl); or Mr. Shinn. Grateful to be alone, and so plausibly alone for the night. *Someone special. In your hotel suite.* Arrangements must have been made through The Studio, which was paying for the suite; through Mr. Z or his office, someone with the authority to direct the Beverly Wilshire to let a visitor into the suite occupied by Marilyn Monroe. It excited her to think that Mr. Z, who'd been her enemy until only just recently, who'd spoken crudely of her as a common tramp, must know her father and know of this imminent reunion and wish both her and her father well. "It's like a happy ending. Of a long confused movie." Before the house lights dimmed and the first blasts of music began, the Blond Actress said to Mr. Z, in the seat beside her, "I understand that I have a special date after the party, in my hotel suite," and shrewd bat-faced Mr. Z smiled his secretive smile, bringing a forefinger to his fleshy lips as Yvet had done to hers. Maybe everyone at The Studio knew? All of Hollywood knew?

They wish me well. Their Marilyn. I love them!

Strange, to be again in Grauman's Egyptian Theatre. Almost, this was a movie scene in itself: *The Blond Actress returning to the very theater in which as a lonely little girl she'd worshiped such blond actresses as herself.* Since those Depression days, Grauman's had been refurbished at considerable cost. For this was another era now, of postwar prosperity. Out of the rubble of Europe and the demolished cities of Hiroshima and Nagasaki, the booming heartbeat of a new world.

The Blond Actress known as Marilyn Monroe was of this new world. The Blond Actress was perpetually smiling, yet without warmth or sentiment or that complexity of the spirit called "depth."

The atmosphere in Grauman's was warmly festive. *Gentlemen Prefer Blondes* was known to be a winner. This wasn't an opening like that of *The Asphalt Jungle* or *Don't Bother to Knock* or *Niagara*, movies that might offend some viewers, and did. *Gentlemen Prefer Blondes* was synthetic and brassy and overproduced, a triumph of glitzy vulgarity, a Technicolor cartoon about winning, American-style, and so it *was* a winner, already booked to open immediately in thousands of movie houses in the United States and destined to make millions here and abroad. "Oh, gosh!—is that *me?*" the Blond Actress squealed, staring up at the gigantic gorgeous doll-woman looming above the audience, in little-girl excitement seizing the hands of Mr. Z and Mr. D. Oh, the magic potion thrumming in her blood! In truth she hadn't a clue what she felt, or if she felt anything at all.

On Broadway, *Gentlemen Prefer Blondes* had been a revue of musical numbers, not a musical comedy. There was no "story" and there were no "characters." The movie was only slightly more coherent but coherence wasn't the point. When Norma Jeane received the script she'd been shocked at how underdeveloped and insipid her character was; she'd wanted more dialogue for Lorelei Lee, a turn or a twist to Lorelei's character, some background, some depth, but of course this was denied her. She'd envied the more adult and more intelligent role of Dorothy but was told, "Look, you're the blonde, Marilyn. You're Lorelei."

The Blond Actress's smile faded as she watched the movie. As euphoria subsided. She didn't want to think what, if he was here in this crowd, her father might be thinking. Foam-rubber Lorelei Lee and her twin-mammalian friend Dorothy mouthing their smart-silly lyrics and moving their bodies suggestively. "A Little Girl from Little Rock." Oh, what if Daddy slipped from the theater without even speaking to her? What if, disgusted (and you could see why), he decided against meeting Norma Jeane, his daughter, after all?

"Oh, Daddy. That thing on the screen, *it isn't me.*"

So strange! The audience adored Lorelei Lee. They liked Dorothy, too—Jane Russell was wonderfully warm, attractive, sympathetic, and funny—but clearly the audience preferred Lorelei Lee. Why? Such rapt, smiling faces. Marilyn Monroe was a winner, and everyone loves a winner.

Oh the irony was, surely these people all knew: Marilyn didn't exist.

I can't fail. If I fail I must die. This had been Marilyn's secret no one knew. After the Operation. After Baby was taken from her. Her punishment was throbbing uterine pain. At first heavy bleeding (she didn't dispute, she deserved), and then a slower blood-seeping, hot damp moisture like tears draining from her womb. *Where no one could see. Her punishment.* Sprayed herself with expensive French perfume somebody'd given her. Staggered from the set to hide in her dressing room in terror of bleeding to death. She wanted them to think she was *temperamental*, maybe; all glamorous stars were, female and male. Not this terror. And waking in the night (alone, the Ex-Athlete gone) when the codeine wore off. *I will create Lorelei Lee out of this sickness.* This was Norma Jeane's great accomplishment, except no one in the premiere audience knew, or could guess; nor would they have wished to know.

Kindly Doc Bob, who knew every detail of the Operation including the patient's hysteria afterward, had prescribed for her codeine tablets for "real or imagined" pain and Benzedrine for "quick energy" and Nembutal for "deep dreamless (and conscienceless)" sleep. Saying in Jimmy Stewart style, "Think of me as your closest friend, Marilyn. In this world and the next." The Blond Actress had laughed, frightened.

He knows me. My insides.

Yet there was the triumphant Lorelei Lee moving beautiful bare shoulders suggestively, tilting her head in that way she'd rehearsed to robot perfection, and cooing in a baby-sexy voice

Men grow cold   as girls grow old
And we all lose our charms   in the end.

How prettily Lorelei Lee sang these mordant lyrics! How radiant her smile! Lorelei sang, who had no voice, but the voice was surprisingly sweet and assured; Lorelei danced and her body, which was not a dancer's body and trained far too late in life, was surprisingly supple. Who could guess the hours, hours, hours of rehearsals? Bloodied toenails, and that sick throbbing in the womb. She sounded like a younger sister of Peggy Lee. But of course she was much more beautiful than Peggy Lee.

"I'm proud of myself, I guess. Shouldn't I be?"

Whispering to Mr. Shinn, who belonged beside her. Gripping her hand. Oh, she'd trusted *him!*

The movie was ending, at last. A triumphant double wedding. Those radiantly beautiful showgirl brides Lorelei Lee and Dorothy, virginal in white. (Were these girls *virgins?* It was a shock, but yes.) Immediate applause. The audience loved it, every slick phony moment of it. The Blond Actress, urged to her feet by tuxedo arms on either side, was crying. Look! Marilyn Monroe was crying genuine tears! So deeply moved. Whistles, cheers, a standing ovation.

For this you killed your baby.

7

The Imperial Suite was on the penthouse floor of the Beverly Wilshire. The Blond Actress, dazed and excited, remained less than an hour at the lavish dinner in her honor, excusing herself to slip away. *Someone special. Come alone!* When finally she arrived at the hotel it was past eleven o'clock. Her heart pounding like a bird's, so rapidly she worried she might faint. At the theater after the warm wonderful tumultuous ovation she and Jane Russell had received, she'd had to stealthily swallow another of Doc Bob's tablets to keep from slumping into premature exhaustion. To keep Lorelei Lee foam-rubber solid, not deflated like a balloon spent and stepped on, on a dirty floor. "Just one more. Just tonight." She promised herself!

She fumbled the key in the lock. Her fingers were icy and brittle. Her voice was frightened—"H-hello? Who is it?"

He was seated on a velvet love seat in a pose of self-conscious relaxation. Like Fred Astaire, though not in a tux and not with Fred Astaire's poise. On a low table before him was a cut-glass vase containing a dozen long-stemmed red roses, a silver ice bucket, and a bottle of champagne. He was as excited as she; she could hear his quickened breath. Maybe he'd been drinking, awaiting her. The white fox stole was slipping from her shoulders. She was in childish terror, she'd be revealed to him only partially clothed. He'd risen awkwardly to his feet, a tall muscular figure with surprisingly dark hair. He said, "Marilyn?" just as the Blond Actress said, "D-daddy?" They hurried together. Her eyes were blinded with tears. She might have stumbled, her spike heels catching in the carpet, but immediately he caught her. She reached out her hands; he gripped them tightly in his. How strong his fingers, how warm. He was laughing, startled by her emotion. He began to kiss her, hard on the lips.

Of course, it was the Ex-Athlete. Of course, this man was her lover. She was crying, and she was laughing. "I'm so h-happy, darling. You're here with me after all." Eagerly they kissed, stroking each other's arms. Oh, it was a dream come true. He was explaining he'd decided to fly back a day early; he'd hoped to make the premiere but couldn't get a flight in time. He'd missed her. She said, "Oh, darling, I missed *you*. Everybody was asking about *you*."

They had champagne and a late supper. The Ex-Athlete claimed not to have eaten since lunch and was ravenous. The Blond Actress picked distractedly at her food. She hadn't been able to eat at the dinner in her honor, anticipating what was to follow; now, giddy with happiness beside the Ex-Athlete, she had no appetite either. Her brain was ablaze, as a house with every room lighted and the shades yanked up to the tops of the windows. The Ex-Athlete had ordered poached pears in brandy for her, cinnamon and cloves. Since their first date at Villars he'd been led to believe that poached pears in brandy were the Blond Actress's favorite dessert. As champagne was her favorite drink and blood-red roses her favorite flower.

Sweetly she called him "Daddy." She'd been calling him "Daddy" for months, in private, since they'd first become lovers.

In turn, the Ex-Athlete called her "Baby."

Another surprise was, he'd brought her a ring. Had this been decided beforehand? A large diamond edged with smaller diamonds. She laughed nervously as he helped push it onto her finger. When had this been decided? He was saying in a low, tense voice, as if they'd been arguing, "We love each other, it's time we were married," and she must have agreed. She heard a frightened whispery voice agreeing. "Oh, yes! Yes, darling." She lifted his hands impulsively, pressed them against her face. "Your hands!—your strong, beautiful hands. I love you." It must have been a script she'd memorized without knowing it.

The Ex-Athlete was sleeping. Snoring. A man chuckling wetly to himself. He lay on his back in boxer shorts (he'd tugged them on, using the bathroom after lovemaking), bare-chested. He was one who sweated in his sleep and who twitched and lurched and ground his teeth. Now he was dodging stealthy phantom balls thrown at his unprotected head. The Blond Actress sometimes comforted her lover at such times but now she slipped from the bed to wander naked across the carpet. She used the bathroom, careful to shut the door before turning on the light. Blinding white tile, mirrors reflecting mirrors. Her Magic Friend staring at her without recognition. *It didn't leave any scar you can see. Not like an appendectomy or a cesarean.* She went then into the adjoining room, the spacious, formally furnished living room of the suite where they'd had their romantic late supper and gotten drunk on champagne and kissed and kissed and made their vows. *Just want to protect you. From those jackals. Want you to be happy.* She believed it might work:

here was a man who loved her more than she loved herself. She meant more to him than she meant to herself. Maybe the key to happiness isn't in your own keeping after all but in another's. She in turn would be the key to this man's happiness. The Ex-Athlete and the Blond Actress. "I can do it! I will."

Suffused with joy she went to stand at a window. It was a tall narrow window like a doorway in a dream. The curtain was of a fine transparent material. A naked woman standing at a sixth-floor window of the Wilshire. How relieved she was, now her life was settled! They would marry; it had been decided. They would marry in January 1954 and they would be divorced in October 1954. They would love each other deeply but blindly and in confusion, and they would hurt each other like wounded animals desperately flailing with claws, teeth. She may have known this beforehand. She may have already memorized the script.

Across the boulevard from the Wilshire the die-hard ragtag band of fans still waited. For what, for whom? It was nearly 2 A.M. There were perhaps twelve or fifteen of them, mostly male. One or two were of indeterminate sex. They'd been roused from their stupor by a sudden movement at the sixth-floor window. With childlike curiosity the Blond Actress peered down at those eager faces both familiar and unfamiliar as faces in dreams we have reason to believe are not our own dreams but dream landscapes through which we travel helpless and enthralled as infants in our mother's arms. Where our drifting mothers bring us, we must go. The Blond Actress saw a tall fattish albino male she'd noticed standing on a bleacher near Grauman's Theatre earlier that evening. He wore a knitted cap on his oblong head and his expression was one of utter rapt reverence. She saw a shorter, hydrant-shaped male with a youthful beardless face and squinty eyes hidden by glasses. He held something precious at chest level—a flashbulb camera? A lanky female with a prominent jaw, bony hands, and long narrow feet in cowboy boots was there, in jeans and a floppy-brim hat; she carried a duffel bag stuffed with belongings. (Was this woman Fleece? But Fleece was dead.) These, and others, held autograph books with plastic covers, and cameras. They moved forward haltingly as if not trusting their eyes. Staring up at the sixth-floor window where the Blond Actress had drawn the filmy curtain aside. "Marilyn! *Marilyn!*" Several reached out toward her while others frantically clicked their cheap cameras. The young man with the video recorder lifted it higher, above his head.

But what image could any camera capture, in the dark, at such a distance? And what were they seeing? A naked woman, calm and radiant and still as a statue? Platinum-blond hair touseled from love. Wetted, slightly parted lips. Those unmistakable lips. Pale bare breasts, shadowy nipples. Nipples like eyes. And the shadowy crevice between the thighs. "Marilyn!"

In this way, the long night was endured.

AFTER THE WEDDING: A MONTAGE

She was studying mime: the primacy of the body and the body's natural intelligence. She was studying yoga: the discipline of breath. She was reading *Autobiography of a Yogi*. She was reading *The Pathway of Zen* and the *Book of the Tao* and she was writing in her journal *I am a new person in a new life! Each day is the happiest day of my life.* She was writing haikus, Zen poems:

River of Night
On and on endless.
And I this eye. Open.

(Though in fact she wasn't insomniac, much. These nights.) She was teaching herself to play the piano. For long dreamy spells sitting at the white Steinway spinet she'd bought from Clive Pearce and had repaired and retuned and moved to her home. The spinet wasn't really white any longer but a subtly discolored ivory. The tone was alternately sharp and flat, depending upon which part of the keyboard you were playing. Mr. Pearce was correct: she'd never played Beethoven's "Für Elise" and never would. Not as "Für Elise" should be played. She liked to sit at the piano anyway, depressing the keys gently, running her fingers up into the treble, down into the bass. If she struck the bass too emphatically she could hear, as if dislodged from watery depths, a man's deep baritone voice; in the treble, a woman's soprano voice in contention. *Did you tell me you had a baby. Did you tell me you had this baby.* And Gladys's words, which thrilled Norma Jeane each time she heard them, *Nobody is adopting my child! Not while I'm alive to prevent it.* She was often held by her husband, who adored her. Held in his arms, which were strong muscled arms. His hands, strong muscled hands. She would have liked to draw him, this handsome muscled man! This kindly daddy man. She would have liked to "sculpt" him. But it was figure drawing she was taking, Thursday evenings at the West Hollywood Academy of Art, not entirely with her husband's approval. And she was learning to cook Italian food: when they visited his family in San Francisco, which was often, her mother-in-law instructed her in the Ex-Athlete's favorite foods, Italian sauces and risottos. She did not read the daily papers, much. She did not read the trade papers, the fan magazines. She did not read the trash tabloids. She saw few Hollywood people. She had a new telephone number and a new address. She'd sent a bottle of champagne to her agent with a note:

Marilyn is permanently on her honeymoon.
Don't pursue & don't interrupt!

She was reading *The Teachings of Nostradamus.* She was rereading Mary Baker Eddy's *Science and Health with Key to the Scriptures.* She was in perfect health and she was sleeping well and she was hoping to become pregnant for the first time, as she told the Ex-Athlete who was her husband who was Daddy and who adored her. He'd rented for her a spacious hacienda-style house north of Bel Air and south of the Stone Canyon Reservoir. The house was set back behind a wall covered with bougainvillea. In the night sometimes she heard fluttery scratching sounds on the roof and against the windows and had the thought *Spider monkeys!* though she knew there were certainly no spider monkeys there. Her husband slept soundly and did not hear these noises, or others. He slept in just boxer shorts, and during the night the curly-kinky-graying hairs of his chest, belly, and groin became moist, and a fine oil oozed through the pores of his skin. It was "Daddy's smell" and she loved it. The scent of him! A man. She was herself fastidious about showering, shampooing her hair, soaking in long therapeutic baths. She seemed to recall that, at the Home, or had it been at the Pirigs', she'd had to bathe in water already used by others, sometimes as many as five or six others, but now she could bathe in her own bathwater for long dreamy spells amid wintergreen salts doing her yoga breathing exercises.

Draw breath deeply in. Hold. Observe breath as it slowly expels. Say to yourself I AM BREATH. I AM BREATH.

She was not Lorelei Lee and could barely remember Lorelei Lee. The movie had made millions of dollars for The Studio and would make more millions and she had received for her effort less than $20,000 but she was not bitter for she was not Lorelei Lee, who lived only for money and diamonds. She was not Rose who had conspired to murder her adoring husband, and she was not Nell who'd tried to murder that poor little girl. If she returned to acting she would return to serious roles exclusively. If she returned to acting perhaps she would become a stage actress. She most admired stage actors because they were "real" actors. Often she hiked or ran along the reservoir. She was conscious of persons watching her sometimes. Neighbors who knew her and the Ex-Athlete's identities but who would not intrude upon their privacy. Not usually! But there were others, dog walkers and house sitters and men with secret cameras. There were individuals seen and unseen. Otto Öse was still living, she believed. Otto Öse scorned her marriage to the Ex-Athlete, she believed. As did her Gemini lovers, who had sworn (oh, she knew!) revenge. As if they had not wanted Baby dead. As if it had not been their Gemini will coercing her. In this season of happiness she had come to accept the fact that life is breathing. One breath following another. So simple! She was happy! Not unhappy like Nijinski, who went mad. The great dancer Nijinski whom everybody adored. Nijinski, who danced because it was his destiny, as it was his destiny to go mad; who said

I weep from grief. I weep because I am so happy. Because I am God.

She tried to watch TV with her husband, who was obsessed with TV sports, but her mind drifted off and she saw herself in a tight-stitched purple-sequin gown being flown through the sky like a statue lowered from an airborne vehicle, she saw her uplifted arms and her hair that looked white whipped in the wind. She would make an effort quickly then to comment on the TV sports action or to ask her husband what had happened. At such times she couched her question in the form, *Oh, what was all that? I missed the fine points, I guess.* During the advertisement break, her husband would explain. By herself she rarely watched TV news for fear of being distressed by the evil of the world. The Holocaust had ended in Europe, now the Holocaust would spread invisibly through the world. For the Nazis themselves had migrated, she knew. Many to South America including (rumor had it) Hitler himself. Prominent Nazis lived incognito in Argentina, Mexico, and Orange County, California. It was rumored, or it was known, that a high-ranking Nazi had

had cosmetic surgery, hair transplants, a total transformation of his identity, and was now involved in Los Angeles banking and "international trade." One of Hitler's most brilliant speechwriters worked incognito for a certain California congressman frequently in the news for his zealous anti-Communist campaign. At the white Steinway spinet that had been given to Gladys by Fredric March she was Norma Jeane and she played children's pieces slowly, quietly. Mr. Pearce had given her Béla Bartók's "Evenings in the Country." The Ex-Athlete had a call from his lawyer; the warning was that she would receive a subpoena. She did not think about this. She knew that X, Y, and Z had been interrogated by Communist-hunting committees and had "named names" and one of the men who'd been injured was the playwright Clifford Odets, but Mr. Odets was not her playwright. She was not thinking about politics but about her breathing, which was a way of thinking about the soul and a way of not-thinking about politics or about the baby scraped out of her womb and into a bucket to be disposed of like garbage and she was not thinking of whether the baby had lived outside her womb for a heartbeat or two or whether it had been killed immediately (as Yvet assured her—*It's always immediate and merciful and is perfectly legal in civilized nations like those of northern Europe*). But usually she was not-thinking of these things as she was not-reading the daily papers or watching TV news. On the far side of the world in Korea, United Nations troops were occupying a ravaged and chaotic landscape, but she did not care to know painful details. She did not care to know of Government nuclear testing a few hundred miles to the east in Nevada and Utah. She may have understood that she was being watched by Government informers and that her career-self Monroe was "on a list," but she did not care to think about it and in any case there were many lists and many names on these lists in the year 1954.

That which we cannot affect, that we must pass by in silence like those whirling spheres of the Heavens.

So spoke Nostradamus. She was reading Dostoyevsky's *The Brothers Karamazov*. She was deeply moved by the character of Grushenka, the child-ish cruel soft-sugary-buxom twenty-two-year-old whose peasant beauty would be short-lived as a flower but whose bitterness would rage through a lifetime. Oh, in another lifetime, Norma Jeane had been Grushenka! She was reading the short stories of Anton Chekhov in fanatic night-long sessions, during which time she seemed to have but the vaguest idea where she was, who she was, and would recoil wincing if touched (by her annoyed husband, for instance) like a snail unprotected by its shell. She read "The Darling"— she was Olenka! She read and wept over "The Lady with the Pet Dog"—she was the young married woman who falls in love with a married man and whose life is forever changed! She read "The Two Volodyas"—and she was the young wife who falls passionately in love with, and out of love with, her seducer husband! But "Ward No. 6" she could not bear to finish.

"This is the happiest day of my life."

She would take with her to Tokyo the purple-sequin gown with spaghetti straps and a rhinestone brooch riding the crest of the right breast like a nipple that her husband the Ex-Athlete liked her in; tight as sausage skin that dress, it fell to just below her knee, not in fact a cheap dress but it certainly looked cheap, and squeezed inside it she looked cheap, like a moderately high-priced hooker, which he liked sometimes, private times, but didn't like at other times. She would take the gown with her to Tokyo in secret, but it wouldn't be in Tokyo she'd wear it.

Were there male models in that figure-drawing class? he joked, in his sidelong way that meant it wasn't a joke; don't be suckered into giving a quick unheeding answer. Her reply was pure Lorelei Lee, which almost he could appreciate; anyway he laughed his barking belly laugh—"Gosh, Daddy! I haven't noticed."

It was the female models that fascinated and frightened.
    Often she stared and forgot to draw. Her charcoal stick faltered and ceased its feathery motions. It happened more than once that the brittle little stick broke in two in her fingers! The models were sometimes young but more often not. One woman must have been in her late forties. Not one was beautiful. Not one was what you'd call pretty. They wore no makeup; their hair was unstyled and often uncombed. They were dull-eyed and indifferent to the dozen students in the class, these "students" of ages ranging from late adolescence to late middle age, arranged about the model in a circle and staring with the earnest intensity of the untalented. "As if we aren't even here. And if we are, we don't matter." One of the female models was potbellied and slack-breasted, with sinewy unshaved legs. One had a face all sharp angles and creases like a Hallowe'en pumpkin, a sickly carroty sheen to her skin and coarse hairs sprouting beneath her arms and at her crotch. There were models with ugly feet, not-clean toenails. There was a model (who reminded Norma Jeane of a scrappy girl named Linda at the Home) with a lurid sickle scar on her left thigh, maybe eight inches long. It fascinated her that such unattractive females would not only dare to remove their clothing in front of strangers but evince not the slightest discomfort at being stared

at. She admired them. She did! But they rarely lingered to talk with anyone other than the instructor. They avoided eye contact at all times. Without glancing at a watch they knew exactly when it was time for a break and a smoke, and at once they slipped on their ratty robes and kicked on their ratty sandals and walked quick and defiant out of the room. If any of the models knew, as the other students did, that the shyly earnest young blond woman their instructor had introduced to them pointedly as "Norma Jeane" was in fact "Marilyn Monroe," coolly they gave no sign. They weren't impressed! (Oh, but they did glance at her, sometimes. She caught them. Darting fish-hooks of eyes that didn't snag in her, at least. Such icy eyes, Norma Jeane didn't dare smile.)

After class one evening Norma Jeane dared to approach the scarred young woman (whose name wasn't Linda) and asked would she like to stop for cof-fee? "Thanks but I got to get home," the model muttered, without meeting Norma Jeane's eye. She was edging toward the door, a lighted cigarette already in hand. Well, would she like a ride home? "Thanks, but I got some-body picking me up." Norma Jeane smiled the dazzling Marilyn smile that rarely failed to get attention but totally failed here. She thought *In fact this is Linda. She knows damned well who I am. Who I am now, and who I was then.* Trying not to sound exasperated or desperate, Norma Jeane said, "I just wanted to say, I really admire you. Being a m-model as you are." The model exhaled smoke. You couldn't see the least sign of irony in her plain shut-up face, yet you knew it was pure irony she exhaled. "Yeah? That's nice." "Because you're so brave." "Brave, why?" Norma Jeane hesitated, still smiling. The Marilyn reflex was so instinctive, a sweet-sensuous stretch-ing of the lips, in fact it was nothing more (Norma Jeane had just read) than the human infant's earliest genetically programmed social reflex, a sweet hopeful smile, a smile to make you love me. "Because you're not pretty. At all. You're ugly. Yet you remove your clothes before strangers." The model laughed. Maybe Norma Jeane hadn't said these words out loud? Maybe this wasn't Linda really, but a sister actress down on her luck, possibly with a drug habit, and a lover who beats her? Norma Jeane said, "Because—oh, I don't know—I couldn't do it, I guess. If I was you."

The model laughed, on her way out. "If you needed the money, Norma Jeane, sure you would. Bet your sweet ass."

"This is the happiest day of my life."

She embarrassed him on their honeymoon by exclaiming these heartfelt words to waiters, hotel doormen, sales clerks, and even the Mexican cham-bermaids, who smiled at the beautiful blond *gringa* without comprehension. "This is the happiest day of my life." There was no doubting she meant it.

For one of the truths revealed in scripture is, Each day is the blessed day, each day is the happiest of our lives. She stroked his face, which seemed to her a beautiful face even when unshaven. She stared in rapture. Like a child wife she tickled the coarse graying hairs on his chest and forearms and playfully squeezed the soft flesh knobs at his waist of which, in his male-athlete vanity, he was embarrassed. She kissed his hands, which embarrassed him too. And sometimes she buried her face in his groin, which wildly excited him. *For nice girls didn't kiss men in that part of their bodies, and she knew it. But did he know that she knew? Maybe she was just so naive!* On the beach beside the greeny-aqua ocean she ran with him in the early morning, surprising the Ex-Athlete that a woman could run so well and for so many strenuous minutes—"Darling, I'm a dancer, haven't you noticed?" But she always tired before he did and stopped to watch him run on.

But she didn't perform oral sex with her husband. Anymore than he did, with a woman now his legal wife. It would be a Hollywood tale told for generations how, in a corridor outside the very courtroom in San Francisco City Hall in which only a few minutes before she'd been married in a brief civil ceremony, she'd slyly telephoned her friend Leviticus with the unprintable news bulletin, "*Marilyn Monroe has sucked her last cock.*"

By which the astonished columnist understood that the Blond Actress and the Ex-Athlete had quietly married after months of fevered media speculation.

Another scoop for Leviticus!

Singing for her husband "I Wanna Be Loved by You."

Repeating it was the happiest day of her life and the man was so moved he could only murmur, almost inaudibly, "Me too."

She was subpoenaed to appear before the Subversive Activities Control Board in Sacramento. The Ex-Athlete instructed her, Just tell the truth. She said, I don't owe those men the truth. He said, If you know Communists, name them. She said, I will not. He said, astonished, You don't have anything to hide, do you? She said, It's my private business what I want to hide and what I want to reveal. She saw that he would have liked to strike her but he did not, for he loved her; he was not a man to strike anyone weaker than himself, especially a woman, and a woman he loved. There was an ugly tale of the Ex-Athlete beating his first wife but that had been a long time ago, the Ex-Athlete had been young then, and hotheaded, and his wife "provoking." Calmly he said now, I don't understand this, and I don't like it. She said, I don't like it either. She may have called him Daddy. She may have kissed him. He may have suffered her kiss in dignified silence. But in the end by way of Studio lawyers' negotiations the nature of the meeting with the "control board" was changed from a public interrogation on the floor of the California legislature to a private hearing and the hearing would be an elegant luncheon in a private dining room at the capitol building. There was no interrogation. There was no confrontation. No press or media people were present. At the conclusion of the three-hour luncheon, the Blond Actress signed autographs for the board members and Studio photographs of Marilyn Monroe, as many as requested.

A pure soul. In mime class we were told that the body has its natural language, a subtle, musical speech. The body predates speech. And often lives beyond speech. We were told to mime our deepest selves.

The young blond woman shrank at first from our eyes. She crouched and hugged her knees. She wore cotton pedal pushers and a man's shirt, and her bleached-bone hair was tied back carelessly in a scarf. Her face was bare of makeup (but we knew that face). She crouched in a corner, her eyes fixed upon an invisible horizon. She began to shuffle forward, awkwardly. She lifted herself slowly like a ray of light. She stretched her arms and stood on her toes until her body was shaking. She then moved slowly about the room, staring at an invisible horizon. She began to dance, soundlessly. As if in a trance she moved her body in slow pained gyrations. She removed her shirt, not knowing what she did. She crossed her arms over her bare pendulous breasts. Under an enchantment she lay down on the floor, curled up like a child, and immediately slept, or seemed to sleep. A long magical minute passed. It was impossible to judge if this was still mime or an authentic abrupt sleep. Yet of course it could be both. After another minute, the mime instructor knelt worriedly beside her and spoke the name she'd given us: "Norma Jeane?"

The young blond woman "Norma Jeane" was deeply asleep. It required some effort to wake her. Sure we knew she was who she was. Her studio/Hollywood name. But the woman's deepest self shone through. A pure soul. It was beautiful, and it had no name.

It was just that he loved her so much. He couldn't bear to see her cheapen herself. Demean and degrade herself. Her name and his. Those photographs and movie stills. Those jackals. And paying her so little, under that contract. Everybody knows Hollywood is an open brothel. Allow them to display her like a common whore. A street hooker. They were married now; she was his wife. What of his family and relatives in San Francisco? What of his embarrassment? His fans? Marrying her for love and in all the papers the shameful fact he'd been excommunicated from the Church. His previous divorce. The Church forbids divorce. For her! For love of her. And displaying herself like meat. Sewn into her dresses. Hips swiveling as she walks. Don't say it's a joke. If it's a joke it's a filthy joke. Breasts spilling out of her clothes. That *Photoplay* award dinner. At the Oscar award ceremony. Said she wasn't going, yet she did. Is that what you are? Meat? Everybody knows what Hollywood is. Her name in the papers. And his. Newlyweds quarreling? In public? Filthy lies. Fucking liar. Never would he raise his hand against any woman. How dare she provoke him.

She was naked, drowsy. Midafternoon and she couldn't seem to fully awaken. The day before at mime class (unless it had been several days ago) she'd fallen into a deep sleep and hadn't been able to shake off the effects of that sleep. If she had Doc Bob's wake-up pills—but she didn't. Her angry husband had snatched them out of her hand and flushed them down the toilet.

Is that what you are? Meat?

Daddy, no! I don't want to be.

Tell them you won't. This new movie. No deal.

Daddy, I have to work. It's my life.

Tell them you want good roles. Serious roles. Tell them you're quitting. Your husband says you're quitting.

Yes. Yes, I will tell them.

She began to cry. But nothing happened. She was frightened, for she had no tears. She wasn't yet thirty years old and her tears were drying up! *I killed my baby*. A tear or two eked out. *My baby? Why?* Yet she could not cry. Someone had rubbed sand into her eyes and coated the interior of her mouth with sand. Where her heart had been, an hourglass of sand, sifting downward.

In fact she was ill. It was an emergency appendectomy.

In her panic she'd thought it was labor; she was having a baby after all. An angry demon baby gnarled and twisted with a head so large it would split her groin in two. And her husband wasn't the father and would strangle her with his strong beautiful hands. Guilty and scared, stricken with pain, and her skin burning, and he'd wakened in alarm to discover her in the bathroom, her bare buttocks on the edge of the white porcelain tub rocking from side to side in agony, naked and sweating and giving off the rank animal smell of physical terror. The Ex-Athlete knew the symptoms. In fact he was relieved to identify the symptoms. He'd had a nearly ruptured appendix himself as a young man. He called an ambulance and she was taken to the emergency room of the Cedars of Lebanon Hospital and a Hollywood tale would emerge from the chaos and confusion of these hours to be avidly recounted through generations of how the resident surgeon, who'd only learned the identity of his famous patient when he stepped into the operating room, discovered, taped to her midriff, this shakily scrawled note.

Most important to READ BEFORE operation

Dear Doctor,

Cut as little as possible I know it seems vain but that doesn't really enter into it—the fact that I'm a *woman* is important and means much to me. You have children and must know what it means—*please Doctor*—I know somehow you will! thank you—for Gods sake Dear Doctor. No *ovaries* removed—please again do whatever you can do prevent large *scars*. Thanking you with all my *heart*.

Marilyn Monroe

Since the night of the premiere of *Gentlemen Prefer Blondes*, which was also the night she'd decided to marry the Ex-Athlete, she had not heard from the man who'd called himself her father.
Your tearful Father.
She'd told no one. She was waiting.

She visited Gladys at the Lakewood Home. She went alone. She had a gleaming plum-colored Studebaker convertible with whitewall tires. She was under suspension from The Studio for refusing a new film so there was no Studio car available to her in any case. The Ex-Athlete offered to accompany her but she refused.
"My mother would only upset you. She's an ill woman."
Never had the Ex-Athlete seen Gladys Mortensen, nor would he.
Except she'd shown him a snapshot dated December 1926. Gladys with her infant daughter Norma Jeane in her arms. The Ex-Athlete stared at an ethereal-looking gaunt-faced young woman with Garbo eyes and fine plucked brows holding in the crook of her arm, as one might hold a novelty of some sort, a plump moist-mouthed baby with a question mark of a dark-blond curl at the very top of her head. Shyly the Blond Actress regarded her husband, whom in many ways she did not know. For to love a man is not to know him but rather to not-know him. And to be loved by a man is to have succeeded in creating the object of his love, which must not then be jeopardized.
"Well! Mother and me. A long time ago."
The Ex-Athlete winced, but why? He studied the sepia snapshot for some

minutes. Whatever words he might have wished to utter of pity, sympathy, confused love, or even hurt, he had not the ability to form.

At Lakewood, the Blond Actress became Norma Jeane Baker, whose arrival was greeted with the usual subdued and respectful excitement. She was wearing shoes with only a medium heel and a tasteful mauve-gray gabardine suit with a boxy, not form-fitting, jacket. She was not "Marilyn Monroe"—you could see at a glance. Yet something of the blond aura of Marilyn accompanied her, like a lingering perfume. She was bringing a gift for the staff: a ten-pound Valentine's Day box of assorted Swiss chocolates. "Oh, Miss Baker! Thank you." "Miss Baker, you shouldn't!" Smiling eyes dropping to her ring finger. For she'd married the world-famous Ex-Athlete since last visiting Lakewood. "Isn't it a lovely day? Will you be taking your mother out this afternoon?" "Come with me, Miss Baker. Your mother is awake and eager to see you." In fact, Gladys Mortensen did not appear eager to see Norma Jeane and very likely didn't know that Norma Jeane was expected. If she'd been told, she'd forgotten. Norma Jeane brought gifts for Gladys too, but fruit rather than candy, a basket of tangerines and shiny purple grapes, and a copy of *National Geographic* because this was a quality magazine with beautiful photographs that Gladys might enjoy, and there was the latest issue of *Screenland* with the Blond Actress on the cover in an elegant restrained pose above the caption MARILYN MONROE'S HONEYMOON MARRIAGE. Gladys glanced at these items, crinkling her nose. Was it candy she'd been expecting?

Norma Jeane embraced her mother gently, not warmly as she'd have wished, for she knew that Gladys would stiffen in such an embrace. Lightly she kissed the older woman's cheek. This was one of Gladys's good days, you could see. Norma Jeane had been told when she'd called that Gladys had had a "bad spell" recently and had "come out of it almost one hundred percent." Her hair had been shampooed that morning and she was wearing the pretty pink quilted robe Norma Jeane had bought for her in Bullock's; it was slightly stained, but Norma Jeane wasn't going to notice. The matching pink slippers had been placed neatly side by side beneath Gladys's bed. On a wall beside Gladys's bureau was something new: a picture of Jesus Christ with his flaming heart exposed, a nimbus of light around his movie-handsome head. A Catholic image? One of the other patients must have given it to her. Norma Jeane sighed, as if staring into an abyss at the bottom of which stood a tiny figure, allegedly her mother.

She was surprised and pleased to see, propped up against a mirror, the framed wedding photo of herself and the Ex-Athlete she'd sent to Gladys. The bride in oyster-white, smiling happily. The groom tall, handsome, with eyebrows so sharply defined they looked like an actor's. Norma Jeane thought *She didn't throw it away! She must love me.*

Gladys chuckled, chewing on a grape. "That man is your husband? Does he know about you?"

"No."

"That's good, then." Gladys nodded gravely.

Norma Jeane saw with relief that her mother was still in that suspended time. If anything, she looked younger. There was a girlish mischievous air about her. When Norma Jeane embraced her she'd felt the frail bird bones. And how delicate the bones of Gladys's face. The mysterious Garbo eyes. That ethereal expression a camera had captured long ago. It had pleased Norma Jeane that, gazing at Gladys as she'd been in 1926, younger than Norma Jeane was now, the Ex-Athlete had been drawn into Gladys's spell. Briefly.

All that remained of Gladys's fastidiously plucked and penciled eyebrows were a few stray gray hairs.

The staff reported to Norma Jeane that in good weather Gladys exercised by walking "nonstop" on the hospital grounds. She was one of the most active of the older patients. Her physical health was generally good. As they talked, Norma Jeane marveled at her mother's cheerfulness. Maybe it was quick and shallow and unreflective but at least she wasn't brooding as sometimes she did. Norma Jeane couldn't help but compare her mother to her new mother-in-law: a short, sturdily built Italian woman with a prominent nose and a shadowy mustache, a great collapsed bosom, a rotund little belly. "Momma" she wanted to be called. *Momma!*

Birdlike Gladys was perched on the edge of her bed, bare feet dangling. She ate grapes noisily, spitting the seeds into her hand. From time to time without a word Norma Jeane reached out, a tissue in the palm of her hand, and took the seeds from her mother. Except for an occasional facial twitch and a peculiar shifting of the eyes, Gladys hardly seemed like a mental patient. Her manner was upbeat and resolutely good-natured. As Norma Jeane's manner, strengthened by Doc Bob's Benzedrine, was upbeat and resolutely good-natured. Gladys spoke of "news in the world"—"more trouble in Korea." Was Gladys reading newspapers? That was more than Norma Jeane had done lately. *This woman is no more mad than I am. But she is hiding. She has allowed the world to defeat her.*

That wasn't going to happen to Norma Jeane.

Gladys changed into slacks and a shirt and Norma Jeane took her outside for a walk. It was a mildly cool, hazy day. The Ex-Athlete spoke of such days as "nowhere and no-time" days. Nothing was scheduled to happen on such a day. No baseball game, no focus of attention. Much of life, if you're retired or on suspension or unemployed or mentally ill, is nowhere and no-time.

"I may be quitting the movies. 'At the height of my fame.' My husband wants me to. He wants a wife, and he wants a mother. I mean—a mother to his children. That's what I want too."

Gladys might have been listening but she made no reply. She pulled away from Norma Jeane, like an impatient child preferring to walk alone. "This is my short cut. Through here." She led Norma Jeane, in her gray-mauve gabardine suit and her new ladylike shoes, through a brick-strewn passageway, too narrow to be an alley, between hospital buildings. Ventilators roared overhead. A virulent odor of hot grease struck with the force of an open-handed blow. Mother and daughter emerged in a grassy area downhill from a broad graveled path. Norma Jeane laughed self-consciously, wondering if anyone was watching. She feared that some members of the staff, including even the doctors, were taking pictures of her at times, without her knowing; to placate them, she'd posed in the director's office with him and a few others, smiling her Marilyn smile. *Is this enough? Please.* Yet when no one was visible with a camera, when no one appeared to be watching, when the vast empty sky opened overhead without even the concentration of the sun, weren't such moments being lost? The precious heartbeats of a life being lost? Wasn't most of life nowhere and no-time and irrevocably lost without a camera to record and preserve it?

"The Studio only offers me sex films. To be blunt! That's what they are. The very title—*The Seven-Year Itch.* My husband says it's disgusting and demeaning. 'Marilyn Monroe' is this foam-rubber sex doll I'm supposed to be, they want to use her until she wears out; then they'll toss her in the trash. But he sees through them. Lots of people have tried to exploit him. He's made some mistakes, he says. I can learn from his mistakes, he says. To him, Hollywood people are jackals. And this includes my agent, and people who claim to be on my side against The Studio. 'They all want to exploit you,' he says. 'I just want to love you.' "

These words vibrated oddly in the air, like dented wind chimes. Norma Jeane heard herself continue, as if Gladys had objected.

"I've been studying mime. I want to begin again, from zero. Maybe I'll move to New York to study acting. Serious acting. Not in movies but onstage. My husband wouldn't object to that, maybe. I want to live in another world. Not Hollywood. I want to live in—oh, Chekhov! O'Neill. *Anna Christie.* I could play Nora in *A Doll's House.* Wouldn't 'Marilyn' be perfect for Nora! The only true acting is living. Alive. In the movies, they splice you together, hundreds of disjointed scenes. It's a jigsaw puzzle but you're not the one to put the pieces together."

Gladys said abruptly, "That bench? I used to sit there. But somebody was killed there."

"Killed?"

"They hurt you if you don't obey. If you don't swallow their poison. If you keep it in the side of your mouth and refuse to swallow. That's forbidden."

Gladys's voice had been shrill and excitable. *Oh no* Norma Jeane thought. *Please no.*

Shielding her eyes and whimpering, Gladys hurried past the bench. This was the very bench daughter and mother had sat on a number of times, overlooking a shallow brook. Now Gladys was speaking of an earthquake. The San Andreas Fault. In fact there had been earth tremors recently in the Los Angeles area, but no earthquake. People came into her room at night, Gladys said, and were making a film of her. And doing things to her with surgical instruments. Other patients were encouraged to steal from her. At the time of an earthquake such things happened because there was nobody to govern. But she was lucky: nobody had killed her. Nobody had smothered her with a pillow. "They respect patients with family, like me. I'm a VIP here. The nurses are always cooing, 'Oh, when is Marilyn coming to see you, Gladys?' I say, 'How should I know? I'm just her mother.' They were asking so much about the baseball player, was Marilyn going to marry him; finally I said, 'Go and ask her yourself, it means so much to you. Maybe she'll make you all bridesmaids.' " Norma Jeane laughed weakly. Her mother was speaking in a low, fast, accelerating voice that signaled trouble. It was the voice of Highland Avenue lifting above the cascading roar of scalding water.

As soon as they'd emerged from the smelly passageway, as if out of the range of authority.

"Mother, let's sit down. There's a nice bench here."

"Nice bench!" Gladys snorted. "Sometimes, Norma Jeane, you sound like such a fool. Like the rest of them."

"It's only a way of t-talking, Mother."

"Then learn a smarter way. You're no fool."

In the cool hazy air that smelled faintly of sulfur they hiked to the farthest corner of the Lakewood grounds, where a twelve-foot cyclone fence loomed above them, screened by a privet hedge. Gladys shoved her fingers through the fence and shook it violently. You could see that this was the object of her swift hike. The panicked thought came to Norma Jeane that she and Gladys were both patients at Lakewood. She'd been tricked into coming here and now it was too late.

At the same time she knew better. Under California law, her husband would have had to commit her. The Ex-Athlete adored her, he'd never do such a thing.

Maybe he'd kill her! With his strong beautiful hands. But he'd never do such a cruel treacherous thing.

"Now I have a husband who loves me, Mother. It has made all the difference in the world. Oh, I hope someday you can meet him! He's a wonderful, warm man who respects women. . . ."

Gladys was breathing quickly, invigorated from the brisk walk. In the past several years she'd become an inch or two shorter than Norma Jeane yet it seemed to Norma Jeane that to meet her mother's steely bemused gaze she had to look up. The strain to her neck was considerable.

Gladys said, "You didn't have a baby, did you? I dreamt it died." "It died, Mother." "Was it a little girl? Did they tell you?" "I had a miscarriage, Mother. In just the sixth week. I was terribly sick." Gladys nodded gravely. She didn't seem at all surprised by this revelation, though clearly she didn't believe it. She said, "It was a necessary decision." Norma Jeane said sharply, "It was a miscarriage, Mother." Gladys said, "Della was my mother and Della was a grandmother and that was her reward at last. She'd had a hard life, I brought her terrible pain. But at last, she was happy." A sly witchy light came into Gladys's eyes. "But if you do that for me, Norma Jeane, I can't promise." Norma Jeane said, confused, "Promise what? I don't understand." "I can't be one of them. A grandmother. Like her. It's my punishment." "Oh, Mother, what are you saying? Punishment for what?" "For giving my beautiful daughters away. For letting them die."

Norma Jeane backed away from her mother, pushing at the air with the palms of her hands as if pushing at a wall. This was impossible! You couldn't talk with a mental patient. A paranoid schizophrenic. Like one of those unnerving improvisations in which the instructor has told one actor certain facts withheld from the other and it's up to the other actor to plunge blindly into the scene.

She would determine a new scene.

Just by moving from one space to another onstage you can establish a new scene. By the force of your will.

She took Gladys's thin, wiry, resistant arm and hauled her back to the graveled path. Enough! Norma Jeane was in charge. She was the one who paid the Lakewood Home's exorbitant fees, and she was designated as Gladys Mortensen's guardian and next of kin. Daughters! There was only one daughter, and she was Norma Jeane.

She said, "Mother, I love you but you hurt me so! Please don't hurt me, Mother. I realize you aren't well but can't you try? Try to be kind? When I have my babies, I will never hurt them. I will love them to keep them alive. You're like a spider in her web. One of those little brown recluse spiders. The most dangerous kind! Everybody thinks 'Marilyn Monroe' must have money but I don't have money really, I borrow money all the time, I pay for you to live here, this private hospital, and you poison me. You eat my heart.

My husband and I intend to have babies. He wants a big family and so do I.
I want six babies!"

Sly Gladys quipped, "How'd you nurse six? Even Marilyn?"

Norma Jeane laughed, or tried to. That *was* funny!

In her handbag she had the precious letter from her father. "Sit down,
Mother. I have a surprise for you. I have something to read to you, and I
don't want to be interrupted."

The Ex-Athlete was away on business. The Blond Actress attended a performance of a play, by a contemporary American playwright, at the
Pasadena Playhouse.

She'd been taken by friends. Every night the Ex-Athlete was away, she
attended a play performance at a local playhouse. In this phase of her life the
Blond Actress had numerous friends in circles that didn't overlap and these
were younger friends, not known to the Ex-Athlete. They were writers,
actors, dancers. One of them was the Blond Actress's mime instructor.

At the Pasadena Playhouse, members of the audience covertly watched the
Blond Actress through the evening. She appeared to be genuinely moved by
the play. She was not dressed glamorously and did not call attention to herself. Her friends sat protectively on either side of her.

It would be reported that, at the end of the play, while the rest of the audience was breaking up, the Blond Actress remained in her seat as if stunned.
She said faintly, "That is true tragedy. It tears out your heart." Later she said,
over drinks, "Know what? I'm going to marry the playwright."

"She had the wildest sense of humor! She'd look grave and little-girl and say
the most outrageous things. An ugly soused pug like W. C. Fields, you expect
the guy to be sardonic. The eyebrows and mustache of Groucho Marx, you
expect something surreal. But Marilyn, she came out with these things spontaneously. It was like something inside dared her, 'Shock the bastards. Shake
'em up.' And she would. And what she said might come back to haunt her,
or hurt her, and possibly she knew this beforehand. But what the hell?"

Back in her room at Lakewood, Gladys crawled weakly onto her bed. She
didn't require Norma Jeane's assistance. She'd been wordless since Norma
Jeane read her the letter in a calm, bell-like, unaccusatory voice, and she was
wordless now. Norma Jeane kissed her cheek and said quietly, "Goodbye,
Mother. I love you." Still Gladys made no reply. Nor did she look at Norma
Jeane. At the doorway of the room Norma Jeane paused to see that her
mother was turned to face the wall. Gazing upward at the lurid bright colors of the Sacred Heart of Jesus.

It had something to do with Easter.

The Blond Actress was brought to the Los Angeles Orphans Home Society in a black limousine with an interior plush and sumptuous as the cushioned interior of a casket. In his uniform and visored cap the Frog Chauffeur was behind the wheel.

For days the Blond Actress had been excited, thrilled. In a way it was like a stage debut. For a long time now she'd intended to return to the Home to visit with Dr. Mittelstadt, who had so changed the course of her life. "To say 'thank you.' "

Maybe (the Blond Actress hoped it would be a natural, unforced gesture) they would pray together in the privacy of Dr. Mittelstadt's office. Kneeling together on the carpet!

Often the Ex-Athlete did not approve of the Blond Actress's public appearances. With husbandly justification, the Ex-Athlete thought that such appearances were "vulgar"—"exploitive"—"unworthy of your dignity as my wife." In this case, however, the Ex-Athlete approved. For years, before and after his retirement from baseball, he'd often visited such children's homes, hospitals, and institutions. Some of these kids, especially the sick, wounded ones, could break your heart, he warned. But it was exhilarating too. You felt you were doing some good. Making some impact. Creating positive memories.

In bygone times Kings and Queens visited such places to anoint the sick, the maimed, the outcast, and the damned but in the United States there were only such individuals as the Ex-Athlete and the Blond Actress and they had to "do their part."

Only just don't let the media swarm all over you, the Ex-Athlete warned.

Oh, yes, the Blond Actress agreed.

A number of Hollywood celebrities had volunteered. The Blond Actress, though officially in disrepute, suspended by The Studio for contractual violation, was one of these. She'd asked to be taken to the Los Angeles Orphans Home Society on El Centro Avenue—"Where I once lived. Where I have so many memories."

Mostly these were good memories. Of course.

The Blond Actress believed in good memories. Sure she'd been an orphan—"Lots of people are!"—and yes, her mother had had to give her up—"It was the Depression. Lots of people were affected!"—yet she'd been well taken care of at the Home. The Blond Actress harbored no bitterness about having been an orphan in the Land of Plenty—"Hey, at least I was alive. Not like in some cruel country like China where girl infants are drowned like kittens."

Headlines in all the papers. Special columns by Louella Parsons, Walter Winchell, Sid Skolsky, and Leviticus. A cover story for *Hollywood Reporter* and for the *L.A. Times Sunday Magazine*. Smaller features syndicated across the nation and in *Time, Newsweek, Life*. Troops of photographers, TV crews. Brief coverage on network TV evening news.

MARILYN MONROE REVISITS ORPHANAGE
AFTER YEARS
MARILYN MONROE "REDISCOVERS" ORPHAN PAST
MARILYN MONROE BEFRIENDS ORPHANS AT EASTER

The Blond Actress would tell the Ex-Athlete she "had no idea" how so much publicity was generated. Other Hollywood celebrities visiting other homes, hospitals, and institutions hadn't generated much publicity at all!

The Blond Actress was feeling as excited and apprehensive as a girl. How many years had it been? Sixteen years! "But I've lived more than one lifetime since then." As the Frog Chauffeur skillfully drove the gleaming black limousine out of affluent Beverly Hills through Hollywood and southward into the interior of Los Angeles, the Blond Actress began to lose her composure. A mild throbbing pain between her eyes grew stronger. She'd been taking aspirin for (to her secret shame) she'd gone beyond Doc Bob's prescribed dosage of the "miracle tranquillizer" Demerol and was determined not to take more. As she neared the powerful presence of Dr. Mittelstadt, as nearing a warming, healing sun, she knew that healing can be only from within. There is no pain and in a sense there is no "healing." *Divine Love always has met and always will meet every human need.*

With the Blond Actress, in a separate vehicle, were several assistants. A delivery van bearing hundreds of gaily wrapped Easter baskets filled with chocolate bunnies and marshmallow chicks and multicolored jelly beans. Virginia baked hams and pineapples flown in fresh from Hawaii. The Blond Actress had volunteered five hundred dollars of her own money (or was it the Ex-Athlete's?) so that she could hand over a check to Dr. Mittelstadt as a "personal gesture of my gratitude."

In fact, hadn't the director of the Home betrayed Norma Jeane in some way? Ceased to write to her, after a year or two? The Blond Actress shrugged this off. "She's a busy professional woman. And so am I."

As the Frog Chauffeur turned the limousine into the orphanage grounds, the Blond Actress began to tremble. Oh, but this wasn't the right place—was it? The grimy red-brick facade had been blasted clean and now looked raw as scraped skin. Where there'd been an open area, now there were ugly Quonset huts. Where there'd been a meager playground, now there was an asphalt parking lot. The Frog Chauffeur drew the limousine soundlessly up to the entrance, where reporters, photographers, and cameramen had gathered in an unruly band. The Blond Actress would speak with the press afterward, these folks were told, but of course they had questions for her now, shouted after her as hurriedly she was escorted inside the building, cameras clicking in her wake like machine guns. Inside, strangers shook her hand. Dr. Mittelstadt was nowhere in sight. What had happened to the foyer? What was this place? A middle-aged man with a fresh-shaven Porky Pig face was leading the Blond Actress into the visitors' lounge, speaking rapidly and happily.

"But where is Dr. M-mittelstadt?" the Blond Actress asked. No one seemed to hear. Assistants were bringing in Easter baskets, hams and pineapples in cartons. An amplifying system was being tested. The Blond Actress was having difficulty seeing clearly through her dark-tinted glasses but didn't want to remove them for fear these avid strangers would see the panic in her eyes. Several times she cried, with her dazzling smile, "Oh, gosh!— it's such an honor to be here. Easter time is such a special time! I'm truly happy to be here! Thank you all for inviting me."

The event passed in a blur. But it was not a swift blur. For some time before the ceremony began, the Blond Actress was photographed for the orphanage "archive." She was photographed with beaming Porky Pig, who removed his bifocals for the shot, and she was photographed with members of the staff, and finally she was photographed with a few children. One of the girls so reminded her of Debra Mae as she'd been at the age of ten or eleven. . . . The Blond Actress wanted to stroke the girl's unruly carroty-red hair. "What is your name, sweetie?" the Blond Actress asked. The girl mumbled a syllable or two, grudgingly. The Blond Actress couldn't quite hear. *Donna*, maybe? Or *Dunna*?—"don't know."

The ceremony was held in the dining room. This vast ugly space, the Blond Actress recalled. Children were marched in, in orderly rows, and made to sit at tables staring at her as if she were an animated Disney creature. As the Blond Actress stood at the microphone reciting her prepared speech her eyes darted about the hall seeking familiar faces. Where was Debra Mae? Where was Norma Jeane? Maybe that was Fleece?—a lanky sullen child, unfortunately a boy.

It would be reported that the Blond Actress, contrary to the expectations of most of the orphanage staff, was a "sweet, kind, sincere-seeming" woman. In the eyes of many she was "almost ladylike." "Not glamorous like her publicity but very pretty. And *built*." She was perceived to be "kind of nervous, with almost a stammer sometimes. (We hoped she didn't overhear some of the kids mimicking her!)" She was admired for her patience with the children who'd gotten overwrought and excited about the Easter baskets and restless and noisy, "especially the Hispanic kids who don't know English."

Some of the older boys were rude and leering, moving their tongues in their mouths suggestively, but the Blond Actress, it was believed, "wisely ignored them. Or maybe she loved it, who knows?"

Despite a painful throbbing in her head the Blond Actress enjoyed giving Easter baskets to the children, who passed before her one by one by one. An infinity of orphans. An eternity of orphans. Oh, she could do this forever! Take Doc Bob's magic medicine and you can do anything forever! Better than sex. (Well, anything was better than sex. Hey, just kidding!) Oh, this was a rewarding and expanding and joyous experience, she'd tell the world if queried. And she would be queried. Interviewed. Her every syllable made worthy by newsprint or film. Wouldn't tell them the girl orphans interested her much more than the boy orphans, though. The boys had no need of *her*. Any female would do for them, any female body, wanting to define themselves as male, therefore superior, one body is like another, but the girl orphans were staring at *her*, memorizing *her*, would long remember *her*. The girl orphans who'd been wounded like Norma Jeane. She saw that. Girl orphans requiring a touch, a quick stroking of the hair, a caress of the cheek, even a feathery kiss. Saying, "Aren't you sweet! I love your braids"— "What's your name? What a nice name!" She told them, with the air of one imparting a secret, "My name, when I lived here, was 'Norma Jeane.' " One of the girls said, " 'Norma Jeane'—oh, I wish that was my name." The Blond Actress framed this girl's face in her hands and astonished everyone who watched by bursting into tears.

She would inquire afterward, What was that girl's full name?

She would send a check to the Home, for a "special clothes and book allowance" for that girl.

If the check, for two hundred dollars, was in fact ever used for this purpose, and not rather dissolved into the Home's budget, she would not learn. For she would have forgotten.

A disadvantage, yet also an advantage, of Fame: you forget so much.

And the check for five hundred dollars she'd made out, impulsively, to *Dr. Mittelstadt*? This the Blond Actress would not remove from her handbag.

The new director of the Los Angeles Orphans Home Society was, in fact, the middle-aged man with the Porky Pig face. And a nice if somewhat garrulous and self-important man he was. The Blond Actress listened to him for some patient minutes before interrupting to ask, now emphatically, what had happened to Dr. Mittelstadt?—and was met with a flutter of eyelids and a pursed mouth. "Dr. Mittelstadt was my predecessor," Porky Pig said, in a neutral voice. "I had nothing to do with her at all. I never make comments on my predecessors. I believe we all do the best we can. Second-guessing isn't my game."

The Blond Actress sought out an older matron, a familiar face. Once-young and now stoutly middle-aged with bulldog jowls yet an eager smile. "Norma Jeane. Sure I remember you! The shyest, sweetest little girl. You had some kind of—was it allergy? Like asthma? No. You'd had polio, and a little limp? No? (Well, you sure don't have any limp now. I saw you dancing in that last movie, as good as Ginger Rogers!) You were friends with that wild girl Fleece? Yes? And Dr. Mittelstadt liked you so much. You were one of her circle." The matron chuckled, shaking her head. It was a movie scene, the Blond Actress returning to the orphanage in which she'd been incarcerated for much of her childhood, and being dealt revelations like playing cards, but the Blond Actress couldn't determine what the mood music was. During the Easter basket ceremony, "Easter Parade" crooned by Bing Crosby had been piped into the dining hall. But now there was no music.

"And Dr. Mittelstadt? She retired, I guess?"

"Yes. She retired."

A furtive look in the matron's eye. Better not ask.

"W-where is she?"

A sorrowful look. "I'm afraid poor Edith is dead."

"Dead!"

"She was my friend, Edith Mittelstadt. I worked with her for twenty-six years, I've never respected anyone more. She never tried to foist her religion on *me*. She was a good, caring woman." The pursed mouth twisted downward. "Not like certain of the 'new breed.' The 'budget-minded.' Giving us commandments like the Gestapo."

"How did Dr. Mittelstadt d-die?"

"Breast cancer. So we learned." The matron's eyes grew moist. If this was a movie scene, and certainly it was, it was also vividly real, and painful; and the Blond Actress would have to command the Frog Chauffeur to stop at a pharmacy on El Centro so that she could hurry inside, plead with the pharmacist to telephone Doc Bob's emergency number, and acquire an emergency Demerol capsule to swallow on the spot. *That was how real it was, mood music or not.*

The Blond Actress winced. "Oh. I'm so sorry. Breast cancer. Oh, God."

Unconsciously, the Blond Actress pressed both forearms against her breasts. These were the famous jutting breasts of "Marilyn Monroe." Today, at the orphanage, as Easter visitor, the Blond Actress was not displaying her breasts in any conspicuous way. Her costume was subdued, tasteful. She'd even worn an Easter hat, with a row of cornflowers and a veil. A sprig of lily of the valley on her lapel. Dr. Mittelstadt's breasts had been larger than the Blond Actress's breasts, but of course they weren't of the same genre as those of the Blond Actress, which were, or had become, works of art. On her grave marker, the Blond Actress joked, just her vital statistics should be engraved: 38-24-38.

"Poor Edith! We knew she was sick, she'd been losing weight. Imagine, Dr. Mittelstadt almost *thin*. Oh, the poor woman must have lost fifty pounds while she was right here in our midst. And her skin like wax. And eyes shadowed. We'd urge her to see a doctor. But you know how stubborn she was, and brave. 'I have no reason to see a doctor.' She was terrified but would never admit it. Maybe you know that Christian Scientists have people who pray over them when they're sick. Or whatever they are, I guess they don't get 'sick.' These people pray, and you pray. And if you have faith, you're supposed to be healed. And this was Edith's way of handling the cancer, you see. By the time we realized the circumstances, what was actually wrong with her, she was already on sick leave. She refused to go to a hospital until the very end. Even then, it wasn't her wish. The tragedy was, Edith felt her faith was inadequate. With cancer eating up her body, her very bones, still that poor stubborn woman believed it was her own fault. The word 'cancer' never crossed her lips." The matron took a deep breath, wiping at her eyes with a tissue. "They don't believe in 'death,' you see. Christian Scientists. So when it happens to them, it must be their own fault."

Bravely, the Blond Actress asked, "And Fleece, what happened to Fleece?"

The matron smiled. "Oh, that Fleece. Last we heard, she'd signed up with the WACS. She got to be a sergeant, at least."

"Oh, Daddy. Please hold me."

In his warm muscled arms. He was startled, a little uneasy, but sure he loved her. Crazy for her. More now than he'd been at the outset.

"I just feel so . . . weak, I guess. Oh, Daddy!"

He was embarrassed, not knowing what to say. Mumbling, "What's wrong, Marilyn? I don't get it."

She shivered and burrowed into him. He could feel her heart beating rapidly as a bird's heart. How to figure her? This gorgeous sexy woman who could talk better in public than he could, any day, one of the most famous females in the United States and maybe the world, and she's . . . hiding in her husband's arms?

He loved her, that was settled. He'd take care of her. Sure.

Though puzzled by this behavior, which was becoming more frequent.

"Honey, what the hell? I don't get it."

She read to him from the Bible. In an eager yearning voice. He guessed it was her girl's voice, rarely heard.

" 'And Jesus spat on the ground, and made clay of the spittle, and he anointed the eyes of the blind man with the spittle, and the blind man's eyes were opened.' " She looked up at him, her own eyes strangely shining.

What was he to say? What the hell?

She read to him some poems she'd written. For him, she said.

In her eager yearning girl's voice. Her nostrils were reddened from a lingering cold, and she was sniffling; with a childlike lack of self-consciousness she wiped her nose on her fingers, so strangely breathless as if poised on the edge of a precipice.

"In you
the world is born anew.
As two.
Before you
there was but one."

What was he to say? What the hell?

She was learning sauces. Sauces! *Puttanesca* (with anchovies), *carbonara* (with bacon, eggs, heavy cream), *bolognese* (with ground beef, ground pork, mushrooms, cream), *gorgonzola* (cheeses, nutmeg, cream). She was learning the pastas and these were words, like poems, that made her smile: *ravioli, penne, fettuccine, linguine, fusilli, conchigli, bucatini, tagliatelle.* Oh, she was happy! Was this a dream? And, if a dream, was it a good dream or not-so-good? The kind of dream that can shift subtly to nightmare? Like pushing open an unlocked door and stepping into an empty elevator shaft?

Waking in an overheated, unfamiliar kitchen. Rivulets of sticky perspiration on her face, between her breasts. She was clumsily chopping onions as someone chattered fiercely at her. Her eyes stung and watered from the onions. Hauling a large iron skillet out of a cupboard. Children running in and out of the kitchen screaming. These were her husband's little nephews and nieces. She couldn't remember their faces and she certainly couldn't remember their names. Minced garlic and olive oil smoking in the skillet! She'd turned the flame too high. Or, thoughts flying skyward out the window, she hadn't been watching the stove.

Garlic! So much garlic. Their food was saturated with it. The smell of garlic on her in-laws' breaths. On the mother-in-law's breath. And bad teeth. *Momma* leaning close. *Momma* not to be avoided. A short jiggling little sausage of a woman. Witchy hook nose and sharp chin. Bosom collapsed into her belly. Yet she wore black dresses with collars. Her ears were pierced, she always wore earrings. Around her fatty neck, a gold cross on a gold chain.

Always she wore stockings. Like Grandma Della's cotton stockings. The Blond Actress had seen photographs of her mother-in-law when she'd been a young woman in Italy, not beautiful but good-looking, sexy as a Gypsy. Even as a girl she'd been sturdy. How many babies had that rubbery little body produced? Now it was food. All was food. For the men to devour. And did they devour it! The woman had become food and loved eating, herself.

Years ago in Mrs. Glazer's kitchen, she'd been happy. Norma Jeane Glazer. Mrs. Bucky Glazer. The family had taken her in as a daughter. She'd loved Bucky's mother and had married Bucky to acquire both a husband and a mother. Oh, years ago! Her heart had been broken but she'd survived. And now she was an adult and had no need of a mother. Not this mother! She was nearing twenty-eight and no longer an orphan girl. Her husband wanted her to be a wife, and a daughter-in-law to his parents. He wanted her to be a glamorous woman in public, in his company; but only in his company, under his close supervision. Yet she was an adult; she had her own career if not an identity. Unless to be "Marilyn Monroe" was the entire career. And possibly the career would not last long. There were days that passed with excruciating slowness (these San Francisco days at her in-laws' for instance), yet years passed rapidly as a landscape glimpsed from a speeding vehicle. No man had a right to marry her and wish to change her! As if to claim *I love you* was to claim *I have the right to change you.* "Why am I any different from him, in his prime? An athlete. You have only so many years." She saw the knife slip from her wet fingers and bounce on the floor. "Oh!—I'm sorry, Momma." The women in the kitchen stared at her. What did they think, she'd tried to stab their feet? Their fat ankles? Quickly she held the knife under running water at the sink and dried it on a towel and returned to her task of chopping. Oh, but she was bored! Her Grushenka heart raged with boredom.

Time for frying chicken livers. That rich sour smell that made her gag.

Every girl and woman in the U.S. envied her! As every man envied the Yankee Slugger.

At the Pasadena Playhouse, she'd known she was in the presence of a great talent. The Playwright whose poetry entered her heart. His was a vision of tragic suffering in the near-at-hand. "Ordinary" life. *You give your heart to the world, it's all you have. And then it's gone.* These words spoken at a man's gravesite, at the very end of the play, suffused with an eerie blue light that slowly faded, had haunted the Blond Actress for weeks.

"I could act in his plays. Except there's no role for 'Marilyn.' " She smiled. She laughed. "That's good. I'll be someone else for him, then."

They were watching her, frying chicken livers. Last time, she'd practically set the kitchen on fire. Was she talking to herself? Smiling? Like a three-year-old, inventing stories. Almost, you didn't want to interrupt. You could scare her, she'd drop the frying fork on your feet.

Feverish and heavy-limbed since she'd given up Doc Bob's prescription drugs. Vowing she'd never take anything stronger than aspirin again; she'd had a close call unable to wake or be wakened for fifteen hours of stuporous sleep, until her desperate husband had been about to call an ambulance and he'd made her promise him *never again!* and she'd promised, and she meant to keep that promise. So the Ex-Athlete would see how serious she was. Not just she was saying no to The Studio, no more Marilyn sex films, but she was a devoted wife, a good woman. The Ex-Athlete would see how she'd been a damned good sport this weekend. Even gone to mass with them. The women. Oh, the Sacred Heart of Jesus! There at a side altar of the cavernous incense-smelling old church. That lurid exposed heart like a part of the body you shouldn't see. *Take of my heart, and eat.*

The Ex-Athlete, the celebrity ballplayer, had been excommunicated for marrying the Blond Actress, yet the archbishop of San Francisco was a family friend and a baseball fan and "maybe, somehow" things would work out. (How? This marriage annulled?) She'd gone to mass with the women. They'd seemed delighted to take her, pretty Marilyn. The only blonde in their dark-haired olive-skinned midst. Taller than Momma by a head. She hadn't brought a suitable hat so Momma gave her a black lace mantilla to cover her hair. Plenty of hot dark Italian eyes drifting onto her and snagging though she'd worn nothing provocative, clothes dull as a nun's. Oh but so bored in church! The Latin mass, a priest's high droning voice, interrupted by bell-ringing (to wake you?) and so *long*. But she'd been a good sport, her husband would appreciate it. And in the kitchen preparing enormous meals and cleaning up afterward while he'd been out on the boat with his brothers or tossing a baseball around at the old school with guys from the neighborhood he needed to pretend were his buddies. Signing autographs for kids or their fathers with that shy-startled smile that made you love him, though it was becoming a familiar smile, not so spontaneous as it might seem. In a movie or a play he might say *I know it's hard for you, darling. I know my family can be overbearing. My mother.* He might say simply *Thank you. I love you!* But it wasn't realistic to expect the man who was her husband to make such a speech, he hadn't the words, never would he have the words, and she dared not supply them.

Don't you condescend to me! Once he'd turned upon her a face of incandescent fury and she flinched before him. And how sexy he was, his blood up.

Oh, but she loved him! She was desperate with love for him. She wanted to have his babies, she wanted to be happy with him—and for him. He'd promised to make her happy. She needed to trust him. The key to her happiness wasn't in her keeping but in his. For if he no longer loved her? The stink of frying liver and its steam were making her head spin. She'd tied her hair back to keep it out of her sweaty face. She perceived her mother-in-law and another of the older female relatives watching her with approval. *She's learning!* they were saying in Italian. *She's a good girl, this wife.* It was a movie scene in a movie of the sort that moves inexorably to a happy ending. She'd seen the movie many times. In this household amid her husband's big noisy family she wasn't the Blond Actress and certainly she wasn't Marilyn Monroe, for no one could be "Marilyn" without a camera to record her. She wasn't Norma Jeane, either. Only just the Ex-Athlete's wife.

It wasn't in secret that she packed the purple-sequin gown to take with them to Tokyo, though he'd accuse her of this. Oh, she swore! Or if it was, if she'd purposefully hidden it from him, it was a secret meant to please him. Like the open-toed ankle-strap spike-heeled silver sandals. And certain items of black lace lingerie he'd purchased for her. She would also bring a blond wig, an almost exact replica of her platinum blond cotton-candy hair, but this wig would be discarded on the evening of her arrival in Tokyo.

Oh, how'd she know she'd be invited by a U.S. Army colonel to "boost G.I. morale" in Korea? She'd swear, at the time she hardly knew where that tragic country was "situated."

In her paperback copy of the classic *The Paradox of Acting*, which someone had given her, she underlined in red ink:

As eternity is a sphere whose center is everywhere and circumference nowhere, so the true actor discovers that his stage is both everywhere and nowhere.

This, on the eve of their departure for Japan.

The Ex-Athlete was a man of so few words, in a sense he, too, was a mime.

For her final mime class (which no one but the Blond Actress knew would be her final class) she portrayed an aged woman on her deathbed. Her fellow students were captivated by her painfully realistic performance, so different from their own breezy stylized mimery. The Blond Actress lay flat on her back in a black sheath to her ankles, barefoot, and lifted herself by degrees through anguish, doubt, and despair, yielding finally to an acceptance of her fate and a joyous awakening to—Death? She lifted and lifted herself until like a dancer she was balanced on the balls of her trembling feet, her arms stretched over her head. For a long ecstatic moment she retained this posture, her body trembling.

You could see her heart beating. Against her breastbone. You could see the life vibrating inside her, on the brink of breaking out. Some of us swore, her skin was translucent!

It wasn't just I was in love with the woman because I'm not sure that I ever was.

What wasn't being said was, he couldn't forgive her for being bored by his family. His family!

He was choked with it. What was unsaid. Unsaid and unforgiven. *His wife was bored with his family and with him.*

Did she think herself superior to them? *Her?*

At Christmas they'd driven up and she'd been quiet, watchful, sweet-smiling, polite. Hardly saying a word. Laughing when others laughed. She was the kind of baby-faced woman both men and women tell their stories to, and she seemed to be listening wide-eyed and impressed, but he, the husband, the only one of them who knew her, could see how her attention was forced, her smile faded, leaving only its lines around her mouth. She knew to defer to his father and to older male relatives. She knew to defer to his mother and to older female relatives. She knew to make a fuss over babies and small children and to compliment their mothers—"You must be so happy! So proud." There was no flaw to her performance but he could see it was a performance and that pissed him. Like taking a few bites of chicken liver, sweetbreads, marinated thin-sliced salmon, anchovy paste, and practically tears in her eyes saying it's delicious but she isn't very hungry right now. Almost a look of panic in her face with so much shouting, laughing, crowding, and jostling, and kids running screaming in and out of the room, and the football game on TV turned up loud for the hard-of-hearing among the men. And afterward she'd apologized to him, leaning against him in that weak guilty way of hers, pressing her cheek against his cheek, saying she'd never had any real Christmas when she was growing up. As if that was the problem.

"I guess I got a lot to learn, Daddy? Huh?"

After the wedding, when you'd expect her to be more relaxed with the family and happy to visit them, she wasn't. Oh, she gave that impression, or tried to. But he, the husband—an athlete trained to read his opponents' deadpan expressions, a batter skilled not only at deciphering a pitcher's every nuance of a twitch but at keeping in his consciousness the exact position of every opposing player on the field relative to one another and to his teammates (if any) on base, and to him—could tell. Did she think he was blind?

Did she think he was just another asshole like the kind she'd "dated" since possibly junior high? Did she think he was insensitive as her, passing off as a joke her vomiting through the night after one of Momma's rich marathon meals? She knew, she was always assuring him, that his family "blames me, a little" for him being excommunicated from the Church. Sure, he'd been divorced, and the Church doesn't recognize divorce, but it was only when he remarried (a divorced woman!) that he violated canon law and had to be excommunicated. She needed to make that up to them, if they doubted her. Doubted her sincerity. Her integrity. Her seriousness about life and about religion. "Maybe I'll convert? To Catholicism? Would you accept that, Daddy? My m-mother is Catholic, sort of."

So she went to mass with them. The women. His mother, and his elderly grandmother, and his aunts. And kids. And both Momma and his aunt complained she was "always craning her neck" — "smiling." Like you don't do in church. Like something is funny? At a side altar when they were coming in she pointed to a statue and whispered, "Why is his heart outside his body?" And that smile, like everything is a joke. "Pappa says it's a scared smile, she's a scared little bird. So she's nervous? People looking at her. Because they do. Knowing she's your wife, and who she is. And she kept pulling the shawl over her head and it kept slipping off like this was an accident and she yawned so much during mass we thought her jaws were gonna break. Then it's communion, and she's going to come with us! 'Aren't I supposed to?' she asked. We told her no, you're not Catholic, are you Catholic, Marilyn? and she said with this hurt little baby pout, 'Oh. You know I'm not.' Sure she's aware of men looking at her, that walk of hers. And she's got her head bowed but her eyes are skittering all over. In the car coming home she says how interesting the service was, like 'service' is some word we're supposed to know. She says this word 'Cath-ol-i-cism' like it's something anybody would know. She says with that breathy laugh 'Oh, that was long, wasn't it!' and the kids laughing at her in the car saying, "Long? That's why we go to nine o'clock mass, that priest is the fast one.' 'Long? Wait'll we take you to high mass.' 'Or a requiem mass!' and everybody laughing at her, and the shawl sliding off her hair that's so slippery and shiny like a dummy's hair in a department store, that's why the shawl don't stay."

In the kitchen, it was true she tried hard. She meant well but she was clumsy. It was easier to take things from her and do them yourself. So she'd get jumpy and nervous, if you came near. She'd let pasta boil to a mush if you didn't watch her every second and she was always dropping things, like the big knife. She couldn't do a risotto, her mind was always drifting off. She tasted something, she didn't know what she was tasting. 'Is it too salty? Does it need salt?' She thought onions and garlic were the same thing! She thought olive oil was the same as melted margarine! She said, 'People make pasta? I mean—not just in a store?' Your aunt gives her a marinated hard-boiled egg out of the refrigerator and she says, 'Oh is this to eat? I mean—standing up?' "

The Ex-Athlete, the husband, listened politely to his mother's litany of complaints, which were riddled with the refrain *Well, it's none of my business.* He would listen, and he would say nothing. His face darkened with blood, he stared at the floor, and when Momma finished he walked out of the room, and in his wake invariably he'd hear in wounded Italian *See? He blames me.*

It offended him more, his bachelor's sense of propriety, that his wife left any room she inhabited a mess, failing to pick up not only after him but after herself. Even in his parents' household. He'd swear she hadn't been so distracted before they were married, she'd been neat and clean and prettily shy about undressing in his presence. Now, he stumbled over clothes of hers he hadn't remembered her owning, let alone wearing recently. Tissues caked with makeup! In their bathroom at his parents' home there were ugly splotches of makeup in the sink, a toothpaste tube missing a top, blond hairs in combs and hairbrushes, and scum in the bathtub for Momma to discover when they left, unless he cleaned it himself. God *damn.*

Sometimes she forgot to flush the toilet.

It wasn't drugs, he was certain. He'd destroyed her cache and read her the riot act and she'd sworn she would never, never swallow another pill—"Oh, Daddy! Believe me." He couldn't figure it: since she wasn't doing a movie why'd she need quick energy or courage? Almost, it seemed it was ordinary life baffled her. Like one of his teammates, only good in the heat of a close game, otherwise a chronic fuckup. She was so earnest, saying, "Daddy, it's so scary: how a scene with actual people just goes on and *on?* Like on a bus? What's to stop it?" And, that wistful little-girl look in her face, "D'you ever think, Daddy, how hard it is to figure what people mean when probably they don't mean anything? Not like a script. Or that the point of something happening is when probably there's no point, it just 'happened'? Like the weather?" He'd shake his head, not knowing what the hell to say. He'd dated actresses and models and party girls, and he'd have sworn he knew the personality type, but Marilyn was something else. Like his buddies said, suggestively, giving him a poke in the ribs to make him blush, *Marilyn's something else, eh?* Those assholes didn't know the half of it.

Sometimes she scared him. Kind of. Like if an actual doll opened its blue glass eyes and you're expecting baby talk but she says something so weird, and possibly so deep, it's like one of these Zen riddles, you can't grasp it. And saying it in the vocabulary of a ten-year-old. He'd try to assure her sure he understood, sort of. "See, Marilyn, you been working nonstop for ten years making movies, almost like me, a real pro; now you're taking a break, it's off-season for you, like for me I'm retired, see?"—but by this time he'd lost the point of what he was saying. He wasn't good at bullshitting. Just he could appreciate the similarity between them. Like when you're a top pro and the eyes of the world on you and it's a tight season including playoffs and the Series, never do you have to cast around for something to think about, let alone *do*. And a game in session consumes those hours of that day as nothing else can, except possibly fighting in a war or dying. "In boxing they say 'That got his attention.' When a guy is hit hard." He told her this meaning to be sympathetic, and she looked at him smiling and confused like he was speaking a foreign language. "It's about attention," he said, faltering. "Concentration. And if you don't have that—" His words drifted off like children's balloons, lacking gravity.

Once, at their place in Bel Air, he'd come upon her in their bedroom and she was hurriedly cleaning the clothes-strewn room, though a maid (he'd hired himself) was due in a few hours. She'd showered and was stark naked except for a towel wrapped like a turban around her head. She acted guilty seeing him and stammered, "I d-don't know how the room got this way. I've been sick, I guess." It was like, he'd come to think, she was two people: the blind-seeming and totally self-absorbed woman who left a mess in her wake and the alert and intelligent and stricken woman, a girl really, her eyes snatching at his like they were two kids together in this predicament maybe fifteen years old somehow waking up married. In that instant her body seemed to him not a woman's beautiful voluptuous body but a responsibility they jointly shared, like a giant baby.

But in his parents' house on Beach Street in San Francisco he felt estranged from her. Even as she gazed at him with her wistful-guilty look. Even as, out of sight of his family, she'd pluck at him with her fingers. *Help me! I'm drowning.* Somehow, this hardened his heart against her. His first wife had gotten along well with his family, or reasonably well. And Marilyn was the dream girl everybody was primed to adore. Yet she shut up like a clam if anybody asked her about being a "movie star," as if she'd never heard of such a thing. Blushing and stammering if anybody spoke of seeing her movies as if she was ashamed of them, which possibly she was. She was tongue-tied with embarrassment when one of the Ex-Athlete's nieces asked innocently, "Is your hair real?" Then, a while later, he'd see a savage look in her face: it was Rose, the bitch. Superior. Scornful. Well, Rose was only a waitress, in that trashy film, and a slut. And Marilyn Monroe—a pinup, a photographer's model, a starlet, and God knows what else.

He'd wanted to belt her. Who did she think she was, looking at his family like that?

He'd never told her, of course: he'd come close to canceling their first date when a friend called to tell him Monroe had been involved with Bob Mitchum, a notorious coke user and a suspected Commie; the story was she'd gotten pregnant and Mitchum had beaten her in a rage and caused a miscarriage.

(Was any of this true? He knew how rumors spread, how people lied. He'd hired a private detective recommended by his friend Frank Sinatra, who'd hired him to check up on Ava Gardner with whom he was crazy in love, but the results were, after a six-hundred-buck fee, "inconclusive.")

One thing was certain. Long before he knew her, she'd posed for nude photos. There was a perennial tale in Hollywood that Monroe had done a few porn films in her late teens, too, but none of these ever surfaced. After they were married, a so-called photography dealer contacted the Ex-Athlete through a business associate saying he had some photo negatives he believed "Miss Monroe's husband would wish to acquire." The Ex-Athlete called the man and asked bluntly was this blackmail? Extortion? The dealer protested it was just a business transaction. "You pay, Slugger. And I deliver."

The Ex-Athlete asked how much. The dealer named a sum.

"Nothing's worth that."

"If you love the lady, sure it is."

The Ex-Athlete spoke quietly. "I can have you hurt. You cocksucker."

"Hey, now. That's not the right attitude."

The Ex-Athlete didn't reply.

The dealer said, quickly, "I'm on your side. I'm an old admirer of yours, actually. And the lady's too. She's a real high-class lady, in fact. About the only one of them with any integrity. The females, I mean." He paused. The Ex-Athlete could hear him breathing. "What I feel strongly is, these negatives should be off the market so they can't be misappropriated."

A meeting was arranged. The Ex-Athlete went alone. For a long time he examined the prints. She'd been so young! Hardly more than a girl. The photos were calendar-art nudes, from the series to which "Miss Golden Dreams 1949" belonged, which he'd already seen in *Playboy*. A few were more frontal, more revealing. A swath of darkish-blond pubic hair, the tender soles of her naked feet. Her feet! He wanted to kiss her feet. This was the woman he loved before she'd become that woman. She hadn't been Marilyn yet. Her hair wasn't platinum blond but a honey-brown shade, wavy and curly to her shoulders. A sweet-faced trusting girl. Even her breasts looked different. Her nose, her eyes. The tilt of her head. She hadn't learned yet to be Marilyn. He realized that this was the girl he truly loved. The other, Marilyn, he was crazy for, or maybe crazed over, but you couldn't trust the woman.

So the Ex-Athlete bought the prints and the negatives and paid the "photography dealer" in cash, so filled with disgust for the transaction he could barely force himself to meet the man's eye. It wasn't just the Ex-Athlete was this girl's husband, he was a man of integrity. What the world knew of him, his manliness, his pride, even his reticence, was true. "Thanks, Slugger. You did the right thing." Like a boxer trained not to lead but to counterpunch, the Ex-Athlete jerked his head up at this sniggering remark and met the eyes of his tormentor, a mollusk-faced Caucasian of no specific age, greasy hair, sideburns, a smiling row of capped teeth, and without a word the Ex-Athlete balled his fist and threw a punch into the teeth, a punch uncoiled from the shoulder, a damned good punch for a guy almost forty, not in top condition, and basically sweet-natured and not a fighter. The dealer stumbled and went down. It happened fast and clean as a home run. Even the beautiful *crack!* of the blow. The Ex-Athlete, panting now, still wordless, nursing his cut knuckles, walked swiftly away.

He'd destroy the evidence. Prints, negatives. Up in smoke.

" 'Miss Golden Dreams 1949.' If I'd met you then."

This episode, the Ex-Athlete played and replayed like a movie. It was his movie, no one else knew. He'd never tell the Blond Actress. Observing her with his family, her forced fading smile, the glaze of boredom in her eyes, he was forced to acknowledge that his generosity, his forgiveness, the affection of his family, his mother's effort, were unappreciated by his wife. Maybe she wasn't on drugs but she was god-damned self-absorbed, selfish. By the end of Sunday dinner she'd disappeared again. Where the hell? The Ex-Athlete saw his relatives' eyes on him as he stalked off to find her. Knowing how they'd murmur in Italian, when he left the room. *It's between him and her, nobody's business. You think she's maybe pregnant?*

In their bedroom, she was doing dance exercises. Lifting her legs, pulling at her toes. She wore a silky rust-orange dress he'd bought her in New York, which wasn't an appropriate costume for doing exercises in, and she was in her stocking feet, and there were snags and runs in her stockings. Across the unmade bed and on the chairs and even the carpet were items of clothing, hers and his, and damp towels, and books—God damn he was fed up with her books, one of her suitcases was stuffed mostly with books, he had to carry the fucker and he resented it. In Hollywood it was an open joke Marilyn Monroe thought she was an intellectual, never graduated from high school even and mispronounced every other word she spoke. "Where'd you go so fast? What's this?" She turned a bright insincere actressy smile on him, and his hand shot out and struck her on the jaw.

Not a fist. An opened hand, his palm.

"Oh!—oh, please."

She stumbled and cringed backward, sitting down hard on the bed. Except for her red-lipstick mouth her face was deathly white and looked like a piece of china in the instant before it shatters. A single tear rolled down her cheek.

He was beside her, holding her. "No, Daddy. It was my fault. Oh, Daddy, I'm *sorry*." She began to cry, and he held her, and after a while they made love, or tried to, except outside the windows, outside the shut door, she could hear murmurous muffled voices, like waves lapping. Finally they gave up and just held each other. "Daddy, forgive me? I won't do it again."

It was the Ex-Athlete who'd been officially invited to Japan, to launch the 1954 Japanese baseball season, but it was the Blond Actress whom reporters, photographers, and TV people were wild to see. It was the Blond Actress whom large crowds were wild to glimpse. At the Tokyo airport, security police held back hundreds of staring yet strangely expressionless and silent Japanese. Only a few called to the Blond Actress, in an eerie, near-uniform chant—"*Monchan! Monchan!*" Some of the younger fans dared to throw flowers, which dropped to the soiled concrete pavement like shot songbirds. The Blond Actress, who'd never been in a foreign country, still less on the far side of earth from her home, gripped the arm of the Ex-Athlete. Security guards escorted them briskly to their limousine. It had not yet dawned on the Blond Actress, though it was insultingly clear to the Ex-Athlete, that the crowds had come out for her and not him. "What is '*mon-chan*'?" the Blond Actress asked uneasily and was told by their escort, with a shivery giggle, "You." "Me? But my husband's the one your country has invited, not me." She was incensed on his behalf; she gripped his hand indignantly. Outside the limo, on either side of the airport access road, more Japanese crowded to see the *monchan* seated stiffly in the rear of the limo behind tinted protective glass. They were waving more vigorously than those inside the terminal had dared to wave, and tossing flowers more vigorously, more flowers, and larger flowers, landing with soft splattering thumps on the roof and windshield of the limo. In eerie near-unison like robots they chanted "Mon-chan! Mon-chan! *Mon-chan!*"

The Blond Actress laughed nervously. Were they trying to say "Marilyn"? This was how "Marilyn" sounded, in Japanese?

At the elegant Imperial Hotel, more crowds waited in the street. Traffic had been blocked off. A police helicopter droned overhead. "Oh! What do they want?" the Blond Actress whispered. This was a mad scene out of a Charlie Chaplin film. A silent-film comedy. Except the crowd here wasn't silent but impatient, clamorous. The Blond Actress wanted to protest; weren't the Japanese supposed to be a restrained people? Bound by tradition, exquisitely polite? Except in wartime, the Blond Actress recalled with horror, oh, remember Pearl Harbor! remember the Japanese P.O.W. camps! Jap atrocities! She was thinking, too, of ol' Hirohito's skull on the radio cabinet. Those empty socket eyes boring into her own eyes if she grew careless. "Mon-CHAN! Mon-CHAN!" came the thunderous chant. The

Blond Actress and the Ex-Athlete, both visibly shaken, were escorted into the hotel while hundreds of Tokyo police struggled to hold back the swarming crowd. "Oh, what do these people want with *me?* I thought this civilization was superior to ours. I was *hoping*." The Blond Actress spoke earnestly but no one heard. No one was listening. The Ex-Athlete's face was heavy and grim with blood. They'd been traveling for so long, his jaws were shaded with stubble.

There were hurried formalities, in the hotel lobby and in the luxury suite on the eighth floor reserved for the Ex-Athlete and his wife. There was a ceremonial greeting by one set of hosts and there was a second ceremonial greeting by another set of hosts. All the while, outside the windows, the chant *Mon-chan! Mon-chan! Mon-chan!* rose from the street below. It had become more demanding, like lapping waves stirred by a sudden wind. The Blond Actress tried to speak to one of their Japanese hosts about Zen poetry and the "stillness at the core of agitation" but the man smiled and nodded so eagerly, making little bows with his head, murmuring agreement, she soon gave up. She was tempted to peer out the window but dared not. The Ex-Athlete, ignoring the crowd on the street below, ignored her as well. Were they trapped in the hotel? How could they venture out onto the street? *Now my punishment is beginning* she thought. *I let them kill my baby. It's followed me here. It wants to devour me.*

She was the only woman in the room. She laughed suddenly and ran into a bathroom and locked the door.

Sometime later she emerged smelling faintly of vomit, shaky and pale except for a fierce red-lipstick mouth. The Ex-Athlete who was Daddy when they were alone together but not Daddy now spoke quietly with her, his arm around her waist. Their Japanese hosts had suggested to him through a translator that, if she'd consent to appear on the balcony for just a few seconds, to acknowledge their presence and accept their homage, the crowd would be appeased and disperse. The Blond Actress shuddered. "I c-can't do that." The Ex-Athlete, deeply embarrassed, tightened his arm around her waist. He told her, haltingly, that he'd be beside her. The Tokyo police chief would precede her on the balcony and explain to the crowd through a bullhorn that Miss Marilyn Monroe was very tired from her plane flight and could not entertain them at the present time but that she thanked them for coming to see her. He would say that she was "deeply honored" to be visiting their homeland. She would then present herself demurely to them, say a few words, smile and wave in a friendly but formal manner, and that would be all. "Oh, Daddy, don't make me," the Blond Actress said, sniffing. "Don't make me go out there." The Ex-Athlete assured her he'd be close beside her. It would be a matter of less than a minute. "This is for them to 'save face.'"

So they can go home, and we can have dinner. You know what that is, 'saving face'?" The Blond Actress eased away from the Ex-Athlete. "Whose face?" The Ex-Athlete laughed as if this made sense, and was funny. Carefully he repeated what his Japanese hosts had suggested, and when the Blond Actress stared at him unhearing, he said again, more forcibly, "Look. I'll be standing right beside you. It's just Japanese protocol. 'Marilyn Monroe' brought them here, and only 'Marilyn Monroe' can release them." The Blond Actress seemed finally to hear this.

She agreed to the request, at last. The Ex-Athlete, face roiled with shame, thanked her. She withdrew to a bedroom to change her clothes and surprised the Ex-Athlete by reappearing so quickly, in a dark tailored wool suit, a red scarf tied around her neck. She'd rubbed rouge onto her cheeks and powdered her face and done something to her hair to make it fuller and more luminously blond than it had been, flattened and disheveled after the long plane flight. All this while the crowd had continued their dirgelike chanting: "Mon-*chan!* Mon-*chan!*" There were sirens. Several helicopters droned overhead. In the corridor outside their suite, a sound of footfalls and men's voices lifted in shouted commands. Was it the Imperial Japanese Army, occupying the hotel? Or did the Japanese Army no longer exist, demolished by the Allies?

The Blond Actress didn't wait to be escorted onto the balcony but stepped quickly forward, followed by the Ex-Athlete. Eight stories below, in the street, spilling out onto the pavement in their privileged position in front of the Imperial Hotel, a small mob of photographers and TV crews were recording the scene for posterity. Spotlights glared out of the night like deranged moons. Through a bullhorn, the chief of Tokyo police addressed the crowd, which was now respectfully subdued. Then the Blond Actress, escorted by the Ex-Athlete, came forward. Shyly she lifted a hand. The vast crowd below murmured. The chanting began again, more musically now, sensuously— "Mon-*chan.* Mon-*chan.*" Smiling, suffused suddenly with a bitter sort of happiness, the Blond Actress leaned both hands on the balcony railing and gazed down into the crowd. *Where there are no faces visible, there's God.* As far as she could see the crowd extended, a great multiheaded beast, rapt and expectant.

"I am—'*mon-chan.*' I love you." The wind blew away her words, yet the crowd listened in hushed silence. "I am—'*mon-chan.*' Forgive us Nagasaki! Hiroshima! I love you." She hadn't spoken into the bullhorn and her husky-whispery words went unheard. Only a few yards above the hotel roof a helicopter skidded by, deafening. In a flamboyant gesture the Blond Actress lifted both hands to her hair, took hold of the luxuriant platinum-blond wig and detached it from her own hair (which was brushed back flat and secured with bobby pins), tore it free, and tossed it to the wind. " 'Mon-chan'—loves you! And you! And you!"

Rapturous the Japanese faces far below, struck dumb by the swath of bright blond hair that for some teasing seconds rode the wind—and a cold northerly wind it was—then began to drop, drifting and turning as in a spiral, gliding laterally like a hawk, to disappear at last into a vortex of upraised yearning hands.

That night, when at last they were alone together, the Blond Actress turned from the Ex-Athlete when he touched her. Bitterly she said, "You never answered me—'Whose face?' "

In her Tokyo journal, this terse notation.

The Japanese have a name for me.
Monchan is their name for me.
"Precious little girl" is their name for me.
When my soul flew out from me.

He didn't want her to go. He didn't think it was a "good idea" at this time.

She asked what was "this time." What distinguished "this time" from another time.

He had no reply. His sullen face resembled his bruised knuckles.

Afterward the Blond Actress would plead: It was purely chance, wasn't it? How could it be her fault?

That in Tokyo, at a party at the American embassy, she would meet this Colonel of the U.S. Army. So suave! And so many medals! The Colonel, drawn to the Blond Actress like every other man in the room, asked her if she would be willing to entertain U.S. troops stationed in Korea?

The time-honored American tradition of "boosting morale" among the enlisted. The time-honored American tradition of Hollywood stars performing gratis before enormous G.I. audiences, their photos in *Life*.

How could the Blond Actress not say *yes*? Excitedly recalling newsreels of the forties: glamorous Rita Hayworth, Betty Grable, Marlene Dietrich, Bob Hope, and Bing Crosby and Dorothy Lamour *entertaining the troops overseas*.

Said the Blond Actress in her little-girl breathy voice *Oh, yes sir, thank you! It's the least I can do*.

Except she wasn't sure why U.S. troops were stationed in Korea? Hadn't there been an armistice the previous year? (And what exactly was an "armistice"?) The Blond Actress told the Colonel she didn't approve of

American-imperialist military intervention in foreign nations but she understood that American G.I.s, far from home, away from their families and sweethearts, must get terribly lonely.

Politics isn't their fault. And it isn't mine!

Fortunately she'd brought the low-cut purple-sequin gown the Ex-Athlete loved her in. And the ankle-strap spike-heeled silver sandals.

Fortunately she could sing by rote, like a big animated doll, songs from *Gentlemen Prefer Blondes.* How many times she'd sung "Diamonds Are a Girl's Best Friend," "When Love Goes Wrong," "A Little Girl from Little Rock." There was the disturbing smoldering-sexy "Kiss" from *Niagara.* And "I Wanna Be Loved by You" and "My Heart Belongs to Daddy." These were painstaking recordings she'd made as Marilyn Monroe that had involved as many as twenty-five sessions apiece, after which The Studio's crafty singing coach dissected the separate pieces of tape and reassembled them to make a perfect seamless recording.

All this flashed through the Blond Actress's mind even as the Colonel spoke. And the realization that, though this was her and the Ex-Athlete's honeymoon, the Ex-Athlete might love her even more if she wasn't always there warming the bench.

Deadpan she told the Colonel *Oh, know what?—I can do some Shakespeare soliloquys. And I can do mime! An old, old woman on her death bed, I performed just last month. How's that sound?*

The look on the Colonel's face. The Blond Actress squeezed his hand; almost she'd wanted to kiss him. *Oh, hey. Just kidding.*

So it happened, the Ex-Athlete would remain alone in Japan. This was his and the Blond Actress's honeymoon but there were professional obligations too—he'd explained to the goddam reporters who trailed him everywhere in public—they had to honor. The Ex-Athlete traveled to exhibition games through all of Japan, without his blond-actress wife but accompanied by an entourage, and everywhere he was honored, tall and gracious, as the Great American Baseball Player. Day following day he was honored at luncheons and interminable multicourse dinner banquets. (Where, sometimes, he'd swear he saw movement in the repulsive delicacies he was expected to eat, Christ how he yearned for a cheeseburger and fries, spaghetti and meatballs, even a gummy risotto!) Maybe a drunken evening with geishas? The least a man deserves, in Japan. A man traveling without his wife, by temperament a bachelor, furious with the wife after whom everybody persists in asking *Where is Mari-lyn?*

When it was he, the Ex-Athlete, who'd been invited to Japan.

He was pissed with her, the more he thought about it. Running off and leaving him. And she'd only pretended, before they were married, she'd liked baseball! He'd been shocked to overhear her tell a Japanese journalist *Every baseball game is like every other baseball game, with some changes each time. Like the weather? One day to the next?*

No, he'd never forgive her. She'd have a lot of making up to do before he did.

Amid a frenzy of photographers and TV crews the Blond Actress was escorted by military personnel on a bumpy flight to Seoul, capital of South Korea, then by bumpier helicopter to marine and army encampments in the countryside. The Blond Actress wore olive-drab army-issue long johns, pants, shirt, windbreaker, and heavy lace-up boots. Her head was protected from icy winds by an army cap buckled beneath the chin. (For, though the time of year was April, this was not April in L.A.!) How like a girl of maybe twelve she looked, except for her gorgeous long-lashed widened blue eyes and lipstick-red mouth.

Was Marilyn scared? Hell, no. She wasn't scared at all. Maybe she didn't know that helicopters have accidents, especially in high winds like we had. Maybe, she even thought, if Marilyn's in the helicopter, it can't crash. Or maybe, like she assured us, in this little-girl voice to die for—If my number's up it's up. Or not.

A corporal, a reporter for *Stars and Stripes*, was designated to accompany the Blond Actress to the camps. For a cover feature, he'd report how the Blond Actress amazed everyone in the helicopter—especially the pilot!—by asking could they please fly low over the camp before landing, so she could wave to the men? So the pilot flies low over the camp and the Blond Actress presses against the glass, waving excitedly as a little girl at a few scattered men who happen to be outside, and glance up, and recognize her. (Of course every guy in the camp knows Marilyn Monroe is due sometime. But not exactly when.)

Do it again, please coos the Blond Actress, and the pilot laughs like a kid and swings the copter around and takes it back over the camp like a pendulum, and the wind shaking us, and the Blond Actress waves at the men again, and already there's a lot more men, and this time the men are waving back, yelling and running after the copter like crazed kids. We're thinking Now we're gonna land, but next the Blond Actress amazes us even more saying *Let's surprise them, huh? Open the door and hang on to me?* and we can't believe what this gorgeous crazy broad wants to do but she's got the idea she needs to do it, like it's a movie scene maybe; she can see how it would play from the ground, the aerial view and the ground view alternating, and it's a suspenseful scene, too, so she lies down on the copter floor and instructs us to grab on to her legs, and suddenly we're all in this movie; we slide the door open partway, and the wind's practically enough to capsize us, but Marilyn is determined, she even takes off her cap—*so they can see who it is!* And she leans out the door, and is almost falling, not scared but laughing at us 'cause we're scared shitless, holding her legs so hard she'd be bruised by our fingers for sure, and it must've hurt, not to mention the icy wind, her hair whipping like crazy, but the pilot does what she requests, by this time he's figuring, like her, like all of us, if anybody's number is up it's up and if not, not.

So we carom over the camp with Marilyn Monroe hanging out of our aircraft waving and blowing kisses to the men, screaming *Oh! I love you! You American G.I.'s!* not once, not twice, but three times. Three times! By this time the entire camp's out: officers, the camp commander, everybody. Guys on K.P., guys in the infirmary in pajamas, guys in latrines stumbling outside and holding up their pants. "*Marilyn! Marilyn!*" everybody's yelling. Guys climb up onto roofs and water tanks and some of them fall and break bones, the poor saps. One guy out of the infirmary slips and falls in the stampede and is trampled. It's a mob scene. Feeding time in the zoo, apes and monkeys. M.P.s have to beat the most reckless guys back from the landing strip.

The copter lands, and there's Marilyn Monroe climbing out flanked by us guys, looking like we'd been electric shocked and loved it. Marilyn's got frostbite-white cheeks and nose and those big bright glassy blue eyes and long lashes and her hair's in wild clumps, that hair of a color we'd never seen before except in movies and you wouldn't think it's real, but it is, and she's got tears in her eyes crying *Oh! oh! this is the h-happiest day of my life* and if we hadn't stopped her she'd have run right out and grabbed guys' hands where they were reaching for her, she'd have hugged and kissed them like she's everybody's sweetheart from back home. The mob would've torn her limb from limb loving her, for sure they'd have torn her wild-beaten blond hair out by the roots, crazy with love for Marilyn, so we had to hold her back, and she didn't fight us but she's saying, like it's a profound Zen truth that hit her square between the eyes *This is the happiest day of my life, oh, thank you!*

Absolutely, you could see she meant it.

THE AMERICAN GODDESS OF LOVE ON THE SUBWAY GRATING

New York City 1954

"Ohhhhh."

A lush-bodied girl in the prime of her physical beauty. In an ivory georgette crepe sundress with a halter top that gathers her breasts up in soft undulating folds of the fabric. She's standing with bare legs apart on a New York subway grating. Her blond head is thrown rapturously back as an updraft lifts her full, flaring skirt, exposing white cotton panties. White cotton! The ivory-crepe sundress is floating and filmy as magic. The dress is magic. Without the dress the girl would be female meat, raw and exposed.

She's not thinking such a thought! Not her.

She's an American girl healthy and clean as a Band-Aid. She's never had a soiled or a sulky thought. She's never had a melancholy thought. She's never had a savage thought. She's never had a desperate thought. She's never had an un-American thought. In the papery-thin sundress she's a nurse with tender hands. A nurse with luscious mouth. Sturdy thighs, bountiful breasts, tiny folds of baby fat at her armpits. She's laughing and squealing like a four-year-old as another updraft lifts her skirt. Dimpled knees, a dancer's strong legs. This husky healthy girl. The shoulders, arms, breasts belong to a fully mature woman but the face is a girl's face. Shivering in New York City midsummer as subway steam lifts her skirt like a lover's quickened breath.

"Oh! *Ohhhhh*."

It's nighttime in Manhattan, Lexington Avenue at 51st Street. Yet the white-white lights exude the heat of midday. The goddess of love has been standing like this, legs apart, in spike-heeled white sandals so steep and so tight they've permanently disfigured her smallest toes, for hours. She's been squealing and laughing, her mouth aches. There's a gathering pool of darkness at the back of her head like tarry water. Her scalp and her pubis burn from that morning's peroxide applications. The Girl with No Name. The Girl on the Subway Grating. The Girl of Your Dreams. It's 2:40 A.M. and glaring-white lights focus upon her, upon her alone, blond squealing, blond laughter, blond Venus, blond insomnia, blond smooth-shaven legs apart and blond hands fluttering in a futile effort to keep her skirt from lifting to reveal white cotton American-girl panties and the shadow, just the shadow, of the bleached crotch.

"Ohh*hhh*."

Now she's hugging herself beneath her big bountiful breasts. Her eyelids fluttering. Between the legs, you can trust her she's clean. She's not a dirty girl, nothing foreign or exotic. She's an American slash in the flesh. That emptiness. Guaranteed. She's been scooped out, drained clean, no scar tissue to interfere with your pleasure, and no odor. Especially no odor. The Girl with No Name, the girl with no memory. She has not lived long and she will not live long.

Love me! Don't hit me.

At the edge of the floating white lights as at the edge of civility there's a crowd, mostly male, a rogue-elephant crowd restless and aroused, gathered behind NYPD barricades since shooting began at 10:30 P.M. Traffic has been blocked off, you'd think this was official business—*Oh, what? a movie being shot? Marilyn Monroe?*

And there, with the other men, anonymous like them, there the Ex-Athlete, the husband. Watching with the others. Excited aroused staring men. Men in a pack. Men through whom, massed, sexual desire passes like an agitated wave through water. There's a smoldering mood. There's an angry mood. There's a mood-to-do-hurt. There's a mood-to-grab-and-tear-and-fuck. There's a festive mood. A celebratory mood. Everybody's been drinking! He, the husband, is one of the pack. His brain is on fire. His cock is on fire. Angry-smoldering blue flames. Knowing how the female will touch and kiss and stroke him with those fingers. Soft breathy guilty voice. *Ohhh Daddy gosh I'm sorry keeping you waiting so long why didn't you wait for me back at the hotel gosh why didn't you?* Until the white lights are extinguished and the men-with-no-faces are gone and as in a cinematic quick cut they're alone together in the suite at the Waldorf-Astoria with quivering crystal chandeliers overhead and a guarantee of privacy and then she'll back away from him begging. That same baby breath. The doll eyes shiny with fear. *No. Daddy, don't. See, I'm working? Tomorrow? Everybody will know if*—But his hand, the husband's hand, will leap out. Both hands. Balled into fists. These are big hands, an athlete's hands, practiced hands, hands with fine black hairs on the backs. Because she's resisting him. Provoking him. Shielding her face against the justice of his blows—*Whore! Are you proud? Showing your crotch like that, on the street! My wife!*—with the force of his final blow sending The Girl with No Name staggering against the silk-wallpapered wall, sweet as any home run.

"MY BEAUTIFUL LOST DAUGHTER"

She would hold it in her trembling hand for some time before opening it. A Hallmark card with a red rose embossed on its cover and the words HAPPY BIRTHDAY DAUGHTER. Inside, a single sheet of paper, typed.

June 1, 1955

My Dear Daughter Norma Jeane,

I am writing to you on your birthday, to wish you a Happy Birthday & to explain I have been ill, but you are in my thoughts often.

It is your 29th birthday! Now you are an adult woman & truly no longer a girl. ~~The career of "Marilyn Monroe" will not continue much beyond age 30 I suppose?~~

I did not see your "new movie"—the vulger title & publicity attending it, giant billbords & posters, & the crude likeness of you posed with your dress lifted for all the world to see your private parts did not make me wish to purchase a ticket.

But I would not criticize you Norma Jeane, for you have your own life. It is a Postwar Generation. You have survived your sick mother's curse to make a career for yourself, for this you are to be commended.

I will say, I had hoped to meet your husband! I have been an admirer of his for many years. Though not a die-hard baseball fan like some. Norma Jeane, I was very disappointed (yet not surprised) that your marriage to this steller athlete ended in divorce & such ugly prying publicity. At least there were no children to reap the shame.

Still I hope to have a grandchild. Someday! Before it is too late.

There is the rumor that "Marilyn Monroe" has been investigated for dealings with Communists & fellow travelers. I hope to God, my dear Daughter, that there is nothing incriminating in your past. Your Hollywood life must have many crevices hidden from the light of day. The "overthrow of the U.S. Government" is a sober threat. If the Red Communists strike a nuclear blow before we can man our weapons, how can our civilization survive? Jew spies like the Rosenbergs would betray us to the enemy, & deserve their death by Electrcution. It is wrong to defend "freedom of speech" as you have done while knowing nothing of the harsh realities of life. Everyone has seen how such traitorous individuals once heralded as "great"—Charlie Chaplin & the Negro Paul Robeson are examples—behave when cornered. But no more of this! My Daughter, when I speak with you in person, I will hope to persuade you of your folly.

Soon I will contact you, I promise. Too many years have slipped away. Even your Mother begins to emerge in my memory as more sick than evil. In my recent illness I began to see that I must forgive her. And I must see you, my beautiful lost Daughter Norma. Before I "embark upon a long journey" across the sea.

Your tearful Father

AFTER THE DIVORCE

"One ticket."

The ticket seller in her booth at the Sepulveda Theater, Van Nuys, chewing spearmint gum, a chunky peroxide blonde with a cast in one eye, like a doll whose head has been playfully shaken, pushed the ticket to Norma Jeane without a second glance.

"This movie is doing pretty well, I guess?"

The ticket seller, chewing spearmint gum, nodded briefly.

"Marilyn Monroe is from Van Nuys, somebody said? Went to Van Nuys High?"

The ticket seller, chewing spearmint gum, shrugged her shoulders. Saying, bored, "Yeah, I guess. I graduated in 1953. She's a whole lot older."

An evening in July 1955. At the suburban movie house where fourteen years before, in her lost girlhood, she and a boy named Bucky Glazer had first "dated." Holding sweaty hands and "necking" in the back of the theater amid odors of greasy popcorn and men's hair oil and women's hair spray. Where Norma Jeane and Elsie Pirig won a twelve-piece set of pale green plastic dinner and salad plates in a delicate fleur-de-lis pattern. The shock of having a winning ticket! Being called up on stage, and everybody applauding! *What'd I tell you, sweetie? It's our lucky night.* Aunt Elsie had been so thrilled she'd hugged Norma Jeane and left a lipstick smear on Norma Jeane's cheek, but it would be the last time Norma Jeane and her Aunt Elsie went to the Sepulveda Theater together.

You broke my heart. No husband ever hurt me that much.

And how many times in this movie house alone or with companions years ago she'd gazed enthralled upon the Fair Princess and the Dark Prince. Her heart yearning for that beautiful fated couple. Yearning to be them. Yet somehow to be loved by them. To be taken up into their perfect world, basking in their beauty and their love, and never was there silence in that world but always music, mood music; never were you in danger of flailing about as in a choppy sea in terror of drowning.

Now above the movie marquee out front there loomed a ten-foot plaster-board blow-up of Marilyn Monroe in her notorious *Seven-Year Itch* pose. Laughing blond Marilyn standing legs apart, her pleated ivory skirt flying up to reveal legs, thighs, snug white cotton panties.

Look at you! Cow. Udders and cunt in everybody's face.

Even Norma Jeane glanced up at the marquee. Seeing and not-seeing in the same instant. *No wife of mine. You hear?* She'd heard. Her ears ringing where he'd hit her and she could hear that ringing still, faintly. Mixed with the quickened pulsing of her blood.

"But he'll never hit me again. No one will."

This was a good time for her. This month. Last month hadn't been so good, and the preceding months. Since the separation and the divorce in October. She'd moved several times. She'd had her telephone number changed even more frequently. Her former husband had threatened her. Her former husband followed her. Telephoned her. She told no one. She could not betray him further. HEARTBREAK OF A NINE-MONTH MARRIAGE. MARILYN'S TRUE STORY. She'd told no one the true story. She was not in possession of the true story. EYEWITNESS ACCOUNT OF "BADLY BEATEN" MARILYN IN NYC HOSPITAL. There'd been no eyewitnesses. Not even the fated couple. She hadn't been taken to a hospital in New York City or anywhere else. The hotel physician had treated her. Ninety minutes later at five o'clock in the morning Whitey had come silently to the luxury suite from which the Ex-Athlete had departed and with his magical hands he'd disguised bruises and even a welt above her left eye. She'd kissed Whitey's hands in gratitude. Seeing her blond beauty restored in the mirror.

If not in her heart, in the mirror. And here was her Magic Friend blond and triumphant looming above the marquee of the Sepulveda Theater laughing as if nothing ugly had ever happened to her, and never would.

". . . went to Van Nuys High. Class of 'forty-seven."

"You sure? I heard it was later."

But I never graduated. I got married instead.

Making her way through the lobby, and maybe there were glances in her direction—she was a stranger after all, and Van Nuys was a small town—but no one recognized her, and would not. No one ever recognized Norma Jeane when she didn't wish to be recognized, sometimes not even troubling to wear a wig for when she wasn't Marilyn, she wasn't Marilyn. But tonight in her curly dark brunette poodle-cut wig, in red plastic harlequin sunglasses and no makeup not even lipstick, in a navy-blue rayon housewife dress with cloth-covered belt and buttons, bare feet in cheap straw ballerina flats. Walking with buttocks pinched together as if she'd had a shot of Novocain in her rear. Unrecognized by the very patrons who were staring at Marilyn Monroe in lobby posters and movie stills and talking of her, the Van Nuys High School girl of the mid-forties, yes but her name hadn't been "Marilyn Monroe" then, what was it?—"She was adopted by some local couple. That guy owns the junkyard over on Reseda. Pisig? But she ran away from home. Pisig maybe raped her, it was all covered up."

Norma Jeane wanted to turn on these strangers and protest *You don't know anything about me, or Mr. Pirig. Leave us alone!*

In fact it was none of Norma Jeane's business what strangers said. No more what they said about her than what they said about anyone or anything else.

The lobby of the Sepulveda hadn't changed much. How vividly she recalled the red fake-velvet walls, the gilt-framed mirrors and red-plush carpeting, a grimy plastic runner from the box office booth to the entrance. The "present features" and the "coming attractions" posters and stills were in identical places on the walls. Sometimes Norma Jeane had slipped into the lobby just to study stills and coming attractions. The world held so much promise! Always new movies, always a double bill. Except if a movie was a colossal hit (like *The Seven-Year Itch*) the bill changed every Thursday. *Something to look forward to. You wouldn't ever want to kill yourself, would you!*

The ticket taker was a teenage boy in an usher's uniform, with mournful eyes and acne-raw cheeks. Norma Jeane felt sorry for him, no girl would want to kiss him. "It's busy tonight. For a week night?" she said, smiling. The ticket taker shrugged and tore her ticket in two and handed her the stub. He mumbled what sounded like "Yeah. I guess."

He was an usher, in the employ of the movie house. He'd seen *The Seven-Year Itch* many times. It had been playing here since mid-June. Glancing at Norma Jeane he'd seen a woman he might've believed to be old enough to be his mother. Why should she be hurt by his indifference? She wasn't.

She was happy! Relieved. That no one recognized her. That she could make her way alone in the world like this. An unmarried woman. A woman alone. Her left hand was bare of rings. The mark of her engagement ring and wedding band on her third finger had faded. She'd removed them that night at the Waldorf-Astoria, with cold cream. Twisting and tugging at the rings until she could force them over her knuckle. Strange that her fingers were puffy, like her face. As if she'd had an allergic reaction.

The hotel physician had given her a Seconal shot to "settle her nerves," for she'd been hysterical and had talked wildly of injuring herself. In the early afternoon of the next day, solicitous Doc Bob had given her another injection of Seconal.

That had been months ago. She hadn't had Seconal injected into her bloodstream since last November.

She didn't need drugs! Sometimes just to sleep. But this was a good time for her. She'd come to understand there must always be good times in life to balance the bad. And this was a good time, for she was settled at last in a rented house at the southeast edge of Westwood and she had friends (not connected with the movies) who cared for her and whom she could trust. Oh, she believed this! And the executives at The Studio loved her again. And forgave her. For the new movie was making even more money for them than *Gentlemen Prefer Blondes*. And her salary was frozen at $1,500. But she would accept this for now. She was grateful to be alive, for now. *Maybe I should kill us both. We'd be better off.* But he hadn't killed her and would not. She was free of him now. She loved him, but she was free of him. She'd never been pregnant with him. He'd never known about Baby. Even if she'd wept in her sleep he'd never known. He'd held her in his arms and she'd called him Daddy and he'd comforted her but he'd never known. In October at last he'd agreed to the terms of the divorce and he'd promised not to harass her but she had reason to believe he sometimes followed her. He was watching her house in Westwood. Or he'd hired somebody. Or there were more than one of them. Unless she was imagining them! Yet she certainly hadn't imagined the man-with-no-face in the metallic-gray Chevrolet coupe who'd driven slowly behind her on her residential street in Westwood, keeping another car between them, then on Wilshire he'd sped up to keep her in view, and she'd tried to remain calm, breathing deeply and counting her breaths as she maneuvered her car through traffic, and seeing an opportunity she cut swiftly into the lot of a drive-in bank and a few seconds later she was executing a U-turn in a side street and she pressed down on the gas pedal not seeing the metallic-gray Chevrolet in her rearview mirror yet easing through a traffic light as it changed from yellow to red and then, laughing, elated as a little girl speeding north on the San Diego freeway, she headed for Van Nuys. "Can't catch me! None of you."

She drove to Van Nuys in a state of exhilaration. She exited the freeway and she drove past Van Nuys High School, which had been enlarged since the war, and she felt nothing, no emotion, unless a small stab of hurt that Mr. Haring had never contacted her after she'd quit school as in a frequent dream of hers she'd imagined her English teacher arriving at the Pirig home and ringing the doorbell and asking an astonished Elsie Pirig if he could speak with Norma Jeane, and there he was sternly admonishing Norma Jeane, asking why she'd quit school without telling him? and so young? with so much promise—"One of my best students, in all my years of teaching." But Mr. Haring hadn't come to save her. He hadn't written to her when she'd become Marilyn Monroe; wasn't he proud of her? Or was he, like her former husband, ashamed of her? "I was in love with you, Mr. Haring. But I guess you didn't love me!" It was a movie scene, yet not an original or convincing one, for there were no adequate words and in her adolescent despair Norma Jeane had been incapable of discovering them.

She drove on. Wiping tears from her eyes, and her heart beating hard. Through the town of Van Nuys, which looked more prosperous than it had been in wartime, more residential housing, more businesses, Van Nuys Boulevard and Burbank and there was Mayer's Pharmacy with a new white slick-tile facade (and was the beautiful beveled mirror still inside?) and in a state of exhilaration and dread Norma Jeane drove to Reseda and past the Pirig house—that house!—covered now in asphalt siding meant to resemble red brick but otherwise unchanged. There, Norma Jeane's attic window! She wondered if the Pirigs still took in foster children. Her nostrils contracted; there was a smell of burning rubber in the air. A hazy discoloration of the air. She smiled to see that Warren Pirig's business had spilled out into a side yard. Junked cars, a pickup truck, and three motorcycles FOR SALE. Norma Jeane had been thinking that the Pirigs, too, had abandoned her, but in fact Elsie Pirig had written to her in care of The Studio and in hurt and anger she'd ripped up the letters. How sweet, her revenge!—"I'm driving past your ugly house right now. I'm 'Marilyn Monroe' now. You're inside, it's suppertime, and I'm not going to stop and visit you. You'd love to see me now, wouldn't you! You'd look at me now, Warren, wouldn't you! You'd offer me a beer out of the icebox, like an adult. You'd be respectful. You'd ask me please to sit down and you'd stare and stare and I'd say, 'Didn't you love me, Warren, just a little? You must have seen how I was in love with *you*.' And I'd be polite to Elsie too. Oh, I'd be gracious! Sweet as The Girl Upstairs in *The Seven-Year Itch*. As if nothing had come between us. I wouldn't stay long, explaining that I had another engagement in Van Nuys; I'd go away promising to send you comp tickets to my next premiere in Hollywood and you'd never hear from me again. My revenge!"

Instead, she'd burst into tears. Wetting the front of her navy-blue rayon housewife dress.

An actress draws upon all she's lived. Her entire life. Her childhood espe-cially. Though you don't remember childhood. You think you do but you don't, really! And even when you're older, in adolescence. Much of memory is dreams, I think. Improvising. Returning to the past, to change it.

But, yes! I was happy. People were good to me. Even my mother who got sick and couldn't be a mother to me, and my foster mother in Van Nuys. One day when I'm a serious actress in plays by Clifford Odets, Tennessee Williams, Arthur Miller, I will pay homage to these people. Their humanity.

"Oh. That's *me?*"

The surprise was, *The Seven-Year Itch* was so funny. The Girl Upstairs who was Tom Ewell's summer-fantasy girl was *funny*. Norma Jeane began to relax. She pressed her knuckles against her mouth, she laughed. Why, she'd been so dreading this, and dreading the sight of herself, it was a reve-lation to her: what Hollywood people and what the critics had said was true.

Marilyn Monroe is a natural comedienne. Like Jean Harlow in her sexy-flaunting roles. Like a little-girl Mae West.

This was the first time she'd seen *The Seven-Year Itch* since the Hollywood premiere in June, when she'd lapsed into a panic-fugue state even before the film began, or maybe she'd been exhausted by melancholy, a combination of Nembutal and champagne and the strain of the divorce, and she'd seen the giant Technicolor screen in a haze as if underwater hearing laughter around her buzzing in her ears and she'd had to fight sleep in her gorgeous stitched-in body in a strapless evening gown so tight in the bust she could barely breathe, her brain deprived of oxygen, and her eyes glazing over inside the ceramic Marilyn mask her makeup man Whitey had sculpted over her sick sallow skin and bruised soul. Made to rise to her feet at the end of the movie, she and her co-star Tom Ewell blinking smiling into an acclaiming audience, she'd only just managed not to faint and afterward would remem-ber little of the evening except she'd gotten through it. And during filming in New York City when her marriage was disintegrating like wetted tissue and afterward in Hollywood at The Studio she'd refused to attend the daily rushes for fear she might see something that would have made it impossible for her to continue. For the Ex-Athlete's judgment was harsh and rang in her ears: *Showing yourself like that. Your body. You promised this movie would be different. You're disgusting.*

But, no! The Girl Upstairs wasn't disgusting. Tom Ewell wasn't disgusting. Their mock-love story was just . . . comedy. And what's comedy but life seen as laughs, not tears? What's comedy but refusing to cry, and laughing instead? Was laughter always inferior to tears? Was comedy always inferior to tragedy? Any comedy, any tragedy? "Maybe I am an actress already? A comedienne?" You had to think, seeing Marilyn Monroe on the screen in this frothy movie, that she was an accomplished actress, fully in control, stealing most scenes with her baby-breathy voice, the wriggly movements of her voluptuous body, her little-girl-innocent face. You perceived The Girl Upstairs through the yearning eyes of Tom Ewell so you laughed at him in his fumbling adolescent fantasy of The Girl who was so near to being won, yet so far; so seemingly available for sex, yet elusive. And this was funny! Thwarted lust in an adult man, a married man, a would-be adulterer, was funny. The audience at the Sepulveda was laughing, and Norma Jeane was laughing. And how good to laugh with others. *It makes us human together. I don't want to be alone.*

Almost, Norma Jeane felt a thrill of pride. There was her blond-actress self on the screen, making strangers relax, laugh, and feel good about human folly, and about themselves. Why had her former husband scorned her talent? And her? *He was wrong. I'm not disgusting. This is comedy. This is art.*

Yet not everybody in the movie house was laughing. Here and there scattered through the rows were solitary men, staring up at the screen with fixed-grin grimaces. One, fattish and middle-aged, a wedge of flesh like a misplaced chin at the nape of his neck, had slipped into a seat close by Norma Jeane, and he was glancing at Norma Jeane even as his attention was fixed upon Marilyn Monroe on screen; not recognizing her, maybe not even seeing her, except as a young woman seated by herself only a few feet from him in a darkened movie house. *He's bringing me into his Marilyn fantasy. He wants me to see what he's doing with his hands.*

Quickly Norma Jeane rose from her seat and took another seat several rows behind and to the side of the solitary man. Near a young married couple who were laughing at the movie. Oh, she felt despoiled! Truly, that was disgusting. Or was it just pathetic. The solitary man with the fleshy neck didn't glance back at Norma Jeane but continued with whatever it was he was doing, slyly, surreptitiously, hunched down in his seat. Norma Jeane ignored him and fixed her attention upon the movie. She tried to recall what she'd been feeling—pride? A sense of accomplishment? Maybe the positive reviews hadn't been exaggerated, Marilyn Monroe really was a gifted comedienne? *Maybe I'm not a failure. No reason to give up. To punish myself.* Yet even as she was smiling at The Girl Upstairs as perceived by sex-starved Tom Ewell, a summer bachelor, Norma Jeane was distracted, thinking how many times as a girl she'd had to move her seat in a theater when she'd come alone to the movies. Gazing with rapture at the Fair Princess and the Dark Prince, she'd had to realize that others, solitary men, were gazing at her. Here in the Sepulveda and elsewhere. Oh, Grauman's on Hollywood Boulevard had been the worst! When she'd been a little girl and lived on Highland Avenue. Lone men in the late-afternoon movies, their eyes snatching greedily at her out of the dark. As if they couldn't believe their good fortune, a little girl unaccompanied at the movies. Gladys warned her not to sit "too close" to men in the theater, but the problem had been: men moved their seats to be close to her. How many times could she change her seat, as a child? Once, at Grauman's, an usher had shone his flashlight on her and scolded her. Gladys had warned her never to speak to men, but what if men spoke to her? She'd instructed her always to walk near the curb on her way home. Out by the streetlights. *So I'd be seen. If somebody tried to grab me. Was that it?*

Norma Jeane settled into her seat, laughing with others, even as she became aware of another solitary man to her left, only two seats away. Why hadn't she noticed him before sitting down? He leaned forward abruptly to peer at her. A man of youngish middle age with round winking glasses and a receding chin, rather boyish features that reminded her of—Mr. Haring? Her English teacher? But he'd lost most of his fair fine hair. Norma Jeane didn't dare look too closely. If this was Mr. Haring, they'd discover each other at the end of the movie; if not, not. Norma Jeane forced herself to smile at the screen in preparation for the next scene. This was the most famous scene in the movie: The Girl Upstairs out on the street, in her ivory crepe sundress with the tight halter top, bare legs, and high-heeled shoes on the subway grating as air rushes up to lift her skirt and traffic on Lexington Avenue virtually stops. Yet the movie scene, Norma Jeane knew, was very different from the publicity stills. In order not to be condemned by the Catholic Legion of Decency, The Studio had censored the scene considerably: The Girl's skirt is lifted only to about knee level, and there are no flashes of the notorious white panties. This was the single scene for which audiences waited, having seen sensational photos reproduced worldwide, the flaring white skirt, the blond head flung back, the dreamy-happy smile of ecstasy, as if the very air were making love to The Girl or, somehow, her hands hidden in her floating dress, she were making love to herself: a pose seen from the front, from the side, from the rear, in three-quarters profile, as many camera angles you might think as there were eyes to perceive her. Norma Jeane waited for this scene, conscious of the solitary man in the seat close by. Could it be Mr. Haring? But hadn't Mr. Haring been married? (Maybe he was divorced, and living alone in Van Nuys?) Would he know her? He must recognize "Marilyn" in the movie, his former student, but would he recognize *her?* It had been so many years. She wasn't a girl now.

So strange! The Girl Upstairs seemed a separate being from the desperately worried, anxious actress who'd portrayed her. Norma Jeane remembered insomniac nights even when she'd taken Nembutal. And Doc Bob prescribed Benzedrine to wake her up. She'd been sick with worry about her marriage. The Ex-Athlete had insisted upon visiting the set, though he hated moviemaking, the tedium of it and what he called, with mind-numbing literalness, "how phony it all is." As if he'd thought movies were *real?* Actors spoke their own spontaneous lines, and didn't follow *scripts?* Norma Jeane hadn't wanted to think that she'd possibly married an ignorant man, not just an ignorant and uninformed man but a stupid man; no, she truly loved her husband, and certainly he loved her. She was the center of his emotional life. His very manhood depended upon *her.* So she had to perform The Girl, she had to perform frothy comedy, quicksilver comedy, even as her husband stood staring, silent and glowering, at the edge of the set. He'd made everybody uncomfortable but there he was, rarely missing a day, though in his professional life as a promoter of baseball and a so-called consultant to sports equipment manufacturers, he should have had plenty to do. Nervous in his presence, Marilyn asked to do retake after retake. "I want to get it *right.* I know I can do better." The director had been exasperated by her sometimes, but he'd always given in. For no matter how good a scene is, can't it be improved? Yes!

As in grim disapproval like Ol' Hirohito on the radio cabinet, the Ex-Athlete stared. Grinding his teeth to think of his family back in San Francisco, his beloved Momma, seeing it. *This trash! Sex trash! After this movie no more, you hear?*

What infuriated him was the ease with which Marilyn and her co-star Ewell got along. Those two, laughing together! When he and Marilyn were alone, she wasn't funny at all; she rarely laughed; he rarely laughed; she tried to talk to him, then gave up and they sat, at dinner for instance, eating silently. Sometimes she even asked if she could read a script or a book! She'd urged him to watch TV, if there was sports or sports news on. Oh, he'd never forgiven her for going off and leaving him in Japan, "entertaining" the troops in Korea. The worldwide publicity that followed, eclipsing the Ex-Athlete in Japan where, though he'd been met by large, admiring crowds, they were nothing like the crowds that greeted Marilyn Monroe. In all, more than one hundred thousand U.S. soldiers were to see her perform, in her low-cut purple-sequin dress and open-toed high heels, singing "Diamonds Are a Girl's Best Friend" and "I Wanna Be Loved by You" outside in subfreezing weather, breath steaming. He'd suspected her of having a brief affair with the adoring young corporal from *Stars & Stripes* who'd been her escort in Korea. He'd suspected her of having an even briefer affair, maybe a single swift fuck, with a young Japanese translator from Tokyo University who, to the Ex-Athlete, looked like an upright eel. In New York, on the movie set, he had strong reason to believe that Marilyn and Tom Ewell slipped away during breaks to make love in Ewell's dressing room. There was a warm sexual-joking connection between those two! The Ex-Athlete wasn't jealous but everybody on the set knew, and probably everybody in Hollywood. They were laughing at him, the wronged husband!

His father and brothers had been frank with him. Can't you control her? What kind of marriage is it, you and *her?*

In the end, he hadn't been able to love her. To make love to her. As a man. As the man he'd been—the Yankee Slugger. And he'd hated her for that too. Most of all for that. *You suck a man dry. You're dead inside. Not a normal woman. I hope to God you never have babies.*

She was protesting why did he hate Marilyn, when he'd loved Marilyn? Why did he hate The Girl Upstairs? The Girl was so sweet and good-hearted and thoughtful and *nice.* Of course she was a male sex fantasy, a sex angel, but it was meant to be funny, wasn't it? Wasn't sex funny? If it didn't kill you? The Girl Upstairs invited you to laugh at her and with her, but it wasn't a cruel laughter. "They like me because I have no irony. I haven't been wounded, so I can't wound." An adult learns irony as he learns hurt and disappointment and shame but The Girl Upstairs can erase that knowledge.

The Fair Princess as a New York career girl of the mid-1950s.

The Fair Princess without a Dark Prince. For no man is equal to her.

The Fair Princess advertising toothpaste, shampoo, consumer goods. It's *funny*, not *tragic*, that pretty girls are used to sell products; why couldn't Otto Öse see the humor in it? "Not everything is the Holocaust." It was in fact (as she'd told Mr. Wilder, the director) a profound and wonderful reversal that in *The Seven-Year Itch* in the invented person of "Marilyn Monroe," Norma Jeane should have the opportunity to relive certain humiliations of her young life, not as tragedy but as comedy.

Now came the skirt-blowing scene! More than four hours of filming in New York, during which her marriage ended, and not a second of that footage was used. The final footage was filmed at The Studio in Hollywood on a private sound stage. No gawking men crowded against police barricades. The skirt-blowing scene was only just playful and brief. Nothing to be shocked by. Not much to titillate. The Ex-Athlete had never seen this scene in the actual movie. The Girl squeals and laughs and beats at her skirt to keep it down, her panties don't show, and—that's it.

"Miss! Miss!" The solitary man seated close by Norma Jeane was hissing at her, hunched low and sly in his seat. Norma Jeane knew she should ignore him but glanced helplessly in his direction, half thinking he was Mr. Haring after all and he'd recognized her, even as she knew, staring at the man's immature, curiously corroded features, the damp blinking eyes behind round lenses, the oily-sweaty forehead, that he was no one she knew. "Miss— Miss—Miss!" He was panting. Excited. Shifting the lower part of his body in the seat, both hands working at his groin partially hidden by a canvas bag or rolled-up jacket, and as Norma Jeane stared in shock and revulsion he moaned softly, his eyes rolled white, the entire row of seats jerked as if somebody had kicked them. Norma Jeane sat in a paralysis of confusion. Hadn't this happened to her once, long ago? Or more than once? And she was thinking *It's him? Mr. Haring? Oh, can it be?* Hunched gnomelike in his seat the man dared to reveal one of his hands to her, held low so that no one else could see, shiny-sticky liquid on the trembling palm and fingers. Norma Jeane gave a little cry of hurt and disgust. Already she was on her feet, walking up the aisle, as the man-who-resembled-Mr.-Haring laughed quietly in her wake, a sound like gravel being shaken blending with the larger, louder laughter of the rest of the audience.

The usher with acne cheeks, lounging at the rear, seeing Norma Jeane striding up the aisle, and the look on her face, said, surprised, "Ma'am? Is something wrong?"

Norma Jeane walked past him without a sidelong glance.

"No. It's too late."

THE DROWNED WOMAN

Was it Venice Beach she'd come to? She knew without seeing.

There was something wrong with her eyes; she'd been rubbing them raw with her fists. Sand in her eyes. And overhead the sky at dawn was breaking like a jigsaw puzzle breaking into pieces. And if loosed, never could they be fitted together again. Why was her blood beating! beating! her heart beating! terrified she could hold it in her hand like a hummingbird.

I didn't want to die, it was to defy death. I didn't poison myself. God dies if he is not loved but I was not loved and I did not die.

It was Venice Beach, the ribbed hard-packed sand and gusts of mist like veils and seaweed like drowsing eels and the first of the surfers strange and silent, too, like sea creatures, streaming water, staring at her. Somebody had torn the front of her cerise chiffon dress, her breasts hanging loose. Nipples hard as pits. Her matted hair and grinning-swollen mouth and the oily Benzedrine sweat coating her body.

Hello there, what's your name? I'm Miss Golden Dreams. Do you think I'm beautiful? desirable? lovable? How'd you like to love me? I know I could love you.

First, she'd driven to the Santa Monica pier. That was hours ago. In chiffon and bare legs and no panties. She'd ridden on the Ferris wheel, she'd paid for a child's ticket and taken a little girl with her, the girl's parents smiling and confused seeming to recognize her but not altogether certain (for there were so many Hollywood blondes) and she'd made the car rock and the little girl squealed in her arms *Oh! oh! oh!* flying into the sky. She wasn't drunk. Smell her breath! Sweet as citrus. If there were needle tracks in her arms, in the soft flesh inside the elbow, she had not injected herself. Parts of her body had gone numb and floated away. Where her brawny ex-husband had squeezed her wrist, her arm, her throat. Strong beautiful fingers. Years ago there'd been one of them who could make love only to her breasts, his swollen eager penis between her breasts, he'd cup her breasts in trembling hands and squeeze himself until with a sob of anguish he came, his semen wetting her but Norma Jeane wasn't there, eyes blank and unseeing as stones. *It doesn't hurt. It's over fast. Immediately, you forget.* She'd asked if the pretty little girl could come live with her for a while. Trying to explain to the parents who were upset after the Ferris wheel ride that they could come to visit too. And why was the Ferris wheel operator angry? No one had been hurt. It was all in play! She gave the man a twenty-dollar bill and his agitation ceased. And the little girl was safe, clutching at the pretty blond woman's hand and wanting never to let go. As another little girl had clutched at her hand. *The stuffed tiger I sewed for Irina. It vanished with her. Where?* These killings in Los Angeles County, there'd been another one last month, a "red-haired model" the papers described her, only seventeen years old. Sometimes the murderer buried the girl in a "shallow grave" and rain washed the sandy soil away to expose the body, or what remained of the body. But no harm had ever come to Norma Jeane. Each of the eight or nine or ten raped-and-mutilated girls was known to her, or might've been known to her, sister starlets at The Studio or sister models at the Preene Agency, or models of Otto Öse's, yet were not ever *her.* What did that mean? That she was destined for a longer life? A life beyond the age of thirty and a life beyond Marilyn?

She'd driven to Santa Monica out of rich residential Bel Air. The hills. A fairy-tale mansion close by the Bel-Air Golf Club. He'd offered to pay for her divorce from the Ex-Athlete. "Mental cruelty." "Incompatibility." It was a bottle-green Bentley thinly scraped along its front left fender where she'd sideswiped a guard rail on the Santa Monica Freeway. Was this a time when Gladys was having shock treatments? Because her own head was feeling hurt, jagged. Her own thoughts were frequently derailed. You could smile at The Girl Upstairs but The Girl Upstairs had a script and never deviated. Most of the laughs were hers. Electroconvulsive shock therapy, it was called. They'd asked Norma Jeane, the next of kin, the legal guardian of the sick woman, for permission to perform a lobotomy. She, the daughter, refused.

A lobotomy can work wonders sometimes on a deranged and hallucinating patient, a doctor assured her. No, but not my mother. Not my mother's brain. My mother is a poet, my mother is an intelligent complex woman. Yes, my mother is a tragic woman but so am I! And so they merely "shocked" Gladys. Oh, but that was at Norwalk, years ago. That wasn't at the more genteel Lakewood Home where Gladys was now.

Mother, he wants to see you! Soon. He will forgive you, he says. He will love us both.

It must mean something, her father had called her "Norma." At first he'd called her "Norma Jeane"; then at the end of his letter he'd called her "Norma." So that would be his name for her when they met and ever afterward: "Norma." Not "Norma Jeane" and not "Marilyn." And of course "Daughter." Finally she'd taken the keys to the Bentley, needing to escape. But he wouldn't report her to the police. His weakness was, he adored her. Grunting groveling Porky Pig little man at her feet. Marilyn's bare feet. He'd sucked her grimy toes! She screamed, it tickled so. He was a good man, a decent man, a rich man. He owned stock in 20th Century-Fox. Not only he'd wanted to pay for her divorce but he wanted to hire a tough private detective (in fact, a moonlighting L.A. homicide detective with a number of "justified kills" on his record) to scare off the Ex-Athlete's private detective. He'd wanted to introduce her to a lawyer friend, to help her form her own production company. *Marilyn Monroe Productions, Inc.* She would escape The Studio and she would break The Studio's stranglehold. As a few years before Olivia De Havilland had sued to break her contract with another studio, and had won. He'd given her a pair of sapphire earrings from Madrid; she told him she never wore expensive jewelry! My Okie background she said. She'd keep the sapphire earrings with other items of expensive jewelry in the toes of slippers and shoes to be found in a closet amid dustballs after her death. But not for a long time. She didn't intend to die for a long time! Not for years.

I'm Miss Golden Dreams. How'd you like to kiss me? All over? Here I am, waiting. Already I've been loved by hundreds of thousands of men. And my reign is just beginning!

This was the night she'd seen *The Seven-Year Itch* at the Sepulveda. Bucky would've loved the movie, laughing and gripping Norma Jeane's hand, tight. And afterward he'd have her wear one of the lacy-sexy nighties and really make love to her, a healthy young married guy horny as hell. But she was through with *that thing up on the screen that isn't me.* She'd made her decision to vanish. Like Harriet taking away Irina. It could happen within an hour. It could happen within a minute! She would vanish from Hollywood and from the Ex-Athlete's surveillance and she would move to New York City and live alone in an apartment. She would study acting. It wasn't too late! She would be anonymous. She would begin again, humbly, as a student.

She would study stage acting. Living theater. She would play in Chekhov, Ibsen, O'Neill. Movies are a dead medium, alive solely for the audience. The Fair Princess and the Dark Prince are alive solely to the audience. Beloved solely by the audience, in their ignorance and need. But there was no Fair Princess, was there? No Dark Prince to save you.

Later, she'd driven to Venice Beach. She would recall her bare foot on the gas pedal, and searching for the brake. But where was the clutch? She'd abandoned the scraped and overheated Bentley on Venice Boulevard, keys in the ignition. On foot, then. Barefoot. Running. She wasn't frightened but exhilarated, running. The front of her pretty dress had been torn. The bearded derelict's rough hands. Now this stretch of beach was home, at dawn. For Grandma Della lived close by. Grandma Della's grave was close by. She and Norma Jeane walked along the beach shading their eyes against the bright glittering waves. Grandma Della would be proud of her, of course; yet she would say *Make your own decision, dear. If you hate your life.* Gulls, shorebirds. They circled above her screaming. She ran into the surf, the first of the waves, always you're surprised at the strength of the surf, the chill of the waves. Water is so thin, trickles through your fingers, how can it be so strong, so hurtful? So strange! She saw in those waves, farther out, something living, a helpless drowning creature, it was her task to save it. Oh, she knew this wasn't right, it was a dream or a hallucination or a spell cast by somebody wicked, she knew this but somehow couldn't *feel that she knew* with any conviction and so she had to act quickly. Was this—Baby? Or another woman's baby? A living creature, helpless, and only Norma Jeane saw, only Norma Jeane could save it. She ran stumbling and staggering into the water and waves socked at her calves, thighs, belly. These were no loving caresses but powerful blows. Rushing up into the deep cut between her legs. She was knocked down, and scrambled to get up. She could see the small struggling creature. It was borne high on the crest of a frothy wave, and then dropped into a shallow; lifted again, and again dropped. Its tiny limbs flailed! She'd begun to hyperventilate. Not enough oxygen. She was swallowing water. Water up her nose. A hand at her throat. Strong beautiful hands. *Better for both of us to die.* Yet he'd let her go—why? Always he let her go, that was the man's weakness, he loved her.

Surfers saved her from drowning.

And kept her secret as she'd begged them.

Just her luck, it was this stretch of Venice Beach where a half-dozen surfers hung out. Some of us even slept on the beach, mild nights. We were fully awake and in the water by dawn riding some rough, serious waves. And there came this distraught-looking blond woman in a torn party dress staggering along the beach. Barefoot, and her hair windblown.

At first we thought somebody must've been chasing her, but she was alone. And suddenly wading into the surf! And these rough waves. She was like a blond doll knocked down and pummeled by the waves and she'd have drowned within minutes except one of the guys got to her in time, leapt off his surfboard and dragged her up onto the beach and straddled her limp body doing artificial respiration as he'd learned in the Scouts, and pretty soon she's coughing, choking, vomiting, and breathing normally again, and back to life again, lucky she hadn't swallowed more water or inhaled it into her lungs.

There's this fantastic movie moment we'd remember all our lives when the blonde's astonished eyes open—glassy-blue, bloodshot eyes—seeing a half-dozen of us standing over her staring at her, recognizing her, or anyway who she's supposed to be. *Oh why?* is the first thing she says in this stricken little voice. But trying to laugh, too. And vomiting again and the guy who'd saved her, a smooth-faced college kid from Oxnard, quickly wipes her mouth with the flat of his hand in a sudden tender gesture like nothing in his nineteen years, and all his life he's going to remember how the near-drowned woman, this famous blond actress, clutches his hand and fumbles to kiss it saying what sounds like *Thank you!* but she's sobbing too hard to be certain, and the surf's too loud, and the kid from Oxnard kneeling beside her in the wet sand has to wonder if he did the wrong thing?

Like she'd wanted to die. And I interfered. But if it hadn't been me it would've been one of the other guys, right? So how was I to blame?

The Playwright and the Blond Actress: The Seduction

In the creative process there is the father, the author
of the play; the mother, the actor pregnant with the
part; and the child, the role to be born.

—Stanislavski,
Building a Character

I

You won't ever write about me, will you? About us.
   Darling! Of course not.
   Because we're special, aren't we? We love each other so much. You couldn't ever make anybody understand . . . how it is between us.
   Darling, I would never even try.

2

He'd written a play, and the play had become his life.

This was not a good thing. The Playwright knew. A work of words, a vessel of mere language, somehow wrapped in with his guts, tangled with the arteries of his living body. In a neutral voice he said of this new work, his first in several years, "I have hope for it. It isn't finished."

Hope for it. Isn't finished.

He knew! No play is the playwright's life, as no book is a writer's life. These are only interludes in the life, as a ripple, a wave, a violent shudder may pass through an element like water, agitating it but without the power to alter it. He knew. Yet he'd labored at *The Girl with the Flaxen Hair* for so long. He'd begun it in college, in its earliest, crudest "epic" version. He'd set it aside in the despair and rapture of first love and he'd written other plays—in the postwar forties he'd become the Playwright!—and he'd returned to it in youthful middle age, having carried *The Girl with the Flaxen Hair*—the handwritten notes, the awkwardly typed drafts, the abortive scenes and the protracted scenes and the lengthy character descriptions and increasingly yellowed and dog-eared snapshots from the twenties; above all he'd carried the chimerical hope of it—from one life to another, from single rooms and cramped apartments in New Brunswick, New Jersey, and Brooklyn and New York City to his current six-room brownstone apartment on West 72nd Street near Central Park, and to summer places in the Adirondacks and on the Maine coast, and even to Rome, Paris, Amsterdam, Morocco. He carried it with him from his bachelor life into a life complicated in unexpected ways by marriage and children, family life in which at the outset he'd rejoiced, as an antidote to the obsessive world inside his head; he'd carried it with him from the eager astonished sexuality of his young manhood to the waning and uncertain sexuality of his fifth decade. The girl of *The Girl with the Flaxen Hair* had been his first love, never consummated. Never even declared.

Now he was forty-eight years old. The girl would be, if still living, in her mid-fifties. Beautiful Magda, middle-aged! He had not so much as glimpsed her in more than twenty years.

He'd written a play, and the play had become his life.

3

Vanished! She withdrew the money she'd saved from checking accounts in three Los Angeles banks. She shut up her rented house and left messages for only a few people explaining she was vanishing from Hollywood and not to miss her, please! And not to look for her. She provided no forwarding address not even to her distraught agent because at the time of her flight she had none. And no telephone number because she had none. Books and papers and a few clothes, she packed hastily in boxes and mailed parcel post *c/o Norma Jeane Baker, General Delivery, New York City, New York.*

Grandma Della said to make my own decision, if I hated my life. But it wasn't life I hated.

4

A dream of Back There. The night before the Playwright and the Blond Actress meet in New York City, in the early winter of 1955, the Playwright has one of his recurring dreams of humiliation.

Those dreams of which, since early adolescence, he has spoken to no one. Dreams he tries to erase immediately upon waking!

In art the Playwright thinks *dreams are profound, life-changing, often beautiful. In life, dreams are of no more significance than a blurred view of Rahway, New Jersey, through the rain-splotched window of a Greyhound bus expelling exhaust on Route 1.*

In fact, the Playwright was born in working-class Rahway, in northeastern New Jersey. In December 1908. His parents were German Jews from Berlin who'd emigrated in the late 1890s with a hope of being assimilated into America, their idiosyncratic Jewish surname Americanized and their gnarly Jewish roots extirpated. They were Jews grown impatient with being Jews even as they were Jews resentfully aware of being the object of the scorn of non-Jews, most of whom they knew to be their inferiors. In America, the Playwright's father would find work in a machine shop in East New York alongside other immigrants, he would find work in a butcher's shop in Hoboken and as a shoe salesman in Rahway, and at last, in the boldest adventure of his maturity, he would acquire a franchise to sell Kelvinator washing machines and dryers in a shop on Main Street, Rahway; the shop came into his hands in 1925 and would provide a steadily rising income until it collapsed in early 1931, when the Playwright was completing his senior year at Rutgers University in nearby New Brunswick. Bankruptcy! Misery! The Playwright's family would lose their Victorian gabled house on a leafy residential street and take up residence in the upstairs of the very building in which the washing machines and dryers had been sold, a property in a depressed section of Rahway that no one wanted to buy. The Playwright's father would suffer from high blood pressure, colitis, heart trouble, and "nerves" through the remainder of his long embittered life (he would endure until 1961); the Playwright's mother would be employed as a cafeteria worker and eventually as a dietitian in Rahway public schools, until the year of miracles 1949 when her playwright son would have his first Broadway success and win his first Pulitzer Prize and move his parents out of Rahway forever. A fairy tale with a happy ending.

The Playwright's dream of Back There is set in Rahway in those years. He opens his eyes appalled to find himself in the kitchen of the cramped flat above the shop on Main Street. Somehow the kitchen and the shop have come together. Washing machines are in the kitchen. Time is askew. It isn't clear if the Playwright is a boy just old enough to feel familial shame, or if he's a Rutgers undergraduate with dreams of being another Eugene O'Neill, or if he's forty-eight years old, his youth mysteriously gone, in dread of turning fifty with no strong, electrifying play in nearly a decade. In the dream, in the kitchen, the Playwright is staring at a row of washing machines, all in noisy operation. Dirty, soapy water is being agitated in each of the machines. That unmistakable smell of backed-up drains, plumbing. The Playwright begins to gag. This is a dream and he seems to recognize it's a dream but at the same time it's so painfully real he will be convinced, shaken, that it must have happened in life. Somehow his father's financial records and his own writing materials have been mixed together and placed imprudently on the floor beneath the machines, and water has slopped over onto the papers. The Playwright must retrieve them. It's a simple task he confronts with dread and disgust. Yet there's a perverse pride in this, for it's the son's responsibility to help his weak, ailing father. He stoops over, trying not to gag. Trying not to breathe. He sees his hand fumbling to take hold of a sheaf of papers, a manila file. Even before he lifts it to the light he can see that the papers are wetted through, ink is smeared, and the documents are ruined. Is *The Girl with the Flaxen Hair* among these? "Oh God, help us." It isn't a prayer—the Playwright isn't a religious man—but a curse.

Abruptly the Playwright wakes. It's his own hoarse breathing he's been hearing. His mouth is dry and sour, he's been grinding his teeth in sorrow and frustration. Grateful to be sleeping alone in his bed in the brownstone on West 72nd Street and out of Rahway, New Jersey, forever.

His wife is in Miami visiting elderly relatives.

All that day, the dream of Back There will haunt the Playwright. Like a bad meal, undigested.

5

I knew that girl! Magda. She wasn't me but she was inside me. Like Nell, except stronger than Nell. Much stronger than Nell. She would have her baby; no one could deprive her. She'd have her baby giving birth on bare floorboards in an unheated room and muffling her cries with a rag.

She'd stanch the bleeding with rags.

Nursing the baby, then. Her big swollen breasts like a cow's, warm and oozing milk.

6

The Playwright went to check the papers on his desk. Of course, *The Girl with the Flaxen Hair* was where he'd left it. More than three hundred pages of scripts, revisions, notes. He lifted it, and one of the yellowed snapshots fell out. *Magda, June 1930.* It was in black-and-white, an attractive blond girl with wide-set eyes squinting in sunshine, her thick hair braided and wound about her head.

Magda had had a baby but it hadn't been his. Except in the play it was his.

7

Eager as a young lover, though no longer young, the Playwright hurried up four steep flights of metal paint-splotched stairs to the drafty loft rehearsal space at Eleventh Avenue and 51st Street. So excited! breathless! So anxious. As he entered the loft into a babble of voices, a haze of faces, he had to pause, to calm his heart. To compose himself.

He wasn't in condition to run up these stairs as he used to.

8

I was terrified. I wasn't ready. I'd been up most of the night. I kept having to pee! I wasn't taking any drugs, only just aspirin. And an antihistamine tablet Mr. Pearlman's assistant gave me, for a sore throat. I believed the Playwright would take one look at me and speak to Mr. Pearlman and that was it, I'd be out of the cast. Because I never deserved to be there, and I knew it. I seemed to know this beforehand. I seemed to see myself going down those stairs. I held the script, and I tried to read the lines I'd marked in red, and it was like I'd never seen them before. My only clear thought was: If I fail now, it's winter here, freezing. It wouldn't be hard to die, would it?

9

The Playwright would resent it, that everybody knew. Except him. The identity of the Blond Actress who'd been cast, for the reading, as his Magda.

Yes, he'd been told a name. A mumbled name. Over the phone. By the artistic director, Max Pearlman, who'd said in his usual hurried, harried manner that the Playwright would know everyone in the cast "except possibly the actress who's reading Magda. She's new to the Ensemble. She's new to New York. I never met her before a few weeks ago when she walked into my office. She's done a few films, and she's fed up with Hollywood bullshit and restless to learn real acting, and she's come to study with us." Pearlman paused. His was a theatrical manner, in which pauses are as significant as punctuation to a writer. "Frankly, she isn't bad."

The Playwright, too much on his mind, the humiliating dream of Back There yet heavy in his gut, hadn't asked to hear the woman's name repeated or to be told anything more about her background. This was to be only an in-house reading at the New York Ensemble of Theatre Artists, the company with which the Playwright had been associated for twenty years; it wasn't a public or a staged reading. Only members of the Ensemble were invited. No applause was allowed. Why would the Playwright pause to ask his old friend Pearlman, for whom he felt little personal warmth but whom he trusted absolutely in all things theatrical, to repeat the name of a little-known actress? Especially an actress not from New York? The Playwright knew only New York.

Too much on his mind! A swarm of gnats, gnat thoughts, buzzed continuously about the Playwright's head, waking hours and often when he slept. In many of his dreams he continued to work. Work, work! No woman had ever been able to compete. A few women had won his body, but never his soul. His wife, long jealous, was jealous no longer. He'd taken little note of her emotional withdrawal, as he'd taken but cursory note that she was often away, visiting relatives. In the Playwright's obsessive work dreams, his fingers plucked at words yet untyped on his Olivetti portable; he strained to hear dialogue of surpassing beauty and feeling yet unarticulated in actual sounds. His life was work, for only work justified his existence; and each hour contributed to, or more often failed to contribute to, the completion of his work.

The guilty conscience of mid-century America. Mercantile-consumer America. Tragic America. For the counterminings of Tragedy strike deeper than the cheap quick fixes of Comedy.

10

In the drafty loft space the reading began. Six actors on folding chairs on a raised platform, in a semicircle beneath bare lightbulbs. A perpetual dripping from a lavatory close by. The accumulating smoke of cigarettes, for some of the actors smoked, and many in the audience of about forty people.

Of the six actors, all but the two eldest, veterans of the Ensemble and of the Playwright's plays, were visibly nervous. The Playwright for all his scholarly-rabbinical reserve had a reputation for being severely critical of actors, exasperated by their limitations. *Don't try to understand me too quickly* he was notorious for having said, more than once.

The Playwright was seated in the first row, only a few yards from the actors. Immediately he began to stare at the Blond Actress. Through the lengthy first scene, in which the Blond Actress as Magda had no speaking role, he stared at her, now recognizing her, a heavy blood blush darkening his face. Marilyn Monroe? Here, at the New York Ensemble? Under the tute-lage of the canny self-promoter Pearlman? This explained the murmurous excitement in the audience before the reading began; an air of anticipation the Playwright hadn't dared to imagine might have to do with him. In fact, the Playwright now remembered having glanced at an item in Walter Winchell's column not long before about the Blond Actress's "mysterious disappearance" from Hollywood, in violation of a studio contract requiring her to begin work on a new film. Beneath an accompanying photo of Monroe was the caption RELOCATED TO NEW YORK CITY? The photo resem-bled an advertising logo, a human face reduced to its predominant features, the heavy-lidded eyes and sultry gash of a mouth in a parody of erotic sup-plication.

"My Magda. Her?"

But the Blond Actress who held the Playwright's script in her trembling hands did not much resemble Marilyn Monroe. After the initial buzz of inter-est, the novelty quickly faded. Members of the Ensemble were actors and professional theater people to whom celebrity was fairly common. And tal-ent, even genius. Their judgment would be impartial and unsentimental.

The Blond Actress was seated in the center of the semicircle as if Pearlman had placed her there for protection. You saw that, unlike the other, more experienced stage actors, she held herself unnaturally still, her shoulders squared and her head, which seemed just slightly oversized, large for her slen-der frame, brought forward. She was nervous, licking her lips compulsively. Her eyes glistened with withheld tears. Her face was a girl's face, the skin markedly pale and shadows beneath the eyes exaggerated by the overhead lights. She wore a cable-knit sweater bleached of all color by the stark light-ing, and dark woolen slacks tucked into ankle-high boots. Her blond hair was plaited in a single short braid at the nape of her neck. She wore no jew-elry, no makeup. *You wouldn't have recognized her. She was no one.* The Playwright felt a stab of resentment, that Pearlman had dared to cast the Blond Actress in his play without more explicitly consulting him. *His* play! A piece of his heart. And the Blond Actress, for better or worse, would draw all the audience's attention.

But when at last the Blond Actress spoke, in Magda's voice, at the start of scene two, she was tentative and searching and it was immediately clear that her voice was too small for the space. This wasn't a Hollywood sound stage with microphones, amplification, close-ups. Her excitement, or her terror, was mesmerizing to the audience as if she'd been stripped naked before them. *She's miscast*, the Playwright thought. *Not my Magda.* He was furious with Pearlman, who leaned against a wall close by, chewing on an unlit cigar and watching the scene with an expression of rapt absorption. *He's in love with her. The bastard.*

Yet the Blond Actress, as Magda, was so appealing! There was a flame-like quivering in her voice, in the very uncertainty of her gestures, that made you sympathize deeply with her: her plight as Magda, the nineteen-year-old daughter of immigrant Hungarians, circa 1925, hired out to work in a suburban New Jersey Jewish household, and her plight as the Blond Actress, a Hollywood concoction and something of a national joke, bravely pitted against New York stage performers in a pitilessly exposed environment.

"Oh, excuse me? Mr. Pearlman? C-can I do this again? Please."

The request was made in naïveté and desperation. The Blond Actress's voice quavered. Even the Playwright, long a stoic of the theater, winced. For at the Ensemble, no actor ever dared interrupt a scene to address Pearlman or anyone; only the director had the authority to interrupt, an authority he exercised with kingly restraint. But the Blond Actress knew nothing of such a protocol. Her New York comrades observed her as spectators at a zoo might gaze at a rare, gorgeous, primitive species of simian ancestor, possessed of speech and yet lacking the intelligence to speak correctly. In the awkward silence the Blond Actress squinted over at Pearlman, with a grimace of a smile and a flutter of eyelids meant perhaps to be seductive, and said again, in a husky, breathy voice, "Oh, I know I can do better. Oh, *please!*" The appeal was so raw, it might have been Magda herself who spoke. Women in the audience who had studied acting with Pearlman and had unwisely fallen in love with him and allowed themselves to be "loved" by him in return, however briefly and sporadically, felt in that instant not a furious rivalry with the Blond Actress but a sisterly sympathy and a fear for her, who was so vulnerable, risking a public rebuke; men stiffened in embarrassment. Pearlman shoved his cigar into his mouth and bit down hard. The other actors stared at their scripts. You could see (so everyone would claim!) that Pearlman was about to say something withering to the Blond Actress, in his terse, cold manner, quick as a reptile's tongue. Yet Pearlman only grunted, "Sure."

I I

Pearlman! The Playwright had known the controversial founder of the New York Ensemble of Theatre Artists for a quarter of a century and had always feared the man, in secret. For Pearlman reserved his deepest respect, whatever the enthusiasms of the day, the week, the season, for dramatists who were dead and "classic." He had been responsible for bringing to postwar New York, in radically spare, politicized productions, García Lorca's *The House of Bernarda Alba*, Calderón's *Life Is a Dream*, Ibsen's *The Master Builder* and *When We Dead Awaken*; he had not only directed but translated Chekhov, daring to present Chekhov as the playwright had wished, not in the dirgelike tones of tragedy but as bittersweet comedy. He would claim to have "discovered" the Playwright though the two were of the same generation and of the same German-Jewish immigrant background.

In interviews that rankled the Playwright, Pearlman spoke of the "mysterious and mystical" collaborative process of the theater in which "part-talents" merge, groping, fumbling, in the way of Darwin's theory of evolution through modification, to create unique works of art. "As if I wouldn't have written my plays without *him*." Yet it was true, the Playwright's early plays had been developed at the Ensemble, and Pearlman had directed the premiere production of the Playwright's most ambitious play, the one for which he'd become famous and to which his name would be forever attached. Pearlman professed himself a spiritual brother of the Playwright's, not a rival; he'd congratulated the Playwright on every award, every honor the Playwright had received, while uttering his cryptic remarks within the Playwright's hearing: "Genius is what remains when reputations die."

Yet, unexpectedly, for he'd been a mediocre actor himself, Pearlman shone most brilliantly as a trainer of actors. The New York Ensemble of Theatre Artists had acquired international fame for Pearlman's intimate workshops and tutorials; he taught both beginning actors, if they were talented, and actors who were already professionals. The Ensemble quickly became a haven for such actors, successful Broadway and television performers who yearned to return to their roots or yearned to acquire roots. The Ensemble's low-rent midtown quarters became a place of refuge, not unlike a religious retreat. Meeting Pearlman had changed the lives of many actors and rejuvenated their careers, if not always commercially. Pearlman promised, "Here at my theater, a 'success' can fail. A 'success' can fall flat on his face or his ass and no reviewer will take note. A 'success' can admit he doesn't know shit about his profession. He can begin again at zero. He can be twelve years old, four years old. He can be an infant. If you can't crawl, my friend, you can't walk. If you can't walk, you can't run. If you can't run, you can't soar.

Begin with the basics. The aim of theater is to break the heart. Not to entertain. Crap TV and the tabloids entertain. The aim of theater is to transform
the spectator. If you can't transform the spectator, give it up. The aim of theater—Aristotle said it first, and Aristotle said it best—is to arouse profound
emotion in the spectator and through this arousal to effect a catharsis of the
soul. If there's no catharsis, there's no theater. At the Ensemble, we don't
coddle you but we'll respect you. If you show us you can open your veins,
we'll respect you. If it's more bullshit praise you want from asshole critics
and reviewers, you've come to the wrong place. I don't ask much from my
actors: just that you scour out your guts." To Pearlman, the most tragic of
all performers was the prodigy who, like the great Nijinski, reaches the peak
of genius in adolescence and is doomed to an equally premature decline.

"The true actor," Pearlman said, "will continue to grow until the day he
dies. Death is just the last scene of the last act. We're in rehearsal!"

The Playwright, given to brooding self-doubt, afflicted with a vanity very
different from Pearlman's, had to admire this man. What energy! What
supreme self-confidence! Pearlman reminded the Playwright of a matador.
He was a short man, not five feet seven; a dandy, without being handsome,
well-groomed, or well-dressed; his skin was coarse and exuded a sweaty,
febrile odor; he combed his thinning hair slickly across his ruddy scalp; in
his early forties, he'd suddenly had his stained front teeth capped so his smile
now glared like reflector lights. Pearlman was notorious for keeping actors
in exhausting rehearsals past midnight, in the days before Equity contracts;
yet he was admired, or at least respected, for never demanding more of anyone than he demanded of himself. He worked twelve-hour, fifteen-hour days.
He freely acknowledged that he was an obsessive; he boasted of being "selec-
tively psychotic." He'd been married three times and had five children; he'd
had numerous love affairs, including a few (it was rumored) with young men;
he was attracted to "the spark within" regardless of an individual's appearance. (So he would insist, in interviews, that his interest in working with the
Blond Actress had nothing to do with the woman's beauty but only with her
"spiritual gift.") Several of Pearlman's acclaimed actors had faces you would
have to call "idiosyncratic"; alone of American theater directors, Pearlman
dared to cast heavyset men and women in his productions if they were qualified; he'd earned some admiration, but mostly derision, for having cast a
large-boned six-foot Hedda Gabler in an Ensemble production of Ibsen's
play—"My point being, Hedda is the lonely Amazon in a world of pygmy
males." Pearlman might be ridiculed, but Pearlman was never wrong.

"It's true. I owe him a lot. But hardly everything."

The Playwright was a tall lanky storklike man. He had a reserved, watchful manner, guarded eyes, and a mouth slow to smile. In the New York the-

ater world he was not a "character," he was a "citizen." A hard worker, a man of integrity and responsibility. Not a poet perhaps (like his rival Tennessee Williams) but a craftsman. One of his few eccentricities was wearing white shirts and ties at play rehearsals, as if rehearsals were nine-to-five work in the mode of his salesman father in the Rahway Kelvinator store. By contrast, Max Pearlman was short and barrel-bodied and garrulous, in slovenly sweaters and trousers lacking belts, on his head a Greek fisherman's cap or a jaunty fedora or, in winter, his trademark black Astrakhan lamb's-wool hat that added several inches to his height. Where the Playwright handed over scrupulously written notes to actors, during rehearsals or following readings, Pearlman engaged in hour-long monologues, fascinating and exhausting his listeners in equal measure. Where the Playwright had a long lean austere face some women thought handsome, like a weathered Roman bust, Pearlman had a face even his mistresses could not call handsome, pudgy and pushed together with bulbous lips and nose. Yet what alert, appreciative eyes! Where the Playwright laughed softly with the air of a boy surprised by laughter in some space (school, synagogue?) in which laughter is forbidden, Pearlman laughed with zest as if laughter was a good thing, therapeutic as a sneeze. Pearlman's laugh! You could hear it through walls. On the noisy street outside the theater, you could hear it. Actors adored Pearlman for laughing at their comic lines though he might have heard them dozens of times; during a play performance, Pearlman's habit was to stand at the rear of the theater well into the play's run, like all devoted, monomaniacal directors so wired into his actors' performances that his face and body twitched in sympathy with them, laughing loudly, the loudest and most contagious laughter in the house.

Pearlman spoke of the Theater as you'd speak of God. Or more than God, for theater was something in which you participated and lived. "Die for it! For your talent! Scour out your guts! Be hard on yourself, you can take it. It's life and death up there on the stage, my friends. And if not life and death, it's *nothing*."

It was what I revered in him. Oh, he could reach right in. . . .

But he exploited you, didn't he? As a woman.

A woman? What do I care about myself as a woman? I never did. . . . I came to New York to learn to act.

Why do you give Pearlman so much credit? I hate it, in interviews, you exaggerate his role in your life. He eats it up, it's great publicity for him.

Oh, but it's true . . . isn't it?

You just want to deflect attention from yourself. It's what women do. Defer to bullies. You knew how to act, darling, when you came here.

I did? No.

Certainly you did. I hate this, too, the way you misinterpret yourself.

I do? Gee. . . .

You were a damned good actress when you came to New York. He didn't create you.

You created me.

Nobody created you, you were always yourself.

Well, I guess I knew . . . something. When I did movies. In fact I was reading Stanislavski. And the diary of, of . . . Nijinski.

Nijinski.

Nijinski. But I didn't know what I knew. In practice. It was just . . . what happened when I had to perform. To improvise. Like striking a match. . . .

The hell with that. You were a natural actress from the start.

Oh, hey! Why're you mad, Daddy? I don't get this.

I'm only just saying, darling, you were born with the gift. You have a kind of genius. You don't need theory. Forget Stanislavski! Nijinski! And him.

I never think of him.

Him messing with you . . . your mind, your talent . . . like somebody's big thumbs gripping a butterfly, smearing and breaking the wings.

Hey, I'm no butterfly. Feel my muscle? My leg here. I'm a dancer.

Bullshit theory is for somebody like him: can't act, can't write.

Kiss-kiss, Daddy? C'mon.

Hey, listen: Mr. Pearlman wasn't my lover really.

What's that mean—"really"?

Oh, he might've done some things but it wasn't. . . . Don't look at me like that, Daddy. That scares me.

What did he do?

Nothing actual.

He . . . touched you?

I guess. How d'you mean?

As a man touches a woman.

Mmmmmm! Like this?

Maybe like this? . . . This?

But Daddy, like I said: it wasn't anything actual, y'know?

Meaning . . . ?

Just something in his office? Like . . . a present to him? He asked to inter-view me. Me! He was skeptical, he said. Why'd a famous movie star want to study at his theater? He thought it was . . . some kind of publicity thing? Like anybody'd care where I went, what I did? Now I'm done with movies? He fired these questions at me. He was suspicious, I don't blame him. I guess I cried. How'd he know "Marilyn Monroe" was anybody real? He expected her, and I walked in.

What kind of questions did he ask you?

My . . . motivation.

Which was?

To . . . not die.

What?

To not die. To keep on. . . .

I hate it when you talk like that. It tears my heart.

Oh, I won't! I'm sorry.

He made love to you, then. How many times?

It wasn't l-love! I don't know. Daddy, gee, this makes me feel bad. You're mad at me.

Darling, I'm not mad at you. I'm just trying to understand.

Understand what? I didn't know you then. I was . . . divorced.

Where did you and Pearlman meet? Not always that smelly office of his.

Oh, it was mainly in his office! Late, after class. I thought . . . well, I was flattered. So many books! Some of them, the titles I could see, in German? Russian? A picture of Mr. Pearlman with Eugene O'Neill. All these won-derful actors: Marlon Brando, Rod Steiger. . . . I saw this book in German I'd read in English—I mean I saw the name "Schopenhauer"—I took it down and pretended to read. I said, "I can sure read Schopenhauer better when he writes in English, than like this."

What did Pearlman say?

He corrected my pronunciation— "Schopenhauer." He didn't believe me that I'd read that book. In any language. I mean I read in that book. A pho-tographer I used to know gave me a copy. "This is the truth of the world, The World as Will and Idea." I used to read it till I felt too sad.

Pearlman was always saying how surprised he was by you. What you're really like.

But . . . what'd that be? What I'm really like?

Just yourself.

But that isn't enough, is it?

Of course it is.

No. It never is.

What do you mean?

You're a writer, because being just yourself isn't enough. I need to be an actress, because being just myself isn't enough. Hey, you won't ever tell people, will you?

I would never speak of you, darling. It would be like flaying my own skin.

You would never write about me, either . . . would you, Daddy?

Of course not!

This . . . with Mr. Pearlman . . . was just something that happened. Like a . . . present to him, to thank him? Like . . . "Marilyn Monroe"? For a few minutes?

You let Pearlman make love to "Marilyn Monroe."

That's maybe what he'd call it. . . . Oh, he wouldn't like this! Me telling you.

Exactly what did he do?

Oh mainly just . . . kissing me. Different places.

With your clothes on or off?

Mostly on. I don't know.

His clothes?

Daddy, I don't know. I didn't look.

And did you have a . . . sexual response?

Probably not. I don't, mostly. . . . Except with somebody I love. Like you.

Keep me out of this! This is about you and that pig.

He wasn't a pig! Just a man.

A man among men, eh?

❦

A man among "Marilyn's" men.

❦

Look, I'm sorry. I'm just trying to deal with this.

Daddy, I remember now! I was thinking of Magda . . . in your play. The gift Mr. Pearlman was giving me. To read a new play by you . . . with real theater actors. The gift you were giving me.

He cast you without consulting me. I never knew. He did all the casting when he directed.

He didn't inform you about me, I know! I was so scared . . . I revered you so.

He said, "Trust me. I've got your Magda."

Did you trust him?

Yes.

Why don't I remember things better, my mind gets stuck on a role I'm doing, and I . . . it's like I'm in two places at once? With other people but not . . . with them. Why I love to act. Even when I'm alone I'm not.

Your gift is so natural, you don't "act." You require no technique. Yes, it's like a match being struck. A sudden flaring flame. . . .

But I like to read, Daddy! I got good grades in school. I like to . . . think. It's like talking with somebody. In Hollywood, on the set, I'd have to hide my book if I was reading. . . . People thought I was strange.

Your mind can get muddled. You're easily influenced.

Only by people I trust.

I've seen that office of his plenty of times. That sofa. . . . Filthy, isn't it? Smelling of his hair oil, cigar smoke, stale pastrami. . . . Squalor is the atmosphere Pearlman thrives in, it's his image. Amid the crass marketplace of Broadway. "Uncompromising." "Incorruptible."

Oh . . . isn't he? I thought you were his f-friend.

When we were subpoenaed—by the House Un-American Activities Committee in 1953—he hired an expensive Harvard lawyer. Not a Jew. Me, I hired a guy from right here in Manhattan, a friend. A "Commie lawyer" he was called. . . . I was the idealist. Pearlman was the pragmatist. Damned lucky I didn't get sent to prison.

Oh, Daddy! That won't happen again. It's 1956 now. We're more advanced now.

He had a sexual response, yes?

Why don't you ask him? He's your friend from way back.

Pearlman's not my friend. He's been jealous of me from the start.

I thought Mr. Pearlman gave you your s-start.

As if I couldn't have had a career without him? That's what he says? Bullshit.

I don't know what he says. I don't know Mr. Pearlman, really. He's got a hundred friends in New York . . . you all know him better than I do.

Do you see him now?

What! Oh, Daddy.

You and him, you're together . . . he looks at you. I've seen it. And you look at him.

I do?

That way of yours.

What way?

That "Marilyn" way.

That's just maybe . . . nervousness.

You don't have to tell me, darling, if it's too painful.

Tell . . . what?

How many times . . . you and him.

Daddy, I don't know. My mind's not . . . an adding machine.

You needed to show gratitude to him.

That's what it was? I guess.

Before you and I met.

Oh, Daddy! Yes.

And it was, how many times? Five, six? Twenty? Fifty?

What?

You know what.

Just . . . four or five times. I'd go into Magda. I wasn't there.

He's married.

I guess.

But, hell. I was married too. Yes?

❧

Did you ever come?

Huh?

Did you ever have an orgasm? With him?

Did I ever . . . oh, gee. Daddy, I didn't know you then. I mean, as a real person. I knew your work. I revered you.

Did you ever have an orgasm with Pearlman? Him "kissing" you.

Oh, Daddy, if I did ever have a—a . . . it was only just for the scene, you know? And then the scene was over.

❧

Now you're mad at me? Don't you love me?

I love you.

You don't! Not me.

Of course I love you. I'd like to save you from yourself, is all. The low value you place upon yourself.

Oh, but already I am saved. Already, my new life with you. . . . Oh, Daddy, you won't write about me, will you? Us talking like this? After I'm— when, maybe, you don't love me anymore?

Darling, don't say such things. You must know by now, I'll always love you.

12

This play that was his life. Yet the Blond Actress, reading Magda in her small breathy impassioned voice, was entering the play and entering his life. The Blond Actress had shifted her terror onto Magda and made Magda come alive.

When Magda spoke with Isaac's parents she was faltering and stammering and her wispy voice was almost inaudible, and you felt embarrassment, that the Blond Actress wasn't equal to the occasion and would give up in another minute; then, in the next scene, when Magda spoke with more assurance, you realized that the Blond Actress had been acting, and that this was what gifted "acting" was—a mimesis of life so intense you experienced it viscerally, as life. In her scenes with Isaac, Magda became animated, even vivacious; what was rare in this drab rehearsal space, as in Ensemble productions generally, the Blond Actress exuded a sudden sexual energy that took both the audience and the other actors by surprise. Certainly Isaac was taken by surprise. The young actor, whom the Playwright liked, talented, sharp, a handsome olive-skinned boy with glasses cast as scholarly-Jewish, was at a loss initially how to play to the Blond Actress's Magda; then shortly he began to respond, awkward as Isaac would have been, and excited as an adolescent boy would have been in such circumstances. You felt the electricity between the two: the earthy Hungarian farm girl with nearly no schooling and the younger suburban-Jewish boy soon to depart for college on a scholarship.

The audience relaxed and began to laugh, for the scene was tenderly comic in a mode unlike anything the Playwright, revered for his seriousness, had ever attempted. The scene ended with Magda's "golden laughter."

The Playwright laughed too, a startled laughter of recognition. He'd ceased taking notes on his script. It seemed that the play, his play, was being wrested from him. That Magda, the Blond Actress's Magda, was guiding it in a direction not his. Or was it?

The reading continued through the play's three acts, bringing Isaac and Magda by quick dramatic jumps into adulthood and into wholly separate lives. The Playwright was thinking how ironic! yet how fitting! the husky flaxen-haired Hungarian girl of memory was being replaced by the emotionally fragile Magda with the platinum-blond braid and brimming-blue eyes. Here was a Magda so vulnerable, so exposed, you dreaded her being hurt. You dreaded her being exploited. Isaac and his parents, suburban New Jersey Jews, privileged and well-to-do in contrast to Magda's impoverished background, were not so sympathetic as the Playwright had intended them. And the fairy-tale plot the Playwright had invented to express the distance between Isaac's and Magda's worlds—Magda becomes pregnant by Isaac;

Magda keeps her secret from Isaac and his parents: Isaac leaves for college and a brilliant career: Magda marries a farmer and has Isaac's child and subsequent children: Isaac becomes a writer, successful while still in his twenties; Isaac and Magda meet at intervals, finally at Isaac's father's funeral; Isaac, for all his supposed brilliance, never knows what the audience knows, what Magda has shielded him from knowing—this plot seemed to him now unsatisfactory, incomplete.

The play's final lines belonged to Isaac, standing in the cemetery, as Magda faces him across his father's grave. "I will always remember you, Magda." The figures freeze, the lights dim and go out. The ending that had seemed so right was exposed now as inadequate, incomplete, for why should we care that Isaac remembers Magda? What of Magda? What are her final words?

The reading ended. It had been an emotionally exhausting experience for everyone. In violation of Ensemble protocol for such informal occasions, many in the audience applauded. A few individuals got to their feet. The Playwright was being congratulated. What folly! He'd removed his glasses and wiped at his eyes with his sleeve, drawn, dazed, smiling in confusion, touched with panic. *It's a failure. Why are they clapping? Is this mockery?* Without his glasses he saw the interior of the loft as a pulsing swirl of novalike lights and blurred motion and darkness. He saw no faces, he could recognize no one.

He heard Pearlman speak his name. He turned away. He must escape! He muttered a few words of thanks, or apology. He couldn't bear to speak with anyone. Even to thank the actors. Even to thank *her*.

He fled. Out of the rehearsal room, down the steep metal stairs. On 51st Street he stepped into a wall of head-hammering cold. He fled to Eleventh Avenue seeking a subway. Had to escape! Had to get home. Or anywhere, where no one knew his name.

"But I did love her. The memory of her. My Magda!"

I 3

You ran away from me! When already I loved you.
When I'd come so far, for you.
When my life was already yours. If you wanted it.
How then could I trust you? Yet I loved you.
Already then I began to hate you.

14

The following evening, they agreed to meet. At a restaurant on West 70th and Broadway. The Blond Actress was the one in pursuit.

He knew! A married man. Yet not a happily married man, not for years. And already (it shamed him to think this, yet it was so) he'd begun to fall in love with her. My Magda.

He'd recovered from his shock of the other evening. In a detached voice he said, "This play. It's become too important to me. It's become my life. For an artist, that's fatal."

The Blond Actress listened carefully. Her expression was somber. Was she holding her dazzling smile in reserve? She'd come to comfort the brooding Playwright. There was the blond promise of infinite comfort. Except he was married, an old married man. He was a wreck! Thinning hair, a look about the eyes like frayed socks, those creases sharp as knife cuts in his cheeks. His shameful secret was, Magda had never stroked those cheeks. Magda had never kissed him. Magda had never touched him. Still less had Magda seduced him. He'd been twelve years old when Magda, brimming with blond vigor and health at seventeen, had come to work for his parents; by the time he'd left for Rutgers, Magda had already departed, married, and moved away. All had been the Playwright's adolescent fantasy of a flaxen-haired girl as different from himself and his people as if she'd belonged to another species. Now Magda as the Blond Actress was seated gravely across from him in a booth in a Manhattan restaurant more than thirty years later, saying earnestly, "You shouldn't say such things! About your beautiful play. Didn't you see, people were crying? It has to be your life, see, otherwise you couldn't love it so. Even if it kills you—" The Blond Actress paused. She'd said too much! The Playwright could see her mind working swiftly. Wondering was he one of those men who resent a woman speaking intelligently? Speaking much, at all?

He said, "It's just that I don't think I will ever finish it now. Some of those scenes were originally written a quarter century ago. Before, almost, you were born." This was spoken lightly and certainly without reproach. But the Blond Actress did look disconcertingly young. And her affect, her manner, her sense of herself were young, even childlike. *So the world won't hurt her as much as otherwise it might.* The Playwright quickly calculated he was twenty years this woman's elder and looked it. "Magda is a vivid character to me, yet I think, to an audience, inconsistent. And Isaac, of course, is too much me. Yet only a fraction of me. The material is too autobiographical. And the parents. . . ." The Playwright rubbed his eyes, which were aching. He hadn't slept much the night before. The folly of his long effort and, more painfully, of his recent successes swept over him.

I have no talent, no gift. I have the panting ardor of a workhorse. Yet in time even a workhorse wears out.

He'd seen how, at the reading, when he'd risen to his feet to escape, the Blond Actress's yearning eyes had snatched at him. He'd wanted to shout, Leave me alone all of you! It's too late.

The Blond Actress was saying, hesitantly, "I had some ideas about M-magda? If you're interested?"

Ideas? From an actress?

The Playwright laughed. His laughter was startled, grateful.

"Of course I'm interested. You're very kind, to care."

The Playwright would not have arranged this meeting. And a romantic meeting it was, excitement and tension and a kind of dread on both sides, in a dimly lit smoky restaurant bar, a secluded booth at the rear. A Negro jazz combo playing "Mood Indigo." And that was the Playwright's mood: indigo. His wife had telephoned from Miami just before he'd left to meet the Blond Actress, hair damp from the shower and jaws pleasantly smarting from being shaved, and he'd been jumpy lifting the receiver in anticipation of—what? The Blond Actress was canceling their date? When she'd only just made it, a few hours before? The Playwright's wife had sounded very distant, her voice crackling with static. Almost, he hadn't recognized it. And what had that voice, with its perpetual edge of reproach, to do with *him?*

The Blond Actress wore her hair still in a single short plait at the nape of her neck. He'd never seen her, in any of her photos, with plaited hair. So this was Magda! Her Magda. His Magda had had much longer hair and had worn it plaited and wound about her head in an old-fashioned style that made her seem older than her years and far more prim. His Magda's hair had been coarse as a horse's mane. This Magda's hair was fine-spun, synthetic, a dreamy creamy blond like a doll's hair; a man naturally wanted to bury his face in it, and to bury his face in the woman's neck, and hold the woman tightly, and—protect her? But from whom? Himself? She seemed so vulnerable, so open to hurt. Risking a rebuff from the Playwright. As she'd risked a wounding public rebuff from Pearlman the night before. The Playwright had heard that the Blond Actress "went everywhere alone" in New York and that this was viewed as an eccentricity, if not a risk. Yet, hair hidden, in dark-tinted glasses, in clothes without conspicuous glamour, the Blond Actress wasn't likely to be recognized. This evening she wore a loose-fitting angora sweater, tailored slacks, and shoes with a medium heel; a man's fedora with a sloping brim shielded much of her face from the eyes of curious strangers. The Playwright had seen her, when she entered the crowded bar, as soon as she'd sighted him at the rear, smiling, removing horn-rimmed tinted glasses and fumbling to shove them in her handbag. The fedora she hadn't removed until after the waiter had taken their orders. Her expression was playful, hopeful. Was this blond girl "Marilyn Monroe"? Or did she simply resemble, like a younger, inexperienced sister, the famous/ infamous Hollywood actress?

It would astonish the Playwright when he came to know the Blond Actress better how, when she didn't wish to be recognized, she rarely was, for "Marilyn Monroe" was but one of her roles and not the one that most engaged her.

While he, the Playwright, was always and forever himself.

No, he would not have arranged this meeting. He would not have acquired the Blond Actress's telephone number, as she'd acquired his, and called him. He knew of her marriage to the Ex-Athlete. All the world knew, at least its rudiments. A fairy-tale marriage that had lasted less than a year, its failure eagerly recorded in the public press. The Playwright recalled having seen in one of the newsmagazines an astonishing photo, taken from the roof of a building, of a mob scene in Tokyo, thousands of "fans" crowding a public square in the hope of catching sight of the Blond Actress. He would not have supposed the Japanese knew much of "Marilyn Monroe" or would have cared. Was this some new lurid development in the history of mankind? Public hysteria in the presence of someone known to be famous? Marx had famously denounced religion as the opiate of the people, now it was Fame that was the opiate of the people; except the Church of Fame carried with it not even the huckster's promise of salvation, heaven. Its pantheon of saints was a hall of distorting mirrors.

Shyly the Blond Actress smiled. Oh, she was pretty! An American-girl prettiness to wrench the heart. And how earnest, telling the Playwright how much she "admired" his work. What an "honor" it was to meet him, and to read the role of Magda. The plays of his she'd seen in Los Angeles. The plays she'd read. The Playwright was flattered but uneasy. But flattered. Drinking scotch and listening. In the bar's festive mirrors the Playwright had passed like a tall wraith. A figure of dignity with something wounded, ravaged, in his face. Slope-shouldered, lanky. Born in New Jersey, having lived most of his life in the New York City area, the Playwright yet exuded an air of the West. He looked like a man with no family, a man with no parents. A not-young hatchet-faced man with creased cheeks and a receding hairline and a watchful manner. When he smiled, it was an unexpected occasion. He became boyish! Kindly. A man of brooding imagination but a man you could trust.

Maybe.

Out of her oversized handbag the Blond Actress took a copy of *The Girl with the Flaxen Hair* and laid it on the tabletop between them like a talisman. "This girl Magda. She's like the girl in *The Three Sisters*? Who marries the brother?" When the Playwright stared at the Blond Actress she said, uncertainly, "They laugh at her? The sash of her dress that's the wrong color? Except, with Magda, it's the way she speaks English."

"Who told you that?"

"What?"

"About *The Three Sisters* and my play."

"Nobody."

"Pearlman? That I'd been influenced?"

"Oh, no, I r-read the play myself, by Chekhov. Years ago. I wanted to be a stage actress first but I needed money, so I went into films. I always thought I could play Natasha? I mean, somebody like me could play her. Because she doesn't belong in a good family and people laugh at her."

The Playwright said nothing. His offended heart beat hard.

Quickly, seeing he was angry, she tried to rectify her mistake, saying with schoolgirl eagerness, "I was thinking, what Chekhov does with Natasha, he surprises you because Natasha turns out so strong and devious. And cruel. And Magda, you know—well, Magda is always so good. She wouldn't be, in real life? I mean, all the time? I mean"—the Playwright could see the Blond Actress shifting into a scene, face animated, eyes narrowed—"if it was me, a cleaning girl—and I used to do work like that, laundry, dishes, mopping, scrubbing toilets, when I was in an orphanage and a foster home in Los Angeles—I'd be hurt, I'd be angry, how life was so different for different people. But your Magda . . . she never changes much. She's *good*."

"Yes. Magda is good. Was good. The original. It wouldn't have occurred to her to be angry." Was this true? The Playwright spoke curtly, but he had to wonder. "She and her family were grateful for her job. Though it didn't pay much, it *paid*."

Rebuked, the Blond Actress could only agree. Oh, now she understood! Magda was superior to her, a higher form of herself. Oh, yes.

The Playwright signaled for a waiter and ordered two more drinks. Scotch for himself, a club soda for her. He wondered if she didn't drink? Or didn't dare? He'd heard rumors. . . . In the awkward silence the Playwright said, trying to keep all irony out of his voice, "And what other thoughts do you have about Magda?"

The Blond Actress sat shyly, touching her lips. She seemed about to speak, then hesitated. She knew the Playwright was angry with her and in an instant had decided he hated her. Whatever sexual attraction he'd been feeling for her welled up in him now as rage. She knew! She was as experienced a female (the Playwright sensed) as a prostitute who'd been put out on the street as a girl, as sensitive to the rapid shifts in a man's attention and in a man's desire. *For her life depends upon it. Her female life.*

"I guess . . . . I said something wrong? About Natasha?"

"Certainly not. It's helpful."

"Your play is nothing like . . . that one."

"No, it isn't. I've never been much drawn to Chekhov."

The Playwright spoke with care. He forced himself to smile. *He was smiling.* Confronted with a woman's obstinacy, as with his wife's, and long ago his mother's. The women he knew were susceptible to single, simple ideas that lodged in their brains like pellets and could not be dislodged by argument, common sense, logic. *I am nothing like the poet Chekhov. I am a craftsman of the school of Ibsen. My feet solid on the ground. And the ground solid beneath my feet.*

The Blond Actress had one more thing to say. Did she dare say it? She laughed nervously and leaned toward the Playwright as if imparting a secret. He stared at her mouth. Wondering what desperate foul things that mouth had done. "One thing I was thinking? Magda wouldn't know how to read? Isaac could show this p-poem to her, he'd written to her, and she'd pretend she could read it?"

The Playwright felt his temples pounding.

That was it! Magda was illiterate.

The original Magda had probably been illiterate. Of course.

Quickly the Playwright said, smiling, "We don't need to talk about my play any longer, Marilyn. Tell me about yourself, please."

The Blond Actress smiled in confusion. As if thinking *which self?*

The Playwright said, "I should call you Marilyn, shouldn't I? Or is that just a stage name?"

"You could call me Norma. That's my true name."

The Playwright pondered this. "Somehow, Norma doesn't seem to suit you."

The Blond Actress looked hurt. "It doesn't?"

"Norma. The name of an older woman, of a bygone era. Norma Talmadge. Norma Shearer."

The Blond Actress brightened. "Norma Shearer was my godmother! My mother was her close friend. My father was a friend of Mr. Thalberg's. I was just a little girl when he died, but I remember the funeral! We rode in one of the limousines, with the family. It was the biggest funeral in Hollywood history."

The Playwright knew little about the Blond Actress's background, but this didn't sound right. Hadn't she just said she'd been an orphan, living in a foster home?

He decided not to question her. She was smiling so proudly.

"Irving Thalberg! The New York Jew-boy genius."

The Blond Actress smiled uncertainly. A joke? A way that Jews can speak of other Jews, familiarly, fondly, even in scorn, and non-Jews dare not?

The Playwright, seeing the Blond Actress's confusion, said, "Thalberg was a legend. A prodigy. Young even at his death."

"Oh, was he? At his d-death?"

"He wouldn't have seemed young to a child. But yes, in the eyes of the world."

The Blond Actress said eagerly, "The funeral service was in a beautiful synagogue—temple?—on Wilshire Boulevard. I was too young to understand much. The language was Hebrew?—it was so strange and wonderful. I guess I thought it was the voice of God. But I've never been back since. I mean, to any synagogue."

The Playwright shifted his shoulders uncomfortably. Religion meant little to him except as a mode of ancestor respect, and that he took with a grain of salt. He wasn't a Jew who believed that the Holocaust was the end of history or the beginning of history, even that the Holocaust "defined" Jews. He was a liberal, a socialist, a rationalist. He wasn't a Zionist. In private he did believe that Jews were the most enlightened, the most generally gifted, the best-educated and best-intentioned people among the world's quarrelsome multitudes, but he attached no special sentiment or piety to this belief; it was only just common sense. "I'm not inclined to mysticism. Hebrew isn't, to my ears, the voice of God."

"Oh—it isn't?"

"Thunder, maybe. Earthquake, tidal wave. A voice of God unhampered by syntax."

The Blond Actress gazed at the Playwright with widened eyes.

Beautiful long-lashed eyes in which you could fall, and fall.

The Playwright signaled for another drink, for himself. He was thinking how like most actors and actresses the Blond Actress appeared younger than she photographed. And smaller in stature. And her head, her beautiful shapely head, too large. For such freaky individuals photograph well; on screen sometimes they appear as gods, who knows why? *Beauty is a question of optics. All sight is illusion.* He wanted not to love this woman. He told himself he couldn't possibly become involved with an actress. An actress! A Hollywood actress! Unlike theater actors, who scrupulously learn their craft and must memorize their dialogue, film actors can get by with virtually no work—brief rehearsals, coached by indulgent directors to utter a few lines of dialogue, to be reshot and reshot and reshot—the most egregiously stupid "act" by reading their lines off placards held up to them off-camera. And some of these "actors" receive Oscars. What a mockery of the art of acting! And then, their private lives. The Playwright recalled having heard rumors of the Blond Actress: her promiscuity before (and during?) her troubled marriage, her drug-taking, her suicide attempt (or attempts), her association with a wild decadent crowd of Hollywood-fringe characters, one of them the alcoholic heroin-addict son of blacklisted Charlie Chaplin.

Now he'd met the Blond Actress, he didn't believe any of this for a minute.

Now he'd met his Magda, he wouldn't believe anything about her not his own discovery.

Shyly she was saying, like a schoolgirl imparting a secret, "What I revered in Magda, she had her baby because she loved it. Before it was born, she loved it! It's only a little scene, when she speaks to it, a soliloquy . . . and Isaac doesn't know, nobody knows. She finds a man to marry so the baby can be born and . . . not given away and scorned. Another girl might have given birth in a secret place and killed her baby. You know, that's what they did in the old days, girls who were poor and not married. My best friend in the orphanage, her mother tried to kill her . . . drown her. In scalding water. She had scars up and down her arms like lacy scales." The Blond Actress's eyes flooded with tears. The Playwright instinctively reached out to touch her hand, the back of her hand.

I would rewrite her story. That was in my power.

The Blond Actress wiped at her eyes, and blew her nose, and said, "Norma Jeane is the name my mother gave me, actually. I mean, my mom and dad. Do you like that better than Norma?"

The Playwright smiled. "A little better."

He'd relinquished her hand. Wanting to take it again, and lean across the tabletop to kiss her.

It was a movie scene: not original, yet so compelling! If he leaned over the tabletop the young blond woman would lift her head wide-eyed in expectation and he, the lover, would frame her face in his hands and press his mouth against hers.

The beginning of everything. The end of his long marriage.

The Blond Actress said, apologetically, "I don't like M-marilyn much. But I can answer to it. It's what most people call me, now. Who don't know me."

"I could call you Norma Jeane, if you prefer. I could call you"—and here the Playwright's voice wavered with the audacity of what he said—"my 'Magda.' "

"Oh. I'd like that."

"My Secret Magda."

"Yes!"

"But maybe Marilyn when others are around. So there wouldn't be any misunderstanding."

"When others are around, it doesn't matter what you call me. You can whistle. You can call me, 'Hey you!' " The Blond Actress laughed, showing her beautiful white teeth.

He was touched to the heart, she'd been made happy so quickly.

The Playwright, too, had been made happy so quickly.

"Hey you."

"Hey *you*."

They laughed together like giddy children. Suddenly shy of each other and frightened. For they hadn't yet touched. Just that brushing of hands. They hadn't yet kissed. They would leave the bar at midnight, the Playwright would see the Blond Actress into a cab and they would then kiss, quickly, hungrily yet chastely, and they would squeeze hands, and look yearningly at each other, and nothing more. Not that night.

In a delirium of emotion the Playwright would walk the few blocks back to his darkened apartment. Happy to be in love, and happy to be alone.

15

Like my Magda, a girl of the people.

No scars on her arms. No scars on her body.

My life would begin again with her. As Isaac! A boy again to whom the world is new. Before history and the Holocaust, new.

In fact even after they became lovers, the Playwright would rarely call the Blond Actress Marilyn in public, for that was the name by which the world familiarly knew her; and he, her lover, her protector, was not *the world*. Nor would he call her, in private, Magda or My Magda. Instead he found himself calling her darling, dear, dear one, dearest. For these tender names *the world* had no right to call her.

Only him.

When they were alone, she would call him Daddy. At first playfully, teasing (all right, yes, he was older than she by almost twenty years, why not make a joke of it), then in earnest and with love and reverence shimmering in her eyes. When they were with others she would call him darling, and sometimes honey. Rarely would she call him by his first name, and never a diminutive of that name. For this, too, was the name by which *the world* knew him.

Inventing a private language, each time we love. The codified speech of lovers.

Oh, but Daddy!—you would never speak of me, would you? To anyone else.

Never.
Or write about me? Daddy?
Darling, never. Haven't I told you?

16

An American epic. At last Pearlman called. Knowing that something was wrong (for his old friend the Playwright had avoided him since the reading) but determined not to give a sign. He talked nonstop for an hour praising and dissecting *The Girl with the Flaxen Hair* and said he hoped the Ensemble might produce it next season and then his voice dropped (exactly as the Playwright anticipated in this scene) and he said, "About my Magda—what d'you think? Not bad, eh?"

The Playwright was trembling with fury. He could bring himself to mutter only a polite assent.

Pearlman said, excited, "For a Hollywood actress. A classic dumb blonde with no stage experience. Remarkable, *I* thought."

"Yes. Remarkable."

A pause. This was an improvised scene, but the Playwright wasn't pulling his weight. Pearlman said, as if they'd been arguing, "This could be your masterpiece, my friend. If we work on it together." Another pause. Awkward silence. "If—Marilyn could play Magda." His pronunciation of "Marilyn" was tender, tentative. "You saw how scared she is. Of 'live acting,' she calls it. She's terrified of forgetting lines, she says. Being 'exposed' on the stage. Everything's life or death to her. She can't fail. If she fails, it's death. I respect that, I'm exactly the same way or would be, except I'm the sanest person I know.

"You learn by your mistakes, Marilyn, I told her. 'But people are waiting for me to make mistakes. They're waiting for me to fail, to laugh at me,' she says. She was so scared before the reading, at our run-through that afternoon, she kept excusing herself to use the bathroom. I said, Marilyn, dear, we're gonna get you a potty for right under your chair, and that cracked her up; she relaxed a little after that. We had two rehearsals. Two! To us that's nothing but to her it must've seemed like a lot. 'I should be better,' she kept saying. 'My voice should be stronger.' True, she's got a small voice. Any theater more than one hundred fifty seats, she wouldn't be heard in the back. But we can develop that voice. We can develop *her*.

"That's my business, I told her. Give me talent, I'm like Hercules. Give me rare talent, I'm Jehovah. 'But the playwright will be there, the playwright will hear me,' she kept saying. That's the idea, Marilyn, I told her. That's what a contemporary play means: a playwright working with you."

"With us, this woman could realize her true talent. In your play, in that role. It's made for her. She's a 'woman of the people' like Magda. See, she's more than a movie star. She's a born stage actress. She's like nobody I've worked with, except maybe Marlon Brando, they're alike in their souls. Our Magda, eh? What a coincidence, eh? What d'you say?"

The Playwright had ceased listening. He was in his third-floor study staring out a window at the cobbled winter sky. It was a weekday. A day of irresolution. Yes but he'd decided, hadn't he? He could not hurt his wife and humiliate her. His family. Could not be an adulterer. *Not for my own happiness. Or even hers.* As five years before, the Playwright had been one of those individuals who'd quietly refused to aid the House Un-American Activities Committee in their persecuting of Communists, Communist sympathizers, political dissenters. He could not inform on acquaintances of whom, in fact, in secret, he didn't approve, reckless men, self-destructive men, Stalinist sympathizers who boasted of a bloody apocalypse to come. He could not inform on acquaintances who might have (oh, he didn't want to think this!) betrayed him, in his place. For his was the intransigence of the ascetic, the monkish, the stubborn, the martyred.

Pearlman, too, had held his ground with HUAC. Pearlman, too, had behaved with integrity. Give the man credit.

Have you fucked her, Max? Or plan to? That's the subtext here?

"If we did the play, Marilyn would be sensational. I could work with her privately for months. Already, in acting class, she's responding. There's an outer shell of her—as in all of us—that has to be penetrated; inside, she's molten lava. Everybody in town would be saying what a risk for our theater, for Pearlman's reputation, and Pearlman would show 'em, Marilyn would show 'em, this could be the stage debut of the century."

"A coup," the Playwright said ironically.

"Of course," Pearlman worried aloud, "she might return to Hollywood. They're suing her, The Studio. She refuses to discuss it but I called her agent out there and the man was frank and friendly enough; he explained what the situation is: Marilyn's in violation of her contract, she owes The Studio four or five movies, she's suspended without pay and hasn't anything saved, and I said, But is she free to work for me? and he laughed and said, 'She's free if she wants to pay the price, or maybe you could match the price,' and I said, What kind of money are we talking here? A hundred thousand? Two hundred? and he said, 'More like a cool million. This is Hollywood, not the Great White Way,' the fucker said, sounding like a young guy, younger than me, laughing at me. So I hung up."

Again, the Playwright said nothing. He felt a small shudder of contempt.

Since that first evening, he and the Blond Actress had met twice. They'd talked earnestly. Yes, they'd held hands. The Playwright had yet to say *I love you, I adore you.* He had yet to say *I can't continue to see you.* The Blond Actress had been brimming with talk but not of her Hollywood past or her financial difficulties at the present time. Yet the Playwright knew, from what he'd heard or read, that Marilyn Monroe was being sued by The Studio.

How little that person, that presence, has to do with her. Or with us.

Max Pearlman continued to speak for another ten minutes, his mood veering from ecstatic and convinced to agitated and doubtful. The Playwright could imagine his old friend leaning back in his ancient swivel chair, stretching his fatty-muscled arms, scratching his hairy belly where his stained sweater rode up his torso, and on the walls of his cluttered and smelly office photographs of such Ensemble-associated actors as Marlon Brando and Rod Steiger and Geraldine Page and Kim Stanley and Julie Harris and Montgomery Clift and James Dean and Paul Newman and Shelley Winters and Viveca Lindfors and Eli Wallach smiling fondly upon their Max Pearlman; one day soon, the beautiful face of Marilyn Monroe to be added to these, the most prized of trophies. At last Pearlman said, "You're taking your play to another theater, eh? That's it?" and the Playwright said, "No, Max. I am not. I just don't think it's finished yet, ready to be performed, that's all," and Pearlman said, explosively, "Shit! Then let's finish it together, let's work on it for God's sake, you and me, and get it into shape for next year. For *her*," and the Playwright said gently, "Max. Good night."

Hanging up then, quickly. And taking the receiver from the hook.

Pearlman was the type to call back and let the phone ring to infinity.

17

Deceit. She, too, had called him. The familiar phone's ringing like a knife blade in the heart.

Hi! It's me. Your Magda?

As if she'd needed to identify herself.

One afternoon picking up the receiver to hear the woman's lovely low breathy-throaty voice, no preamble to her singing:

"You ain't been blue
No, no, no
You ain't been blue
Till you've got that mood indigo."

His wife, Esther, had returned from wherever she'd been. Miami.

In his face, in his grieving guilty eyes, she saw.

This awkward, improvised scene: the Blond Actress's words thrumming in his ears, in his groin, in his soul, the remembered scent of her, the promise of her, the mystery of her, in comic collision with a frowning Esther and her suitcases thudding in the front hall, the hall of this cramped old brownstone impossibly narrow because the Playwright's books overflowed in teetering pinewood bookshelves into every part of the household, not excluding the bathrooms, and there was the Playwright stooping to lift the suitcases, and somehow a Neiman-Marcus shopping bag spilled at his feet. "Oh, clumsy! Oh, look what you've done."

True! He was clumsy. Not a graceful man. Not a romantic man. Not a lover.

He'd begun to call her *Dear, dear one*. Not yet *darling*. Oh, not yet *darling!*

Holding hands, gripping hands. In their shadowed jazz-club rendezvous. Where no one recognized them. (In fact, did no one recognize them? A middle-aged bespectacled stork of a man with a luminous young woman gazing adoringly up at him?) A few kisses. Yet not yet a deeply passionate kiss. Not a kiss that was a prelude to lovemaking.

Please understand: my life is not my own. I have a wife, I have children and a family. I could hurt others by loving you. But I can't hurt others! I prefer to hurt myself.

And the Blond Actress smiled, and sighed, and so beautifully improvised her half of the scene. *Oh gosh. I understand, I guess!*

His wife was saying, brightly, "Miss me?"

"Of course."

"Yes." She laughed. "I can see."

Since the night of the play reading, and all that it had revealed to the Playwright of his folly and the futility of his labor, he'd been unable to concentrate on his work. He'd hardly been able to sit still. Mornings, he went for long windblown walks to the far side of the park and back; the cold was a corrective to his fevered state. He wandered the drafty corridors of the Museum of Natural History where, as a boy, Isaac-like, he'd dreamt and brooded and lost himself in the austere impersonality of the past. What a mystery, that the world precedes us, gives birth to us, seems for a brief while to cherish us, then sloughs us off like outgrown skin. Gone! Fiercely, he thought *I want my passage here to be remembered. To be worthy of being remembered.*

The Playwright understood that the Blond Actress did not want to be his equal. Shrewdly he perceived that she was reliving a role she'd once played, maybe more than once, and for which she'd been rewarded: she was the girl child; he was the older male mentor. But did he want to be this woman's mentor/father, or did he want to be her lover? To the Blond Actress, the two were possibly identical. To the Playwright, there was something perverse about being both, or seeming to be both. *She can only love a man she imagines to be her superior. Am I that man?* He knew his failings! Of the Playwright's critics, he was himself the harshest. He knew how painstaking and tentative he was in composition; how he lacked the genius of poetry that is quicksilver, magic, unwilled. The Chekhovian moment that flashes out of the seeming ordinary, as out of an empty sky. A sudden peal of laughter, an old man's snoring, the death stink of Solyony's hands. *The sound of a string breaking that dies away sadly.*

He could not have created Chekhov's Natasha. He could not have understood even that his "girl of the people" was too good, and so not credible, except the Blond Actress had seen it by instinct. In his doggedly crafted plays there were no such Chekhovian flashes, for the Playwright's imagination was literal, at times clumsy; yes, he acknowledged his clumsiness, which was a form of honesty. The Playwright would not bend truth even in the service of art! Yet he'd been rewarded for his work; he'd received a Pulitzer Prize (which had had the unexpected result of making his wife both proud of him and resentful of him simultaneously) and other prizes; he would be honored as a major American dramatist. For his work could wrench hearts, even as Chekhov's work did. And the work of Ibsen, O'Neill, Williams. Perhaps in its very homeliness it more powerfully wrenched the American heart. When he was feeling hopeful he told himself that he was an honest craftsman who built sturdy seaworthy vessels. The lighter, sleeker, more dazzling crafts of poet playwrights flew past, but his reached the same harbor as theirs.

He believed this. He wanted to believe!

Your wonderful work. Your beautiful work. I admire you so!

A beautiful young woman, saying such things to him. Speaking sincerely. With the air of one imparting an obvious truth. She'd gone to the Strand Bookshop to buy those out-of-print plays of his she hadn't yet read, back in her old life.

She was living in the Village. She'd sublet a flat on East 11th Street from a theater friend of Max Pearlman. She never spoke of her "old life." The Playwright would have liked to ask her: Were you wounded when your marriage collapsed? When your love collapsed? Or does love never "collapse," only just fade gradually away?

I honor marriage. The bond between a man and a woman. I believe it must be sacred. I would never violate such a bond.

Gazing at him with her lovelorn smiling eyes.

He was deeply touched by her, as by a lost child. An abandoned child. In that voluptuous body. Her body! When you came to know Norma Jeane (as

The Playwright would think of her, though rarely call her: it wasn't his privilege somehow) you saw how, to the woman, her body was an object of curiosity. It seemed at times her odd wish to bring the Playwright into collusion with her, into a shared understanding. Other men were sexually attracted to her, because her body was all they could see; he, the Playwright, a superior man, knew her differently and could never be so deceived.

Was she serious? The Playwright laughed at her, gently.

"You must know you're a lovely woman. And that isn't a debit."

"A what?"

"A debit. A shortcoming, a loss."

The Blond Actress nudged his arm. "Hey. You don't need to flatter *me*."

"I'm flattering you by suggesting that, in all frankness, you're a beautiful woman? And that it's no handicap?" The Playwright laughed, wanting to squeeze her arm, her wrist; wanting to make her flinch just a little, to acknowledge the simple truth of what he said. She could not wish him not to be a man! Even as, presenting herself to him as she did, childlike, yearning, wistful, seductive, she was so clearly arousing him to sexual desire.

Unless maybe he was imagining it. Her campaign to make him love her. To leave his wife, love her. Marry *her*.

Hadn't the Blond Actress said she lived for her work, and she lived for love. And she wasn't working at the present. And she wasn't in love at the present. (Lowering her eyes, her quivering eyelids. Oh, but she wanted to be in love!) With touching earnestness she told the Playwright, "The only meaning of life is s-something more than just you yourself? In your own head? In your own skeleton? In your own history? Like in your work, you leave something of yourself behind; and in love, you are elevated to a higher level of being, it isn't just *you*." She spoke so passionately, the Playwright half wondered if these weren't words she'd memorized. The naïveté, the idealism— was she echoing one of Chekhov's fiercely intelligent yet fatally deluded young women? Nina of *The Seagull*, or Irina of *The Three Sisters*? Or was she quoting from a source closer to home, dialogue the Playwright himself had written years ago? Yet there was no doubting her sincerity. They were together in a shadowy booth at the rear of a Sixth Avenue jazz club in the West Village and they were holding hands and the Playwright was a little drunk and the Blond Actress had had two glasses of red wine, she who rarely drank, and her eyes were brimming with tears for a crisis of some kind was approaching, now that the Playwright's wife was returning home next day. "And if you're a woman, and you love a man, you want to have that man's baby. A baby means . . . oh, you're a father, you know what a baby means! It isn't just *you*."

"No. But a baby isn't *you*, either."

The Blond Actress looked so confused, so oddly hurt, as if rebuked, the

Playwright slipped his arm around her shoulders and held her, for they were huddled on one side of the booth; no longer did they meet chastely with a tabletop between them. The Playwright wanted to hold the Blond Actress in his arms and she would lay her head against his chest, or bury her warm teary face in the crook of his neck and shoulder, and he would console her and protect her. He would protect her against her own delusions. For what is delusion but the prelude to hurt. And what is hurt but the prelude to rage. He knew, as a parent, that a child can enter your life and rend your life in two, not make it whole; he knew, as a man, that a child can intrude in a seemingly happy marriage, a child can alter if not irrevocably destroy the love between a man and a woman; he knew, as one who'd lived as a mature citizen for decades, that there is no romance in parenthood, or even in moth-erhood, only just a heightening of life. When you are a parent, you are yet still *you*—now with the new and terrifying burden of being a parent. He wanted to kiss the fluttering eyelids of this beautiful young woman so mag-ical to him, so mercurial, and say, Of course I love you. My Magda. My Norma Jeane. How could a man not love you? But I can't. . . .

I can't provide what you require. I am not the man you seek. I am a flawed man, I am an incomplete man, I am a man whom fatherhood has not appre-ciably altered, I am a man fearful of hurting, humiliating, angering his wife, I am not the savior of your dreams, I am no prince.

The Blond Actress protested. "My mother and me, when I was a baby, were like the same person. . . . And when I was a little girl. We wouldn't need to talk, even. She could send her thoughts to me, almost. I was never alone. That's the kind of love I mean, between a mother and a baby. It takes you out of yourself, it's *real*. I know I would be a good m-mother because—don't laugh at me, hey?—I see a baby being pushed in a carriage, it's all I can do to hold myself back from reaching in and kissing it! 'Oh, gosh!' I'm always saying. 'Oh, can I hold your baby? Oh, he's so beautiful!' I start to cry, I can't help it. You're laughing at me! It's the way I am, I always loved kids. When I was a kid myself, in foster homes, I'd be the one to take care of the babies. Just kind of sing to them and rock them, y'know? Till they fell asleep. There was this little girl, her mother didn't love her, I took care of her a lot, I pushed her stroller in the park—this was later when I was maybe sixteen— I sewed her a little stuffed tiger toy with material from a dime store, I loved her so. But it's a boy baby I hope I have, y'know why?"

The Playwright heard himself ask why.

"He'd be like his father, that's why. And his father, he'd be somebody I was crazy for, you can bet he'd be a wonderful man. I don't just fall for any-body, y'know?" The Blond Actress laughed breathlessly. "Most men, I don't even *like*. And you wouldn't either, honey, if you were a woman."

They were laughing together. The Playwright was sick with desire. He heard himself say, "You would make a wonderful mother, dear. A born mother."

Why, why was he saying this! An improvised scene, and the vehicle careening out of control, and nobody to grab the wheel.

Drunken driving!

Lightly yet sexily the Blond Actress kissed the Playwright on the lips. A wave of sick exhilarated desire in his groin, in the pit of his belly, suffused his body.

Hearing himself say, in a raw, tender voice, "Thank you. My darling."

18

The Adulterous Husband. He didn't want to exploit the Blond Actress. She was a child, so trusting. He wanted to caution her *Beware of us! Don't love me.*

By "us" he meant both himself and Max Pearlman. All of the New York theater community. The Blond Actress had journeyed here as to a shrine, to redeem herself in art.

To sacrifice herself for art.

The Playwright hoped she hadn't journeyed here to sacrifice herself for him.

His predicament was, he hadn't ceased loving his wife. He wasn't a man to take marriage casually, like so many men of his acquaintance. Even men of his generation, from Jewish-liberal-family-oriented backgrounds like his own. He hated the careless, jaunty amours of the satyr Pearlman; he hated it that Pearlman was so readily forgiven, by women he'd treated shabbily, and by his own attractive but now middle-aged wife.

Not once had the Playwright been unfaithful to Esther.

Even after his rapid ascendancy to a modest sort of fame, in 1948. When, to his shock, chagrin, embarrassment, he'd experienced a quickening of female interest in him: intellectual women, Manhattan socialites, divorcées, even the wives of certain of his theater friends. At universities at which he was invited to speak, at regional theaters where his plays were being performed, invariably there were these women, bright, animated, attractive, cultured, Jewish and non-Jewish, academic women, literary women, the wives of well-to-do businessmen, many of them middle-aged, moist-eyed over male genius. Perhaps he'd been drawn to some of these women out of boredom and loneliness and the usual frustration with his work, but never had he been unfaithful to Esther; there was this grim dutiful accountant's side to him, committed to facts. He hadn't been unfaithful to Esther, surely that should mean something to her?

My precious fidelity. What hypocrisy!

He hadn't ceased loving Esther and he believed, despite her anger and resentment, she hadn't ceased to love him. But they felt no quickening of desire for each other. Oh, no quickening even of interest! Not for years. The Playwright lived so much inside his head, other people were often unreal to him. The more intimate, the less real. A wife, children. Now grown children. Grown-distant children. And a wife at whom—literally!—he sometimes failed to look even when speaking with her. ("Miss me?" "Of course." "Yes, I can see.") The Playwright's life was words, painstakingly chosen words, and when not words typed out singly with two quick-darting forefingers on an Olivetti portable, his life was meetings with producers and directors and actors, auditions and play readings and workshops and rehearsals (culminating in dress rehearsal and "tech") and previews and opening nights, good reviews, not-so-good reviews, good box office, not-so-good box office, prizes and disappointments, a fever chart of continuous crises not unlike the careening course of a downhill skier through an unknown terrain, rocks amid the snow, and either you're born to this crazed life and are thrilled by it, however much exhausted by it, or you are not born to such a life, and exhaustion is most of what you feel, and finally you wish to feel nothing. The Playwright had not wanted to marry an actress or a writer or a woman of artistic ambition, so he'd married a handsome energetic good-natured young woman from a background similar to his own with a degree from Columbia Teachers College. Esther had taught junior high math briefly when they were first married, capably but without enthusiasm; she'd been eager to marry and to have children. All this in the early thirties, a lifetime ago. Now the Playwright was a distinguished man and Esther was one of those spouses of distinguished men of whom neutral observers remark *Why? What did he ever see in her?* At social gatherings, the Playwright and his wife would not have naturally gravitated toward each other, would not have naturally fallen into conversation, would perhaps have merely glanced at each other, smiled, and moved on. No one of their mutual friends would have introduced them to each other.

It wasn't a tragedy! Only just, the Playwright believed, ordinary life. Not life dramatized on the stage.

The Playwright didn't care to think how long it had been since he and Esther had made love or even kissed, with feeling. Where Eros has departed, a kiss is the oddest gesture: numbed lips touching, pressing: *why?* The Playwright knew, if he embraced Esther, she would stiffen in irony and say, "Why? Why now?"

Hardly could her husband say *Because I am falling in love with another woman. Help me!*

Still, he believed their love hadn't ceased but had only faded. Like the dust jacket of the Playwright's first book, a slender book of poems published when he'd been twenty-four years old, to reviews of praise and encouragement and sales of 640 copies. In his memory, the dust jacket of *The Liberation* was a beautiful cobalt blue and the lettering canary yellow, but in fact, as he had occasion to notice now and then, always to his surprise, the front cover had been bleached by the sun almost white, and the once-yellow letters were nearly unreadable.

There was the book jacket in memory, and there was the book jacket a few feet from the Playwright's desk. You could argue that both were real. Only just that they existed in separate times.

Hesitantly the Playwright said to the woman with whom he lived in the handsome old brownstone on West 72nd Street amid overflowing bookshelves, "We never talk much any longer, dear. I was hoping, now that—"

"When did we ever talk much? You talked."

This was unfair. In fact, it was inaccurate. But the Playwright let it pass in silence.

Saying, another day, "How was St. Petersburg?"

Esther stared at him as if he'd spoken in code.

On the stage, language is code. The text's true meaning lies beneath the text. And in life?

The Playwright, sick with guilt, called the Blond Actress to break off their meeting that afternoon. It was to have been his first visit to her sublet flat in the Village.

Recalling those lurid soft-porn scenes in *Niagara*. The astonishing spread legs of the blond woman, the V of her crotch almost visible through the sheet drawn up to her breasts. How had the filmmakers gotten such scenes past the censor? Past the Legion of Decency? The Playwright had seen *Niagara* alone, in a Times Square movie house. Just to satisfy his curiosity.

He hadn't seen *Gentlemen Prefer Blondes* or *The Seven-Year Itch*. He wouldn't have cared to see Marilyn Monroe in comic roles. Not after *Niagara*.

Carefully he explained to the Blond Actress that he couldn't see her for a while. Maybe in a week or two. Please understand.

In her husky-cheerful Magda voice the Blond Actress said yes, she understood.

19

The Ghost Sonata. The Playwright and his wife Esther attended the opening of a production of Strindberg's *The Ghost Sonata* at the Circle in the

Square on Bleecker Street. Many in the audience were friends, acquaintances, theater associates of the Playwright's; the director of the production was an old friend. The theater held only about two hundred seats. Shortly before the lights dimmed there were excited murmurs among the audience and the Playwright turned to see the Blond Actress coming down the center aisle. At first he believed she was alone, for always the woman seemed to him alone, in his memory alone, so strangely, luminously alone, with her vague sweet wistful smile, her quivering eyelids, her air of having wandered in by chance. Then he saw that she was with Max Pearlman and his wife and their friend Marlon Brando; Brando was the Blond Actress's escort, talking and laughing with her as they took their seats in the second row. What a vision: Marilyn Monroe and Marlon Brando. Both were dressed informally, Brando with a stubbled chin, shaggy hair past his ears, a worn leather jacket, and khaki trousers; the Blond Actress wrapped in her dark wool coat purchased at an Army-Navy surplus store on Broadway. She was bareheaded; her platinum hair, darkening at the roots, glowed.

The Playwright, six feet two, shrank in his seat hoping not to be seen. His wife nudged him and said, "Is that Marilyn Monroe? Are you going to introduce me?"

THE EMISSARY

The Gemini have said they miss their Norma, and the baby.

In the claw-footed tub with gleaming brass fixtures, the Dark Prince, naked. In the steaming bathwater she'd lavishly sprinkled with fragrant salts, as you would prepare the bath of a god. To welcome the Dark Prince. To honor the Dark Prince. *I love a man* she'd confessed suddenly to him. *I am so deeply in love with a man for the first time in my life, I want to die sometimes! No, I want to live.* Chastely the Dark Prince kissed her on the brow. Not as a lover. For the Dark Prince could not love her. Had loved too many women and had sickened of the love of women, of even the touch of women. She believed that the Dark Prince gave her his blessing in this way. *Just to live* she said *and to know he's living, too. That we might love each other someday as man and wife.* The Dark Prince had grown contemptuous of Caucasian females, yet her he called *Angel.* From the first he'd called her *Angel.* By none of her names did he call her except *Angel.* Telling her now, sly-slurred words and his beautiful cruel eyes brought close to hers *Angel, don't tell me you believe in love? Like in an afterlife?* And quickly she said, confused *Oh d'you know that Jews don't believe in an afterlife like Christians do? I just learned that today.* The Dark Prince said *Your lover's a Jew, eh?*

and quickly she said *We are not lovers. We love each other from a distance.* The Dark Prince laughed, saying *Keep that distance, Angel. And you'll keep your love.* She said *I want to be a great actress, for him. To make him proud of me.* The Dark Prince was swaying on his feet. Tugging at his shirt, which he'd sweated through. Already he'd removed his ratty leather jacket and dropped it onto the carpeted floor of her sublet flat on East 11th Street. The Dark Prince may not have known his precise whereabouts. He was one of those whom others tend to, as handmaids and lackeys. The Dark Prince was fumbling at his belt and at his fly, which was partly unzipped. *I need to take a bath* the Dark Prince declared. *I need to cleanse myself.* It was an abrupt and unexpected demand but she was prepared for the abrupt and unexpected demands of men.

Helping this man into the bathroom at the rear of the flat and turning on the gleaming brass faucets and gaily sprinkling bath salts into the tub and into the gushing steaming water to welcome him, to honor him. The Dark Prince was an emissary from her past and she was terrified of the message he might be bringing her for they'd first met years ago when she'd been Norma living with the Gemini before she'd made *Niagara* and become "Marilyn Monroe" and of that era she did not wish to think, and perhaps could not think clearly, chattering to the Dark Prince as women do to make a kind of movie music to dispel the terror of silence. When she turned, she saw to her shock that the Dark Prince had stripped himself clumsily bare. Except for his socks. He was panting from just this exertion. He'd been drinking for hours and he'd smoked a thin parchment cigarette with a virulent-sweet smoke, offering it to her (who declined), and now he was panting and flush-faced and his eyes clouded. His trousers, soiled shorts, and sweaty shirt in a tangle at his feet, kicked aside.

She smiled, frightened. She had not expected this. The Dark Prince's body was so—profound! It was a body only partially and teasingly exposed in the eight remarkable movies that had made the Dark Prince the most revered film actor of the era: a beautifully sculpted male body with distinct chest muscles, perfectly shaped male breasts and nipples like miniature grapes, a peltlike covering of dark hairs in a swirl at his chest and thickening at his groin. The Dark Prince was thirty-two years old and at the height of his male beauty: within a few quick years his skin would lose its arrogant glisten, his body would grow flaccid; within a decade he would be visibly overweight, potbelly and jowls; within two decades he would be frankly fat. In time, the Dark Prince would become obese as a balloon mannequin blown up by a bicycle pump in willful mockery of this young self. Staring at him she thought *If only I could love him! If he might love me. We are free to love and to save each other.* The Dark Prince's penis dangled swollen and sullen amid the frieze of groin hair, semierect, stirring; at its tip there gleamed a solitary pearl drop of moisture. She stumbled backward, colliding with a towel rack. The faucets gushed water, the fragrant water steamed. Still she was smiling, panicked. For there was a script for this scene. *He will want me to kiss that off. That is what they demand. He will take me by the nape of my neck.* For where was Mother? In another room. In bed. Asleep, and moaning in sleep. Just Norma Jeane and a swaying-drunk naked man, a man with an erect bobbing penis, kindly crinkled eyes, and a kissable mouth as Gladys wryly acknowledged *As long as he gets his way, oh sure he's a prince.*

Instead, the Dark Prince pushed past Norma Jeane to the tub, lowering his bare buttocks hard against the porcelain rim. Amid the fragrant rising steam helpless and peevish as a young child *Angel c'n you help me, these fuckin'*—

It was his socks he meant, he couldn't bend to remove them by himself.

(Such sorry episodes the Sharpshooter would record. The Sharpshooter would indicate no moral judgments in his meticulous reports for that was not the Sharpshooter's task. In the service of the Agency. In such matters of suspected subversive activities, threats to the national security of the United States. *For where there is an innocent citizenry there will be nothing to hide. There will be no guilt. All citizens will be informers and no professional Sharpshooters required.*)

She was his Magda, his! She would telephone her lover. She would weep over the phone *I love you, please come to me now! Tonight.* The Jews are an ancient people, a nomadic people blessed and accursed by God. Their history is yet a history of god-men: Adam, Noah, Abraham the father god of all. A lineage of men. Men who understood the weakness of women and could forgive them. *I forgive you! For being a coward. For not daring to love me as I love you.*

Oh, yes, she'd seen the Playwright in the theater on Bleecker Street. Certainly she'd seen him. She'd known he would be there, in fact. For a woman new to this city she knew many things; she had many new friends to tell her things; how many strangers yearned to be her friend, men and women of good reputation eager to walk beside "Marilyn Monroe" in public and be photographed with her.

Yes, I saw you. Saw you look away and deny your Magda.

In the musty-smelling little theater on Bleecker Street stiff and cringing beside his wife. That woman, his wife!

I'm Miss Golden Dreams. I'm the one a man deserves.

Never would she telephone her lover! Not the Playwright she admired above all men. He was her Abraham: he would lead her into the Promised Land.

She'd been baptized a Christian and would unbaptize herself and become a Jew. *In my soul I am Jewish. A wanderer seeking my true homeland.* He would see how serious she was, how dedicated to her profession. For acting is both a craft and an art and she meant to master both. She was an intelligent young woman, a woman of pride and honor and shrewd common sense. A man like the Playwright could not love her otherwise. A man like the Playwright would flee from her otherwise. See how level-headed, his Magda: so far from bitterness and female hysteria, she changed into a quilted dressing gown and as the Dark Prince bathed at the rear of her sublet flat in the claw-footed antique porcelain tub with the gleaming brass fixtures she curled up on a sofa to copy into her journal verses from *The Song of Solomon*. At the Strand Bookshop she'd bought a copy of The Hebrew Bible and was astonished yet relieved to discover that it was the Old Testament merely under another name.

Let him kiss me with the kisses of his mouth: for thy love is better than wine.

Behold, thou art fair, my love; behold, thou art fair; thou hast doves' eyes.

The voice of my beloved! behold, he cometh leaping upon the mountains, skipping upon the hills.

For lo, the winter is past, the rain is over and gone;
The flowers appear on the earth; the time of the singing of birds.

I sleep, but my heart waketh: it is the voice of my beloved that knocketh, saying, Open to me, my sister, my love, my dove, my undefiled.

I opened to my beloved: but my beloved had withdrawn himself, and was gone: my soul failed when he spake: I sought him, but I could not find him; I called him, but he gave me no answer.

She must have slept. Her head so heavy! All that lay before her, the effort of the remainder of a life.

Yes, she would return to Hollywood; she would contract for another film. How could she avoid it, she had no money; for the Playwright's divorce, and for their life together, she would need money; and money was available for Marilyn Monroe if not for her. As Marilyn then she would return to the City of Sand. *This I knew beforehand. Without knowing that I knew.*

Yet she would return knowing far more about acting than she'd known in the past. For months studying with Max Pearlman, her exacting tutor. For months humbled and eager as a bright child being taught the rudiments of reading and writing and speaking.

You have the promise of a great actress he'd said.

If it was not true, she would make it true!

The Dark Prince was the greatest American actor of his time, as Laurence Olivier was the greatest British actor of his time. To the Dark Prince, his genius seemed to mean very little; his success had aroused him to contempt, not gratitude. *I will not be that way. Where I am blessed, I will bless.*

She must have slept for now she woke suddenly. A sensation of sick dread swept over her. It was 3:40 A.M. Something was wrong. The Dark Prince! He'd been in her bathroom for hours.

In the claw-footed tub in tepid bathwater there he lay, the back of his lolling head against the porcelain rim, the Dark Prince with slack mouth, spittle on his chin, eyes half shut and showing only a clouded crescent of gray, like mucus. His hair was damp and his head sleek as a seal's. The body that had seemed so beautifully sculpted to her only a few hours ago was now strangely bent, the shoulders rounded and chest collapsed, a ridge of fat at the waist, his penis shrunken to a stub of flesh lifting wanly upward in the scummy water. Oh, he'd vomited in the water! Skeins and puddles of vomit surrounding him. *Yet he was breathing, he was alive. That was all that mattered to me.* She managed to wake him. He shook off her hands and cursed her. He heaved himself to his feet, slopping water onto the tile floor, and cursed again, losing his balance and almost falling in the slippery porcelain tub so that she had to catch him to keep him from cracking his skull, and held him in her arms, which trembled with strain; for the Dark Prince was a heavy man, not tall but compact and muscled. She pleaded with him, she begged him to be careful, he called her *cunt!* (but without knowing her, he could not mean insult to her) but gripped her hard, and after some minutes she managed to maneuver him out of the tub, sitting again on the rim swaying and mumbling and his eyes shut, and she soaked a washcloth in cold water and gently wiped his face and did what she could to wipe patches of vomit from his body, still she was concerned that he begin to vomit again, he might collapse and die for his breath came erratically, his mouth slack and fallen, and he seemed not to know where he was, yet after several applications of the washcloth he revived to a degree and got to his feet, and she wrapped him in a bath towel and led him into the bedroom, her arm around his waist, his pale hairy legs and bare feet dripping water, she was laughing gently to assure him it was all right, he was safe with her, she would take care of him; stumbling then and cursing her again *cunt! stupid cunt!* he fell sideways onto the bed with such violence that the springs creaked loudly and she was in terror he'd broken this bed which did not belong to her, the handsome antique brass bed of a well-to-do woman friend of Max Pearlman residing in Paris. Next she lifted his feet, his feet that were heavy as concrete bricks, and positioned his damp head on a pillow, all the while murmuring to him, comforting him as she'd done with the Ex-Athlete sometimes and with other citizens of the City of Sand; she was feeling better now, more optimistic now, Norma Jeane Baker was by nature an optimistic girl, hadn't she sworn herself to eternal optimism crouched on the roof of the Home staring at the lighted RKO tower miles away in Hollywood, *I pledge! I vow! I will! I will never give in!* and now it dawned on her that their ugly ignominious scene was in fact a movie scene; its contours if not its details were familiar, and in a way romantic; she was Claudette Colbert, and he was Clark Gable; no, she was Carole Lombard and he was Clark Gable; there was a script for this situation, and if neither of them knew it they were gifted actors and might improvise.

The Dark Prince in my bed. Oh, he was a close friend, he told me to call him Carlo. But were we lovers? I don't think so. Were we?

Immediately he began to snore. She drew bedclothes up over him and cuddled quietly beside him. The remainder of this nightmare night passed in swift jumps and cuts. She was exhausted from the hope and strain of her New York life; her life that was to redeem her. Five-hour workshops several days a week at the Ensemble, and hours of intense private tutoring with Max Pearlman or with one of his aggressive young associates; her love for the Playwright and her anxiety that he should escape her, and then she must die; such failure as a woman would condemn her to death for hadn't Grandma Della spoken in scorn of her own daughter Gladys, who'd lacked the ability to keep a husband, even a sugar daddy to support her? Della wheezing and laughing *What good is it being a fallen woman and a slut if at the age of thirty you're empty-handed?* And Norma Jeane would be thirty in a few months.

She settled her head cautiously on the Dark Prince's shoulder. He didn't shove her away. He slept fitfully but deeply, as men do. Ground his teeth, jerked and kicked and sweated, until by dawn he'd dampened the bedclothes and smelled as if he hadn't bathed at all, a smell that made Norma Jeane smile thinking of Bucky Glazer, his swampy armpits and dirt-webbed feet. This time, with her new husband, she would make none of the mistakes she'd made in the past. She would make the Playwright proud of her as an actress and she would make him love her all the more as his wife. They would have babies together. Almost, she could imagine herself pregnant already. *In the peacefulness of that night, toward dawn, Baby again came near, and forgave me.*

Otto Öse had cruelly predicted for her a junkie's death in Hollywood but that was not to be her fate.

. . .

Midmorning, she woke and dressed as quietly as possible while the Dark Prince continued to sleep, and went out to a grocer's on Fifth Avenue to buy fresh eggs, cereal, fruit, and Java coffee beans, and when she returned the Dark Prince was waking, wincing as light struck his bloodshot eyes but otherwise in reasonably good condition, surprising her with his humor, his wit; he told her the stink of his body repelled him and he needed to shower, and lurching into the bathroom another time he laughed at her concern, and she stood at the door listening in dread of another catastrophe but heard nothing more jarring than the *thud!* of the bar of soap which clumsily the Dark Prince dropped several times. Afterward, toweling his hair dry, the Dark Prince poked through her closet and bureau drawers looking for men's clothes, a change of underwear and socks at least. But found nothing. And in the kitchen accepting from her only a glass of ice water, which he drank cautiously as a man walking a tightrope with no net beneath. Norma Jeane was disappointed he wanted nothing to eat. He wasn't giving her a chance! Bucky Glazer and the Ex-Athlete had both been excellent breakfast eaters. She herself was drinking only black coffee to liven her nerves. How handsome the Dark Prince was, even with his bloodshot eyes and wincing headache and what he called "intestinal flu." In his soiled clothes of the previous day, unshaven, and his damp hair carelessly combed. He was calling her *Angel* and thanking her. She stroked his hand, smiling sadly as he spoke with unconvincing eagerness, like a character in an Odets play, of their one day doing a play together under Pearlman's auspices, or possibly a movie together if they could get the right script (for he, too, despising Hollywood, yet needed Hollywood money); she was thinking how ironic, neither would recall with any degree of clarity what had happened the previous night except to know that some measure of tenderness had passed between them. Maybe she'd saved his life, or he'd saved hers? And so they were bound together, if only as sister and brother, for life.

After I died, Brando would give no interviews about me. He alone of the Hollywood jackals.

It was as the Dark Prince prepared to leave her that he recalled the message he'd been instructed to bring.

"Angel, listen: I ran into Cass Chaplin recently?"

Norma Jeane smiled faintly. She said nothing. She was trembling and hoped her friend wouldn't notice.

"I hadn't seen him or Eddy G for maybe a year. You hear things about them, y'know? Then I ran into Cass at somebody's house and he told me, next time I saw you, he had a message for you."

Still Norma Jeane said nothing. She might have reasonably said, *If Cass has a message for me, why doesn't he deliver it himself?*

"He said to me, 'Tell Norma, *The Gemini miss their Norma, and the baby.*' "

The Dark Prince saw the look on her face and said, "Maybe I shouldn't have relayed that message? That fucker."

Norma Jeane said goodbye and walked hurriedly into another room.

She heard her companion of the previous night call after her, hesitantly. "Hey, Angel?" But he didn't follow her. He knew, as she knew, that the scene was over; their night together was done.

Brando and I never did a film together. He was too powerful an actor for Monroe. She'd have been broken by him, like a cheap doll.

Yet the scene with the Dark Prince wasn't entirely over.

Late that afternoon she would return from an acting workshop to discover what seemed to her, in the first startled, stunned moment of stepping into her living room, a sepulchre of flowers. There were several floral displays, of predominantly white flowers: lilies, roses, carnations, gardenias.

So beautiful! But so many.

The gardenia smell was nearly overwhelming. Her eyes stung with tears. She felt a swirl of nausea.

Wanting to think the flowers were from the Playwright, her lover begging her to forgive her. But she knew they were not.

They were from the Dark Prince of course. Her lover who could not love her.

He'd carefully printed in red ink on a heart-shaped card the message

ANGEL
I HOPE IF ONLY ONE OF US MAKES IT
ITS YOU

YOUR FRIEND CARLO

"Dancing in the Dark"

A middle-aged tattered coat upon a stick. God, he'd come to despise himself!

Yet: clenching his gloved fists staring across the expanse of fresh-fallen powdery snow. There, as in a musical comedy in which sound, color, movement are highlighted, was the Blond Actress ice-skating with a young actor from the New York Ensemble. In fact, it was the actor who'd played his Isaac. His Isaac, ice-skating with his Magda. Almost, it was more than a playwright could bear.

If the two kissed? As he watched?

The rumor was of her and Marlon Brando too. Of that, he could not allow himself to think.

She'd had so many men. So many men had had her.

It had been relayed to the Playwright by mutual friends that the Blond Actress would soon be leaving New York for Los Angeles; strengthened by months of intensive work at the Ensemble, she would be resuming her career as a film actress. But not on the old terms. The Studio had not only forgiven Marilyn Monroe but had capitulated to a number of her demands. It was to be Hollywood history. Marilyn Monroe, so long despised in the industry, had beaten The Studio! Now she would have project approval, script approval, director approval. Her salary was raised to $100,000 per movie. *Why? Because there was no blonde they'd been able to invent to take her place. Who'd made so many millions of dollars for them, so cheaply.*

He wasn't jealous of the Blond Actress, he wished her well. That deep sadness in her eyes. As in the eyes of his Magda of thirty years ago that he, blinded by adolescent infatuation, hadn't understood.

On the ice rink in Central Park amid dozens of colorfully attired skaters of all ages the Blond Actress in dark glasses, a white angora cap pulled down snug around her ears to hide every strand of hair and a matching muffler around her neck, was skating! She who claimed never to have skated on ice before, only just roller-skated as a girl in southern California.

Where she came from, the Blond Actress said with a wink, there was no ice. Ever.

You could see her tentativeness on skates. As other, more experienced skaters breezed past. Her ankles were weak; she was always about to lose her balance. Pumping her arms, laughing and teetering and about to fall except her companion deftly caught her, an arm around her waist. Once or twice, despite his gallantry, she sat down hard on the ice but only laughed and with his help scrambled up again. She dusted off her bottom and continued. Skaters glided around her, past her; if anyone glanced at her, it was only to see a pretty creamy-skinned girl in very dark glasses, wearing a minimum of makeup. Or no makeup at all. She wore her heather-colored cable-knit sweater and dark slacks of some warm plush material the Playwright hadn't seen before, and white leather ankle-high rental skates. If new to ice-skating, the girl was obviously a natural athlete, possibly a dancer. That suppleness in her body. That energy! One moment she was clowning to disguise her awkwardness, the next moment she'd become graceful, skating hand in hand with her companion. The young man was a skilled skater, with long elastic legs and a sure sense of balance; he wore wire-rimmed glasses that gave him, like the Playwright at his age, a boyish-scholarly-Jewish look, darkly attractive. Except for earmuffs, his head was bare.

It was mid-March, and still very cold in New York City. A northeast wind out of the blinding-blue sky.

Heartsick, lovesick, the Playwright watched. He'd been unable to stay away. Unable to remain in his study, at his desk. Sick with yearning. (Yet had he the right to involve the Blond Actress in his life? He was again being investigated by the House Un-American Activities Committee; it was not an investigation so much as a persecution, a harassment; he had to hire a lawyer, and he had to pay legal fees that were tantamount to fines; the new chairman of the committee had taken a special dislike to the Playwright since he'd seen a play of his allegedly "critical of American society and capitalism." It was known that the Playwright's F.B.I. files were "incriminating." The Playwright was one of a "cadre of New York-born left-leaning intellectuals.")

The Blond Actress skated, and the Playwright watched. To his credit (he was thinking) he made no effort to hide. He was not a man to hide. And what purpose in hiding? Seventy-second Street was close by the Park and he often walked here; frequently, needing to clear his head, he tramped through the snow on days when most of Central Park was deserted. Watching the skaters made him smile. He'd loved to skate as a boy. And he'd been surprisingly good. As a young father living in the city he'd taught his children to skate on this very rink, years ago. Suddenly it didn't seem so long ago.

The Blond Actress on the glittering ice, laughing and shining in the sun.

The Blond Actress who loved him in a way that no woman had ever loved him. Whom he loved as he'd loved no other woman.

Monroe! A nympho.

Who says? I heard she does it for money. She's desperate.

She's frigid, hates men. She's a lezzie. But yes, she does it for money when she can get her price.

The Playwright stared smiling at his Magda on the ice, and his Isaac gripping her hand. His heart pounded with a kind of pride.

He wondered that the other skaters and the numerous spectators didn't recognize her. Stare and point and applaud.

He had the impulse to lift his hands and applaud.

Had she noticed him yet? Had Isaac noticed him? The Playwright stood in full view, a familiar figure to them both. The Playwright who had created them. His Magda, his Isaac. She was a girl of the people; he was a boy of European Jewry eager to become "of the people," eager to become American, eager to erase all dreams of Back There.

Maybe in fact the Playwright was a Holocaust survivor. Maybe all living Jews were. It was not a fact of which the Playwright wished to think there in the bright blazing sunshine of a late-winter afternoon in Central Park.

There he stood tall as a totem figure at the edge of the flagstone terrace past which skaters glided in long looping circles around and around the rink. A music box of animated figures! The Playwright whom strangers frequently recognized in Manhattan. In his dark trench coat, dark wool Astrakhan hat. Thick-lensed glasses. As the Blond Actress and her companion skated past, hand in hand, talking and laughing, the Playwright refused to turn aside or even to lower his eyes. On this terrace in warm weather there was a popular outdoor café to which the Playwright frequently came, midafternoons, for a break from his work. In winter the wrought-iron tables and chairs remained. He would have dragged a chair to the edge of the terrace and sat but he was too restless. That music! "The Skater's Waltz."

He would marry her after all, if she would have him. He could not let her go.

He would divorce his wife. Already in his heart they were divorced. Never would he touch her again, never kiss her again. The thought of that woman's aging raddled flesh repelled him. Her angry eyes, her hurt mouth. His manhood had died with her but would be resurrected now.

He would rend his life in two for the Blond Actress.

I would rewrite the story of both our lives. Not tragic but American epic! I believed I had the strength.

There he was, renting skates! Nothing to it. Shoving his feet into the shoes, lacing them tightly up. And on the ice, his ankles weak at first, stiffness in his knees at first, but quickly his old skills returned; he felt a boy's thrill of simple physical exertion. He was skating boldly counterclockwise against the gliding skaters. He looked like a man who knew what he was doing, not a muddled older man flailing his arms to keep his balance. The amplified music was now "Dancing in the Dark." A song written by a Jew yet how American-assimilated it seemed, like all the great tunes of Tin Pan Alley. A song of romance and mystery if you listened closely to the lyrics.

Skating toward the Blond Actress he smiled happily. He had no doubt! This was a scene of a kind the Playwright himself could not have written for it lacked irony, subtlety. She'd drawn him out of his snug airless study on 72nd Street. She'd drawn him to her; he had no choice. Smiling like a man wakened by sunshine, who'd fallen asleep in the dark.

"Oh, gosh! Oh, *look*."

The Blond Actress saw him now and was skating toward him, radiant with happiness. Not since he'd been a young father and his children had greeted him with such expressions of rapture, as if they'd never seen anyone so wonderful, nor so unexpected, had he felt this privileged and this happy. The Blond Actress would have collided with him except he caught her and held her up. They swayed together on the glittering ice. They were drunken lovers together. Gripping each other's hands, laughing in delight. The young actor who'd played Isaac hung back discreetly, rueful but smiling, too, for he knew himself privileged to see this meeting as he would be privileged to portray it to others, to tell and retell the historic occasion of the Playwright and the Blond Actress so publicly in love on the ice-skating rink in Central Park that day in March.

"Oh! I love you."

"Darling, I love *you*."

Reckless and daring in her skates the Blond Actress stood on tiptoe to kiss the Playwright full on the mouth.

And that night in the sublet flat on East 11th Street, the Blond Actress, naked, after lovemaking trembling with emotion, and her cheeks shining with tears, took both the Playwright's hands in hers, caressed his fingers and lifted them to her lips, and covered them with kisses. "Your beautiful hands," she whispered. "Your beautiful, beautiful hands."

He was deeply moved. He was stricken to the heart.

They would be married in June, soon after his divorce from his wife, and after the Blond Actress's thirtieth birthday.

THE MYSTERY.
THE OBSCENITY.

The intersection between private pathology and the insatiable appetite of a capitalist-consumer culture. How can we understand this mystery? This obscenity.

So the grieving Playwright would one day write.

But not for a decade.

CHERIE 1956

I love Cherie! Cherie is so brave.

Cherie never drinks out of fear. Never swallows pills. For if Cherie begins, she knows how it will end. Where it will end.

The place Cherie came from she's terrified she will return. I shut my eyes and saw a sandy bank, a shallow muddy creek and a single tall spindly tree with exposed, ropy roots like veins. The family was living in a battered trailer in a mound of rusted cans and vines. Cherie with her younger brothers and sisters. Cherie was the "little mother." Singing to them, playing games with them. She'd had to drop out of school aged fifteen to help at home. Maybe she'd had a boyfriend, an older guy in his twenties. He broke her heart but not her pride. Not her spirit. Cherie sews toys for her brothers and sisters and mends the family's clothes. Her *chanteuse* costumes will break your heart, so much clumsy darning. Even the black-net stockings are darned! Cherie wasn't platinum blond, her hair was dishwater blond. She had a healthy color then, spending so much time outdoors, now she's sickly pale. Pale as the moon. Maybe anemic? This cowboy Bo takes one look at her and knows she's his Angel. His Angel! Might've always been anemic, and her younger brothers and sisters too. Vitamin deficiency. One of her brothers was retarded. One of her sisters was born with a cleft palate and there wasn't money to correct it. As a girl Cherie listened to the radio a lot. Sang with the radio. Country-and-western songs mostly. Sometimes she'd cry, her own singing broke her heart. I saw her lifting a baby with a soaked diaper to carry into the trailer to change. Her mother watched TV a lot when the set worked. Her mother was a heavy, sallow-skinned woman in her forties, a drinker with a puckered collapsed face like raw dough. Cherie's father was gone. Nobody knew where. Cherie was hitchhiking to Memphis. There was a radio station she listened to, she hoped to meet one of the disc jockeys. She had a two-hundred-mile journey. Thought she'd save bus money and got a ride with a long-distance trucker. You're a pretty girl, he told her. About the prettiest girl ever climbed into this cab. Cherie pretended to be deaf and dumb, retarded. Gripping her Bible.

He looked at her so funny, she was scared and started singing Bible songs. That sobered him up, fast.

How Cherie ended up age thirty in a tavern in Arizona singing "Old Black Magic" off-key to drunken cowboys who don't listen to her, who knows!

Pursued by a cowboy crazy for her. His *Angel.* Always yelling, clumsy as a young bull. She's terrified of him but will love him, marry him.

Have his babies she'll sing to, and play games with. And sew little toys and clothes for.

Daddy, I miss you! It's so far away here.

Darling, I'll be flying out to see you next week. I thought you liked it there? The mountains—

The mountains scare me.

I thought you said they were beautiful.

Something has happened, Daddy.

Darling, what? What has happened?

I . . . don't know.

Do you mean on the set? The director, other actors?

No.

Darling, you're frightening me. Are you—unwell?

I don't know. I don't remember . . . what "well" is.

Darling Norma, dearest girl, tell me what's wrong.

Darling, are you crying? What is it?

I . . . don't have the words, Daddy. I wish you were here.

Is somebody being cruel to you? What is it?

I wish we were married. I wish you were here.

I'll be there soon, darling. Can't you tell me what's wrong?
  I think . . . I'm afraid.
  Afraid of . . . ?

Darling, this is terribly upsetting. I love you so. I wish I could help you.
  You do help, Daddy. Just by being there.
  You're not . . . taking too many pills, are you?
  No.
  Because it's better to be a little insomniac, than—
  I know! You told me, Daddy.
  You're sure no one has hurt you? Offended you?
  I guess I'm just . . . afraid. My heart beats so hard sometimes.
  You're excited, darling. That's why you're an excellent actress. You immerse yourself in your role.
  I wish we were married now! I wish you could hold me.
  Darling, you're breaking my heart. What can I do for you?

What are you afraid of, dear one? Is it anything in particular?
  You won't ever write about me, will you?
  Darling, of course not. Why would I do such a thing?
  It's what people do. Sometimes. Writers.
  I'm not other people. You and I are not other people.
  I know we're not, Daddy. But sometimes I'm just so afraid. I don't want to sleep. . . .
  You're not drinking, are you?
  No.
  Because you can't tolerate alcohol, darling. You're too sensitive. Your metabolism, your nerves—
  I don't drink. Only champagne, to celebrate.
  We'll be celebrating soon, darling. There'll be so much to celebrate.
  I wish we were married now. I don't think I'd be afraid then.
  But what are you afraid of, darling? Try to tell me.

I can't hear you, darling. Please.
  I think . . . I'm afraid of Cherie.

Cherie? What?

I'm afraid of her.

Darling, I thought you loved that role.

I do! I love Cherie. Cherie is . . . myself.

Darling, Cherie may be a part of you, but only a part. You're so much more than Cherie ever could be!

Am I? I don't think so.

Don't be ridiculous. Cherie is a comic-pathetic woman. Cherie is a sweet naive Ozark girl with no talent. She's a singer who can't sing, a dancer who can't dance.

She's so much braver than I am, Daddy. She doesn't despair.

Darling, what are you saying? You don't despair! You're one of the happiest people I know.

I am, Daddy?

Certainly you are.

I make you laugh a lot, don't I? And other people.

You certainly do. One day the world will recognize you as a marvelous comedienne.

They will?

They certainly will.

You liked me as Magda, didn't you? I made you laugh, and maybe I made you cry? I didn't ruin that role.

Darling, you were excellent as Magda. You were a far richer Magda than I'd created. And Cherie will be an even more brilliant performance.

Sometimes I don't know what people mean: "Performance."

You're an accomplished actress, you "perform." As a dancer dances on stage, and walks off. As a pianist performs, a public speaker. Always, you're greater than your roles.

People laugh at Cherie. They don't understand.

They laugh because you're funny. You make Cherie funny. The laughter isn't cruel, it's sympathetic. They see themselves in you.

Laughter isn't cruel? Maybe it is.

Not when the performer controls it. You're the performer, and you're in control.

But Cherie doesn't know she's funny. She thinks she will be a star.

That's why she's funny. She's so . . . unconscious.

It's all right to laugh at Cherie because she's "unconscious?"

Darling, what are we arguing about? Why are you so excited? Of course Cherie's funny, and touching too. Bus Stop is a very funny play, and it's touching, too. But it's a comedy, and not a tragedy.

The ending. . . .

Well, it's a happy ending, isn't it? They get married.

There's nobody else for Cherie. Nobody else to love her.

Darling, Cherie is a character in a play! A play by William Inge!

No.

What d'you mean, no?

Cherie, Magda . . . the others. They aren't just roles.

Of course they are.

They're in me. I'm them. They're actual people in the world, too.

I don't understand you, darling. I know you don't believe such a thing yourself.

If they weren't actual somewhere, you couldn't write about them. And nobody would recognize them. Even if they look different.

Dearest, all right. I think I know what you mean. You have a poet's sensibility.

What's that mean, I'm a dumb blonde? A dumb broad?

Darling, please!

A stupid cunt, I've been called.

Darling—

I love Cherie! I don't love "Marilyn."

Darling, we've discussed this. Don't upset yourself.

But people laugh at Cherie like they have a right. Because she's a failure. "Can't sing, can't dance."

Not because she's a failure. Because she has pretensions.

She has hope!

Darling, it's not a good idea for us to talk like this. So far from each other. If I were there—

You laugh at Cherie, people like you. Because she has hope and she has no talent. She's a failure.

—I could explain better. I love you so much, I can't bear it when we misunderstand each other.

It's just that I love Cherie and want to protect her. From a woman like "Marilyn" she'd be compared to, y'know? That's when people laugh.

Darling, "Marilyn" is your stage name, your professional name, not a person. You speak as if—

Sometimes at night when I can't sleep, it's clear to me. Where I made my first mistake.

What mistake? When?

The moon is so bright here it can hurt your eyes. The air is so cold. Even if I draw my blinds and cover my eyes, I know I'm in a strange landscape, even at night.

Would you like me to come sooner, darling? I can.

I told you, we drove to Sedona the other day? That's north of Phoenix. It was like the beginning of the world. Those red mountains. And so empty. And quiet. Or maybe it was the end of the world. We were time travelers and traveled too far and couldn't return.

You said it was beautiful—

It would be beautiful, at the end of the world. The sun will be all red and fill most of the sky, they say.

This mistake you mentioned—

Never mind, Daddy. I didn't know you then.

There are mistakes in every career, darling. It's the things we do right that count. Believe me, darling, you've done many, many things right.

I have, Daddy?

Of course you have. You're famous: that must count for something.

What does it count for, Daddy? Does it mean I'm a good actress?

I think so, yes.

But I'm a better actress now. Since New York.

Yes. You are.

Does it mean I should be proud of myself?

I think you should be proud of yourself, yes.

Are you proud of yourself, Daddy? Your plays?

Yes. Sometimes. I try.

I try, too. Daddy, I do!

I know you do, darling. That's a good, healthy thing.

It's just that everybody watches me now, waiting for me to slip. They didn't used to. I wasn't anybody then. Now I'm "Marilyn" and they're waiting. Like in New York. . . .

Darling, you were fine in New York. It was your first time acting before a live audience and everyone was impressed and enthusiastic. You know that.

But I was so scared. Oh, God, I was so scared.

That's stage fright, dearest. We all have it sometimes.

I don't think I can live with it. It makes me so exhausted.

If you act on stage, you'll have weeks of rehearsals. Six weeks minimum. Nothing like that reading.

Daddy, I wish I could sleep at night but . . . I'm afraid of my dreams. The moon is so bright, and the stars. I'm used to the city. If you were here, Daddy, I know I could sleep! I could love love love you and boy! would I sleep.

Soon, darling. I'll be there soon.

Maybe I wouldn't ever wake up, I'd sleep so hard.

You don't mean that, darling.

No, I don't, because I can't leave you. Once we're married, I never want to spend a night away from you.

You won't have to. I'll see to that.

Daddy, did I tell you there's this rodeo scene in the movie? Cherie's there, in the bleachers. It's hard for her to climb up in her high heels and tight skirt. Her skin's so pale. We made her pale, a special chalky-white makeup for me, not just my face but everywhere you can see on me. She's the only one in the crowd who looks like . . . this strange sad moon-pale thing. A female. The other women wear slacks and jeans, like men. They're having a good time.

Doesn't Cherie have a good time?

She's this freak, *she can't have a good time. I was climbing up the bleachers, the sun was so bright I got dizzy and started vomiting. Not on camera!*

Sick to your stomach? Darling, are you ill?

It's Cherie, how tense she is. Because she knows people laugh at her even if, like you say, she's "unconscious."

I didn't mean "unconscious" in any derogatory way, darling. I was just trying to explain—

I don't want to be ashamed all my life. There's people who laugh at me. . . .

The hell with them. Who are they?

People in Hollywood. Anywhere.

Look, Time *magazine is doing a cover story on Marilyn Monroe, for God's sake. How many actresses, how many actors, have been on* Time's *cover?*

Daddy, why'd you say that!

What? What's wrong?

Oh, I told them it's too soon! I told them, I didn't want it yet. I'm not that old—

Of course you're not old. Not old at all.

—it should come when I'm ready. When I deserve it.

Darling, it's an honor. Just don't take it too seriously. You know what publicity is. This is publicity for Bus Stop. *Your "return to Hollywood." It can only help, not hurt.*

Daddy, why'd you bring that up? I didn't want to think about that now.

I'll read the story before you see it, I promise. You won't need to see even the cover if you don't want to.

But people will see it. All over the world. My face on the cover! My mother will see it; oh, what if the reporter says awful things about me? About my family? About . . . you?

Darling, I'm sure that won't happen. This will be a celebratory story, "The Return of Marilyn Monroe to Hollywood."

Daddy, I'm just so scared now! I wish you hadn't said that.

Darling, I'm sorry. Please. You know I adore you.

I won't be able to sleep now. I'm so scared.

Darling, I'll fly out as quickly as I can. I'll make arrangements tomorrow morning.

It's worse now. It's worse than it was. There are six hours I have to get through, before I can be Cherie again. I'm going to hang up now, Daddy. Oh, I love you!

Darling, wait—

Summoning Doc Fell to her motel room. No matter the hour of night. Doc Fell smiling with his emergency medical kit.

A red-desert landscape. By day, an overexposed print. By night, a sky punctuated with lights like distant screams. You wanted not just to hide your eyes but press your hands over your ears.

What was happening in Arizona on the *Bus Stop* location, what had happened in Los Angeles, what she could not tell her lover was a strangeness too elusive to be named.

It had begun on the long flight westward. After she'd said goodbye to the Playwright at LaGuardia and kissed, kissed, kissed him until both their mouths were bruised.

The task before him was divorce. The task before her, returning to "Marilyn Monroe."

Or it had begun on the long flight west. The plane flying ahead of the sun. Several times she asked the stewardess (who was serving drinks) what time it was in Los Angeles and when they would be arriving and how should she set her watch? She could not seem to calculate if they were time-traveling into the future or into the past.

The *Bus Stop* screenplay with its numerous revisions and inserts and X'd-out passages. She'd seen the play on Broadway starring Kim Stanley and secretly believed she'd be a much more convincing Cherie. *But if you fail. They're waiting.* She'd brought with her also the oversized secondhand copy of *The Illustrated Origin of Species* by Charles Darwin. There were profound truths here! She was eager to learn. The Playwright seemed to be impressed with her knowledge of books but sometimes he smiled in a way that meant she'd said something wrong or mispronounced a word. But how do you know what words sound like, from just reading? Those names in Dostoyevsky's novels! Those names in Chekhov! There was a certain grandeur in such names, uttered in full.

She was the Fair Princess returning to the cruel kingdom that had sent her into exile. Yet, as the Fair Princess, she was forgiving of course.

"So *happy*. So *grateful*. It's time for 'Marilyn' to return to work!"

"What feud? Oh there's no feud! I love Hollywood, and I hope Hollywood loves *me*."

"An individual, like a species, must adapt or perish. To a changing environment. And the environment's always changing! In a democracy like ours . . . so many discoveries in science alone. One day soon, a man on the moon." She laughed breathlessly, for all things were revealed to her, microphones shoved into her face. "One day the mystery of mysteries, the origin of life. Why I'm naturally optimistic."

"Oh, yes, like Cherie, my film character. A sweet little honky-tonk *chanteuse* stranded in the Wild West. But a born optimist. A born American. I love her!"

Yet, disembarking at Los Angeles International Airport! She may have panicked slightly, refusing to leave the plane. Emissaries from The Studio came aboard. So many people were awaiting the arrival of Marilyn Monroe: photographers, reporters, TV crews, fans. A roaring as of a waterfall sounded in her ears. It was Honolulu, it was Tokyo. Two hours and forty minutes would pass before the Blond Actress could be escorted to a limousine and driven swiftly away. In the background glimpses of the frightened faces of ordinary travelers caught in milling crowds and police barricades. An earthquake? A plane crash? An A-bomb attack on Los Angeles? *This is in mockery* she thought. In the morning papers there were front-page photos, articles.

MARILYN MONROE RETURNS TO HOLLYWOOD.
MOBS AT AIRPORT.
MARILYN MONROE TO RESUME FILMS.
MARILYN "HOME AGAIN, HAPPY"

In photos there was the Blond Actress replicated like a figure reflected in multiple mirrors. Front, profile, left side, right side, smiling, smiling more radiantly, blowing kisses, kissy-kissy mouth. An enormous bouquet in her arms. Also on the front page of the *Los Angeles Times* were articles reporting the meeting of British Prime Minister Anthony Eden and Soviet Prime Minister Nikolai Bulganin, and the meeting of President Eisenhower with a representative of the recently formed Federal Republic of West Germany. There was a human interest story on the families of the "top classified" scientists involved in the recent testing of an H-bomb (10 million tons TNT equivalent!) on Bikini atoll in the South Pacific. Mudslides in Malibu "claiming" three lives. An "orderly" NAACP picketing in Pasadena led by the Reverend Martin Luther King.

In mockery of me she thought. *Of what I am.*

Marilyn Monroe had a new agent, Bix Holyrod, of the Swanson Agency. She had a team of lawyers. She had a "money man." With her advance from signing the *Bus Stop* contract, she made the first installment of what would be in time a $100,000 trust fund for her mother, Gladys Mortensen. She had a press secretary provided by The Studio. She had a makeup man, a hairdresser, a manicurist, a skin-hair-health expert with a degree from UCLA, a masseur, a costumer, a driver, and a "general assistant." She was temporarily housed in luxurious Bel-Air Towers near Beverly Boulevard, where often she would wander confused and lost unable to locate the entrance to Building B. She had difficulty with the keys, which often she misplaced. In the furnished apartment provided her there were a housekeeper and a part-time cook who addressed her in reverent whispers as "Miss Monroe." Beneath the fragrant flower scent (for the apartment was always filled with floral displays) a subtle scent of fungicide. She kept none of these floral displays in her bedroom, knowing they would use up her oxygen. There were a half-dozen telephone extensions in the apartment but the phone rarely rang. All of Marilyn's calls were screened for her. When she lifted the phone receiver to make an outgoing call the line was often dead, or it crackled in that way (the Playwright had told her) that meant her phone was being tapped. She was careful to keep venetian blinds drawn in all the windows. The apartment was on the third floor of the building and vulnerable. She asked her housekeeper to sew tags onto every item of her clothing and to keep a careful laundry list for she'd been told (by Bix Holyrod, who thought it was funny) there was a lucrative black-market trade in Marilyn Monroe undergarments. She attended luncheons and dinners in her honor. She excused herself in the midst of such events to telephone the Playwright in New York City, in his new quarters, a small walk-up apartment on Spring Street. One of the most lavish of the dinner parties for Marilyn was hosted by Mr. Z, who had now a new magnificent Mediterranean villa estate in Bel Air and a new young wife, bronze-haired, with breasts like armor. Mr. Z had aged surprisingly well. He seemed in fact to be younger than she recalled. Though shorter than she ("my major asset, Marilyn") by several inches, with a small hump between his shoulder blades, Mr. Z now boasted flowing white hair of the kind called leonine and his eyes were those of an Old Wise Man. Mr. Z was a Hollywood pioneer, a living "chunk of history."

As always, Mr. Z and Marilyn Monroe exchanged comedy banter to which others listened enviously.

"D'you still have The Aviary, Mr. Z? Those poor dead birds!"

"I'm a collector of antiquities, dear. I think you have me confused with another mentor."

"You were a taxidermist, Mr. Z. Many of us were in awe of your hands."

"I have the most selective private collection in the country of Roman busts and heads. Shall I show you?"

A limousine brought her to such dinners in the wealthy residential hills above Los Angeles and to daytime appointments. Interviews, photo sessions, preproduction meetings at The Studio. She saw with a stab of shock that her driver was the Frog Chauffeur. *So I had not imagined him after all. None of that, I'd imagined.* The Frog Chauffeur seemed not to have aged either. His stiff, perfect posture, his soft puckered spotted darkish skin and shiny protuberant eyes. Yet veiled eyes. A visored cap, a dark green uniform with brass buttons like Johnny of Philip Morris but unlike that rascal Johnny, whose falsetto call was a summons to the blood of how many billions of nicotine-addicted Americans for much of the twentieth century, the Frog Chauffeur was silent. The Blond Actress smiled at him without subterfuge. "Why, h'lo there! Remember me?" She was trembling, yet determined to be sunny and forthright for we all wish to be spoken well of, by such individuals as the Frog Chauffeur, after our deaths. "Once, you drove me to the Los Angeles Home for Orphans. What a time we had! And other places." In the rear of the limousine the Blond Actress, behind dark-tinted windows driven about the City of Sand *while my heart was in New York with my lover soon to be my husband who would write the true story of my life, in which I am an American girl-of-the-people, a heroine.* At the same time, exhausted and mildly drunk ("Marilyn Monroe" drank only champagne, and of champagne only Dom Perignon), she smiled to think *There was once a handsome young prince under a cruel spell in the guise of a frog. Only if a fair young princess kissed him could the spell be broken and the handsome young prince and the fair young princess would wed and live happily ever after.*

In the midst of such a wonder tale she fell asleep. At their destination the Frog Chauffeur would rap on the glass divider to waken her, reluctant even now to utter any word.

"Miss Monroe? We are here."

Usually it was The Studio to which she'd been brought. The immense empire behind walls; through a sentry-guarded gate. Where hardly a decade ago "Marilyn Monroe" had been born. Where the destiny "Marilyn Monroe" had been forged. Where, decades earlier, the fated lovers who were the parents of "Marilyn Monroe" had presumably met. She was Gladys Mortensen, a film cutter but an extremely attractive young woman. He was—(in all sincerity the Blond Actress told interviewers who persisted in asking after her mysterious father that the man was still living, yes; he was in contact with her, yes; he was known to her, yes; yet not wishing to be known to the world "and I respect his wishes").

Her old dressing room, formerly that of Marlene Dietrich, was in readiness for her. Floral displays awaited. Stacks of mail, telegrams, touchingly wrapped little gifts. She opened the door and shut it in a swirl of nausea.

Doc Bob was gone from The Studio, vanished as if he'd never been. There was a rumor he was serving time for manslaughter in San Quentin. ("A girl died on him, and he refused to dump her body as ordered.") A new doctor, Doc Fell, had taken over his office. Doc Fell was tall and craggy-browed with Cary Grant good looks and a forceful bedside manner. He would impress his patients with his knowledge of Freud; he spoke familiarly of libido, repressed infantile aggression, and the discontents of civilization—"To which we all contribute, and from which we all suffer." Doc Fell would be in attendance on the *Bus Stop* set and would later fly to Arizona on location. Often in the moon-bright insomniac night Cherie would summon Doc Fell in pajamas and Cary Grant dressing gown to her motel room desperate to sleep. *Only just this once. Once more. I won't make a habit of it, I promise!* Doc Fell was a priest who in an emergency had the authority to inject liquid Nembutal directly into a vein; it would happen that Doc Fell's mere touch, his thumb searching for a vein in the tender inside of Cherie's forearm, was already a relief. *Oh, God! Thank you.*

At first on the set of *Bus Stop* there was an atmosphere of magic and good-will. She was Norma Jeane who was "Marilyn" who was "Cherie" to her fingertips. She was an actress who'd been trained at the New York Ensemble as a Method actress; she was the embodiment of Stanislavski's stagecraft and wisdom. *Always you must play yourself. A self smelted in the furnace of memory.* She knew Cherie down to the smallest mend and tatter of Cherie's pathetic-glamorous *chanteuse* costumes. She knew Cherie as intimately as she'd known Norma Jeane Baker of the Preene Agency, Miss Aluminum Products 1945, Miss Southern California Dairy Products 1945, Miss Hospitality at ten dollars a day, eagerly smiling, smiling to be loved. Oh, look at me! Hire me. She was the happiest she'd been in any screen role. For never until now had she actually chosen a role. Like a brothel girl who had to accept any client forced upon her or be beaten up, she'd had to accept from The Studio any role forced upon her. Until now. *I'll make you love Cherie. I'll break your hard hearts with Cherie.* She was able to believe in herself and to concentrate as she'd never before concentrated. Pearlman's admonitions rang in her ears like the pronouncements of Jehovah. *Deeper! Go deeper. To the very root of motivation. Into memory buried like treasure.* The Playwright's kindly forceful paternal voice rang in her ears. *Don't doubt your talent, darling. Your incandescent gift. Don't doubt my love for you.* Oh, she didn't doubt!

The director was a distinguished man hired by The Studio because she had requested him. He was not a Studio hack. He was a theater artist highly regarded by the Playwright, quirky and independent-minded. He listened carefully to his leading lady's suggestions and was clearly impressed with her intelligence, psychological insight, and acting experience as she discussed at length her film character Cherie; how Cherie had to be costumed and lighted and made up, her hair, the very tincture of her skin. ("I want a pellagra look, sort of moony-green. Just the suggestion, I mean. It must be subtle as a poem.") Of course, the director owed his job to this leading lady and that might have tempered his attitude; he did not glance aside with a smile or pointedly humor her as other directors had done. Yet in his very attentiveness there was something disturbing. He seemed to her too scrupulously polite; too much in awe of her; even wary of her. The way he stared when she came on the set as Cherie in her showgirl costume, tops of her breasts exposed and legs in black fishnet stockings, like a man in a dream. She hoped to God the man wasn't in love with her.

Here was some good luck! Better than maybe she deserved. The *Time* cover story was sheer Marilyn, and not *her*.

Jesus I had no idea Monroe was so . . . charismatic. That woman was fascinating as a dancing flame. On the set and off. Sometimes I'd be staring at her and wouldn't know where the hell I was. I'd been directing a long time and immune to female beauty I'd have thought and certainly to sexual attraction but Monroe was beyond female beauty and way beyond sex. Some days, she just burned with talent. In her there was a fever raging to get out. You could see it was genius and maybe genius turns to sickness if it can't get out, which I guess eventually happened with her, the way she went to pieces those last years. But I had Monroe in her prime. There was nobody like her. Everything she did as her character was inspired. She was so insecure she'd ask to reshoot, and reshoot, and reshoot and she'd make it perfect. When she got a scene perfect, she'd know. She'd smile at me, and I'd know. Still, some days she was so scared she'd be hours late on the set. Or couldn't make it at all. She had every kind of sickness: flu, strep throat, migraine, laryngitis, bronchitis. We went way over budget. In my opinion, it was worth every penny. When Monroe was in her element she was like a diver plunging into deep water; if she stopped to breathe, she'd drown. I guess I was in love with her. I was frankly crazy for her. It stunned me I'd been thinking this crude dumb broad all wiggly tits and ass and this angel Marilyn Monroe glides in and takes my hands and tells me it's not much of a script, it's slick and shallow and corny, but she's gonna rescue it and she's gonna break my heart, and God, she did.

They didn't even nominate her for an Oscar that year. Everybody knew she deserved it for Bus Stop. *Fuckers!*

.   .   .   .

Something was happening, she'd told her lover, but she dared not tell him how longer and longer each morning it was required to summon her Magic Friend out of the mirror.

Where once as a girl she'd only needed to glance into the glassy depths and there came her pretty smiling Friend-in-the-Mirror eager to be kissed and embraced.

Where once as a photographer's model she'd only needed to pose as required. In the postures suggested. Drifting into a trance as her Magic Friend emerged.

Where once as a film actress she'd only just needed to show up on the set, go to her dressing room and be prepared, and before the cameras an inexplicable magic occurred, a rush of blood to the heart more powerful than sex. Speaking her lines, which she'd memorized without trying, often without knowing she'd memorized, excited and scared coming alive in her borrowed body, she was Angela, she was Nell, she was Rose, she was Lorelei Lee, she was The Girl Upstairs. Even on the subway grating, the Ex-Athlete a witness to her degradation, she'd been thoroughly The Girl Upstairs luxuriating in her being. *Look at me! I am who I am.*

Yet so strangely now, in what she believed to be the role of her career, the beginning of her new career as a serious screen actress, she was overcome with doubt. She was anxious, she was sick with dread. Dragging herself from bed only when her door was sharply rapped, only when she was already late for the morning's shooting. Staring at herself in the mirror: Norma Jeane and not "Marilyn." Sallow skin and bloodshot eyes and the beginning of something fatally puffy around her mouth. *Why are you here? Who are you?* She could hear low, muffled laughter. Jeering male laughter. *You sad, sick cow.*

Longer and longer time was required to summon "Marilyn" out of the mirror.

She confessed to Whitey, her makeup man, who knew her more intimately than any lover or husband could know her, "I've lost my courage. The courage of being young."

Whitey's response was invariably reproachful.

"Miss Monroe! You are a young, young woman."

"These eyes? No, I'm not."

Whitey peered into the mirror eyes with a faint shudder.

"When I get finished with those eyes, Miss Monroe, then we'll see."

Sometimes Whitey worked his magic and this was so. Sometimes not.

At first on the set of *Bus Stop* it required a little more than the amount of time you'd reasonably expect for the Blond Actress to be prepared for the cameras. This young woman was so naturally beautiful, such soft luminous skin, such quick eyes, she might almost face the cameras with a light dusting of powder, lipstick, and rouge. Then by quick degrees it began to require pointedly more time. Was Whitey losing his touch? The actress's skin wasn't right, her makeup would have to be removed gently with cold cream and reapplied. Sometimes the hair wasn't right. (But what could possibly be wrong with *hair*?) Dampened and reset and again dried with a hand blower. As Norma Jeane sat motionless before the mirror, eyes lowered in prayer.

Please come. Please!

Don't abandon me. Please!

The very one she'd scorned. This "Marilyn" she despised.

The Playwright flew to Arizona to be with her. Though his life was in tatters. Though (he was in dread of telling her) he'd been issued a subpoena to appear again in Washington in the Caucus Room of the Old House Office Building, to explain his involvement in possible "subversive" and "clandestine" political activities as a young man.

He was shocked to find the Blond Actress so distraught, so . . . unlike herself. There was nothing of the girl with the flaxen hair and golden laughter in her now.

Oh, help me. Can you help me?

Darling what is it? I love you.

I don't know. I want Cherie to live so badly. I don't want Cherie to die.

His heart was stricken with love of her. Why, she was just a child! As dependent upon him as one of his own children, years ago. Yet more dependent, because the children had had Esther, and Esther had been closer to them always.

In her bed in the motel, shades drawn against the desert glare, they lay for hours. Whispering together, kissing and making love, and giving solace, she as much to him, for his soul was ravaged without her, he too was fearful of the world. In a dreamy twilit sleep they could lie for hours. They imagined (but perhaps this wasn't imagination) they entered each other's dreams, as if entering each other's souls. *Just hold me. Love me. Don't let me go.* The surreal desert landscape, red rock mountains and ridges like craters of the moon. The night sky, vast and intimidating and yet exhilarating as the Blond Actress had described it.

I feel as if I could be healed, with you. With you here. If we were married. Oh, when can we be married! I'm so afraid something will happen to prevent us.

His arm around her waist, he talked to her of the night sky. He said what came into his head. He spoke of a parallel universe in which they were already married and had twelve children. He made her laugh. He kissed her eyelids. He kissed her breasts. He raised her hand to his mouth and kissed the fingers. He told her what he knew of the constellation Gemini—for she'd told him she was a Gemini—the Twins: not warring twins but loving twins, loyal and devoted to each other. Even after death.

It was noted how, within a day of the Playwright's arrival, the Blond Actress began to revive. The Playwright, already a hero to some, became yet more a hero. It was as if the Blond Actress had had a blood transfusion. Yet the Playwright wasn't drained of strength but appeared invigorated, rejuvenated, as well. A miracle!

They were so in love, those two. Just to see them together . . . the way she held on to his arm, looked up at him. The way he looked at her.

What was the Playwright's secret? He reasoned with the Blond Actress as no other man had. Yes, he'd held her and comforted her; yes, he'd babied her as other men had done; but he'd also talked frankly with her. She liked that! Telling her sternly that she had to be realistic. She had to be professional. She was one of the most highly paid women performers in the world and she'd contracted to do a job. What had emotions to do with it? What had self-doubt to do with it? "You're a responsible adult, Norma, and must behave responsibly."

Silently she kissed him on the lips.

Oh, yes. He was right.

Almost, she wished he would seize her arm and shake her, hard. As the Ex-Athlete had done, to awaken her.

The Playwright warmed to his subject. He'd begun his playwriting career composing monologues, and the monologue was most natural to him as a form of speech. Hadn't he warned her against too much theory? "I've always believed you were a natural actress, darling. Intellectualizing can only cripple you. In New York you obsessively prepared for acting classes, you exhausted yourself after a few weeks. That's a sign of an amateur. A zealot. Maybe it's a sign of talent, but I don't think so. In my opinion it's much better for an actor to retain an edge of something raw and unexplored in a character. That was John Barrymore's secret. You're a friend of Brando's? That's one of Brando's techniques, too. Even to not completely know your lines, to be forced to invent, in the idiom of your character. A brilliant stage actor never gives the same performance twice. He doesn't recite lines, he speaks them as if he's hearing them for the first time. This is advice Pearlman should have given you, but you know Max: that pretentious Stanislavski 'method.' Frankly, it verges on bullshit. What if a hummingbird becomes conscious of its beating wings, its flight pattern, could it fly? If we become conscious of every word we utter, could we speak? Forget Pearlman. Forget Stanislavski. Forget bullshit theory. The danger for the actor is to overrehearse and burn out. There've been productions of my plays where the director pushed the actors too hard; they peaked before opening night, lost their momentum, and went flat. This has happened with Pearlman. People boast of him there's 'blood on the floor of his rehearsal rooms'—more bullshit. You were claiming, darling, that you knew Cherie from the inside? Like a sister? Maybe that wasn't altogether a good thing. Maybe it wasn't even true. You should have acknowledged that Cherie is mysterious to you. As you'd told me Magda was so much more than I'd known. Why not let Cherie breathe a little? Trust to Cherie to surprise you, tomorrow on the set."

Another time, silently, trembling in gratitude, the Blond Actress stood on tiptoe to kiss the Playwright on his lips.

Oh, yes. Thank God. He was right.

There came pellagra-pale platinum-blond Cherie onto the set next morning in her tacky black-lace blouse, tight black satin skirt with a wide, tight black belt, and black-mesh stockings and spike-heeled black sandals. Sooty eyes, a luscious red baby-mouth, tremulous and contrite. Here was Marilyn on time! No, here was Cherie. We stared at this gorgeous woman gnawing at her bitten thumbnail like a girl in acting class, or like an actual simple-hearted girl, knowing damned well she's been bad and she's waiting to be scolded.

She'd been trailing her bedraggled feather boa along the floor just like Cherie. She spoke in Cherie's earnest Ozark drawl, so soft a voice we almost couldn't hear. "Oh, gosh. I'm so sorry. I beg your forgiveness. I did what Cherie wouldn't have done, I lapsed into despair. I wasn't a responsible member of this production. I'm so ashamed!"

What the hell. We immediately forgot our hurt, our anger, our frustration with her. We burst into spontaneous applause. We adored our Marilyn.

Things are going very well now with my new movie after a shaky start. It is called "Bus Stop." I hope you'll like it!

She was in the daughterly habit of sending postcards to Gladys at the Lakewood Home. She'd sent cards from New York City.

I love this city. It's a true city, not like the City of Sand. If ever you would like to visit me here, Mother, I could arrange it. Planes fly all the time back & forth.

It made her uneasy to telephone Gladys, since departing Los Angeles. She believed that Gladys blamed her for abandoning her. Though on the phone, Gladys was unaccusing. Norma Jeane had called her from New York when she'd first fallen in love with the Playwright and knew she would marry him and he would be the father of her babies.

> *I have new wonderful friends here one of them a world-famous acting teacher and another a distinguished Pulitzer Prize-winning American playwright. I have seen some of my friend from Hollywood Marlon Brando.*

She'd told Gladys about buying books at the Strand. It was a used-book store and she'd searched for some of Gladys's old books but hadn't found them. *A Treasury of American Poetry.* Was that the title? She'd loved that book! She'd loved Gladys reading poetry to her. Now she read poetry to herself, but in Gladys's voice. To such remarks, Gladys would reply, almost inaudibly *That's nice, dear.*

So she didn't call Gladys any longer, only just sent picture postcards of the Southwest.

> *Someday when I'm rich we can visit here. It's "the end of the world" here for sure!*

So fearful was Norma Jeane of seeing daily rushes, so in dread of discovering that Marilyn had let her down, she had no idea what *Bus Stop* was becoming apart from her scenes. And her scenes were shot and reshot so many times, so suffused with the strain of her performance, and her heart knocking against her ribs, she had no idea how they might appear to a neutral observer. Like Cherie she plunged ahead, blind and "optimistic." She would trust, as her lover advised, to instinct.

So Norma Jeane didn't see *Bus Stop* in its entirety, from its noisily comic opening to its sentimental-romantic ending, until a preview at The Studio in early September. She wouldn't see how brilliantly she'd portrayed Cherie until then, months afterward. By then a married woman. Sitting with her husband's hand gripping hers in the darkened preview room in the first row of plush seats. In a haze of Miltown and Dom Perignon. Norma Jeane was "Marilyn" but calmly sedated. The crises of the previous spring in Arizona were as remote to her as the crises of a stranger. It was a shock to her that *Bus Stop* had turned out so well. As Cherie, she'd given the most inspired performance of her career. Out of terror still another time she'd risen to an achievement of which she need not be ashamed but possibly even proud. Yet it seemed to her an ironic victory, like that of a swimmer who only barely manages to cross a turbulent river that nearly drowns her. The swimmer staggers to shore; the audience that has risked nothing bursts into applause.

And so the audience in the preview theater burst into applause.

The Playwright held her protectively, his arm around her shaking shoulders. "Darling, why are you crying?" he whispered. "You were wonderful. You are wonderful. Listen to the response here. *Hollywood adores you.*"

Why was I crying? Maybe because in actual life Cherie would've been drinking, a lot. She would've been missing half her teeth. She would've had to sleep with the bastards. It didn't make any sense she could avoid them except the screenplay was sentimental and corny and in 1956 you couldn't risk getting an X-rating from the Legion of Decency. In actual life Cherie'd have been beaten and probably raped. She'd have been shared by men. Don't tell me the Wild West wasn't like that, I know men. She'd have been used by them until she got knocked up or her looks went or both. There wouldn't have been any good-looking yokel-cowboy Bo to throw her over his shoulder and carry her away to his ten-thousand-acre ranch. She'd have been drinking and taking drugs to keep going until the day she couldn't get up from bed any longer, couldn't even get her eyes fully open, and after that she'd be dead.

THE (AMERICAN)
SHOWGIRL 1957

Miss Monroe! This is your first visit to England. What are your impressions?

It was the Kingdom of the Dead. Whose inhabitants moved soundless as ghosts. Faces pale as the opalescent sky and misty shadowless air. And she among them, the (American) Blond Actress, beneath that same spell.

On these isles in the North Sea it was as likely to be winter as spring. There was no predicting one day to the next. Crocuses and daffodils bloomed in bright brave colors in a bone-piercing cold. The sun was a faint crescent in the mist-sky.

Soon, you ceased to care.

"Darling, what's wrong? Come here."

"Oh, Daddy. I'm so homesick."

The Prince and the Showgirl. Her co-star was the renowned British actor O.

She was the (American) showgirl. In a traveling troupe in a mythical Balkan country. Busty, and swivel-buttocks in shiny satins. When first you see the Showgirl, hurriedly taking her place in a line to curtsy to the mono-cled Grand Duke, one of her shoulder straps breaks and her gorgeous inflated bosom is virtually exposed.

"It's cheap. It's vaudeville. It's the Marx Brothers."

"Darling, it's *comedy*."

The Blond Actress was a plucky Irish-American platinum blonde from Milwaukee, Wisconsin. She was Cinderella, she was the Beggar Maid. Whose improbable knowledge of the German language complicates the flimsy cobweb of a plot. O was the prig Prince Regent. Played by the renowned British actor with the zest and subtlety of a wind-up toy.

"What is it, his acting? Parody? I don't understand."

"I don't think he means his performance to be parody, exactly. He interprets the script as drawing-room comedy, which means a certain stage style. A certain air of the artificial. He isn't a Method actor—"

"He's sabotaging the film? But why? He's the director!"

"Darling, he isn't 'sabotaging' the film. His technique is just different from yours."

The Prince and the Showgirl were fated by the script to *fall in love* in this fairy tale. Except their *falling-in-love* was no more credible than love between two life-sized animated dolls.

"He's contemptuous of his role. And of me."

"That can't be true."

"Watch him! His eyes."

Through O's lusterless monocle eye she was forced to see herself: the busty American actress, the cotton-candy fine-spun platinum-blond hair and glossy red lips and shivery mannerisms. The Showgirl was an outspoken young woman of the (American) people, the Prince was the reticent, tradition-bound (European) aristocrat. Off the set, O was coolly polite, even gracious to the Blond Actress, but on the set, before the cameras, he scorned her. She was as out of place amid these Academy-trained Shakespearean actors as poor Cherie the *chanteuse* would have been.

Marilyn Monroe was the (American) cash cow in O's Brit fantasy of wealth via Hollywood. O's contempt for Hollywood and for "Marilyn" was a smell her desperate perfumes couldn't disguise.

The way O uttered "Mari-lyn."

O, as director of the doomed movie as well as leading man. His Brit accent like a knife striking china.

Addressing her as you might address a retarded child. Yet without smiling. "Mari-*lyn*. My dear, can you speak a little more clearly? More coherently."

She would not reply. He might have leaned over and spat into her face. She was Norma Jeane Baker trussed up in a dress baring much of her bosom, her scalp stung from that morning's peroxide touch-up, mind slow as a winding-down alarm clock. Suddenly sunk in a dream. Four hours, forty minutes late that day. Coughing, so scenes had to be reshot. She fumbled her lines; she'd begun to forget the simplest dialogue. Where once she'd memorized so easily. Where once she'd memorized even other actors' dialogue. The pores of her forehead and nose oozed grease through the thick pancake makeup.

O stared at her through the monocle. Removed the monocle and forced a grimace of a smile.

You could see he meant this to be witty. Drawing-room witty.

"Mari-lyn, dear girl. Be sexy."

The previous week she'd been ill with a stomach flu. Vomiting through the night. The Playwright was her nurse, her devoted and anxious husband. She'd lost six pounds. Her costumes had to be readjusted. Her face was thinner. Would the scenes she'd already done have to be reshot? Last week she'd been able to work only a single full day, morning to late afternoon. The other actors regarded her with wary sympathy. *As if my sickness might be catching. Oh, I wanted them to love me!*

It was an exquisite revenge. American-girl revenge. The renowned British actor O had expected emotional outbursts, crude hysteria; he'd been warned that the Blond Actress was "difficult." He had not expected so passive and lethal a revenge.

Thinking I was dumb-blond Desdemona. My secret is, Marilyn is Iago!

She crept away to hide. She laughed. No, she was frantic with hurt, confusion.

"It's O who is making me sick. He's put a curse on me."

"Don't think that way, darling. He does admire you—"

"When he has to touch me, his skin crawls. His nostrils contract. I see it."

"Norma, you're exaggerating. You must know—"

"Look, do I *stink?* What is it?"

Fact is, Marilyn, here's a man who doesn't desire you. A man you've failed to seduce. Who'd as soon fuck a cow as you. One in millions.

The Playwright! What was he to think, and what was he to do?

This woman his wife. The Blond Actress, *his wife.*

Here in England he was beginning to comprehend the nature of the task before him. As an explorer on foot begins to comprehend, as terrain shifts and a new, abrupt, stunning, and unexpected vista opens before him, the challenge that lies ahead.

He'd become so swiftly her nurse! Her only friend.

Yet he was a friend to O too. He'd long been an admirer of O. His plays were not suitable for an actor of O's background and training; still the Playwright revered O and was grateful for O's company and conversation. He supposed that O had agreed to undertake this project primarily for the money; yet he believed that O was too professional an actor, and too decent a man, not to perform to the very best of his ability.

As a man of the theater the Playwright had been prepared to be fascinated by moviemaking and to learn what he could. In fact he'd begun writing a screenplay, his first.

A screenplay for the Blond Actress his wife.

But moviemaking shocked and confused him. He hadn't been prepared for the commotion, the incessant busyness. So many people! The brightly lit space in which actors performed was surrounded by a bevy of technicians, cameraman, the director, and his assistants. Scenes were begun and interrupted and begun again and interrupted and again begun and interrupted; scenes were shot and reshot; there was a fanatic, frantic concern with makeup and hair; there was an artificial dreamlike quality to the enterprise, a cheapness and shoddiness of the spirit that offended him deeply. He began to understand why O, trained as a man of the theater, performed so oddly, so archly, for the camera. The Prince was wholly artificial while the Showgirl was "natural." It seemed sometimes as if the two were speaking different languages; or that two radically different genres, drawing-room comedy and a type of realism, had been yoked together. In fact, of the cast only the Blond Actress seemed to know how to play to the camera while behaving as if she were playing to the other actors; but her confidence had been shaken so early in the production, her girlish enthusiasm dampened by O's chill, she, too, had been thrown off stride.

"Daddy, you don't understand. This isn't the theater. It's . . ."

The Blond Actress's voice trailed off. For what, in fact, was she trying to say?

Later that night, coming to him and tugging at his arm as if she'd been preparing these lines to recite. "Daddy, listen! What I do is, I tell myself I'm alone. And there's this other person with me, or maybe more than one person? I don't know who they are but there's a purpose. To us being there. Why we're there in that place that's meant to be a room, or we could be outdoors or in a car, there's a logic to it? We figure out why we're there and what we mean to each other by playing out the scene." She smiled anxiously at him. How badly she wanted him to understand; his heart was touched. He stroked her feverish cheek. "See, Daddy, like you and me right now? We're alone here together, and we're making sense of why. We fell in love . . . and we came together to make sense of why. It isn't like we can know ahead of time. We can't! We're in a circle of light and outside us is darkness and we're alone together in the sea of darkness like we're floating in a boat, see? We'd be frightened of this except there is a logic to it. There is! So even when I'm scared, like I guess I am here in England, with people hating me. . . . Stanislavski says, 'This is solitude in public.' "

The Playwright was astonished by his wife's impassioned words though he hadn't understood most of what she'd said. He held her tight, tight. Her hair had been newly bleached at the roots and hairline that morning and exuded a harsh sickening chemical odor that made the Playwright's nostrils contract. This odor, the Blond Actress had long since ceased to smell.

Now in the Kingdom of the Dead she began to sink. The very marrow of her bones turned to lead. In this chill undersea kingdom with its fish inhabitants hideous to her.

They hate me. Their eyes!

The Playwright was O's emissary as he was, or hoped to be, O's friend. Both the Playwright and O the renowned British actor were men married to "temperamental" actresses.

She heard jeering laughter! The Playwright pronounced, like a straight man in a Marx Brothers movie, "Darling, no. It's just the plumbing."

The plumbing! She had to laugh.

"Darling, what's wrong? You're frightening me."

The Blond Actress dreamt of lead pythons shuddering to life close beside her bed. In these sumptuous quarters in an old stone house in the kingdom of perpetual damp. It was true, the aged pipes groaned, writhed, spat. Jeering laughter was communicated through such pipes as through a speaking tube. The Playwright was alternately concerned, cajoling, impatient, patient and pleading, and on the verge of threatening, and again concerned, anxious, sympathetic and cajoling, impatient, and patient and pleading on the verge of desperation.

Norma darling there's been a car waiting for you downstairs for an hour why don't you get up   take a shower and dress   Shall I help you darling please wake up

She pushed him away, whimpering. Her eyelids were stuck shut. The voice came to her muffled as through cotton batting. A voice she recalled dimly having loved once as, hearing an ancient recording, you recall the mysterious emotions that recording once stirred.

Later, as the afternoon quickly waned and the cotton batting voice grew more urgent *Darling this is serious   you're frightening me   everyone's hopes are on you don't let them down*

Sunk in a dream. Oh, she'd ceased to be anxious! The new medication seeped into her bones' marrow and held her fast.

The Playwright was frantic; what to do? What to do?

In this chill inhospitable place so far from home. In this borrowed old stone house where the plumbing shrieked and the single-pane windows leaked a perpetual mist.

Those unmistakable symptoms: glassy bloodshot eyes. If he lifted one of her eyelids with his thumb, she was unseeing. His thumb left an indentation in her puffy flesh that was slow to fill in. *Like the flesh of the dead.*

When she did manage to get up, she moved awkwardly and seemed uncertain of her balance. She sweated, yet she was shivering. And her breath like copper pennies held in the hand.

Why was he thinking, panicked, of Bovary's dying? The hideous protracted agony. The protruding tongue, the beautiful pale-skinned woman contorted in death. The black liquid running from Bovary's mouth when she died.

The Playwright was ashamed of himself thinking such thoughts.

Why did I marry her! Why did I imagine I was strong enough!

The Playwright was ashamed of himself thinking such thoughts.

I love this woman so much. I must help her.

Ashamed of himself, searching the silk compartments of her suitcases for pills.

These, her "surplus" pills. Her cache he wasn't supposed to know about, she'd smuggled in secret to England.

She kicked at him, furious and weeping. Why didn't he leave her alone for Christ's sake?

Let me die! It's what you all want, isn't it?

You made of the smallest issues a test of my loyalty. Our love.
Smallest issues! You didn't defend me against that bastard.
It wasn't always clear who was in the wrong.
He despised Marilyn!
No. It was you who despised Marilyn.

Except if Daddy could make her pregnant she would love Daddy again.

How she yearned for a baby! In her nicest dream the rumpled pillow was a baby, soft and cuddly. Her breasts were swollen and aching with milk. There was Baby just outside the circle of light. There was Baby with glistening eyes. There was Baby smiling in recognition of his mother. There was Baby, needy of her love, and her love alone.

She had made a mistake, years ago. She had lost Baby.

She had lost little Irina, too. Hadn't saved Irina from her Death Mother. None of this could she explain to her husband, or to any man.

How many times curling in her husband's arms, removing his glasses (as in a movie scene, and he was Cary Grant) to kiss and cuddle and with girlish-shy audacity stroking him through his trousers to make him hard as no girl had ever done (was this possible?) to him in quite this way. *Oh, Dad-dy! Oh my.*

Yes she'd forgive him if he made her pregnant. She'd married him to become pregnant and to have his child, a son by the American Playwright she revered. (His published plays on bookshelves in stores. Even in London! She'd loved him so. So proud of him. Wide-eyed, asking what does it feel like to see your name on a book jacket? To glance at a shelf in a bookstore not expecting to see your name on a book spine, then to see it; what does that feel like? I know I would be so proud, I would never again be unhappy or unworthy in my life.)

Yes she'd forgive him. For siding with the Brit O who hated her and with all the goddam company of Brit actors who condescended to her.

Yet he continued to plead. To reason. As if this were a matter of logic.

Darling you have a fever   you haven't eaten   Darling I'm going to call a doctor

So she returned to the set. This was work to her now, this was duty and obligation and expiation. Silence at her entrance!—as in the aftermath, or the anticipation of, a cataclysm. Somewhere at the rear of the sound stage someone clapped harshly, in irony. And how long, how painstakingly long to summon gorgeous Marilyn out of the dressing room mirror, not one but two hours, Whitey's skilled priest-hands working, finally, their magic.

Frankly, it astonished us. This weak, tentative person. We were all so strong, and except for her looks she had nothing. Then, in the daily rushes, in the finished film, we saw an entirely different person. Monroe's skin, her eyes, her hair, her facial expressions, her body that was so alive. . . . She'd made of the Showgirl an actual living person, where the script provided so little. She was the only one of us who'd had any experience making movies, we were all duds beside her. We were dressmaker's dummies uttering perfectly enunciated perfectly empty English speech. Oh yes certainly we'd hated Monroe at the time we knew her but afterward seeing the movie we adored her. Even O, he had to admit he'd completely misjudged her. She virtually eradicated him, in every scene they shared! Monroe saved the ridiculous movie when we'd believed she was the one causing its ruin; now isn't that ironic? Isn't that strange?

Yet again that damned drawing-room interior. Oh, it was hell to her, this stage set. The prig Prince and the Showgirl are alone together at last and the prig Prince hopes to seduce the Showgirl but the Showgirl is evading seduction and there is the damned curving staircase to be ascended, descended, ascended, and again descended in her low-cut tight-waisted satin gown the Showgirl must wear through how many scenes of this slow joyless fairy tale she'd come to loathe. The Showgirl as the Beggar Maid. The Showgirl as the Female Body. Worst of all, the Showgirl wasn't allowed to dance! Why?— it wasn't in the script. Why?—it wasn't in the original play. Why?—it's too

late now, it would cost too much. Why?—it would take you forever to perform those scenes, Marilyn. Why?—just learn your lines, Marilyn. Why?—
because we loathe you. Why?—because we want your American money.

In this Kingdom of the Dead where a spell was laid upon her.

I miss my home! I want to go home.

Suddenly on the staircase the Showgirl fell, hard. Her high-heeled shoe
catching in the hem of her gown. She grunted, falling. She'd swallowed several Benzedrines to counteract the Nembutal and the Miltown and she'd had
gin in her hot tea and the Playwright had not known (he would afterward
claim) and she'd fallen on the curved staircase and there were cries on the
set and the young cameramen rushed to help her. The Playwright who'd been
anxiously watching at a short distance now rushed to help her in a torment
of love kneeling over her.

Her pulse! Where was her pulse!

A few yards away on the landing above stood the costumed prig Prince
staring through his monocle.

"It's the drugs. Get her stomach pumped."

Never would they forgive him.

THE KINGDOM
BY THE SEA

I

It was an enchanted isle to which he brought her, Galapagos Cove on the Maine coast forty miles north of Brunswick.

Though they'd been married for more than a year and had lived in many places, she was yet his girl bride. Yet to be completely won.

He loved that in her, that edgy air of discovery, surprise, delight. He was not fearful of her moods, he had made himself master of her moods.

Seeing the house he'd rented for them for the summer, and the view of the ocean beyond the house, she'd been excited, childlike. "Oh! This is so beautiful. Oh, Daddy, I don't ever want to leave."

There was a strange child's pleading in her voice. She hugged him and kissed him, hard. He felt the warm yearning life in her, as years ago he'd felt the warm yearning life of his children when he held them. Sometimes the love came so strong, and the sense of responsibility, he was physically shaken. His very identity seemed to him obliterated.

He stood tall and proudly smiling out upon the rocky shore below the cliff and upon the vast open water of the Atlantic as if he owned these things. This was his gift to his wife. And it was taken as a gift, prized as a love offering by her. Wind made the waves turbulent this afternoon. Light reflected off the water like metal. Now slate-gray, now cloudy blue, now dark bitter green, trailing seaweed and froth, always shifting. The air was fresh and briny and wet with windborne spray as he remembered it, and the sky was a pale fading blue like a watercolor riddled with vaporous swift-scudding clouds. Yes, it was beautiful; it was his to bestow; his heart expanded with happiness and anticipation.

They stood shivering in the ocean wind of early June. Arms tight around each other's waist. Overhead, gulls reeled with flapping wings and sharp piercing cries as if furious that their territory had been violated.

The ring-billed gulls of Galapagos Cove, like old thoughts.

"Oh, I *love you*."

She spoke these words so fiercely, smiling up at him, her husband, you would believe she'd never spoken these words before.

"*We* love you."

Taking his hand and pressing it against her belly.

A warm rounded belly; she'd been gaining weight.

Baby was two months, six days in the womb.

2

He stroked and kissed and pressed his cheek against her naked belly, in bed. Marveled at the pale skin stretched tight as a drum so early in the pregnancy. How healthy she was, brimming with life! She meant to nourish Baby in the womb, she followed a strict diet. She took no pills now except vitamins. She'd retired from her career *in the world* (as she spoke of it not disdainfully or with regret or anger but matter-of-factly as a nun might speak of her past, now repudiated secular life *in the world*) to cultivate a true life in marriage, and in motherhood. He kissed her, he pretended to hear Baby inside, a phantom heartbeat. No? Yes? Drawing his hand across her belly, lightly touching the zipper scar from an appendectomy she'd had a few years before. *And how many abortions has she had. The rumors told of her! To which I refused to listen, even before falling in love with her. I swear.* His need to protect her was a need to protect her from even her own recollection of a past confused and careless and promiscuous and yet innocent as the past of a wayward child.

Losing himself in a trance of wonderment at the beauty of her body. This woman his wife. His!

The exquisite soft skin, the living envelope of her beauty.

Like the sea, this beauty changed constantly. As if with light, gradations of light. Or the moon's gravitational pull. Her soul, mysterious and fearsome to him, was like a sphere precariously balanced atop a jet spray of water: tremulous, ever-shifting, now rising, now descending, now rising again. . . . In England she'd wanted to die. If he had not summoned a doctor, more than once. . . . At the time of her collapse, following the completion of the movie, she'd been haggard, ravaged, looking her age and more; yet back in the States, within weeks she'd made a complete recovery. Now, two months pregnant, she was the healthiest he'd ever seen her. Even her morning bouts of nausea seemed to cheer her. How normal she was! And how good, being normal! There was a simplicity and a directness in her now he'd seen before only when she'd read the part of Magda in his play.

Away from the city. Away from the expectations of others. The eternal eyes of others. Pregnant with his child.

I have done this for her. Returned her to life. If only now I'm equal to it. Becoming a father again, after so many years. At almost fifty.

3

The Playwright had often come to Galapagos Cove in the summer, with another woman. A former wife. When younger. He frowned, remembering. But what was he remembering? Not quite remembering. Like searching through old yellowed papers, drafts of plays he'd written quickly in a fervor of inspiration, then laid aside; then forgot. You can't believe in the fervor of such inspiration that you will ever feel differently, let alone that you will forget. He sighed, uneasy. He shivered in the damp ocean air. No, he was happy. His new young wife was climbing down to the pebbly shore, agile and just slightly reckless, as a willful child. He'd never been happier, he was certain.

The gulls' cries. What had stirred these unwanted thoughts?

4

"Daddy, come *on*!"

She'd climbed down the cliff amid slippery mossy rocks and ocean debris. Excited as a little girl. The beach was more pebbly than sandy. Frothy waves broke at her feet. She seemed not to mind that her feet were getting wet. The cuffs of her khaki trousers wet and smeared with mud. Her pale hair was whipping in the wind. Tears glistened on her cheeks, her sensitive eyes watered easily. "Daddy? Hey." The surf was so noisy, her words were almost inaudible.

He hadn't liked to see her climbing down there but he knew better than to caution her. He knew better than to reestablish the unhealthy bond between them, of his wife's willful self-hurting behavior and his paternal reprimands, threats, dismay.

Never again! The Playwright was too smart for that.

He laughed and climbed down after her. The wet, slick rocks were treacherous. Spray blew into his face, covering his glasses with moisture. The cliff dropped about fifteen feet, not far, but tricky to manage without slipping. He was astonished she'd climbed down so quickly, nimble as a monkey. He thought *I don't know her, do I!* It was a thought that came to him swift and unbidden a dozen times a day, and at night when he happened to wake to hear her moaning softly beside him, whimpering or even laughing in her sleep. His knees were stiff and he nearly sprained his wrist, catching himself when he lost his balance. He was panting, his heart pounding in his chest, yet he was smiling happily. He too was agile, for a man his age.

In Galapagos Cove they would be mistaken for father and daughter, until their identities became known.

At the Whaler's Inn farther north along the coast where he would take her for dinner that evening. Holding hands by candlelight. A pretty young blond woman with delicate features, in a white summer dress; a tall, slope-shouldered older man, polite, soft-spoken, with furrowed cheeks. *That couple. The woman looks familiar. . . .*

He jumped down beside her, his heels sinking in the pebbly sand. The noise of the surf was deafening. She slipped her arms around his waist, tight; against his skin, up inside his sweater and shirt. They were wearing matching navy-blue cable-knit sweaters she'd ordered for them from an L. L. Bean catalog. They were panting and laughing with a curious kind of relief, as if each had barely escaped harm: yet where had been the harm? She stood on her toes and kissed his mouth hard. "Oh, Daddy! Thank you! This is the happiest day of my life."

Absolutely, you could see she meant it.

5

It was known locally as the Captain's House, sometimes the Yeager House, built in 1790 for a sea captain on a bluff above the ocean. A tall scrubby hedge of lilac screened it from the traffic, heavy in summer, of the country highway Route 130.

The Captain's House was an old New England saltbox of weathered wood and weathered stone, with steep roofs and narrow mullioned windows and oddly narrow, low, rectangular rooms; the upstairs rooms were small and drafty; there were stone fireplaces large enough to stand inside, and worn brick hearths; bare floorboards covered with braided rugs, endearingly old and faded as if testaments to time. The baseboards and staircase railings were hand-molded. The furnishings were mostly old, antique, eighteenth-century New England hand-made chairs and tables and cabinets, flat surfaces, plain straight lines, an air of Puritan canniness and restraint. In the downstairs rooms there were paintings of sea scenes and portraits of men and women so awkwardly rendered they had to be authentic "folk art"; there were hand-sewn quilts and needlepoint cushions. There were numerous antique clocks: grandfather's and ship's clocks, glass-encased German clocks, music-box clocks, clocks finished in porcelain and black lacquer grown clouded with time. ("Oh, look! They've all stopped at different times," Norma said.) The kitchen and bathrooms and electrical outlets were reasonably modern, for the property had been many times renovated, at considerable cost, but the Captain's House smelled of age, of the ravages and wisdom of Time.

Especially the low, windowless, dirt-floored cellar. You had to descend into it on wooden steps that swayed beneath your weight, shining a flashlight into the cobwebbed dark. There was an oil furnace there, fortunately unused in summer months. A powerful odor of something sweet and dank, like rotted apples.

But why descend into the cellar? They would not. They sat for a while on the screened-in porch overlooking, at a short distance, the ocean; they drank lemon-flavored club soda and held hands and talked of the months ahead. The house was very quiet: the telephone wasn't yet connected, and they fantasized having no telephone—"For why? For other people, wanting to call *us*." But they would have a telephone of course. They could not avoid a telephone: the Playwright was deeply, passionately committed to his career. Next, they went upstairs and unpacked their things in the largest, airiest bedroom, with a stone fireplace and a swept brick hearth and new-looking floral wallpaper and a view of the ocean over the tops of juniper pines. Their bed was an old four-poster with a carved walnut headboard. In a dressmaker's oval mirror, their smiling faces. His forehead, nose, and cheeks were sunburnt; her face was pale, for she'd shielded her sensitive skin from the sun with a wide-brimmed straw hat. She rubbed Noxzema into his smarting skin, gently. And were his forearms burnt too? She rubbed Noxzema into his forearms and kissed the backs of his hands. She pointed to their faces in the oval mirror and laughed. "They're a happy couple. Know why? They've got a secret." She meant Baby.

In fact, Baby was not a complete secret. The Playwright had told his elderly parents and several of his oldest friends in Manhattan. He'd tried to keep an air of pride out of his voice; still more, an air of concern, and embarrassment. He knew what people would be saying, even people who liked him and wished him well in his new marriage. *A baby! At his age! That's a man for you. A man with a gorgeous young wife.* Norma had told no one yet. As if the news were too precious to be shared. Or she was superstitious. ("Knock on wood!" was one of her frequent remarks, uttered with a nervous laugh.)

Norma would call her mother in Los Angeles sometime soon, she said. And maybe Gladys could visit, later in her pregnancy. Or when Baby was born.

The Playwright had yet to meet his mother-in-law. He was self-conscious, envisioning a woman not much older than he was.

They lay for a while in the late afternoon, fully clothed except for their shoes, on the four-poster bed; it had a horsehair mattress, comically hard and unyielding. They lay with his left arm beneath her shoulders and her head on his shoulder in their favored position. Often they lay like this when Norma was feeling weak, or lonely, or in need of affection. Sometimes they drifted into sleep; sometimes they made love; sometimes they slept and then made love. Now they lay awake listening to the quiet of the house, which seemed to them a layered, complex, and mysterious quiet; a quiet that began in the windowless dirt-filled cellar that smelled of rotted apples and lifted, through the floorboards, through the varied rooms of the house, to the part-finished attic above their heads, lined with a surprising metallic-silver insulation like Christmas wrapping paper. The Playwright envisioned, as Time lifted from the earth, it became airier, less condemning.

Beyond the mysterious quiet of the Captain's House which was theirs until Labor Day was the rhythmic pounding of the surf, like a gigantic heartbeat. From time to time, on the far side of the house, traffic on the country highway.

He thought she'd drifted off to sleep but her voice was wide-awake and excited. "Know what, Daddy? I want Baby to be born here. In this house."

He smiled. The baby wasn't due until mid-December, when they'd be back in Manhattan in their rented brownstone on West 12th Street. But he wouldn't contradict her.

She said, as if he'd spoken aloud, "I wouldn't be afraid. Physical pain doesn't scare me. Sometimes I think, it isn't even real, it's what we expect it to be, we tighten up and we get scared. We could get a midwife for me. I'm serious."

"A midwife?"

"I hate hospitals. I don't want to die in a hospital, Daddy!"

He turned his head to look at her, so strangely. What had she said?

6

Yes but you killed Baby.

She had not! She had not meant to.

Yes you meant to kill Baby. It was your decision.

Not the same baby. Not this baby. . . .

It was me of course. Always it is me.

She knew she must avoid the dirt-floored cellar that smelled of rotted apples. Baby was already there, waiting for her.

7

How happy she was! How healthy. The Playwright's spirits lifted in the Captain's House. In this summer place by the sea. He was more in love with his wife than ever. And so grateful.

"She's wonderful. Pregnancy agrees with her. Even morning nausea, she's cheerful about. She says, 'This is how it's supposed to be, I guess!' " He laughed. He so adored his wife, he had a tendency to mimic her light, lilting, lyric voice. He was the Playwright: the subtle, and not-so-subtle, distinctions between voices fascinated him. "Except, if I have one regret—time passes so quickly."

He was talking on the phone. In another room of the spacious house, or in the back yard in the overgrown garden, she was singing to herself, utterly preoccupied, and would never have heard.

Of course, he'd been worried. If not worried, "concerned."

Her emotions, her moods. Her fragility. Her fear of being laughed at. Her fear of being "spied upon"—photographed without her knowledge or consent. It had been a nightmare to him, her behavior in England. Her behavior for which he'd been as wholly unprepared as an explorer in the Antarctic equipped for a summer stroll in Central Park. The only women he knew intimately were his mother, his former wife, his adult daughter. All were capable of emotional outbursts of course and yet all behaved within the compass of what might be called fair play, or sanity. Norma was as different from these women as if she belonged to another species. She struck out at him blindly, yet woundingly.

Let me die! It's what you all want, isn't it?

The Playwright would think how, in a play, such an accusation would have a ring of truth to it. Even as the accusation was strenuously denied, the audience would understand. *Yes, it's so.*

Yet in actual life the strategies of drama were not applicable. In the extremities of emotion, terrible things were said that were not true and were not meant to be true, only just the expression of hurt, anger, confusion, fear; fleeting emotions, not obdurate truths. He'd been deeply wounded and had had to wonder: did Norma really believe that others would have liked her to die? Did she believe that he, her husband, would have liked her to die? Did she want to believe that? It sickened him to think that his wife whom he loved more than he loved his own life should believe, or wish to believe, such a thing of him.

Yet here in Galapagos Cove, far from England, these ugly memories didn't intrude. Rarely did they speak of Norma's career. Of "Marilyn." She was Norma here, and would be known locally by that name. She was happy, and healthier than he'd seen her; he didn't want to risk upsetting her by talking of finances, of business, of Hollywood, or her work. It impressed him that she had the power to so completely shut out that part of her life. He didn't believe any man in her position could do so, or would wish to do so. Certainly he himself could not.

But, of course, the Playwright's career didn't terrify him. His public identity was agreeable to him. He was proud of his work and hopeful of the future. For all his reserve and irony he acknowledged he was an ambitious man. Smiling to himself, thinking yes, he could use a little more acclaim and a little more income.

The previous year, with a play on Broadway and regional productions of earlier plays throughout the United States, he'd made less than $40,000. Before taxes.

He'd refused to answer questions put to him by the House Un-American Activities Committee. He'd refused to allow "Marilyn Monroe" to be photographed with the committee chairman. (Though he'd been told that the committee would "go easy" on him if such a photo session could be arranged. What blackmail!) He'd been found in contempt of Congress and sentenced to a year in prison and fined $1,000 and his case was being appealed and was certain, his lawyers said, to be overturned; yet in the meantime he had legal fees to pay and no end in sight. HUAC had been harassing him now for six years. It was no accident that the IRS was auditing his income. And he had alimony payments to make to Esther, he meant to be a decent, generous ex-spouse. Even with "Marilyn Monroe's" income, they hadn't much money. There were medical expenses, and with Norma's pregnancy and the baby's imminent birth there would be more.

"Well. It's a theme of my plays, isn't it? 'For mankind, economy is destiny.' "

Norma seemed truly to have repudiated her career. She might have a gift for acting but she hadn't, she said, the temperament or the nerves. After

The Prince and the Showgirl she refused even to think of making another movie. She'd escaped, she said, with her life—"but only just barely."

So she made a joke of the nightmare in England. Slyly and elliptically and without seeming to know, or to allow that she knew, the gravity of what had really happened. *Her stomach pumped. A lethal amount of drugs in her blood. The British doctor querying him, was his wife consciously suicidal.* No, Norma didn't know. And he had not the heart to tell her, or the courage.

He dreaded spoiling her recovery. Her new happiness.

When she'd learned she was pregnant, she'd returned from the doctor's office to seek out her husband (in his study at home, where he worked most days) and whisper the news in his ear. "Daddy, it's happened. It's happened to me at last. *I'm going to have a baby.*" She'd held on to him, weeping. With joy, with relief. He'd been stunned, yet happy for her. Yes, of course he was happy for her. A baby! A third child of his, born in his fiftieth year; at a time in his career when he felt himself stalled, uninspired. . . . But yes of course he was happy. He would never allow his wife to guess that he wasn't as happy as she. For Norma had tried so hard to become pregnant. She'd talked of little else; she'd stared trancelike at babies and small children in the street; almost he'd begun to pity her and to dread her frantic lovemaking. Yet it had turned out well after all, hadn't it? Like a neatly constructed domestic play.

The first two acts, at least.

As wife and mother-to-be, Norma had found her finest role. It was not a Marilyn Monroe glamour-girl role. Yet it was one for which, physically, she seemed fated. She walked about naked boasting that her breasts were growing even larger and harder. She was proud of her stomach swelling "like a melon." Since coming to Maine she laughed spontaneously for no reason except she was happy. She prepared most of their meals at home. She brought fresh-brewed coffee and a single flower in a vase to the Playwright in the late morning where he worked in an upstairs bedroom of the Captain's House overlooking the ocean. She was gracious if oddly shy with his friends when they came to visit; she listened eagerly as women spoke to her of their pregnancy and childbirth experiences, of which they were happy to speak, and at length; the Playwright heard his wife tell one of these women that her own mother had once told her she'd loved being pregnant, it's the only time a woman truly feels at home in her body, and in the world—"Is that true?" The Playwright hadn't lingered to hear the answer; he wondered what such a revelation meant, for a man. *Are we never at home in our bodies? In the world? Except in the act of sexual intercourse, transmitting our seed to the female?*

It was a grim, truncated identity! He didn't believe such lurid sex mysticism for a minute.

Norma was the most devoted mother to a baby yet unborn. She would not allⁿ anyone to smoke in Baby's vicinity. She was always jumping up to en windows or to close windows against a draft. She laughed at herself but could not stop. "Baby makes his wishes known. Norma is just the vessel." Did she believe this? Sometimes fighting nausea she ate six or seven times a day, small but nutritious meals. She chewed her food thoroughly to a pulp. She drank a good deal of milk which, she'd said, she'd always hated. She'd acquired an appetite for oatmeal with raw brown sugar, coarse-ground brown bread, very rare steaks leaking blood, raw eggs, raw carrots, raw oysters, and cantaloupes eaten virtually through their chewy rinds. She devoured mashed potatoes with ice-cold chunks of unsalted butter out of a mixing bowl, with a big spoon. She cleaned her plate at mealtimes, and often his. "Am I your good girl, Daddy?" she asked wistfully. He laughed and kissed her. Recalling with a stab of pleasure that years ago he'd kissed his young daughter to reward her for such accomplishments as cleaned plates.

When his daughter had been two, three years old.

"You're my good girl, darling. My only love."

He liked it less, though he kept his feelings totally to himself, that Norma had acquired from a Christian Science reading room on lower Fifth Avenue in Manhattan a slew of materials including books by Mary Baker Eddy and a publication called *The Sentinel* in which true believers shared testimonies of their prayer-and-healing experiences. As a rationalist, a liberal and a Jew-agnostic, the Playwright felt only contempt for such "religion" and could but hope that Norma took it very lightly, in the way she skimmed the dictionary, encyclopedias, secondhand books, even clothing and seed catalogs as if seeking—what? Some stray wisdom to be put to use for Baby's well-being? He was particularly touched by Norma's long lists of vocabulary words, which often he found about the house in odd places like the bathroom, on the cracked porcelain rim of the old tub, or on top of the refrigerator, or on the top step of the cellar stairs, absurd and even archaic words neatly printed in a schoolgirl hand: *obbligato, obcordate, obdurate, obeisance, obelisk, obelize.* ("I didn't graduate from high school like you and your friends, Daddy! Let alone college. What I'm doing is, I guess—I'm studying for my finals.") She wrote poetry, too, curled up for long dreamy hours in a window seat of the Captain's House, at which he would never glance without her permission.

(Though he wondered what his Norma, his barely literate Magda, could possibly be writing!)

His Norma, his Magda, his bewitching wife. The synthetic Marilyn hair was growing out at the roots; her true hair was a warm honey-brown, and wavy. And those sumptuous big-nippled breasts, enlarged for an infant's nursing. And the fever of her kisses, and her hands in an ecstasy of gratitude caressing him, the male, the father-of-the-baby. Outside his clothes and inside. Running her hands swiftly up inside his shirt, down inside his trousers, as she leaned against him kissing him. "Oh, Daddy. *Oh.*"

She was his geisha. ("I met them in Tokyo once, those geisha girls. They're classy!")

She was his shiksa. (The very word tentative and salacious in her mouth, never quite accurately pronounced—"That's why you love me, I guess? Daddy? 'Cause I'm your blond *shik-sta?*")

He, the husband, the male, was both privileged and overwhelmed. Blessed and frightened. From the first, their first touch, their first unmistakable sexual touch, their first real kiss, he'd felt that there was a superior power in the woman seeking to flow into him. She was his Magda, his inspiration, and yet—so much more!

Like lightning, this power. It could justify his existence as a playwright and as a man, or it could destroy him.

One morning near the end of June, when they'd been living in the Captain's House for three idyllic weeks, the Playwright came downstairs much earlier than usual, at dawn, wakened by a passing thunderstorm that had shaken the house. Yet, within minutes, the worst of the storm seemed to be over; the house's windows were illuminated by a quickly dawning gauzy-ocean light. Norma had already slipped from the four-poster bed. Only her scent remaining on the bedsheets. A strand or two of her hair, glinting. Pregnancy made her drowsy at unpredictable times, she napped like a cat whenever sleep overtook her; but always she woke at dawn, or even earlier, when the first birds began to sing, stirred by Baby into action. "Know what? Baby's hungry. He wants his momma to *eat.*"

The Playwright walked through the downstairs of the old house. Bare feet on bare floorboards. "Darling, where are you?" A man of the city, accustomed to despoiled city air and the incessant city noises of Manhattan, he breathed with satisfaction and a kind of proprietary joy this fresh chilly ocean air. There, the Atlantic Ocean! *His* ocean. He'd been the first person (he believed) to bring Norma within sight of the Atlantic; certainly he'd been the first to travel with her across the Atlantic, to England. Hadn't she whispered to him, how many times in their most intimate embraces, her cheeks damp with tears *Oh, Daddy. Before you I wasn't anyone. I wasn't born!*

Where was Norma now? He paused in the living room, a long narrow space with an unaccountably uneven floor, to stare outside at the breaking sky. How powerful such visions must have seemed to primitive man, as if a god were about to appear, presenting himself to mankind. The sky of dawn, at the ocean's edge. A blaze of spectacular light. Fiery, golden, shading in the northwestern sky into the bruising dark of thunderclouds. But the thunder-clouds were being blown away. The Playwright, staring, wondered if Norma too had been drawn to this sight? He felt a stirring of pride, that he, her husband, could offer her such gifts. She seemed to have no ideas of her own of where to travel. There were no such morning skies in Manhattan. No such morning skies in Rahway, New Jersey, in even the innocence of childhood. Through rain-splashed windowpanes the light of dawn was refracted onto the wallpapered interior of the living room in wisps and curls of flecked fire. As if light were life, living. The single carved mahogany grandfather clock that Norma had managed to rouse into life was calmly ticking, its smooth dully gleaming gold pendulum keeping an unhurried beat. The Captain's House was a snug ship floating on a grassy-green sea, and the Playwright, the man of the city, was himself the Captain. *Bringing my family into safe harbor. At last!* The Playwright in the innocence of male vanity. In the blindness of hope. Feeling in that instant as if he'd penetrated the opaque layers of Time to realize a communion with generations of men who'd lived in this house through the decades, husbands and fathers like himself.

"Norma, darling? Where are you?"

A vague idea she might be in the kitchen, he'd imagined he heard the refrigerator door open and shut, but she wasn't there. Was she outside? He went out onto the screened-in porch where the floor matting, some sort of braided bamboo, was wet; droplets of water gleamed like jewels on the green tubular porch furniture. He could see Norma nowhere in the back lawn and wondered if she'd gone down to the pebbly beach. So early? In this chill, and wind? In the northern sky the thunderous storm clouds had been beaten back. Most of the sky was now a brilliant bronze-gold, cobwebbed with flamey orange. Oh, why was he a "man of letters"—why not an artist, a painter? A photographer? One to pay homage to the beauty of the natural world, not to pick and poke and fuss over human foolishness and frailty. As a liberal, a believer in mankind, why was he always exposing mankind's failings, blaming governments and "capitalism" for the evil in man's soul? But there was no evil in nature, and no ugliness. *Norma is nature. In her, there can be no evil, no ugliness.* "Norma? Come look. The sky . . . !" He returned to the darkened kitchen. Through the kitchen and the laundry room in the direction of the garage, but there before the door to the garage was the cellar door, ajar; and a woman's figure in white just inside in the shadows, seated or crouched on the top step. The cellar light, operated from a switch, was very feeble; if you intended to go into the cellar, you needed a flashlight. But Norma hadn't a flashlight and evidently didn't intend to go down into the cellar. Was she talking to someone there? To herself? She was wearing only her diaphanous white eyelet nightgown, and her hair, dark at the roots, was disheveled. He was about to speak her name another time when he hesitated, not wanting to startle her, and in that instant she turned, her azure eyes widened even as the pupils were dilated, unseeing. He saw that she held in both hands a plate and on the plate there was a chunk of raw hamburger, leaking blood; she'd been eating the hamburger from the plate, like a cat, and licking the blood. She saw him, her staring husband. She laughed.

"Oh, Daddy! You scared me."

Baby was soon to be three months in the womb.

8

She was so excited! Guests soon to arrive.

His friends. His friends from Manhattan who were intellectuals: writers and playwrights, directors, dramaturges, poets, editors. She felt (oh, it was silly she supposed!) that simply being in the vicinity of such superior people couldn't help but have a beneficent effect upon the baby in her womb. Like the solemn recitation of vocabulary words she meant to memorize. Like passages from Chekhov, Dostoyevsky, Darwin, Freud. (In a used-book store in Galapagos Cove, in fact somebody's musty, crazily cluttered cellar, she'd found a paperback copy of Freud's *Civilization and Its Discontents* for sale for fifty cents—"Oh, this is a miracle. Just what I've been looking for.") There was a nourishment of food, and there was a nourishment of the spiritual and the intellectual. Her mother had brought her up in an atmosphere of books, music, superior people if only just Studio employees in relatively low-paying positions, people like Aunt Jess and Uncle Clive, and her own baby would be far better nourished, she would see to that. "I've married a man of genius. Baby is the heir of genius. He'll live into the twenty-first century, with no memory of war."

The Captain's House, on two acres of land above the ocean. It was a true honeymoon house. She knew it could not be, but she fantasized Baby born in this house, in the four-poster bed, delivered (by a midwife?) with as much pain and blood as necessary, and Norma would not scream, not once. She had the uneasy memory (she'd told only Carlo, who'd seemed to believe her, saying yes he'd had the identical experience) of her own mother screaming and screaming in agony at her birth, the physical horror of it, like maddened pythons grappling with one another; she wanted to spare Baby such an experience, and a cruel memory to endure through his life.

Guests soon to arrive for the weekend! Norma Jeane had become so domestic, so thrilled to be domestic; it was no screen role she'd ever played, yet it was the role for which she'd been born. Far more the housewife-hostess than the Playwright's first wife (he'd told her) and she liked it, he was surprised and impressed. Marrying a temperamental actress, what a risk! A blond "sexpot" and "pinup"—what a risk! She meant to make her husband understand she was no risk, and it was deeply gratifying to her, he'd come ·to understand. She knew how his friends had taken him aside to exclaim, "Why, Marilyn is lovely! Marilyn is adorable. And nothing like what anyone might expect." She'd even heard a few of them marvel, "Why, Marilyn is *intelligent*. And *well read*. I've just been talking with her about. . . ." Now some of them knew to call her not Marilyn but Norma. "Why, Norma is remarkably well read! She's read my latest book, in fact."

She loved them, her husband's friends. Rarely did she speak to them unless they spoke to her first and drew her out. She spoke softly, hesitantly, uncertain how to pronounce sometimes the simplest words! Shy and tongue-tied as with stage fright.

Maybe she was a little scared, and tense. And Baby in her womb gripping her tight. *You won't hurt me this time will you. Not do what you did last time?*

She was outside on the lawn. Barefoot, in not very clean sailcloth slacks and one of her husband's shirts tied up snug beneath her breasts, to bare her midriff; her floppy-brimmed straw hat tied also, beneath her chin. She had that eerie ticklish sensation that meant (maybe) someone was watching her. An aerial shot, from the second floor of the Captain's House. From the Playwright's study where he'd placed a desk near a window. *He loves me. He does! He would die for me. He's said so.* She liked it that her husband was watching her but she didn't like it he might be writing about her for she reasoned *For a writer, first you see, and the next thing you write. Like a recluse spider, stinging 'cause it's his nature.* She was cutting flowers to put in vases. She walked diffidently in her bare feet because there were unpredictable things in the tall grass: parts of children's toys, broken bits of plastic and metal. The owners of the Captain's House were good, gracious people, an older couple who lived in Boston and rented out their house, but the previous tenants had been careless, even slovenly, maybe there was malice to it, tossing bones off the screened-in porch onto the lawn below, for barefoot Norma to tread upon and wince.

But she loved this place! The weathered old house like a storybook house high above her, for the lawn steeply slanted. The property that ran to the cliff, and below to the rocky beach. She loved the peace here. You could hear the surf, and you could hear the traffic on the highway out front, but these sounds were muffled, in a way protective. There was no raw silence. There was no glaring-white silence. As in the hospital when she'd awakened in that Kingdom of the Dead thousands of miles away. And a Brit doctor in a white coat, a stranger to her, gazing at her as if she were meat on a slab. He would ask in the calmest voice if she was aware of what had happened to her; if she recalled the number of barbiturates she'd ingested; if she had intended to do grave injury to herself. He would call her Miss Monroe. He would remark that he had "enjoyed certain of her movies."

Mutely she'd shaken her head. *No no no.*

How could she have meant to die! Without having her baby, and her life fulfilled.

Carlo had made her promise, last time they'd spoken on the phone, she'd call *him*, as he would call *her*. If either of them was thinking of taking what Carlo called "the big baby-step into the Unknown."

Carlo! The only man to make her laugh. Since Cass and Eddy G had departed from her life.

(No, Carlo wasn't Norma's lover. Though Hollywood columnists had linked them and run photos of them together twined arm in arm and smiling. *Monroe and Brando: Hollywood's Classiest Couple? or "Just Good Friends"?* They hadn't made love in Norma's bed that night but the omission was only just technical, like forgetting to seal an envelope you've mailed.)

Norma had a hoe from the garage and a badly rusted, cobwebby clipping shears she'd found in the cellar hanging from a hook. Their guests weren't due until early evening. It wasn't yet noon and she had a luxury of time. She'd made a vow when they'd first moved into the Captain's House that she would keep the beds neatly weeded but, damn!—weeds grow *fast*. In her head, rhythmically as she worked, a poem grew sudden and weedlike.

WEEDS OF AMERICA

Weeds of America we dont die
Burdock crabgrass thistle milkweed
If yanked out by the roots we DONT
If poisoned we DONT
If accursed we DONT
Weeds of America know what?
WE ARE AMERICA!

She laughed. Baby would like this poem. The simple silly beat. She'd compose a tune for it on the piano.

Amid the overgrown flower beds were several pale blue hydrangea plants, newly in bloom. Norma Jeane's favorite flower! Vividly she remembered, in the Glazers' back yard, hydrangea in bloom. Pale blue like these, also pink and white. And Mrs. Glazer saying, with that curious solemn emphasis with which we commonly speak as if the very banality of our words were a testament to our authenticity, and a plea that these words endure beyond our frail, failing lives, "Hydrangea is the *nicest flower*, Norma Jeane."

9

Nothing is more dramatic than a ghost.

The Playwright had always wondered what T. S. Eliot meant. He'd always rather resented the remark, for his plays had no ghosts.

He was watching Norma on the back lawn cutting flowers with a shears. His beautiful pregnant wife. A dozen times a day he lost himself in contemplation of her. There was the Norma who spoke to him and there was the Norma at a short distance from him. The one an object of emotion, the other an object of aesthetic admiration. Which of course is a type of emotion, no less intense. *My beautiful pregnant wife.*

She was wearing her wide-brimmed straw hat to protect her sensitive skin from the sun, and slacks, and a shirt of his, but she was barefoot which he didn't like, and she wasn't wearing gardening gloves which he didn't like. Her soft hands were growing calluses! The Playwright wasn't watching Norma deliberately. He'd been gazing out the window at the ocean, and the sky pebbled with clouds of varying degrees of translucence and opacity, and he'd been feeling pleasantly excited about his work, stray scenes and drafts of a new play, or maybe these would feed into the screenplay (never had he attempted a screenplay before) which might one day be a "vehicle" for his wife. And she'd appeared below, in the lawn. With a hoe, a clipping shears. She worked clumsily but methodically. She was thoroughly absorbed in what she did, as she was thoroughly absorbed in her pregnancy; the certainty of her happiness suffused her body like a powerful interior light.

He dreaded something happening to her, and to the baby. He could not bear to think of such a possibility.

How healthy she seemed, like a Renoir woman in the prime of her physical female beauty. But in fact she wasn't strong: she came down easily with infections, respiratory ailments, blinding migraine headaches, and stomach upsets. Nerves! "Except not here, Daddy. I have a good feeling about *here*."

"Yes, darling. So do I."

He watched her, leaning on his elbows. On a stage, each of her clumsy-graceful gestures would signal meaning; offstage, such gestures pass into forgetfulness and oblivion, for there is no audience.

How long could Norma endure the category of *non-actor*? She'd repudiated Hollywood films but there remained the stage, for which she had a natural talent; perhaps a genius. ("Don't make me go back, Daddy," she'd begged, pressing into his arms, naked in his arms in bed, "I never want to be *her* again.") The Playwright had long been fascinated by the strange mercurial personality of the Actor. What is "acting," and why do we respond to "great acting" as we do? We know that an actor is "acting" and yet—we wish to forget that an actor is "acting," and in the presence of talented actors we quickly do forget. This is a mystery, a riddle. How can we forget the actor "acts"? Is the actor "acting" on our behalf? Is the subtext of the actor's "acting" always and forever our own buried (and denied) "acting"? One of Norma's numerous books she'd brought with her from California was *The Actor's Handbook and the Actor's Life* (of which the Playwright had never heard before), and every page of this curious compendium of seemingly anonymous epigraphs and aphorisms had been annotated by her. Clearly, this book was Norma's Bible! The pages were dog-eared, water-splattered, falling out. The publication date was 1948, an unknown press in Los Angeles. Someone who called himself "Cass" had given it to her—*To Beautiful Gemini-Norma with Starry Undying Love*. On the title page Norma had copied an aphorism, now in faded ink.

The actor is happiest only in his sacred space: the stage.

Was this true? Was it true for Norma? It was a bitter revelation to any lover, if true. A bitter disclosure for any husband.

"But the truth of an actor is the truth of only a fleeting moment. The truth of an actor is 'dialogue.' "

This, the Playwright felt more certainly, was true.

Norma had finished cutting flowers and was headed back to the house. He wondered if she would glance up and acknowledge him and there was a fraction of a second when he might have drawn back out of sight but, yes, she glanced up and waved to him; and he waved back, smiling.

"My darling."

Strange how it had passed through his mind, that remark of T. S. Eliot. *Nothing is more dramatic than a ghost.*

"No ghosts in *our* lives."

The Playwright had been wondering, since England, what Norma's future would be. She'd repudiated acting and yet: how long could she remain, not-acting? A housewife and soon a mother, with no career? She was too talented to be content with private life, he knew. He was certain. Yet, he conceded, she couldn't return to "Marilyn Monroe"; one day, "Marilyn" would kill her.

Still, he was writing a screenplay. For her.

And they needed money. Or would, soon.

He went downstairs, to help her in the kitchen. There was Norma breathless with her bouquet, a light film of perspiration on her face. She'd picked pale blue hydrangea and a few stems of red climber roses, their leaves stippled with a black fungus. "Look, Daddy! Look what I have."

Friends of his were coming from Manhattan to visit. Drinks on the screened-in porch, dinner afterward at the Whaler's Inn. The Playwright's shy, gracious wife would have placed vases of flowers through the house, including the guest bedroom.

"Flowers make people feel *welcome*. Like they're *wanted*."

He was filling vases with water and Norma was beginning to arrange the flowers, except something was wrong, the hydrangeas kept falling out of the vases. "Darling, you've cut the stems a little too short. See?" It wasn't a reprimand, certainly not a criticism, but Norma was deflated at once. Her happy mood was crushed.

"Oh, what did I. . . . What?"

"Look. We can repair the damage, like this."

Damn! He shouldn't have used the word "damage." This crushed her further, she shrank back like a struck child.

The Playwright arranged the hydrangea blossoms in shallow bowls, flower heads floating. (The blossoms were past their peak. They wouldn't survive for more than a day. But Norma hadn't seemed to notice.) The awkwardly cut red climber roses, their stippled leaves trimmed, were then woven through the hydrangeas.

"Darling, this is just as beautiful, I think. It has a kind of Japanese effect."

From a few yards away Norma had been watching him, her husband's deft hands, in silence. She was stroking her belly, her lower lip caught in her teeth. She was panting and hadn't seemed to hear the Playwright's words. Finally she said, doubtfully, "It's all right to do it, like that? Flowers like that? So short? Nobody will l-laugh at that?"

The Playwright turned to look at her. "Laugh? Why would anybody laugh?"

His expression was incredulous. Laugh at *me*?

IO

He would seek her out in the kitchen alcove where she was hiding.

If not the kitchen, the garage.

If not the garage, the top of the cellar steps.

(What a dank, smelly place to hide! Though Norma wouldn't admit to hiding.)

"Darling, aren't you going to come sit with us? On the porch? Why are you here?"

"Oh, I'm coming, Daddy! I was just . . ."

Greeting their guests and hurrying away almost immediately to leave him with his friends, shy as a feral cat. Was this a form of stage fright?

He wouldn't chide *Norma, don't give them fuel to talk about us!*

Meaning *To talk about you.*

No, he was warm, sympathetic, husbandly, smiling. Making of the famous shyness of Marilyn Monroe a gentle domestic joke. He found her in the kitchen alcove absorbed in the task of flattening grocery bags. Their visitors were exploring the house, stepping out onto the screened-in porch. The Playwright kissed his wife's forehead, to calm her. A faint chemical odor lifted from her hair when she perspired though she hadn't bleached her hair in months.

Careful to speak gently. Not critically. He saw their dialogue before him as if he'd written it himself.

"Darling, it isn't necessary to make so much of this visit. You seem so anxious. You know Rudy and Jean, you've said you like them—"

"They don't like me, Daddy. They've come to see you."

"Norma, don't be ridiculous. They've come to see us both."

(No: he must keep all incredulity from his voice. He must speak to this childlike woman as long ago he'd spoken to his very young, very vulnerable children who adored yet feared their daddy.)

"Oh, I don't blame them! I don't blame *them*. See, you're their friend."

"Of course I've known them longer than you've known them, half my life in fact. But—"

She laughed, shaking her head and holding up her hands, palms outward. It was a gesture of both appeal and surrender. "Oh, but—why would these people, these smart friends of yours, he's a writer and she's an editor, why would they want to see *me*?"

"Darling, just come, will you? They're waiting."

Again she shook her head, laughing. She was watching him sidelong. How like a frightened cat, frightened for no reason, about to bolt, and dangerous. But the Playwright refused to confirm her absurd suspicions and pleaded with her quietly, gently, drawing a thumb across her forehead, stooping to lock his gaze with hers in that way that sometimes worked upon her like a kind of hypnosis. "Darling, just come out with me, eh? You're looking very very beautiful."

She was a beautiful woman frightened of her own beauty. She seemed to resent it, that her beauty might be confused with "her." Yet, he'd never known any woman so anxious, when meeting strangers, about her appearance.

Norma had been listening and considering. At last she shivered, and laughed, and rubbed her sticky forehead against his chin, and took from the refrigerator a large heavy platter of raw vegetables geometrically arranged by color and a sour cream dip she'd prepared. It was a spectacular platter and he told her so. He carried drinks on a tray. Suddenly, it was all right again! It was going to be fine. As on the set of *Bus Stop* he'd seen her panic and freeze and back off, and yet after a while she'd return, and there was Cherie more intense, more alive, more flamelike and convincing than ever. Their friends Rudy and Jean, admiring the view of the ocean, turned now to see the handsome couple approach. The Playwright and the Blond Actress. The woman who wished to be known as "Norma" was radiantly beautiful (no avoiding this cliché, as both Rudy and Jean would report) with the fresh, creamy-translucent complexion of early pregnancy; her hair was a darker blond, shimmering and wavy; she was wearing a floral print sundress with splashy orange poppies that flared at the hips and was cut low to reveal the tops of her swelling breasts; she wore spike-heeled open-toed white pumps and she smiled at them as if dazed by flashbulbs, and in that instant she stumbled on the single but fairly steep step down onto the porch and the platter slipped from her hands and crashed to the floor, vegetables, dip, and broken crockery flying.

I I

You made of the smallest issues a test of my loyalty. Our love.
    Smallest issues! You mean my life.
    And your life too became an issue. Blackmail.
    You never defended me, mister. Never against any of those bastards.
    It wasn't clear who needed defending. Always you?
    They despised me! Your so-called friends.
    No. It was you who despised yourself.

I 2

Yet she adored his elderly parents.
    And to his surprise, his elderly parents adored her.
    At their first meeting, in Manhattan, the Playwright's mother, Miriam, took him aside to squeeze his wrist and murmur in his ear, in triumph, "That girl is just like me at her age. So *hopeful*."
    That girl! Marilyn Monroe!
    It would turn out, to the Playwright's surprise and belated chagrin, that

neither of his parents had ever felt "warm" toward his first wife, Esther. More than two decades of poor Esther, who'd given them grandchildren they adored. Esther, who was Jewish and of a background very like their own. While Norma—"Marilyn Monroe"—was the quintessential blond shiksa.

But the year of their meeting was 1956, not 1926. Much had changed in Jewish culture, and in the world, in the intervening years.

The Playwright had noticed, as Max Pearlman had pointed out, how women often took warmly to Norma, quite in reverse of expectations. You would anticipate jealousy, envy, dislike; instead, women felt a curious kinship with Norma, or "Marilyn"; could it be, women looked at her and somehow saw themselves? An idealized form of themselves? A man might smile at such a misapprehension. A delusion, or a confusion. But what can a man know? If anyone resisted Norma, it was likely to be a certain kind of man; one sexually attracted to her, yet wise enough to know she would rebuff him. What strategies of irony bred out of threatened male pride, the Playwright well knew.

Wasn't it true, if the Blond Actress hadn't been so clearly attracted to him, the Playwright might have spoken dismissively of her?

Not bad for a film actress. But too weak for the stage.

So it happened that the Playwright's mother adored the Playwright's second wife. For there was shyly smiling Norma, a girl seemingly young enough, and younger-enough looking, to stir in the seventy-five-year-old woman nostalgic memories of her own bygone youth. The Playwright heard his mother confide in Norma that, at Norma's age, she'd had hair just like Norma's—"That shade exactly, and wavy." He heard her confide in Norma that her first pregnancy, too, had made her feel "like a queen. Oh, for once!"

Norma never worried that her in-laws, who weren't intellectuals, might laugh at her.

In the kitchen in Manhattan, and at the Captain's House. Miriam chattering away, and Norma murmuring agreement. Miriam instructed Norma in preparing chicken soup with matzoh balls and in preparing chopped liver with onions. The Playwright had no great craving for bagels and lox, but these "favorites" of his turned up frequently at Sunday brunch. And borscht.

Miriam made borscht with beets, but sometimes with cabbage.

Miriam prepared her own beef stock. She would claim it was "just as easy" as opening a dozen cans of Campbell's.

Miriam served borscht hot or chilled. Depending on the season.

Miriam had an "emergency borscht" recipe using Berber's canned sieved beets for infants. "Not much sugar. Lemon juice. And vinegar. Who's to know?"

Their borscht was delicious as any borscht in memory.

13

The Ocean

I broke a mirror
& the pieces
floated to China.

Goodbye!

14

There came the terrible July evening when Norma returned from a trip into town and he, her husband, saw Rose in her place.

Rose, the adulterous wife of *Niagara*.

He was only imagining it of course!

She'd taken the station wagon to drive to Galapagos Cove, unless it was to Brunswick. She was going to buy groceries, fresh fruit, or items from the drugstore. Vitamins. Cod-liver oil capsules. To strengthen her white blood cells, he'd thought she said. She talked frequently of her condition; in a sense, it was her only subject. *A baby growing in the womb. Preparing to be born. What happiness!* There was a Brunswick obstetrician she'd begun seeing every other week, a professional acquaintance of her Manhattan obstetrician. Or maybe she'd gone to have her hair "done," or her nails. Rarely did she shop for clothes (in Manhattan, she was always being recognized and would then flee the store), but now that she was pregnant and beginning to show, she spoke wistfully of needing new things. Maternity smocks, dresses. "I'm afraid you won't love me, Daddy, if I don't look nice? Or will you?" She'd driven away after preparing lunch for him and hadn't returned by 3 P.M.

The Playwright, lost in his writing, in a trance of inspiration (he who rarely managed to write more than a page of dialogue a day, and that provisional, crabbed, and grudging) had scarcely noticed his wife's absence until the phone rang.

"Daddy? I know I'm l-late. I'm on my way home, though." She was breathless and contrite and apologetic. He said, "Dearest, don't hurry. I was a little concerned, of course. But drive carefully." The coastal highway was narrow and curving and sometimes even in daylight swaths of fog drifted languidly across it.

If Norma had an accident, at such a time!

She was a cautious driver, so far as the Playwright knew. Behind the wheel of the old Plymouth station wagon (which seemed to her big and unwieldy as a bus) she hunched forward, frowning and biting her lower lip. She tended to apply the brakes too quickly, and jarringly. She tended to overreact to the presence of other vehicles. She had a habit of stopping for traffic lights well out of the intersection, as if she feared hitting the pedestrians even when her car was stationary. But she never drove more than forty miles an hour even on the open highway, unlike the Playwright, who drove much faster, and absentmindedly, with a certain New York masculine swagger, talking as he drove, sometimes lifting both hands from the steering wheel as he gestured. It was his belief that Norma was far more to be trusted behind the wheel than he!

But now he'd begun consciously to wait for her. Impossible for him to return to work. He would wait for another two hours and twenty minutes.

The drive from Galapagos Cove to the Captain's House took no more than ten minutes. But had Norma called from Brunswick? In his confusion he couldn't recall.

Several times he imagined he could hear her turning up the steep graveled drive to the house. Driving into the garage in that cautious way of hers. The crunching of the gravel. The slam of the car door. Her footsteps. Her whispery voice lifting through the floorboards—"Daddy? I'm back."

Unable to resist, he hurried downstairs to check the garage. Of course, the Plymouth wasn't there.

On his way back he passed the cellar door, which was ajar. He slammed it shut. Why was that damned door always open? The latch caught securely, it must have been that Norma left it open. Up from the dirt-floored cellar lifted a rich, sickish odor of decay; of earth, rot, and Time. He shuddered, smelling.

Norma said she hated the cellar—"It's so *nasty*." It was the one thing about the Captain's House she disliked. Yet the Playwright had the idea she'd explored the cellar, with a flashlight, like a willful child determined to seek out the very things that frighten her. But Norma was a woman of thirty-two, hardly a child. To what purpose, scaring herself? And in her condition.

He could never forgive her, he was thinking. If she brought harm to their happiness.

At last, after 6 P.M., the phone again rang. He fumbled to lift the receiver at once. That faint breathy voice. "Ohhh, Daddy. You're m-mad at me?"

"Norma, what is it? Where are you?"

He couldn't keep the fear out of his voice.

"I got kinda stuck with these people . . . ?"

"What people? Where?"

"Oh, I'm not in any trouble, Daddy. Just I got kind of—What?" Some-one was speaking to her and she answered, holding her palm over the receiver. The Playwright, trembling, heard raised voices in the background. And loud thumping rock-and-roll music. Norma came back onto the line, laughing. "Ohhhh, it's wild here. But these are real nice people, Daddy. They kinda speak *French*. There's these two girls? Sisters? Identical *twins*."

"Norma, what? I can't hear you. Twins?"

"But I'm on my way home *now*. I'm gonna make us a supper. I promise!"

"Norma—"

"Daddy, you love me, huh? You're not mad at me?"

"Norma for God's sake—"

At last, at 6:40 P.M., Norma drove the station wagon up into the drive. Waving at him through the windshield.

He was waiting for her and his face was taut with waiting. It would seem to him that he'd been waiting a full day. Yet much of the sky was still bright, summery. Only at the eastern horizon, at the ocean's distant edge, dusk had begun like a dark stain rising into thick wedges of cloud.

There came Norma hurrying. This was The Girl Upstairs. Unless it was Rose masquerading as The Girl Upstairs.

In her wide-brimmed straw hat that tied demurely beneath the chin. In a maternity blouse embossed with pink rosebuds, and a pair of somewhat soiled white shorts. She slung her arms around the Playwright's stiffened neck and kissed him wet and hard on the mouth. "Oh, gosh, Daddy. Am I *sorry*."

He tasted something ripe and sweet. There were stains at the corners of her mouth. Had she been drinking?

She was fumbling for grocery bags in the rear of the Plymouth and the Playwright took them from her without a word. His heart beat in fury that was in fact the aftermath of dread. If something had happened to Norma! And their baby! She'd become the center of his life without his realizing.

How he'd been bemused, pitying. Having heard tales of Norma's previous husband. The Ex-Athlete hiring private detectives to spy on her.

Now she was home and unharmed and laughing and apologetic. Watching him, her frowning husband, sidelong. Telling him a lengthy disjointed story he could not be expected to unravel of having picked up girl hitchhikers out on the highway and driving them into Galapagos Cove where they were headed, and from there to somebody's house and they'd talked her into staying for a while. "See, they all knew who I am, they called me 'Marilyn,' but I kept saying 'No, no, I'm not her, I'm Norma'—it was like a game, I mean we were laughing a lot—like my girlfriends back in Van Nuys, in high school, I miss." These twin sisters were "real pretty" and lived with their divorced mother in a "sad, ratty old trailer" in the country and one of the girls, Janice, had a three-month baby named Cody—"the father, he's in the merchant marine and wouldn't marry her, just *sailed off* into the blue." Norma spent some time at the trailer and then they all went somewhere else in the station wagon and then—"Daddy, know what? We ended up at that big Safeway store, you know? All of us including the baby. 'Cause they needed so many things just to *eat*. I spent every penny." She was apologetic, telling this story; yet she was defiant. She was a contrite little girl, yet she wasn't contrite in the slightest, she was in fact proud of her little escapade. Not saying *It's Marilyn's money, Daddy. I'm gonna do with it what I want.*

Sighing, as if in wonder. "Every last penny in my *wallet*. Gosh!"

The Playwright was being made to think how deeply and helplessly he loved this woman. This strange, mercurial woman. Now she was pregnant with his child. And he had not truly wanted another child. In Manhattan, at the New York Ensemble and in theater circles, he'd seemed to know her; now, he wasn't so sure. At the start of their love affair she'd seemed to love him more than he'd been prepared to love her; now, they loved each other equally, with a terrible hunger. But never until today had the Playwright considered there might be a time when he loved Norma more than she loved him. How could he bear it!

Putting things away in the kitchen, Norma was watching him sidelong. In a play, as in a film, such a scene would contain a powerful subtext. But life rarely conformed to art, especially the forms and conventions of art. Though Norma painfully reminded him of Rose in *Niagara*, leading her besotted husband Joseph Cotten by the nose. (Or by another part of his male anatomy.)

Norma told her story, her soft breathy voice quavering with excitement. Was she lying? He didn't think so. It was such an innocent, guileless story. Yet her excitement was such, she might as well be lying. It would be an identical thrill. *She's been unfaithful to me. She's gone outside the marriage.* He saw with a stab of horror that her white shorts were stained, smears of what might be menstrual blood, oh, God, did that mean a miscarriage was beginning?—and Norma didn't seem to know?—except, seeing his face, she looked down at herself and laughed, embarrassed. "Oh, gosh! We were eating raspberries. We all made pigs of ourselves, I guess." Still the Playwright was stricken. His lean face, tanned from summer, had gone ashen. His thick-lensed glasses slipped on his nose. Norma had removed a quart of raspberries from a bag and now gave some of the berries to the Playwright to eat, lifting them to his mouth. "Oh, Daddy, don't look so sad, just *taste*. They're delicious, see?"

It was true. The raspberries were delicious.

15

It wasn't enough to underline these prophetic words in *Civilization and Its Discontents*. Norma was compelled to copy them into her notebook.

We are never so defenseless against suffering as when we love, never so helplessly unhappy as when we have lost our loved object or its love.

16

THE KINGDOM BY THE SEA

There was once a Beggar Maid
In a Kingdom by the Sea.
A spell was cast over her—
"The Fair Princess must you be."

Oh but the Beggar Maid cried,
"This is a cruel curse."
The wicked godmother laughed,
"Yet things will get worse."

A Prince spied the Princess
A-walking in the glen.
He said to her, "Are you lonely?
Are you needful of a friend?"

The Prince courted the Princess
Through many a night and a day.
The Princess loved the Prince
And yet—what could she say?

"I am not a Fair Princess,
I am but a Beggar Maid.
Would you love me if you knew?"
The Prince smiled at her, and said . . .

Curled up in a window box in Baby's Room at the top of the stairs, dreamy, so happy, wiping tears from her eyes, and the vast cavernous sky looming above her and the dirt-floored cellar so far below she could hear nothing of its murmurous muffled speech, Norma Jeane tried, and tried, so hard!—but was never to complete the rhyme.

17

Baby's Room. She knew of course that the baby would be born in Manhattan. In Columbia Presbyterian Hospital. If all went as scheduled. (December 4 was the magical date!) Still, here in the Captain's House in Galapagos Cove, Maine, so much solitude and such dreamy happiness through the summer, she'd created a fantasy nursery into which she placed items purchased in local antique shops and roadside flea markets. A wicker rocking cradle for Baby, creamy-white and decorated with blue morning glories. (Wasn't it nearly identical to Gladys's cradle for *her*?) Little stuffed toys, hand-sewn. A "genuine American Shaker" baby's rattle. Old children's books, fairy tales, Mother Goose, talking animals, in which she could lose herself for long entranced hours. *Once upon a time* . . .

In Baby's Room, Norma Jeane curled up in the window box and dreamt her life. *He will write beautiful plays. For me to act in. I will mature into these roles. I will be respected. When I die, nobody will laugh.*

18

Sometimes there came a knock at the door. She had no choice but to invite him in. Already he'd have opened the door and stuck his head inside. Smiling. *In his eyes such love! My husband.*

In Baby's Room she wrote in her schoolgirl journal that was her secret life. Jottings to herself, poem fragments. Vocabulary lists. In Baby's Room, Norma Jeane curled up in the window box, reading Mary Baker Eddy's *Science and Health* and the fascinating (if true!) testimonies of *The Sentinel*; reading books she'd brought to Maine from Manhattan, though knowing the Playwright didn't always approve of these books.

The Playwright believed that a mind like Norma's ("susceptible, sensitive, easily influenced") was like a well. Precious, pure water. You don't want to contaminate it with toxic elements. Never!

The knock at the door, and already he'd have opened it, smiling at her but his smile faded when he saw (she didn't dare try to hide it from him) what she was reading.

One afternoon, *The Shame of Europe: A History of the Jews of Europe.*

(At least it wasn't one of Norma's Christian Science publications, which her husband truly abhorred!)

The Playwright's response to such books, her "Jewish" books, was complex. His face would twitch in a reflexive smile, almost a smile of fear. Certainly a smile of annoyance. Or hurt. It was as if unwittingly (oh, she didn't mean this! she was *so sorry*) she'd kicked him in the belly. He would come to her and kneel beside her and leaf through the book, pausing at certain of the photographs. Her heart beat quickly. She saw in the faces of the photographed dead the features of her own living husband; even, at times, his quizzical expression. Whatever emotions this man was feeling, which were beyond her ability to imagine (if she were a Jew, what would she feel at such a time? she believed she could not have borne it), he would hide from her. True, his voice might quaver. His hand might shake. But he'd speak to her calmly in the tone of a man who loved her and only wished her, and their baby, well. He would say, "Norma, do you think it's a good thing, in your condition, to upset yourself with these horrors?"

She would protest, faintly. "Oh, but I w-want to know, Daddy. Is that wrong?"

He would say, kissing her, "Darling, of course it isn't wrong to want to 'know.' But you already know. You know about the Holocaust, and you know about the history of pogroms, and you know about the blood-drenched soil of 'civilized' Christian Europe. You know about Nazi Germany and you even know how indifferent Britain and the U.S. were about saving the Jews. You know generally, if not in exhaustive detail. You already know, Norma."

Was this true? It was true.

The Playwright was the master of words. When he entered a room, words flew to him like iron filings to a magnet. Norma Jeane, faltering and stammering, hadn't a chance.

He might speak then of "horror pornography."

He might speak of "wallowing in suffering"—"wallowing in grief."

Cruelly he might speak of "wallowing in others' grief."

Oh, but I'm a Jew too. Can't I be a Jew? Is it only how you're born? In your soul?

She listened. She listened gravely. Never did she interrupt. If this were acting class she'd hold the offensive book against her breasts and her quickened heart, it wasn't acting class but she might hold the offensive book against her breasts and her quickened heart; better yet she might shut the book and push it from her across the worn plush cushion of the window seat. At such times contrite and humbled and hurt but not wounded for she knew she had no legitimate right to be wounded. *No, I'm not a Jew. I guess.*

It was only that her husband loved her. More than love, he adored her. But he feared for her, too. He was becoming possessive of her emotions. Her "sensitive" nerves. (Remember what "almost happened" in England?) He was her elder by eighteen years, of course it was his duty to protect her. At such times he was touched by the magnitude of his own feeling. He saw tears glistening in her beautiful slate-blue eyes. Her quivering lips. Even at this intimate moment he would recall how the director of *Bus Stop* who'd been in love with her had marveled at Marilyn Monroe's ability to cry spontaneously. *Monroe never asked for glycerine. The tears were always there.*

Swiftly now the scene became an improvisation.

She was saying, stammering, "But, Daddy—if nobody does? I mean, now? Shouldn't I have to?"

"Have to—what?"

"Know about it? Think about it? Like, on such a beautiful summer day? Up here, by the ocean? People like us? Shouldn't I l-look at the pictures, at least?"

"Don't be ridiculous, Norma. You don't 'have' to do anything."

"What I mean is, there should always be somebody seeing these things, see what I mean? Somewhere in the world. Every minute. Because what if— they're forgotten?"

"Darling, the Holocaust isn't likely to be forgotten. It isn't your responsibility to remember it."

He laughed, harshly. His face was heating.

"Oh, I know! That sounds so vain. I mean"—she was apologizing, and yet not apologizing—"I guess I mean—what Freud said? 'No one who shares a delusion ever recognizes it as such'? So you could have a delusion that other people were doing what you need to do, so you didn't need to do it? Right at that time? See what I mean?"

"No. I don't see what you mean. You're wallowing in others' grief, frankly."

"That's what it is?"

"There's an element of the ghoulish in this, darling. I know plenty of Jews who wallow in it, believe me. The rotten luck of history given a cosmological spin. Bullshit! But I didn't marry a ghoul." More excited than he knew, the Playwright suddenly smiled horribly. "I didn't marry a ghoul, I married a *girl*."

Norma laughed. "A girl not a ghoul."

"A pretty girl, not a ghoul."

"Ohhh—can't a ghoul be pretty, too?"

"No. A ghoul can't be pretty. Only a girl."

"Only a girl. Okay!"

Lifting her face to be kissed. Her perfect mouth.

Improvising, you don't know where you're headed. But sometimes it's good.

"He doesn't love me. It's some blond thing in his head, he loves. Not *me*."

19

In fact she crept away like a kicked dog. And Baby in her womb, shrunken in shame to the size of a thumb.

Afterward, always they made up. Hours later, in their four-poster bed in the night. The comically hard horsehair mattress, the creaking bed springs. These were exquisite times which the Playwright would recall throughout his life, stunned by the power of physical love, sexual pleasure, to reverberate through time long after the individuals who generated such love out of their yearning, anguished bodies have died.

She would be Rose for him, if it was Rose he wished.

Oh, she was his wife, she would be anyone! For him.

She kissed, kissed, kissed his breath away. She sucked his tongue into her mouth. Ran her hands over his body, his lean angular body beginning to go slack at the waist and belly, boldly she kissed his chest, the fuzzy hairs of his chest, kissed and sucked his nipples, laughed and tickled and stroked him hard. Her deft hands. Practiced (it excited him to think this, whether it was true or not) as a concert pianist running his fingers over the keyboard, playing scales. She was Rose of *Niagara*. The adulterous wife, the murderous wife. The blond woman of surpassing beauty and sexual allure he'd gazed upon years ago, long before even the possibility of knowing her. And what a fantasy, to imagine he might know *her*! When he'd identified with the betrayed, impotent husband Joseph Cotten. Even at the end of the movie he'd identified with Cotten. When Cotten strangles Rose. An eerie dreamlike scene, of mute strangulation. A ballet of death. The expression on Monroe's perfect face when she realizes. *She is going to die! Her husband is Death!* The Playwright, staring up at the flickering screen images in silence, had been moved as never before by any film. (He tended to speak dismissively of film as a medium.) Never had he seen any woman like Rose. He'd seen the movie alone in a Times Square theater and he believed that there could be no man in the audience who felt otherwise than he felt. *No man is equal to her. She has to die.*

In their bed in their summer house above the ocean at Galapagos Cove she lay upon him, his wife, his pregnant wife, and fitted herself to him. Her sweet baby breath. Her sweet sharp strangulated cries—"Oh, Daddy! Oh, God!"—he would not know whether feigned or genuine. Never would he know.

20

He pushed open the bathroom door not knowing she was inside.

Her hair in a towel, naked and flat-footed, stomach bulging, she turned to him startled. "Oh! Hey." In the palm of one hand several pills, and in her other hand a plastic cup. She popped the pills into her mouth quickly and drank and he said, "Darling, I thought you weren't taking anything? Any more?" and she said, meeting his eyes in the mirror, "These are vitamins, Daddy. And cod-liver oil capsules."

21

The phone rang. Few had their number here in Galapagos Cove, and the sound of the ringing telephone was jarring.

Norma answered. Her stricken face. Wordless, she handed the receiver to the Playwright and walked quickly out of the room.

It was Holyrod, the Hollywood agent. Apologizing for calling. He knew, he said, that Marilyn was not considering films at the present time. But this was a special project! Titled *Some Like It Hot*, a madcap comedy about men disguised as women with the lead role expressly written for "Marilyn Monroe." The Studio was eager to finance the project and would pay Marilyn a minimum of $100,000—

"Thank you. But we've told you: my wife isn't interested in Hollywood at the present time. She's expecting our first baby in December."

What pleasure in these words! The Playwright smiled.

Our first baby. Ours!

What pleasure, though they would soon be in need of money.

22

DESIRE

Because you desire me
I am not

This, Norma shyly showed to her husband for he'd often said he would like to see her poetry.

He read this little poem and reread it and smiled in perplexity having expected something very different from her. Something that rhymed, surely! Now, what to say? He wanted to encourage her; he knew how abnormally sensitive she was, how easily her feelings were bruised. "Darling, this is a strong, dramatic beginning. It's very . . . promising. But where does it go from here?"

Quickly Norma nodded as if she'd been anticipating such criticism. No, it wasn't criticism of course, it was encouragement. She took the poem back from him and folded it up into a small square and said, laughing in the manner of The Girl Upstairs, " 'Where does it go from here?' Oh, Daddy. You're so right. The riddle of all our lives, I guess!"

23

In the near distance, beneath the floorboards of the old house, a faint plaintive sound like mewing, whimpering. Crying *Help! Help me.*

"There's nothing there. And I don't hear anything. I know."

24

It was late July, late one afternoon. A male friend of the Playwright had come up from the city and the two were out together fishing for bluefish. Norma was alone in the Captain's House. *Alone with Baby: just us.* She was in good spirits, she'd never felt healthier. She had not gone into the cellar, nor even glanced down the stairs, for days. *Nothing there. I know!* "It's just that, where I come from, there aren't cellars? No need."

She was in the habit, alone in the house, of speaking aloud.

It was Baby she addressed. Her closest friend!

That was what Nell the babysitter had lacked, in her own being: a baby. "Why she'd wanted to push that little girl out a window. If she'd had a baby of her own . . ." (But what had happened to Nell? She'd failed to slash her throat. They'd led her away to confinement. Without a struggle she'd surrendered.)

Late July, late one afternoon. A mild muggy day. Airless. Norma Jeane entered the Playwright's study feeling a tremor of excitement like one trespassing. Yet the Playwright wouldn't mind if she used his typewriter. Why would he mind? This was not an improvised scene exactly for she'd planned it. She intended to type out a letter to send to Gladys in Lakewood, making a carbon copy. That morning she'd awakened with a jolt realizing that Gladys must miss her! She'd been away, in the East, so long. She would invite Gladys to come visit them here in Galapagos Cove! For she was certain that Gladys was recovered enough now to travel, if she wished; this was the view of her mother she'd presented to the Playwright, and it was a view she thought reasonable. The Playwright had said how interesting Gladys sounded, how he'd like to meet her. Norma Jeane would write two letters, making carbon copies of both. One to Gladys and one to the director of the Lakewood Home.

Of course, she would tell only Gladys that she was expecting a baby in December.

"At last, you'll be a grandmother. Oh, *I* can't wait!"

Norma Jeane sat at the Playwright's desk. The camera would hover close about her, peering down. She loved her husband's old faithful Olivetti with its frayed ribbon. Papers strewn across his desk *so real* like the scattered thoughts of genius. Maybe these were notes, sketches? Fragments of dialogue? The Playwright rarely spoke of his work-in-progress. Superstitious probably. But Norma Jeane knew he was experimenting with two or three projects at the same time, including his very first screenplay. (*She'd* been able to do this for him, she was so pleased and so proud.) Searching for a clean sheet of paper when her eye involuntarily skimmed—

X.: Know what, Daddy? I want Baby to be born here. In this house.

Y.: But darling, we've planned—

X.: We could get a midwife for me! I'm serious.

(X., excited & eyes dilated; holds her belly with both hands as if it is already swollen)
On another page, with numerous corrections—

X. (angrily): You didn't defend me! Not ever.

Y.: It wasn't clear who was in the wrong.

X.: He despised me!

Y.: No. It was you who despised yourself.

Y.: No. It is you who despise yourself.

(X. can't bear it that any man might look upon her without desire.
She is 32 yrs old & fears her youth is passing)

25

Where do you go when you disappear? She'd been hearing that sound in the cellar. She told him with averted eyes, knowing he did not believe her, did not wish to believe her. He touched her to comfort her and she stiffened. "Norma, what?" She could not speak. He went away to investigate the cellar, using the flashlight, but found nothing. Still, she heard the sound. A faint plaintive mewing, whimpering. Sometimes a scuffling sound. A sound of clawing, agitation. She recalled (had this been a dream? a movie scene?) a baby's single scream. Early in the mornings and during the day when she was alone downstairs and often in the middle of the otherwise quiet night when she woke in a sweat with a sudden acute need to use the bathroom. She thought it might be a stray cat or a raccoon—"something trapped down there. Starving." It filled her with horror to imagine that a living creature might be trapped in that hideous cellar as in a pit. The Playwright saw that she was truly agitated, and he meant to placate her fear. He didn't want her poking around in the cellar herself, in that depressing dark. "I forbid you to go down there, darling!" He'd discovered that joking with his wife was the shrewdest strategy: in this way he co-opted her commonsense Norma-self against her irrational Marilyn-self. Holding his nose against the smell (more than rotted apples it had now a meaty-rancid stench mixed with smells of earth and Time), he descended again into the cellar and probed the flashlight beam into all the corners and returned to her panting and irritable (for it was an unfairly hot, humid day, for the Maine coast) and wiping cobwebs from his face but gentle with Norma insisting no, there wasn't anything down there, nothing he'd been able to discover; nor had he heard the sounds she claimed to hear. Norma seemed placated by this report. She seemed relieved. She lifted his hand impulsively to her mouth and kissed it, embarrassing him. His hand wasn't clean!

"Oh, Daddy. Guess you have to humor a pregnant woman, huh?"

In fact Norma had been feeding feral cats in the back yard since the second week they'd moved here. Against the Playwright's better judgment. At first just one cat, a skinny black tom with bitten ears; then another joined the tom, a skinny but very pregnant calico; soon there were as many as a half dozen cats waiting patiently at the back door to be fed. The cats were strangely silent and crouched separate from one another; they kept their distance as Norma set down their dishes, then hurried in to eat, swift as little machines, and as soon as they finished eating they trotted away without a backward glance. At first Norma had tried to befriend them, even to pet them, but they hissed at her and shrank away, baring their teeth. Since there was an outdoor entrance to the cellar it wasn't unreasonable to think that one of the cats might have gotten inside and become trapped. If so, the creature hid itself from the Playwright, who'd come to rescue it.

"Darling, maybe you should stop feeding those cats," the Playwright suggested.

"Oh, I will! Soon."

"More and more of them will be showing up. You can't feed the entire Maine coast."

"Daddy, I know. You're right."

Yet she continued, through the summer, as he'd known she would. How many scrawny, starving cats showed up each morning to be fed by her, he didn't want to know. *Her strange stubbornness. Her powerful will. The man knew himself obliterated by her, in essential things. Only in surface matters was he triumphant.*

He was upstairs at his desk writing these words or words very like these when he heard a cry. "I knew. I knew what it would be."

He ran downstairs to find her lying at the bottom of the cellar steps, moaning and writhing. The flashlight, fallen from her hand, casting its tunnel-like beam into the cellar's depths as into an oblivion of unshaped, undefined shadow.

She screamed for him to help her, to save the baby. As he stooped over her she clawed at his hands, pulling at his hands. As if wanting him to deliver the baby.

He called an ambulance. She was taken to the Brunswick hospital.

A miscarriage in the fifteenth week of pregnancy.

The date was August 1.

THE FAREWELL

We began to die then, didn't we? You blamed me.
  Never. Not you.
  Because I failed to save you and the baby.
  Not you.
  Because I wasn't the one to suffer. To bleed out my guts.
  Not you. It was me. All that I deserved. I killed Baby once, Baby was already dead.

She, the stricken woman, was hospitalized for a week. She'd hemorrhaged severely and had nearly died in the emergency room. Her skin was a lusterless waxy-white, there were deep circles beneath her eyes, bruises and lacerations on her face, throat, upper arms. She'd sprained a wrist in her fall. She'd cracked several ribs. She'd had a concussion. There were sharp, shallow lines beside her stunned eyes and slack lips. When her terrified husband had first seen her unconscious on a gurney in the emergency room he'd believed she must be dead; that body was a corpse. Now in her hospital room closed to all visitors but him, propped up against pillows, in glaring white, IV tubes in both her arms and a breathing tube in her nostrils, she looked like the survivor of a disaster: an earthquake, a bombing raid. She looked like a survivor who would have no language in which to express what she'd survived.

She's aged. Her youth has vanished at last.

She was "under observation" because, as the Playwright was informed, she'd raved in a delirium of killing herself.

Yet, how festive the patient's room! Filled with flowers.

Though this patient was under an assumed name. A name in no way resembling any name of her own.

Such beautiful floral displays, no one on the staff at Brunswick General had ever seen before. Spilling out of the room and into the visitors' and nurses' lounges.

Of course, Brunswick General had never had a Hollywood celebrity patient before.

Of course, press and photographers were forbidden. Yet, a photograph of **Marilyn Monroe** would appear on the front cover of *The National Enquirer*, the stricken woman in her hospital bed, glimpsed through a doorway at a distance of about fifteen feet.

MARILYN MONROE SUFFERS MISCARRIAGE IN 4TH MONTH OF PREGNANCY. "SUICIDE WATCH."

Another similar photograph appeared in the *Hollywood Tatler* along with an "exclusive bedside telephone interview" with Monroe, by the columnist who called himself, or herself, "Keyhole."

These outrages, and others, the Playwright would keep from her.

On the phone he would say, talking eagerly, compulsively, to friends in Manhattan: "I'd been belittling Norma's fear. I can't forgive myself now. No, not about her pregnancy: she wasn't at all afraid of having a baby. I mean her fascination with the Holocaust, with 'being a Jew.' Her fascination with history. Now I see that her fear wasn't exaggerated or imagined. Her fear is an intelligent apprehension of—" He paused, confused. He was breathing quickly and on the verge of breaking down, as several times publicly he'd broken down since the catastrophe, not knowing what word he sought. In this time of distress, the Playwright, the master of language, had lost much of his power; to himself he seemed a small child struggling to express concepts that floated in his brain like great soft balloons that, as you reach for them, elude you. "Others of us learn to gloss over this fear. This tragic sense of history. We're shallow, we're survivors! But Marilyn . . . I mean, Norma . . ."

Oh, God, what did he mean?

. . .

Much of the time in the hospital she was silent. She lay with her bruised eyes half shut like a body floating just beneath the surface of the water. A mysterious potion dripped into her vein and from her vein coursed to her heart. She breathed so shallowly, he couldn't be certain she was breathing at all and if he slipped into a light hypnotic doze, a veil of white flashing over his brain, for he was an exhausted man, a not-young man, a man who would lose most of the surplus fifteen pounds he'd gained since his marriage, he woke in a panic that his wife had ceased breathing. He held her hands, securing her to life. He stroked her limp unresisting hands. Her poor, hurt hands! Seeing with horror that her hands were rather small stumpy hands, ordinary hands, with broken, dirt-edged nails. Her hair, her famous hair, darkening at the roots, dry and brittle and beginning to thin. Quietly he murmured as at child's bedside, "I love you. Norma darling. I love you," in the certitude that she must hear him. She must love him, too, and would forgive him. And then suddenly in the evening of the third day she was smiling at him. She clutched at his hands and seemed suddenly revived.

The genius of the actor! To summon energy out of what unspeakable depth of the soul. We can't comprehend you. No wonder that we fear you. On a farther shore we stand, stretching our hands to you in awe.

"We'll try again, won't we, Daddy? And again, and again?" She began to speak rapidly, who had not spoken for days. She was fierce and pitiless. Her sick eyes glistened. He, her husband, wanted to shield his eyes from her. "We won't ever give up, Daddy? Will we? Ever? *Promise?*"

The Afterlife

1949–1953

Death came unexpectedly, for I wanted it.

—Vaslav Nijinski,
Diary

In Sympathy

My Beautiful Lost Daughter —

Having heard of your tragic loss I wish to offer you my heartfelt condolences.

The death of an unborn soul may lodge more painfully within us than any other for the innocence is unsullied.

Dear Norma, I heard of your most recent sorrow in a time of sorrow of my own for my beloved wife of many years has passed away. I am awaiting a period of calm before considering what direction my life must now move in. I am not a young (nor a very well) man. I am probably going to sell my house & property (far too lavish for a solitary widower nearing 70, with ascetic tastes). I live near Griffith Park with a southward view of Forest Lawn Memorial Cemetery where beloved Agnes is buried & where a plot awaits me one day. ~~It is too sad and lonely~~

Dear Daughter, the thought has come to me: It may be that your life has so changed, you would wish to live with me. My house is spacious I assure you, realtors call it a mansion.

I heard of your sorrow in a vulgar way I'm afraid. In a "gossip column" in the *Hollywood Tatler*. (At the barber's) Of course, it has
been in the press by now. And also of your current "marital strain."

Your talent for the screen would seem so much greater, dear Daughter, than your talent for life. ~~Your unhappy mother I came to believe~~
~~carried poison in her loins like the brown recluse spider~~

But I did not send this card of sympathy to you, to chide. Forgive me,
my dear! And bless you.

I do not see your films but see your beautiful face often & wonder
you appear so untouched but the soul does not show in the face
always, I suppose. ~~Perhaps at age 33 in a woman~~ —

I hope to contact you soon, dear Norma. Forgive an aging man his
recalsitrance to reawaken old hurts.

Your repentent and loving Father

SUGAR KANE 1959

I wanna be loved by you   *nobody else but you*   *I wanna be loved by*
you   *nobody else but you*   *I wanna be loved by you*   *nobody else*
but you   *I wanna be loved by you*   *alone*   she was trapped in
this! she was trapped in *I wanna be loved by you nobody else but you I*
wanna   be   loved   by   you   alone   she   was   drowning!
smothering!   *I wanna be kissed by you*   *nobody else but you*   *I*
wanna be kissed by you alone   she was Sugar Kane Kovalchick of Sweet
Sue's Society Syncopaters   she was dazzling-blond Sugar Kane girl
ukulelist   she was the female body   she was the female buttocks,
breasts   she was Sugar Kane dazzling-blond girl ukulelist fleeing male
saxophonists   her ukulele was pursued by male saxophones   she
would not be able to resist!   again & again & always & they loved her
for it   *I wanna be loved by you*   *alone*   it was happening again,
it was happening always & forever   it was happening another
time   *I wanna be loved by you nobody else*   *but you*   she was
cooing & smiling into the audience strumming the ukulele they'd taught her
to play & her fingers moved with surprising dexterity for one so doped &
drugged & terrified even as her gorgeous kissable mouth stammered *I*
wanna! I wanna! I wanna be loved!   just another variant of the sad, sick
cow but they adored her & a man was falling in love with her on

screen   *I wanna be kissed by you   alone*   but was this funny? was this funny? was this funny? why was this funny? why was Sugar Kane funny? why were men dressed as women funny? why were men made up as women funny? why were men staggering in high heels funny? why was Sugar Kane funny, was Sugar Kane the supreme female impersonator? was this funny? why was this funny? why is female funny? why were people going to laugh at Sugar Kane & fall in love with Sugar Kane? why, another time? why would Sugar Kane Kovalchick girl ukulelist be such a box office success in America? why dazzling-blond girl ukulelist alcoholic Sugar Kane Kovalchick a success? why *Some Like It Hot* a masterpiece? why Monroe's masterpiece? why Monroe's most commercial movie? why did they love her? why when her life was in shreds like clawed silk? why when her life was in pieces like smashed glass? why when her insides had bled out? why when her insides had been scooped out? why when she carried poison in her womb? why when her head was ringing with pain? her mouth stinging with red ants? why when everybody on the set of the film hated her? resented her? feared her? why when she was drowning before their eyes?   *I wanna be loved by you boop boopie do!* why was Sugar Kane Kovalchick of Sweet Sue's Society Syncopaters so seductive?   *I wanna be kissed by   nobody else but you   I wanna! I wanna! I wanna be loved by you   alone*   but why? why was Marilyn so funny? why did the world adore Marilyn? who despised herself? was that why? why did the world love Marilyn? why when Marilyn had killed her baby? why when Marilyn had killed her babies? why did the world want to fuck Marilyn? why did the world want to fuck fuck fuck Marilyn? why did the world want to jam itself to the bloody hilt like a great tumescent sword in Marilyn? was it a riddle? was it a warning? was it just another joke?   *I wanna be loved by you"   boop boopie do   nobody else but you   nobody else but you   nobody else*

This curse of a compulsion! It was the Beggar Maid's punishment.

On the set came spontaneous applause. It was Monroe's first full day, she'd been sick & absent & rumors circulated & there was her tall pale bespectacled husband in attendance like a mourner & yet she'd sung "I Wanna Be Loved by You" to win their hearts, they loved their Marilyn didn't they! Yearning to love their Marilyn! W led the applause, which was his prerogative as director, & others joined in eagerly praising the blond actress & she was staring at the floor & biting her lower lip till almost it bled her sedated heart yet beating hard in an effort to know if these people were consciously lying or were themselves innocently deceived & waiting for them to cease she said calmly

"No. I want to try again."

And again the absurd little ukulele like a toy instrument, an emblem of her toy-life & blond toy-soul & again the suggestive-seductive big-doll body movements like Mae West & Little Bo Peep in lurid commingling. The camera was a voyeur adoring Sugar Kane's fattish body & the joke of it must be (between camera & audience) that Sugar Kane is too dumb to comprehend the joke's on her, Sugar Kane must play it straight to the very death   *I wanna be loved by you   nobody else but you   I wanna be loved by you   alone*   seeing the protruding unblinking all-knowing eyes of the Frog Chauffeur in the rearview mirror of the studio limo, he who was the Beggar Maid's kinsman & knew her   *I wanna be loved by you nobody else but you I wanna be loved by you by you I wanna be loved by you I wanna be boop boopie do! boop boopie do! I wanna be*

"No. I want to try again."

And gradually Sugar Kane's performance sharpened, from within she had a sense of its refinement by degrees though Sugar Kane was but a sex cartoon in another sex farce imagined by men for men for the laughing enjoyment of men   Sugar Kane who is "Jell-O on springs"   this role an insult & deeply wounding to Monroe & yet: Sugar Kane was written for her & who was Sugar Kane except the blond actress?

"No. I want to try again."

I wanna be loved by you   by you by you   Not sharply! she hadn't spoken sharply she was certain. Her hairdresser & Whitey her makeup man were witnesses. She listened to herself hearing her throaty-whispery-Marilyn voice at a distance like a telephone voice & she was certain she hadn't spoken sharply to W, she would keep *sharp* in reserve. Still there was the threat of *sharp*. Since she'd returned to The Studio, the rumor was. The promise of *sharp*. As the glinting edge of a pristine razor blade is a threat & a promise of *sharp*. Saying to W the distinguished director whom The Studio had hired to please her, "Look, mister. You have Marilyn Monroe in this ridiculous film so use her, don't fuck her up. And don't try to fuck with her, either."

It was like she'd died and come back to us this different person. They say she'd lost a baby boy. And she'd tried to kill herself. Drowning in the Atlantic Ocean! Monroe always had guts.

After their unwanted & distracting applause, next take was a disaster & she forgot her lines & even her fingers betrayed her plucking wrong notes on the ukulele & she burst into sobs strangely without tears & pounded at her thighs in her silky-tight Sugar Kane costume (so tight she couldn't sit down on the set & could only "rest" in a hollowed-out apparatus devised for such circumstances) & began to scream like a creature being killed & in a fury tore at her newly bleached fine-blown hair brittle as spun glass & would have raked her nails across her sweet-baby cosmetic mask of a face except W himself rushed to prevent her. "No! Marilyn, for God's sake." Seeing in Monroe's crazed eyes his own looming fate. Doc Fell, resident physician, never far from the sound stage & from Monroe, was summoned & quickly appeared & with a nurse-assistant led his hysterically weeping patient away. In the privacy of the star's dressing room once the dressing room of Marlene Dietrich who knew what magic potion was injected straight into the heart?

I live now for my work. I live for my work. I live only for my work. One day I will do work deserving of my talent & desire. One day. This I pledge. This I vow. I want you to love me for my work. But if you don't love me I can't continue my work. So please love me!—so I can continue my work. I am trapped here! I am trapped in this blond mannequin with the face. I can only breathe through that face! Those nostrils! That mouth! Help me to be perfect. If God was in us, we would be perfect. God is not in us, we know this for we are not perfect. I don't want money & fame I want only to be perfect. The blond mannequin Monroe is me & is not me. She is not me. She is what I was born. Yes I want you to love her. So you will love me. Oh I want to love you! Where are you? I look, I look & there is no one there.

She'd driven in a borrowed car east on the Ventura Freeway to Griffith Park & to Forest Lawn Cemetery (where I. E. Shinn was buried & to her shame she'd forgotten where!) & gone for hours & no one knew & a blinding migraine coming on & still she drove & drove through miles of residential neighborhoods thinking *So many people! so many! why did God make so many!* not knowing exactly what she sought, whom she sought, yet confident she would recognize her father if she saw him. *See?—that man is your father, Norma Jeane.* More vivid to her mind, which was slipping and skidding like ice cubes tossed across a polished floor, than any person of her present-day life, this *father.* She could not allow herself to think he might be tormenting her. That his letters were not loving but cruel. Toying with her heart.

My Beautiful Lost Daughter.

Your repentent and loving Father.

Toying with Norma Jeane as she'd observed in horror from a window of the Captain's House the skinny but so-pregnant calico cat toying with a baby rabbit down on the lawn, allowing the dazed & bleeding & whimpering creature to drag itself a few inches in the grass & then pouncing upon it in glee

& tearing & biting with carnivore teeth & again allowing the dazed & bleeding & whimpering creature to drag itself a few inches & then pouncing upon it until at last all that remained of the baby rabbit was the lower torso & legs still twitching in terror. (Her husband had not allowed her to intervene. It was only just nature. A cat's nature. It would only upset her. It was too late, the rabbit was dying.) No. She could not bear to think so. She would not think so. "My father is an aging, ailing man. He doesn't mean to be cruel. He's ashamed to have abandoned me as a child. Leaving me with Gladys. He wants to make restitution. I could live with him and be his companion. A distinguished older man. White-haired. Well-to-do, I guess; but I could support us both. MARILYN MONROE AND HER FATHER——— He would accompany me to openings. But why doesn't he declare himself? Why is he waiting?"

She was thirty-three years old! It crossed her mind that her father was ashamed of Marilyn Monroe & reluctant to publicly acknowledge their relationship. He called her only Norma. He spoke of not seeing Monroe's films. It crossed her mind too that her father might be waiting for Gladys to die.

"I can't choose between them! I love them both."

Since returning to Los Angeles to begin work on *Some Like It Hot*, she'd seen Gladys only once. Though Gladys had presumably known about her pregnancy, she had not told Gladys of the miscarriage and Gladys had not inquired. Most of their visit was walking on the hospital grounds, to the fence and back.

"My loyalty is to Mother. But my heart is *his*."

In such a state, she became lost in the hills above the city. She was lost in Forest Lawn Cemetery & she was lost in Griffith Park & finally she was lost in the suburb of Glendale & even if she'd returned to Hollywood & Beverly Hills she could not recall exactly where she was living. Courtesy of Mr. Z & The Studio. It was a small but tastefully furnished house not far from The Studio but she could not remember where. At a Glendale drugstore (where they recognized her, God damn she could see, staring & whispering & grinning & she was exhausted in rumpled clothing & no makeup & bloodshot eyes behind dark glasses) she telephoned Mr. Z's office pleading like Sugar Kane & a driver was sent to bring her back to the house which at first she didn't recognize, on Whittier Drive, flaming bougainvillea & palm trees & she'd had to be assisted to the door which was opened abruptly & there stood a tall furrow-faced anxious man of middle age with thick-lensed glasses & she seemed in her confusion & blinding migraine unable to recognize him.

"Darling, for God's sake. I'm your *husband*."

Thirty-seven takes of "I Wanna Be Loved by You" before Monroe was satisfied she couldn't do any better. A number of the takes seemed to W and others nearly identical yet to Monroe there were small distinctions &

these small distinctions were crucial to her *as if her life depended upon it & to oppose her was to threaten her very life & the woman would respond in panic & rage.* Everyone was exhausted. She was herself exhausted but satisfied, & was seen to smile. Cautiously W praised her. His Sugar Kane! Cautiously taking her hands & thanking her as often he'd done during *The Seven-Year Itch* filming & she'd responded with smiles & giggles of gratitude but now Monroe stiffened & drew back as a cat might, not liking at that moment to be touched, or to be touched by him. Her breath was quickened & fiery. W would claim it was combustible! W was a distinguished Hollywood director who'd directed this difficult actress in the earlier comedy which had been a commercial & critical success in 1955 & The Girl Upstairs a comic triumph but still Monroe didn't trust him. It was only three years later but Monroe was so greatly changed W would not have known her. She wasn't The Girl now. She wasn't looking to him for approval & praise now. She wasn't married to the Ex-Athlete now, & hiding her bruises & once on location in New York she'd broken down in W's arms, sobbed as if her heart was broken, & W had held her like a father holding a child & he'd never forgotten the tenderness & vulnerability of that moment but Monroe had clearly forgotten. The truth was, Monroe didn't trust anybody now.

"How can I? There's only one 'Monroe.' People are waiting to see her humiliated."

In her dressing room at The Studio sometimes she slept. The door locked, & DO NOT DISTURB posted, & one of them who adored her, often Whitey, keeping guard. Slept in only underpants & her breasts bared & body covered in sweat & smelling from the panic attacks & vomiting to exhaustion & the liquid Nembutal pulsing through her heart was so powerful she was drawn gently downward into a warm sheltering muck of dreamless sleep & the terrible racing of panic subsided & soothed & *if my heart stops one day this is a risk I must accept* & her frayed soul mended in sleep of how many hours, sometimes as many as fourteen, sometimes only two or three, except then waking in confusion & fear not knowing where she was, not after all in the dressing room at The Studio but in Baby's Room at the summer house she had never once entered after the miscarriage, or an unknown room in a private home or even a hotel room & she was Norma Jeane waking to a scene of devastation wrought by a stranger, a madwoman who had dumped makeup jars & tubes onto the floor, powder & talcum, yanked clothes off hangers in a heap in the closet, & sometimes her favorite books, pages torn from them & scattered, & the mirror cracked where a fist had been pounded against it (yes, Norma Jeane's fist would be bruised) & once there was crimson lipstick smeared across the mirror like a savage shout & she rose shakily to her feet knowing she was responsible for cleaning this devastation, she would not wish others to see it, what shame, the shame of being Norma Jeane the daughter of a mother sent away to Norwalk & everybody knowing, the other children knowing, alarm & pity in their eyes.

In the shuttered bedroom at the rear of the house on Whittier Drive a man was saying tenderly *Norma you know I care for you so much* & she was saying *Yes I know* & her mind drifting onto Sugar Kane & the next morning's shoot which was a love scene between Sugar Kane & a man who adored her (in the movie) played by C who (in life) had come to despise Marilyn Monroe. Her childish selfish behavior, repeated failure to arrive at the sound stage on time & once there her inability to remember lines out of spite or stupidity or were the drugs destroying her brain forcing C & the others into retake after retake & C knew his performance in the film was deteriorating daily, & the director W would favor Monroe in the final cut because Monroe was the major attraction, the sick bitch. And so C despised her & at their climactic kissing scene how he'd wish to spit into Sugar Kane's phony ingenue face for by this time the mere touch of Monroe's legendary skin revulsed him & C would be Monroe's enemy for life & after her death what tales C would tell of her! And so before the cameras next morning these two must kiss in a simulation of passion & even affection & the audience must believe & this prospect she was contemplating even as a man was speaking with her, pleading, *What can I do to help you, darling? To help us.* She recalled with a stab of guilt that this man who wished to comfort her, this quiet decent balding man, was her husband. *What can I do to help us, darling? Only tell me.* She tried to speak but there was cotton batting in her mouth. He was saying, stroking her arm *It seems every day since Maine we're growing more distant* & she murmured a vague reply & he said in anguish *I'm so worried about you, darling. Your health. These drugs. Are you trying to destroy yourself, Norma? What are you doing to your life?* & last she pushed him away saying coldly *But what business of yours is my life? Who are you?*

Stage fright. The Beggar Maid's curse! To repeat to repeat to stammer & repeat & begin again & again begin & stammer & repeat & retreat & lock herself away & return at last only to repeat & repeat repeat to get it perfect to get whatever it is perfect to get perfect what is not perfectable to repeat & repeat until it was perfect & unassailable so when they laughed they would be laughing at a brilliant comic performance & not at Norma Jeane, they would not be aware of Norma Jeane at all.

. . .

Stage fright. This is animal panic. The actor's nightmare. A rush of adrenaline so strong it can knock you off your feet & your heart is racing & so much blood pumping through it you're in terror it might burst & your fingers & toes turn to ice & there's no strength in your legs & your tongue is numb, your voice is gone. An actor is his voice & if his voice is gone he's gone. Often there's vomiting. Helpless & spasmodic. Stage fright is a mystery that can hit any actor at any time. Even an experienced actor, a veteran. A successful actor. Laurence Olivier, for instance. Olivier was incapable of acting on a stage for five years in the prime of his career. Olivier! And Monroe, hit by stage fright in her early thirties, really hit, in front of movie cameras & not even live audiences. Why? It's always explained that stage fright must be a simple fear of death & annihilation but why? why would so general a fear strike so randomly? why for the actor specifically, & why so paralyzing? why this panic at this time, why? will your limbs be torn from you, why? your eyes gouged out, why? guts pierced, why? are you a child, an infant to be devoured, why, why, why?

Stage fright. Because she could not express anger. Because she could express beautifully & subtly all emotions except anger. Because she could express hurt, bewilderment, dread, & pain yet could not convincingly present herself as an instrument of such reactions in others. Not on stage. Her weakness, her quavering voice if she lifted it in anger. In protest, in rage. No but she couldn't! And someone would shout at the back of the rehearsal space (this was in Manhattan, at the New York Ensemble; she wasn't miked), *Sorry Marilyn can't hear you.* The man who was her lover or who had wished to be her lover, like all her lovers a man possessed of the certainty that he alone knew the secret of undoing the puzzle, the riddle, the curse of Monroe, told her she must learn to express anger as an actress & she would then become a great actress or would at least have a chance to become a great actress & he would guide her career, he would choose her roles for her & direct her, & he would make her into a great actress of the theater; teasing & chiding her even as he made love to her (in his peculiar slow & bemused & almost abstract way never ceasing to speak except at the very moment of climax & then but briefly, as in a parenthesis) that he knew why she wasn't able to express anger, and did she? & she shook her head wordlessly no, & he said *Because you want us to love you, Marilyn   you want the world to love you & not destroy you, as you'd wish to destroy the world, & you fear us knowing your secret isn't it so?* & she'd fled him, & loved his friend the Playwright, & would marry the Playwright who knew her as his Magda, who would know her scarcely at all.

. . .

Stage fright. When she fell, striking her belly on the steps, when the bleed-ing began, the contractions in her womb & somehow she was lying upside down & her legs twisted beneath her screaming in pain & terror & her boast of having no fear of physical pain was revealed as the reckless boast of an ignorant & doomed child, & her wickedness would be punished, losing this baby she loved, oh she'd loved more than life itself yet had not the power to save. *So Sugar Kane recalls & freezes midway in a comic recognition scene kissed by C as a female impersonator before a nightclub audience.*

She'd freeze   she'd walk off the set staggering like a drunk woman sometimes she'd shake her hands at the wrists so hard, it was like a hurt bird trying to fly   she wouldn't let any of us touch her if the husband was there she wouldn't let him touch her   the poor bastard   in this shimmering mostly transparent gown they'd concocted for Monroe showing these mam-moth boobs & the twin cheeks of her fantastic jelly-ass & the dress dipped low in the back showing the entire back to practically her tailbone   there was this tragic terrified woman emerging out of Sugar Kane   like a con-fectioner's sugar mask melting & it's Medea beneath   it was a sobering sight   Monroe would press her hands against her belly   sometimes her head, her ears, like her brain was going to explode   she'd told me she feared a hemorrhage   I knew she'd had a miscarriage in the summer, in Maine she'd said *You know it's just a network of veins? arteries? holding us together? & if they burst & start bleeding?*   In the rushes there was this entirely different person   there was the true Monroe I always thought   "Sugar Kane" by any other name   If she'd have let herself be just "Marilyn" she'd have been all right   Yes I hated her then   I'd have fantasies of strangling the bitch   like in *Niagara* but looking back I feel differently   all my years of directing, I guess I'd never worked with anyone like Monroe   she was a puzzle I couldn't solve   she connected with the camera, not with the rest of us   she'd look through us like we were ghosts   maybe it was Monroe beneath that made Sugar Kane spe-cial   she had to get through Monroe, to get to Sugar Kane who's all sur-face   maybe what's "surface" has to be achieved by going deep   by being badly hurt & by hurting others

There was a rumor, Marilyn & Doc Fell "had a thing going." We'd hear gig-gling in her dressing room, & the door shut.
    DO NOT DISTURB.

There was a rumor, Marilyn & W "had a thing going, & it went sour." We'd hear W cursing her, not to her face but her departing back. He'd try to call her on the phone, when she was late for work or wasn't showing up, & couldn't get through to her, sometimes she'd be five hours late, six hours late, or wouldn't come at all. W's back trouble began with *Some Like It Hot*, it went into spasms. One of us, W's assistant, was sent to fetch her at her trailer (we were on location then at Coronado Beach for the "Florida" sequence) & there was Sugar Kane all made up & costumed in her bathing suit, she'd been ready an hour or more & we'd been waiting & she was just standing inside in this strange urgent way reading something it must've been sci-fi called *Origin of Species* & W's assistant said, "Miss Monroe? W is waiting" & not missing a beat or even glancing at him Marilyn says "Tell W to fuck himself."

Her starlet start. Monroe was both shrewd & practical. Dividing her numerous drug prescriptions (Benzedrine, Dexedrine, Miltown, Dexamyl, Seconal, Nembutal, etc.) among several drugstores in Hollywood & Beverly Hills as she divided herself among several doctors each unknowing & unsuspecting (at least, they would so claim after her death) of the others. But her favorite drugstore, she would say in interviews, would always remain Schwab's. "Where Marilyn got her starlet start with Richard Widmark staring at her ass."

Not sweet Sugar Kane but that tramp Rose sprawling naked & languid across the disheveled sheets of an unmade bed in the cinderblock Sunset Honeymoon Motel off the Ventura Freeway. Rose yawning & brushing her platinum-blond peroxide hair out of her face. That dreamy look of a woman who's been with a man, whatever the man has done to her or with her, whatever she's actually felt with him or pretended to have felt or might feel hours later, in her own bed elsewhere, in dreamy retrospect. In the adjoining bathroom a man, also naked, was pissing noisily into a toilet bowl & the door not half closed. But Rose had turned on the TV & watched as the screen cleared to show the likeness of a smiling blond girl, photographer's model age twenty-two, resident of West Hollywood, & her body had been found in a culvert near a railroad track in East Los Angeles, she'd been strangled & "sexually mutilated" & undiscovered for several days. Rose stared at the smiling blonde & herself smiled. When Rose was nervous or confused, Rose smiled. It gives you time to think. It throws the other guy off. But what was this? Some kind of ugly joke? *The blond girl was Norma Jeane. At that age.* Otto Öse must have given them Norma Jeane's picture.

They'd given this dead girl a different name. It wasn't Norma Jeane's name or any of her names.

"Oh, God. Oh God help us."

Yet the thought came to her. *She knows who she is, now. She's a body in the morgue.*

The pissing man, whoever he was, she wouldn't share either the murder news or the revelation.

This man she'd picked up at Schwab's at breakfast for sentimental reasons though even with that face & big burly body he wasn't an actor, & his precise identity she would not know. He had not recognized her as Rose Loomis or even as Monroe, it wasn't a day in which in fact she was "Monroe." He was standing now at the bathroom sink running water noisily from both faucets & talking to her in a loud-pitched voice like somebody on TV. She made no effort to listen. It was empty movie dialogue, a way of filling out the scene till it ended. Or she'd already sent the guy away & the noise of the faucets & of plumbing was from the adjacent room. No, he was still here, wide-shouldered & freckles across his back like splotches of dried sand. She would ask his name & he would tell her & she would forget & would be embarrassed to ask him another time & could not recall if she'd told him *My name is Rose Loomis* or possibly *Norma Jeane* or even *Elsie Pirig*, which was a name comically jarring to the ear, yet no man ever laughed. The dead girl might've been *Mona Monroe*. In the car she'd driven & he'd noticed her wedding band & made a comment almost wistful & she'd quickly explained she was married to The Studio, she was a film cutter & he seemed actually impressed & asked if she saw "movie stars" on her job & she said no, never; only on film, cutting & splicing film, & they were nothing but images on celluloid.

It was a later time. The freckled man had vanished. The TV screen was a blizzard of crooked & quavering lines & when the lines were transformed into human faces they were not faces she recognized, the strangled Mona Monroe had vanished & a boisterous quiz show was under way. "Maybe it hasn't happened yet?"

Suddenly she felt happy again, & hopeful.

The wronged husband. Returning to him in early evening, whoever he was, this man, the semen of another man leaking from her cunt & the stink of the other's cigarette smoke (Camel's) in her matted hair, she who did not smoke, she might have expected if this was a movie scene, & ominous movie music beneath, that there would be a dramatic exchange, a confrontation; in the days of the Ex-Athlete, a savage beating & possibly worse. But this wasn't the movies. This was nothing like the movies. This was but the borrowed house on Whittier Drive shuttered against the pitiless sun & the silent wounded figure with his carved-wood face, he whom she'd once so much admired & now could barely tolerate, a man as out of place in southern California as any New York Jew waking to the Land of Oz; a co-actor cast with her in a prolonged scene meriting no more notice than any co-actor in any such scene to be endured on the way to another, more exciting scene: in this case a long steaming-hot soaking bath & the door locked against husbandly intrusion for she was so terribly tired, so tired! pushing from him with averted face & wishing only to pass out by languorous degrees in the marble bath sipping gin (out of Sugar Kane's very flask, she'd brought home with her) & dialing Carlo's private number (but Carlo was on location somewhere making a new film, & Carlo was newly in love) without success, then lapsing into reverie searching for a vision to make her smile & laugh for she was Miss Golden Dreams & not morbid-minded by nature, that's not the American-girl way, & she thought of how at The Studio that morning they'd have been awaiting her—"Marilyn Monroe"—& making their usual frantic telephone calls until such time that it would become clear, to even the most hopeful among them, that "Marilyn Monroe" would not be coming that day to impersonate & demean herself; & W would have to film around her another time. W, daring to give her direction! Oh, it was funny! She laughed aloud, envisioning the misery of pretty Brooklyn-boy C, who'd made it known he hated Monroe's guts, forced to stand around in makeup & high heels & female drag like a cross between Frankenstein & Joan Crawford, & if the *wronged husband* hovered anxiously outside the locked door heard this shrill girlish laughter maybe he'd interpret it as happy?

The wronged husband. "I only just wanted to save her. I wasn't thinking of myself, those years. My pride."

The Magic Friend. Three miles away at The Studio they were beginning another vigil awaiting Monroe who'd assured them through her agent that she would certainly be arriving for work that day, she'd been ill "with a virus" but was now nearly recovered; filming was to begin at 10 A.M. & not earlier in concession to Monroe who, a notorious insomniac, often failed to get to sleep until 4 or 5 A.M. & already it was 11 A.M. & would soon be noon & blazing sun outside the shuttered house & the phone began to ring & the receiver left off the hook & in a bedroom at the rear she stood, & sat, & paced, & peered into the mirror awaiting the arrival of her Magic Friend, she was not too proud to whisper, "Please. Please come." Already at 8 A.M. she'd begun her vigil waking dazed & sober & with but a vague memory of the previous day & the cinderblock motel & determined now to make amends & at first she'd been patient & not anxious or alarmed, calmly cleansing her face with cold cream & rubbing in moisturizer, "Please. Please come." Yet the minutes passed, & the Magic Friend did not appear.

And soon she was an hour late at The Studio, & soon she was two hours late, & minutes passed cruel as the ticking of the grandfather clock in the Captain's House chiming the quarter hour even as her living baby hemorrhaged out of her in a mass of clots & clumps like something but partially digested & she knew the truth of it: her womb was poisoned, & her soul. She knew she did not deserve life as others deserve life & though she had tried, she had failed to justify her life; yet must continue to try, for her heart was hopeful, she meant to be good! she'd contracted to play Sugar Kane & she would do a damned good job! & by noon she'd begun to be frantic & amid a flurry of calls it was arranged that Whitey, Miss Monroe's personal makeup man, would come to the house on Whittier Drive & do a prelimi-nary makeup before the actress left the privacy & sanctuary of her house, for she had not the courage otherwise, & what relief to see Whitey! beloved Whitey! tall & grave & sacerdotal bearing his makeup kit that contained far more jars, vials, tubes, pastes & powders & paints & pencils & brushes & creams than she possessed; what joy to see Whitey in this place of dishevel-ment & dismay; almost, she would have seized & kissed Whitey's hands, except knowing that Monroe's faithful circle of assistants preferred their mistress aloof to them, as their rightful superior.

Seeing her misery, & the absence of all magic from her wan, sallow, fright-ened face, Whitey murmured, "Miss Monroe, don't be upset. It will be all right, I promise." It was said of Monroe, on the set, that, some days, she spoke in an addled way, as if words confused her; Whitey now heard his mis-tress stammer, "Oh, Whitey! Must 'Sugar Kane' want to get there, more I'm meaning than life itself!" & knowing exactly what his mistress meant, Whitey instructed her to lie down on the hastily made-up bed & begin her yoga breathing exercises (for Whitey, too, was a practitioner of yoga, of the school called Hatha Yoga) & thoroughly relax the tension in her face & body & he vowed he would conjure up "Marilyn" within the hour, & this they tried, gamely they tried, but Norma Jeane found the position uncomfortable atop her bed, the heavy brocade spread drawn up over rumpled sheets smelling of night panic, too much a ritual of death she felt it, this prone pos-ture, herself in the mortuary & her embalmer laboring over her with pastes & powders & pencils & tubes of color, her lover embalmer, her first hus-band who'd broken her heart & denied her Baby, how then was she to blame that Baby was gone; in that posture tears began to leak from the corners of her eyes & Whitey murmured, "Tsk! Miss Monroe." She felt too a hideous sensation of her skin slack on her bones & the cheeks rubbery & yielding to a new tug of gravity—Otto Öse had teased her, she had a round boneless baby face that would soon sag—& at last Whitey himself conceded, his magic was not working. Not yet.

So Whitey led the trembling Beggar Maid to the vanity with its triumvi-rate of mirrors & white lights where she cringed hopeful in her black lace bra & black silk half-slip like a supplicant in prayer, & Whitey's gentle but practiced hands removed the failed makeup with cotton swabs & cold cream & there came damp warmed gauzy cloths like bandages to soothe her skin that had become roughened, coarsened as if by some cruel caprice of the previous night (or had it been the wide-shouldered freckled lover, a giant troll who'd rubbed his stubbled jaws against her sensitive skin?) & Whitey somberly & without haste began his rites a second time, with the application of astringent, & moisturizer, & foundation makeup, & blusher, & powder, & eye shadow, & eye pencil, & mascara, & the blue-red lipstick devised for Sugar Kane though the film was in black & white & could not show her to her full advantage; & as the minutes passed, there emerged out of these mirrors a familiar if elusive presence, at first no more than a winking glisten of the eyes, then a twitching of the lips in that teasing-sexy smile, & the beauty mole was made to appear, no longer at the left corner of her painted mouth but now an inch or so lower, beneath the lip; for so Sugar Kane's face had been designed in a way subtly different from previous Monroe faces in previous films; & both mistress & servant began to feel a quickening of excitement—"She's coming! She's almost here! Marilyn!"—like the tension before a thunderstorm or the sensation following an earthquake tremor, the awaiting of the next tremor, the next jolt; & finally as Whitey fussily erased, & redid, the brown arching eyebrows, in bold contrast to the pale hair, there emerged laughing at the Beggar Maid's fears the most beautiful face she'd ever seen, a wonder of a face, the face of the Fair Princess.

To the legendary Whitey, Monroe would give a number of gifts, the most prized of which was a heart-shaped gold tie clasp inscribed

> TO WHITEY WITH LOVE
> WHILE I'M STILL WARM!
> MARILYN

Like flies crawling over something sweet & sticky, the way women's eyes crawled over C. An actor so handsome, made up as female in *Some Like It Hot,* still C looked handsome & not lurid & ludicrous as as you'd expect. C, the sullen one. C, Sugar Kane's nemesis. C had had too many women. He'd gorged himself, & he'd vomited. Monroe was no more tempting to C than a puddle of fresh vomit. When C kissed Monroe, his mouth tasted of bitter almonds & she'd pushed from him panicked & fled the set accusing he'd put poison on his lips!—so it would be rumored. C would tell the rueful tale of, at their early meetings, preproduction, joking & teasing with Monroe about their upcoming love scenes, which were numerous; in one lengthy scene aboard a yacht, C would lie flat on his back pretending impotence while Sugar Kane lay upon him kissing & nuzzling in her effort to "cure" him, a scene to be eased past the censor only under the pretense it was comic & farcical; & at those early meetings C had liked Monroe well enough, never would C have anticipated what misery lay in store. One of their scenes, & this not complicated, would require sixty-five takes. Day following day, C & others would wait for hours for Monroe to show up, & sometimes fail to show up altogether. Filming to begin at 10 A.M. might begin at last at 4 P.M. or at 6 P.M. C was a man of pride, & ambitious for his career, & could not give up this gem of a role (in a film that would be his best, & make him the most money) & so his rage at Monroe. Yes, he could acknowledge Monroe was distraught & a little crazy (she'd had a miscarriage, her marriage was falling apart) but what was that to him, a man fighting for his life? *With a woman in that state it's you or her* he might've confided in the husband if they'd been friends; but they weren't. C was particularly cruel mimicking Monroe's addled words & confused stammering, how one day when he'd been made to wait for her for five hours—five hours!—& Monroe had at last appeared, fragile & breathless & without apology, she'd turned upon him & W with a bitter smile & said, "Now what you know is how it's a woman! *Laughed at.*"

Forever it would be asked of W what was it like, working with Monroe in this late stage of her brief career, and W would say simply, "In life, the woman was hell and in hell; on film, divine. There was no connection. No more mystery to it than that."

Yet that day Sugar Kane arrived triumphant on the set, no more than four hours late; & they'd been shooting around her, & making some progress; & there came Sugar Kane sweet & breathless & this time apologetic & rueful; begging them to forgive her, especially C, whose hands she clutched with hands so icy cold, C had to suppress a shudder; & unaccountably, Sugar Kane would perform through four or five pages of script without a single blunder; that very love scene, protracted & embarrassingly intimate, aboard the yacht. So many kisses! Sugar Kane in her most suggestive see-through costume, the back cut so low & loose practically the tops of her buttocks were visible, a cooing simpering sexy-funny blond doll, lying atop C & wriggling, & C was astonished, this difficult scene between two actors who hated each other's guts would play so convincingly & smoothly; he could not believe that at the conclusion Monroe would not say, "No. I want to try again." Instead, Monroe smiled. *Smiled!* The scene would remain intact, as is, perfectly performed in a single take. A single take! After the nightmare of repetition of previous days & weeks! C would wonder if this miracle was a signal that Monroe had recovered overnight from an actual illness; or, more likely, she'd played the scene brilliantly in a single take simply to demonstrate that, yes, she could do it. When she wished.

Yet even C & others who hated Monroe had to concede she was terrific that day. We applauded, so grateful she'd returned, if only for a brief while. We adored her, or yearned to. Our Marilyn!

Always you were watching me. Coward! After she'd been discharged from the Brunswick hospital. He'd brought her back to the Captain's House, which was not their home. Never again would she enter Baby's Room. Baby's precious things were given to the girl Janice, for her baby. Never again would she pass by the shut door to the cellar but she would insist to the Playwright she was fine, she was happy, she was recovering and not "morbid minded" & he'd believed her as surely she believed her own adamant words & one night in muggy August he woke from sleep to the noise of plumbing in the old house & his young wife gone from their bed yet not in the bathroom adjoining their bedroom; he found her in another upstairs bathroom running scalding water into a tub, naked & trembling crouched beside it, her muscular haunches, her glistening eyes, & he had to grab her in his arms to prevent her climbing into this water, this water so hot steam had coalesced in globules on the bathroom's mirrors & fixtures, & she struggled with him saying the Brunswick doctor had told her to "douche" to purify herself & that was what she meant to do & he saw in her eyes the glisten of madness & did not recognize her & again they struggled, how strong this woman was, even in her weakened state, his Magda! Of course she was not his Magda, she was no one he knew. Later she would say to him bitterly, "That's what you want, isn't it? Me gone" & he, her husband, would protest, & she would shrug & laugh, "Ohhhh, Daddy"—this term of endearment now mockery in her mouth since the miscarriage—"why not tell the truth, for once?"

Impossible to know the simplest truths. Except that death is no solution to the riddle of life.

(These words he'd written, & would write; words as solace, & as penitence; in time, words of exorcism; & never again would she ask of him with begging eyes *Daddy you won't write about me will you?* Never again.)

Premiere Night! In Sugar Kane's sugary cadences the Zen wisdom came to her, uttered through a mouthful of Dom Perignon. "Ohhhh my God! Oh, I get it! Those cats! They were the ones." Not until opening night of *Some Like It Hot.* Not until a hiatus of how many insomniac-drugged nights & days, weeks & months of consciousness frayed & soiled as a towel in a broken towel dispenser, & one ER admission (in Coronado Beach, where her heartbeat quickened into tachycardia & C of all people loathing the mere touch of MM's skin was the one to lift her from the sun-burning sand where she'd fallen). In the long elegant black-gleaming Cadillac limousine with legendary Hollywood film pioneer & philanthropist Mr. Z seated to her right & the gaunt furrow-browed man who was her husband seated to her left. "Those cats. I f-fed. Oh!" She spoke aloud & no one heard. She had entered a phase of life where often she spoke aloud & no one heard. Makeup & costuming at The Studio had required six hours, forty minutes. She'd been delivered sometime after 11 A.M. semiconscious. Doc Fell had medicated her in the privacy of her dressing room; her whimpers & muffled cries of pain they'd worked into a routine that sounded, to others' ears, like gaiety, hilarity. She shut her eyes & the long piercing needle was sunk into an artery in her inner arm; sometimes in her inner thigh; sometimes in an artery just below her ear & hidden by her fluffy platinum hair; sometimes, riskier, in an artery above her heart. "Miss Monroe, only just hold still. *There.*" What kindly falcon's eyes, a beak of a nose. Her Doc Fell. In another movie, Doc Fell would be Marilyn's suitor & eventually her husband; in this movie, Doc Fell was a rival to the actual husband who, grimly disapproving of his wife's medications, knew nothing, or very little, of the rival. Doc Fell was one of those like Whitey zealously involved in the public presentation of MARILYN MONROE & presumably drew a sizable paycheck from The Studio. She feared him as she would never fear Whitey, for Doc Fell held the power of life & death over his subjects.

"One day soon I will break off with him. With all of them. I *vow.*"

This was the actress's truest wish & intention. In Norma Jeane's schoolgirl journal she inscribed it.

This opulent Hollywood premiere! How like the glorious golden age of Hollywood! The Studio was lavishly honoring *Some Like It Hot*, which had turned out, to the astonishment of all industry insiders, to be a success. Advance word in the trade was another blockbuster MARILYN MONROE smash hit for The Studio. Preview audiences loved it. Reviewers loved it. Exhibitors throughout the U.S. were competing to book it. Yet the blond actress's memory of the film was discontinuous as a dream many times interrupted. No single line of Sugar Kane's remained in her memory except, ironically, the very one she'd fumbled through sixty-five legendary takes: "It's me, Sugar." Which somehow she'd misspoken as "It's, Sugar, me." "Sugar it's me." "S-Sugar, it's me?" "Sugar! It's *me.*" "It's Sugar, me." "It's m-me? Sugar?" Yet all was forgiven now. They wanted to love their Marilyn & Marilyn was again lovable. Three years away from Hollywood & MARILYN IS BACK! The Magi had been trumpeting & blazoning & heralding her return for months. TRAGEDY & TRIUMPH was the revelation. MISCARRIAGE IN MAINE. (From the purview of southern California, miscarriage-in-Maine certainly made sense.) TRIUMPH IN HOLLYWOOD. (Hollywood was the place for triumph!) Asked how did she feel, Marilyn replied in her sugary-sweet-sexy-whispery voice, "Oh, I just feel so privileged? To be alive?"

This was her truest belief. In Norma Jeane's schoolgirl journal she inscribed it.

Along the brightly lit Boulevard. A procession of gleaming black studio limousines. A motorcade of Hollywood royalty. LAPD officers on horse-back. Police barricades, flashbulbs, & the myriad winking flashes of binoc-ulars & even telescopes trained upon her from the crowd. *And the Sharpshooter among them invisible in black shirt & jacket & trousers crouched patiently behind a window of a rented room in a stucco-facade building in the hire of the Agency observing her (& her Commie husband) through the scope of his high-powered rifle* of which, in her festive mood, she was determined not to think.

For why?

"Some things reside only in your imagination. It's called 'paranoia.' Oh, you just *know*."

This wisdom, she'd inscribed in Norma Jeane's schoolgirl journal.

Thousands of people lining the Boulevard on this balmy southern Califor-nia evening, pressing up against LAPD barricades to stare in wonderment at the motorcade! seething & murmuring & cheering in ecstatic waves! They were awaiting famous faces, & the face (& body) of MARILYN MONROE most eagerly. "Mari-*lyn*! Mari-*lyn*! Mari-*LYN*!" came the chant. If only the limo were open, & the blond actress could stand & be seen more clearly by her thousands, hundreds of thousands of fans! But the gaunt furrow-browed man who remained her husband would not have allowed such a folly, & perhaps even Mr. Z & the other Studio bosses would have forbidden it, fearing dan-ger to their fragile property. *Monroe wasn't going to last much longer. That was obvious. Grable lasted twenty years and Monroe won't last ten. Fuck!*

In wonderment she was staring back at the fans. So many! You would not think that God had made so many of these.

Suddenly seeing a scattering of feral-cat faces & grinning carnivore teeth. The snubbed noses of cats & erect, pointed ears. Those cats! At the Cap-tain's House. The horror of it struck her: "They were the ones, they wanted Baby dead. The very cats I f-fed." She turned to the gaunt furrow-browed man beside her uncomfortable in his tuxedo & would have told him of her discovery but could not think how to express it. He remained the master of words. She, an intruder in his imagination. *He resents me. Resents loving me. Poor sap.* She laughed. Sugar Kane was a girl ukulelist & girl singer & her simplicity was a delight on screen even as in "real life" such simplicity would be a sign of mental deficiency; how much easier, & how much more they will love you, if you can be Sugar Kane without irony for once. "I can do it. Just watch. Sugar Kane without irony. Marilyn without tears." The furrow-browed man in the boiled-looking tux leaned toward her indicating he hadn't heard what she'd said amid the screams & cheers & noise of the police bullhorns & quickly she murmured what sounded to his ear like *Wasn't-talking-to-you.* No longer did she call this man to whom she'd been married for more years than she could recall "Daddy" & yet she seemed incapable of devising another name to call him. There were spells when she did not remember his name, not even his last name; she would try to think of a "Jewish" name & would be confused. Less frequently now did he call her "dearest," "dear one," "darling," & the very name "Norma" on his lips sounded alien. She would overhear him on the telephone speaking worriedly of "Marilyn" & understood that, to him, she had become Marilyn; there was no Norma remaining; possibly she'd been Marilyn to him all along.

"Mari-*lyn!*" "Mari-*lyn!*" "Mari-*LYN!*" Her kinsmen!

Oh, God, she'd been stitched so tight in her Sugar Kane gown she could hardly breathe, tight as sausage skin, her breasts jutting out as if about to burst with milk; & her cushiony buttocks poised on the very edge of the limo seat where she'd been positioned (since she couldn't sit back like the men, the entire dress would explode at the seams). That day she'd been unable to eat & had had no nourishment except black coffee & medication & several quick swallows of champagne from a bottle she'd smuggled into the limo— "Just like Sugar Kane, eh? A girl's weakness."

She was feeling good now. Bubbly & floating. She was feeling strong now. She wasn't going to die for a long long time. She'd promised Carlo & Carlo had promised her. *If ever you're thinking seriously of it. Call me at once.* She'd memorized Brando's private number. She would not be capable of recalling any telephone numbers including her own yet she would recall to the end of her life Brando's private number. "Only Carlo understands. We share the same soul." She hadn't liked it, though, that Carlo had been an emissary for the Gemini. She didn't like it, Carlo was of their dissolute Hollywood fringe circle. Cass Chaplin! Eddy G, Jr.! She believed it was ominous, she never heard of them. No one spoke to her of them. *How many people know? Of the Gemini. Of Baby.*

But why think of such morbid-minded things? Her own husband, an intellectual & a Jew, had counseled her not to be ghoulish. Not ghoulish but girlish! This was a time of celebration. This was Sugar Kane's night of triumph. Sugar Kane's night of revenge. The fans weren't assembled here along Hollywood Boulevard & side streets to catch a fleeting glimpse of Marilyn's male co-stars C & L, admirably as they'd performed in the movie, no they were not; they were were gathered here tonight to see MARILYN. As the limousines drew nearer Grauman's, the site of the premiere, there was a quickening beat to the air, the noise became deafening, the gigantic heartbeat of the crowd accelerated. She'd begun to recognize, here and there, individuals in the crowd. Troll people, those creatures of the under-earth. Hunchbacked gnomes & beggar maids & homeless females with mad eyes & straw hair. Those among us mysteriously wounded by life. Disfigured faces & shrunken limbs & glaring-glistening eyes & holes for mouths. She saw a hulking fattish albino male with a knitted cap pulled down tight on his oblong head; she saw a shorter male with youthful bearded face & glittering eyeglasses holding aloft with trembling hands a video recorder. At the curb stood a stunted woman in dressy attire, tufts of dyed carroty-red hair lifting from her scalp & protuberant watery eyes, taking pictures with a box camera. Close by, a face molded carelessly out of clay or putty, lopsided, with shallow indentations for eyes and a small fishhook mouth. So many! And there, suddenly, a woman in her mid-thirties who looked familiar, lanky, attractive, in men's clothing, with shining agate eyes & frizzed brown hair beneath a cowboy hat, waving energetically at her. Was it—? Fleece? After all these years, Fleece? Alive? Norma Jeane awoke from her trance at once. "Fleece? Oh, Fleece! Wait—" Norma Jeane clawed at the limo door, which was locked; tried to roll down the window, as Mr. Z protested. In her excitement she scrambled onto Z's bony knees—"Fleece! Fleece! Meet me at the theater—" but already the limo had moved past.

So like royalty she was borne along the Boulevard, to the premiere. Where a cataclysm of lights awaited. Where a crimson carpet lay upon the pavement. Applause washed around her like a maddened surf as she emerged from the limo waving, smiling her dimpled smile as the chant increased in volume—"Mari-*lyn*! Mari-*lyn*!" The crowd adored her! Their Fair Princess who would one day die for them.

"Oh, hey! Oh, I love you! Love love love you all!"

Inside the theater, there was more applause. Marilyn waved and blew kisses and walked without leaning on an escort's arm in her spike-heeled shoes, in her stitched-in skin-tight Sugar Kane gown. Mr. Z in tux & luminous lizard-skin observed the ecstatic blond actress with surprised approval; the tall gaunt furrow-browed man who remained her husband observed her with alarm. Where was the tense, distracted, deeply unhappy woman about whom everyone had been so worried? About whom so many rumors in Hollywood had circulated? No sign of her here! For here was "Sugar Kane," Marilyn's very essence. W & C & others of the battle-weary production crew watched the actress with astonishment as she shook hands, was embraced & kissed, smiled sweetly & joyously, engaged in reasonably coherent speech, for here was a Marilyn Monroe they would swear they'd never once seen during the making of the movie. *Jesus, was that one sweet! and gorgeous! and I got stuck, poor sap, kissing the other.*

Like a blur the film passed before her eyes. Though greeted with enthusiasm & continuous laughter. From the madcap Keystone Kops opening to the final classic line of Joe E. Brown—"Nobody's perfect." The audience loved *Some Like It Hot* & most of all the audience loved MARILYN MONROE returned to them in her prime (yes, it did seem so! despite the rumors) & were eager to forgive their wayward star as MARILYN MONROE was eager to be forgiven.

At the film's end, more applause. The massive interior of Grauman's was filled with waterfalls of applause. Cherie, that earnest *chantoose*, had never received acclaim like this. W the distinguished director (looking now not exhausted but positively beaming) & his three distinguished actors were being honored by the crowd, yet of these MARILYN MONROE was clearly the center of attention. *The fact was, you never looked at anybody else if you could look at Monroe.* Gaily she rose to her feet & sweetly accepted the applause like waves washing over her. "Oh, this is so w-wonderful. Oh, gosh, thank you!"

It hasn't happened yet? I am still alive.

Sure, we invented MARILYN MONROE. The platinum-blond hair was The Studio's idea. The *Mmmm!* name. The little-girl baby-voice bullshit. I saw the tramp one day on the lot, a "starlet" looking like a high school tart. No style, but Jesus was that little broad built! The face wasn't perfect so we had the teeth fixed, & the nose. Something was wrong with the nose. Maybe the hairline was uneven & had to be improved by electrolysis, unless that was Hayworth.

MARILYN MONROE was a robot designed by The Studio. Too fucking bad we couldn't patent it.

"Congratulations."

"Marilyn, congratulations."

"*Marilyn baby!* Con-grat-u-la-*tions*!"

Though she couldn't remember *Some Like It Hot* except as an undersea creature with eyes no more than primitive photosensitive protuberances in its head might recall the ocean floor across which, driven by desperate appetite, it scuttled. *I'm here, I'm still alive.* She laughed so happily, people stared, smiling. Her husband stared, gravely. Many mouthfuls of champagne the blond actress swallowed, some of which leaked out of her nostrils. Oh, so happy! She would be observed late in the evening speaking with Clark Gable handsome & "mature" in his tux & smiling in gentlemanly mystification at her girlish stammer—"Ohhh, Mr. G-gable. I'm so embarrassed. You saw the movie? That fat blond thing up on the screen, that wasn't *me*. Next time, I promise I'll do better."

RAT BEAUTY

What a sleek hot-skinned little rat beauty *she* was. No one like her in all of Hollywood.

Ohhhh, God. The Blond Actress got high staring & *staring*.

Essence of Brunette. No need to bleach her pubic hair, eh? The Blond Actress's dark sister.

Yet in her presence, the Blond Actress was shy. It was the Brunette who approached her smiling & seductive. Both women had come to the party (in a Venetian palace of a house overlooking a Bel Air canyon & in the near distance mists as of Shangri-La) without male escorts. (Yet both women were married. Or were they?) The hot-skinned little rat beauty from rural North Carolina. The L.A.-born Okie meringue beauty. The one talked & smoked & laughed like a man from the gut, the other emitted faint breathy laughing noises as if not knowing what they were & meant. Oh, the Blond Actress was tongue-tied & stammering & too tall; & heavier than the Brunette by twenty pounds. *What a sad, fat cow I am.*

They were on a balcony. Night air & mist. The Brunette was saying, "Why take it so seriously?—acting."

Had they been discussing this subject? What subject? The Blond Actress was confused.

Was she drunk? At the long long dinner she'd been toasted, for *Some Like It Hot* was a hit. Another hit for MM. A masterpiece & MM's best performance. She wasn't drunk though she'd had (how many?) glasses of champagne that evening. And before dinner, at somebody's house? Nor had she had medication, she could recall. Not since whenever it had been, in somebody's car.

The Brunette had soared to fame & notoriety years before the ascension of Marilyn Monroe & yet was not much her elder.

Saying, "Acting, the movies, it's mostly shit," & the Blond Actress protested, "Oh, but!—it's my l-life," & the Brunette said in derision, "Bullshit, Marilyn. Only your life is your life, Marilyn." It would not escape the Blond Actress that her dark-mirror sister had been sent to her, an emissary, to deliver a profound truth; yet it was not a truth the Blond Actress could accept. She winced & said, almost pleading, "Please? Don't call me 'M-marilyn'? Is that to mock?" & the Brunette stared & contemplated her for a poignant movie moment as if pondering *Is she deranged? or only drunk?* Such rumors you heard in Hollywood, of MM. She said, "Why do you say 'Is that to mock'? I don't understand." The Blond Actress said eagerly, "You could call me 'N-norma.' We could be friends." How wistful, the Blond Actress's voice. "Sure, we could be friends. But Norma's a bad-luck name." (Meaning Norma Talmadge had died a junkie's death not long ago.) The Blond Actress said, hurt, "I think it's a beautiful name. It's for Norma Shearer who was my godmother. It's *mine*." "Sure, Norma. Anything you say." "But it *is*." "Right. It *is*." All evening at the dinner table they'd been eyeing each other, assessing. Their mega-millionaire producer host had seated the Blond Actress & the Brunette at opposite ends of the table, as ornamentation. The Blond Actress in sexy white silk low-cut to her navel & the Brunette swathed in elegant purple. The Blond Actress reticent & the Brunette a raconteur like a man. *Except for her size & body & that face, she's a man. Oh, God.* It was said of this Hollywood actress that she fucked like a man. Took sex where & when she wanted, like a man. (But which man?) She'd been married young & divorced & married & divorced; married to famous wealthy men & she'd walked away from marriage like one slipping out a back door unencumbered & without regret & no backward glance. *Women don't behave this way!* How many times she'd had abortions it was speculated. She boasted she had no maternal instinct. Was she a secret lesbian, or not-so-secret. She'd become one of the world's highest paid film actresses yet liked to shock by saying frankly, "Y'know, I don't know a shit about acting. I've brought nothing to this business. I don't respect it. It's a living. You don't have to get down into the actual dirt like in porn or turning tricks." It was said of the Brunette beauty that she walked through her film roles performing scene after scene in whichever order the director directed, with few retakes. If it was good enough for the director, it was good enough for her. She rarely read a script through & knew & cared little of her co-actors' roles. She memorized her lines by scanning them swiftly while being made up & costumed. She had a passion for gambling & a gambler's quick cunning shallow mind. She had a perfect body, not so busty as the Blond Actress, nor with the Blond Actress's billowy rear. She had a perfect face with defined cheekbones, subtly heart-shaped, a delicately cleft chin, & lustrous dark eyes. You saw that face & thought of Botticelli. You thought of classic Greek sculpture. Certainly you didn't think of Hollywood CA in 1960 & still less did you think of Grabtown NC in the early 1920s. *If I could be this woman! Yet myself, inside.*

The Blond Actress heard herself saying in a raw scratchy adolescent voice, "See, I'm an actress? It is my life! That's why I want to do my best. It's my best self that is the actress." With bemused disdain the Brunette lit a cigarette as a man might light it, one-handed, not with a lighter but with a match expertly struck, & exhaled smoke, making the Blond Actress's eyes tear & saying, not unkindly, very like an elder sister, "Your best for who, Norma? For the fans? The Studio bosses? Hollywood?" The Blond Actress said, "No! For—" *For the world. For time. To outlive me.* She faltered, eyes widened in perplexity, alarm. "For—" The Brunette's beautiful long-lashed eyes were so fixed upon her, so seductive. Hypnotic. She was trembling & could not think. In a rush of recollection with the force of a Benzedrine hit she saw Harriet's imperturbable dark gaze, & tendrils of smoke rising across that face. *My dark seductive sister. My rat sister.* The Brunette was saying, "Why get so agitated? You're MONROE. What you do is MONROE. Every movie you make from now on can be a box-office failure, but you're MONROE for life. You'll be MONROE after life. Hey." Seeing the look on the Blond Actress's face. *But I'm alive! I'm an alive woman.* "Nobody can play the blonde like you. Always there's a blonde. There was Harlow, and there was Lombard, and there was Turner, and there was Grable; now there's Monroe. Maybe you'll be the last?" The Blond Actress was confused. What was the subtext here? Or was there no subtext? Some evenings, if she'd been awake too long, now her husband-the-playwright (as Hollywood deferred & condescended to this mystery man) had departed for New York City at her behest, & again she was living alone in Hollywood like one floating on an iceberg in the midst of a turbulent ice sea, not just her spoken words but her thinking became scrambled. She could feel thoughts cracking & breaking apart. Out of the anguish of ceaseless thinking & self-blaming there had arisen the antidote for anguish, which was disintegration & madness & that blasted-clean look of Gladys Mortensen's gaze & this Norma Jeane both knew & refused to know; this was the secret subtext of her life. The Brunette may have guessed some of this. The Brunette was powerfully attracted to the Blond Actress. The way, as a girl living on her family's rundown farm in North Carolina, she'd been attracted to wounded things: the young chicken, once beautifully feathered, now missing feathers & pecked at & bleeding & doomed, having aroused the mysterious fury of other chickens; the runt of a sow's litter, unable to nurse & doomed to be trampled, pummeled, even devoured by other pigs. . . . So many of these, the wounded. You wanted to save them all. As a child, you wanted to save them all.

The Brunette said, "Hollywood pays. That's why we're here. We're higher-class hookers. A hooker doesn't make a romance of hooking. She retires when she's saved enough. Movies aren't brain surgery, honey. Not delivering babies." Babies? What had this to do with babies? The Blond Actress said, confused, "Oh I'd be—I'd be ashamed, talking like that." The Brunette laughed. "There's nothing much that can shame *me*." Yet the Blond Actress persisted. "Acting is a l-life. Not just for money. It's—you know. An art." She was embarrassed to speak so passionately. The Brunette said sharply, "Bullshit. Acting is only acting."

But I want to be a great actress. I will be a great actress!

Pitying her maybe. Seeing that look in her eyes. The Brunette changed the subject & began to speak of men. Witty & cruel. Men they knew in common. Studio bosses, producers. Actors & directors & screenwriters & agents & the shadowy shifting inhabitants of the fringe culture. Sure, she'd fucked Z "on my way up. Who hasn't?" She'd fucked, years ago, "that sexy little dwarf-Jew Shinn" & she missed I. E. even now. There was Chaplin. In fact, there was Charlie Sr. and there was Charlie Jr. There was Edward G. Robinson Sr. and there was Edward G. Robinson Jr. "Those two, Cass & Eddy G: your buddies too, Norma, eh?" There was Sinatra, she'd been married to for a rocky few years. Frankie, who'd lost her respect when he'd tried to kill himself with sleeping pills. "For love. For *me*. Somebody called an ambulance, not me, & they saved him. I told him, 'You shithead. Women take sleeping pills. Men hang themselves or blow out their brains.' He'll never forgive me, but other women, even more he'll never forgive." The Blond Actress said hesitantly how much she admired Sinatra's singing. The Brunette shrugged. "Frankie isn't bad. If you like that American white-guy crooning crap. Me, I go for down-dirty Negro music, jazz & rock. As a fuck, Frankie was OK. If he wasn't drunk or doped. He was wired. A quivery skeleton with a hot prick. But nothing like his wop buddy what's-his-name—you were married to him, Norma, for a while. In all the papers, we read about you two." Nudging the Blond Actress, winking. " 'Yankee Slugger' he liked me to call him. Got to hand it to the wops, eh? At least they're men."

The look on the Blond Actress's face. From some distance, this was being observed & preserved & one day would be replayed in indistinct yet classic black & white. The sexy rat-beauty Brunette in purple silk laughing & taking hold of the Blond Actress's stricken baby face in both hands & kissing her full on the mouth.

Essence of Brunette, essence of Blonde.

Monroe wanted to be an artist. She was one of the few I'd ever met who took all that crap seriously. That's what killed her, not the other. She wanted to be acknowledged as a great actress and yet she wanted to be loved like a child and obviously you can't have both.

You have to choose which you want the most.

Me, I chose neither.

THE COLLECTED
WORKS OF MARILYN
MONROE

SEX is NATURE & I'm all for NATURE
   I am MARILYN   I am MISS GOLDEN DREAMS
   I believe no SEX is wrong if there's LOVE in it
   no SEX is wrong if there's RESPECT in it   no SEX is wrong if there's SEX
in it   you sure can't get SEX from CANCER   I mean you can't get CAN-
CER from SEX
   The human body, nude, is BEAUTIFUL
   I've never been ashamed of posing NUDE
   People have tried to make me ashamed but I do not & I will not
   All my shyness & fears went away when I removed my clothes
   You sure know who MARILYN is when MARILYN removes her clothes
   I wished to run naked in church before God & mankind
   See I wouldn't be ashamed why would I for God created me as I AM
   God has created us as WE ARE

I see you looking at my perfect body   I see you loving my perfect
body   like it is your own body   & in a vision it came to me   in
MARILYN you can love your own PERFECT BODY   that is why MARILYN came
into this world   that is why MARILYN exists

I am Miss Golden Dreams   the most famous nude pinup in the History of Mankind   I would say that is an honor isn't it   I love you looking at me   I hope you will never stop   I believe that the human body is BEAUTIFUL & nothing to be ashamed of   at least if you are a beautiful desirable woman   & YOUNG

I am Miss Golden Dreams   what is your name?

I am Miss Golden Dreams   I'd say that is quite a responsibility isn't it

I am Miss Golden Dreams   tell me what you like best & I will do it   I will keep every secret of yours   I will adore you   only just love me & think of MARILYN sometime? promise? *sad, sick cow   piece of meat   cunt that's dead inside*

I'm not bitter   for they are telling me I am HISTORY

You wouldn't be bitter if you are HISTORY   any of you

A MAN would not be bitter if entering History!   nor should a WOMAN

Break my heart, better than break my nose   (you bastards)

Revenge is SWEET   (& I need to acquire that taste)

Oh hey! let's be HAPPY TOGETHER please   that is why we EXIST

In a vision it came to me   that is why we EXIST

SEX is NATURE & I'm all for NATURE   aren't you

Fact is you can't get sex from cancer I mean

can't get death from cancer

I mean death from sex   you CAN'T   else in Hell we'd be created like we are   NATURE is the only God   I was craeted by NATURE as I am   I   mean   I   was   created   as   this   I   was craeted   crated   kreated   craeated   as MARILYN   & could not be anyone else from the beginning of Time   I believe in NATURE   I believe I mean I am NATURE   We are all NATURE   You are MARILYN too if you are NATURE   That, I believe   *We may look with some confidence to a secure future of great length   & as NATURAL SELECTION works solely by & for the good of each being all corporeal & mental endowments will tend to progress toward perfection   There is grandeur in this that from so simple a beginning countless forms most beautiful & most wonderful have been & are being evolved*

I'm having such a good time in life, guess I'm gonna be punished!

THE SHARPSHOOTER

The secret meaning of the evolution of civilization is
no longer obscure to us who have pledged our lives
to the struggle between Good and Evil; between the
instinct of Life and the instinct of Death as it works
itself out in the human species. So we vow!

—Preface,
The Book of the American Patriot

It was my daddy's pioneer wisdom. *There is always something deserving of
being shot by the right man.*

When I was eleven my daddy first took me out onto the range to shoot
butcher birds. I date my lifelong respect for firearms & my prowess as a
Sharpshooter from that time.

Butcher bird was Daddy's name for hawks, falcons, California condors
(now almost extinct), & golden eagles (ditto) we would shoot out of the sky.
Also, though scavengers (& not predators actively threatening our barnyard
fowl & spring lambs), Daddy despised turkey vultures as unclean & disgusting creatures there could be no excuse for their existing & these ungainly
birds too we would shoot out of trees & off fence railings where they perched
like old umbrellas. Daddy was not a well man, suffering the loss of his left
eye & "fifty yards" (as he said) of ulcerated colon as a result of War injuries,
& so he was filled with a terrible fury for these predator creatures striking
our livestock like flying devils out of the air.

Also crows. Thousands of crows cawing & shrieking in migration darkening the sun.

There are not enough bullets for all the targets deserving, was another of
Daddy's firm beliefs. These I have inherited, & Daddy's patriot pride.

Those years, we were living on what remained of our sheep ranch. Fifty acres, mostly scrubland in the San Joaquin Valley midway between Salinas to the west & Bakersfield to the south. My daddy & his older brother who'd been crippled in the War, though not Daddy's war, & me.

Others had deserted us. Never did we speak of them.

In our Ford pickup we'd drive out for hours. Sometimes rode horseback. Daddy made a gift to me of his .22-caliber Remington rifle & taught me to load & fire in safety & never in haste. For a long time as a boy I fired at stationary targets. A living & moving target is another thing, Daddy warned. Aim carefully before you pull any trigger, remember someday there's a target that, if you miss, will fire back at you & without mercy.

This wisdom of Daddy's, I cherish in my heart.

I am overcautious as a Sharpshooter, some believe. Yet my belief is, where a target is concerned you may not get a second chance.

Our barnyard fowl, chickens & guineas, & in the fields spring lambs were the *butcher birds'* special prey. Other predators were coyotes & feral dogs & less frequently mountain lions but the *butcher birds* were the worst because of their numbers & the swiftness of their attacks. Yet they were beautiful birds, you had to concede. Red-tailed hawks, goshawks & golden eagles. Soaring & gliding & dipping & suddenly dropping like a shot to seize small creatures in their talons & bear them aloft alive & shrieking & struggling.

Others were struck & mutilated where they grazed or slept. The ewes bleating. I'd seen the carcasses in the grass. Eyes picked out & entrails dragged along the ground like shiny slippery ribbons. A cloud of flies was the signal.

Shoot! Shoot the fuckers! Daddy would give the command, & at the exact moment we both shot.

They praised me for my age all who knew me. Sharpshooter they called me & sometimes Little Soldier.

The golden eagle & the California condor are rarities now but in my boyhood we shot many of these & strung up their carcasses in warning! *Now you know. Now you are but meat & feathers, now you are nothing.* Yet there was beauty in contemplating such powerful creatures of the air, I would have to concede. To bring down a golden eagle as Daddy would say is a task for a man & to see its golden neck feathers close up. (To this day I carry with me, in memory of my boyhood, a six-inch golden feather close to my heart.) The condor was an even larger bird, with black-feathered wings (we'd measured once at ten feet) & vivid white underwing feathers like a second pair of wings. The cries of these great birds! Gliding in wide circles & tilting from side to side & what was strange in such creatures was how, feeding, they might be joined by others swiftly flying from far beyond the range of a man's vision.

Of the *butcher birds* it was goshawks I shot the most of, as a boy. For there were so many & when their numbers were depleted in our vicinity I would go in search of them, farther & farther from home, in ever-widening circles. Choosing to travel cross-country, I would ride a horse. Later, when I was old enough to have a driver's license & the price of gasoline not yet too high, I would drive. A goshawk is gray & blue & their feathers like vapor so that drifting against a filmy sky they would vanish & reappear & again vanish & reappear & I would become excited, knowing I must fire to strike a target not only speeding but not visible & yet this I would do, by instinct, sometimes missing (I concede) but often my bullet struck its target to yank the soaring creature from the sky as if I held an invisible string attached to it & had such power over it, unknown by the goshawk & unguessed, I might yank it down to earth in an instant.

On the ground, their beautiful feathers bloody, & eyes staring open, they lay still as if they'd never been alive.

Butcher bird now you know—I would speak to these calmly.

Butcher bird now you know who has dominion over you, who cannot fly as you fly—never would I gloat, almost there was a sadness in my speech.

For what is the melancholy of the Sharpshooter, after his beautiful prey lies crumpled at his feet? Of this, no poet has yet spoken, & I fear none ever will.

Those years. I lived in that place yet spent long days roaming & often slept in the pickup, following I know not what thread of unnamable desire drawing me sometimes as far south as the San Bernardino Mountains & into the vast desert spaces of Nevada. I was a soldier seeking my army. I was a sharpshooter seeking my calling. In the rearview mirror of the pickup a fine pale-powdery ascension of dust & in the distance before me watery mirages that beckoned & teased. *Your destiny! Where is your destiny!* Driving with my rifle beside me on the passenger's seat, sometimes two rifles, & a double-barreled shotgun, loaded & primed to be fired. Sometimes in the emptiness of the desert I would drive with boyish bravado, my rifle slanted at an angle on the steering wheel as if I might fire through the windshield if required. (Of course, I would never do such a self-destructive thing!) Often I would be gone for days & weeks & by this time Daddy was dead & my uncle elderly & ailing & there was no one to observe me. Not *butcher birds* exclusively but other birds too became my targets, primarily crows, for there are too many crows in existence, & such game birds as pheasants & California quail & geese, for which I would use my shotgun, though I did not trouble to search out their carcasses where they fell stricken from the air.

Rabbits & deer & other creatures I might shoot, yet not as a hunter. A Sharpshooter is not a hunter. With binoculars scanning the range & the

desert, seeking life & movement. Once I saw on a mountainside in the Big
Maria Mountains (near the Arizona border) what appeared to be a face—a
female face, & unnatural blond hair, & unnatural red mouth pursed in a
teasing kiss—& though trying not to stare at this apparition I was helpless
before it, & my pulses pounded, & my temples, & I reasoned it was but a
billboard & not an actual face & yet it teased & taunted so, at last I could
not resist aiming my rifle at it as I went slowly by, & fired a number of times
until the terrible pressure was relieved & I'd driven past, & no one to witness. *Now you know. Now you know. Now you know.*

Soon after that my excitation was such, I was drawn to target-shoot sheep
& cattle, even a grazing horse, provided the countryside was empty of all
witnesses. For *how easy to pull the trigger* as they would tell me one day in
the Agency. There is a sacred wisdom here, I believe it is a pioneer wisdom.
Where the bullet flies, the target dies. Subtle as poetry is *What is the target
is not the question, only where.* Sometimes I would sight a vehicle far away
on the highway scarcely more than a speck rapidly approaching & if there
were no witnesses (in the Nevada desert, rarely were there witnesses) at the
crucial instant as our vehicles neared each other I would lift my rifle & aim
out my rolled-down window & taking into account the probable combined
velocities of both vehicles rushing together I would squeeze the trigger at the
strategic moment; with the supreme control of the Sharpshooter I would not
flinch, though the other driver might pass close enough by for me to see the
expression on his (or her) face; I would proceed onward without slackening
my speed, nor increasing it, observing calmly in my rearview mirror the target vehicle swerving from the highway to crash by the roadside. If there were
witnesses what were they but *butcher birds* gazing down at such a spectacle
from their high-soaring heights; & *butcher birds* despite the keenness of their
eyes cannot bear witness. These were in no way personal vengeful acts, only
the instinct of the Sharpshooter.

Shoot! Shoot the fuckers! Daddy would command, & what could a son
do but obey.

It was in 1946 I would be hired by the Agency. Too young to have served
my country in wartime, I pledged to serve my country in these interludes of
false peace. For Evil has come home to America. It is not of Europe now or
even of the Soviets exclusively but has come to our continent to subvert &
destroy our American heritage. For the Communist Enemy is both foreign
& yet close to us as any neighbor. This Enemy can indeed be the neighbor.
Evil is the word for the target as it is said in the Agency. *Evil is what we mean
by our target.*

ROSLYN 1961

"I can't memorize the words by themselves. I have to memorize the feelings."

The Misfits would be the Blond Actress's final film. There are observers who claim she must have known this, you can see it in her face. Roslyn Tabor would be her strongest screen performance. *Not a blond thing! A woman, at last.* Roslyn confides in a woman friend she always ends up back where she's started & Roslyn speaks wistfully of her mother who "wasn't there" & her father who "wasn't there" & her handsome ex-husband who "wasn't there" & Roslyn who's an adult woman over thirty & not a girl confesses on the brink of tears *I miss my mother* & we know that this is the Blond Actress speaking. She speaks of not having children & we know that this is the Blond Actress speaking. She never finished high school. She feeds a hungry dog & she feeds hungry men. She nurses men. Wounded, aging, grief-stricken men. Sheds tears for men incapable of shedding tears for themselves. Screams at men in the Nevada desert, calling them *Liars! Killers!* She convinces them to free the wild horses they've lassoed. Wild mustangs that are themselves, wild lost wounded male souls. Oh, Roslyn's their shining madonna. Intense & breathless & luminous as one at the brink of a precipice. Saying *We're all dying aren't we. We're not teaching each other what we know.* Roslyn is the Blond Actress's invention & her screen speech a mimicry of the Blond Actress's private speech & if the playwright husband who wrote the screenplay & appropriated his wife's speech & certain painful circumstances of her life wished also to appropriate her soul, the Blond Actress would not so accuse him. No., *We exist for each other & in each other. Roslyn is your gift to me as Roslyn was my gift to you.*

Now that she no longer loved him.

Now it was only poetry that bound them. A poetry of speech, & a yet more eloquent poetry of gesture.

She'd been unfaithful to him, he supposed he knew.

With whom, how many, when & how & with what degree of emotion, passion, or even sincerity he would not wish to know. He was a caretaker husband now, a famous actress's nurse. (Yes, he felt the irony: in *The Misfits,* luminous Roslyn is everybody's nurse.) He was uncomplaining, stoic, resigned, & when he could not help himself he was hopeful. For that much remained of his youthful ambitious self. He would be faithful to her until she rejected his very touch. He would love her long after. For had she not carried his baby killed in the womb, were they not now linked for life in a way too deep & profound & sacred to be named? She was no longer his Magda, nor was she his Roslyn, he knew!—yet he would care for her & he would forgive her (if she wished forgiveness; this wasn't certain). Guardedly he asked, "Are you certain you want to do this film, Norma? You're strong enough?"—meaning by this without drugs this time, without killing herself as helpless he would have to watch; & hurt, angry, she told him, "I'm always strong enough. None of you know *me.*"

We run carelessly to the precipice, after we have put something before
it to prevent our seeing it.

These words, copied in Norma Jeane's schoolgirl journal.
She wasn't sure she understood. Did Carlo mean this to apply to *her?*
He'd given her Pascal's *Pensées* before she left for Reno, on location for *The Misfits.* Carlo-not-her-lover-who-yet-loved-her.

"My little gal Angela, all growed up, eh?"
Who but H had been hired to direct *The Misfits!* H the distinguished director of *The Asphalt Jungle.* The Blond Actress revered H, whom she had not met in ten years. *He gave me my start. He gave me my chance.* She'd planned to hug the older man when they met but his lined face, whiskey breath, & paunch discouraged her; his rude staring eyes more bloodshot than her own.

H had observed the Blond Actress's career with bemused skeptical interest as a father might observe from a distance the life of a bastard daughter or son: misbegotten offspring for whom he need feel no paternal responsibility, only just a wayward elliptical connection. At their initial meeting in Hollywood the Blond Actress was shy & may have flinched as H took both her hands in his & squeezed them, hard. That hearty gravel voice, that male manner a woman can't determine is he mocking or affectionate or somehow both? She would call him "mister," wanting to defer to him. He would call her "honey" as if unable to recall her name. He would speak more respectfully to her husband the playwright. He would make her uneasy pointedly looking her over, as a worldly man known for his appreciation of both horse-and woman-flesh. He would make her yet more uneasy by recalling her audition for *Asphalt Jungle*—"You got to be Angela just by walking away." The Blond Actress asked what did he mean?—she'd auditioned like anyone else except she'd lain on the floor to speak Angela's lines because Angela was supposed to be lying on a sofa; & H laughed & winked at Z (they were in Z's opulently furnished office at The Studio, signing contracts) & repeated—"No, honey. You got to be Angela just by walking away." A sick wave of hurt washed over the Blond Actress. *He means my ass. The bastard.*

The Blond Actress could not now recall her Angela self very clearly. To recall Angela would be to recall Mr. Shinn, whom she had betrayed, unless he'd betrayed her. To recall Angela would be to recall Cass Chaplin when they'd been new young lovers. *My soul mate* Cass had called her. *My beautiful twin.* She would not wish to recall herself before Angela, the yet-unnamed starlet who'd been summoned to Mr. Z's office to see the Aviary.

Z's office was in another building on The Studio lot now. The furnishings in this office were Asian: thick-piled Chinese rugs, brocaded sofas & chairs, & on the walls antique scrolls & watercolors of exquisite natural scenes. Z was known in the industry as the man who'd invented MARILYN MONROE. In interviews Z boasted quietly of keeping "my girl" on contract when other executives including the then-president of the company had wanted to terminate her. ("Why? You won't believe it: they didn't think she could act, & they didn't think she was attractive.")

The Blond Actress heard herself laugh, flirtatious & friendly. She'd been feeling good that day. That was one of her good days. And she looked good. It was her fervent belief that *The Misfits* would be a great classic movie & that the role of Roslyn would be her salvation. It would make people forget Sugar Kane & The Girl Upstairs & Lorelei Lee & the others. *Not a blond thing! A woman, at last.*

"Well. I'm not Angela any longer, Mr. H. I'm not Marilyn Monroe either, not in this movie."

"No? You look like Marilyn Monroe to me, honey."

"I'm Roslyn Tabor."

This was a good answer. She could see H liked it.

There's a kind of horse, could be a pure Thoroughbred, requires the whip to run his best. That's me. I was in debt and I needed to be bailed out and this deal came along and Monroe was part of it. I didn't respect her as an actress. I hadn't seen most of her films. I didn't think I could trust her, or even like her. I never had patience for suicidal neurotics. Kill yourself if you're going to, but don't botch life for other people. That's my belief.

People said I was crazy for her, and people said I was hard on her and caused her to crack up. The hell with that. You could see in her eyes what the story was. Permanently bloodshot, capillaries burst. We couldn't have filmed Misfits *in color if we'd planned to.*

Reno, Nevada. It's a film in black & white like memory. A film of the forties, not of the sixties. Dead actors! And already posthumous in the telling.

The Blond Actress instructed herself *I will be professional in all ways.*

The Blond Actress & the playwright husband she no longer loved yet who continued doggedly (it would be remarked upon by witnesses) to love her lived, in Reno, in what would be Reno-*Misfit*-hell, in a suite of rooms on the tenth (top) floor of the Zephyr Hotel, so named for Zephyr Cove. On the first day of shooting, due on the set at 10 A.M., already by 9 A.M. the Blond Actress had hidden away in a locked bathroom incapable of forcing herself to contemplate the frightened apparition in any mirror & she would turn away from the door even her faithful Whitey, who begged Miss Monroe to allow him to *try.* She was sheer emotion. She was sheer nerves. Not a coherent thought! Hadn't slept all night; or, if she had slept intermittently, possibly now she was still asleep, her barbiturate-stunned brain in a sleep state though her eyes were open & she'd managed to crawl from bed & into the bathroom. And she refused to unlock the door. And the playwright husband begged. And the playwright husband threatened to call the front desk of the hotel, to ask that the door be removed from its hinges. The Blond Actress screamed at them to go away & leave her & blocks away on the set arriving at 11:15 A.M. the playwright husband made excuses for her—*Marilyn has a migraine*—*Marilyn has a fever*—*Marilyn will be here this afternoon she promises*—& the distinguished director H grunted & said little except he'd film around Roslyn that morning & in private saying he hoped to Christ if Monroe was going to crack up it would be sooner, not later.

Locked away in a room of the Zephyr Hotel in Reno, Nevada. A view of sun-blinded streets & neon casino signs—$$$—& in the distance a mountain range called the Virginias, dusty-diaphanous as a stage set faded of all color. It was an era in which Reno, Nevada, was the divorce capital of the United States & so it was logical that Roslyn was here & would be divorced—"freed"—in this desert city. Oh, she was Roslyn! She would be Roslyn to her fingertips. *This is the role of my life. Now you will all see what I can do.* Only just, she was feeling shaky. Trying to read the script & her vision was blurred. Already it was noon & she'd been due on the set at 10 A.M. & she believed she might yet prepare herself to arrive on the set by mid- or late afternoon & hoped that H would be sympathetic. *He will, he likes me! He's like a father to me. He gave me my start.*

In this stark pitiless sun she wore dark glasses everywhere & shrank from photographers & reporters waiting like vultures in the lobby of the Zephyr or out on the street. The set was closed to them but not public places. H complained that Monroe brought with her packs of dogs like a bitch in heat & the less she gave them, the more they wished from her, & harassed others including him. *How is Marilyn? How is her marriage?* Fine white cracks had appeared at the corners of her eyes & framing her mouth & those eyes once so blue & beautiful were now a fine network of burst capillaries so that the eyeballs were discolored as if with jaundice not even a twelve-hour sleep might heal. *Lucky this movie isn't in Technicolor, huh?*

You no more could predict what might emerge from that luscious Marilyn mouth than you could guess, or estimate, all that'd gone into it.

She'd told H & the others, all of them men, that she was Roslyn Tabor. "I know Roslyn. I love her." This was both true & not-so-true. For Roslyn is only what men see. What about a Roslyn the men never see? She'd told H that Roslyn's dialogue was poetic & beautiful & yet she wished for Roslyn to do more in the movie apart from consoling the men & wiping their noses & making them feel admired & loved; why couldn't Roslyn be the first person the audience sees in the movie, Roslyn emerging from a train, Roslyn driving a car into Reno, Roslyn in motion & active—not, as it was, Roslyn near-invisible behind an upstairs window as a man casts his eyes upward, in search of her; & the next scene, Roslyn peering worriedly into a mirror as she applies makeup. "The hell with windows, mirrors. Makeup! Let's see Marilyn—I mean R-roslyn—full on." The more she thought about it, the more she wanted some of Roslyn's corny lines cut, no matter if they had been penned by a Pulitzer Prize–winning playwright. She wanted new dialogue. And why couldn't Roslyn herself cut the trapped horses free at the end of the movie? "Roslyn could do it just as well as the cowboy. Monroe, not Gable. Or both—Monroe & Gable? See?" She'd grown excited trying to explain the logic & how it was movie logic, the Fair Princess & the Dark Prince united to cut free the mustangs; sure, Gable could keep the stallion for himself to free, & she could free

the others—"Why the hell not?" H stared at her as at a madwoman &
yet called her honey to placate her.

"Just give Roslyn more to *do*," she'd pleaded.

Into their bemused male silence.

To the press it would be leaked that Marilyn was "being difficult" even
before production of *Misfits* began. Marilyn was "making her usual outrageous demands."

Yet she would not be cheated of Roslyn & of the strongest performance
of her career. Roslyn was an older sister of Sugar Kane, except no madcap
comedy & quivering musical numbers. No ukulele & luscious love scenes.
Roslyn was painful because "real" & yet (as any woman in the audience
would recognize immediately) only just a "real dream" (a man's dream). To
become Roslyn, she could not remain Norma Jeane; for Norma Jeane was
smarter & shrewder & more experienced than Roslyn; Norma Jeane was better educated, if only self-educated. When Roslyn's lover Gay Langland speaks
of her approvingly—"I don't like educated women; it's nice to meet a woman
who has respect for a man"—Norma Jeane would have laughed in the man's
face, but Roslyn listens & is flattered. Oh, the male things said of Roslyn to
flatter & seduce & confuse! "Roslyn, you have a gift for life." "Roslyn, here's
to your life, I hope it goes on forever." "Roslyn, why are you so sad?"
"Roslyn, you just shine in my eyes." "Roslyn, you've got to stop thinking
you can change things." *Oh, yes, I can change things. Just watch me!*

The phone was ringing. Like hell she'd answer it. She would wash her face
& douche her eyes with cold water & swallow a painkiller or two & throw
on makeup, & a blouse & slacks, & her dark glasses, & leave the Zephyr by
a rear exit, through the kitchen; she had a friend in the kitchen (she was a girl
who'd always have a friend in a hotel kitchen), & she would arrive on the set
unexpected by 3:20 P.M., now that she was feeling so much better, & her
strength flooding back at the thought of the looks on their faces, the bastards.
(Except Clark Gable; she revered Clark Gable.) She would become Roslyn:
shampooed & set shimmering-blond hair, makeup to accentuate her moon-
white skin, & tight white V-neck dress decorated with cherries. The Fair
Princess, in the Nevada desert city! To the amazement of the *Misfits* crew she
would put in what remained of the first day of filming & she would demand
as many takes as required for her initial scene (at the vanity mirror, talking
wistfully about her impending divorce with an older woman) until her Norma
Jeane armor was worn down & tremulous fearful forgiving Roslyn emerged.
She would impress H, who was not an easy man to impress; H who'd so condescended to her, ten years before, H who didn't respect her, H the renowned
director who was hoping, she knew damned well, that Monroe would crack
up early on so he could cast another, more malleable actress in her place.

"But there's only one Monroe. That, the fucker must know."

It was a miracle sometimes. That's a cliché but happens to be true. Monroe would show up hours late and the rumor might be she was in the Reno hospital (tried to kill herself the night before!) yet suddenly there she'd arrive sweet and shy-seeming & stammering apologies, and a cheer would go up no matter we'd all been cursing the bitch. When Monroe arrived you saw she was no bitch only a force of nature like a high wind or lightning storm, you saw she was in the grip of this force of nature herself and you were eager to forgive her; even her co-star Gable with his ailing heart said she couldn't help it, he didn't like it but he understood. And Whitey and the Monroe crew went to work on her like resuscitating a corpse and transformed this white-skinned blond woman you'd almost not recognize into Roslyn the angelic beauty; and it would happen many times during the weeks of the filming, too many times maybe; and not always a cheer would go up, and not always the bitch was transformed into the angel, but usually. The thing Monroe projected through the camera—none of us could figure it out. We'd seen plenty of actors and actresses and nobody like Monroe. See, there were days she'd seem flat and almost ordinary except for that moon-white skin and she'd interrupt a scene and ask to begin again like an amateur & most scenes she'd demand to do over and over and over a dozen times, twenty times, thirty times, and you could see only the smallest change from take to take yet somehow it added up, Monroe was building up, getting steadily stronger as her co-actors weakened and became exhausted, poor Clark Gable who wasn't young, who had hypertension and a bad heart, but Monroe was impervious to such exhaustion; as she was impervious to other people; and impervious to H hating her guts; or maybe she believed, maybe Marilyn always believed, everybody had to love her, she was so pretty and this orphan waif you absolutely had to love. There was a Marilyn slogan she'd infected us all with, she said it so often— *If your number's up it's up, and if not, not.* This was appropriate for Reno, Nevada, we thought. So it seemed not to matter how late Monroe arrived to work, or how distraught or dazed, once she emerged from her dressing room made up and costumed and actually acting it was like another self inhabited her, and she'd become Roslyn, and how could you blame Roslyn for some crap Marilyn had done? You couldn't. You would not wish to. And whatever the thing was she projected on the set, through the cameras, at the rushes you'd stare almost in disbelief thinking *Who the hell's that? That stranger?*

Absolutely, Monroe was the only one of her kind.

This was *before.* What would happen *hadn't yet happened.*

In a waking dream of excitement & hope she was gliding barefoot through the upstairs of the Captain's House. The ill-fitting floorboards & crooked windows & beyond, an opaque-misty sky. She knew it hadn't happened yet because Baby was snug inside her beneath her heart. A special purse—a pouch?—beneath the heart. Baby had not yet departed. One day (she'd imagined this elaborately!) Baby would be an actor, & would depart upon his mysterious actor journeys, breaking with whoever he'd been, but that was far into the future, & this was a dream to comfort, wasn't it? Baby had not yet left her in clots & rushes of dark uterine blood. Baby was the size of a medium cantaloupe swelling her belly in a way she loved to stroke. *And somehow this was linked to my good feeling about Roslyn & the film, now we were in the third week.* And (this was confusing!) it might have been in Baby's dream not her own (for babies too dream in the womb; Norma Jeane had dreamt her entire life sometimes, she believed, in Gladys's womb!), she entered barefoot the long narrow chilled workroom of the man with whom she lived, the man to whom she was married, the man believed to be Baby's father, & saw papers scattered across his desk; she knew—she knew!—she should not examine these papers for they were forbidden to her; yet like a bold, naughty girl she took them up & read; & in her dream these words were not visual but spoken in men's voices.

DOC: Mr ————, I'm afraid I don't have very good news for you.

Y: What—is it?

DOC: Your wife will recover from the miscarriage though there may be occasional pain & spotting. But . . .

Y (trying to remain calm): Yes, Doctor?

Doc: I'm afraid her ~~reproductive organs~~ uterus is badly scarred. She's had too many abortions—

Y: Abortions?

DOC (embarrassed, man-to-man): Your wife . . . seems to have had a number of rather crude abortions. Frankly, it's a miracle she ever conceived at all.

Y: I don't believe this. My wife has never had—

DOC: Mr. ————, I'm sorry.

Y exits (quickly? slowly? a man in a dream)

LIGHTS DOWN (not blackout)

END OF SCENE

Marilyn was so outrageous! The things she'd say. Knowing we couldn't quote her in our straitlaced publications so she'd come out with the wildest

remarks, for instance when she and Gable were doing *The Misfits* there was
lots of media interest and *Life* flew me out to Reno to interview her and her
co-stars and director and playwright husband, all men, and we were arranging to meet in a Reno bar and I made some half-assed joke like you do when
you're nervous, asking how'd I recognize her, what would she be wearing,
and Marilyn doesn't miss a beat; in this breathy-cooing voice she whispers
over the phone, "Oh hey!—you can't miss Marilyn, she'll be the one with
the vagina."

*Maybe all there is is just the next thing   maybe all there is is just the next
thing   maybe all there is   is just   just the next just the next
thing   maybe all there is   is just the next   maybe all there is
is   is just   is just the next thing*   Roslyn's words stuck in her head
& she could not stop repeating them *Maybe all there is is just the next
thing*   like a Hindu mantra & she was a yogin murmuring her secret
prayer   *Maybe all there is is just the next thing*
    She thought, That's a comfort!

Stinging red ants crawled inside her mouth as she lay in a paralysis of phenobarbital sleep. Her mouth was open, at a slant. The ants must've been tiny
red Nevada-desert ants. Stung and discharged their toxins and were gone.
But later, Whitey asked worriedly, "Miss Monroe, is something wrong?" for
the Blond Actress was wincing as, while he made her up, she tried to drink
her usual steaming-hot black coffee with a tablet or two of codeine dissolved
in it, and she whispered to Whitey in a voice he almost couldn't hear, Whitey
who could hear his mistress's words not only hoarse and croaking across a
room but miles and eventually years distant from the actual woman, "Oh,
Whitey. I d-don't know." She laughed, then began without warning to cry.
Then stopped. She hadn't any tears! Her tears were dried up like sand! She
poked a forefinger gingerly into her mouth and touched the stinging sores.
Some were canker sores and others were tiny blisters.
    Sternly Whitey said, "Miss Monroe, open up and let me look."
    She obeyed. Whitey stared. A dozen one-hundred-watt lightbulbs framing
the mirror made the scene bright as any film set.
    Poor Whitey! He was of the tribe of trolls in the employ of The Studio,
under-earth folk, yet grown to an unusual height of over six feet; with massive shoulders and upper arms and a doughy-kindly face. A whitish fuzz covered his head, which was the shape of a football. His colorless eyes were
myopic yet possessed a reassuring ferocity. Except for these eyes, you would
not have thought that Whitey was an artist. *Out of mud and colored paints
he could fashion a face. Sometimes.*
    In the Blond Actress's service this expert cosmetician had grown stoic;

always he was a gentleman, hiding from the Blond Actress's anxious eye any visible signs of concern, alarm, repugnance. He said quietly, "Miss Monroe, you'd best see a doctor."

"No."

"Yes, Miss Monroe. I'll call Doc Fell."

"I don't want Fell! I'm afraid of him."

"Another doctor, then. You must, Miss Monroe."

"Is it—ugly? My mouth?"

Whitey shook his head mutely.

"Things have bitten my mouth. The inside. While I was asleep I guess!"

Whitey shook his head mutely.

"Or it could be, I guess, something in my blood? Allergy? Reaction to medication?"

Whitey stood in silence, head bowed. In the brightly lit mirror, his eyes did not lift to meet his mistress's.

"Nobody's kissed me for a long time. Not deeply I mean. Not as a l-lover I mean. I can't blame a poison kiss, can I." She laughed. She rubbed her eyes with both fists, though her eyes were sand-dry.

Silently Whitey slipped away to fetch Doc Fell.

When the men returned, they saw that the Blond Actress had laid her head on her arms. She was slumped forward as if unconscious and breathing shallowly. Her silvery hair had been shampooed and styled in preparation for Roslyn. She hadn't yet been fitted for her costume and was wearing a soiled smock and slacks, and her muscled dancer's legs were white and bare and twisted oddly beneath her. So shallow and erratic was her breath, Doc Fell would experience a moment's panic. *She's dying. I will be blamed.* But he was able to revive her, and would examine her mouth, and scold her for mixing medications against his orders, and for betraying him with other doctors, and he would provide further medication to heal the sores, unless the sores were past healing. Then Whitey would return to the challenge of her face. He would remove the makeup he'd put on, cleanse her skin gently, and begin again. He would chide her—"Miss Monroe!"—as her eyes slipped out of focus and her mouth, even as he penciled in bright lipstick, grew slack. On the set they'd been awaiting Roslyn for two hours, forty minutes. Repeatedly with dogged masochistic rage H would send an assistant to the Blond Actress's dressing room to see how much longer it might be. Whitey murmured diplomatically, "Soon. We can't be hurried, you know." The imminent scene was more complex than previous scenes because it involved a good deal of blocking, four actors, music and dancing. The men would gaze upon Roslyn with an intensity of passion borne of their frustration, misery, rage; the camera would record devotion, hope, love shining in their eyes like reflectors. The scene belonged to Roslyn. Roslyn would drink too much and dance alone displaying her beau-tiful-waif body and she would run outside into the romantic dark and embrace a tree in a "poetic" moment and the Dark Prince would proclaim *Roslyn you have the gift of life, here's to your life I hope it will go on forever.*

The estranged husband. "Y'know, mister?—nobody likes being *spied on.*"

Loving her was the task of his life and he'd come to feel in this sun-glaring desert city that he might not, for all his devotion, be equal to the task. *The Misfits* was to have been his valentine to her and now the tomb of their marriage. He had wished to enshrine her luminous beauty in Roslyn and could not see how he'd failed, or why he must fail; yet she was increasingly impatient with him, even rude to him, as her work with her screen lover Gable deepened. *Am I jealous? If that's all, so ignoble, maybe I can live with it.* Yet she continued to take drugs. Too many drugs. She lied about her drugs, to his face. She had built up so deadly a tolerance she could chew and swallow codeine tablets even as she talked, laughed, "did Marilyn" with oth-ers. They would say, "Marilyn Monroe is so *witty*!" They would say, "Mar-ilyn Monroe is so—*alive*!" While he, the somber husband, the husband of four years, the husband-who-seems-too-old-for-Marilyn, the censorious husband, stood to the side, observing.

"Fuck, I told you: I don't like being *spied on.* You think you're so perfect, mister, go look in the *mirror.*"

Her brain was broken like a cheap wind-up clock yet she was desperate to improve her mind. Desperate!

Not just *Origin of Species* she'd been reading & annotating for months. Now this book Carlo had given her. Oh, she was so moved by Pascal! So long ago, such thoughts, it didn't seem possible, the story of *Origin of Species* was things improving, more refinement in time, "reproduction with modification" for the better, & yet: Pascal! In the seventeenth century! A sickly man who would die young, age thirty-nine. He had written her own deepest thoughts she could never have expressed even in rudimentary stammering speech.

Our nature consists in motion; complete rest is death. . . . The charm of fame is so great that we revere every object to which it is attached, even death.

These words of Pascal, copied in red ink in Norma Jeane's schoolgirl journal.

Carlo had inscribed the little book *To Angel with Love from Carlo. If only one of us makes it. . . .*

"Maybe I could have his baby someday? Marlon Brando."

She laughed. Oh, it was a crazy thought but . . . why not? They wouldn't have to be married. Gladys hadn't been married. The Dark Prince was better off not married. She was thirty-four years old. Two or three more years of childbearing.

The lovers kissed! Roslyn & the cowboy Gay Langland.

"No. I want to try again."

Again, the lovers kissed. Roslyn & the cowboy Gay Langland.

"No. I want to try again."

Again, the lovers kissed. Roslyn & the cowboy Gay Langland.

"No. I want to try again."

These were new lovers. Clark Gable who was Gay Langland who wasn't young, & Marilyn Monroe who was Roslyn who was a divorcée past the bloom of first youth. *Long ago in the darkened theater. I was a child, I adored you. The Dark Prince!* She had only to shut her eyes & it was that long-ago time in the movie house to which she would go after school on Highland Avenue & pay for her solitary ticket & Gladys would have warned her *Don't sit by any man! Don't speak to any man!* & she lifted her eyes excited to the screen to see the Dark Prince who was this very man who kissed her now & whom she kissed with such hunger, the hot stinging agony of her mouth forgotten; this handsome dark man with the thin-trimmed mustache now in his sixties, now with lined face & thinning hair & the unmistakable eyes of mortality. *Once, I believed you were my father. Oh tell me, tell me you are my father!*

This movie that is her life.

These were new lovers & the feeling between them delicate & evanescent as a spider's web. Sleeping Roslyn in bed her beautiful body covered only by a sheet & her lover Gay leaning gently over her to wake her with a kiss & Roslyn quickly rose to slip her bare arms around his neck & kiss him in return with such yearning that, for the moment, the hot-stinging agony of her mouth & the terror & misery of her life were forgotten. *Oh, I love you! Always I have loved you!* She saw again the framed photo of this handsome man on Gladys's bedroom wall. It was a long-ago time yet so vivid! The building was The Hacienda. The street was La Mesa. It was Norma Jeane's sixth birthday. *Norma Jeane, see?—that man is your father.* Roslyn was naked beneath the sheet, Gay was dressed. To be naked onscreen & against a crumpled crimson velvet cloth is to be exposed & vulnerable as a sea creature prized out of its shell & if the soles of your feet are exposed, what shame! And the dark erotic thrill of such shame. When they kissed, Roslyn shivered; you could see her pale skin lift in goose pimples. Stinging red ants! The tiny sores would course through her veins & blossom in her brain & destroy her one day but not just yet.

A kiss should hurt. I love your kisses, that hurt.

Monroe was superstitious and rarely saw daily rushes, but that evening she came by with Gable and the scene came on and we were astonished at how it played. H took Monroe aside and loomed over her gripping her hands and thanking her for her work that day. Jesus that was good, he said. It was so subtle. It was beyond sex. She was a real woman in the scene, and Gable a real man. You ached for them. None of the usual movie bullshit. H had had a few whiskeys and was in a repentant mood for he'd been cursing Monroe behind her back for weeks and making us laugh describing the ways he'd have liked to murder her. "If ever I doubt you again, honey, give me a good swift kick in the ass, eh?"

Monroe laughed mischievously. "How's about a good swift kick in the balls?"

You're my friend, Fleece—aren't you?

Norma Jeane, you know I am.

You've come back into my life for a reason.

I always knew you.

You did! I loved you so.

I loved you too, Mouse.

We were going to run away together, Fleece.

We did! Don'tcha remember?

I was afraid. But I trusted you.

Oh, Mouse, you shouldna. I wasn't never good.

Fleece, you were!

To you, maybe. But not in my heart.

You were kind to me. I never forgot. That's why I want to give you things now. And in my will.

Hey, don't talk like that. I don't like fucking talk like that.

It's just realistic, Fleece. In this movie I'm making, a cowboy tells me *We all got to go sometime.*

Shit! Why's that funny?

I didn't mean to laugh, Fleece. I laugh sometimes . . . I don't mean.

I don't get why it's funny. You seen dead people? I have. I seen 'em up close. I smelled 'em. They ain't funny, Norma Jeane.

Oh, Fleece, I know. It's just *We all got to go sometime* is a cliché.

A what?

Something been said before. Lots of times.

That's why it's funny?

I wasn't really laughing, Fleece. Don't get angry.

Everything's been said before by somebody, that don't mean it's right to be laughed at.

Fleece, I'm sorry.

In the Home, you were the saddest little thing. Cried every night like your heart was broken & wet your bed.

No, I didn't.

The girls who wet their beds, they had to have oilcloth instead of a bottom sheet. Didn't smell too good. That was always little Mouse.

Fleece, that isn't true!

Hell, I was mean to you. I shouldna.

Fleece, you weren't mean to me! You protected me.

I protected you. But I was mean to you. I liked to make the other girls laugh.

You made me laugh.

I feel bad, Norma Jeane. I took your Christmas present from you that time & you cried.

No.

Yeah, I had it. I ripped the damn tail off it. The reason I think I did, I was jealous of it.

I don't believe that, Fleece.

That little striped tiger I ripped the tail off. I had it in my bed for a while & later I threw it away. I was ashamed I guess.

Oh, Fleece, I thought you l-liked me.

I did! I liked you the best. You were my Mouse.

I'm sorry I left you. I had to.

Is your mother still alive?

Oh, yes!

You'd cry a lot. Your mother gave you away.

My mother was sick.

Your mother was crazy & you hated her. Remember, you & me were gonna go kill her where she was locked up at Norwalk.

Fleece, that isn't true! That's a terrible thing to say.

We were gonna burn it down. We were.

We were not!

She wouldn't let you be adopted. That's why you hated her.

I never hated my mother. I l-love my mother.

Don't worry, "Marilyn." I won't tell anybody. That's our secret.

It isn't a secret, Fleece. It isn't true. I always loved my mother.

You hated her so, she wouldn't let you be adopted. Remember? Nasty old witch wouldn't sign the papers.

Fleece, I never wanted to be adopted! I had a m-mother.

Hey: I been in Norwalk myself awhile.

Norwalk? Why?

Why d'you think, dummy?

Were you—sick?

Ask 'em. They do what the fuck they want with you, you can't stop 'em. Fuckers.

You were in—Norwalk? When?

How in hell I know when? A long time ago. There was the War, I signed up with the WACS. I was trained in San Diego. I was shipped out to England. Me, Fleece, in England! I got sick, though. I had to be sent back to the States I guess.

Oh, Fleece. I'm sorry.

Hell, I don't look back. I'd dress like a man, nobody bothered me mostly. Unless something got fucked up.

I like the way you look, Fleece. I saw you right away, in that crowd. You could be a good-looking guy. I like that.

Yeah but I don't have a prick, see? If you have a cunt & not the other, you have to do what the pricks want. I'd use my knife on them if I could. I wasn't a shrinking violet. I'm scared of more things now than I was then. I wanted beauty in my life. I lived in Monterey, in San Diego, & in L.A. I followed your career.

I was hoping you would, Fleece. All the girls.

I knew you right away. "Marilyn." I saw *Don't Bother to Knock* & wanted you to push that little brat out the window. I don't like children! In *Niagara* I couldn't believe how grown up you were, & beautiful. It excited me, though, when he strangled you.

Fleece! That's a strange thing to say.

I only just tell the truth, Norma Jeane. You know Fleece.

That's why I love you, Fleece. I need you in my life. Just to be in my life. See? We can talk once in a while.

I could be your driver. I can drive a car.

I'm Roslyn now. This woman in the movie I'm doing. I'm not an actress, just a woman. I try to be good. I've been hurt by men, I'm divorced. I'm not bitter, though. I'll find my way. I live in Reno, I mean as Roslyn. But I never gamble in the casinos, I'd only just lose.

I could be your driver, I said.

The Studio provides a driver, I guess.

I could be Marilyn's bodyguard.

Bodyguard?

You think I'm not strong? I am. Don't underestimate me, Norma Jeane. I'm not—

This knife? I carry this knife. I'm protected from any fucker fucking with me.

Oh, Fleece.

What? This scares you?

Oh, Fleece, I guess I . . . I don't like a knife.

Well, this is my knife. This is my protection.

Fleece, I think you should put that knife away.

Yeah? Where? Put it away where?

In a—where you took it out of.

The blade? I should put the blade—where?

Fleece, don't scare me. I n-never meant—

You look kind of scared, Marilyn. Jesus.

I'm not. I'm only just—

Like I'd hurt you? Norma Jeane? *You?* I'd never hurt you.

Oh, I know that, Fleece. I hope so.

My little Mouse.

It just makes me n-nervous. A knife like that.

I'm not afraid to use this to protect myself. I could protect you.

I know you could, Fleece. I appreciate that.

Somebody comes up to Marilyn & says something rude, or pushes against her. I'll be your bodyguard.

I don't know, Fleece.

There's those who want to hurt Marilyn. I could protect you.

I don't know, Fleece.

Hell you don't know! That's why you wanted me back.

Fleece, I—

OK I put the knife away, OK there ain't no knife. Never was no knife. See?

Thank you, Fleece.

I always knew you, Norma Jeane. I never forgot you. I saw you were Marilyn, for all of us.

Kissing Fleece, did I dare kiss Fleece or it was a dream of kissing Fleece & being kissed by (& bitten by!) Fleece, & my lips raw afterward, swollen. Kissing Fleece like inhaling ether. So fierce & orangey-smelling & my heart brimmed to bursting.

oh God thank You.

The anniversary. Their fourth. Came & went unheralded.

The estranged husband. Discovered it wasn't only Gable she was entranced by (& possibly fucking) there was the yet more enigmatic Montgomery

Clift. Alcoholic and charmingly deranged and his handsome face ravaged and scarred from a motorcycle accident that had nearly killed him the previous year; a Benzedrine/Amytal junkie (by syringe?); a recluse in his trailer like a willfully absent Dionysus hiding out with his perpetual grapefruit and vodka and insolent young lover and refusing most interviews and even to venture forth into the "ghastly" Nevada sunshine until nighttime. Many in the *Misfits* crew were making book that Clift would not finish the film and was a higher risk even than Monroe. "Know why I love Monty Clift? He's a Gemini." "A what?" "A Gemini like me." The husband would not be jealous of a doomed homosexual actor, he had too much pride. She saw the hurt in his eyes and touched his arm. (Her first touch in days.) Suddenly she was Roslyn, blond healing beauty in soft focus. "Oh, hey, what I mean is: I don't know if Monty's born under my actual sign, I mean he's like my twin? There's people who're like your twin, you meet? Montgomery Clift is mine."

The husband had come to fear Clift as a mystery deeper than even his wife, whose suicidal malaise (he was certain) had only to do with the loss of their baby. That terrible day in Maine that had changed their lives forever. A woman's perpetual and exhausting grief.

A woman is her womb, isn't she?

If not her womb, what is a woman?

Since Maine, their relations had permanently altered. Since Nevada, she no longer welcomed him into her bed. Yet he knew she wanted a baby as desperately as ever; perhaps more desperately, now she'd had another birthday and her health was increasingly unstable. As the doctor had predicted she had frequent uterine pain, "spotting" that terrified her. Her menstrual periods were as painful as ever, and irregular.

Of course he'd never told her what the doctor had said. Her "scarred" uterus. Her "crude" abortions.

That would be his, the husband's, secret. That he knew, and that she could not know what he knew.

If not her womb, *what is a woman*?

At the happy ending of *The Misfits*, Roslyn and her cowboy lover Gay Langland speak of having children. (No matter the disparity in their ages.) After the trauma of the lassoed and finally released mustangs, they are driving "home." They are guided by a "north star."

If I couldn't give you a baby in life, Norma, I will give you a baby in this dream of you.

Did it matter that the Blond Actress regarded him, the master of words, with scorn? In the daily rushes, Roslyn was all shimmering sensitivity. Those who abhorred the Blond Actress were seduced by Roslyn. It would be acknowledged that Roslyn was the most subtle, the most complex, the most brilliant of all screen performances by Marilyn Monroe; even in the midst of filming, with disaster a possibility at any hour, this fact was known. Roslyn was like a beautiful vase that has been broken and shattered yet by patience, craft, and cunning meticulously restored, fragment by fragment, bit by bit, with tweezers and glue, you see only the restored vase and have no knowledge of the shattered vase, still less of the monomaniacal energy that has gone into its restoration. The illusion of wholeness, of beauty. Delusion?

I'm losing her. I must save her. The estranged husband would not have wished to admit even to himself that he'd abandoned his playwriting career. His deepest self. His life in New York City among his theater friends whom he respected as he could not respect filmmakers. H he recognized as a genius of a kind; yet not his kind, for he required solitude, inwardness, a probing of the imagination, not an aggressive prodding. He'd become, in the West, a servant not only of the Blond Actress, who devoured those in her service with the greed of the perpetually ravenous, but of The Studio; he, too, was on their payroll, he too was "for hire." He told himself it was only temporary. He told himself that *The Misfits* would be a masterpiece that would redeem him. An act of husbandly love that would save his marriage. Yet his soul was elsewhere: in the East. He missed his book-crammed steam-heated little apartment on 72nd Street, he missed his daily walks into Central Park, he missed the quarrelsome company of Max Pearlman. He missed his younger self! Strange that plays of his were being performed, but these were plays he'd written years before; he wasn't involved in their productions and would have had no time had he been asked. He'd become a classic while still alive: an alarming fate. Like Marilyn Monroe idolized by millions of strangers even as the woman herself was vomiting into a toilet, the door ajar so that he, the despairing husband, the revulsed husband, was obliged to hear and yet not to question.

"Nobody likes to be *spied on*, mister: got it?"

And another time he'd found her in the steamy bathroom shaving her legs, her hand so shaky or her vision so blurred she'd nicked and cut herself, her dead-white skin, her slender beautiful legs, and was bleeding from a dozen miniature wounds. Almost sobbing in her rage at his concern, the very look on her face: "Get out of here! Who asked you! Go to hell out of here! I'm so ugly? So disgusting? Jewish men despise women, that's your problem, mister, not mine."

He'd left her, screaming at him. He'd shut the door. Maybe she'd seen something in his face more than husbandly concern.

From that time he watched her covertly, without comment. He would have wanted to tell her *I won't judge you. I only just want to save you.* He'd permanently set aside his dramatic work. All that remained of years of writing were fragments, sketches. Scenes that began and ended on a single sheet of paper. He'd abandoned *The Girl with the Flaxen Hair*. No longer could he believe in his naive vision of Magda, "the girl of the people." As the Blond Actress had shrewdly seen, Magda would have been so much angrier than he knew. But he couldn't envision his Magda that way. He couldn't envision his adolescent Isaac self any longer. His dreams of Back There had long since ceased. Back There had meant emotional upset, yet inspiration for his writing; since marriage to the Blond Actress, little of his previous life remained. Rahway, New Jersey, had become more distant to him now than the miseries of London during the filming of *The Prince and the Showgirl*, when he'd given up even trying to write in order to care for his disintegrating wife. (He couldn't begrudge her the surprising success of Monroe's performance in that waxworks of a film. Critics had adored her. She'd even won an award from the Italian film industry! Not even a booby prize for him.) Yet he could not write about her and their marriage. Except in private, in secret. *Never would I expose her. Betray her. I will not.*

For the truth was, he still loved her. He was waiting to again love her. Even if she repudiated him publicly. Even if she filed for divorce.

Covertly he watched her, without comment or judgment. *She is deceiving herself. She isn't Roslyn. She's fighting for her life to wrest this movie away from the male actors. Her rivals.* The Blond Actress perceived herself and was perceived by the world as a victim, yet in her innermost heart she was rapacious, pitiless. He'd seen her reading Darwin's *Origin of Species* with such intensity you would think she was reading of her own future. Marilyn Monroe, reading Darwin! No one would believe it. Now she was reading Pascal's *Pensées*. Pascal! (Where'd she get this book? He'd been astonished to see her extract it out of the chaos of one of her suitcases, leaf through it, and begin to read, where she stood, frowning and moving her her lips.) But rarely now did she speak with him about her reading, and if she still wrote poetry she didn't show it to him. She no longer read Christian Science material. She'd left her books on Jewish history and the Holocaust behind in the Captain's House.

A bloody pulp soaking into the dirt floor of the cellar.

In Reno, her most intense rivalry was with H. For H was one of those men who seemingly felt no desire for Marilyn Monroe. She complained of H. "Everybody says he's a genius. Some genius! What he loves is gambling and horses. He's in this project for the money. He doesn't respect actors."

The playwright husband asked, "Why are we in this project?"

"Maybe you for the money. Me, I'm fighting for my life."

There's a curse on the actor, always you are seeking an audience. And when the audience sees your hunger it's like smelling blood. Their cruelty begins.

. . .

H shouted one day, "Marilyn, look at me!" and she wouldn't. "Look at *me*." They were on location in the desert outside Reno for the rodeo scene. A blinding-hot day, temperature must've been 100 degrees Fahrenheit. There was H, paunchy and soaked in sweat and those glaring-bulging eyes of mad Nero sculpted by a bemused and mock-reverent hand. Heaved himself out of his chair and broke into a run like a steer and actually grabbed her wrist as we stared; we would have liked to see Monroe thrown to the burning sand, such grief Monroe had been causing us for days and days in this hellhole of shimmering sun (in late October) but Monroe turned and struck at him, clawed him quick as a cat. H would claim *The animal rage in that woman! Scared the shit out of me.* H outweighed Monroe by possibly one hundred pounds but H was no match for Monroe. She broke loose and ran away and slammed into her trailer (where there was an air-conditioning unit); then a few minutes later surprised us all by returning, makeup freshened, hair nicely brushed, for Whitey and the crew were always in attendance, and there came Roslyn smiling like the cat that's had the cream.

What she showed me was she wasn't Roslyn. She was nothing to do with Roslyn. Roslyn who loves these men, these losers, and nurses them. She could play Roslyn like a virtuoso musician plays his instrument. No more. She wanted me to know. Only then she could finish the scene.

Fleece! She'd known it might be a mistake but what the hell, it's like watching your hand toss a pair of losing dice. You have to watch.

She'd bought a plane ticket for Fleece to come to Reno for a week to stay at the Zephyr Hotel to keep her company when she was blue & to watch the filming of *The Misfits*. Shake hands with the legendary Clark Gable! Montgomery Clift! Her husband disapproved. Fleece wasn't "stable," he said, you could see that at thirty feet, & she retorted, "Am I stable? Is 'Marilyn'?" He said, "The issue isn't you. The issue is this person you call 'Fleet.' " "Fleece." (He'd met Fleece briefly in Hollywood, on a sidewalk. Sulky Fleece in soiled suede cowboy hat, electric-blue satin shirt, tight black jeans showing the V of her skinny crotch & fake palomino-hide boots. She'd shaken the playwright's hand with exaggerated courtesy & called him "sir.") Norma Jeane said, "Fleece is the only one who knows *me*. Who remembers Norma Jeane from the orphanage." The husband said gently, "But why is that a good thing, darling?"

Norma Jeane stared at him, unable to speak.

Darling. Hadn't she killed this man's love for her, by now?

Fleece had been excited about coming to Reno as a special guest of Marilyn Monroe. But she'd turned in her plane ticket & came instead by

Greyhound bus. In the Zephyr, she would run up a room service bill of over three hundred dollars in three days, much of it for liquor. She would badly damage the room with spillage & cigarette burns; she would fall asleep in the tub while running bathwater & the water would overflow onto the floor and through the floor into the room below. (These hotel damages, Norma Jeane would pay.) She would pawn the gold Bulova wristwatch Norma Jeane impulsively gave her, removed from her wrist (a gift from Z inscribed *To My Sugar Kane*). She would pawn several items from her hotel room including a brass lamp in the shape of a rearing horse smuggled from the hotel in a shower curtain. She would lose literally every penny of the one-hundred-dollar "stake" provided by Norma Jeane in the casinos. She would not visit the set of *The Misfits* once. She would kiss Norma Jeane fully & fiercely on the mouth in the very presence of the playwright husband, who was himself mildly drunk or pretending to be so. She would abruptly leave the married couple in the midst of dinner in a Reno restaurant & would subsequently be arrested early the following morning in a casino bar for causing a disturbance & slashing a blackjack dealer & a security guard with a knife & she would be jailed on several charges including assault with a deadly weapon until Marilyn Monroe of all people (the tabloid *National Enquirer* would publish the lurid scoop featuring a large photo of the dazed-looking Marilyn in dark glasses & smeared lipstick mouth trying to shield her eyes from the camera flash) came to post her one-thousand-dollar bail bond. Shortly afterward she would disappear from Reno, probably by Greyhound, leaving only a scribbled note for Norma Jeane pushed beneath her hotel door.

DEAR MOUSE

LIVE FOREVER IN **MARILYN** FOR US!

YOUR FLEECE LOVES YOU

The estranged husband. Heard a scratching at the door. In the night. They were in separate rooms in the suite, he on a sofa and she in the bedroom insomniac and drinking Dom Perignon and reading and inscribing in her battered journal in a shaky hand *Between us and heaven and hell there is only life, the frailest thing in the world* until her eyes would not focus and later then trying to get out of bed—and such a high bed!—her legs so weak she had to crawl like a baby to the door but it was the wrong door, not the bathroom door; he would find her naked (always she slept naked) whimpering and clawing at the door and discover to his alarm and disgust she'd soiled herself and the carpet. Not for the first time.

Maybe all there is is   just the next thing

This time Marilyn came out alone, with us, visiting the bars and casinos, and in the Horseshoe Casino there was H at the craps table and called us over. H was a compulsive gambler and like all such his anxiety wasn't losing but being out of the game and having to leave the casino and return to his hotel room alone. H drunk and in a maudlin mood now *The Misfits* had only another week or so of shooting on location and he was telling himself it might be a masterpiece or maybe it was an utter flop. H took up Monroe's hand and kissed it. Those two! They fought so much on the set neither could truly recall, meeting like this, who'd gotten the shitty end of the stick that day, who owed who an apology, or maybe they were even for once. H was up a few hundred at the craps table and staked Monroe to fifty bucks, and Monroe said in this baby voice she never gambled 'cause she'd only just lose, knowing the house odds were against her, and H cut her off like a director will, not realizing he's being rude, saying, "Honey, just throw the fucking dice," and Monroe laughed this nervous little squeaky laugh like a single throw of the dice was her life at stake, and she threw and won; it had to be explained how she'd won (craps is a complicated game); she smiled at the people clapping for her but told H she wanted to quit while she was ahead, for sure she'd lose if she tried again, and H looked at her surprised, saying, "Honey, that isn't Marilyn. Not the Marilyn I know. That's fucking poor sportsmanship, we're only just getting started." Monroe looked scared. (There were plenty of people gawking and some even snapping pictures but it wasn't these people she was scared of. Strangers gawking at her, whispering to themselves *That's Marilyn Monroe!* made her feel safe and protected.) She said, "What? You play till you lose? I don't like that." H said, "That's right, honey. You play till you have nothing left to lose."

That was what they did, those two, that night at the Horseshoe Casino our last week in Reno, Nevada.

The estranged husband. He would say, he would allow himself in the carelessness of grief to be quoted, "I gave her *The Misfits* and she left me anyway, I love her and don't understand."

The fairy tale. Some movies you make and forget even as you're making them and won't bother to see even the previews, and some movies you feel such anguish for, you'll never forget and see numberless times and come to love and in retrospect convince yourself you'd loved the hour-by-hour experience of making the movie as in retrospect you might wish to convince yourself you'd loved the hour-by-hour experience of your own mysterious life, at its conclusion. So we loved the fairy tale of *The Misfits*. We loved Monroe and Gable loving each other. The Fair Princess and the Dark Prince they were, strolling in the desert dusk, whispering and laughing together. Monroe had her arm linked tight through Gable's. She was a brash little girl leaning into the crook of his arm. Now he'd aged into his sixtieth year Gable was revealed to be solid as rock. He had a broad big alert face lined and creased like a weatherworn rock. That thin mustache. That quizzical half smile.

Did you think Gable wasn't real? Gable can't die like any of you, of a heart attack in a few weeks?

Now that Monroe had aged into her thirty-fifth year you saw she would never be The Girl again and her hair appeared prematurely white, wispy-white in the lengthening shadows and her eyes!—those yet-beautiful eyes always watering and shifting out of focus (never detected by the camera; the camera was forever Monroe's lover) as if even as you spoke with her you were not-there for her, as in a dream sudden images appear imposed upon others and fade and are gone without memory, and yet most of the time Monroe would reply coherently and often she was witty, cheerful, "doing" Marilyn to make you smile. In this scene the Fair Princess in shirt and slacks and boots and the Dark Prince in cowboy attire and a hat amid the sharp fragrance of sagebrush. It was a stark clear night. The movie music so subdued almost you can't hear it. In the distance you could see the glow of Reno like a strange undersea phosphorescence.

She was saying, "Funny how we end up!" and he was saying, "Honey, don't talk like that. You're far from ending up." She said, "I mean here in the Nevada desert. Mr. Gable—" "Haven't I told you to call me 'Clark,' Marilyn. How many times?" "C-clark! When my mother was a little girl, she used to pretend you were my father," she said eagerly, and realizing her error amended, "I mean when *I* was a little girl, my mother used to pretend you were my father." Gable snorted with laughter that may have been genuine. He said, "That long ago!" She protested, tugging at his arm, "Oh, hey. It wasn't that long ago I was a little girl, Clark." Good-naturedly he said, "Hell, I'm an old man, Marilyn. You know that." "Oh Mr. G-gable you'll never be old. The rest of us come and go. I'm just a blonde. There's so many blondes. But you, Mr. Gable, will be forever." She was pleading with him, and Clark Gable was gentleman enough to grant her the possibility. "Honey, if you say so." His several heart attacks had left him with a shaken sense of his own mortality and yet he had not protested like the others the delays in filming and the ceaseless stress caused by Monroe's unpredictable behavior. *She's not a well girl. She'd be well, if she could.* He would not much complain of filming in searing-hot desert temperatures and as Gay Langland he would choose to perform many of his character's strenuous action shots and in an accident find himself dragged by a rope behind a truck traveling at thirty-five miles an hour. Oh, Gable knew he was mortal! Yet he had a new young wife. His wife was pregnant. Wouldn't that mean he would live for many years, to see his child grow up?

In old Hollywood, it would.

The fairy tale. The Blond Actress would herself come to believe in this fairy tale a man had written for her as a love offering. She would come to believe not just that luminous Roslyn could save the small herd of wild mustangs but that wild mustangs might be saved. These horses, only six remaining of how many hundreds and one of them a foal. A foal galloping anxiously beside its mother. Lassoed and roped by the desperate men, yet they might be saved from death. From the butcher's knife and being ground into dog food. Here is no romance of the West or even of manly ideals and courage but a melancholy "realism" to thrust into an American audience's faces! Roslyn alone would save the mustangs with her slow-gathering female fury. Roslyn alone would run into the desert in an action blocked out with care by the Blond Actress and her director that would allow her to express, at the top of her lungs, her fury at manly cruelty. ("But I don't want close-ups. Not of me screaming.") She would scream at the men *Liars! Killers! Why don't you kill yourselves!* She would scream in the emptiness of the Nevada desert until her throat was raw. Until the interior of her sore-pocked mouth throbbed with pain. Until more capillaries burst in her straining eyes. Until her heart pounded close to bursting. *I hate you! Why don't you die!* She may have been screaming at those men of her life whose faces she retained or she may have been screaming at those men lacking faces, constituting the vast world beyond the perimeters of the crimson velvet backdrop and the blinding-bright photographer's lights. She may have been screaming at H who had eluded her charm. She may have been screaming into a mirror. She'd told Doc Fell she would not need any medication that morning (after even the stupor of the phenobarbital night) and aroused now to pity, horror, rage by the spectacle of the trapped horses she had not needed any drug. She believed she would never again need any drugs. What power! What joy! She would return to Hollywood alone, and she would buy a house, her first house, and she would live alone, and she would do only work she wanted to do; she would be the great actress she had a chance of becoming; she would no longer be trapped by men; she would no longer be cheated of her truest self. The Blond Actress was expressing anger, rage. At last. Except (all observers would claim) it wasn't the simulated expression of anger and rage but genuine passion ripping through the woman's body like an electric current.

"Liars! Killers! *I hate you.*"

Weeks behind schedule. Hundreds of thousands of dollars over budget. The most expensive black-and-white feature film ever made.

"We owe it all to our Marilyn. Infinite thanks."

This time there would be no lavish premiere for a Monroe movie.

No royal motorcade making its way along Hollywood Boulevard past thousands of screaming fans. No gala celebration at Grauman's. No sparkling Dom Perignon foaming and overflowing down the Blond Actress's bare arm. By the time the film was released Clark Gable would have been dead for several months. Monroe would have been divorced for nearly as long. *The Misfits* would be a box-office failure. It was a film disliked by The Studio that had produced it, though it would receive intelligent, respectful reviews and the performances of Gable, Monroe, and Clift would be praised. It would be damned as special, "artistic." It had a stubborn integrity. The characters resembled broken-down actors. Famous faces yet not themselves. You looked at Gay Langland and thought *Wasn't he once Clark Gable?* You looked at the blond Roslyn and thought *Wasn't she once Marilyn Monroe?* You looked at the battered rodeo performer Perce Howland and thought *My God! He used to be Montgomery Clift.* These are people you knew when you were a kid. Gay Langland was a bachelor uncle of yours; Roslyn Tabor was a friend of your mother's, a small-town divorcée. Small-town wistfulness and lost glamour. Maybe your father was in love with Roslyn Tabor! You'll never know. The rodeo performer was a drifter, sad-eyed, skinny, with a ruined face. You'd see him in the early evening outside the bus station smoking and casting ghost-eyes in your direction. *Hey: do you know me?* These were ordinary Americans of the fifties yet mysterious to you because you knew them long ago when the world was mysterious and even your own face, contemplated in a mirror, in for instance the cigarette vending machine of that bus station or in the water-specked mirror above a lavatory sink, was a mystery never to be solved.

Living in the house at 12305 Fifth Helena Drive, Brentwood, Norma Jeane would one day realize, "All that Roslyn was, was my life."

CLUB ZUMA

Hey? Who?

Astonished to see her Magic Friend up there onstage & the dance performed in front of mirrors. Flashing/gyrating lights. "I Wanna Be Loved by You." MARILYN MONROE in the white crepe sundress with the halter top, swirling pleated skirt, & white panties exposed as an updraft of air lifts the skirt. The audience screams. Shapely legs spread. Arching her spine squealing with delight & the crowd whistles, cheers, thumps fists & feet amid a haze of blue smoke & deafening music. *Oh why'd they bring me here, I don't want to be here.* Shining platinum-blond hair on the dancer's bobbing head. MARILYN MONROE look-alike except the white clown face is longer & the jaw more prominent, & a bigger nose. But the red-luscious mouth & blue-shadowed eyes sparkling like rhinestones. And big breasts in the halter top. The dancer begins to strut, stomp, wriggle in her spike high heels, to shake big boobs & ass. Mari-*lyn*! Mari-*lyn*! the crowd loves her. *Oh please I wish you wouldn't. We're more than just meat to be laughed at. We are!*

This night smelling of jasmine & Jockey Club cologne & there's Norma Jeane cringing in dark glasses, white silk turban hiding her hair & white silk pasha trousers & a man's striped jacket belonging to Carlo. *Oh why'd he do this. Why'd he bring me here I thought he loved me?* The dancer is skillful, contorting her mammalian body in the accelerating beat of copulation. Pelvis like an air hammer. Moist pink tip of tongue between her lips. Panting, moaning. Caressing her big bouncy breasts. The audience loves this! Can't get enough! *Oh why? Make them laugh at us?* The dancer is coked to the gills you can see her white eyeballs & sweat gleaming on her chest streaking the white clown makeup like exposed nerves. Can't stop that rhythm! The crowd is insatiable. Like fucking. Rhythm builds, can't stop. The dancer in the mirrors stripping off her elbow-length white gloves, tossing them into the frenzied crowd. *I wanna be loved be loved by you by you by nobody else but you.* Removing stockings & tossing. Removing the halter top—*Ohhhh!*—the crowd in Club Zuma goes crazy. Club Zuma on the Strip hazy-blue with smoke. Carlo's Moroccan cigarettes. Carlo laughing with the rest. The dancer struts amid swirling smoke & deafening music holding her enormous bouncy breasts like foam rubber, neon-pink nipples the size of grapes & next the pleated skirt is torn off & tossed & she's shimmying her plump ass & turns her back to the screaming audience stoops & spreads cheeks—*Ohhhh!* the audience groans, yells—the dancer now nude gleaming in powdery-caked oily-white sweat on her pimply back & turning at last in triumph to reveal the long slender penis taped to the shaved pubis with flesh-colored adhesive & this adhesive she/he unfurls with a scream *wanna be loved be loved be loved be loved* & now the crowd in Club Zuma has truly gone crazy, screaming at the dancer & frantic bobbing penis semi-erect

MARI-LYN!   MARI-LYN!   MARI-LYN!

DIVORCE (RETAKE)

> Once a part is prepared and elaborated in all its
> details . . . the actor will always play it correctly
> even if uninspired.
>
> —Michael Chekhov,
> *To the Actor*

I

"I'm sorry. Oh forgive me! I c-can't say anything more."

In this newsreel known as the Divorce Press Conference the Blond Actress, tastefully dressed in black, is white-skinned as a geisha. Like Cherie in *Bus Stop* she appears so much paler than her companions, she might be a mannequin or a clown. Her lips have been outlined in a purplish-red pencil to make them appear larger and fuller than they are. Her eyes, seemingly reddened from weeping, have been carefully made up in pale blue eye shadow and dark brown mascara to match her eyebrows. Her hair as always is platinum blond, with a high glossy sheen. This is MARILYN MONROE and yet a hurt, confused woman. Her manner is both agitated and eager-to-please. As if in the midst of uttering crucial words to be recorded by dozens of journalists she's forgetting her lines. She's forgetting who she is: MARILYN MONROE. She's wearing an elegant black linen suit with a pale diaphanous scarf knotted at her throat, dark-tinted stockings, and black high-heeled shoes. No jewelry. No rings: her shaky hands are conspicuously bare of rings. (Yes: she threw her wedding ring into the Truckee River in Reno, Nevada, like the divorcée Roslyn Tabor. A revered old Reno custom!) It's startling to see MARILYN MONROE appearing fragile and not busty; the assembled media people have been informed that she's recently lost "between ten and twelve pounds." She is "suffering mental anguish" since her Mexican divorce from her playwright husband of four years and since the "tragic death" of her friend and co-star Clark Gable.

Like a widow. You want to impress these cynics as a widow suffering irrevocable loss, not a divorcée relieved to be free of a dead marriage.

Though she manages to stammer more or less coherent answers to questions about Clark Gable—how close a friend was he, what of accusations made by the actor's widow that MARILYN MONROE was directly responsible for Gable's heart attack, so delaying and complicating the production of *The Misfits*, causing such stress et cetera—she will not discuss her former husband. Either of her former husbands. The Playwright and the Ex-Athlete. Except to say in a whispery voice, so quiet her words must be repeated by her divorce attorney who stands beside her, the Blond Actress leaning on his arm, she "infinitely respects" them.

Be natural. Say what you feel. If you don't feel anything say what you'd imagine you might feel if you weren't sedated with Demerol.

"They are g-great men. Great Americans. I revere them as human beings of fame and achievement in their fields though I c-could not remain married to them as a woman." She begins to cry. She lifts a clutched tissue—no, it's a white handkerchief—to her eyes. A brassy-voiced female reporter for one of the tabloids dares to ask if MARILYN MONROE feels she has "failed as a wife, a woman, a mother" and there's a collective gasp from the assemblage at such audacity (just the question everyone was dying to ask!); the Blond Actress's attorney frowns, a press representative/media consultant from The Studio who stands close behind her frowns, clearly the Blond Actress isn't required to answer so rude a question, but bravely, lifting her stricken eyes to search out her persecutor, she says, "All my life I have t-tried not to fail. I have tried so hard! I tried to be adopted out of the orphanage. That's the Home, on El Centro Avenue. I tried to excel in sports in high school. I tried to be a good housewife to my first husband who left me at the age of seventeen. I've tried so hard to be a good actress, not just another blonde. Oh you know I've tried, don't you? Marilyn Monroe was a pinup, you r-remember I was a calendar girl, nineteen years old, I was paid fifty dollars for 'Miss Golden Dreams' and it almost ruined my career, it's said to be the best-selling calendar photo in history and the model received only fifty dollars for it back in 1949, but I'm not b-bitter. I'm upset I guess but I'm not b-bitter or angry or—I just keep thinking about what might have been, having a b-baby and—oh and Mr. Gable is gone and Marilyn Monroe is even being blamed for that!—though I loved him—as a friend—though he'd had heart attacks before—oh I miss him!—I miss him I guess more than I miss my marriage—my marriages—"

No more. The mood we want is elegiac, not melodramatic. If the genre is tragic it's classic, Greek: the bloody messes are offstage and only reflection remains.

"I'm sorry. Oh, forgive me! I c-can't say anything more." She is crying seriously. She hides her face. Camera flashes have been intermittent and continuous through the press conference and now dozens of cameras flash simultaneously; the effect is of a miniature A-bomb! The Blond Actress is escorted by her two male companions to a waiting limousine (the Divorce Press Conference has been staged on the front lawn of the Beverly Hills residence in which the Blond Actress is currently residing, courtesy of her agent Holyrod or maybe Z of The Studio or "a Marilyn film devotee") and the media people, disappointed at the brevity of the press conference, press forward now, lunging out of control like maddened dogs, a pack of journalists, columnists, radio people, photographers, camera crews, many more than the select few invited for this exclusive event; the newsreel sound track picks up isolated frenzied shouts—"Miss Monroe, one more question please!"—"Marilyn, wait!"—"Marilyn, tell our listeners in radioland: will Marlon Brando be your next?"—and despite several Studio security guards fending off the crowd, a wily little Italian-looking reporter with satyr ears manages to slip under the attorney's arm and thrusts a microphone into the Blond Actress's face with such violence he strikes her very mouth (and chips a front tooth!—to be repaired by a Studio dentist) shouting in accented English, "Mari-*lyn*! Is't true you hava many times tried to *suicide*?" Another audacious party, apparently not a bona fide journalist, brawny and sweatily gleaming with up-tufted hair like a toothbrush and a face that appears boiled-looking on film, manages to thrust an envelope at the frightened Blond Actress which she takes, seeing it's addressed to MISS MARILYN MONROE in red ink and attractively decorated with several red Valentine hearts.

Then the Blond Actress is in the limousine. The rear door is shut. The windows are dark-tinted, impossible to see through from the outside. Her escorts speak sharply to the crowd—"Give the girl a break, will you!"—"She's suffering, you can see!"—and climb into the limousine and it moves off, slowly at first, for photographers are blocking the street; then it's gone. The crowd in its wake still clamoring for attention and cameras still flashing until the newsreel breaks off.

2

"Am I d-divorced now? Is it over?"

"Marilyn, you were divorced a week ago. Remember? In Mexico City? We flew down together."

"Oh, I guess. It's all over then?"

"All over, dear. For the time being."

The men laughed as if the Blond Actress had uttered witty lines.

They were in the rear of the speeding limousine behind dark-tinted windows. No longer on camera. It should have been *real life* but it did not seem real. It was no easier to breathe now, or to focus her eyes. Her front teeth ached where a hard object had struck her but she told herself it had been an accident, the reporter hadn't meant to hurt her. Her attorney whose name she didn't immediately recall and the Studio PR man Rollo Freund were congratulating her; she'd performed beautifully in a stressful situation. *It was my real life. But yes it was a performance.*

"Excuse me? I'm d-divorced, now?" She saw by their faces she must've asked this question already and knew the answer. "Oh, I mean—will I have more papers to sign?"

Always, more papers to sign. In the presence of a notary.

MARILYN MONROE signed such documents averting her eyes. Better not to know!

In the speeding limousine that was a kind of Time Machine. Already she was forgetting where she'd been. She had no idea where she was being taken. Maybe there was more publicity to do for *The Misfits*. "Rollo Freund" was in fact "Otto Öse" and maybe he was still a girlie photographer? She was too tired to sort it out. She fumbled in her handbag for a Benzedrine tablet to wake her up but couldn't find any. Or her fingers were too clumsy. Oh, she missed sinister Doc Fell now he was gone! (Doc Fell, resident physician at The Studio, had vanished from The Studio. A new physician resembling Mickey Rooney had taken his place. There was a cruel rumor circulating in Hollywood that Doc Fell had been found dead seated on a toilet in his Topanga Canyon bungalow, trousers around his ankles and a syringe in his scarred arm; in some versions of the story he'd died of a morphine overdose, in other versions of a heroin overdose. A tragic end for a physician who resembled wholesome Cary Grant!)

She was clutching the Valentine envelope in her fingers. For months she'd been nervously awaiting another letter from her father but supposed this would not be it. "I'm so lonely. I don't understand why I'm so lonely when I've loved so many people. I loved girls in the Home, my sisters!—my only friends. But I've lost them all. My mother hardly seems to know me. My father writes to me but keeps his distance. Am I a leper? A freak? A curse? Men say they love me but who's it they love? 'Marilyn.' *I* love animals, especially horses. I'm helping some people in Reno start a fund to save the wild mustangs of the Southwest. I wish no animals ever had to die. Except natural death!"

One of the men cleared his throat and said, "Your interview is over now,

Marilyn. Why don't you relax." She was trying to explain how unfair, how unjust it was to be blamed for Clark Gable's death—"When I was the one who loved him. So much! He was the only man I've ever truly admired. My m-mother Gladys Mortensen knew Mr. Gable a long time ago when they'd both been young and new to Hollywood." Another time she was gently told, "The interview is over, Marilyn." She said as if pleading, "Why love goes wrong, it's a mystery. I didn't invent that mystery, did I? Why am I to blame? I know you're supposed to play the dice until you lose. You're supposed to be brave, a good sport. I'm going to try. Next time I'll be a better actress, I promise."

The men were fascinated by this famous film actress. Seeing close up how her face was a girl's innocent face beneath that crust of theatrical makeup. Such makeup is ideal for photography but jarring to the naked eye. They noted how pathetically she was clutching the Valentine envelope, as if a message from an anonymous fan, a declaration of love by a stranger, might save her life. "Don't stare at me, please! I'm not a freak. I don't care to be memorized for anecdotal purposes. Nor do I want to sign any more legal documents. Except for my mother's trust fund. To keep her at the Lakewood Home after I'm"—she paused, confused: what did she mean to say?—"in case something unexpected happens to me." She laughed. "Or expected."

Both men quickly protested she shouldn't speak like that. MARILYN MONROE was still a young woman and would live a long, long time.

3

This strange thing! "Wish I had somebody to *tell*."

Rollo Freund, the press representative/media manager hired by The Studio to oversee their star MARILYN MONROE was no one else but Otto Öse! Returned to her, after more than a decade.

Yet the man refused to acknowledge he'd once been Otto Öse. As Rollo Freund he claimed to be a "native New Yorker" who'd migrated to L.A. in the late fifties to pioneer in a new science called "media management." Within a few years he'd become so successful, the film companies were bidding for his services. For those megastars (like MARILYN MONROE) who seemed always to be involved in sensational publicity and scandal, stars possibly inclined to self-destruction, an expert media manager was a necessity. Otto Öse, or Rollo Freund, was tall and brooding as Norma Jeane remembered, and as thin, with a hawkish, pockmarked face, a drooping left eyelid that gave him a perpetually ironic look, and those curious thornlike scars on his forehead. *His crown of thorns. Him, Judas*! His once-black hair had faded to the color of used steel wool and now covered his bony skull in a peculiar oleaginous fuzz. He must have been in his fifties. He hadn't aged so much as calcified. His small shrewd eyes seemed to peep at you, watery and alert, out of an imperturbable plaster mask. His teeth had been beautifully capped, Hollywood style. *The ugliest man I've ever seen. Yet not dead!*

Rollo Freund drove a bottle-green Jaguar and dressed in expensive shark-colored suits custom made (as he boasted) by "my tailor in Bond Street, London." These suits fitted his pencil-thin body so tightly he had to sit bolt upright in a posture familiar to the Blond Actress when she was sewn into her straitjacket gowns. When first introduced she'd been sharp-eyed Norma Jeane and not the sweetly myopic and self-absorbed Blond Actress and she'd recognized Otto Öse at once though he'd grown an ashy goatee and was wearing amber-tinted steel glasses and one of his custom-made suits. She'd stared at this man in astonishment. She stammered, "But don't we know each other? Otto Öse? I'm Norma Jeane, remember?"

Rollo Freund, like any practiced liar or actor, regarded this remark with equanimity. He was not one to allow any situation involving him to be commandeered by another. He smiled politely at the clearly confused woman. " 'Oz'? I'm afraid I'm unacquainted with any 'Oz.' You must be mistaking me for another man, Miss Monroe."

Norma Jeane laughed. "Oh, Otto, this is ridiculous. Calling me 'Miss Monroe.' You know me, Norma Jeane. You're the photographer who took my picture for *Stars & Stripes* and you're responsible for Miss Golden Dreams—you paid me fifty dollars!—and you haven't changed so much I can't recognize you. You'd have to be more than dead, Otto, for me not to recognize you." Otto Öse, or Rollo Freund, laughed heartily as if the Blond Actress had uttered one of her witticisms. She said, pleading, "Please, Otto. You must remember. I was Mrs. Bucky Glazer in those days. Wartime. You discovered me and changed my l-life." *Ruined my life, you bastard.* But Otto Öse, or Rollo Freund as he insisted upon being called, was too canny to be seduced even by the Blond Actress.

She had to admire him. What a character!

It was 1961 now, and in Hollywood, as elsewhere, it was no longer a traitorous thing to be or appear to be Jewish. The era of Red Scare anti-Semitism had subsided; hatred of Jews had gone underground or had become more subtly codified, a matter of country club memberships and neighborhood restrictions, not a matter of blacklists and "Commie" persecution; the Rosenbergs had long since been electrocuted and their martyred zeal gone to ashes; Senator Joe McCarthy, the Attila of the right wing, had died and been dragged by devils down into the raging Catholic hell he'd hoped to evoke on earth for others. Otto, or Rollo, made no secret of seeming Jewish; he spoke with a New York Jew inflection that sounded, to Norma Jeane's ear, she who'd lived with a New York Jew for four years, not entirely convincing. Yet when they were alone together Otto, or the intrepid Rollo, refused to acknowledge their shared past. Norma Jeane said, "I get it, I think. 'Otto Öse' was blacklisted so you changed your name?" Still the man shook his head, as if mystified. "I was born Rollo Freund. If I had my birth certificate with me, I'd show you, Miss Monroe." Always he called her "Miss Monroe" and, in time, "Marilyn." These names in his mouth sounded subtly mocking. Hadn't he once accused her of selling herself like merchandise? Hadn't he once predicted for her a lonely junkie's death? He'd said the female body is a joke. He loathed women. Yet he'd introduced her to the writing of Schopenhauer, he'd given her *The Daily Worker* to read. He'd introduced her to Cass Chaplin, who'd made her, for a time, so happy. "Oh, Otto. I mean, Rollo. I won't torment you. I'll be Marilyn."

She had to admire the media manager for his skill in organizing the Divorce Press Conference and for orchestrating it, in the borrowed house, like a director. He'd carefully blocked out not only MARILYN MONROE's movements, as she left the house to face the press, but her attorney's and his own as well. Even the security guards were rehearsed. "The tone we want to avoid is melodrama. You'll dress in black linen, I've ordered just the perfect costume for you from Wardrobe, and you'll look like a widow. You want to impress these cynics as a widow suffering irrevocable loss, not a divorcée relieved to be free of a dead marriage." They were in Z's office when Rollo Freund made this speech. She'd been drinking vodka and the Blond Actress laughed in her new gut-laughter way, like a North Carolina farm girl who didn't give a shit for the film industry or her own beauty or talent. "You said it, Rollo. A dead-doornail marriage. A fucking boring old dead-doornail marriage to a boring old dead-doornail (if kind and decent and 'talented') husband. Help!" When the Blond Actress sailed into one of her riffs, like Fred Allen, Groucho Marx, the late W. C. Fields, observers stared at her in a kind of shock. Rollo Freund and his male companions laughed nervously. MARILYN MONROE was frequently the only female at such gatherings, if you didn't count secretaries and "assistants"; as she'd have specified, the "only practicing vagina"; men were wary of seeming to encourage her though they certainly stared avidly at her, memorizing and storing up anecdotes; for was it true, MARILYN MONROE never wore underwear? (it was! you could see!) and went for days without bathing (she did! you could smell her talcumy sweat). But the men never laughed more than briefly.

You didn't want to encourage Monroe. With a hysteric an outburst is only a fraction of a second away. Handle with kid gloves. Never forget this sleek blond pussy has claws.

Sitting that afternoon on Z's plush sofa, leaning forward and clasping her hands around her crossed knees. Her manner was schoolgirl earnest in the way of a contract-player starlet. She spoke soberly. "When did I agree to a 'divorce press conference'? Divorce isn't a tragedy maybe but it's a private sadness. Four years of marriage to a man and I can't—" She paused, trying to think. Can't what? Can't remember why the hell she'd ever married the playwright? A man nearly old enough to be her father and in temperament old enough to be her grandfather? Not one of the ribald-jolly Jews (like Max Pearlman she'd adored) but a rabbinical-scholarly Jew? Not her type at all? Can't remember his name? "I can't understand where I m-made my mistake so how can I learn from it? There's this French philosopher says 'Heart, instinct, principles.' Shouldn't I be guided by mine? I'm a serious person really. Why don't we cancel it? I'm just feeling so sad and, I don't know, *retreating*."

Z and the other men stared at the Blond Actress as if she'd spoken in a demon's tongue, unknown to their ears. Rollo Freund smoothly leapt in, seeming to agree with her. "You feel genuine emotion, Miss Monroe! That's why you're a brilliant actress. That's why people see in you a magnified image of themselves. Of course they're deluded, but happiness dwells in delusion! Because you live in your soul like a candle that lives in its own burning. You live in our American soul. Don't smile, Miss Monroe. I'm serious, too. I'm saying that you are an intelligent woman, not just a woman of 'feeling'; you're an artist, and like all artists you know that life is just material for your art. Life is what fades, art is what remains. Your emotions, your anguish over your divorce or Mr. Gable's death, whatever—" with an airy impatient gesture taking in all of the world she'd inhabited in thirty-five years or even envisioned: the very memory of the Holocaust evoked out of much-thumbed secondhand books rescued from a used-book store, vessels of Jewish fortitude and suffering and eloquence even in suffering, the stale-rancid odors of the California madhouses of her mother's captivity, all the memories of her personal life, as if they were of no more significance than a screenplay—"you may as well see your trauma as a newsreel, because others will."

"Newsreel? What newsreel?"

"The press conference will be taped. Not just by us, but by the media of course. Parts of it will be played and replayed. It will be a precious document." Seeing the Blond Actress was shaking her head, Rollo Freund continued, with passion, "Miss Monroe. You may as well concede the ultimate form of your raw emotions. Actual life is but the means of achieving form."

Norma Jeane was too shaken to protest. Staring at her old friend Otto, who'd never been her lover or even, in fact, her friend. He was all she had from the days of her youth. She said in her Marilyn voice, so soft and whispery it was almost inaudible, "Oh. I guess. You argue so forcefully. I surrender."

4

And what was in the Valentine envelope?

Seeing her stricken face, Rollo Freund quickly took it from her. "Oh, Miss Monroe. *Sorry.*"

It was a square of white toilet paper upon which someone had carefully block-printed, in what appeared to be actual excrement,

WHORE

MY HOUSE. MY JOURNEY.

The scene must be properly lighted. Beyond the
stage there is unacknowledged darkness.

—From *The Actor's Handbook
and the Actor's Life*

12305 Fifth Helena Drive, Brentwood California

Valentine's Day 1962

Dear Mother,

I just moved into my own house!
I am furnishing it & I am SO HAPPY.

It's a small house Mexican style. So
charming. Hidden & private at the end
of this street & a wall partway around.
Wood-beamed ceilings & a large living
room (with a stone fireplace). The kitchen
is not very modern but you know me,
I'm not Homemaker of the Year exactly!

The big surprise is, behind my house
there is a swimming pool. It's *big*. Imagine!
When we lived in the Hacienda, & on Highland, that one day we would have a house
in Brentwood with a pool.

I am divorced now. You didn't ask about
the baby. I'm afraid I lost the baby.
I should say the baby was taken from me.
~~It was an accident I think~~
I wasn't well for a long time & lost
touch with people.

Now I am VERY WELL. I hope to bring
you home to visit with me soon.

I am "in retreat" from life. Theres a
French philosopher says the unhappiness
of human beings is not being able to stay
in one small room. I walk through these
rooms singing!

I had to borrow $$$ to make this purchase,
I confess. I cried when I signed the
papers. Because I was SO HAPPY. Owning
my first house.

Wish I had more $$$ to show for my long
years of work. Broke into films in 1948
& have only about $5000 saved. I'm
ashamed when others have made so much $$$
from Marilyn. The real estate agent who
sold me this house was surprised I could tell.

Hey I'm not bitter of course! Not me.

Mother, I can't wait to show you my
special surprise for you. It's our piano!
Our white Steinway spinet, remember? Once
belonged to Fredric March. I'd put it in
storage after my first marriage ended & now
it's here. In the living room. I try to
play every day but my fingers are "rusty."
Soon I will play "Für Elise" for you.

There's a room for you here, Mother. Just
waiting. ~~I think it must be time~~
I plan to furnish the house with authentic
Mexican things including tiles. I will travel
soon to Mexico with a friend. Will you be my
friend, Mother?

I have other news, Mother.
I hope you won't be upset. But, I have been
in contact with Father. After all these years,
imagine! Nobody more surprised than me.
Father lives near Griffith Park. I have not yet seen
his house but hope to soon. He said he followed
my career for years & admires my work esp.
The Misfits which he belives is my best (I agree).
Father is a widower now. He speaks of selling
his big house. Who knows what our future will be!

Sometimes I feel I am a widow. Strange there is
no word for a mother who has lost her baby. Not
in English anyway. (Maybe in Latin?) This is a
harder loss than a divorce for sure.

Sometimes I feel I am riding the Time Machine,
don't you? That scary story you read to me.

Oh Mother, I'm not critical but—
it's hard to talk to you sometimes!
On the phone I mean. You don't try to raise
your voice to be heard. I guess that's the
problem? Last Sunday my feelings were hurt,
you left the receiver dangling & walked away?
The nurse apologized. I told her no, I was
just worried you were (1) angry with me (2) unwell

However you know, mother You can come stay here
as long as you wish. On medication, much can
be done. I have a new doctor here & new medication. I am prescribed for "chloral hydrate"
to help me sleep & calm my nerves. If there
are voices

This doctor says there are miracle drugs now
to control the "blues." I said, oh if the
blues go, what about blues music? He asked
is the music worth the agony & I said that
depends upon the music & he said life is more
precious to retain than music, if a person is
depressed her life is endangered & I said
there must be a middle way & I would find that
way.

One day in this house on Helena Drive there will
be grandchildren for you, Mother, I promise.
We will be like other Americans! Life Mag.
asked could they photograph MARILYN MONROE in
her new house & I said oh no not yet, I don't
feel it's mine yet exactly. I have surprises
for you all!

(Who knows maybe Father will join us. That's
my secret wish. Well, "it's a wonderful life"
as they say.)

Mother, I am SO HAPPY. I cry sometimes, I am
alone & so happy. My heart can reach out to
those who have hurt me, & forgive.

On a tile outside my front door there's a
Latin saying CURSUM PERFICIO (translated means
"I am finishing my journey").

Mother, I love you.

Your loving daughter

THE PRESIDENT'S PIMP

Sure he was a pimp.

But not just any pimp. Not him!

He was a pimp *par excellence*. A pimp *nonpareil*. A pimp *sui generis*. A pimp with a wardrobe, and a pimp with style. A pimp with a classy Brit accent. Posterity would honor him as the President's Pimp.

A man of pride and stature: the President's Pimp.

At Rancho Mirage in Palm Springs in March 1962 there was the President poking him in the ribs with a low whistle. "That blonde. That's Marilyn Monroe?"

He told the President yes it was. Monroe, a friend of a friend of his. Luscious, eh? But a little crazy.

Thoughtfully the President asked, "Have I dated her yet?"

The President was a wit. A joker. A quick study. Away from the White House and the pressures of the Presidency, the President was known to enjoy a good time.

"If not, make the arrangements. Pronto."

The President's Pimp laughed uncertainly. He was not the President's only pimp, of course, but he had reason to believe that he was the President's favored pimp. He was certainly the President's most informed pimp.

Quickly telling the hot-blooded President that the sexy blonde was a "poor risk" for a relationship. Notorious for—

"Who's talking about a relationship? I'm talking about a date in the cabana there. If there's time, two."

Uneasily, in a lowered voice, conscious of many admiring eyes upon them as they strolled poolside smoking their after-dinner cigars, the President's Pimp informed the President, as the F.B.I. would have done if consulted, for their files on MARILYN MONROE A.K.A. NORMA JEANE BAKER were bulging, that Monroe had had a dozen abortions, she snorted cocaine, mainlined Benzedrine and phenobarbital HMC, and had had her stomach pumped out a half-dozen times in Cedars of Lebanon alone. It was public knowledge. In all the tabloids. In New York, she'd been committed to Bellevue streaming blood from two slashed arms, carried inside on a stretcher stark naked and raving. This had been in Winchell's column. In Maine a couple of years ago she'd had a miscarriage, or tried her own abortion and it misfired, and had to be fished out of the Atlantic by a rescue squad. And she hung out with known and suspected Commies.

See? A poor risk.

"You know her, eh?" The President was impressed.

What could the President's Pimp do but nod gravely. Tugging at his collar movie style to indicate sweaty nervousness, which, in fact, he was feeling. The President's favorite pimp was an in-law of the President and his wife might give him royal hell and put a new lien on his credit if he dared introduce the President to the sexpot Marilyn Monroe, who was a junkie, a nymphomaniac, suicidal, and schizzy.

"But only indirectly, chief. Who'd want a close contact with her? Monroe has had relations with every Jew in Hollywood. She slept her way up from the gutter. Lived with two notorious junkie fags for years and serviced their rich friends. Monroe's the origin of the Polish sausage joke, chief, you've heard?"

But the freckle-faced boy President, youngest and most virile in our history, scarcely listened. Staring at the woman known as Marilyn Monroe, who'd been drifting uncertainly about the terrace like a sleepwalker, vaguely smiling, and that look about her, or perhaps it was an aura, of such extreme vulnerability, such not-thereness, others kept their distance too, watching. *Unless this was my dream they could see into?* The Blond Actress on the moonlit terrace swaying at the edge of the shimmering aqua pool, eyes shut, mouthing the words to a recording of Sinatra's "All the Way." Platinum hair glowing like phosphorescence. Red-lipsticked mouth a perfect sucking O. She wore a teasingly short terry-cloth beach robe borrowed from her host whose name just possibly she'd forgotten, and this was tied tight around her waist; she appeared to be naked beneath. Her legs were a dancer's legs, slender and hard-muscled, but the upper thighs were beginning to show fatal white striations in the flesh. And her skin was starkly white, like an embalmed corpse's, drained of blood.

Yet the President trailed after her, that look in his eyes unmistakable. A parochial schoolboy bent upon mischief. Boston-Irish bulldog charm. Fierce in loyalty to family and friends, fierce in enmity to all who crossed him. In all scenes the President was the leading man, the actor with the script; everyone else improvised sink or swim. The President's Pimp could only say, vehement and pleading, "Monroe! She's screwed Sinatra, Mitchum, Brando, Jimmy Hoffa, Skinny D'Amato, Mickey Cohen, Johnny Roselli, that Commie 'Prince' Sukarno, and—"

"Sukarno?" Now the President was impressed.

The President's Pimp could see that things had gone too far for intervention. It was often thus. He could only shake his head and murmur, ungallantly, that if the President became involved with Monroe it would be wise to use protection for the woman was known to be infected with VD of the most virulent strain, when to get her ex-husband the Commie Jew off HUAC's hook she'd flown to Washington to screw McCarthy; this was common knowledge in all the tabloids. . . . The President's Pimp was himself a good-looking man of still youthful middle age with graying temples, intelligent if self-loathing eyes, and puffy jowls. His face looked as if it had been poached in a milky sauce. At Trimalchio's banquet he would have played Bacchus the Reveller, vine leaves and ivy twined about his head, smirking and simpering among the drunken guests, though frankly (he knew) he was getting too old for the role. In another decade he'd have the red-glazed eyes of the perpetual souse/junkie and a tremor in both hands like Parkinson's but not just yet. Oh, the President's favored Pimp had his pride! Wouldn't stoop to a lie even out of terror of his wife. "As to whether or not you've dated this person Marilyn Monroe, chief, to the best of my knowledge you have not."

At that moment, as if on cue, Marilyn Monroe glanced nervously in their direction. Tentatively, a little girl not knowing if she's liked or disliked, she smiled. That angel face! The President, smitten, was all business muttering in the Pimp's ear, "Make the arrangements, I told you. Pronto."

Pronto! White House code for *within the hour.*

THE PRINCE AND THE
BEGGAR MAID

Would you love me if you knew? The Prince smiled at me and said. . . .

He said he knew, he knew what it was to be poor! to be bone-aching poor
and in terror of what's-to-come!—not in his own lifetime, his family is
wealthy as everybody knows, but in his Irish ancestors' past, the sorrow of
oppression by the English conqueror. Like beasts of the field they worked
us, he said. Starved us to death. His voice quavered. I was holding him tight.
This precious moment. He whispered, Beautiful Marilyn! We are soul mates
beneath the skin.

His skin coarse-freckled and hot to the touch as if sunburnt. Mine smooth
and thin and eggshell-pale and, where a man grips me in the forgetfulness of
passion, easily bruised.

These bruises proudly worn like mauled rose petals.

This, our secret. Never will I reveal my lover's name.

He knew he said what it is to be lonely. In his large family there was loneliness growing up. I was crying to think he understood! Understood *me*. He,
of a great American name. A tribe of the blessed. I told him I revered him so
I would never ask anything of him after this night except to think of me now
and then. To think of MARILYN with a smile. I revered his family, I said. Yes,
and his wife, too, I revered, so beautiful and poised, so gracious. He laughed

sadly, saying, But she can't open her heart like you, Marilyn. She lacks the gift of laughter and warmth you possess, dear Marilyn.

So quickly we fell in love!

For sometimes it's so. Though unspoken.

I said, You can call me Norma Jeane.

He said, But you are MARILYN to me.

I said, Oh, do you know MARILYN?

He said, Wanted to meet MARILYN for a long long time.

Cuddling together on tossed-down beach towels and terry-cloth robes smelling of damp and chlorine on the floor of the bathhouse. Like naughty children laughing together. He'd brought with him a bottle of scotch whisky. And the party spilling out of the beautiful glass house onto the poolside terrace only a few yards away. I was so happy! where only an hour before I'd been so sad! wishing I hadn't been talked into coming to this weekend party but had stayed home in my house I love, my little Mexican house on Fifth Helena Drive. But now so happy, and giggling like a little girl. *He is a man who makes a woman feel like she's a true woman. Like no man I have ever met. A figure of History.* Making love with him, my Prince. How quick and hard and excited like a boy. Though his back was not strong, cervical spine strain he said, temporary, nothing for me to be concerned about, oh, but you were a war hero, I said, oh God how I revere you! My Prince. We were drinking, he would lift the bottle to my lips for me to drink, though I knew I should not, not with my medication, but I could not resist, as I could not resist his kisses; who among women could resist this man, a great man, a war hero, a figure of History, a Prince. And his hands a boy's eager hands, so urgent! We made love again. And again. A wildness came over me. I did feel something, a tinge of pleasure: like a flame being scratched out of a match, quick, fleeting, gone almost immediately yet you know it's there and may return. How long we were hidden away in that bathhouse, I don't know. Who knew we'd slipped away from the party, I don't know. The President's brother-in-law had introduced us; Marilyn, he'd said, I'd like you to meet an admirer of yours; and I'd seen him, my Prince, staring smiling at me, a man women adore, that look of ease and lightness in a man who knows he is adored by women, his very desire like a flame that women will stoke, and quench, and stoke, and quench, through a lifetime. And I laughed; suddenly I was The Girl Upstairs. I was not Roslyn Tabor, I was not a divorcée. I was not a widow. I was not a grieving mother who'd lost her baby in a fall down cellar steps. I was not a mother who'd killed her baby. I had not been The Girl Upstairs for a long time but in my white terry-cloth robe and bare legs I became again The Girl Upstairs on the subway grating. (No, I would not wish the Prince to know my true age: soon to be thirty-six. And not a girl.)

He winced, his back was hurting. I pretended not to notice but settled myself on top of him, fitted myself to him, my slightly sore vagina, my empty womb this man might fill, his penis so hard and eager; I was gentle as I could be until nearing the end he grabbed my hips and ground himself against me whimpering and moaning almost out of control so I worried he would hurt himself, his back, as he was hurting me, his hands gripping my hips so hard, and I was whispering *Yes yes like that like that yes* though rivulets of sweat ran down my face and my breasts, he was biting my breasts, biting the nipples, *You dirty girl* he was saying, moaning, *dirty cunt, I love you dirty cunt*; and soon it was over and I was out of breath and hurting and trying to laugh as The Girl would naturally laugh and I heard myself say, Ohhhh! I'm almost afraid of you I guess! which is what men like to hear; I caught my breath and said, If I was Castro ohhhh! I'd be real afraid of you; I was The Girl dumb-blonde style saying Hey, where's those Social Security men that follow you around? (for suddenly I realized that those men, plainclothes officers, must be close outside the bathhouse guarding the door and a wave of shame passed over me I hoped to God they hadn't been listening or worse yet watching with some sort of surveillance device as sometimes even in my house with the drapes drawn, and in the bedroom thick black drapes stapled to the window frames, I seemed to know I was being spied upon and my phone tapped), and he laughed and said, You mean Secret Service men, MARILYN, and we broke up laughing, whisky-laughing; I was the girl from North Carolina who didn't give a shit, laughing from the gut as a man laughs. Oh, it felt good. The tense moment was past as if it had never been, already I was forgetting the names, the ugly words he'd called me, my Prince, shortly I would forget that I'd forgotten anything and by next morning I would recall only kisses, a fleeting match flame of sexual pleasure, the promise of a future. My Prince was saying MARILYN you're a genuinely funny woman, I'd heard you were bright quick intelligent fan-tas-tic (he was tonguing my breasts, tickling) and I said, Oh Mr. P-president, know what? I write my own lines, too. He said Mmmm! you have the nicest lines in show biz MARILYN. I said, stroking his thick hair, You can call me Norma Jeane, that's what people call me who know me, and he said, What I'm going to call you, baby, is whenever I get the chance. *Pronto!*

I said, My Pronto! That's the word for you, eh?

A single dim light was burning in the bathhouse. It was a dank smelly place. Through a louver-shuttered little window I could see, at a sharp angle upward, the desert moon. Or was it a blurry light in a palm tree behind the pool? The desert night! Almost I thought I was in Nevada again, I was Roslyn Tabor in love with Clark Gable soon to die and I was sick with guilt still married to a man I didn't love. I was not drunk but could not have said where

I was exactly. Where I would be sleeping that night, and with who. Or would I be alone? And how I would get back home again. Back to Los Angeles the City of Sand, back to Brentwood to 12305 Fifth Helena Drive. For always you have this terrible fear, how to get back home? even if you know where home is. The Prince was wiping briskly between his legs with a towel saying he hoped he could see me soon again, he was leaving Palm Springs pronto in the morning to return to Washington but he'd be in contact, I said Would you like my unlisted telephone number Mr. President? and he laughed and said There are no unlisted telephone numbers MARILYN and I said soft and breathy as a high school girl I would fly east if he wished it, your wish is my command Mr. President, I said, joking, kissing his flamey face, he liked that I could see; he said there'd be a first-class ticket provided and we could meet in Manhattan at a certain hotel, also he'd be in California for fund-raisers et cetera, his sister and brother-in-law had a beach house in Malibu. I said, Oh yes I would l-like that. I mean, I would love that.

What did my Prince tell me, my secret I will never reveal.

Framing my face in his hands, oh I hoped I was beautiful for him and not sweaty, my makeup smeared, hair sticking to my forehead which is the way it felt, but he was speaking sincerely, from the heart I could tell as he spoke in his public addresses, and we all loved him; he said, There's something in you none of them has, MARILYN. No woman I know. You're alive to be touched. To be breathed on like a flame. Alive to be hurt, even! It's like you open yourself to hurt, no woman I know is like you, MARILYN. No screen image or photograph has shown your soul MARILYN as I have seen it this night.

A final kiss and my Prince was gone.

The Prince would leave the bathhouse fully dressed and the blond Beggar Maid he'd been with would remain behind for ten minutes at his suggestion, but his bodyguards didn't wait around for her, only the President's Pimp waited for her, at a discreet distance on the other side of the pool; and when at last she emerged, dazed-looking, stumbling, carrying her high-heeled shoes, the terry-cloth robe haphazardly tied about her, the President's Pimp approached her in his suave manner saying with a smile, Miss Monroe! The President wanted you to have this small token of his esteem. It was a silver-foil rose (the Pimp had found discarded on a table, a decorative touch on a bottle of wine he'd appropriated and stuck through the lapel of his jacket) and it would be observed how the world celebrity MARILYN MONROE blinking dazedly at the President's Pimp took the fake rose from his fingers and smiled. "Oh! It's beautiful."

She sniffed its tinny fragrance and was happy.

The Beggar Maid
in Love

Yet if the Prince didn't call, as he'd promised?

If she waited, and waited, and waited, and he didn't call? And others in her snarled and blurred life called in the intervening weeks, and never him? And at last when almost she'd given up hope a call from a mysterious individual ———— (a name that meant nothing to her in her agitation) in (she was given to assume) the very White House. (One of the President's assistants?) And soon afterward the President's brother-in-law who lived in Malibu called to invite her for the weekend.

Just a small intimate gathering, Marilyn.

Very elite. Just private people.

Casually she asked, "And he—he'll be there?"

Sexy-suave brother-in-law to the President said, casually too, "Hmm. Says he'll try his damnedest."

Marilyn laughed excitedly. "Oh. I know what that means."

I know he has many women. He's a man of the world.
I am a woman of the world. I'm not a child!

A weekend came, spun past, and was gone. She could recall but fragments as in a film collage. *Is this happening to me? Is this me? Or was it?*

Unlike movies, there were no retakes. You had but one chance.

Those giddy times, telephone ringing, her private private line, and the mysterious ————— (in Washington) asking would she be home to take a call at 10:25 P.M. that night? And laughing, having to sit, she felt so weak, "Will I be h-home? Hmm!" It was The Girl, naive and funny. Warm sweet witty Girl Upstairs who wrote all her own lines. "How'll I know for sure till ten-twenty-five P.M. gets here?"

A bemused murmur at the other end. (Or did she imagine?)

And so she would wait, and wait. But it was not waiting that exhausted and humiliated but waiting that thrilled. Waiting that gives you a reason to be happy, joyous, smiling, singing and dancing all day. And promptly at 10:25 P.M. the telephone rang and she lifted the receiver to say in a breathy baby voice, *H'lo?*

His deep voice, unmistakable. Her Prince.

H'lo? Marilyn? I've been thinking about you.

I've been thinking about you, Mr. P.-for-Pronto!

Making him laugh. God it's good to hear a man laugh. The power of a woman isn't sex but the power to make a man laugh.

If I could be out there with you darling d'you know what I'd be doing?
Ohhh. No. What?

ᔐ

There were occasions when the President's brother-in-law telephoned to suggest he drop by to see her for a drink or take her out for a drink, or for dinner; they had "confidential matters" to talk over, he said; and quickly she said no she didn't think so. Recalling the man's eyes on her in Palm Springs, that look of frank assessment. Not a good idea, she said, right now. The President's brother-in-law said in the affable way of a man to whom sexual conquests or refusals bore approximately the same emotional weight, Another time then, darling. Nothing crucial about tonight.

She'd heard, they pass women among them.

More accurately, the women were passed down. Models, "starlets." From the Prince/President down to his several brothers, his brothers-in-law, and his buddies.

Yet thinking *Not me! He wouldn't, me.*

Last time he'd called, a brief breathless conversation, he'd sounded sleepy and sexy and he'd repeated those magical words she'd come to wonder if she had imagined or heard long ago in a movie otherwise forgotten. *Something in you none of them has. No woman. Alive to be touched. Like a flame. No woman I know is like you, Marilyn.*

She believed this might be so. Oh, but she believed he might believe it was so! *It's like saying he loves me. Except in not those words.*

The Beggar Maid waited. She was faithful in waiting.

Word came that Cass Chaplin was hospitalized. In a detox clinic in Los Angeles. She had a panicked hour when she came close to telephoning, to inquire. Thinking then *No. I can't. Can't get involved with them. Not now.* She wondered if Cass and Eddy G were still so intimate.

God, she missed them. Her Gemini lovers. Through two boring marriages to good decent heterosexual men.

The beautiful boys Cass and Eddy G! She'd been their Norma, their girl. She'd done what they told her to do. Possibly they'd hypnotized her. If she'd remained with them, and had their baby? She might still have had a career as "Marilyn Monroe." But it was a long time ago. Baby would be eight years old now. *Our child. But accursed.* She could not clearly recall why Baby had died, why Baby had had to die, why Marilyn had killed him. A few months ago she'd seen a photo of Cass Chaplin in the tabloid *Tatler* and was shocked at how her former lover had aged, shadowy pouches beneath his eyes and creases beside his mouth. His beauty in ruins. The camera's flash had caught him in a moment of rage, a fist raised, mouth twisted in an obscenity.

But now I have a worthy lover. A man who appreciates my worth. A true soul mate.

Oh, even if it was Irish blarney, and she didn't doubt it was, ninety percent of it, still it was the Prince's blarney and not a Hollywood junkie's.

So strange! In reply to her letter to Gladys she'd written with such affection, there came a typewritten note, the words crowded into the center of a much-folded sheet of paper.

> Aren't you ashamed Norma Jeane, I read about Clark Gable   they are saying you killed him contributed to his "fatal heart attack" Even the nurses here are disgusted. That is how I learned of it.

Yet one day, if I'm invited to the White House. Mother might come with me. It might make all the difference to her as to any American mother.

She was seeing a psychiatrist. She was seeing an analyst. She was seeing a "psychic health adviser" in West Hollywood. Twice a week she visited a physical therapist. She'd begun again to take yoga classes. Sometimes, those endless nights when she knew she could not allow herself to swallow enough chloral hydrate to put her to sleep for more than a few hours, she called a masseur who lived in Venice Beach. In her imagination he was one of those surfers who'd saved Norma Jeane from drowning a long time ago. A giant, a bodybuilder. But gentle. Like Whitey, Nico adored her without desiring her; her body was to him but a material like clay to be kneaded, serviced, for a fee.

"What I wish I could do, Nico, know what?—wish I could leave my body with you. And I could go—oh, I don't know where!—somewhere *free*."

Sniffed its tinny fragrance and was happy. Returned from Palm Springs to Brentwood in the hidden-away hacienda on Fifth Helena Drive (a strange name! she'd asked the real estate agent what it meant but the woman didn't know), she'd put the silver-foil rose in a crystal vase and set the vase on the white Steinway spinet where it glowed even in shadow. The rose. His rose! Because it was silver foil and not a living rose, it could never rot and die; she would keep it forever as a memento of this great man's love for her. *Of course he would never leave his wife. His Catholic family, his upbringing. I would not expect that. He is a figure of History.* The acknowledged leader of the Free World. Waging a war in Vietnam. (So close to Korea! Where MARILYN MONROE had entertained the troops so famously.) Close to invading Communist Cuba. Oh, the President was a dangerous man to make an enemy of. She was proud of him, thrilled for him. His image was in newspapers and on TV continuously. The male world of history and politics, the world of ceaseless strife. And joy in that strife. What is politics but war by another means. The aim is to defeat your adversary. Survival of the fittest. Natural selection. Love is a man's weakness. Blond Marilyn wanted to assure her Pronto that *hey, she understood.*

It was the silver-foil rose that drew her to the piano. Seated at the keyboard in the silent house shuttered against the pitiless sun. Depressing chords uncertainly, shyly. In that way of one who fears trying to play piano after a long hiatus because she knows her modest skills have badly atrophied. She'd never really played "Für Elise" and never would. Even more she feared the tissue memory in her fingertips would trigger in her brain memories of lost time, too painful now to recall. *Mother? What did you want from me I could never give you? How did I fail? I tried so hard.* She wondered if, if she'd played piano better for Mr. Pearce and sung better for poor Jess Flynn, her childhood would have turned out differently? Maybe her miserable lack of talent had contributed to Gladys Mortensen's madness. Maybe something in Gladys had simply snapped.

Still, Gladys had seemed to absolve her of blame. *Nobody's fault being born, is it?*

Still, she was feeling optimistic. In this house, her first house, she would begin to play piano again. She would take piano lessons again, soon. When her life was better in order.

Waiting for the Prince to summon her. Well, why not?

Almost without knowing what she did that spring, in the way of a whim, she accepted a new film. The Studio had been pressing her. Her agent had been pressing her. At the time of her divorce she'd been discussing with Max Pearlman the possibility of her performing in a play at the New York Ensemble, it would not be *The Girl with the Flaxen Hair* after all but it might be Ibsen's *A Doll's House* or Chekhov's *Uncle Vanya*, but to Pearlman's disappointment she could not seem to commit herself to any date. She was enthusiastic as a young girl when they spoke, yet weeks passed and he would not hear from her or Holyrod; if he telephoned they rarely returned his calls; the project had languished. *Because I am too frightened. Can't face a living audience.* In a dream she'd been so paralyzed with terror acting in a play she'd lost control of her bladder and wakened urinating in her bed.

"Oh my God. Oh, not *this*."

Recalling the urine stink of Gladys's mattress at Lakewood.

And so in the confusion of her thoughts she would recall, as if it had actually happened, wetting herself in New York, in a rehearsal hall. "Oh gosh I s-stood up, and the back of my dress was wet and sticking to my *legs*. Ohhhh."

This story of The Girl's, she would not tell in the White House.

A *rendezvous. So romantic!* Not in California but in New York when the President was visiting. *In utmost secrecy of course* she understood.

Yes, but she had to work. She hadn't married a wealthy man, she'd married for love. *Each of my marriages, for love. But I'm not discouraged. Oh yes I'd try again!* She had to work, and she wasn't in a position, after *The Misfits* (*The Misfire* as Z called it) to be demanding about scripts. She told her agent, "Oh but Roslyn T-tabor was my strongest performance, wasn't she? Everybody said so," and Rin Tin Tin barked in a way that, if you didn't know Hollywood, you might've thought meant amused, and said, in his reasonable-agent voice, "Yes, Marilyn. Everybody said so," and she said, "But you don't think so? Don't you think so?" and Rin Tin Tin said, in that new way of his she'd begun to hear more frequently since *The Misfits*, as if humoring her, "What does it matter what I think, dear Marilyn? It's what millions of Americans think, lining up like sheep to purchase tickets at the box office. Or not lining up," and she said, hurt, "But *The Misfits* hasn't done badly, has it? Know who's seen it? And l-loved it? The President of the

United States! Imagine!" and Rin Tin Tin said, "The President should've brought some of his friends," and she said, "What's that mean? Oh, what are you s-saying?" and Rin Tin Tin said, relenting, in a more or less normal human voice, "Marilyn dear, it didn't do badly. No. For a film without Marilyn Monroe it would've done pretty well," and she didn't ask *What's that mean?* because she knew exactly what it meant. She said, biting at her thumbnail, her face heating as if she'd been slapped, "So it doesn't matter, does it! I can 'act,' and people have acknowledged it. But it doesn't matter. People scorned Marilyn all these years for being a blond sexpot who couldn't act; now they scorn Marilyn for not making a bundle at the box office, huh? Now Marilyn is box-office poison," and Rin Tin Tin said quickly, alarmed, "Marilyn, of course not. Don't say such a thing, anyone might overhear." (They were talking on the phone. She was in her hideaway hacienda, blinds drawn against the glare.) "Marilyn Monroe *is not box-office poison*—" and Rin Tin Tin paused so she could hear a vibratory hum, unspoken.

Not yet.

On the mantel in her shadowy living room were two slender statuettes. One from the French film industry, the other from the Italian film industry. Awarded to MARILYN MONROE for her outstanding performance in *The Prince and the Showgirl*. ("Oh, why'd they 'honor' me for *that*? Why not for *Bus Stop*? Damn!") But she'd never received any award for her acting in the United States, not even an Academy Award nomination for *Bus Stop* or *The Misfits*. What The Studio was sensibly demanding (as Rin Tin Tin explained, unless it was bat-faced Z who explained) was a return to sure-fire MARILYN MONROE sex comedy like *Some Like It Hot* and *The Seven-Year Itch*, for why the hell should Americans shell out hard-earned cash to see mopey movies that depress them? Movies like their own fucked-up lives? What's wrong with a few belly laughs? A stirring of the groin? Eh? Gorgeous blonde, scenes in which her clothes are falling off, air drafts blowing her skirt up to her crotch. In this terrific new property, *Something's Got to Give*, there'll be skin-tight costumes and an airhead blonde who'll be photographed swimming in the nude. Fan-tas-tic!

Hey I love to act. Truly, acting is my life! Never so happy as when I'm acting, not living.
Oh, what'd I say? Oh well, you know what I mean.
(Why am I so afraid, then? I will not be afraid.)

So she accepted the role. Immediate Studio press releases to all the papers! Thrilled, MARILYN MONROE to be back again, working again. Not until then did she read the script, *Something's Got to Give* delivered to her door by a sweaty mustached boy on a bicycle and sat by the pool (stippled with palm fronds, beetle shells, what looked like skeins of human sperm) reading it and an hour afterward could not remember a word. A mass of clichés. Idiotic dialogue. She wasn't even sure which role was hers. The name was changed every few pages. "I g-guess Marilyn's the cash cow for this? The come-on for investors?" Now she was speaking with Rin Tin Tin in person, he was young-middle-age, paunchy, with a loose-fishy look in the jowls and eyes squinty as her own. Telling her that, look, she had only to show up on the sound stage for this movie, mouth the lines they provided for her and forget about prepping, driving herself into a nervous breakdown and making everybody's life hell. "Just show up, be sexy and funny like Marilyn used to be, and have a little fun for a change, anything wrong with that?" Heard herself say, incensed, "Oh yes? Well, there's some shit even Marilyn won't eat."

Heard herself say, next morning dialing the agency's number, "Well, maybe. I need the money I guess?"

Never would it be very real to her. The last film with which MARILYN MONROE would be associated.

The President and the Blond Actress: The Rendezvous

In the week following Easter 1962 the summons came!

"Did I doubt him? I did not."

Please dress inconspicuously Miss Monroe she'd been told. A male voice, unidentified, on the phone. There had been a series of telephone messages, some straightforward enough and others coded. She sensed she was embarking upon *the most exciting and profound adventure of my life as a woman.* So she'd prepared herself privately for the experience. No professional makeup man, no costumer from Wardrobe. She'd purchased new clothes (on credit, Saks Beverly Hills) in understated cream and heather tones; her platinum-blond hair was freshly brightened but partly hidden beneath a stylish cloche hat. Only her lipstick was bright but isn't lipstick meant to be bright? It was a Lorelei Lee look but her manner would be gracious and restrained *as befits a friend of the president and that man an American aristocrat.* Yet the Secret Service men who were her escorts regarded her with shocked disapproving eyes that shifted to indignation and disgust like coagulation. "You were expecting maybe Mother Teresa?"

She was The Girl who wrote her own lines. Sometimes, no one laughed or even acknowledged hearing.

The Secret Service men were Dick Tracy and what was his name, the little man with the wife Maggie—oh, yes: Jiggs. Strange escorts to bring Marilyn Monroe to a secret rendezvous in the elegant C Hotel on Fifth Avenue, Manhattan!

Soberly she told herself *These men have pledged their lives for their President. In the event of bullets, they will shield his body with their own.*

To fly from Los Angeles to Manhattan within the space of a few hours is to be hurtled rapidly forward in time. Yet, arriving several hours later in the day of your embarkment, you can't shake off the feeling that you've arrived in past time. Years ago?

My Manhattan life. Married life. When?

She never thought of the Playwright. A man with whom she'd lived for five years. Her agent had sent her a page torn from *Variety*, a positive but qualified review of *The Girl with the Flaxen Hair*. She'd stopped reading at the words *what is lacking in this earnest production is a genuinely mesmerizing Magda. For such a role to be credible, one would need. . . .*

In Manhattan there were ginkgo trees in bud, and on Park Avenue daffodils and tulips so beautiful, but was it *cold*! The Blond Actress felt the shock, a reproach to her California blood; she hadn't brought sufficiently warm clothing for her romantic overnight visit to Manhattan. This was a different season. The very light looked different. She was feeling shaky, disoriented. *But spring is April isn't it?* and realizing a syntactical error *April is spring isn't it, I mean.* They were in the bulletproof limousine moving soundlessly north on Park Avenue and the larger of the Secret Service men, the sharp-jawed humorless fellow who put her in mind of Dick Tracy, said tersely, "This *is* spring, Miss Monroe."

Had she spoken aloud? She hadn't meant to.

The other Secret Service escort, stumpy, doughy, with a bland potato face and empty white eyes, a dead ringer for Jiggs, sucked at his lips and stared glumly ahead. These were plainclothes police officers. Possibly they resented today's Presidential mission. The Blond Actress would have liked to explain. "It isn't sexual. Between the President and me. It has little to do with sex. It's a meeting of our souls." The limo driver must have been another Secret Service officer, grim-faced as the others, wearing a fedora. He'd barely nodded at Miss Monroe at the airport. He bore an uncanny resemblance to the comic-strip character Jughead.

Gosh it's scary sometimes! Comic-strip people populating the world.

The day before by special-delivery bicycle messenger there'd come the Blond Actress's first-class airline tickets (purchased for her under the code name "P. Belle," which she'd been given to know, by way of the President's brother-in-law, meant "Pronto's Beauty") and during the flight from West Coast to East Coast she had reason to suspect that the pilot and his crew were aware of her connection with the White House. "Not just I'm

'Marilyn.' But this special day. This special flight." In the perversity of her happiness it seemed to her the airliner must crash! Yet it did not. The flight was intermittently turbulent but otherwise uneventful. Oh, there was Dom Perignon, Miss Belle. Especially for you, Miss Belle. She'd been given two seats to herself at the front of the first-class cabin. Treated like royalty. The Beggar Maid as the Fair Princess. Oh, she was deeply moved. A stewardess assigned to watch over her, to see that no one disturbed the Blond Actress traveling incognito lost in a dreamy reverie of *A rendezvous. With him.* They had spoken only three times on the phone in the intervening weeks and then but briefly. Except for the President's likeness in the newspapers and on TV (which now she watched, nightly) she would perhaps not remember what he looked like; for in the uncertain light of the bathhouse (Bing Crosby's Palm Springs house, near the golf course, wasn't that where they'd met?) he might have been any man of youthful middle age and vigor with a handsome boyish American face and a powerful sexual appetite. That morning she'd medicated herself with Miltown, Amytal, and codeine (one tablet, for she seemed to be running a mild fever) in careful dosages. This was a time in her life, she would have sworn it would be a temporary time, when she was seeing two, three, perhaps four doctors and each man in presumed innocence of the others' existences supplied her with prescriptions. *Just to help me sleep, Doctor! Oh, just to help me wake up. And to calm my nerves like ripped silk.*

Doctor, no, of course I don't drink.

Don't eat red meat it's too coarse for my stomach to digest.

At LaGuardia on shaky legs she'd been the first to disembark. "Miss Belle? Let me assist you." A stewardess led her along the tunnel ramp from the plane and there at the gate were waiting two grim unsmiling men in sharkskin suits and fedoras and she felt a stab of panic *Am I under arrest? What will happen to me?* She was The Girl, smiling inanely. Her hands shaking, almost she dropped her overnight bag, and the larger of the Secret Service officers took it from her. They called her "Miss Monroe" and "ma'am" as if in shame and mortification of being heard even by her, their charge. Pointedly they averted their policeman eyes from her fuchsia mouth and generous bosom of which they did not approve, the coldhearted bastards. *Just jealous aren't you. Of your boss. 'Cause he's a real man, huh?* But she was determined to be sweet to them. Chattering in the sunny-friendly way of The Girl as the silent men escorted her briskly through the airport (attracting the startled stares of many individuals but lingering for none) to a waiting limousine. The vehicle was sleek and blackly gleaming and large enough inside to seat a dozen persons. "Ohhh. Is this bulletproof, I hope?" She laughed nervously. Settling herself on the plush rear seat, tugging her skirt below her knees, all female perfumy excitement as the Secret Service men sat on either side of her, against the windows. She wondered if the President had instructed them to shield her from bullets, too? Did that come with a Presidential summons? "Gosh, all this attention makes me feel like an R.I.P."—laughing nervously into their male silence—"no, I mean V.I.P. That's what I mean?"

Doughy-faced Jiggs grunted what might've been amusement. Though maybe not. Dick Tracy in profile gave no sign of hearing.

She thought *These men. These three. They're carrying guns!*

Well, she was hurt. A little. For clearly they disapproved of her beautiful creamy-white-and-heather-colored cashmere knit suit from Saks Beverly Hills, the low neckline, the prominent bust and shapely hips. Her dancer's legs. Feet in open-toed alligator pumps, four-inch heels. She'd painted her finger- and toenails a tasteful frost hue. Bright fuchsia lipstick and blond-blond hair and the unmistakable Marilyn radiance beating off her unnaturally white skin like white-painted stucco in tropical heat. Yet these men disapproved of her as a woman, as an individual, and as a historical *fact*. She hoped she wouldn't make a wrong move somehow and they'd draw their guns and shoot her?

How uneasy the Blond Actress was made in the thirty-sixth year of her life, in the prime of her celebrity, by men who gazed upon her without desire. *Oh, but why? When I could love you so.*

Dick Tracy was telling the Blond Actress, with averted eyes and a priggish grim satisfaction, that the President's plans had been suddenly changed and so her plans would be changed. There was an emergency situation calling him back to the White House and he would be flying out that afternoon. He would not after all be staying the night in New York. "Your airline ticket, ma'am"—he was handing her the packet—"for your return to Los Angeles this evening. You will take a taxi from the hotel to La Guardia, ma'am." Through a roaring in her ears the Blond Actress was able to think with surprising clarity, in self-consolation *My lover is not a private citizen, he is a figure of History.* Murmuring only, "Oh. I see." She couldn't hide that she was surprised, hurt. Disappointed. The Girl was only human, wasn't she? But refusing to give Dick Tracy the satisfaction of asking what the emergency was and being told it was classified information.

The limousine turned onto a side street. Headed toward Central Park. She heard a childlike voice inquire, "I g-guess you can't tell me what it is? The emergency? I hope it isn't a n-nuclear war! Something nasty in the Soviet Union!" and as if on cue, though quietly, without gloating, Dick Tracy said, "Miss Monroe. Sorry. That's classified information."

Another disappointment: the limousine pulled up not in front of the famous old C Hotel on Fifth Avenue but at a rear entrance, in a narrow alley behind the massive landmark building. The Blond Actress was given a raincoat to slip on over her clothing, a cheap wrinkly-plastic black garment with a hood to hide the cloche hat and her hair; she was furious but complied, for this was turning into a familiar sort of movie scene, mild slapstick comedy, and no scene lasts more than a few minutes. Oh, how eager she was to escape these cold men and press herself into the arms of her lover! Next, Jiggs dared to hand her a tissue requesting her to please remove the "red grease" from her mouth, but she was indignant and refused. "Ma'am, you can put it back on again inside. As much as you wish." "I will not," she said. "Let me out of this car." She did remove from her handbag a pair of very dark glasses that hid half her face.

Jiggs and Dick Tracy conferred in grunts and must have decided she was sufficiently disguised to walk a distance of perhaps twenty feet, for they unlocked the limousine doors and cautiously climbed out and escorted the Blond Actress in her absurd hooded raincoat through a rear entrance in a ventilator blast of hot rancid cooking odors, and quickly inside she was ushered into a freight elevator to be carried creakily upward to the sixteenth penthouse floor where the door opened and she was urged out, in haste—"Miss Monroe, ma'am"—"Step along please, ma'am." She said, "I can walk by myself, thank you. I'm not crippled"—though stumbling a little in her high-heeled shoes. They were Italian-made, the most expensive shoes she'd ever owned, with V-pointed toes.

The Secret Service men knocked on the door of the appropriately named Presidential Suite. The Blond Actress was stricken with a sudden unease. *Am I female meat, to be so delivered? Is that what this is? Room service?* But she'd removed the raincoat and handed it to her escorts; the slapstick-comic scene had ended. The door was opened by another frozen-faced Secret Service officer, who admitted them with no more than a curt nod at the Blond Actress and a muttered expletive—"Ma'am!" From this point onward the scene would move in a swerving zigzag course as if the camera were being jostled. The Blond Actress was allowed to use a bathroom—"Should you wish to freshen up, Miss Monroe"—and in the elegantly appointed gilt-and-marble cubicle she checked her makeup, which was holding up fairly well, and her eyes, her large frank wondering crystal-blue eyes, the whites still discolored from myriad broken capillaries slow to heal, and the faint white lines beside her eyes she hoped a gentler bedroom light would not expose to her lover's scrutiny. The President would be forty-five years old on May 29, 1962; the Blond Actress would be thirty-six years old on June 1, 1962; she was a little old for him, but perhaps he didn't know? For Marilyn did look good! looked the part! Perfumed and primped and primed and her body shaved and the hair on both her head and her pubis recently bleached, hateful purple paste stinging her sensitive skin, so she was looking the part, the platinum-doll Marilyn, the President's secret mistress. (Though she'd had a bad spell on the plane. Vomiting into the miniature toilet in the miniature lavatory despite the fact she hadn't been able to eat in twenty-four hours. Having to repair damage to her makeup with a shaky hand while peering into a poorly lighted mirror.) Yes, and she had to admit she was "feeling kind of sad" to be told so rudely that her tryst with the President would be truncated; their rendezvous was to have been for a full night and a day. The Blond Actress swallowed a Miltown tablet for her nerves; and, for quick energy and courage, a Benzedrine. She used the toilet and washed herself between the legs (in Palm Springs, the lusty President had kissed her lavishly there, as elsewhere on her body); she would not notice, in a wastebasket beside the toilet, crumpled wads of damp toilet paper not unlike those she was dropping into the basket, and tissues blotted with a chic plum-colored lipstick. *No! Would not notice.*

"This way, ma'am." A Secret Service officer whom she hadn't seen before, with an overbite like Bugs Bunny's and something of that cartoon character's springiness of step, escorted her along a corridor. "In here, ma'am." Breathless then the Blond Actress found herself entering a spacious but dimly lighted bedroom as one might enter a dimly lighted stage whose dimensions are lost in shadow. The room was as large as her Brentwood living room and furnished in what her unpracticed eye supposed were authentic French antiques. Some kind of antique, at least. What luxury! What romance! Underfoot, a thick-piled oriental rug. The heavy brocaded drapes of several tall narrow windows were drawn against the acidic sunshine of April in Manhattan as her own bedroom drapes were drawn against the warmer sunshine of southern California. There was a commingled odor in the room of tobacco smoke, burnt toast, soiled linens, bodies. On the canopied four-poster bed there sprawled the naked President, telephone resting on his chest as he spoke rapidly into the receiver; amid rumpled bedclothes and disheveled pillows he lay, his prince's face sulky and flushed and so handsome! How could any First Lady be cold to *him*?Embarking upon a stage with only a fellow actor with whom to play the scene. The dimensions of the stage, as of the vast murmurous audience, unknowable. *I stepped into History!*

But it was a scene already begun. Beside the President, on the bed, was a silver tray bearing china plates dirtied with coagulated egg yolk and scorched toast crusts, coffee cups, wineglasses, and a depleted bottle of burgundy. The President, a forelock of graying-brown hair over one eye. His handsome manly body was covered in a fine glinting-brown fuzz that thickened on his torso and legs; it looked almost as if he wore a vest. Pages of the *New York Times* and *Washington Post* were scattered across the king-sized bed and, precariously balanced against an upended pillow, was an opened bottle of Black & White scotch whisky. Seeing the Blond Actress make her entrance, a vision of creamy hues and radiant fuchsia smile, the President swallowed hard, smiled eagerly, and beckoned her to him, even as he held the receiver to his ear. His limp penis stirred too in an acknowledgment of her beauty among its tangle of bristly hairs like a large affable slug that would grow larger. Now here was a greeting worthy of a three-thousand-mile pilgrimage!

"Pronto. *Hiya*."

The Blond Actress, removing her cloche hat and shaking out her fine-spun platinum hair, laughed gaily. Oh, this was a scene! She felt her nervousness drain away, her anxiety. If there was an audience, the audience was invisible; the stage floated upon darkness; the lighted space belonged to her and to the President exclusively. What surprised her was the tone: for this was a funny, droll, relaxed meeting, an encounter of such erotic ease that a neutral observer would be led to believe that the President and the Blond Actress had many times met in rendezvous like this, had for many years been lovers. The Blond Actress, who felt so little sexual desire, inhabiting her voluptuous body like a child crammed into a mannequin, stared in wonderment at the President. *The most attractive man I've ever loved! Except for Carlo maybe*. She would have leaned gracefully over to kiss the President in greeting, except he held the damned receiver against his mouth and was murmuring, "Uh-huh. Yup. Gotcha. OK. Shit." He gestured for her to sit beside him on the bed, which she did; he embraced her playfully with a bare muscled leg and with his free hand stroked her hair, her shoulders, her breasts, the shapely curve of her hip, with the expression of an awestricken adolescent boy. He whispered, half in pain, "Marilyn. You. Hel-*lo*." She whispered, "Pronto. Hel-*lo*." With a low groan he murmured, "Am I glad to see you, baby. This has been one hell of a day." She said, in a breathy warm rush she was certain the First Lady with her patrician poise could not have imitated, "Oh, gosh, I've been told, darling. How can I help?" With a toothy grin, the President took her hand that was caressing his unshaven jaw and closed the fingers around his now-upright penis; this was abrupt but not unexpected; in Palm Springs, she'd been a little shocked by the man's boldness, yet there was solace in such immediate intimacy, wasn't there; you eliminated so much and were rewarded with so much, so quickly. Gamely the Blond Actress began to stroke the President's penis, as one might stroke a charming but unruly pet while its owner looked on proudly. Yet, to her annoyance, the President didn't hang up the phone.

The conversation not only continued but shifted to another degree of seriousness; another party must have come onto the line, with more urgency, a White House adviser or cabinet member (Rusk? McNamara?). The subject seemed to be Cuba. Castro, the President's glamorous Cuban rival! The

Blond Actress felt the thrill of the challenge though not yet knowing any facts. She recalled the handsome bearded Cuban revolutionary on *Time*'s cover a decade before; within recent memory, Castro had been a hero in the United States in many quarters. Of course, his image had radically shifted and he was now one of the Communist enemy. And only ninety miles from U.S. territory. Both the youthful President and the even younger Castro were actors of a romantic, heroic mode; both were self-styled "men of the people," vain and self-displaying and merciless with their political enemies, idolized by their followers, who would forgive them anything; the one, the American President, committed to protecting "democracy" globally; the other, the Cuban dictator, committed to that extreme form of political and economic democracy called communism, which was in fact totalitarianism. Each man was the son of a wealthy family yet would publicly align himself with the "people"; one would eloquently criticize "Republican business ties" and the other would lead a bloody revolt against capitalism, including American capitalism. It was part of the Castro fable that the dashing Cuban in army fatigues and combat boots disdained security measures; though under constant threat of assassination, Castro eluded his bodyguards to mingle with the idolatrous "masses." The American President yearned to be so courageous, or to be so perceived! Both men had been brought up Catholic and trained by Jesuits and may have been infused from boyhood with the Jesuitical sense of being above not God's law but man's, and if God doesn't exist, who gives a damn about man's law?

The President's handsome face turned ugly. The President cursed Castro in a way shocking to the Blond Actress: should she, an ordinary citizen though a loyal Democrat, be a witness to such remarks? Or were they being made partly for her benefit? The scene throbbed with sex. The Blond Actress had gradually ceased stroking the President out of a realization that he was distracted and not thinking of her at all. *It's Castro. His rival.* With dismay she noticed the dirtied plates, the smears of plum lipstick on a pillow. Briskly she began to tidy up. *The June Allyson of sexpots, was Marilyn.* She set the tray aside, not wishing to examine the wineglasses closely. Moved the scotch bottle to the bedside table and before she knew what she did, though her head was buzzing from the combination of Dom Perignon and her medication, she took a swig of the whisky. How it burned going down! She hated the taste. She coughed, sputtered. She took a second swallow.

Past three o'clock already!—the President would be leaving their rendezvous soon. How soon, the Blond Actress hadn't been told. Still the conversation continued. The Blond Actress gathered that the Russians and the Cubans were conspiring together—"Payback for the Bay of Pigs, eh? We'll see!" The Blond Actress began to tremble inwardly for the President was speaking of—nuclear missiles? Soviet missiles? In Cuba? She wanted to press her hands over her ears. She didn't want to eavesdrop; she didn't want to risk the President's rage; she could see that the President was hot-tempered as the Ex-Athlete and of a similar masculine type. Anger aroused him sexually, and so anger was pleasure to him. He saw her staring at him, his penis bobbing like an angry head, and said, "Baby. C'mon." The President tugged at her hair. Pulled her toward him to kiss her roughly even as he gripped the phone receiver in a practiced way between his neck and shoulder. Out of the receiver's plastic interior a miniature male voice droned. The President whispered, "Don't be shy." As in a movie scene hastily rehearsed, the Blond Actress kissed him and fondled him and stroked his hair, knowing what she was expected to do, what the script demanded of her, but resisting.

"Baby . . . ?"

Gently at first, but with the assurance of a man accustomed to getting his way, the President gripped the Blond Actress by the nape of her neck, guiding her head toward his groin. *I won't. I'm not a call girl. I'm*—in fact, she was Norma Jeane, confused and frightened. She could not recall how she'd gotten to this place, who'd brought her here. Was it Marilyn? But why did Marilyn do such things? What did Marilyn want? Or was it a movie scene? A soft-porn film? She'd declined all offers but possibly it was 1948 again and she was unemployed, dropped by The Studio. She shut her eyes, trying to envision the very hotel room in which she'd found herself, a luxury room, she was playing the part of a famous blond actress meeting the boyishly handsome leader of the free world, the President of the United States, for a romantic rendezvous, The Girl Upstairs in a harmless soft-porn film, just once, why not? She fumbled for the whisky bottle another time and the President relented, allowed her a drink. The fiery liquid burned but comforted, too.

Any scene (so long as it's a scene and not life) can be played. Whether well or badly it can be played. And it won't last more than a few minutes.

No argument! These lovers were never to argue.

There was the Blond Actress naked entwined in a man's naked limbs. She could breathe now. She'd managed to overcome a powerful wave of nausea. She'd been in terror that she might vomit, gagging, no sensation worse than helpless gagging, in this bed of all places! *in this man's arms.* She apologized for coughing but couldn't seem to stop. Swallowing the male's semen is in homage to the male, but was ever anything more disgusting; yes but if you love the male, the man, shouldn't you? love his cock, his semen? Her jaws ached, and the nape of her neck where he'd gripped her, so hard at the end as his hips bucked she'd been in terror that he would break her neck. *Dirty girl. Dirty cunt. Oh, baby. You're fan-tas-tic.* In soft-porn films the scenes are crudely spliced together, no one cares much for continuity or narrative logic, but in actual life a sex scene may shift to another mode quite naturally, and now the telephone conversation with the White House was over, now the receiver was back on the hook, now the President could speak to the Blond Actress there was the anticipation on her part that he would speak to her and when he did not, when he simply lay panting, a forearm flung over his sweaty forehead, she heard herself say, in desperation for lines, any lines, since she had no script, "C-castro? He's a dictator? But, Pronto, should the Cuban people be punished? This embargo? Oh gosh won't that make them hate us all the more? And then—" These startling words, uttered in the seismic upheaval of the king-sized canopied bed, were lost amid the ravaged sheets and pillows; the President no more acknowledged hearing them than he would have acknowledged the noise of antiquated plumbing elsewhere in the suite, a toilet flushing. Since his agitated climax, the President hadn't touched the Blond Actress; his penis lay limp and spent amid the bristly groin, like an aged slug; his face had taken on the tone of a rueful maturity; he wasn't an American boy any longer but a patrician patriarch; but, since she was still naked, she would remain The Girl.

She tried to speak again, possibly to apologize for offering her uninformed opinion, or maybe in breathy Girl coquettishness she meant to reiterate it, and saw herself, on the escalator, suddenly falling. Or maybe he was pressing on her windpipe. A salty-tasting palm over her mouth and an elbow against her neck. She was too weak to protest. She lost consciousness and was wakened sometime later (she could gauge it was perhaps twenty minutes later, some of the stickiness in the bedclothes had coagulated) to another man, a stranger, vigorously mounting her; a man in a hurry, like a jockey on a filly; a man in a white shirt smelling of starch; a man naked below the waist, his penis thrusting blindly at her, and into her, the cut between her legs, the emptiness between her legs that hurt, and she pushed at him feebly trying to murmur *No! no please! this isn't fair.* She loved the President and no other man, this was an unfair use of her love. A man pumping away inside her when she couldn't wake up and (possibly it was the President clean-shaven now?) thrusting himself into her with the dogged and inexplicable air of a man kicking into hard-packed sand.

Then it was later, and somebody was trying to revive her. Shaking her. Her head lolling on her shoulders. Bloodshot eyes rolled back into her skull. In the near distance her lover's voice cold with fury *For Christ's sake get her out of here.*

It was later still. An ornate little bedside clock chimed the hour of four-thirty. Voices issued overhead. "Miss Monroe. This way. Ma'am, do you need assistance?" No she did not! God damn she was fine. Unsteady on her bare feet and haphazardly dressed, but she was fine, a little dizzy, but shook off unwanted hands on her. In the gilt-and-marble bathroom. In the mirror blazing with light that hurt her eyes. There was her Magic Friend sallow-skinned and exhausted, a crust of puke lining her lips. She stooped to rinse her face and started to pass out but the cold water revived her and she was able to pee into the toilet, a scalding flaming pee, she whimpered so loudly there came a swift rap on the door—"Ma'am?"—and hurriedly she said no, no, she was fine, no don't come inside, no please.

The lock had been removed from this door, and why?

On the counter were her purse and overnight bag. With shaking hands she removed the stained clothing she'd hastily struggled into, thinking they would turn her directly out onto the street, and changed into a silk dress, this a rich royal purple of the hue the Brunette Actress from North Carolina had worn with such style. She wouldn't trouble with stockings. Must've left her garter belt in the bedroom. As long as she had her expensive Italian pointytoed shoes, what the hell. She slapped on makeup, smeared bright fuchsia lipstick on her swollen mouth, rummaged for her cloche hat and pulled it down to hide her matted hair. A girl dumb as Sugar Kane deserves a beating. As she was leaving the suite by a side entrance, Dick Tracy to her left, Bugs Bunny to her right, both men gripping her by the upper arm, she happened to see through a part-opened door the President!—her lover!—she'd had reason to believe had already left the suite. He was wearing a beautifully fitted dark pinstripe suit, a white shirt, and a silver-checked tie; his jaws were freshly shaven and his hair was damp from the shower; he was talking and laughing with a red-haired young woman in what appeared to be jodhpurs; wasn't that what you called a riding costume?—jodhpurs. The President and the red-haired girl spoke with an identical Boston-lockjaw accent and the Blond Actress stared at them, her heart beating hard. Oh, she wasn't jealous! This girl might be a relative of his, a friend of the family. She called out softly, "Oh, excuse me?" meaning to slip into the room to say goodbye to the President and to be introduced to the red-haired girl, but Dick Tracy and Bugs Bunny yanked her away with such violence she worried her arms were loosened from their sockets. The President was staring at her. His face flushed with anger to the hue of rare-cooked beef. He strode to the door and shut it in her face.

She tried to defend herself against her captors. One of them shook her and the other slapped her and her mouth was bleeding. "Oh! My new dress." It was Dick Tracy with his grimacing razor jaw. "You're not hurt, ma'am. That's red grease from your mouth, ma'am." She began to cry. She was bleeding through her fingers. One of them pressed upon her, in disgust, a wad of toilet paper. They were hurrying her along a corridor. She was crying, threatening she would tell how they'd treated her, she would tell the President, the President would have them fired, and there came doughy-faced Jiggs with eyes now fixed upon her, not blank and lacking pupils any longer, warning, in a mean voice, "Nobody threatens the President of the United States, lady. That's treason."

She would awaken when the plane landed at Los Angeles International Airport. Her first thought was *At least they didn't shoot me. At least.*

WHITEY STORIES

In the mirror, Whitey was crying!

She stammered, "Whitey, what—is it?"

Stricken with guilt, knowing it must be in pity of her. Her makeup man wept in pity of her.

It was late. A morning in April, unless a morning in May. In the third week of the filming. No: it must be later, a week or two later. At first she'd believed this was her day off, then realizing her mistake when the intrepid Whitey arrived promptly at 7:30 A.M. as evidently they'd planned. The masseur Nico had left not long before. A coincidence, or maybe not a coincidence since they were both Geminis; Nico the masseur was an insomniac too. Nico at night, Whitey at daybreak. She would never plead with them *Don't tell my secrets oh please?* They knew her naked, not nude.

Now Whitey was crying, oh why?

Oh she was to blame—was she? She knew.

It was late! Always it was late. She knew without squinting at her watch that it was late. Though the drapes were drawn, grimly stapled to the windowsill, all sunshine banished. She would scream in agony if, having slipped at last into an approximation of sleep, she had to endure the thinnest sliver of sunshine entering her bedroom, piercing her eyelids like needles and returning her to heart-pounding wakefulness. Nico stumbled in the dark, good-natured if sometimes clumsy; Whitey, whose arrival signaled the end of night, was obliged to switch on a low-wattage bedside lamp and given permission by his mistress to do so. On extreme mornings, Whitey brought his kit to her bedside and gently began the preliminaries (deep-cleansing astringent, ointments, and moisturizer) while she lay flat on her back, eyes shut, floating in dreamy shadow. But this had not been one of the bad mornings, had it?

Still, Whitey was crying. Though stoically, as a man will cry; trying not to wince or grimace, only tears streaking his cheeks and betraying his sorrow.

"Whitey? What's w-wrong?"

"Miss Monroe, please. I am not crying."

"Oh, Whitey, that's a—fib. You are too crying."

"No Miss Monroe I am *not*."

Whitey, so stubborn. Whitey the intrepid makeup man. How long ago that morning he'd begun his procedure, she couldn't clearly recall except to know it must be two hours at a minimum for she'd consumed six cups of hot black coffee laced with painkiller and a little gin (a custom picked up in England during the filming of another jinxed movie), and Whitey himself had consumed a quart bottle of unsweetened grapefruit juice (drunk Whitey-style straight from the bottle, Adam's apple bobbing). Whitey who would never say to his mistress *Miss Monroe what has happened to you since your trip to New York in April, oh what has happened!* Whitey so taciturn for others as for himself.

Whitey's deft fingers and cotton swabs soaked in astringent. His soothing ointments, his eyelash curlers and tweezers and tiny brushes and colored pencils, his pastes, rouges, powders working their magic, or almost working their magic. This morning he'd been laboring for hours and she was only partway MARILYN MONROE in the mirror. On such jinxed mornings she could not leave her house, she dared not leave the safety of her bedroom, until MARILYN MONROE was present. She did not require MARILYN MONROE to perfection, but a respectable and recognizable MARILYN MONROE. An individual of whom it could not be said by any stunned witness on the street, at The Studio, on the sound stage *Oh my God is that Marilyn Monroe? I didn't recognize her!* The actress was running a temperature of 101 degrees Fahrenheit, a viral infection raging in her blood. Her head felt as if it were filled with helium. So much powerful medication, and still the fever held. Maybe she had malaria? Maybe she'd contracted a rare disease from the President? (Maybe she was pregnant?) One of her Brentwood doctors told her she should be hospitalized, her white blood count was low, so she'd stopped seeing him. She preferred psychiatrists who never examined her but prescribed pills for her: their interpretation of her problem was theoretical, Freudian. Which is to say mythical, legendary. *Anyone beautiful as you Miss Monroe has nothing to be unhappy about. And talented, too. I think you know this, yes?* Two days the previous week and three days in succession this week Whitey had called The Studio to inform C, the director, that Miss Monroe was ill and could not come to work that day; other days she arrived hours late, coughing, with reddened eyes and runny nose, or, astonishingly, as the luminous-beauty MARILYN MONROE.

The very sight of MARILYN MONROE on the set, sometimes the production crew burst into relieved cheers and applause. More recently, dead silence.

C, the celebrated Hollywood hack. C, who despised and feared MARILYN MONROE. C, who'd signed onto the project in full knowledge of what might lie in store but who needed the work, the money. She would claim with some justice that C was punishing her by continually shifting her scenes, tossing out entire sections of the banal and hackneyed script of *Something's Got to Give* and ordering overnight revisions. Each time MARILYN MONROE was prepared to do a scene she was greeted with new dialogue. Her character's name had been changed from Roxanne to Phyllis to Queenie to Roxanne. She'd said to C with a shuddery little Marilyn laugh (they'd been on speaking terms at the time), "Oh, gosh! Know what this is too damned much like? Life."

That morning in the mirror MARILYN appeared only to retreat at once like a teasing child. She emerged, and she receded. She hovered and fled. Somewhere in the glassy depths of the mirror she resided, and had to be coaxed out. Norma Jeane's Magic Friend in the Mirror she'd once adored but now knew she could not trust. Nor could poor Whitey trust her. Whitey who was far more patient than Norma Jeane and less easily discouraged. For suddenly, as Whitey inked her eyelashes, there might appear sly MARILYN, crystal-blue eyes sparkling with life; she winked and laughed at them both; yet minutes later, after a coughing fit, the MARILYN eyes had vanished, and in their place Norma Jeane stared in dismay and self-loathing. Saying, "Oh, Whitey. Let's give up."

Whitey ignored such remarks as unworthy of her, and of him.

Always, Norma Jeane kept her voice from betraying despair. It was the least she could do for Whitey, who adored her.

Poor Whitey had grown stout and ashy-skinned and -haired in the arduous service of MARILYN MONROE. His epicene body was large and softly pear-shaped and his head, a handsome head with noble features, was disproportionately small, set upon massive sloping shoulders. His eyes had grown to resemble his mistress's, the eyes of an aged child. One of the tribe of troll people, he was proud, stubborn, and loyal. If sometimes he stumbled on the cluttered bedroom floor (strewn with discarded clothing, towels, paper plates, food containers, books and newspapers, and unwanted scripts forwarded by her agent, like beach debris in the aftermath of a storm) she might hear him swear softly to himself, as a normal person would do, but he would never chide her, and she believed he didn't judge her. (Norma Jeane had gradually wearied of cleaning up after Marilyn. Her messy habits were so clearly faults of character, irremediable! The Studio had arranged for a housekeeper to tend to Miss Monroe's house, and to Miss Monroe their investment, but Norma Jeane asked the woman not to return after less than a week—"You can stay on salary. But I need to be alone." She'd discovered the woman looking through her closets and drawers, reading her journal, examining the silver-foil rose on the piano.) Whitey was her friend, dearer to her than the nocturnal Nico. She was leaving Whitey a surprise in her will: a percentage of future royalties of Monroe films, if there were to be royalties in the future.

Still, Whitey was blinking tears from his eyes. The sight of him was upsetting.

"Whitey, what's wrong? Please tell me."

"Miss Monroe. Look at the ceiling, please."

Stubborn Whitey stooped over his work, frowning. Applying dark brown liner to her eyelids, with a treacherously sharp pencil; brushing the curled eyelashes with mascara. His breath smelled fruity and warm as a baby's. When finally he finished this painstaking work he straightened and looked away from the mirror. "Miss Monroe, I'm sorry for my weakness. It's just my cat Marigold died last night."

"Oh, Whitey. I'm so sorry. Marigold?"

"She was seventeen years old, Miss Monroe. Old for a cat, I know, but she never seemed old! Until almost the hour she died, in my arms. A beautiful silky long-haired calico, a stray who came to my back door all those years ago, motherless and abandoned and starving. Marigold slept on my chest most nights and was my companion always when I was home. She had such a sweet loving disposition, Miss Monroe. Such a hearty purr! I don't see how I can live without her."

This lengthy speech by Whitey, who rarely spoke more than a few words and those quietly, astonished Norma Jeane. In her MARILYN makeup and platinum hair she felt stricken with shame. She would have clutched at Whitey's hands except, hiding his teary face, he'd drawn away. He stammered, "She just so s-suddenly died, you see. And now she's gone. I can't believe it. And almost a year to the day after my mother."

Norma Jeane stared at Whitey's averted face in the mirror. She was too stunned to react. Mother? Whitey's mother? She hadn't known that Whitey's mother had died; hadn't known that Whitey had a mother. Norma Jeane was one who prided herself on knowing and caring about assistants. She remembered their birthdays, she gave them gifts, and listened to their stories. Their stories which were of little significance in the public world were far more meaningful to her than her own stories, which were of exaggerated significance in that world. How to respond to Whitey's grief? Obviously, Marigold's death was foremost in his thoughts; it was Marigold he'd slept with, and Marigold he wept over; yet Norma Jeane had to speak of his mother, didn't she? How strange that Whitey had never mentioned his mother's death at the time of that death. Not a word. Not a hint! He'd never mentioned his mother to Norma Jeane at all. To commiserate with both his losses now would be to trivialize the mother's death.

Yet it was Marigold's death that was making Whitey cry.

At last Norma Jeane said, ambiguously, "Oh, Whitey. I'm so sorry." It would have to do for both.

Whitey said, "Miss Monroe, I promise it won't happen again."

He wiped his face and returned to work. Whitey would summon forth a dazzling and young-looking MARILYN MONROE to arrive on the set of the doomed *Something's Got to Give* several hours late, but to arrive! As he completed his skillful powdering and primping, Norma Jeane thought uneasily *But this was a story already. A Russian story. A carriage driver begins to cry, his son has died and no one will listen? Oh why can't I remember!* It frightened her that, since her angry lover had shut his door in her face, she was forgetting so much.

Another Whitey story. One day Whitey was giving his mistress a facial in her dressing room at The Studio. A mud pack smelling of nasty muck and ditch water but she liked the smell, it was a smell that suited Norma Jeane. She found the drying-tightening sensation of the mud pack peaceful too, hypnotic and consoling. She was lying on a chaise lounge covered in towels, her eyes protected by damp pads. That day she'd been brought to The Studio groggy and sedated. She'd been delivered to her crew of assistants like an invalid, MARILYN MONROE in fact newly released from Cedars of Lebanon (bladder infection, pneumonia, exhaustion, anemia?) and that day at The Studio she was scheduled for publicity stills exclusively, no speaking, no acting, no reason for anxiety, and so she'd lain back as Whitey applied the mud pack and quickly drifted into sleep like one deprived of her troubling senses *the girl who sees too much and a crow comes to peck out her eyes, a little girl who hears too much and a big fish walking on his tail comes to gobble up her ears* and after a while she'd wakened and sat up excited and confused and removed the pads from her eyes and saw herself—her mud face, her naked and appalled eyes—in the mirror and screamed and Whitey came running, his hand on his heart, asking what was wrong Miss Monroe, and Miss Monroe said, laughing, "Oh gosh, I thought I was dead, Whitey. Just for a second." So they laughed together, who knows why. Amid the clutter of gifts in this dressing room of MARILYN MONROE that had once been the dressing room of MARLENE DIETRICH there was an opened bottle of cherry-chocolate liqueur and from this each had several swallows and laughed again, tears in their eyes, for a female in a mud pack is a comical sight, mouth and eyes untouched by mud but defined by mud, and Norma Jeane said in her shivery MARILYN voice that meant she was serious, no joking, no flirting or banter, and don't repeat this please, "Whitey? Promise me? After I'm"— hesitating to say *dead*, even *gone*, out of delicacy for Whitey—"will you make Marilyn up? One final time?"

Whitey said, "Miss Monroe, I will."

"HAPPY BIRTHDAY MR. PRESIDENT"

She'd been dreaming she was pregnant with the President's baby but there was something wrong with the President's baby, they would charge her with manslaughter, the drugs she'd been taking so the fetus was misshapen in the womb, no larger than a seahorse floating in that liquid darkness, and in any case the President though a staunch Catholic in horror of abortion as of contraception wished strongly to prevent a national scandal and so the misshapen fetus would have to be surgically removed from her, *Hey: I know this is a crazy dream* she'd wake every half hour shivering and perspiring and her heart knocking in terror one of them (Dick Tracy, Jiggs, Bugs Bunny, the Sharpshooter) had entered her house in stealth to chloroform her (as they'd chloroformed her in the C Hotel and delivered her comatose in the crinkly black hooded raincoat to her return flight to L.A.) so she dialed Carlo's number in desperation, though knowing that Carlo wouldn't answer, but dialing Carlo's number was in itself a consolation, like prayer, her pride wouldn't allow her to consider how many other women, and men, were dialing Carlo's number in the exigency of night terror too banal to be named, but later that day when she was entirely awake and conscious and aware of her surroundings, *This is real life! not the stage* the telephone rang and when she lifted the receiver saying in The Girl's breathy welcoming voice, "Hi there?

H'lo? Who's it?" (her number was unlisted, only parties dear to her or crucial to her career had this number) hearing the clicking-crackling of the line that meant the phone was being tapped, the monitoring equipment in a van around the corner or parked unobtrusively in a neighbor's driveway, but she hadn't any proof of course, didn't want to exaggerate, certain of the drugs exacerbated nerves, suspicions, diarrhea, light-headedness and vomiting and paranoid thoughts and emotions. *But what is imagined might already have happened.*

And later that day, as dusk softened the contours of things, a watercolor-apocalyptic sky overhead, she was lying on a plastic lounge chair by the pool (in which she would never once swim) and glanced up to see him, not the President but the President's brother-in-law who resembled the President, the men as alike as blood brothers, and he smiled at her, saying, "Marilyn. We meet again." This genial unctuous ex-actor who (she'd come to learn, to her embarrassment) was known fondly in certain quarters and contemptuously in others as the President's Pimp. *He is the devil. But I don't believe in the devil do I?* She was in a vulnerable mood. She'd been reading Chekhov's *The Three Sisters* imagining she might play Masha; she'd been approached by a well-regarded theatrical director in New York to perform in a six-week limited-run production and her optimistic heart urged her *Why not? I can whistle, like Masha!* for she'd matured into Masha, she was maturing into tragedy, though her pessimist-realist heart knew *You will only fail again, don't risk it.* The MARILYN MONROE successes that constituted her career had the taste of failure in her mouth, a taste of wetted ashes, but here suddenly was an emissary from the President "gobbling her up with his eyes," MARILYN MONROE in a black bikini reading *Chekhov: Major Plays* what could be funnier, if only he had a camera, Jesus! He could imagine the President his drinking/fucking buddy cracking up over that one.

Asked MARILYN for a drink and she went to fetch it for him (barefoot and her ass jiggling in the skinny black thong and her boobs the most amazing he'd ever seen on any *Homo sapiens* female), and when she returned he sprang upon her the surprise: MARILYN MONROE was being invited to sing "Happy Birthday" to the President at a gala birthday salute to be held in Madison Square Garden later that month, it was to be one of the great fundraisers in history and for a damned worthy cause, the Democratic Party, the party of the people, fifteen thousand paying guests and more than a million dollars hauled in for next November's elections and only the very special very top-talented American entertainers were being invited to participate, only special friends of the President including MARILYN MONROE. She stared. No makeup, a scrubbed plain-pretty look, and her hair in pigtails, looking so much younger than almost thirty-six, wistful and plaintive and saying shyly, "Oh but I thought he didn't l-like me anymore? The President?" The President's brother-in-law seemed astounded. "Doesn't like *you*? Are you serious, Marilyn? *You*?" When she didn't reply, biting at a ragged thumbnail, he protested, "Honey, you must know we're all crazy for you. For Marilyn." Doubtfully, as if thinking this might be a trick, she said, "You—you are?" "Absolutely. Even the First Lady, the Ice Queen as she's fondly called. Loves your movies." "*She* does? Oh. Gosh." He laughed, finishing his drink, a scotch and soda prepared as ineptly as a child might prepare it, and in the wrong kind of glass and the rim chipped. " 'See no evil, hear no evil.' My strategy, too."

She couldn't fly to New York in the midst of making a movie, she said. She was close to being fired from this project, she said. Oh, she was sorry, she knew this was an honor, a once-in-a-lifetime honor, but she couldn't risk being fired and frankly she couldn't afford it. She wasn't Elizabeth Taylor making one million dollars for her movies; she was lucky to make one hundred thousand and saw so little of that after expenses and agents' fees and God knew who else was sucking her dry, oh she was ashamed almost, she hadn't much money. Maybe he could explain to the President? This house she loved was costing her, she couldn't really afford it. Plane tickets, hotel expenses, a new dress, oh gosh she'd have to wear a special dress for the occasion, wouldn't she, that would cost thousands of dollars, and if she went to New York in violation of her contract with The Studio they wouldn't pay for the dress of course, as they wouldn't defray her expenses, she'd be on her own entirely; no she couldn't afford it, an honor of a lifetime but no: she couldn't afford it.

Anyway I know he hates me. He doesn't respect me. Why should I be exploited by that gang!

The President's Pimp took her hand and kissed it.

"Marilyn. Until we meet again."

It would cost five thousand dollars.

She didn't have five thousand dollars but (she'd been promised!) the organizers of the Birthday Salute to the President would defray her expenses including the dress so there she was being fitted, excited nervous giddy as any American high school girl trying on her prom dress. And what a prom dress! A very very thin "nude" fabric like gossamer magically covered with hundreds—thousands?—of rhinestones so MARILYN MONROE would shine—glare—glitter—seem virtually to explode in the deliriously swirling spotlights of Madison Square Garden. She would be nude beneath the dress, of course. Absolutely nothing beneath. MARILYN MONROE guaranteed. Assiduously she'd shaved her body hairs, preparing herself smooth as a doll. Oh, that old bald floppy-footed doll of her childhood! Except nothing about MARILYN MONROE is floppy, not yet. So the jammed-in cheering crowd would stare at her, at the President's gorgeous wind-up sex doll, an inflatable platinum-blond doll she appeared, they would stare and imagine what they couldn't in fact see, and in imagining it they would see it, *a shadowy cunt! a shadowy cut! a shadowy nothingness* between the female's luscious creamy-pale thighs! as if this shadow were the very eucharist, fraught with mystery. As it happened, the emcee for the Birthday Salute was none other than the President's handsome brother-in-law or, as he was known more intimately, the President's Pimp, mellow and beaming in his tuxedo, rousing the clamorous crowd to a fever pitch of cheering roaring applauding whistling stomping enthusiasm for MARILYN MONROE the President's whore.

So drunk, Marilyn had to be aimed from backstage and practically caught by her underarms by the broadly grinning emcee and walked to the microphone. So tightly stitched into that ridiculous dress and in her spike-heeled shoes she could barely walk, in mincing baby steps. So terrified, despite being drunk and coked to the gills, she could barely focus her eyes. What a spectacle. What a vision. The audience of fifteen thousand affluent Democrats roared their approval. Unless their good-natured derision. *Mari-lyn! Mari-lyn!* This incredible female was the grand finale of the birthday salute and well worth waiting for. Even the President, who'd dozed off during some of the salutes, including heartfelt gospels sung a cappella by a mixed Negro chorus from Alabama, was roused to attention. In the presidential box above the stage there lounged the handsome youthful President in black tie, feet up on the rail, an enormous cigar (Cuban, the very best) between his teeth. And what milk-white chunky teeth. He was staring downward at MARILYN MONROE this spectacle in mammalian body and glittery "nude" dress. Had Marilyn time to wonder if the President would fly to Los Angeles to help celebrate her birthday on June first, an intimate celebration possibly, no, not likely she had time to wonder, for she found herself standing at the microphone dazed and vacuously smiling licking red-lipstick lips as if trying desperately to remember where she was, what this was, glassy-eyed, swaying in spike-heeled shoes, beginning at last after an embarrassingly long pause to sing in the weak, breathy, throaty-sexy MARILYN voice

HAP	py	birth	day	to YOU		
Happy		birth	dayyyy	to	YOU	
H-Hap	py	bir	th	day	mis	ter
PRES	i	dent				
Hap	py	BIRTH	day	TOYOU		

Somehow these gasped syllables emerged despite the terrible dryness of her mouth and the roaring in her ears and the blinding swirling spotlights as she stood holding the microphone, now clutching desperately to keep from falling, and giving her no assistance was the emcee in his tux standing behind her clapping vigorously and wolf-grinning at her backside in the shimmering dress; there were some who would claim that MARILYN turned lovesick eyes toward the President lounging like a spoiled young prince in the box above her, her sexy-intimate nursery-rhyme song was clearly for him alone, except the President was in a party mood, not a sentimental mood, the President was flanked by raucous male buddies including his rival brothers and the First Lady was notably absent, the First Lady disdained rabble-rousing occasions like this vulgar fund-raiser in Madison Square Garden, much preferring genteel company to this crowd of party hacks and politicos, these crude characters! As the President gazed down at MARILYN MONROE cooing seductively to him, one of his buddies nudged him in the ribs *Hope she fucks better than she sings Prez* and the witty Prez muttered around his cigar *No but, fucking her, you don't have to listen to her sing*, which cracked up everybody in the box. In fact, MARILYN MONROE managed to get through not one but two precarious choruses of "Happy Birthday" attentively observed by the vast crowd as a tightrope walker on a high wire stricken suddenly with vertigo might be observed by a hushed audience waiting for her to fall, yet she sang without hitting a single false note (it seemed) or stammering or losing her way and brought the audience to their feet to join in a joyous finale wishing the President "Happy Birthday." *Marilyn was fabulous that night a fantastic performer nobody like Marilyn the guts required to stand in front of fifteen thousand people knowing you've got no talent* looking like a drowned woman though beautiful in that dead-white way of hers, a corpse floating just below the surface of water *so sweet that night we fell in love with her all over again Marilyn in this weird dazzle-gown she'd been stitched into like a sausage and it surprised us, she almost could sing in this wistful ghost voice.* And suddenly it was over. She was squinting out at them, these strangers who adored her. Clapping and screaming for her. And the President and his companions vigorously clapping too. Laughing and clapping. Oh, they liked her! They respected her. She hadn't journeyed in ill health and terror for nothing. *This is the happiest day of my life* she was trying to explain *now I can die happy, I am so happy oh thank you!* trying to explain to the crowd but the laughing emcee in his tux was urging her away, Thank you thank you Miss Monroe, an assistant emerged from backstage to escort Miss Monroe away, poor dazed woman leaning on a stranger's arm *You could see she was sick, drained, she'd given everything she had it was pitiful to observe* she was leaning on a man's arm, might have sunken to the floor to sleep except he said gently *Miss Monroe? you don't want to lie down here* and there she was breathing hard hanging on to the doorframe, then leaning heavily against the bathroom counter, she was alone, she was fighting waves of nausea, in her bathroom at 12305 Fifth Helena Drive staring at her haggard face in the mirror, she'd never left home? she'd never flown to New York City, to sing "Happy Birthday" to the President? yes but it was days later, she'd been fired by The Studio and was being sued for one million dollars (according to *Variety*) but she'd had her moment in history, there was the fabulous "nude" rhinestone dress hanging in her closet, such a beautiful dress requires a fabric hanger not a wire hanger but she hadn't one, or if she had one somewhere she had no idea where, oh God she was appalled seeing that many of the rhinestones had fallen off, and the dress had cost so much, and they would never "defray" her expenses. Oh, she knew!

SPECIAL DELIVERY
3 AUGUST 1962

There came Death hurtling toward her yet she was unable to know in what form, and when.

That evening following the news of Cass Chaplin's death.

Hanging up the receiver numbly after being informed she'd sat for a long time unmoving, tasting something brackish and cold at the back of her mouth. *Cass is gone! We never said goodbye.* He'd been thirty-six years old, her very age. Her twin. Obituaries would not be kind to Charlie Chaplin, Jr., son of the Little Tramp.

"Am I to blame? It was so long ago."

To feel guilt would be a luxury now. To feel alive!

It was Eddy G who'd called. Eddy G sounding drunken and belligerent and immediately recognizable.

Her first instinct was to demand how did you get this number, this is an unlisted number, recalling then the President correcting her *There are no unlisted numbers.* In paralyzed silence she listened knowing Eddy G would be calling her only to report the death of Cass Chaplin, just as Cass would have called her only to report the death of Eddy G.

So Cass is the first of us! The Gemini.

She'd always thought of Cass secretly as the father of Baby.

Because she'd loved him more than she'd been able to love Eddy G.

Because he'd entered her life before Marilyn. When she'd been "Miss Golden Dreams" and all the world before her.

Am I to blame? We all wanted Baby dead.

Cass had died, Eddy G was saying, early that morning. The medical examiner estimated between 3 and 5 A.M. In a place on Topanga Drive where he'd been staying, and Eddy G visited sometimes.

It was an *alky* death not a *junkie* death, Eddy G informed her.

Norma Jeane swallowed. Oh, she didn't want to know this!

Eddy G continued, his voice quavering; you could see the actor working up to his buried emotion, his fury, beginning quietly, a deceptive calm, then you build, a clenching of the jaws, a thickening of the voice. "He was on his back in bed and out cold, and he'd been drinking, mostly vodka, and some mushy stuff might've been egg rolls and chow mein, and he started to puke, too weak to turn on his side and nobody was with him, so he choked in his puke and strangled. Classic alky death, huh? I found him when I came over this morning around noon."

Norma Jeane was listening. She wasn't sure what she'd heard.

Hunched forward now, a fist jammed against her mouth.

With boyish urgency Eddy G was saying (as if this was really why he'd called, not to hurt Norma, not to upset her), "Cass left a memento for you, Norma. Most of his things he left for me—see I was his good buddy, never let him down, so he left most of his things to me—but this memento, 'This is for Norma someday,' he'd say. It meant a lot to him. 'Norma always had my heart,' he'd say."

Norma Jeane whispered, "No."

"No what?"

"I d-don't want it, Eddy."

"How d'you know you don't want it, Norma? If you don't know what it is?"

She had no reply.

"Right, baby. I'll send it. Look for special delivery."

There came death hurtling toward her and at last in the waning light of what had been (she assumed, she hadn't gone outdoors, nor had she opened most of her blinds) a day of smothering heat there was Death ringing her doorbell, and the dread of waiting was over, or would soon be over. Death smiling showing white chunky teeth, wiping his sweaty forehead on his sleeve, tall lanky Hispanic boy in a Cal Tech T-shirt. "Ma'am? Package." His bicycle was ugly and stripped bare and would propel him through clogged traffic and she smiled to think of him, a stranger, bearing Death to her, and oblivious of what he brought her. He was employed by Hollywood Messenger Service and smiling hoping for a generous tip at this Brentwood address and she didn't want to disappoint him. Taking from his hand the lightweight package, wrapped in candy-cane striped tinsel with a dimestore satin bow.

"MM" OCCUPANT
12305 FIFTH HELENA DRIVE
BRENTWOOD CALIFORNIA
USA
"EARTH"

She heard herself laugh. She signed "MM."

The delivery boy didn't say that's your name, ma'am? that's a strange name? Didn't recognize "MM" evidently.

In her clothes that were laundered but not ironed, bare feet with chipped pink-polished toenails, matted and uncombed hair dark at the roots hidden by a towel turban. In her very dark oversized sunglasses whose lenses drained the world of color like a photo negative.

She said, "Wait? Just a m-minute."

She went to search for her purse, and where was her wallet not in her purse, oh where had she put it, she hoped it hadn't been stolen like the previous wallet, so much taken from her, misplaced, lost, despoiled, and she carried the tinsel-wrapped package as if it were nothing out of the ordinary, just a delivery she'd been expecting whose contents she knew, biting her lower lip beginning to perspire searching for the damned wallet amid a confusion of items in the shadowy living room, a lampshade still in its cellophane wrapping on the sofa, Mexican-weave wall hangings purchased early in the summer and yet to be hung, ceramic vases glazed in earthen colors, oh where was her wallet? containing her State of California driver's license, her credit cards, what remained of her cash? and in the bedroom with its sharp medicinal odor laced with perfume, spilled powder, the rot of an apple core that must've rolled beneath her bed the other night, at last in the kitchen she found what she was looking for, fumbling through the expensive calfskin wallet a present from a forgotten friend to locate at last a bill, and hurrying back to the front door with it, but—

"Oh. I'm sorry."

The Hispanic delivery boy had vanished on his chunky bicycle.

In the palm of her hand, a twenty-dollar bill.

It was the little striped tiger.

The stuffed child's toy. The one Eddy G had stolen for Baby.

"Oh my God."

So long ago! She'd pulled away the tinsel paper with trembling fingers and at first she'd thought—oh, this was crazy but she thought the tiger might be the one stolen from her at the Home, Fleece had said she'd stolen it out of jealousy but maybe (maybe!) Fleece had been lying; then she'd thought possibly it was the tiger she'd sewed for Irina with dime-store materials, and Harriet had never thanked her; though knowing of course it had to be the tiger Eddy G had grabbed out of a window display. She remembered that store vividly: HENRI'S TOYS. HANDMADE TOYS MY SPECIALTY. Eddy G had frightened her by smashing the window and stealing the little striped tiger because Norma Jeane had expressed a wish for it, for herself and for Baby.

This child's toy she stared at, her heart beating so hard she felt her body shake. Why had Cass wanted her to have it? For all that it was a decade old it looked new. It had never been hugged and soiled by any child. Cass must've tossed it into a drawer, his memento of Norma and of Baby, but he'd never forgotten it.

"But you wanted Baby dead too. You know you did."

She examined the card Eddy G had included with the toy. Unless this was something Cass had typed out in anticipation of his death.

To MM IN HER LIFE, YOUR TEARFUL FATHER

"We Are All Gone Into the World of Light"

The Ghost Spinet. Swiftly she could act when required. When time was running out. Two or three telephone calls & the white Steinway spinet was delivered to the Lakewood Home to be placed in the visitors' lounge in the name of GLADYS MORTENSEN. Gladys seemed confused when the honor was explained to her but in this new phase of her life (she was sixty-two hadn't tried to escape the Home or caused disturbances among her fellow patients or the staff hadn't tried seriously to kill herself in years had become a model/stabilized patient) she was willing to be made happy, or to seem to be made happy, as a child may respond with smiles to the expectations of adults; refused to sit at the piano as urged but she touched the keys shyly, played several chords in the careful reverent way her daughter did. Norma Jeane saying to the Director & admiring staff *It's a precious instrument I've tried to keep perfectly tuned, isn't the tone beautiful?* & they assured her it was beautiful & much appreciated. This was an unrehearsed scene in every particular yet it went well. Surprisingly well. The Director expressed his gratitude & more of the staff than she'd remembered & several of Gladys's friends among the patients smiling & lucid & staring at her their blond visitor whom they now openly called Miss Monroe & it seemed to her both silly & pointless to insist upon her true name. In the visitors' lounge amid heavy pieces of furniture the graceful little piano gleamed ghostly as a remembered piano.

She was saying *Music is important for sensitive souls, lonely souls, oh music has meant so much to me* these lines banal & comforting & the Director warmly took her hand for the second or third time clearly not wanting his celebrity visitor to leave just yet.

But she had another appointment she explained, saying goodbye to her mother & kissing her & though Gladys didn't respond with a kiss or a hug in return she did smile, allowing herself to be kissed & hugged by her daughter—*This is how a mother behaves, I acknowledge that*—probably it was her medication, yet how much more merciful & humane these powerful tranquillizers than a lobotomy or shock treatments & above all preferable to raw unmediated emotion, & Norma Jeane promised to call soon & next time to visit longer & walked swiftly away replacing her dark glasses so they wouldn't see her eyes, but one of the younger nurses dared to walk with her out to the parking lot, a nervous smiling blonde like a young June Haver, too shy to speak of Marilyn Monroe but saying she'd taken piano lessons for five years & she'd give lessons to the patients. *A white piano, gosh! I thought they were only in movies* & Norma Jeane said *It's an heirloom it once belonged to Fredric March* & the young nurse crinkled her face & asked *Who?*

The Fireplace. So he'd hated her & she would accept his hatred as once she'd accepted his love, basked in his love & betrayed him & she saw the justice of it, possibly it was laughable, a joke, if her detractors knew they would laugh *Cass Chaplin was writing Monroe weird letters pretending to be Monroe's old man & she believed him; this went on for years.* These letters so treasured by her & kept in a little safe protected from fire, flood, earthquake, & the ravages of Time & without allowing herself to glance at them another time these letters typed & signed *Your tearful Father* she burned in the stone fireplace of the house at 12305 Fifth Helena Drive. *The first & last use to which Monroe would put the fireplace.*

The Playground. In fact there were several playgrounds, in Brentwood within walking distance, in West Hollywood, & in the city, for she'd been wary of being noticed, being observed & identified as in Manhattan she'd been identified in Washington Square Park years ago observing the children at play & laughing & asking their names, & it was all right then in those months before Galapagos Cove & the fall into the cellar; but now, the earth having shifted on its axis, now she was wise & cautious & rarely returned to a playground more frequently than once every two weeks or ten days. The children she came to recognize though she did not watch them overtly. She would bring a book or a magazine or her journal. She would sit near the swings, facing the front of the slide & the monkey bars & teeter-totters.

She would accept it that someone might be watching her (not a mother or a nanny) from a short distance training his sights upon her & secretly photographing or filming the scene. The Sharpshooter in his van or a private investigator (hired by the Ex-Athlete, still in love with her & bitterly jealous?) & she could not protect herself except by hiding forever in that house & this she refused. For the playgrounds, the children drew her. She loved to hear their excited cries & laughter & their names pronounced by their mothers repeatedly as it's said we pronounce the names of lovers simply to hear the names, the sounds; if it happened spontaneously that someone spoke to her, that a child ran near her, a ball rolled past her, she glanced up & smiled & yet would not wish to make eye contact with any adult even in her disguise for fear *This woman looking like Marilyn Monroe I swear except older & thinner & lonely seeming in the park today!* Though still in the right circumstances, if a child ran near & the mother/nanny was a safe distance away she might say *Hi! What's your name?* & let it happen if the child paused to tell her, for some children are friendly & sociable & others are scared as little mice. She would not give the stuffed toy tiger to any child. She would not approach a mother or nanny or baby-sitter & say *Excuse me this belonged to a little girl who outgrew it, would you like this? It's clean! spotless! handsewn!* She would not say even in a fever dream *Excuse me this belonged to a little girl who died would you like this? Oh please will you take this.* She had too much pride & feared being rebuffed. She could not bear being rebuffed. So her strategy was, she drove to a playground in Los Angeles where children were Caucasian, Negro, Hispanic, & she left the little striped tiger toy on a picnic table near the sandboxes where the youngest children played & she drifted away without looking back & driving home to Brentwood she felt enormous relief, she was able to breathe freely & deeply & smiled thinking of a little girl discovering the toy. . . . *Mommy look!* & the mother would say *But who's it belong to, that belongs to somebody,* & the little girl would say *I found it, Mommy, it's mine* & the mother would ask around *This yours? This belong to you?* & so the scene would play itself out as scenes do, in our absence.

The Time Traveler. It was a time of discipline. It was a time she could not repeat & therefore sacred in its particulars. She was writing in her journal, a poem & a fairy tale. Her schoolgirl notebook had long ago been used up, the little red diary a woman who'd loved her had given her, each page covered in Norma Jeane's script, & loose sheets of paper now inserted. On one of these new sheets she carefully transcribed, copying the faded ink of an early page *So I traveled, stopping ever & again in great strides of a thousand years or more, drawn on by the mystery of the Earth's fate, watching with a strange fascination the sun grow larger & duller in the western sky, & the*

life of the old Earth ebb away. At last, more than thirty million years hence,
the huge red-hot dome of the sun had come to obscure nearly a tenth of the
darkling heavens. . . . A bitter cold assailed me. Still, she was alive.

Chloroform.. It was a dream & therefore not real. She knew. No evidence
otherwise. She wasn't hallucinating. Chloral hydrate was the safe sedative.
She wasn't in that state of mind. She'd put away the telephone as you would
put away temptation. Shut up inside a bureau drawer. And if it rang, like the
cry of a baby. Not to be tempted to answer for there was no one with whom
she wished to speak except he who would never telephone her. And she had
too much pride to call a certain number she'd vowed she would never. If by
mid-July it was obvious she'd ceased menstruating it must be for some other
reason & she was obliged to know that reason. She examined her breasts:
these were/were not the breasts of a newly pregnant woman. She associated
such breasts with the smell of the Atlantic Ocean. Galapagos Cove vivid to
her/remote as a movie she'd seen long ago in a heightened state of aware-
ness, arousal. She asked one of the doctors & he said we'll have to do a pelvic
examination Miss Monroe & a pregnancy test of course & he'd sounded
grave & quickly she'd said Oh but I don't have time today. Never returned
to him. (She had a terror, these doctors & analysts! *One day they will betray*
me. Their patient. They will tell the world Monroe's secrets & what secrets
they don't know they will invent.)

She understood what menopause was & wondered in clinical fascination
Has it begun? So soon? Confusing her age (thirty-six) with her mother's age
(sixty-two). At first glance you'd think one number was double the other but
it wasn't. Yet both were born under the sign of Gemini, there was that fatal
connection. And that night there came someone, it must have been more than
a single individual, yet she was aware only of one, entering her house by a
rear door, & as she lay in her bed naked beneath a single sheet unable to
move her muscles rigid & paralyzed with animal fear a wadded cloth soaked
in chloroform was pressed over her mouth & nose & she could not struggle
to free herself to save herself & could not draw breath to scream & she was
carried from the house to a waiting vehicle & borne away to an operating
room where a surgeon removed the President's baby (under the pretext it
was misshapen & could not survive) & when she woke fifteen hours later
exhausted & bleeding from the womb thick brackish blood soaking the sheet
& mattress where she slept naked & her lower belly throbbing with cramps
her first thought was *Oh Christ what an ugly dream* & her second thought
was *It had as well be a dream, no one would believe me anyway.*

White Bathing Suit 1941. "This poor sweet dumb kid. Sure we all knew her.
She had a new bathing suit, it was white & glamorous, one-piece, crossed

straps in front & an open back & the kid had this gorgeous knockout figure & curly hair down her back but the bathing suit was made of cheap material, & when she went into the water (this was at Will Rogers Beach) it turned almost transparent, you could see her pubic hair & her nipples & she didn't seem to notice running & squealing in the surf & Bucky turned bright red & flustered & must've said something to her finally because he got her calmed down & put a towel around her waist & made her wear one of his shirts, so big on her it looked like a tent billowing. She got embarrassed then & never said a word more that day. We never laughed at her to her face but we laughed a lot, it was quite a joke among us; when Bucky & his girl Norma Jeane weren't around we'd laugh like hyenas."

The Poem.
   River of Night

   & I this eye, open.

At Schwab's. She'd been off Nembutal for months. She'd been taking moderate doses of chloral hydrate prescribed by two doctors & had plenty of that at home, fifty capsules at least. She had a new prescription from a new doctor for Nembutal which she took to Schwab's that night to be filled & waited while it was being filled, seventy-five tablets because she was going to be out of the country traveling for weeks & while waiting she moved restlessly around the brightly lit drugstore avoiding only the magazine counter & lurid displays of *Screen World, Hollywood Tatler, Movie Romance, Photoplay, Cue, Swank, Sir!, Peek, Parade* et cetera in whose pages MARILYN MONROE lived her comic-book life & the young woman cashier would recall *Sure we all knew Miss Monroe. She'd come in here late at night. She said to me Schwab's is my favorite place in all the world, I got my start in Schwab's guess how, and I asked how and she said, Some man noticing my ass, how else? and laughed. She wasn't like the other big stars who you never see, who send in servants. She came in herself and she was always alone. No makeup and you'd hardly know her. She was the most alone person I ever knew. That night it was around ten-thirty. She paid with cash counting out the bills and change from her wallet. She got mixed up counting and had to start over. She always smiled at me and had something friendly to say like we were girls together and that night was no exception.*

The Masseur. At midnight there came Nico she'd nearly forgotten, & she met him at the door & apologized for not calling but she wouldn't be needing him that night & she insisted upon paying him, a handful of bills he would count later & discover to his astonishment nearly one hundred dollars far

more than his usual fee & when he asked should he return the following night
she said possibly not, not for a while, & Nico asked why & she said laughing *Oh Nico, you've made my body perfect.*

The Elixir. Of these mysterious powders & liquids she would make an elixir
delicious to her as Dom Perignon, & as intoxicating.

The Fairy Tale.

THE BURNING PRINCESS

The Dark Prince took the Beggar Maid by the hand
& commanded her *Come with me!*

The Beggar Maid knew not but to obey, she was
dazzled by the beauty of the red sun
shining upon the waters of the world.

Trust me! said the Dark Prince.
& so she trusted him.

Obey me! said the Dark Prince,
& so she obeyed him.

Adore me, said the Dark Prince,
& so she adored him.
Follow me, said the Dark Prince,
& so I followed him.
Eagerly despite my fear of heights I climbed the
notorious ladder of 1001 rungs
& each rung rimmed with flame.

Stand here beside me! said the Dark Prince
& so I stood beside him
though frightened now &
wishing to be home.

On the high platform swaying in the wind
high above the cheering crowd
the Dark Prince took up the magic wand
of the Impresario.

I said, But who are you? & he said
I am your beloved.

I had been bathed in perfumed waters
& the impurities of my body drained from me,
the crevices of my body carefully cleansed.
The unsightly hair on my skull had been bleached
of all color & made to be fine as silk
& the hairs of my body had been plucked
& my body covered in a fragrant oil to give me power
to withstand pain others could not bear.

It was a magic oil, the Impresario promised.
Coated on the body it mingled with the oil of the body
to produce a film of invulnerability like a shell
& though thin as the translucent membrane of an egg
it would burn & burn & not cause pain.

Said the Impresario, Here is the Elixir to drink.
& I held the goblet in my hand that shook
& high above the cheering crowd I hesitated
& The Dark Prince commanded, Drink!

I trembled with fear.
I tried to speak, the wind blew my words away.

Here. At the edge of the platform, said the Impresario.
Drink of the Elixir I command you.

I want to turn back, I said.
The wind blew my words away.

Drink, and you will be the Fair Princess!
Drink, and you will be immortal.

I drank of the Elixir.
It was bitter & made me choke.
Finish the Elixir, said the Impresario.
To the last drop.

& so I finished the Elixir,
to the last drop.

Now you will plunge forward, said the Impresario.
Now you are the Fair Princess
& immortal.

The Impresario worked the crowd to a frenzy.
Far below, there was a tank of water for me to dive into.
Far below, a band was playing circus music.
The crowd was becoming impatient.

The Impresario lighted a torch.
The Impresario worked the crowd to a frenzy.
You will feel no pain, the Impresario said.

I was hypnotized by the flames—
I could not look away.

The Impresario brought the torch to my head
& at once my hair was aflame
& my naked body aflame.
I lifted my arms my head flaming
spires of flame.

The crowd was hushed now
a great beast staring.
Such pain as I felt was more than I could feel.
Such pain!
My hair afire, my belly afire, my eyes afire,
I would leave my burning body behind.

Dive! commanded the Impresario. Obey me!

I dived from the platform into the tank of water far below.
I was a burning jewel, a comet hurtling earthward.
I was the burning Princess, immortal.
I dived into the dark, into night.
The last thing I heard was the maddened screams of the crowd.

I ran along the beach barefoot & my hair whipping in the wind.
It was Venice Beach, it was early morning, I was alone &
the burning Princess was dead.

& I was alive.

The Sharpshooter. In dark clothing & his face masked the Sharpshooter entered the secluded Mexican-style house at 12305 Fifth Helena Drive from the rear. He had a key provided him by the informer R. F. The Sharpshooter was one who acted upon orders & those orders having to do with physical facts, evidence. He was not one to interpret. Not even his own actions would he interpret. He was without passion & without pity. Gliding weightless through the darkened house as any butcher bird through the air. In a mirror he would see no reflection. The beam of his narrow flashlight was no wider than a pencil but powerful & unwavering. The Sharpshooter's will was powerful & unwavering. *Evil is a word for the target. Evil is what we mean by our target.* He would not know if the Agency had sent him on this mission to protect the President from the President's blond whore who had threatened him & in this way threatened "national security" or whether he would this night execute such actions that, when revealed to the public, would damage the President for being associated with the blond whore. For the Presidency & the Agency were not invariably allies; the Presidency was an ephemeral power, the Agency a permanent power. The Sharpshooter knew of this female's long involvement with subversive organizations in America & abroad & of her marriage to a Jew subversive & her sex liaison with the Communist Sukarno of Indonesia (an encounter in the Beverly Hills Hotel, April 1956) & her public defense of such Communist dictators as Castro; he knew, what would have enraged him if he'd been a man of passion & not calculation, that the female had signed inflammatory petitions challenging the power of the very State to which he had pledged his life. Yet he would not speculate. He would gather evidence in a valise & deliver it to be examined & destroyed by his superiors. He would destroy no evidence himself. Incriminating diary entries, documents, & potential (or actual) blackmail materials the Sharpshooter would know nothing of. The first of these items was a silver-foil rose covered in dust, in a vase in the living room; this, he placed in his valise. Next, a diary or journal into which numerous sheets of paper had been inserted, on a small dining room table untidy with books, scripts, newspapers, dirtied cups & glasses & plates. He leafed swiftly through this notebook knowing it was evidence & must be confiscated. Words arranged as "poetry" in an earnest schoolgirl hand.

There was a bird flown so high
He could no longer say, "This is the sky."

If the blind man can SEE
What about ME?

To My Baby

In you,
the world is born anew.

Before you—
there was none.

Baby! That sounded dangerous for someone.

The Japanese have a name for me.
Monchan is their name for me.
"Precious little girl" is their name for me.
When my soul flew out from me.

Japs! That didn't surprise him.

    Help help!
Help I feel Life coming closer

He smiled. He slipped a hand inside his jacket, to finger the six-inch golden-eagle neck feather carried in an inside pocket against his heart. Next, he came upon lists of words, clearly code words, in that same earnest school-girl hand to deceive. *Obfuscate obdurate plangent assurgent excoriate palingenesis/metempsychosis* These materials the Sharpshooter placed carefully in his valise for experts to decode, analyze, & in time destroy. For all that came into the Agency as evidence would be shredded in the Agency's immense grinding machines or consumed by incinerator. (Did this apply to agents themselves, one day to be erased from the Agency's files? Not a patriot's question.)

All that would remain would be reduced to a file & that file enigmatic in its brevity & language, indecipherable even by the majority of agents. The Sharpshooter then proceeded to the darkened bedroom at the rear of the house. Here, the subject herself lay in bed seemingly asleep. Judging by her hoarse & irregular breathing the Sharpshooter could trust she was deeply unconscious. His informer R. F. had so assured him, the blond actress slept a drugged sleep each night & would not easily awaken. The Sharpshooter though by August 1962 a seasoned professional & hardly a roughhewn lad riding the range in his dad's pickup, twenty-two rifle cocked to fire, felt nonetheless a stab of excitement in the presence of prey. And this prey, the notorious Blond Actress. For always the prey like this female is "unconscious": unknowing & ignorant. *Never is the target personal. As evil is never personal.* The President's whore was a junkie & alcoholic & such a death would not be unexpected in Hollywood & vicinity. On her bedside table a sordid array of pill bottles, vials, a glass partly filled with a cloudy liquid. In this room a small window air conditioner hummed & vibrated but was inadequate to purify the rich rank female odor & that of spilled powder & perfume, soiled towels & bed linens & something sharply medicinal that made his eyes water; he was grateful for the close-woven mask over his mouth & nose shielding him from despoiled air.

The subject would offer no resistance. R. F.'s word confirmed.

The woman lay naked beneath a single white sheet as if already on the coroner's slab. This sheet clung damply to her fevered body outlining belly, hips, breasts in a way both exciting & repugnant to observe. Beneath the sheet the legs spread lasciviously, one knee partly raised. In rigor mortis such a raised knee! One of her breasts, the left, was nearly bared. The Sharp-shooter would have wished to cover it. The platinum hair matted like doll's hair & ghost-pale almost invisible against the pillow. Her skin too was ghost-pale. In life the Sharpshooter had many times seen this female & was struck always by the white skin & the unnatural smoothness of that skin. And what the world called in craven servitude *Beauty*. Even as the great birds of the air golden eagles & goshawks & others were beautiful in flight & yet might be reduced to mere meat, carcasses to be strung up on posts. *Now you see what you are. Now you see the Sharpshooter's power.* As if the female could hear his thoughts her eyelids quivered but the Sharpshooter had no true fear; in such a state a subject might open her eyes & yet not see, for she was beset by dreams & distant from her surroundings. Her mouth was slack as a gash cut into her face & muscles in her cheeks twitched as if she were trying to speak. In fact she groaned softly. She shivered. She lay with her left arm flung above her head, framing her head. Her armpit exposed, & dark-blond soft-curly hairs glinted in the beam of his flashlight, repugnant to him. From the valise he removed a syringe. It had been prepared for him by a physician in the employ of the Agency, filled with liquid Nembutal. Though the Sharp-shooter wore gloves they were latex gloves thin as any a surgeon might wear. In no haste the Sharpshooter circled the bed determining from which angle he would strike. He must strike swiftly & unerringly as directed. Ideally, he might straddle his target. Yet he could not risk waking her. Finally he stooped over the unconscious woman at her left side, & as she drew a deep heaving breath & her rib cage rose, he sank the six-inch needle to the hilt into her heart.

Hacienda. In the darkened movie house! It was her happiest time. Recognizing Grauman's Egyptian Theatre years ago when she'd been a little girl. Those afternoons she hadn't been lonely when Mother was at work for she sat through double features & memorized all she could to tell Mother & Mother was captivated by her breathless accounts of the Dark Prince & the Fair Princess & sometimes asked her to tell more. In Grauman's, she was not to sit near men. Solitary men. And so that afternoon in a row close by two older women with shopping bags she knew she would be safe, & so happy! Though the movie ended with the Fair Princess dying, her golden hair spilled over a pillow & the Dark Prince brooding above her & when the lights came up the women were wiping at their eyes & she wiped at hers, & wiped her nose on her hands, though already the beautiful dead face of the Fair Princess was fading, an image on a screen of less substance than the whirring of a hummingbird's wings.

Quickly she left the movie house before anyone could speak to her as sometimes they did, & it was dusk & streetlights burning & surprisingly windy & damp for she was dressed lightly, her legs bare & exposed, short cotton sleeves baring her arms as if she'd dressed or been dressed in another season. She made her way home along the Boulevard remaining near the curb as Mother instructed. There were few vehicles on the street; a trolley rattled noisily by, but no one appeared to be inside. She could not lose her way, she knew the way. Yet at Mother's apartment building she saw it was THE HACIENDA & not the other; & she knew she'd become confused in time. This was not Mesa Street but Highland Avenue; yet it was Mesa Street for there was the Spanish-style stucco building with the green awnings Gladys said were eyesores & the corroded fire escapes Gladys joked would crash beneath anybody's weight if there was a fire. THE HACIENDA with its front stoop brightly lit blindingly lit as a movie set & surrounding the entrance was darkness & suddenly she was afraid.

Keep your concentration Norma Jeane   don't be distracted   the circle of light is yours   you enclose yourself in this circle   you carry it with you wherever you go   Norma Jeane was on the stairs & Gladys had come to meet her, Gladys was smiling & in a happy mood. Her lips were reddened & her cheeks & she smelled of something flowery. So Gladys was younger. What was to happen had not yet happened. Gladys & Norma Jeane giggling like naughty girls. So excited! So happy! There was a surprise for Norma Jeane up in the apartment. Her heart was beating like a hummingbird held in the hand & frantic to escape. There, movie posters on the kitchen walls, Charlie Chaplin in *City Lights* & his eyes staring at her. Beautiful soulful dark eyes staring at Norma Jeane. But Gladys's surprise was in the bedroom, Gladys tugged at Norma Jeane's hand, & lifted her to look at the handsome smiling man in the picture frame who seemed in that instant to be smiling at her. "Norma Jeane, see?—that man is your father."

ABOUT THE AUTHOR

JOYCE CAROL OATES is a recipient of the National Humanities Medal, the National Book Critics Circle Ivan Sandrof Lifetime Achievement Award, the National Book Award, and the PEN/ Malamud Award for Excellence in the Short Story. She is also the recipient of the 2018 Los Angeles Times Mystery/Thriller Award for *A Book of American Martyrs* and the 2019 recipient of the Jerusalem Prize for the Freedom of the Individual in Society.

She has written some of the most enduring fiction of our time, including the national bestseller *We Were the Mulvaneys* and the *New York Times* bestseller *The Falls,* which won the 2005 Prix Femina. She is the Roger S. Berlind '52 Professor in the Humanities Emeritus at Princeton University and has been a member of the American Academy of Arts and Letters since 1978.